Dorset Libraries
Withdrawn Stock

THE WATERS RISING

Sheri S. Tepper

Copyright © Sheri S. Tepper 2010
Map by Tracy Pollock, Springer Cartographics LLC
All rights reserved

The right of Sheri S. Tepper to be identified as the author of
this work has been asserted by her in accordance with the
Copyright, Designs and Patents Act 1988.

First published in Great Britain in 2011 by Gollancz
An imprint of the Orion Publishing Group
Orion House, 5 Upper St Martin's Lane, London WC2H 9EA
An Hachette UK Company

A CIP catalogue record for this book is available
from the British Library

ISBN 978 0 575 09493 2 (Cased)
ISBN 978 0 575 09495 6 (Trade Paperback)

1 3 5 7 9 10 8 6 4 2

Printed in Great Britain by CPI Mackays, Chatham ME5 8TD

The Orion Publishing Group's policy is to use papers that are
natural, renewable and recyclable products and made from wood
grown in sustainable forests. The logging and manufacturing
processes are expected to conform to the environmental
regulations of the country of origin.

www.orionbooks.co.uk

My gratitude to LuAnn Breckenridge
who proofread, shook her head,
allowed "This could be better said."
And would not let me just play dead.

Cast of Characters

Abasio—a wanderer with a mysterious mission

abbot, the—leader of Wilderbrook Abbey

Alicia—Duchess of Altamont, holder of the Old Dark House, daughter of Mirami

Bang, Mrs.—servant of Genieve

Bartelmy Fletcher—Woldsgard youngster, crossbowman, part of Xulai's escort

Bear—"Great Bear of Zol," a Tingawan warrior appointed to guard Xulai

Benjobz—owner of an inn and a pond called Benjobz

Belika—aunt of Nettie Lean, a convenient person for Nettie to have known of

Big Blue—a horse with a history

Black Mike—a smith, driver, fixer, part of Xulai's escort

Bright Pearl—a Tingawan girl of no particular importance

brothers—Rahas, Pol, Aalon, and others; interchangeable functionaries of the abbey

Brother Derris—a very individual functionary

Chamfray—Mirami's chamberlain and close associate

Crampocket Cullen—penny-pinching steward of Woldsgard

Dame Cullen—Crampocket's wife, a managerial type

Dobbich—servant of Genieve

Falyrion—Duke of Kamfels, Mirami's first husband

Falredi—Falyrion's son with his first wife

Farrier brothers—Willum and Clive; drivers, workmen from Woldsgard, part of Xulai's escort

Gahls—king of Ghastain, Mirami's second husband

Genieve—Falredi's older sister, onetime sweetheart of Justinian

Ghastain—historic personage, conquerer, despot, Huold's lord

Hallad, Prince Orez—descendant of Huold

Horsemaster—master of most everything in Woldsgard

Huold the Heroic—historic personage, heavily mythologized; Ghastain's companion, Lythany's father

Hulix—son of Mirami and Falyrion; he became Duke of Kamfels after Falredi's death

Jenger—Alicia's consort of a certain sort

Justinian—Duke of Wold; husband of Xu-i-lok, the Woman Upstairs

Lok-i-xan, Prince—most important man in Tingawa; father of Xu-i-lok, the Woman Upstairs

Lythany—historic personage; Huold's daughter, ancestress of Justinian and Orez

Mirami, Queen—widow of Falyrion; fourth wife of King Gahls; mother of Alicia, Hulix, and Rancitor

Naila—first wife of Falyrion, mother of Falredi and Genieve

Nettie Lean—seamstress, lady's maid, part of Xulai's escort

Oldwife Gancer—Xulai's nursemaid when she was a baby and part of her escort

Orez—the name of Hallad's mother's family, from whom the lands of Orez were inherited

Pecky Peavine—a farmer and drover, Bartelmy's cousin, part of Xulai's escort

Precious Wind—the Norland name of a Tingawan woman, Xu-xin, guardian of Xulai

prior, the—elder brother, second in command at Wilderbrook Abbey

Rancitor, Prince—son of King Gahls and Queen Mirami, half brother of Hulix and Alicia

sisters—Tomea, Solace, and other abbey functionaries

Wainwright—chief craftsman of Wold, particularly of rolling stock

Wordswell—elder brother, librarian in charge of the vast Wilderbrook Abbey library

Xulai—"Precious Hope." A Tingawan girl appointed as Xakixa, soul carrier, for Xu-i-lok

Xu-i-lok—Tingawan princess, daughter of Lok-i-xan, wife of Justinian; also called "the Woman Upstairs"

Places: Rivers, Roads, Mountains, Towns

Ghastain: Any country or area at one time conquered by Ghastain. Since this included a great deal of territory, most of the conquered peoples simply continued using the names they had used before they were conquered, and Ghastain did not linger long enough in any one place to notice. Ghastain's original lands were far south and east of Norland.

Norland: A vast conquered area north of Ghastain's original homeland, including Wold, Kamfels, Altamont, Orez, the Highlands of Ghastain, the King's Highland, Elsmere, Merhaven, and a good deal of other, unmapped territory.

Wold: In the northwest of Norland, a pastoral duchy surrounded by mountains and cliffs, with Orez to the west, the Highlands of Ghastain to the east, Kamfels to the north, and Altamont to the south. It has one major river, the Woldswater Running, rising from streams in the north and ending in Lake Riversmeet. It has two major roads—the Wolds Road, paralleling the Woldswater, and the King's Road, crossing from east to west at Lake Riversmeet—plus many narrow roads connecting villages and giving access to various forest areas. It has several sizeable towns, including Hay, Harness, and Hives, plus a plethora of small villages. Its capital is at Woldsgard, in the north, and this citadel is surrounded by a market town.

Kamfels: Kamfels is a forested duchy with many fisheries. It is bounded by Ragnibar Fjord on the south, the sea on the west, the trackless forests on the north and east. It has several towns, at the ocean side, and numerous crofts and mills on the mountains. Its capital is at Kamfelsgard. Under Hulix, its present duke, it has acquired a reputation for bellicosity.

Altamont: Altamont is bounded by Wold on the north, the Icefang Mountains on the west, the area around Lake of the Clouds on the south, and the great cliffs on the east. It is a hereditary duchy occupied by farmers in the valley, foresters on the western mountains, miners (at a previous time), and some freshwater fisheries at Lake of the Clouds. Its villages are scattered, it has no towns, and many of its people have moved south, away from Altamont and into the upper reaches of Elsmere.

Orez: Orez includes the large island of Elsmere, the fiefdoms along the opposite shore, and a very large tract of country from the Great Dune Coast inland to the mountains. Much of it is unoccupied and those who live there are intensely independent, well armed, and fierce. It is ruled by Hallad, Prince Orez, who inherited the lands from his mother's people. He is half brother to Ghals, by far the better half. The fiefdoms lying on the west slope of the Icefangs are, south to north:

Wellsport: ruled by the Port Lords

Marish: ruled by Earl Murkon of Marish, Prince Orez's second son

Chasmgard: ruled by Defiance, Count Chasm, Prince Orez's eldest son

Combe: ruled by Hale Highlimb, called Treelord

Vale: ruled by the Free Knights, horse breeders

The Dragdown Swamps: This area includes the western slope of the King's Highland south of the great falls, plus the western end of the Eastern Valley, all of it previously riddled with old mine shafts and tunnels that flood in wet weather and are a source of difficulty for travelers.

The Big Mud: A vast area of mire, a swale of enormous extent that accumulates water during wet seasons and seldom dries to any great extent. People attempting to cross the Big Mud are often lost. The Big Mud has recently been invaded by the waters rising and is now a swamp populated by swamp creatures, including many birds.

The Great Dune Coast: An area of sand dunes along the eastern shore of the Western Sea, inhospitable, dry, constantly subject to storms. It is traversed, north to south, by one long, straight road, maintained by Hallad, Prince Orez, and the Council of Elsmere.

Elsmere: A city and port on the north coast of the Bay of Elsmere. Known for its fisheries and for ocean trade. It is protected from the strife often found in the north by its remoteness from other large population centers.

Merhaven: A duchy to the east of Elsmere, small, self-contained, consisting largely of fishing villages and farms. Genieve is Duchess of Merhaven, though she never uses the title.

The Highlands of Ghastain: A huge mesa thrust up when the skystone fell, surrounded by precipitous cliffs, drained through the King's Cut and the Eastern Valley by the river Wells and to the south through various rivers flowing into the Big Mud. The northwest quadrant of the highlands is known as the King's Highlands.

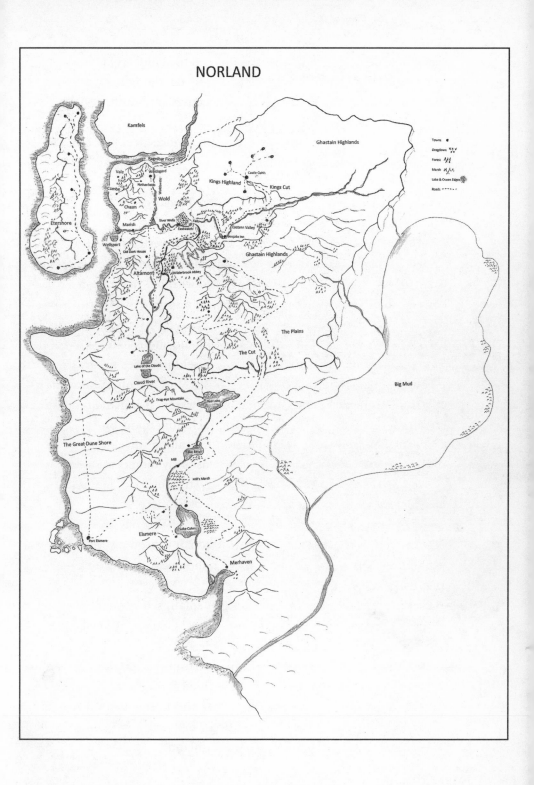

The Woman Upstairs

"IF YOU LOOK OVER YOUR LEFT SHOULDER," SAID the horse, "you can see the towers of King Gahls's castle on the highlands."

The wagon driver replied, speaking very softly, "Blue, if you look over your right shoulder, across the water, you might catch a glimpse of a dozen or so of Hulix's archers with arrows nocked."

"Ahhhh," murmured the horse, plodding resolutely forward. "That would be Hulix, Duke of Kamfels, son of Queen Mirami."

Abasio, the driver, resolutely keeping his eyes forward, yawned and stretched, giving no indication he had seen the archers. Among Abasio's former friends and companions it was generally supposed that archers who had taken the trouble to paint their hands and faces to match their leafy surroundings were less likely to shoot a passerby if the passerby didn't notice them. Being noticed could be considered an insult. "He is indeed the son of Queen Mirami." Abasio yawned again, loosening his jaw, which had been tightly clenched. "In order to allay suspicion, I am about to sing something pastoral and suggestive of bucolic innocence."

"Something half-witted and full of tra-la-las," sneered the horse, sotto voce, "and hey-nonny-nonnies."

"Very probably," said Abasio, clearing his throat.

> *Hey—oh, the wagon pulls the horse,*
> *Or else the horse the wagon,*
> *And no one really knows what force*

By which the which is draggin'.
For time can run from front to back
And sometimes even sidewise,
And oceans have the liquid knack
Of often running tidewise. . .

"Neigh, neigh," offered the horse, "ti-i-idewise."
The singer continued:

Though who does what and what was where
Are matters that can lure us,
With riddles so arcane and rare
That none know how to cure us,
Let's not waste life deciphering,
Let lore and logic scatter,
Let love and beauty rapture bring,
And meaning will not matter!

His voice, a pleasant baritone, after engaging in a number of fal-de-lals and triddle-de-dals, faded into a silence that did not so much fall as insinuate itself.

"Are they gone?" the horse whispered.

"Seemingly," replied Abasio, throwing a surreptitious glance across his shoulder where the water-filled gap had widened considerably between them and the archers. "Either they or we have gone, yes."

"It was all those neighs that did it," the horse said, approaching a curve in the road. "They decided we were not dangerous because I kept de-neighing it. Whaagh?" Blue snorted in astonishment, stopped dead, glaring ahead in dismay. What had been a road was, for a considerable distance, underwater.

Abasio heaved a sigh and leapt from the wagon seat. Once level with the horse he could see that small stones emerged from the water's surface here and there. Fallen branches at the edges lay partly submerged but not afloat. "It's shallow," he said, leaning away from the wagon to look ahead. "The road comes out of it just at the end of the curve."

"I suggest you wade," the horse remarked. "Let's keep as much weight off the wheels as possible." He put his shoulders into the collar and heaved, moving briskly through the swale, the wheels making ripples that sloshed against Abasio's boots as he moved alongside, ready to push if necessary. They came out of the water onto an uphill road freshly cut from the forest. Rounds of new wood, sawed off flush with the ground and scarred with wheel and hoof tracks, showed where trees had been. Branches, some still with leaves attached, were piled in the forest on the uphill side, though the large timber had been hauled away. Downward to their right—where the old road had been—water rippled softly under the stroke of the wind, its shivering surface flecking the valley with darting glints of sun gold.

"It's the waters rising. So they say," Abasio commented resentfully.

"We should have gone down the other side of the fjord."

"Where we'd definitely have encountered the inimical duke himself. If we'd survived the encounter, we'd have had to take the ferry to get to Krakenholm," said Abasio. "You may recall what happened the last time we put you on a ferry."

"It was windy. There were waves."

"You were seasick," said Abasio. "I was only thinking of your welfare." He tugged very slightly on the reins to signal a momentary halt and did a few knee bends to give the appearance of a man stiffened by hours of driving, though he had been asleep inside the wagon until recently. Big Blue had slept the previous night while Abasio had kept watch, so today the horse had followed the road while the man slept. The lands of both King Gahls and the duke of Kamfels were reputedly unfriendly to travelers, but there had been no alternative to trespassing on one or the other.

"How much farther to Woldsgard?" the horse asked.

"Not far. You can see a couple of fingers of the Hand of Wold just over the rise, a little to the left."

The horse raised his head, peering. Indeed, above a jagged sawed tooth of stone, four slightly separated fingers thrust monstrously into the air. One could imagine the rest of the hand, a right hand, palm forward, thumb jutting to the north, the whole conveying the word "stop" as clearly as though it were being shouted.

"It's only one big tower," remarked Abasio, who had taken the halt as an opportunity to pee into the brush at the side of the road and was now rearranging his clothes. "One big one with five smaller ones at the top. No one knows if the architect intended it to look like a hand or whether it just turned out that way."

"Unfriendly, either way," said the horse around a succulent tuft of grass.

"Not according to what I hear," Abasio replied, making a quick circuit of the wagon to be sure all the baskets, pots, and vats were tightly attached. Usually they hung loosely, the whole equipage jangling like a kitchen in a high wind. Coming through the king's lands and those of Hulix, his stepson, horse and driver had chosen quiet. "The Duke of Wold is said to be a good, kind, and honorable man, though a very sad one."

He climbed into his seat once more and they proceeded westward along a road that continued to edge upward wherever the terrain made it possible. Below them, on the right, the water-filled fjord had grown too wide for a bowshot to be of any consequence; on the left, the mountainside into which the road had been cut became steeper. By late afternoon, they rounded a final corner and moved out from among the trees onto a flat, square monolith half a mile across. Abasio leapt down to inspect the vaguely rectangular outcropping beneath them, like some monstrous gravestone. They had entered a third of the way down the eastern side of the rock. The high point was ahead, a little to their left, the southwestern corner, buried in the mountain, and from there the massive pavement sloped diagonally all the way to the northeast corner, which was marked only by a cluster of small tiled roofs, wavelets shuddering along their eaves. A good bit higher and farther west, a shabby cluster of newer buildings crouched uneasily beside a floating pier where a dilapidated ferry teetered on the wavelets, certainly empty, perhaps abandoned.

"Krakenhold," said Abasio in some wonder. "I thought it was larger."

"It was larger," the horse snorted. "The larger part is now drowned. I don't see anything on the other side."

Abasio stared slit-eyed across the water. "That's Ragnibar Fjord, and there used to be something called Ghost Isle on the far side. Evidently it's drowned, too. There's still the ferry, though, so there must be somewhere on the far side it can tie up."

A line of ashen clouds edged across the western sky; the northern shore, if there was any, lay very low upon the waters. Abasio kicked at the black rock beneath them: basalt, virtually immune to the elements. The western edge plunged into a vertical wall, blocking any farther travel to the west. Anyone going on from here would have to go north on the ferry or south, where a narrow, topless tunnel had been cut through the jagged upper edge of the tilted slab they stood upon.

"I was told about this," Abasio remarked, striding toward the cut, horse and wagon following. "It's called the Stoneway. It seems to have acquired a few more stones along the way, fallen from the mountain." He went ahead, kicking small rocks away from the wheels and protecting various items of the wagon's paraphernalia that threatened to be brushed off by the uneven walls on either side. "The woman who first built Woldsgard had it built. Her name was Lythany. She was Huold's daughter."

"That would be Huold the Heroic."

"Very probably." Abasio stopped for a moment, looking at the tool marks on the sides of the cut, following their lines upward to the sky, considering the work involved, the years it must have taken. The shadowed, stony pipe itself would be well lit only when the sun was directly above, though it rose steeply into sunlight at the far end. Several hundred paces later they rattled across the last of the rock and emerged onto a gravel road.

"Grim in there," said Abasio, not looking back.

"Blood in there," replied the horse. "People died making that cut."

"Dwarves, do you think?"

The horse shrugged and rested his chin on the man's shoulder when Abasio came forward to assess the view. Mountains closed from either side behind them. They stood at the narrow end of a widening green valley that fell away into the distant, hazy south. With Abasio walking beside him, the horse tugged the wagon into easy, downslope movement. Several chattering streamlets trickled toward them, joining at either side of the road into brooks plunging away to the south. Before the sun had sunk much farther the right-hand stream had found a rocky culvert and ducked under the road to join the left-hand stream, which gradually became a modest and rather talkative river. The great hand they had seen earlier, somewhat less forbidding when seen from the side, was surrounded by greenery and its fingertips were identifiable as the conical roofs of five separate towers. Within another hour, as the sun dipped behind the mountains, they approached a rustling crowd of fruit trees behind a low stone wall, the tree shadows mottling the roadway before them.

"Apples," said the horse, breathing deeply and approvingly. "I smell apples!"

Directly before them a particularly old and massive tree leaned across the wall, and Abasio pulled gently on the reins as they approached it.

"Hello," he said to the tree. "What are you doing there?"

A brown branch uncurled itself and peered at him between two lower limbs. "Watching."

"Not for me," Abasio said. "I didn't even know I was coming."

"I was watching for what I was waiting for." The small brown person uncoiled herself further and stepped onto the wall. "Your horse talks."

"Ah, yes," said Abasio. "Strictly speaking he is not *my* horse, though we do travel together. And though it's true that he speaks, I'd prefer that you not mention it to anyone. Talking animals are more or less customary where I come from, but I don't notice many of them around here." He blinked. He saw a child. But he also saw something . . . as though the child stood within some larger, older embodiment, crystalline, barely visible . . . invisible. He blinked again. It was gone. One of those temporal twists that sometimes proved true? Or not?

The child murmured, "I wouldn't talk about it. People would just laugh at me."

"Do they do that a lot?" he asked, rubbing his eyes. He wasn't in the habit of seeing things, but he had definitely seen something.

"No," she replied after a moment's consideration. "Mostly they don't talk to me at all. My teacher, the Great Bear of Zol, says you have to be very careful of some horses, especially their back ends, but yours seems nice."

"His name is Big Blue, or just Blue. My name is Abasio."

"Abasio. I'm called Shoo-lye," she said. "It's spelled with an X in front, but in our language that's pronounced like an SH. Xulai."

"Your language. And what might that be?"

"Tingawan."

"Ah. From over the Western Sea. And how do you happen to be here in the land of Wold, so far from the Ten Thousand Islands?"

She stared at him wonderingly. "Not many people know about

Tingawa. I was sent from there. I am the Xakixa, soul carrier, for the Woman Upstairs. You probably don't know what that is . , ."

Abasio smiled. "As it happens, I do. I have read of the custom. Yours is a very responsible duty. And the Woman Upstairs? That would be the wife of the Duke of Wold, am I right?"

The girl went suddenly rigid, as though overcome by a sudden awareness of guilt. "I shouldn't have told you. Why did I do that! I'm not supposed to talk about . . . I never talk about . . ."

"It's all right," snorted the horse. "Don't worry about it. Everyone tells him things, but he doesn't tell people's secrets. He just goes hither and thither helping out . . . orphans?"

"Blue!" said Abasio, somewhat discomfited. "Really!"

"Well, you do," said the horse in a strangely puzzled voice. He stared at the person on the wall. "You do."

"Oh," cried the girl, her face lighting up in joyous wonderment. "Then you *are* the one I was waiting for! I prayed to Ushiloma, protector of the motherless, to send me someone!"

Abasio went from the wagon step to the wall top, where he sat down beside her. "Life has taught me that almost anything is possible. For example, it is possible I will trade this horse in for a donkey. Or perhaps a yak. Something less given to making spontaneous and gratuitous commitments."

The girl laid her hand upon his arm pleadingly.. "Oh, I don't know what a yak is, but please don't. He . . . he sounds very sensible. I get very tired of never talking about anything. I don't have many people I can talk to. Oldwife Gancer, she was my nursemaid when I was really little, but she's not exactly a friend, more like a, a granny, I guess. Bartelmy is probably the youngest one who's actually friendly. He helped me pick out my horse and taught me to ride, but he's not someone I'd talk to about *her, the princess*. Besides, Oldwife says he's a little more fond of me than he should be, being as I'm a Xakixa for a princess and he's just a bowman for my cousin, though I don't know what that has to do with anything because he's very nice and kind. And the children around the castle, well, for some reason, the little ones think I'm too old, but the older ones say I'm too babyish, and the grown-up ones all have their own problems, or they keep trying to educate me, and sometimes I feel words wanting to come out all on their own but there's no one

there to . . . do you understand me? I'd love to have a horse to talk to.
Don't you find him a lot of company? Besides, if you help out orphans,
I am one, and you really are the one intended to help me. Probably."
The words had come in a spate, a gush, as from an overloaded heart.

"Possibly," said Abasio. "Only possibly." He put his arm around the
child's shoulders and hugged her lightly, suddenly removing the arm as
though the embrace had been . . . what? Inappropriate? Certainly not.
He liked children, and she was just a child. Of course, no one had *said*
there would be a *child*. What had he expected?

"While you two converse, I think I'll have a few mouthfuls of grass,"
said Blue, dragging the wagon to the side of the road.

Abasio held Xulai away from him. Seeing the streaks of tears on her
cheeks, he wiped her face with his kerchief. Her crow-black hair, full of
blue lights in the even-glow, was pulled together in a thick braid that lay
across her left shoulder and hung to her waist. Her neck and face were
pale nut brown and her face seemed to be at least half eyes, dark and
huge, either far too old or far too young for someone her size. Or she
herself was far too small, perhaps, for someone sounding as mature as
she did. "How old are you?"

"I think seven or eight maybe. I'm not sure."

"And what kind of help did you pray for?"

She sighed deeply, the words coming slowly, hesitantly: "The Woman
Upstairs is very sick and she hasn't really talked to anyone for a long
time, in words, out loud. But she talks to me—kind of in my head. Do
you understand?"

Abasio nodded. Oh, yes. He understood very well. He, too, often carried on lengthy conversations with someone very dear to him, someone
who spoke to him in his head.

The child picked uneasily at the hem of her shirt, this small movement obviously substituting for some other, much more expressive
gesture she could not allow herself to make. "She wants me to do something for her. And I've tried, I really have. But I got so scared. I couldn't
get there, I couldn't do it. So . . . I prayed for Ushiloma to send somebody to go with me."

He stared at his boots, finding himself faced with a not unusual
problem: deciding what was appropriate. Was this request for assistance
something that was "meant," that is, a fate-laden task put in his way by

someone or something other than this surprising female because *it* or *they* intended for him to do something about *it* or *her*? Did he, in fact, believe in such things? Did he believe in *it* or *them*? Or was this merely an accidental meeting that provided an opportunity to do something helpful or, conversely, totally unhelpful because of this . . . person's bad judgment, or his own? Or was it one of those dreadful nodules in space-time in which interference of any kind would do more harm than good? Or vice versa?

"Tidewise . . . ," neighed Blue, sotto voce.

Abasio avoided the questions. "What does she want you to do?"

"Go into the woods after dark and fetch something, and it's not long until dark . . ."

He thought about this for some time. "How many times has the Woman Upstairs asked you to do this?"

"Twice," Xulai confessed, staring at her boots. "Yesterday and the day before, but the shadows stopped me. They're full of writhey things that curl like snakes. And last night there was something huge that crunched as it came at me! I got partway, I really tried, but I was so scared I couldn't . . . I couldn't move!"

"Has she ever suggested you take someone with you?"

There was a lengthy silence. "She never really said *not to* . . ."

"She probably never said to tie bells to your feet and beat a drum on the way there, either, did she?"

Xulai felt her eyes filling. "No."

"Have you done other things for her?"

"Oh, yes, many things."

"Did she ever ask you to do anything that hurt you?"

She shook her head, seeming reluctant to do so.

Abasio took a deep breath. "Then, scared or not, if she's your friend you have to trust her. She needs you to do this thing and she needs you to do it by yourself."

Her eyes filled with tears, and she started to climb back into the tree.

"Bastard," said the horse, quite audibly.

"What I *will* do," said Abasio to the girl's back, "is provide some help . . ."

She stopped moving.

"I'll give you two things. I'll give you some good advice and some assistance. Now listen to me. No, come back down here on the wall and really listen, don't just pretend you're listening while you're planning to fall apart! There. Now breathe. Again. No, not hu-uh-hu-uh-hu-uh, like a panting puppy dog! Breathe, deeply, and listen! When you set out to do this thing tonight, you will have to *think*. Haven't people talked to you about thinking, using your head?"

She shivered, her face suddenly fierce with anger. "No! They tell me not to! I am not supposed to think! I am supposed to do what they tell me to do and not worry about it. Worrying about things might . . . it might get me into trouble."

"Aaah," said Blue very softly. "That would explain things."

Abasio glared at the back of Blue's ears, which twitched. "Well, for the time being, forget any advice that includes not thinking. Instead of concentrating on how scared you are, you will have to move up into your brain and think. The answer to being frightened is often right there in your head, when and where you need it, if you merely look for it. Stop shaking! There. See? You can stop when you *think* about it! Now, I do not mean you should merely take a quick glance around and then have a fit of hysterics! I mean look for the solution with everything you've got, eyes, nose, ears, everything!

"As for the other thing, I *will be there* to keep an eye on you to be sure nothing happens to you. *You may trust me to do this.* I won't be holding your hand; I will be nearby, but you have to do the task alone because that's what the lady asked you to do. Right?"

"Right," she barely managed to say as she turned.

"Just a moment. I need to know where you set out from. And when."

She gestured with a trembling hand toward the castle wall above the trees. "I go out through the kitchen garden and the poppleberry orchard through the little stoop gate in the back wall. I go as soon as it is really dark." She trudged away, pausing to look back in case he'd changed his mind, but he was just sitting there on the wall, staring at his boots. They weren't ordinary boots, being very long and made of red leather. Nothing about the man was ordinary. Though he wasn't really tall, not so tall as her guard, the Great Bear of Zol, the wagon man seemed taller and his shoulders were exceptionally broad for so slender a person. His hair was dark, rather curly, with just a few silver hairs above his ears where a stray lock fell at each side, curling under the lobes at the corners of his jaw, which was square and determined looking, beneath a mouth that was just the opposite, what she thought of as a listening mouth, the lips not pinched, but always just a tiny bit open, as though expecting to hear something. Add the alert brown eyes that seemed to be looking at the world very carefully, and he reminded her more of the Duke of Wold's hunting dog than of any other person. Even his strange wagon was extraordinary, festooned with odd things, sacks of dried plants and bundles of roots, and it was hung all over with a jangle of ladles and vats that should have clanked like an armorer's workshop as the wagon had come toward her if it hadn't all been tied down. She didn't even know why she had asked him to except that Ushiloma might have sent him. It wasn't as though she knew him. If he wouldn't help her, the whole thing seemed dark and desperate and terrible, except he'd said . . . he *had* said he'd look out for her. He had said to *trust him, he would be there.* The horse was watching her, however. His head was cocked as though he wanted to ask a question, as though he knew exactly what the trouble was. He saw her watching. He nodded at her. No, he nodded at someone slightly above her head. She turned to look behind her. No one. Perhaps both the man and the horse were strange!

She comforted herself with the possibility that the Woman Upstairs wouldn't ask her again. Since Xulai hadn't been able to do it in two tries, maybe the woman wouldn't ask her again. She really hoped, really did, that the woman would forget about it. Head down, she trudged through the apple orchard toward the guardhouse at the stable gate. Once inside the walls, she turned right, past the stables, full of the sound and smell of horses, harness oil, and hay, then to the lower wall that enclosed the kitchen garden and across it to the wing of the castle that held kitchen and storerooms and laundry and stillroom and smokehouse and servants' quarters and all suchlike *inferior offices,* which is what Crampocket Cullen, the steward of Woldsgard, called them. The cistern and two of the wells were at the far side of the kitchen garden beside the low wall that separated the garden from the poppleberry trees, and beyond the trees was the tall castle wall. Everything would be locked and guarded from sundown on, but just now the place was empty as a beer keg after the footmen had been at it. Everyone had had supper, and all the dinnertime mess had been cleaned up and everything put away. In Wold, days started and ended early.

She kicked dried leaves aside, following the cabbage path to the kitchen well and cistern. The little kitchen door she always used was well hidden behind a fat buttress that went halfway up the tower wall. Almost nobody knew about it, and nobody else ever used it. It was narrow and inconvenient and the door swelled shut whenever it rained and it was Xulai's secret.

It had been dry lately, so the door opened easily. Inside, on the right, was the back of a cupboard. If one knew the trick, one could get into the cupboard and from there into the big kitchen. On the left, a narrow slit between the stones had a panel that slid sideways, letting her onto what she called the "sneaky staircase." The stonemasons had built it into the wall when the castle was erected. The steps were narrow as the door, every one was a different height and shape, they were hard to climb and easy to trip over, and they went off in all directions: up and down, over and under, sometimes branching off to make side trips into unexpected places like the dungeons or the bird lofts or across the top of the armory. The staircase often provided Xulai a shorter though more difficult route to wherever she was going, and she rehearsed her excuses as she climbed: how frightened she was, how black the night, how terrible the darkness! All too quickly she was at the first landing, where a panel hidden behind a tapestry opened into the great hallway.

She pushed the panel soundlessly, just far enough to peep through the crack at the edge of the tapestry. One of the footmen, the mean one who always called her "dwarf" or "midget" or asked her if she'd been "shrunk in the wash," was snuffing the dozen or so candles that had dripped themselves into stumps on the heavy, curly iron stand beside the door into the room occupied by the Woman Upstairs. He muttered as he worked, his remarks obviously directed at the other footman, the fatter, greasier, lazier one lolling in a gilded chair he had already worn half the gold off of. Rabbity little snores fluttered between his moist pink lips and his pleated neckpiece was all slobbery.

"Useless," said the mean footman, dropping the last candle stub into his basket and replacing the dozen with a single thick candle that would burn all through the night. "If the duke saw you here, sleeping, he'd roast your fat haunches and feed you to the dogs!"

The sleeper showed no sign of having heard. The worker made no attempt to wake him. The one always talked; the other always slept. Behind them the door to the lady's room stood slightly ajar as it always did, in case she spoke, or murmured, or moaned—much good would it do her—though she had made no sound at all for a very long time. The candle gatherer took his time at his job, using his dagger to pry the wax drippings from the intricate windings of the candle stand, catching them in the basket. The candle maker could use the unburned wax over and over again, and it was not right to waste the bee's labor; so said the beekeeper.

The job took a while, and it was some time before the talker's footsteps dwindled away down the hallway, allowing Xulai to slip out into the silent hallway and through the open door of the bedroom. The castle was built of gray stone: iron gray, ash gray, silver gray, variously mottled, flecked and striped, laid with no attempt at pattern but with a fine discrimination as to fit. The mortar joints were so thin as to be almost invisible, so that the rooms appeared to have been carved in one piece, out of the core of the mountain. In this room, the lower parts of the outer walls were covered with rich tapestries that kept out the cold. The great gilded bed stood with its curtains almost closed to hold in the warmth of the braziers burning at head and foot. The room had unusually large windows, but since late afternoon they had been masked by closed shutters and heavy draperies. Xulai knew this as she knew everything about this room except why the Woman was here and why the whole of Wold was centered on this room. Were there other places in the world where women were cursed, women who could not speak, who lay silent for years while their husbands mourned endlessly and the world went on without them?

Nowhere else! Only here at Wold! The Woman Upstairs lay like a statue on a tomb, but her bed was smooth with soft linens, her pillows fluffy with down, her coverlet embroidered in gold. A thick cushion lay on the floor beside the bed, and it was there that Xulai knelt, tasting blood on her lip where she had bitten it, her face already wet with guilty tears.

She hoped, she prayed, the Woman would not ask her to go again. She hoped, she prayed, perhaps the Woman would not even speak. She touched the quiet hand. . .

And the Woman spoke! Silently, in her mind, only a few words.

"Xulai! You must. There is no more time. Only tonight or all is lost! I am lost!"

Xulai recoiled as though she had been slapped across her face. She felt a silence so deep it was like an abyss to the center of the earth, the word "lost" echoing forever downward, each echo striking at her heart like the clangor of a great bell.

There was nothing Xulai could say. She had never heard anger, terror, hopelessness, from the Woman Upstairs, never, never before! All the excuses she'd been practicing on her way up the stairs withered into nothing. All her delays crumbled and she was thrust onto her feet as though someone had lifted her from her knees and pushed her! She fled, hearing the repetition of that word. Lost! Echoes thundering down the abyss. Lost! The hammer at her heart. Lost! Her feet pattered into the hall where the footman still slept, through the hidden door onto the back stairs, down the stairs, gaining speed as she went, leaping, two and three steps at a time like a cliff goat fleeing an ice panther, a rabbit fleeing a hound, a child fleeing terror, except that her desperation took her toward the terror rather than away from it.

At the bottom of the stairs she caromed off a pillar as she changed directions, the clatter of her shoes loud in her ears as she went out her hidden door into the kitchen garden. There the gravel scattered behind her as she fled past rows of turnips and onions, almost colliding with the orchard wall. She darted through that gateway into the moon shadows of untrimmed poppleberry trees, their tangled branches wrestling with one another in the light wind. Then she was at the tall outer wall, the one the watchmen walked at night, at the big gate, barred and locked against the world but holding at its side a tiny stoop gate, one large enough only for a child, or a man so hunched over he would be unable to attack or to defend himself as he entered. Though she had prayed that she would not have to use it, the key to the little gate was already in her hand. The lock clicked; the gate swung open and shut. This time she did not hear the tiny metallic sound of the gate relocking itself, the sound that twice before had held a knife-edged snick of inevitability, cutting off all hope. Over the panicky thudding of her heart she did not hear the gate open and close again behind her.

The moonlit path stretched across open ground to the forest edge, where a sparse stand of oak saplings, their leaves dried and rattling, gradually gave way to the somber darkness of ancient pines. Near the last of the oaks, half-hidden by the evergreens, a tall pillar of white stone loomed pale against the shade. There she stopped, throwing a frantic look over her shoulder. She could not remember coming through the kitchen garden, she could not remember unlocking the gate, yet how could she have come this far without unlocking the gates? Above and behind her, Woldsgard Tower thrust its prodigious arm into the darkness, the five clustered bird lofts at its top holding back the moonlit clouds in the east. Lights burned up there in the lofts, softly yellow, and she choked down a customary sorrow at the thought of the one who lit them and watched there through the night. No time for sorrow. No time. *Lost, everything lost.*

She had come this far twice before, she reminded herself. The first time, her journey had ended in panicked flight back to the safety of the walls when the white stone had spoken to her. The Woman Upstairs had said nothing about speaking stones. The second time, the stone had been blessedly silent and she had gone farther into the wood, though threatened at every step by the same shadows that were piled around her tonight. They lay under the trees like pools of troubled smoke, moving uneasily as though something hungry swam within them. The thought of the possible swimmers shriveled her heart, which caught; her throat, which closed; her eyelids, which squeezed themselves shut.

"*Think,*" the wagon driver's voice whispered in her mind. "*Just think.*"

Slowly, she forced both jaws to unclench, eyelids to open, hugging herself tightly. *I'll be very, very quiet. I won't brush against anything. If I don't bother them, they won't bother me.*

A fine resolution, but it was no more helpful than in the past. As she moved down the path the shadows came with her: charred stumps of twisted darkness seeming to writhe in agony like burning creatures, sinuous ropes of tarry blackness that oozed serpent-like from crevices in the rock. Last time she had actually heard them hissing. "Think!" the man had said. Very well, she would think. She would think about being . . . furious! She was not accustomed to anger, but she knew how it felt. She was angry at the sleeping footman who was supposed to keep watch. Angry at the other one who called her names and laughed at her when she cried. Angry at Great Bear, who always, always told her to be quiet and not ask questions. Angry at herself for the strange feelings she had some of the time. Most of the time. So she would be angry! Let the shadows bite her. Let them kill her! Being killed could be no worse than hearing the Woman Upstairs saying, *"Xulai! You must do this. My soul hangs upon your loyalty. I am lost if you do not do as I have bid you."*

"But, but," she had planned to say, "but Great Bear told me . . ." Great Bear, though he was afraid of nothing, had taught Xulai that fear was appropriate, that she should be afraid of many things: the rear ends of horses; dogs one had never met before; armored men with their visors closed, all in a great rush to get somewhere without looking down. Even as she remembered these warnings, she knew she would rather face an army of murderous horses, furious men, and ravening dogs than spend one more moment among these rippling, crouching, slithering shapes that stopped her breath and froze her legs into immobility.

Except for that voice! Always before, always, it had been calm, gentle, loving, without harshness, without threat. Tonight it had spoken with tortured despair. It had panted, begged, almost screamed in her mind, inexpressibly agonized, at the very end of its strength. It had said that this was the last, the only time left, or she was lost. Again the word rang, reverberating. *Lost . . . lost . . . lost . . .*

"Think!" the wagon man had said. Why else had he come if Ushiloma had not sent him? She *must* have sent him, so Xulai had to pay attention. Think! No one speaking as the Woman had spoken could be that tired and go on living. Not the bravest or the finest. No one could ask for help from that agony and not be answered. No one. It would be better to die than to fail! She said it over and over in her mind, *Not this time, no, no, not this time, I will not, I will not fail . . .* , the words like a drumbeat, moving her feet in time, repeating, over and over again, until she looked up in surprise to find herself already at the second stone, the place she had been last night when she had heard something huge crunching toward her through the trees. She had run, then, for the second time, weeping at her cowardice. The Woman Upstairs asked for so little, so very little, and she had failed . . .

She fed her anger with shame. Very well! Let the monster come if it would. Let it squash her if it would. She bit her tongue until the blood came, tasted it, focused every nerve on the taste of it, praying to Ushiloma, protector of the motherless, to carry her onward, to that place she had her eyes fixed upon, that faint gloss of light upon stone, that pale patch among the ferns where the moon struck a glint from the third and last pillar. Tonight the first and second stones had not spoken at all. Perhaps they were holding their tongues, trying to help her, listening to her prayers.

Ushiloma, dandeoras eg bashlos, bunjimar. Aixum! Great Mother who watches over the motherless, you have sent help. I hear! She repeated it silently, focusing on that vagrant moon-gleam, that evanescent glimmer that came and went behind the screen of branches: there it was, within reach, the third pillar, the last one. The distance from the second stone to the third could be no more frightening than the way from the castle wall to the first pillar. Think! She had done that twice and survived it! She had gone to the second stone and survived it! Tonight she had to finish it or declare her love, her sworn duty, her very reason to have been a specious, trivial thing.

Tasting blood once more, she heaved several short, gasping breaths, stiffened her legs, and stepped purposefully along the path, refusing to creep, keeping her eyes fixed on the moon-glossed reflection, no matter how often she lost it behind a frond of fern, behind a needle spray of pine, in momentary darkness when a shred of cloud covered the light. She might lose it a hundred times, but she would find it again, she would go on walking, there it was again, and she would . . .

And without knowing how she had managed it, she was at the edge of the clearing where the temple stood, its bulk elaborated with carved shapes that were barely discernible beneath centuries of moss. A lump had formed in her throat and she tried to swallow it, but it would not go down. What came next? She was actually here! What came next?

"Make your obeisance to the third stone and ask permission to go on." That's what the Woman had said, days ago.

More falling than kneeling, she laid her forehead on the ground, feeling the impress of dried needles, old leaves, something soft and unpleasantly squishy on her forehead that stuck there when she lifted her head. "I, Xulai, come at the order of my kinswoman, Xu-i-lok, the Woman Upstairs. I beg you let me pass to the shrine."

"Speak up, child," said the stone. "Can't hear a word you say!"

She had been prepared for it to say something, but speaking up was impossible. She had used up all the voice she had. The stone was very tall, though only the gods of stone knew where its ears were. If it had ears. Or a mouth. She bit down on her tongue once more, tasted blood once more, and forced herself to stay where she was.

Think! The answer might be there if she would just think. What should she think? Think about what the stone had said, or how it had said it. That would do. The stone had spoken without menace. Its tone had been inoffensive, even kindly. Kindliness should be met with good manners. Precious Wind, her teacher, had spent years teaching her good manners, and they were all there, in her head, ready for use when needed! Still, she had to swallow several times before she could say the words a little louder.

"Ah. Well," the stone murmured when she had spoken, "go on then! About time *someone* came to fetch it."

Xulai rose, brushed the squishiness off her forehead with the back of her hand, bowed again to emphasize how well mannered she intended to be, and returned to the path. The third pillar had been the last; the shrine itself was just over the bridge that crossed the water she heard chattering nearby.

"Just a moment," said the stone.

She turned back, mouth open, suddenly fearful and furious, both at once. What now? Couldn't they just let her get on with it?

"You didn't say thank you," said the stone.

Taking a deep breath, she dropped to her knees once more, pressing her forehead to the ground. "May I offer thanks, a multitude of thanks, oh stone."

"Very pretty," said the stone. "Not that I need a multitude, but it's nice to know some children still know their manners. Precious Wind has done a good job with you! Go on now."

Xulai set her feet on the path, noticing with some surprise that she was not trembling. Her feet moved quite solidly and steadily. Indeed, she felt . . . what? Not quite cheerfulness. But the stone had been approving! Approval was *good*. Even better was being reminded of Precious Wind! No one in the whole world was more calm and poised and well mannered than Precious Wind. And, *thinking* about it, as the wagon man had bid her, if the stone knew Precious Wind, then the stone knew about Princess Xu-i-lok, who had advised her to make the obeisance but had forgotten to say anything about stones that talked, though, again, if Xulai had *thought* about it at the time, she would have noticed that she was to ask permission. *Well, if one asked permission, presumably permission would have to be granted, and if not in speech, then how?* So it was clear, if one *thought* about it, that the Woman Upstairs had implied that the stones would speak.

Perhaps the stone even knew who Xulai was, or what she was, which would be a good sign, almost an omen, for it would mean Xulai wasn't really alone out here.

The sound of water had grown louder. Ahead of her a streamlet came chattering from the left, bickered its way around a mossy boulder, and continued alongside the pathway, still fussing with itself.

"Nan subi dimbalic, Poxiba. E'biti choxilan, landolan," Xulai murmured to herself in Tingawan before restating the idea in the language of Norland. "No bad creatures, elder kinswoman. Just the company of the water as it talks to itself." Imagining herself accompanied by a group of elders was a way she had invented of keeping herself from feeling too lonely. Over the years, she had created a whole family of elders in her head, some of them quite ancient and wise. They all had names and histories and sayings, their considerable wisdom accumulated from many sources, some of them unlikely. It suddenly occurred to her that having all that wisdom in her mind might have helped more if she'd paid more attention to it! Why was she such a baby?

A dozen paces ahead of her, the brook squabbled with another boulder that forced it to turn right under the stone bridge that led onto the paved forecourt of the temple itself. All of it—bridge, forecourt, and temple—was swaddled in moss velvets and liverwort lace with ferny frills around the edges, having become, so Xulai told herself in sudden surprise, as much a living being as it was dead stone. Why, at any moment, it might creak up from its foundations and stumble off into the trees, its dappled hide dissolving into the fabric of the forest.

The thought stopped her only for a moment, and she was actually smiling as she hurried the dozen long steps that took her across the arched bridge. From the forecourt, two hollowed granite steps ascended to the temple floor. Several paces within the temple, a few more steps would gain the altar platform, which Xulai circled carefully while keeping her eyes away from the carvings around its edge. Even veiled in moss, they could catch hold of one's eyes, captivate one, melt a person down into the stone to become one with it, or so the Woman Upstairs had said, though that threat had not greatly bothered Xulai. Things one was instructed *not* to look at were far less fearful than things that forced themselves upon unwilling eyes.

From the far side of the bridge, Abasio, who had followed her closely each trembling step of the way, heard a sound behind him. He slipped between two trees into a web of darkness, leapt over the quarrelsome streamlet, and circled the temple with a few long, careful strides. From among the trees behind the temple, he saw Xulai drop to her knees. Now what? She was trembling, her eyes shut, thinking. "Good for you, girl," he murmured to himself. "Good for you, little maiden!"

The Woman Upstairs had said, *"In the floor behind the altar. A triangular stone, small, not heavy, but you'll need something sharp to pry it up with."*

Her fingers closed on the awl in her pocket. She had taken it from the shoemaker's stall just as he had been closing his booth for the night. Just before suppertime the castle yard bustled and echoed in a confusion of men shouting, wagon wheels grinding on the stones, horses clopping toward the stables, women screeching for their children. The shoemaker, dressed all in shiny leather like a cricket, had been eager to get home to his new wife. He wouldn't look for the awl until morning, and by then, Xulai would have pushed it back through a hole in the shutter. If she ever got back to the castle. If she could find the right stone, one triangular stone among a great many stones that looked more or less triangular.

"Oh where?" she whispered. "Where?"

"Think!" said the voice of the wagon driver, as though from beside her ear. *"Think!"*

She thought, *Stone,* and there it was: one that glowed and trembled, almost calling her by name! Xulai inserted the awl at one edge and pried it up. The cavity below held a small wooden box. She thrust it into her pocket, at the same instant hearing voices! People! At least two of them on the path and coming quickly toward the temple.

She replaced the stone and quickly scuffed dirt into the cracks around it, scattered a few pine needles over it, and moved away from the altar. She could not go back the way she had come. She had been told not to leave the path. There was no path! The only shelter was among the shadows she had been so frightened of . . .

The voices came closer. She tried not to breathe, suddenly realizing the awl was not in her hand, not in her pocket. Then, suddenly, an arm was around her, a voice in her ear.

"Shh. Here's your awl. Slip under my cloak. Be still."

Abasio! She scrambled against him, burrowing into the darkness of his cloak, letting him cover her like a cloud as he crouched, then lay in the darkness between the trees, among the leaves, ferns before their faces, her body between his side and his cloak, his arm holding her gently there, invisible. She sighed, drawing closer to him, feeling his warmth.

"What was that?" demanded a high, imperious voice.

"Some beastie." This was a deeper voice, smooth and oily, like the slosh of pig slop in the bucket. "That's what woods are full of, lovely lady. Lots of little beastie creatures hunting their dinner."

Xulai felt a dark-sleeved arm cover her face, felt Abasio's head close beside hers, his slitted eyes peering at the newcomers from a face he had painted dark with mud. Something moved on her hand. She opened one eye to see two tiny black eyes, a wriggly nose, two fragile ears like new leaves, a striped back beneath a curved tail: a chipmunklet, scarcely bigger than her thumb. It sat on the edge of her sleeve and peered intently at the noisy intruders beyond the temple.

"So, where is this night wanderer?" the high voice queried, a voice of ice and knives and shattered glass. "Where is she, Jenger?"

The man answered soothingly, "Duchess, lovely one, I think your informant is mistaken. There's no reason for children to come out here at night. Orphaned children wander during wars or famines, of course, but there's no war or famine at Woldsgard. As we have been told"—he chuckled, a thick, glutinous sound that was not really one of amusement—"Justinian, Duke of Wold, houses and cares for his people well. There are none without a roof over their heads and a hearth to warm themselves by."

The woman sneered. "So the duke is a fool, wasting his substance on nobodies. Well, he should be more careful about the people he puts beneath his roof! One of them is mine, and she tells me she has seen a child come out of the castle at night and enter the woods."

"How old is this roaming child supposed to be?"

"I don't know," the woman answered angrily. "That's what I'd like to find out. My spy looks down from a great height. She says it's a child, could be any age at all. Perhaps a ward or by-blow of the duke's?"

"And you care about this for some reason?"

"My own reason, Jenger. If she's only a toddler, I care little. She'd be a pawn at best. But I would care greatly if she were a game piece held in reserve, someone much older than that."

Xulai trembled, the words echoing in her ears. *Much older than that . . . I would care greatly.* The couple approached, climbing the stairs to the altar.

"How strange," said the man. "Look at the patterns carved here . . ."

As he spoke, the altar stones began to glow, faintly, like coals kept from a long-spent fire.

The woman growled, "Dolt! Fool! Pull your eyes away and keep them so. This is a shrine of Varga-Grag, hag goddess of all earthly desolations. You have no business being here, looking at it." She gave a croaking rasp of barely suppressed laughter. "For that matter, considering my allegiances, neither have I. Neither my mother, the queen, nor I would be welcome."

The man laughed, unembarrassed. Neither of the intruders seemed to notice how the glow from the stones brightened as they turned away and walked around the altar to stand behind it, staring directly toward Xulai. "Your pardon, ma'am. Our being in this particular place is the result of following a path, but . . . this is where all paths end."

Xulai almost stopped breathing. She could feel the speaker, feel his presence oozing toward her as he peered into the darkness. The chipmunk had crept beneath her curled hand and was looking out between her fingers at the man, a dark silhouette against the bloody glow from the temple stones, brighter now. Xulai's companion closed his arm about her, only a bit, just enough to reassure her. Something hard lay along his side, and she realized he wore a sword. He was armed! Mere peddlers were not usually armed.

The man near the altar went on: "There's not even a game trail among the trees back here. Wherever your child may be, he or she is not here. If you want me to bring some men and search the woods around here in daylight, I'll be happy to lead them, though we would need the duke's permission since we'd be trespassing."

"Which is why we've been camped down the road and have come

alone," the woman snarled, raising her hand to thrust aside one of the low branches that overhung the platform. "The Duke of Wold won't know we're trespassing. Never mind. I'll have my grubby little spy, Ammalyn, follow the child next time she ventures here."

The man asked, "Why do you think this thing you want is here at all? Why do you think she ever had it? Or are you really seeking the miraculous device that Huold is said to have left in these lands? Wasn't that somewhere in Marish, on the other side of the Icefang range?"

The woman said impatiently, "Huold's device was something else entirely. Everyone has a story about that thing. It is even rumored that Justinian found Huold's device and gave it to that woman as a betrothal gift, but that's merely another old tale grafted onto a new occasion. No, the thing I seek is a more recent thing, a powerful device of some kind that was in that woman's keeping! She must have brought it with her from Tingawa."

"And you know this how?"

"Because she isn't dead, Jenger! I would have succeeded in killing her long ago if she did not have some powerful protection! She must have brought it with her!"

Abasio's arm tightened around Xulai to prevent her moving, for she had trembled in both horror and anger at the woman's words.

The man said, "But neither her protection nor Huold's talisman is as old as this shrine."

"No. These desolation shrines were built by the Forgal people who survived the end of the Before Time, well before Huold was born."

"Then what made you think the thing you want could be here?"

"Only the rumor of a child sneaking about. I have a man loitering near the castle to learn what's happening, what's being said. He knew we were nearby. Ammalyn told him to tell me about this child. It occurred to me the woman might have sent a child to hide something, and the something might be what I'm looking for."

"It doesn't sound very likely."

"The woman I'm killing all too slowly has done many unlikely things, Jenger. Besides, I have a talent. I can smell the heat of power, smell it like the smoke of a distant campfire. Whoever holds it, my nose will find them and they will lead me to it. No matter how many men and how much time it takes."

"Why does it matter to you?" he said, again soothingly.

Her voice was furious. "Because the Sea King's ambassador told me the Sea King will buy Huold's device. The Sea King will buy *anything* of value to Tingawa. The reward is very great. A very great payment indeed."

"And what is that?"

She turned to face him, her eyes glinting red, reflecting the glow of the stones, or perhaps, Xulai thought suddenly, they were lit by the same fire that lit the altar stones, ancient evil, heaped like eternal coals, ready to spring into flame if they were fed.

"The Sea People have taken the Edgeworld Isles, Jenger! What they found there is beyond imagination. They found ease machines! Ease machines in vaults below the great library, and books that tell about them and how to use them!"

The tall man's face betrayed something very like fear. "From the Before Time? How could things like that have stayed hidden?"

"The Sea People's hearing is different from ours. They hear with echoes. They heard the vault, the hollowness! They knew it was there and needed only to find the way to it. There was much delving, Jenger, much exploration, but they found the vault full of machines!"

"But I thought you already had machines. You said—"

"There are a few little ones at the Old Dark House. Enough to kill that woman of Woldsgard, if used correctly. I confess to a mistake with that one . . ."

"You? I don't believe that," he said caressingly.

"Yes. I did. It was decades ago, I was much younger, and I cursed her hastily, badly. However, when I sent the curse, I made copies of the sending, many of them, and eventually they'll do the job. She can't go on fighting them forever! Ammalyn tells me she can't even speak anymore."

"And that's the only machine you have?"

"I have three others: one to find people, one to send sounds and sights, one to make speaking mirrors—as you well know—but nothing really powerful."

"I thought it was your magic that's killing her."

She laughed, genuinely amused. "Don't be silly, Jenger. There's no such thing as magic. No. My favorite machine makes lovely curses, invisible clouds of very small, powerful killers. I can make the cloud and keep it alive in a special kind of vial. Then, if I get close enough to the person and release the cloud, the cloud will find that person among all the peoples who may be near, no matter where the person is hidden, so long as I release it nearby!"

"Any person?" he said in a choked voice.

"Any person I choose—if I have their code. That's what the books call it, the code."

"What code?"

"The code of themselves! The code that makes each of them unique. It's in their fingernails, in their skin. It's in their spit on the rim of a wineglass. That's where I got the code of the princess, while she was at the court of King Gahls. I made my cloud and I carried it here to Woldsgard, near the castle. And once my cloud had settled upon her, she was doomed. The very cells of her body have been slowly, inexorably destroyed by my cloud." She laughed again. "Clouds, I should say. In her case, I have to keep releasing them. It is almost like magic, isn't it?"

Xulai, staring, saw a malevolent vapor spread from the woman's mouth, smelled something vile. She held her breath so she would not inhale, for she knew she would choke if she breathed that laughter. Abasio's arms tightened around her as they watched the woman laughing and swaying on her feet as though dancing. "Like your pigeons, Jenger. Like your homing pigeons at the tower. My curses will find their roost in one person only, one in the whole world."

Above her, a branch, red-lit from the glowing altar below, moved, as though thrust by a puff of wind. It danced above the woman's head, moved down toward her hair as though to caress her. She, laughing, reached up to thrust it away. "But the machines I have are useful only for killing one person at a time, or finding someone who wishes not to be found or watching people who are far away. The ones the Sea King has found, the ones in vaults . . . ah. Worlds can be moved with those, and once we have them, Jenger, no power in the world will stand against us."

She took his hand and tugged him almost gently away, around the altar, their footfalls retreating over the bridge, their voices fading. Beneath Xulai's hand, the chipmunk grasped her little finger with all four paws and clung to it as she rose, its beady eyes fixed on something behind her. She followed its gaze to the many pairs of eyes in the forest around her, close to the ground, red disks in the darkness, reflecting the bloody light still emanating from the altar. They were chipmunk hunters, no doubt. Xulai lowered the little creature into her pocket, feeling it settle into a corner, taking up residence.

"You have found a friend," Abasio whispered. "Such little creatures are good friends. They can hide and hear and remember. You also should remember what the woman said. There was a spy who looked down from a great height, and her name was Ammalyn."

Xulai whispered her reply. "She's a scullery maid. From down in the scullery, she could spy only dirty pots, but from her bedroom, high up under the roof, the windows look down upon the orchard, the wall, and beyond the wall to the forest. If she has seen me go past the wall, she will also see me returning. That is, if I use the path, and the Woman Upstairs told me not to leave the path."

"Well and well, your Woman Upstairs hadn't expected trespassers to be abroad in the night. We'll find a solution to that. Let us wait until that red light fades. I do not trust it."

"Is it evil?"

"It is said by those who made a study of such things that those upon whom the red light falls will die within the year." He shook his head slowly. "In this case, one might hope, but it's only a saying."

They waited. The red light faded slowly, dying reluctantly, exactly like the coals of a fire. When it was dark, they moved up toward the altar, and as Xulai went up the step she saw something moving in the air before her eyes, a cobweb, a tendril. "Can you reach that?" she asked him, pointing.

"A lock of hair? No, not so much as a lock, only a few hairs pulled out by their roots. Long ones, from the woman." He lifted them from the branch where they were caught and passed them to her. Xulai stood, staring at them for a long moment, trying to remember everything the woman had said. Ah, yes. She took a handkerchief from her pocket, wound the hairs around her fingers, and folded the linen square around them, replacing it in her pocket. Tomorrow she would tell the Woman Upstairs about having the hair . . .

With Abasio's hand on her shoulder, she passed the third pillar and the second, both silent. From the first pillar they could see the castle wall and the orchard gate, closed.

"Someone is watching from a window," she whispered. "So if I go back the way I came, she'll see me. But if I go some other way, I may run into those people. They may even be waiting for me . . ." Her voice trailed into silence.

"So," said the chipmunk. "What are you going to do?"

"I don't know." She almost wept, finding in that moment no wonder left over to spend on a talking chipmunk.

"Stop that!" the chipmunk ordered. "It's always easier to whine than to do something, but something must be done! Now, figure it out. Think! *Velipe vun vuxa . . .*"

"*Duxa vevo duxa,*" Xulai said, finishing the saying. " 'Wisdom comes from putting little things together.' That's what the Woman Upstairs says, but how did you know, chipmunk?"

"An interesting saying indeed," said Abasio, strangely moved. He wanted to sweep this little one up and carry her away into safety and did not trust the feeling! As though some monitor upon his shoulder cautioned him. He said, instead—as he would have said to a much older woman—"Do you think she talked merely to exercise her tongue? Words are useful tools only when one does something with them!"

Xulai felt suddenly angry. "I don't have any little things to put together!"

"Don't be stupid," said the chipmunk. "The world is full of little things. You seem to be a little thing; so am I."

This, she found, was a surprising new thought. Of course she herself *was* a little thing—or was considered to be so by too many people—but the surprising thought was that the Woman Upstairs might actually have meant these particular words to be useful! Putting little things together. Actually, the Tingawan words meant "Wisdom comes from piling nothing much on nothing much." Well, starting with herself, she could put herself on a path, which might be little enough. Then she'd need a way to discover whether the people were still around, then. . .

"Path," said chipmunk, reading her intention. "To the right."

She examined it. Yes. Very narrow and dark and tree covered, so that no one could see her from above. She moved toward it. Caught in a twig, at eye level, was a bit of cloth.

"A little thing," she murmured. "The woman went this way."

"And?" demanded the chipmunk.

"She went," Xulai said. "The threads are trailing away from me, so she was moving away."

"So, if you move slowly?"

"I won't catch up to her. Or him."

"You might get lost," the chipmunk jeered.

"No," she replied. "The path is just at the edge of the trees. I can see the castle wall."

Suddenly the tall white stone beside her asked, "Abasio, is Xulai taking the chipmunk home with her?"

"Would she be wise to do so?" asked Abasio.

"I'm afraid my cats . . . ," murmured Xulai. "They'll . . ."

"Nothing of the kind," said the stone. "The creature will be quite all right in your pocket. Take it. Keep it safe. Nice to hear of you again, Abasio. It's been too many years since the great battle at the Place of Power. Some of my fellow watchers were there."

Xulai's pocket squirmed briefly, as though in agreement. Xulai, though she realized the stone and her companion were not strangers to one another, was too weary even to wonder at it. What Ushiloma did was goddess business, and Xulai was not required to understand it. Instead, she merely moved onto the new path, so concentrated upon listening that she scarcely noticed the tripping roots and snatching briars. She was no longer fearful, only desperately weary. All that was important was getting back to the Woman Upstairs.

Soon the path swerved around the tower, and Xulai stopped, staring at the level, bare ground between the trees and the tower. It was kept that way by the groundsmen so as to give no cover to possible attackers. Not that there were attackers, nor had there been for almost a hundred years, but Justinian, Duke of Wold, Lord Holder of Woldsgard Castle, stayed in readiness, when he could spare time from his grief. From here, she could see nothing of the upper part of the castle except the tower itself. The watcher could not possibly see her.

She raced to lean against the wall, looking upward. "If I can't see the roof, the roof can't see me," she muttered to Abasio, who replied by patting her shoulder. Staying close to the stones, she circled the wall tower, checked again to be sure the roof was out of sight, then stayed close to the wall until she reached the tiny gate and inserted the key. Here she and her companion were sheltered from above by the tangled branches, the fruit-bearing tendrils now bare but still contending with one another in the breeze. The key clicked; she went through, Abasio stooping behind her, and the gate locked itself. Xulai murmured thanks to each tree as it sheltered them from the spy above, all the way to the kitchen garden. Even from here she could not see the high windows.

"Why are the poppleberries in a separate orchard?" the man murmured.

"They pick on other trees," whispered Xulai. "They beat all the leaves and fruit off. If you want to pick the fruit for jelly or pies, they will pop you unless you have a woodsman standing by, threatening them with an axe! No one knows who first found them or created them. They've just always been here . . ." Her voice faded as they approached the kitchen door, which was waiting unlatched, as she had left it. Inside, she turned wearily toward the stairs, saying, "Please, will you come with me?"

"If you like," he replied in a subdued voice. "If you don't think the lady will mind."

She led the way, too tired to comment at Abasio's muttered curses as he struggled with the uneven stairs. "What in the name of artistry was this leg trap built for?"

"A way for the workmen to get things into parts of the castle that are hard to reach," she murmured. "So my cousin says."

"Your cousin?"

"The duke." She took a deep breath. Perhaps it was time for explanations. "He says I am to call him cousin. I am of his wife's family. Everyone speaks of 'the Woman Upstairs,' but she is really Princess Xu-i-lok, wife to His Grace the Duke of Wold, seventh daughter of Prince Lok-i-xan, Tingawan ambassador to the court of King Gahls and head of Clan Do-Lok. Though she merits both great respect and watchful people to serve her day and night, just you watch! The footman will be asleep outside her door, slumped in his chair and snoring like an overfed dog. It is a good thing Wold is at peace. Once His Grace the duke goes up to the bird towers at night, even the watchmen on the outer walls sleep more than they watch."

Abasio smiled to himself. She sounded like a fully mature and offended mistress of the castle, but she was proven right, for the footman still slept. They crept past him into the lady's room. Xulai dropped to her knees in the somber shade of the hangings, near one of the braziers, its charcoal glowing red beneath the smoke hood, its suspended chimney leading up into the darkness where it found a vent to let the smoke out. The heat was welcome against Xulai's face. She leaned against the high mattress and searched the still face before her. No change. Never any change. Not anymore.

Abasio soundlessly closed the door behind them and came to join her where she knelt beside the great bed. She whispered, "It has been a long time since the princess has been able to speak aloud, but I remember everything she ever said to me, no matter how long ago it was." She took the woman's hand in her own and leaned forward to put her lips close to the woman's ear. "Princess. I have it. I will hide it and keep it safe as you have asked."

She waited for a moment. There was no motion in the face or behind the closed lids of the eyes, but the hand she held moved to squeeze her own, so slightly the movement would have been invisible to anyone watching.

Suddenly, his eyes wide, Abasio stirred. He heard . . .

"Xulai," the woman spoke in her mind. "There is no time left to hide it. Open it now."

Wonderingly, Xulai stared at his face. "You heard her!"

He nodded, putting a finger before his lips. She pulled the box from her pocket and set it on the bed, prying up the close-fitting lid. Inside, cushioned in lamb's wool, was an orb the size of a large grape, delicately patterned in blues and greens. It might have been made of glass, perhaps? Or perhaps it actually was a kind of fruit? And yet . . . it seemed large. In her sight it expanded, becoming huge, as though she looked at the world from a great distance. Surely those blue areas were seas, and the green ones were forests. Surely those white things were clouds . . .

The chipmunk came from her pocket, sat on her shoulder, and peered. Xulai reached for the orb, then drew back as the voice of the Woman Upstairs spoke in her mind: "Take it. Put it in your mouth, child. Don't be afraid! Quickly!"

Xulai froze in place. She had heard the words, actually heard them, as though they had been called loudly but from an infinite distance. Abasio put his hand on her shoulder and shook her, very slightly. She stared at the orb, measuring it with her eyes. The chipmunk crept toward the orb, sniffing at it.

"It's too big," she whispered, to the walls, to herself, perhaps to the chipmunk.

"It isn't really," Abasio said firmly.

"Yes, it is," Xulai asserted angrily. Not for someone grown-up, perhaps, but for her, it was too big.

"Just put it in your mouth for a moment," the chipmunk told her. "To warm it. Poor thing's cold!"

Xulai stared at it.

Abasio said lightly, teasingly, "Pretend it's a sugar drop. You've eaten sugarplums bigger than that. Chipmunk is right. Warm it up."

He watched as her lips closed around it.

The thing in her mouth came alive in an instant. It was like a squirming tadpole, a slippery fish, and she gagged, trying to spit it out. Abasio put his hands across her lips, hugged her tightly, for she was a good deal stronger than she looked. She squirmed as she felt the thing dive down her throat, vanishing like a frog into a pond.

"Not too big?" queried the chipmunk, cocking its head to one side. "Not at all."

She glared at it, forgetting the woman, forgetting herself in sudden anger, snarling, "It wasn't your mouth it was squirming around in!" She put her hands to her sides, thrust them under her dress, felt her stomach. Not a flutter, nothing there to say she had swallowed some lively thing. Except a kind of creeping warmth, a feeling of . . . well, the way she felt sometimes when Precious Wind let her have a few sips of wine. Soft inside. Warm. Really wonderful.

Abasio heard words, fleetingly, a whisper. *"Friend. We hoped you would come in time. Thanks."*

Stunned, but conscious of the girl's anger, he managed to whisper, "Xulai, it was what she wanted, what she needed." He put his hand on her shoulder and shook her. "Look at her, Xulai. *Look at her!*"

Before her on the bed the woman lay unchanged, except . . . except that her lips were very, very slightly curved upward in the ghost of a smile. Xulai took the lax hand in her own, waited for words in her mind, looking at the curved lips, definitely a smile. No words came. She leaned forward to feel the woman's breaths upon her cheek, softly, barely, a long, long time between. As she knelt there, a quiet wind came into the room. The fire blazed up. The wind circled, as though it were searching for something, then gathered itself from all corners of the room and gusted into the fireplace, the flames leaping up behind it as it fled up the chimney and away from Woldsgard toward some other, more suitable place.

"Ah," whispered Abasio. "Look, sweetheart. The pain is gone. Look at her."

And it was true. The pain was gone. The face was peaceful. The hand she held had relaxed; the lines were gone from her face; the room was changed. All the strain, the hurt was gone. The room, too, was at peace.

"Tranquil," said Abasio in a strange, choked voice. "She is full of quiet. We can let her sleep."

After a silent time Xulai rose, the chipmunk still on her shoulder, and they left the silent room. They passed the footman where he slept snoring in his chair and went down the wicked stairs and out into the kitchen garden.

Abasio held out his hand. "I've taken shelter in the courtyard with the other travelers. I can find my way there. Give me the awl you borrowed from the shoemaker . . ."

"How did you know I did?"

"I saw you take it. I followed you here when you left. I'll return it. Sleep well."

As he turned away, she saw tears on his face. He felt pity for the princess, no doubt, for he was a kind man. "Abasio," she called. He turned, leaned down toward her. She reached up and kissed his cheek. "You were kind, and she called you friend. Thank you."

She turned back toward the stairs as he, moving as though under some compulsion of quiet and necessity, found his way through the interior gates leading to the courtyard, where he pushed the shoemaker's awl through a gap in the shutters of the stall. He managed to exchange casual greetings with a sergeant who moved slowly across the paved area from wall to wall, checking on the guards. There were other wagons and several peddlers bedded down in the area near the stable, and he wended his way among them to the paddock where Blue, who was spending the night among other horses and mules, came to push his head over the railing and whisper, "Is the woman all right?"

"I think . . . the princess was helped," whispered Abasio.

"I meant the . . . little one," said Blue, gazing at Abasio's face, which held a strange expression, something with traces of amazement and fear and gratification. People had such trouble with their faces. They often said too little or too much.

Abasio took a deep breath. "She has done what she had to do, just in time."

"We came as fast as we could."

"I know. I think this was the night we needed to be here. It's just . . . I didn't realize the person they spoke of was a child."

Blue did not reply for a moment. "Perhaps so. People don't always tell everything, you know. Mostly they don't. Who was the person who told you to come here, anyhow?"

"You saw him. He was also Tingawan, I think. That part fits."

"I thought he was rather ordinary looking, but you said he was *strangely compelling.*"

"We would hardly have made this journey had he not been."

"You said she did whatever it was just in time?"

"Yes," said Abasio, wiping tears from his face. "I'm sure it was."

"But you're troubled. Why?"

"Blue, I don't know. She went to find something, she found it, brought it back, was told to swallow it. None of my business, but there I was, urging her on to swallow it because I heard this voice . . . tortured, it was. But so . . . determined, needful, imperious! As though the fate of the world hung on it." He laughed, shaking his head.

"The younger one swallowed it?"

"Yes. And once she had done it, there was a kind of peace that came, exalted, ecstatic, whatever. All I can compare it to . . . think how one feels at the end of a dreadful day. You know: fighting bandits, maybe wounded, bleeding, stung by flies, everything happening in a half-frozen marsh where you can't sit or stand or lie down, and every time you dispose of one enemy, two others pop up, and you're soaking wet, and shaking with cold, and then somehow at the end of the day you're brought to a warm room with a place to wash, with food and a jug of something soothing to drink, and you can lie down on a comfortable bed and it's safe to sleep. You know that feeling."

"Except for the jug, yes. Substitute oats, add a groom with a curry comb, and I know exactly."

"Well, that's how she felt, and I knew it, and it made me incredibly sad."

"Sad? Why?"

"We'll probably know by morning."

XULAI HAD GONE UP THE stairs, two floors above the place where the Woman Upstairs slept, and there she examined the box that the strange thing had come in. It was tiny, beautifully carved all over with designs of fish and shells and seaweed and waves. The hinges were invisible and the handle was carved in the shape of a leaping dolphin. Now it was empty. After a moment's thought, she took her handkerchief from her pocket and unfolded it to disclose the long, black hairs within. There were a dozen of them, perhaps more; the duchess's hair, with little bulbs of tissue at the roots. She placed the handkerchief in the box, wrapped the box in a scrap of linen from her quilt bag, and thrust it into a niche behind a tapestry where she kept her private treasures.

"Now I can quit being afraid," she said firmly as she sat upon her bed and unlaced her shoes. "It's done. There's nothing else I'm afraid of. She won't ask me to do anything else, and now it's done, she's feeling better."

"Many things you'll be afraid of," said the chipmunk, who was now sitting on the foot of her bed. "But, as you proved tonight, with thought, with concentration, fear can be overcome."

Though the creature had spoken several times, she thought the words were only in her mind. Little animals did not speak. They were too timid, perhaps, as she was, but she was too tired to worry about it. She struggled to keep her eyes open long enough to take off her cloak and lay it across the bed. If chipmunk wanted to wander, let chipmunk wander. The cats slept in the kitchen where it was warmer. The covered jar on her table still had one nut cake in it. She put a piece of it into the cloak pocket, somewhat reluctantly. If chipmunk was hungry, let chipmunk eat, though it hardly deserved such generosity. Why did it have to tell her she was going to be afraid all over again when she'd just conquered a present fear! It wasn't her fault she was timid! Everyone, all the time, told her to be timid!

"What does that mean?" the chipmunk asked from her pillow. "Timid? As timid as a chipmunk perhaps?"

"I suppose," she said, so near to sleep that she could as well have dreamed the conversation.

"Really? When those people came toward us in the woods, I took refuge under your hand. Would you say that was timid? Or would you agree that it was a sensible reaction to a very real threat? Would you have preferred me to be brave? I might have challenged that big man to battle, chittered at him in my most threatening tones, and kicked pebbles at him with both back feet! Oh yes, one knows very well how *that* would have come out!"

Xulai dreamed that she giggled, very slightly.

"Timidity has its place," said the chipmunk in a didactic tone. "Hiding in a hole in a rock or tree, staying in darkness and shadows, hiding behind or under things is an excellent tactic, particularly good for small and inoffensive creatures. Step number one in survival training is always hiding. More active tactics come later."

"Like what?"

"Fading into the background. Protective coloration. Misleading the eye. Oh, many, many other things. Believe me, there are more ways than one to fool a cat."

Xulai wondered if that were true. She had never really tried to fool a cat, though she thought it might be amusing to try. Perhaps Bothercat could be convinced there was something malignant in her left sleeve, something that he should stay away from. Sometimes he was with her in the stable and they fell asleep in the loft with him often curled up on top of her left arm. She woke with a useless appendage, all full of pins and needles. Could she teach him to leave her arm alone? Trying might be more difficult or troublesome or frightening than it was worth.

"Frightening!" exclaimed the chipmunk, who seemed quite capable of reading her mind. "Well, let me tell you, the world can be thoroughly frightening in most of its parts, all of which can be dealt with! When you have thoroughly mastered the art of being unnoticed, perhaps we will take up the study of misdirection . . ."

Though Xulai tried to listen, the warm feeling that had come after swallowing the . . . what? Egg? Seed? Whatever it was, the warm feeling had lasted and a gentle tide of sleep came all at once. Soothed by chipmunk chatter, she floated away on it without a thought.

THE COUPLE WHO HAD TRESPASSED in the woods of Woldsgard returned to their camp. Though it was placed in a quiet glen with ready access to water, though it was well enough hidden that she feared no interlopers, Alicia, Duchess of Altamont, could not fall asleep. It had been a long day, a tiring day, but her mind would not shut itself off and let her go. Instead she lay in a strange half-drowsing state, her mind drifting among half-remembered things that had happened long ago when she was a child. Tonight, she smelled tar, and sun on timber. She heard a huge chain creaking and the slosh of water. She was in a favorite place of her childhood, in Kamfels, well hidden under the pier, directly across the narrow fjord from Krakenholm.

The sloping ground under the end of the pier was dry and warm. Stout wooden posts made walls on two sides, the massive timbers of the pier made a roof over her head—even when rain fell, this secluded place usually stayed dry—and at the far end there was room between the posts for her to sneak out without getting her feet wet. Once beneath the pier, she could stand up without bumping her head, but grown-ups couldn't. She had gathered some old crates and baskets and piled them toward the back, with room behind them to hide in, so if anyone even started to come under, they wouldn't see her at all.

She liked it because she could hear everything people said and did: the guardsmen shuffling their feet, talking, sometimes calling out to their replacements at the end of their duty. Across the water she could see Krakenholm, where the ferry was moored. When people needed to cross from the Kamfels side, they took the hammer chained to the post and rang the bronze bell that hung above, on the pier itself. The bell was large, with a sonorous tone that echoed between the walls of the mountains on the far side. When people wanted to cross from Woldsgard to Kamfels, they hammered on the door of the ferryman's house. His house had two holes in the wall with a long loop of chain going in one hole and coming out the other. The bottom floor of his house held a treadmill that pulled the chain in an endless circle. When the ferry was loaded with men or horses, the donkeys on the treadmill made the wheel go around; the wheel pulled the chain; the chain moved the ferry across the fjord. When people needed to go back, the donkeys faced the other direction and made it come back again. Alicia had seen the inside of the house, so she knew how it worked. When the ferry was being used, she could hear the people getting on and off, their conversations, all kinds of things. Usually it was not very interesting, but sometimes the things they said were strange and mysterious. Those were things she would talk to her mother, Mirami, about. Sometimes Mirami laughed at the things she heard.

Today, one of the guardsmen was new, some farmer's son who was full of questions about Kamfels.

"So the ruler here is Duke Falyrion, is it? I thought that was the son."

"The duke is Falyrion, the boy's Falredi."

"The boy, he'll inherit the dukedom, right?"

"Right. He's the child of the duke's first wife, Naila. The duke's second wife is Mirami, and she has children, too: a girl and a boy. Boy's named Hulix. The girl's called Alicia."

"So Hulix'd be duke if anything happened to Falyrion and Falredi, right?"

"Right. Boy's younger than the girl, but sons inherit in Kamfels. Leastways . . ."

"Leastways what?"

"Hulix would inherit unless somebody decides he's not really Falyrion's son."

There was a silence, then the young one said, "You mean . . ."

"I don't mean anything. Don't repeat this. You'll hear it said because it's often bein' said. You can't help what you hear, but you can help what you say. You don't repeat it because if you're heard saying it by the wrong person, you'll lose your head over it."

There was a nervous shuffling overhead, the younger voice saying, "Well, maybe it'd be better if you hadn't told . . ."

"If you don't know what you aren't supposed to know about, boy, how do you keep from knowing it when somebody says it? Heh? It's better to know what to say, and that's easy: you don't know anything about it. So, anybody says something about who inherits, you just say, 'I don't know anything about it.'"

"Oh."

"That's right. Oh."

Alicia's eyes had opened wide. Of course Falyrion was Hulix's father, and Falyrion was her father. He was handsome and tall and he loved her and she loved him. He even told her that he liked having a daughter instead of another clumsy boy. He gave her wonderful gifts: a music box that played over a hundred tunes. A puppet theater. Of course he was Hulix's father and her father. What was this guardsman talking about!

The memory came back to her every now and then. She had overheard other conversations later, more important ones, more enlightening ones, but that was the memory that had given her the strange feeling inside her chest as though her heart had forgotten how to beat. That was the memory that kept coming back, even though she had tried different remedies, oak gall and sage smoke and oil of lavender. She remembered every word, just the way she had heard it: the footsteps echoing through the timbers, the cries of the gulls on the fjord—Falyrion, her father, said the gulls came all the way up from the ocean because it was shallower here and the salmon fish were closer to the surface of the water. She remembered the smell of the oil the guardsmen used on their boots. She remembered that Hulix would inherit if he was Falyrion's son, and she remembered exactly what she had thought at the time. Who else could be his father? He was her brother, and if he wasn't Falyrion's son it would mean she wasn't Falyrion's daughter and she knew she was! He was her father! Who else could her father be? Usually, when Alicia didn't understand something, she asked her mother about it. Mirami knew everything, though some things Alicia overheard made her angry. That time, though Alicia couldn't explain why, she had thought it might be better not to ask her mother.

XULAI WAKENED EARLY, WELL BEFORE the maids appeared with warm water and long before the hour when Precious Wind usually swept in, comb and brush in one hand, pail of warm water in the other. Precious Wind had begun neatening Xulai when Oldwife couldn't manage the stairs anymore. Xulai missed Oldwife, though Precious Wind got the neatening done much more quickly than Oldwife ever had. For a moment, Xulai wondered if she'd dreamt last night's happenings, but when she fished the box from its hiding place behind the tapestry, it confirmed what had happened. She had found something. She had swallowed it. Would it be digested? Would it come out whole, as some things did when swallowed? The hostler's boy had swallowed a ring once, and it had come out whole, though filthy. His mother had been very angry.

"It simply needed a warm resting place of some kind," the chipmunk said from beside her ear on the pillow. "If it needs to get out, it will probably slip out of your ear while you're asleep. And you needn't wait for hot water and Precious Wind. Though you've been trained to be timid—overtrained perhaps—don't you think you're old enough to get yourself dressed?"

Not waiting for Precious Wind was a completely new idea. She wondered why she had never thought of it herself. When she dipped into the icy water from the ewer she decided that was the answer. Though it was only early autumn, the nights were already cold. Shivering, she pulled on her chemise, drawers, undershift, stockings, and shoes. When she thrust her head through the neck of the undershift, bits of briar and leaf scraped out of her hair to litter the floor, something the chipmunk had no doubt noticed since he or she had shared the pillow last night. So chipmunk knew Xulai's hair would require some explanation! He could have told her! Though, perhaps, he had told her, in a way, by suggesting she not wait for Precious Wind. *Thinking* led to all kinds of ideas like that.

She leaned over, letting her hair hang straight down, a black curtain that reached to her toes, as she combed through it again and again until it crackled and sparked.

She checked in the little mirror Precious Wind had given her. The long sweep of blue-black hair was free of trash, but her dark eyes had sleep caked around them and there was a definite smutch of something icky on her forehead. The icy washcloth got rid of both, though it set her shivering again. She would not wash her ears. If she tried, they would freeze and fall off! Some people might look better if their ears did fall off, but Xulai's ears weren't bad. Not too big and ugly like some people had. It was nice not to be ugly, though some ugly people were very interesting. She rather liked the color of her skin. It wasn't as dark as Precious Wind's, but it wasn't as pale as that of most of the people in the castle. Some of these Norlanders were frog-belly-colored.

Carrying her warm woolen skirt and her cloak (thinking, meanwhile, that perhaps she should think of the cloak as the chipmunk's cloak, since chipmunk seemed determined to live in it), she went down the hall to the necessary office that protruded from the side of the curtain wall over the moat. The moat was fed by the river, which carried all the waste away, and in winter the wind came up from the surface of the water to freeze her bottom. Even this early in the fall, the wind was chill. Finally, skirt securely belted and cloak around her shoulders, she went down the two flights to the kitchen, where a fire-warmed seat in the inglenook waited for her. Every morning she sat there to eat oat cakes with jam, or porridge with honey and cream, or new-laid eggs and buttered toast.

This morning, however, she was stopped at the door by the sight of Cook leaning over the table in the center of the room, tears dripping from her eyes into a puddle on the scrubbed wooden surface. Xulai had never seen Cook weep over anything, and she hovered in the doorway, uncertain whether to go in or go back.

Cook looked up, wiped her eyes, shook her head slowly, side to side.

"What is it?" asked Xulai, though she was immediately certain that she knew what it was, what it had to be.

Cook cleared her throat. "Sadness, child. Sadness. The Woman Upstairs . . ."

"The princess Xu-i-lok," said Xulai very carefully, pronouncing each syllable clearly.

"The princess Xu-i-lok," parroted Cook obediently. "Oh, the poor precious thing. When the nurses went in this morning, she was gone, child. She died last night."

Xulai was silent. For a long moment, her mind was completely empty. Had she known, really? Had she lied to herself when she thought the princess was sleeping? Or had it happened later? Had Abasio known? Almost certainly he had known. That was why he had told her to look at the princess's face. To see it at peace. To see the pain gone. She had only been waiting for Xulai to complete her task, then she had let the pain go. She had quit fighting it. And that was why Abasio had cried. Why? He didn't even know her.

"*No,*" said a voice in her mind. "*But he knows you.*"

Xulai turned and went back upstairs to her room, and there she allowed herself to weep as she could not recall ever having wept before. She was not interrupted. Precious Wind didn't bother her. Great Bear stayed away. Nobody bothered her. It was as though they had decided she should have this time to herself, so she had it and wept.

Even in the midst of it she reminded herself to thank Abasio. Whether Ushiloma had sent him or not, he had helped her, he had helped the princess, and those who help should always be thanked, in one way or another.

SEVERAL DAYS LATER, IN THE Old Dark House, the Duchess of Altamont learned the duke's wife had died. She had arrived home only the evening before and was told by a passing traveler, so she knew the woman had died the very night she, Alicia, had been there. During the day that followed, she felt joyous, really joyous, as though she had swallowed a balloon and might float away at any moment. When her maid sloshed tea into the saucer, Alicia only slapped her a few times instead of having her whipped. She actually thanked a footman for holding the stirrup of her horse. She and Jenger rode together south along the road that led, eventually, to the Lake of the Clouds, and she teased him about something or other and laughed with him.

"Have you let Hulix know?" Jenger asked.

She sat very still. Hulix. Her face darkened as though a shadow had crossed it.

Jenger read the expression on her face. "I'm sorry," he said quickly, abjectly. "I've said something wrong."

"When Falredi died, Hulix became duke of Kamfels," she said.

He did not trust himself to speak as he could not think of anything it would be safe to say. He was silent, head slightly cocked, waiting for her to head them down whatever dark road her thoughts might lead to.

"I was older than Hulix! I took care of all the details. I should have been duchess then. He was only a boy, but he became the duke."

He thought furiously. "On several occasions I've heard your mother, the queen, say that titles don't matter. She says only power matters."

"Yes," she muttered. "But I wanted the title." She turned her horse, her face twisted with hatred. He let his horse fall behind and followed her without speaking. When she was in a mood like this, it was better not to speak at all.

She said something he could not hear. He rode up beside her and said, "Sorry, ma'am, I couldn't hear."

"I said Falyrion, my father, was the duke. When he died, Falredi became the duke. That day, when he became the duke, I asked him if I would be duchess if he died. He said no, Hulix would be the next duke, because he was a boy. He said the only way I could become a duchess was if I married a duke, if any duke would have me. He was wrong. I did become a duchess, of Altamont. I have a title. I proved he was wrong."

He said nothing. What was there to say? Yet, he had to say something. She would insist that he say something eventually. Not answering would be taken as agreeing with what young Falyrion had said.

"I have no idea why he should have said anything like that," he blurted at last. "It makes no sense at all. Of course you have the title."

After a time her face cleared a little. "Of course," she said. "Falyrion said I could never have a title because bastards can't have titles. It makes no sense at all. Hulix has the title. If I was a bastard, so was Hulix, and he couldn't have been the duke, either."

THE ROAD FROM WOLDSGARD CASTLE came across the bridge and down from the height on which the castle stood, winding between the rough stone walls that divided orchards and pastures, the little river that filled the moat running beside it. When the castle road reached the level land of the valley, it joined the wider Woldsroad, which ran south, parallel to Woldswater Running. If followed two or three days' journey south, Woldsroad led to Lake Riversmeet, the lake where the Woldswater and river Wells ran together, where the roads crossed and led away in all directions: south past the Old Dark House and on to the Lake of the Clouds, east to the highlands of the king, west to Wellsport and the sea. Today the journey would be much shorter than that.

First in line was the catafalque, drawn by four black horses with purple plumes nodding above their heads. Then the carriage in which the Duke of Wold rode alone, then the other carriages and wagons, half a dozen, carrying those of the castle folk who had served the princess. Xulai was riding with Precious Wind and Great Bear, and Abasio had joined them as well, seemingly having struck up a friendship with the Tingawans over the last day or so. Certainly his own clattery wagon would have been unsuitable for such an occasion. For over an hour the horses drew them along among pastures tall with sun-glittered grasses and late flowers, scattered here and there with herds of cattle or sheep or goats under the eyes of quiet dogs and their herdsmen, who took off their hats and bowed their heads as the procession went by. In Wold it was said that the dogs owned the herdsmen, not the other way around, and certainly it was the dogs who demanded quiet reverence from the flocks as the procession passed, for the sheep stood facing the road in long rows, their heads bowed.

To their left, eastward, unfenced meadows stretched from the road to the Woldswater, a ribbon of silver glitter rimming the green. On their right, down from the western heights of the Icefang range, streamlets hurried to join the river, some crossed by shallow, splashy fords, others by sturdy timber bridges that thundered hugely under the hooves of the horses.

After the seventh such crossing, the catafalque turned west into a road that ran upward across green meadows into a valley extending into the mountains. On each side, the meadows gradually gave way to gray cliffs that grew higher the farther into the mountain they went, sheltering the valley on either side and joining at the western end in a vast, towering arc. Between the arms of this great escarpment a tall, sprawling gray building stood among gigantic, white-bolled trees.

"Netherfields," said Abasio. "I am told this is where the duke's parents lie, and theirs before them back to the time of Lythany, Huold's daughter. Here Xu-i-lok will lie now, and when the time comes, here the duke will lie beside her."

Xulai murmured, "What people keep this place? I have never met anyone at the castle who mentioned working at Netherfields."

It was Precious Wind who answered. "No. The people who keep this place are brothers and sisters from Wilderbrook Abbey. It lies some distance east of us, across the river Wells and upward, upon the heights beyond the great falls. They come here a year at a time, some to maintain this holy place, some to say their prayers and perform the rites that have been performed here for a thousand years or more, some armed men to protect the others, and when their term of service is over, they return to the abbey and another group comes to replace them. The place is never untenanted, never unguarded."

The gray building looked large even at a distance, and it proved to be both larger and farther away than it had appeared. It was some time before the catafalque went through the heavy gate in the surrounding wall and drew up in the forecourt. The abbey doors, tall doors made of heavy planks strapped with iron, stood open at the foot of the square tower. Outside them, eight gray-robed and hooded brothers stood, moving immediately toward the catafalque to take up the coffin. Others, white-garbed men and women, moved behind them, singing words Xulai did not know in a strange melody that she had never heard. They went up the steps, through two sets of doors, and into a long room, arched high, with colored windows at the very tops of the arches, so angled that sunlight fell upon the floor and upon their bodies as they moved along it, jeweling them with multicolored light. On the walls were carved figures of those who had ruled in Wold, silently guarding the crypts below the floor. One of these had already been opened, its great slab of stone lying at one side, the leathern lifting straps folded neatly atop it.

The bottom of the crypt had been strewn with fragrant herbs and the walls of the crypt had been newly whitewashed. These pale surfaces too were stroked with rainbow colors from the high windows, jeweled shards of light falling upon stone, upon robes and faces, upon the white coffin being carried down the aisle. Xulai, as was proper for a soul carrier and as she had been instructed by Precious Wind, laid her hands upon the coffin for a long moment while trying to think of nothing at all. When she stepped away, the coffin was lowered, and the duke knelt beside the opening to drop an offering of flowers together with the glittering golden crown made in the shape of a branch of fluttering leaves. This crown of golden leaves was reserved for the Duchess of Wold. His people knelt around him, murmuring prayers to this deity or that helpful spirit as they were moved to do. From somewhere above them a high voice began to sing, soon joined by others, a hymn in that same unknown language. Though her head was bowed and her eyes closed, Xulai felt her spirit floating upward, lifted and made buoyant by the song. She had thought she would cry, but she could not cry while the music went on. It was too soon over.

Those who had borne the coffin were joined by as many more to draw the heavy stone into place, its surface already carved:

Here lies Princess Xu-i-lok of Tingawa,
Wife of Justinian, Duke of Wold.

Young in years but old in wisdom;
Her soul is in the keeping of her people.

"I will remain here tonight," the duke said to no one in particular, his voice choked and indistinct. "Xulai, you will return with your protectors and the Wold folk."

And so it ended. Great Bear gathered her up as though she were an armload of laundry; behind her she heard the ponderous shrieks as the straps were removed and the stone was levered into place. Precious Wind followed them out to the small carriage where a small group waited for her: young Bartelmy Fletcher, with a flower in his hand for her. Oldwife Gancer. Her friend Nettie Lean, the seamstress. Cook. Abasio. While Abasio looked on, Xulai allowed herself tears on Oldwife's shoulder, a tentative hug from Nettie, another from Bartelmy. Then everyone was packed up again, Bear clucked to the horses, and they led the other wagons back the way they had come, a little more quickly on the return, for the horses were eager to get back to Woldsgard and Horsemaster.

"What was that language the people were singing?" Xulai asked.

"An Old Tongue," replied Precious Wind. "One of the many that were spoken during the Before Time. They make a study of such things at the abbey. The music, too, was from the Before Time. I am told even the abbey does not know what the words mean, but since they were written in letters still used in Norland, they can be pronounced. The words and the music are so fitted together that the meaning seems plain."

"To lift up the soul," murmured Xulai.

"Certainly," Precious Wind agreed. "To lift up the soul."

To lift it from the princess and to place it onto me, thought Xulai, thinking that she should feel a great deal heavier and surprised that she did not.

It was the thought of heaviness that moved her to consider what had actually happened the night she had carried out the princess's wishes. The time since then had been full of duties and responsibilities, there had been no time for consideration, but that word, "heaviness," now sent her mind back to the quiet, candlelit room where the princess had died.

The princess had been frantic. She had wanted Xulai to find, bring, and then swallow a thing. The princess had died of a curse. So it was said. So the duchess herself had said, there in the woods. Xu-i-lok had known a curse had come upon her, known from the beginning that someone sought her death, not only of the body but of the self, the soul, the being.

If one were cursed, perhaps one would want to put one's soul beyond reach. And perhaps, if one were dying, one would want to be sure that soul was given to the carrier who would have the strength to take it home.

Was that what it had been? She caught Abasio's eyes on her, serious and quiet.

"I never knew her," he said, speaking directly to Xulai. "But I imagine she was a quiet woman of great dignity who never spoke of things better left unsaid."

Precious Wind nodded, and Oldwife Gancer echoed the notion. "You speak truly, sir. She spoke often of important matters, of things we needed to think of and consider, but she never spoke of things better left in silence."

"A trait we might all seek to emulate," said Precious Wind.

"Yes," murmured Abasio, his eyes on Xulai's face. "Yes, that is true."

Xulai took a deep breath. "I will try to behave as she did. In her honor."

Abasio smiled, an almost invisible smile. Nothing more was said until they reached Woldsgard, and even then, they spoke only of ordinary things. Abasio took his meal with Great Bear and Precious Wind. Xulai had guessed why. Abasio was determined to make close friends of Xulai's people and do it as quickly as he could. She was glad he took his supper with them that night while she had her own supper in the kitchen. She did not feel like talking and retreated to her bed when she had finished, sleeping through all the night, as though there were not enough sleep in the world to rest her heart.

The Journey

"WHEN WILL HE TELL HER?" DAME CULLEN ASKED the cook.

"Shh," Cook replied. "She can hear you."

Dame Cullen turned, her glance scraping the table's wood to its grain, the wall's stone to its heart, finding nothing there to warrant her attention, a rare occasion, for the wife of Crampocket Cullen was as dedicated to the welfare of Woldsgard as was the steward himself. Neither of them need look far to find faults in others' care of the place. Pinch-lipped, Cook nodded toward the chimney corner, where only Xulai's knees could be seen, the rest of her hunched and snuggled into the warmth of the curved inglenook, a bowl of oatmeal in her lap. Across from her sat Abasio, whose presence Dame Cullen thought it impossible to account for.

"Hmph," said Dame Cullen, casting one of her most reproving sneers in Abasio's direction. "For years I've wondered why she isn't out playing with the other children. Our children not good enough for her?"

"The duke keeps her close because of why she came here," said Cook sharply. "The princess was cursed; Xulai came because of that. Keeping her safe is the point of it; good or bad enough doesn't enter in."

"Well then, when will he tell her?"

"Tonight, I should imagine," said Cook very softly.

Dame Cullen never spoke softly. "Young for what's coming, the dwarfish thing."

Abasio considered the unpleasant words had been directed at him as much as at anyone and he replied, his voice slow, authoritative, and quietly admonitory. "Not dwarfish, madam. The Tingawans are said to be slow growing, long of life, slow to age, which may prove to be a good thing, considering the years that may pass before the way to the west will be peaceful enough that Xulai can fulfill her task."

Dame Cullen, who found sources of insult as easily as she imagined cobwebs in corners, tossed her head and swept out of the kitchen, her stiff skirts scurrying along the floor like the scuttle of a dozen rats. In the chimney corner with the chipmunk half-hidden in a fold of her skirt, Xulai suddenly saw and heard the rats, the lead rat insistent upon the cadence, his whispery squeak keeping his fellow rats in step until they reached Dame Cullen's bedchamber. She looked up to meet Abasio's eyes.

He winked at her and asked, "Do you hear them? When she gets upstairs, they'll all come rushing out, gnashing their yellow teeth and scaring her half to death."

"Oh, I heard them," said the chipmunk. "An army of them."

Xulai's jaw dropped, though only a little. Things had become stranger than usual during the past few days. Had the chipmunk actually spoken? In the woods, she was sure it had. Later she thought she'd imagined it. Had Abasio given her a vision? She thought so, but she could have imagined that, too. She had been almost sure she had imagined it, but then, how to explain that Abasio imagined the same thing? Or could it be his imagining, which he had somehow put into her head? Some imaginings did persist. For example, sometimes when she looked into water, she imagined she could swim into its depths without needing air. Sometimes when she looked at herself in a mirror, she imagined she saw someone else, someone older, larger, and very powerful! Those imaginings were more than a little frightening. She had never mentioned them to Bear or Precious Wind. They would tell her to stop imagining any such thing. But she rather enjoyed the thought of Dame Cullen being attacked by an army of rats. She had no right to suppose that Xulai didn't want to play with other children, for she did want to! At least, she had wanted to—some years ago.

There had been a time when she had watched them from behind a window shutter, little groups of them moving about, full of self-importance, almost always with a studied confidence that Xulai believed they must have learned somewhere, from someone. In their movements, their voices, each of them seemed to know exactly what was appropriate, what came next, a calm assurance that had baffled Xulai. In time, she had come to understand that they were pretending! Each of them was being someone else! This one was father, that one mother, this one the guest invited to tea. Or, again, that one was a nameless assassin, this one a Wold warrior, the third one a Wold friend who arrived in time to save his companion's life. As soon as Xulai figured it out, their confidence was understandable. They were not being themselves at all; they were not subject to agonies of self-betrayal, to having forbidden thoughts, feelings, and dreams, persistent anxiety and fear of failure. They were being *other* people, people who weren't real, and whatever poise they might have lacked in their own lives could be pretended in another life with great virtuosity. How wonderful to be someone other than oneself! Someone who couldn't be hurt, or killed, or lost in some terrible spasm of obliteration that she knew existed, that she had always known existed though she could not remember being told. No one had told her. She just knew.

Once she knew what they were doing, she had tried to join them, but only a few times, for she could not fit in. She lacked the words to describe what she played at. What did she know of fathers, heroes, or assassins, of warriors and friends? Then, too, it did not help her that all the children seemed slightly afraid of her, or of what she was said to be. In the mythology of Norland, only the Wasting God carried souls, but the souls he carried were only the leftover, twisted, rotten ones. All truly virtuous souls were snatched into the pastures of paradise as they drew their last breaths. There they were replanted to bloom endlessly as flowers under perfumed skies. Though Xulai was obviously not twisted, ancient, and evil, as was the Wasting God, she was still tainted by association.

But none of that mattered now. Precious Wind and the Great Bear of Zol had told her a thousand times that death changes and upsets things. If the princess's death had not prepared Xulai for change, certainly the funeral would have done so, and if that hadn't done it, Abasio's continued presence would have, all by itself. Yesterday he had put his hand on her shoulder, leaned close to her ear, and told her firmly that he was staying with her. Wherever she was going, he was going also, he said. He had also said he didn't know why, in particular, but sometimes he decided to do things without knowing why, just for the nicanotch of it.

"Nicanotch?"

"The whatever. In lieu of a swear word. Obscenity. Scatological comment. Nicanotch."

"I may be a very long time," she said. "Won't you be homesick?" Xulai was already homesick, and it was on her mind.

"Will I be homesick?" he had repeated in a thoughtful voice. Well, would he? "Home was a farm I had been eager to leave from the time I was old enough to walk. Home was a city so filthy, so violent, and so torture ridden that I sometimes shudder when I remember it. Home was a few good friends or, rather, good fellows who could be depended upon if one were under attack, though—for the most part—if they had shared one thoughtful new idea among them, it would have surprised me greatly. Home was a long journey into new lands to the south while people died all around me, cut down like a harvest of grain. Home was one woman, one woman I loved, love, gone now, leaving only her speaking, thinking spirit behind. Home held another woman I had been with but never met, but who, I was assured, would raise my son to heroic stature by sheer force of will. Home was that son, not yet born when I left, a son I unintentionally fathered though I was unconscious before, during, and for some time after the act. Home was a war in which too many good men and creatures died, irreplaceable men, irreplaceable creatures, irreplaceable love."

She felt shattered, unaccustomed to being given so much, so truly, though she had understood it completely! His words made her feel as though she was not a child at all! "So, I guess you're not homesick."

"I've never really found a home," he said quite honestly. "So, you're right. I don't suppose I'll be homesick."

"Well then, you need to come with me to see what the duke, my cousin, has to say." Since she was the princess's Xakixa and her duty had officially begun, the duke would certainly have something to say. It would have surprised her if he had not, though no more than her constant state of surprise at being where she was and doing whatever it was she was supposed to do.

"Why did they pick me to be Xakixa?" she had repeatedly asked Bear and Precious Wind over the years.

The answer had never changed: "They needed someone of her lineage who could be away a long time. You're of the same family as the princess; you were an orphaned child without people to worry over you; who better to send far away for what might be a lifetime?"

To which Precious Wind sometimes added, "When the princess fell ill, no one thought that the sickness was necessarily fatal. It was while the matter was still uncertain that they sent me to bring you from Tingawa. Back then, they really thought you might be with her for a very long time."

"Bear didn't come until later, did he?"

"No, Bear was sent later. To help me care for you and protect you."

Xulai knew she must have been very young when she came to Wold, for she had no memories of Tingawa at all. Her earliest memories were of farms and fields and certain places in and around Woldsgard Castle, of Oldwife Gancer, of Precious Wind, of the princess, who had then been in full command of her mind and voice, though her body was already very weak and frail. Woldsgard Castle had been her world, her home. The princess had been the sun that warmed that world. Her family had been a small one: Oldwife Gancer. The princess. Bartelmy, maybe. Bear, though Bear was more like the weather than he was like family: changeable day by day. Justinian, Duke of Wold.

She knew the duke less well than the others. His portrait on the great staircase wall showed him as a powerful, handsome man with golden hair and neatly trimmed beard, piercing eyes, a mouth both stern and kindly. He was now thin, gray, and sorrowful, his eyes bleary from being too often buried among books in his vast library or sequestered among his birds in the tower. He had always treated Xulai kindly, though never too intimately, as though her close company was too remindful of the long dying that had brought her there. Somehow, Xulai had understood this from the beginning. She did not count his reserve as a slight toward herself.

Though many had loved the princess, only Justinian and Xulai and a few others really mourned her. Most of the people of Wold had done their mourning years ago, when it became known she was dying, but as Precious Wind had said even then, "Long dying outlasts grief." The dying had been long, years long, continuing as seasons passed and returned and passed again. Near the end of those years the princess had lain silent, eating nothing except the broth and gruel spooned down her throat, supposedly insensible of the world around her, balanced on the brink of mortality like a lone, frail tree at the crumbling edge of an abyss.

Xulai, perhaps only Xulai, had known the tree was not as frail as it seemed. There, above that everlasting chasm, Princess Xu-i-lok had driven the fibers of her life deep within the stone, spending her waning strength to stay alive until Xulai would become old enough and brave enough to complete the task the princess had given her, the task of hiding or keeping safe the thing in the box. Xulai had become fully aware of this only in the last two days, and she was now overcome with guilt at that knowing.

Had she known the princess was only holding on until Xulai returned from the temple? If so, should she have made herself go to the temple sooner and ended the princess's pain? Or should she have delayed, just to keep the princess alive? Which would have been the proper choice? Precious Wind said there was always a proper choice, though Bear disputed that.

"Sometimes any choice is a bad choice, only slightly better, if at all, than doing nothing," he said sometimes when a quandary presented itself. "Ofttimes I know I can do only this or that, and I will regret either!"

Without mentioning either the princess or her own late-night quest into the forest, and certainly without mentioning what had happened in the princess's room when she and Abasio had returned, Xulai had probed at Precious Wind, hoping for some enlightenment. "Someone should have told me what was expected of me. I'm supposed to be a soul carrier, but no one has ever explained anything about it!"

"There is little enough to explain," Precious Wind had replied. "When a Xakixa arrives after a death, he or she keeps watch beside the tomb for three days, announcing from time to time, in formal language, that he or she is the Xakixa, so the soul will know whom to attach to. That is considered sufficient. When the Xakixa arrives before the death, as you did, it is obligatory to visit the dying regularly and to lay hands upon the coffin for the same reason."

"As if telling the soul you're still there?" asked Xulai doubtfully.

"Something of the kind. In any case, you have done what is required."

Nothing was said about hiding anything, finding anything, swallowing anything at all. Nothing was said about searching through darkness for some kind of hibernating jeweled pollywog! Bear and Wind knew nothing about that, and this morning, when Xulai had suggested discussing it with them, it was Abasio's counsel (as well as that of the chipmunk) that she say nothing at all about it, at least not yet. If the princess had kept silent, then Xulai should keep silent.

The princess had not been taciturn. She had been fond of sayings, *"fumitos"* in Tingawan, pithy adages that held more wisdom than they seemed at first to do. *"Velipe vun vuxa duxa vevo duxa"* was one. "Wisdom grows from piling nothing on nothing." Or *"Pontos potentos al axis alentos,"* which meant "The first place to hunt for information is in your own head." In the last few days, Xulai had realized this was simply a longer way of saying what Abasio said more briefly: "Think!"

"I don't understand *'Pontos potentos . . .'* at all," Xulai had grumbled long ago.

"Oh, you really do," the princess had responded. "Suppose I need to know something about horses. Do I go out onto the parapet and shout into the air, 'I need to know about horses'?"

"No. You would go find Horsemaster."

"And where did you find that name, Horsemaster?"

"In my head."

"Right, and if you had not known that name, you would have known some other name of someone you could ask. Instead of sitting about saying 'I don't know,' you can always start with something you do know to find out things you don't. *'Velipe vun / em euxati nun / corusus apun / zusa paflotun.'* 'All wisdom grows / from curiosity seeds / planted in pots / full of ignorance.' *Paflotun,* ignorance, is far better fertilizer than false certainty, which allows nothing to grow at all."

"What about that other one, about connecting nothings?"

"Suppose I lost a bracelet. Then I saw a certain page flush deep red and begin to sweat when it was mentioned. Then later I saw him sneaking into the stable and coming out with dirt on his hands; what would you suppose?"

"That perhaps he took it," said Xulai. "And hid it in the stable somewhere."

"I am so glad you said *perhaps.* You would not know that for sure, but *devo,* piling, *duxa devo duxa,* little bit on little bit, assembles possibilities," said the princess. "One should explore all the possibilities, though one may neither accuse nor exonerate until one knows for sure . . ."

There were years of the princess's *fumitos* in Xulai's head. Even when the princess could no longer speak aloud, Xulai had visited, sitting close, stroking the princess's single long braid as it faded over the years from jet, to ash, to silver. She had spent hours chattering like a magpie about utterly boring and inconsequential things: the kitchen cat's latest kittens in their box beneath the stove; the tree in the orchard she had climbed to pick fruit so Cook could make a tart for dinner; the new surcoat Nettie Lean, the seamstress, was making for her. Her mouth had grown numb with chatter designed to bore the serving woman sitting nearby, bore her until she fell asleep or went for a walk or decided to visit the privies. If Xulai babbled long enough, the watchers always did one or the other.

Then Xulai could lean forward to the woman's ear and say what she had really come to say.

"I have done as you asked, Xu-i-lok. The Duchess of Altamont went by today in her carriage. I watched from a tree in the orchard. When she had gone, I collected dust from the tracks the wheels of her carriage had made. I have it with me."

"Cast it on the red coals of the fire and say the words I taught you."

Xulai took her handkerchief from her pocket, fluttered the dust that it held onto the fire, and murmured the words. At once, the room lightened and the air lifted as though a gentle breeze had blown through to make the fire burn brighter. Xulai returned to the bed and leaned forward until her forehead touched the forehead of the sleeper, making her mind empty as a broken bowl so the woman's words could come into it.

"Take the little knife I gave you and gather some rosemary from the kitchen garden, some yew from the cloister. Get a bit of chalk from your classroom. Put them in my hands. Tonight, before dark, take them from my hands, draw a line from side to side on each windowsill and threshold in this room; lay a sprig of rosemary at one end of each line, a sprig of yew at the other."

That evening, while the footman was having his supper downstairs, Xulai sneaked into the woman's room and did as she had been told. On the following morning, she heard Dame Cullen say to Cook, "The nurse says *she* had a good night last night, free of those terrible dreams that make her tremble and moan. Her face is quite peaceful this morning."

Then Xulai knew she had helped create barriers against a harassing evil that came through windows and doors. Were these barriers merely symbolic? Perhaps. Did they have intrinsic efficacy? Perhaps. Whichever it might have been, she learned quickly and applied what she knew relentlessly, *"duxa de duxa,"* piling little thing on little thing to make a larger understanding. Chalk, for example. Chalk was made up of the shells of millions of tiny creatures that had lived in the Far Before Time. Chalk's very essence was one of attenuation, of existence stretched over time. The essence of rosemary was healing. The essence of yew was threefold: power in the wood, poison in the berry, panacea in the bark. The essence of chalk and herbs together weakened evil intentions and kept them at bay, though whether this was intrinsic or merely a conduit for some other power, she didn't know.

She had learned how to defeat evil by putting bits of image-bound mirror at windows where the evil would be trapped by its own reflection and held there until Xulai gathered the shards in a basket of osier (itself emblematic of life) and cast them surreptitiously in the farrier's forge. There, the glass melted into lumps with the evil trapped inside. The lumps could later be scratched out of the ashes and put somewhere as remote and unreachable as possible, for they could be destroyed only by a power greater than that held by the sender. The princess, in her weakness, no longer held such potency. Still, she said, even a mountain may be worn away by a constant fall of rain. Each bit of foulness was worth catching and hiding away, day after day, for even these tiny shards reduced the power of the sender over time.

Almost always it was a woman who was an Evil Sender (though the princess used the Tingawan phrase, *um zagit-gao*). The *gao*, the sender, expected her *zagit* to return to her strengthened by the accomplishment of its work. *Zagit* meant evil, or pain, or death. Whichever the sender intended might return if it had been unsuccessful, just as it went, with no loss to the *gao*. If it did not return at all, however, the *gao* was weakened, if only a tiny bit. Each time Xulai gathered the melted bits of glass and dropped them into an unused well, or into some bottomless crack in a rock, she received comfort and love from the Woman

Upstairs. Each time, she could scarcely believe in receiving such kindness from someone so ill.

Xulai had never before spoken to anyone of what happened between herself and the princess. She had never asked anyone what the illness was. She had heard the curse whispered of, but no one in the castle had spoken openly of it—not until now, after the curse had killed and was done with.

"Well. Presumably done with," Abasio had said doubtfully when she told him of it. "I would like to know more, much more, about it. Who would I ask?"

"Precious Wind," Xulai had replied. "She might know."

Now, leaving the kitchen with Abasio, Xulai thought it would be a good time for him to meet Wind and Bear. She had planned to meet them in the solar this morning, for things were changing, Bear had said, and they had to make plans.

Upstairs, in the little corner room that always caught the morning sun, she introduced him without preamble. "This is my friend Abasio." Having mentally tried to explain him to herself, she had decided not to try to explain him to anyone else.

The two Tingawans looked him over without expression. Abasio merely stood, perfectly relaxed, neither fidgety nor presumptuous, awaiting their verdict.

"Where from?" asked Bear eventually.

"Some years ago I was east of here, past the first range of mountains, past the desert that lies east of them, over the second range of mountains, the Great Stonies, and down onto the plains beyond. There were cities there then."

"And now? What happened to them?"

"Gone, mostly, struck by a plague. The restorers have been busy since. They're still planting trees where the cities were. They've brought back animals and birds. The plague killed most of the warlike people; the ones who are left are peaceable. The Edges are still there. Those are places around the old cities where the Old Sciences are still understood."

"Dangerous?" murmured Bear.

Abasio shook his head. "I think not. The people in the Edges have a noninterference doctrine. They know what they know; they pass it on to their children; they preserve their knowledge, but they don't bother anyone else with it. They have one unbreakable rule: they must understand everything a discovery is capable of before they use it in any way. If it can hurt, they don't use it."

"There's been a lot of talk about the waters rising."

Abasio shrugged. "The Edgers told me the waters will keep coming. They said that when the earth was formed, the aggregation included several huge ice comets. They were mixed and surrounded by a lot of stone, so there were reservoirs of water deep inside the planet that nobody knew were there. Recently, they've found a way out. There's a country called Artemisia, south of the mountains. The Big River used to run through there and the land went on south a long way before it came to a part of the ocean they called the Gulf. Now over half that land is gone. Of course, it was lowland to begin with. I haven't been to the East End of this continent, but I've heard about it. All the cities that used to be along the eastern shore are underwater now, or with their tops sticking out. There's people living in the tops of the old buildings. They go back and forth in boats. Down below, in the parts below water, they farm oysters and mussels."

Bear snorted. "We hear about other places. I'm not sure I believe it."

Abasio regarded him thoughtfully. The people in the courtyard had told him that Bear disbelieved most things he hadn't seen for himself—except that the winning card was destined for his hand. Bear was said to be a dreadful and losing wagerer. "You don't need to go far to learn the truth of it, just to Ragnibar Fjord, between Wold and Kamfels. I've seen old maps, really old maps. You know there's an ocean west of the Icefang Mountains where there used to be farmland stretching westward for hundreds of miles?"

"We do know that," said Precious Wind, quelling Bear's snort before it sounded.

"An earthquake went right down that whole side of the continent, split a piece of it off, and the ocean came in. What's now Ragnibar Fjord used to be a river canyon flowing to the west, into the sea. The river made a dogleg north for a way, then went west to the ocean. The ocean flooded up that river canyon, kept coming south, around the bend, then it's turned east for a few miles."

"Where Krakenholm is," said Bear.

"No. *Past* where Krakenholm *was*," said Abasio. "I was there a few days ago. Now the buildings at Krakenholm are underwater. Somebody's built new ones on the higher rock, but they don't look permanent to me."

"How far?" asked Precious Wind, her eyes wide. "How far east have the waters gone?"

"Miles back into the hills. The track I followed was above the river, but they've built a new road for some miles east of Krakenholm. Before I got quite that far, I was watched by some nervous bowmen. Hulix's men, I'd guess. The Stoneway, the way through the wall . . ."

"What about it?"

"When the water gets to the top of the Stoneway, you'll have ocean running down the valley instead of a river."

"Except that most of Wold will probably already be underwater as the sea moves east from Wellsport." Precious Wind stared out the window. "I have been told that this happened in the Before Time, this great surge of waters, shortly before the hot times came, before the Big Kill and the Time When No One Moved Around."

"I've been told the same," said Abasio. "Back then, it was a matter of ice melting and then freezing again. This time there's a lot more water, and as it flows out of the deep caverns, the earth will collapse into them, leaving only water, that's all."

Bear made an impatient gesture at what he regarded as so much nonsense. "So, how'd you come all that way?"

"The old maps say the desert is a low place. When I started out, I figured if water got that far, it had filled the desert, so I didn't go that way. I went north, along the east edge of the mountains, until there was nothing but forests. People call it trackless, but it's not. There's trails there, even roads some places. People still trade and travel and wander. There's blowholes and hot springs jumping out at you, true, but most places people have put up warning signs. Other places there's signs saying which trails are safe. People are generally helpful; they're eager for news, always."

Precious Wind asked, "Do you know which of the old lands are gone?"

"On this continent, by the old names? Some. There was a place called Florda, and it's gone. There were three places along the water west of Florda and they're all gone. George's and Mispi's and Albambas, something like that. The ocean comes way up into the land along there, and there's fish! My heaven, are there fish! Conkrodiles, too. Or maybe alley gators. Never did know the difference. Both eat you as soon as say good morning to you. The way we know about them and the fish and all is from the boat people, and there are more of them every year. They'll decide on a place, maybe a hundred boats or more of them. They'll link themselves together with ropes and give the place a name. They'll live there for a year or two, until the fishing gets slim, then one night they'll untie the ropes, pull up anchors, and go off in all different directions. Later they'll gather up in different sets of boats and call it something else. Some say it's a courting move, to remix their families genetically every so often."

Bear demanded, "And so, what do you do?"

Finally, Bear had come to the question he'd been headed for all along. Abasio had been expecting it. "I do two things. One way I earn money or trade for goods is by being a dyer. I make fancy cloth for women's clothes, sometimes men's, too, depending on how people dress wherever I am. I do cloths for dining tables or napkins, sometimes curtains or fabric for fancy furniture. Second thing I do is—you ever hear of a newspaper?"

Great Bear shook his head.

"Back in the Before Time, before the Hot Times and the Big Kill and the Time When No One Moved Around, every day somebody would write down everything interesting that happened and they'd print copies of the writing and go around the town selling copies to everyone so they'd know what was happening. That was a newspaper. They had other ways of doing it, too, but they were ease-machine ways, so we can't have those ways anymore. Me, and others like me, we're it. We like to travel and we like to find out what's happening and we like to tell people about it. Like if you were going east past the second range of mountains, you'd probably give me a bit of money or some food or supplies as a thank-you when I made it a point to tell you there were griffons there, plus a few giants and more trolls than I'd be comfortable with unless I had a small army with me."

"Magic," sneered Bear.

"From what I know, more likely genetics," said Abasio. "Mixing it up under conditions leading to mutation. And very few of them are able to reproduce themselves. I've never seen a female giant, for example, but the male ones must have mothers somewhere. They live a good long time. I'd guess giants are a grizzly bear–human sex-linked cross overdosed on human growth hormone, if you'd feel happier about those words. Trolls probably had some genetics from way back, elephant, maybe, or something from the prehistoric past when beasts were huge. Could be accidental, or . . ."

"Or?" asked Bear.

"Or somebody could be doing it. They knew how, in the Before Time."

There was a lengthy silence.

"If you can explain trolls, how about curses?" asked Xulai when the silence became boring.

"What about them?" asked Abasio.

"I was in the inglenook and I heard Cook say the princess was cursed," Xulai announced, trying to sound calm and uninvolved in the matter.

Precious Wind raised her head to cast an appraising look at Xulai. "Yes, it was a curse. And it's all right to weep for her, Xulai."

As though Precious Wind's words had turned a faucet, Xulai's tears spilled. Ignoring the wetness that slipped over her cheeks and dripped from her jaw onto her lap, she said, "Dame Cullen asked who had done it. I think I know who it was. I know the princess was fighting against it. I helped her when I could."

"Of course you did, Xakixa. So did the duke. So did I."

Only rarely did Precious Wind call her Xakixa, and never when other people were about. The role of a Xakixa was very much a Tingawan thing, not something one bandied about among the locals.

"She taught me things," Xulai said, gulping.

"Such as?" asked Bear.

"She taught me that chalk has tenacity, endurance, intractability, that yew has strength to resist unnatural invasions of the body—"

"Which we should not discuss where anyone can overhear," interrupted Bear, who had been sitting in the open window, drinking tea. He got up and pulled it shut.

Precious Wind went to close the door. "What we do, we do silently.

It's best not to set these Norlanders thinking we are much different from themselves. Misunderstanding between us and them can happen too easily. Our sages have said that what may be considered sacred in one land is considered foolishness in a second, barbarous in a third, and heretical in a fourth. And in those first and fourth kinds of places, their officials don't mind executing anybody so foolish or barbarous as to question divinity or heresy." She stared hard at Abasio, as though ready for an argument.

He said mildly, "I've known that to happen, yes."

"They wouldn't think such things foolish if we could show them it really works," Xulai interjected.

Precious Wind shook her head. "We couldn't show them, because the kind of thing you're talking about doesn't work unless a powerful intention unites all the elements. You could put the physical elements in place as Xu-i-lok told you to, but without a source of power, it would not work."

"Why did *that person* wish her dead?" Xulai asked.

Bear, rising, frowned at Precious Wind as he nodded in Abasio's direction. Xulai knew he felt they shouldn't talk about things with him in the room. She started to object.

Precious Wind did it for her, smiling at Abasio. "He's all right, Bear. He doesn't know if he's here for some reason, but he's not inimical. When he showed up, I made inquiries. He's said to have saved the world from being wiped out by resurrected ease machines."

"Not just me . . . ," objected Abasio. "I only helped . . ."

Precious Wind shook her head kindly at him. "People tell stories about you."

Great Bear frowned in irritation. He didn't like being contradicted at the best of times, but he satisfied himself with a relatively quiet snort.

"If we want to discuss what's going on, we must go back a number of years," murmured Precious Wind, settling herself comfortably, as for a long story.

"Falyrion, the Duke of Kamfels; his wife Naila; and their two children, Falredi and Genieve, were close friends with Justinian's parents and Justinian himself. There was a good deal of visiting back and forth. I understand that at one time, it was even thought possible that someday Justinian and Genieve might be married.

"Then Falyrion's wife Naila died suddenly, leaving Duke Falyrion a widower. Not long after, somehow, the widower Falyrion met a woman named Mirami. She was the heiress to Altamont, very young, about Genieve's age, very beautiful, fascinating by all accounts, and they ended up getting married."

"How did Genieve and Falredi feel about that?" Abasio asked.

"Falredi had his own interests, his own friends. Genieve, I recall hearing, spent most of her time after her father's second marriage making long visits to friends of her mother's. Eventually she married someone from Elsmere, I believe.

"Meantime, however, Mirami bore Falyrion a daughter, Alicia, and two years later, a son, Hulix. Then, while Hulix was still just a toddler, Falyrion, Duke of Kamfels, died suddenly. His son Falredi became Duke of Kamfels. A few years after that, Falredi also died. Hulix succeeded him in assuming the title.

"When that happened, Mirami left Hulix in Kamfels while she and Alicia went to live in Ghastain, with friends of hers. Hulix was only five at the time, so Mirami left her chamberlain, Chamfray, to serve as steward of Kamfels until Hulix was old enough to rule by himself.

"Mirami was only in her twenties, a very beautiful woman. She must be around fifty now, but we are told she is still a very beautiful woman. At any rate, her friends introduced her at court. King Gahls saw her, married her, and she bore him his only son: Rancitor.

"Then, one day when Justinian, Duke of Wold, was visiting the court of King Gahls, as he did occasionally, to be diplomatic and show respect, Crown Prince Rancitor, who was then a boy of twelve, told the duke he should consider marrying Alicia, the Duchess of Altamont, Rancitor's half sister. She was, I suppose, in her mid or late twenties then."

" 'Consider marrying,' " snorted Bear. "It was a command."

Precious Wind made a face at him and continued. "It's true that when royalty suggests something, the timorous take it as a command. The duke has never been timorous, and he could not follow the suggestion anyway, for, as he explained to the child-prince, he had recently been betrothed to Princess Xu-i-lok, youngest daughter of Prince Lok-i-xan, Tingawan ambassador to the court of King Gahls. The wedding date had been set."

Bear stretched and decided to take part in the discussion. "Child or not, Rancitor knew very well that they were betrothed. He also knew that for us Tingawans pledging troth is more important than the rite of marriage itself. The betrothal involves our family and tribe, and our money, and our property, and our succession to family title, as I very well know! When one becomes betrothed, everything important is already done. The wedding is just a time for feasting and moving furniture!"

Precious Wind nodded. "True, the betrothal was talked of widely. Everyone thought it astonishing that a mere duke of a barbarian country had become the accepted betrothed of Tingawan royalty!"

"Barbarian?" said Abasio, head tilted in question.

Precious Wind said, "Any cultured Tingawan would consider Norland a barbarian land. Many people here do not read; they have no orchestras, no choruses; there is no such thing as a museum; dance and drama do not exist; and except in the Tingawan embassy, there was not a bathhouse in all of Wold until Justinian built one for his wife!"

Xulai, who much enjoyed cavorting with Precious Wind in the great steaming tub in the bathhouse, said, "I didn't know that!"

Precious Wind patted her hand and went on. "The duke had met the princess at the court of King Gahls during a great reception given for the Tingawan ambassador." She smiled, a bit sadly. "It was one of those fatal meetings that are later immortalized in both history and fable. Generations to come will read of it."

Though Precious Wind had said this quietly, and though her face was still, Xulai felt the words like hammer blows. She knew Precious Wind. She was saying that something had happened that was more important than a mere romance, something of portent.

Precious Wind turned to look directly into Xulai's eyes, nodded slightly, and went on: "Their fates were cast with their first glance at each other, and the duke went to the ambassador on his knees to ask for her. There were lengthy negotiations."

"Negotiating what?" Xulai asked.

"Everything," growled Bear, throwing up his hands. "On Wold's side: dowry. On Tingawa's side: wife-price. That's another of our differences. In Norland, women are so little valued, a man must be paid to a take a wife; in Tingawa, women are so greatly treasured, a man must pay dearly to get one, as I have good reason to know!" Bear still owed a large part of the bride-price for his own betrothed, and getting it by wagering had proven unprofitable.

Precious Wind took up the story. "The ambassador, Lok-i-xan, had already allowed his six elder daughters to become first wives to nobles of leading Tingawa clans, and he had obtained sisters or cousins of these highborn men as wives for all six of his sons in Clan Do-Lok. In this manner, Prince Lok-i-xan had already made a dozen alliances with wealth and power, enough to satisfy his ambitions several times over."

"What were his ambitions?" Xulai asked.

Bear answered. "Clan Do-Lok has been a century putting its alliances together. We are far too lowly to be told anything about them, though everyone knows Clan Do-Lok now heads the roll of great clans in Tingawa. Only the emperor ranks higher, and even he rules only as allowed by Do-Lok."

Precious Wind nodded in agreement. "This marriage of his youngest daughter evidently fit into Do-Lok plans well enough, though Tingawa made it look like a sizeable concession. Perhaps they felt that a seventh daughter was worth building good relationships with barbarian Norland. At any rate, the ambassador said, so let it be."

"Mirami was a widow with children," said Abasio, returning to the earlier subject. "Why would a king marry someone with a family to complicate the succession?"

Bear laughed. "It was his fourth marriage. During the preceding five years, he had had three noble, virginal wives in a row, each of whom died without producing any children at all. Perhaps that was enough excuse for choosing a wife who had proven herself capable . . ."

"Not to mention expeditious," murmured Precious Wind, "as regards fecundity."

Abasio murmured, "Since the king had been unable to impregnate his three former wives, I am surprised there weren't some questions as to who actually, ah . . ."

"Sired either the Kamfels or Gahls offspring?" Precious Wind finished his question. "There may have been whispers, but the queen has several faithful and very dangerous gentleman advisers who are known to react violently against anyone speculating on the queen's virtue. If anyone thought of doing so, chances are the matter remained unspoken—or was spoken of only once by someone who subsequently went away on a long, long journey."

Xulai had been trying to remember where this conversation had begun. "I asked about curses . . ."

"Which led us to Alicia, who is half sister to the crown prince," Precious Wind agreed. "From the time he was born, she had been his constant playmate and companion. Rancitor grew to love Alicia more than anyone. In fact, when he was about six or seven, he asked his father to award her the duchy of Altamont, which was at the time ownerless."

Abasio looked up sharply. "A six-year-old thought of that?"

"Not very likely, is it?" Bear grumped. "The king was so besotted with having a son he didn't ask whose idea it was. It may well have been Alicia's idea; more likely hers than her mother's. It's rumored the queen had a prior claim to Altamont through a former association with the Old Dark Man, and she wasn't delighted at its having been given to Alicia . . ."

"Especially since the queen knew nothing about it until it was done," said Precious Wind. "Alicia was only eight when she came to court, only fourteen when she became Duchess of Altamont."

"And this was how long ago?" Abasio asked.

Precious Wind returned to her stitchery, ignoring the question. "It was five or six years after she became Duchess of Altamont that she proposed marriage to Justinian through the mouth of her half brother, the crown prince."

Abasio ran his fingers through his hair and made a face. "I have to confess complete ignorance about Altamont."

Bear leaned forward to grasp a charred stick from the fire and draw with it upon the hearthstone. "Here is Wold, shaped rather like a square. The square is split from north to south by Woldswater Running and is limited on the east by the great cliffs and on the west by the peaks of the Icefang range; from those peaks the mountains slope westward almost to the sea. On that western slope, from mountain to sea, from south to north, lie the fiefdoms of Wellsmouth, Marish, Chasm, Combe, and Vale, all of them owing allegiance to Etershore-Across-the-Water, where the king's younger half brother, Prince Orez, rules his own lands, left to him by his mother."

Bear thumped his stick on the hearth. "Back to this land of Wold: the northern end is much higher in altitude than the southern end. The northern edge is completely taken up with an arc of tall peaks between us and Ragnibar Fjord, cut only by the Stoneway and curved like an upside-down U. From there the mountains make the rest of the U, marching southward on both east and west. On the east they rise as great cliffs to an immense tableland called the Heights of Ghastain, which is partly occupied by the King's Highland, a slightly lower, better-watered section to the south. On the west the Icefang range shuts us off from the sea."

Abasio nodded. "The same earthquake that split off Etershore pushed the Icefangs higher."

Bear went on, "And is said to have elevated the Heights of Ghastain, yes. Small streams begin in the cliffs and in the mountains, streams that run into the valley of the Wold from the north, the east, and the west, joining together to become Woldswater Running."

He moved his stick to the middle of the square and ran it southward. "The Woldswater continually gains strength as it flows south . . ." He made a circle with the stick. "And here, near Wold's southern boundary, is Lake Riversmeet, where the Woldswater is joined by the river Wells. The Wells rises in many small streams on the Heights of Ghastain and flows into the King's Highland, which is like a tilted platter, higher on the north and around the edges. Over the ages the Wells has cut through the south edge of the highland and has meandered about, creating a wide, fairly flat and fertile valley almost a third of the way down through the eastern heights . . ."

Precious Wind said, "The people of Wold usually call it the Valley of the Wells, or sometimes the Eastern Valley. From there the Wells drops down to meet the Woldswater and from there it runs west to the sea."

"Which is not so far as it used to be," said Abasio. "I've been told the waters rising has brought it a good way east of Wellsport. The onetime swamps of Marish are now an ocean inlet."

Bear stared at him silently for a moment. "You have good informants."

"As I've said, people travel, they spread the news."

Bear returned to his lesson. "Now we come to the duchess. Not far south of the river Wells begin the lands of Altamont, rising toward the south, where Alicia occupies the Old Dark House."

"Not a castle?" Xulai asked.

Precious Wind answered, "It is a gard, or fortress as they're named here, but it's called the Old Dark House by anyone who knows anything about Altamont. Those lands were owned by the Old Dark Man for a hundred years or more."

"The Old Dark Man?"

"He was called a wizard, a warlock, a devil. His people feared him. He was seldom seen. When he was seen, people said he was eight feet tall and thin as a rail and black as night, with a long, gray beard. The Old Dark Man." Precious Wind pinched her lips together. "Some say Mirami was his daughter. Some claimed it was Alicia who was his daughter, but he had disappeared years before Alicia was born. She didn't actually leave Ghastain to live in the Old Dark House until she was a good deal older."

Bear went on, "The east part of Wold, beyond Woldswater Running, is mostly farm country until it gets to the eastern edge where the cliffs rise up. One section of the cliffs, near the river, is where the only road ascends to the valley above, a region now occupied by refugees from the islands conquered by the Sea People."

"Yes," said Abasio. "I'm told the refugees roost like swallows! I heard about them on my travels. I even met a few who had come up the fjord and were hunting in the forests to the north. Odd folk, but pleasant enough. Is the area they have settled part of Wold?"

"It should be," said Precious Wind. "It's north of the Wells, which is sometimes considered to be the line between Wold and Altamont."

Xulai murmured, "Justinian, Duke of Wold, says the line is farther south than that."

"It may well be." Precious Wind shrugged. "More interestingly, the plunge of the Wells over the cliffs gives Wold possession of the greatest waterfall in the world."

"Before it falls anywhere," interrupted Bear, thumping charred marks on the floor, "it has to wind about a good deal through the whole length of the Eastern Valley."

"Beyond which lie the Great Stony Mountains and the grasslands where I was born, and such of the endless forests as have not been swallowed by the sea." Abasio sighed. "I have heard much of that area but have never seen it."

Precious Wind mused, "You've seen the north. We've been told there is nothing but forest, trees going north and east as far as anyone has ever traveled, and west through scattered islands around the north end of the seas."

Abasio nodded. "Well, that's mostly true, but as I said, it's full of trails that are well used and there are many little towns, fisheries on the rivers, farms with sheep and cattle on the heights. The monsters I saw in the east have not come there. The northlands have only normal dangers: wolves, bears, some particularly large and vicious eagles, and occasional bands of cutthroats who would rather steal sheep than raise them."

"Which doesn't concern the king," said Bear. "He seems to be living happily on the Highlands of Ghastain."

Xulai looked up. "This is the same Ghastain that Huold followed?"

Precious Wind said, "Ghastain was a semi-mythical warrior. When Ghastain overran this part of the world—I do not say conquered, for there was no real force to oppose him—he called it Norland, because it was *north* of Ghastain's homeland. On most old maps, Norland begins far north of Kamfels and stretches south far past Elsmere. On the west, it extends from beyond Etershore and the Great Dune Coast farther east than anyone has a map for. 'The Heights of Ghastain' is merely a label identifying the huge, high tableland included in that area. King Ghals *claims* to rule all the territory of Norland, but, in fact, he actually *holds* only that small part of it included in the King's Highland, or, if one is generous, the part of the tableland north of the Eastern Valley. Holding all of Norland would take a huge army and a good deal of effort. The king is not really an energetic ruler."

Abasio had a puzzled look. "But twenty years or so ago, when Tingawa sent an embassy to Norland, it presented itself to King Gahls."

"True," said Precious Wind. "But prior to that time, it had also presented itself to each of the principalities or duchies within Norland. Tingawa was very careful to reach out to Hallad, Prince Orez, and to the Dukes of Wold and Kamfels."

"You say Ghastain was semi-mythical . . . ," said Xulai. "And Huold?"

Precious Wind smiled. "Both really did exist, Xulai, but it is unlikely Ghastain was the mighty warrior legend tells us of. If one overruns an unarmed village of fewer than one hundred people, many of them children, and then calls it the 'Great Battle of Lake Cohm,' we may be excused for thinking hyperbole may be involved. Ghastain did have a friend and supporter named Huold."

Xulai asked tentatively, "Wasn't he said to have some powerful device?"

Bear grinned widely, shaking his head. "That's the legend, yes. In Ghastain's last great battle with the Sea People, Huold was carrying some miraculous device that had belonged to Ghastain. No one knows what it was."

Abasio was once again staring at his boots, from which he seemed to gather some unspoken intelligence. "Is Justinian the only great land-holder who's not related to the king or to Mirami?"

"Ah, well, my friend," Precious Wind remarked with a sly smile. "You cleave to what may be the heart of a trouble. It is true that Justinian, Duke of Wold, counts Wold as part of Norland. Also, Hallad, Prince Orez, counts the isle of Etershore, his fiefdoms on the west of the Ice-fangs, and quite a large chunk of country down the Dune Coast—all collectively known as Orez—as part of Norland. Falyrion, Duke of Kam-fels, always counted the lands to our north as part of Norland. However, each of these places has always passed from prince or princess, from duke or duchess, to an appropriate heir, and each has always ruled in-dependently rather than at the pleasure of the so-called king, whoever he might have been."

"Couldn't Duke Falredi have been succeeded by his sister?" asked Abasio.

Precious Wind frowned. "Justinian, Duke of Wold, says Genieve could have been legitimate heiress of Kamfels only if there had been no male heir: that is, if Hulix were not Falyrion's son. In that case, King Gahls would have respected her right to the duchy. As the situation is now, however, the king likes having both Altamont and Kamfels more closely tied to Ghastain." Her nose twitched as though she smelled something vile. "And with Mirami whispering in his ear, he will likely not be satisfied with anything less than complete power over all Nor-land. And now Justinian's wife is dead and Wold has no heir."

"Yes," murmured Abasio. "Now the princess is dead. Was she sick the whole time they were married?"

Bear nodded slowly. "On the morning of her wedding day, Princess Xu-i-lok fell ill and the wedding did not take place."

Precious Wind said, "The princess rallied, however, and it was thought she would recover. During that seeming recovery, Justinian and Xu-i-lok were quietly married, here at Woldsgard, by two priests, one from Wilderbrook Abbey and one of our own religion attached to the Tingawan embassy. These dual rites were performed to forestall any talk of impropriety in either Tingawa or Norland, for even the court of King Gahls submits to the sacerdotal rulings of the abbey . . ."

"On some matters," sniffed Bear.

"True," Precious Wind admitted sourly. "The princess's father, Prince Lok-i-xan, witnessed and approved of both ceremonies. Shortly thereafter, the sea war worsened, and he had to return to Tingawa. It was he who later appointed Xulai as his daughter's Xakixa."

Abasio asked, "You speak often of this war with the Sea People. Has anyone ever figured out why the war happened at all?"

"Ah," murmured Precious Wind. "It's a great mystery."

"They hold us responsible for something or other," said Bear. "A debt going back to the Big Kill, maybe before that. Perhaps over land . . ."

"I find it difficult to believe it's a matter of land," Precious Wind commented. "The Sea People don't occupy land. They don't have legs, after all. They don't breathe air."

"It was said on the islands that Prince Lok-i-xan had met with the Sea People and agreed to some kind of settlement, but that settlement was somehow delayed or disrupted," said Bear.

"Do they make demands? Do they take hostages?" Xulai asked.

"No and yes," said Bear. "Sometimes they take hostages to make fishermen stop fishing in certain places. More often, they just sink the fishing boats, though they don't stop rescuers from saving the sailors. Sometimes they demand that people quit spilling things into the sea, like the poisonous tailings from some mines or the filth from some cities."

"But why stop all ships from going across the sea to Tingawa?"

Bear shrugged. "As Precious Wind has said, it's a mystery."

Xulai sat in silence for a long moment, finally asking: "How old was I when you brought me here?"

"Oh, a mere baby," said Precious Wind, peering at her from below tented brows. "You were an orphan child of Clan Do-Lok, so young as to be barely able to say 'horsey' or 'kitty.' Bear arrived when you were a bit older."

"Am I carrying Xu-i-lok's soul now?" Xulai had been holding this question unasked for some days, but she uttered it now in an innocent tone, as though it were not really important.

Precious Wind looked out the window at the sky. "We don't know, though it is probable you are," she said at last.

Bear shrugged. "I thought it might be different with princesses, but I guess it's the same. The truth is, no one ever knows until a Xakixa returns to Tingawa. It is after the return that the lantern light comes on . . ."

"Lantern?" Xulai demanded.

"Ah," murmured Precious Wind. "The name of each family member is carved on an individual stone tablet, and the tablet holds a lamp. If someone dies at home, the lantern lights itself. If someone dies far away, when the Xakixa returns home, bearing the soul, the lamp above that person's name lights itself. Prior to that time, one just doesn't know. There have been cases where lamps lit themselves, years, even generations later, and in those cases, it is known that the soul found its own way home. Until the lamp lights itself, one has to accept that the soul is on its way."

"Exactly," said Bear, turning to grin at Xulai, his eyes crinkled into mere slits, his neck muscles bulging, his eyebrows rising up at the outer ends to lose themselves in his hair. Aside, perhaps, from Abasio, whom Xulai considered very handsome, and Xulai's young friend Bartelmy, Bear was the handsomest man Xulai had ever seen, except when he laughed. Then he looked like a monster mask, all teeth, eyebrows, and looming muscle. Even at his quietest, there was always something a little uncertain about Bear.

Nonetheless Xulai returned Bear's smile while receiving a glance from Abasio that said: *They're not lying, but there's something weird going on.*

Abasio lowered one eyelid. A half wink, one that promised conversation later.

Xulai thought, *What do we call this kind of deceit? Not sleight of hand. Sleight of tongue, perhaps? Tortuosity. Blabification? They're protecting me, but they don't say why. They know I won't question them. They taught me not to. One day, though . . .* One day she and her guardians would tell one another the truth. Not now. Without these two, she would have had no family at all. Better to keep silent about one's doubts at the moment. *Legami durs kannak e'burs.* Tiny roots break great stones. The two Tingawans were her great stones. She could not eat away at them with even the smallest roots of doubt. Not Precious Wind, slender as a willow, with silken almond skin and long black hair swimming with blue lights; not Great Bear, with his fierce eyes and curling mouth, his body apparently made entirely of blades and stone. Except for Bear's gambling and Precious Wind's emphasis upon self-discipline, she could find no fault with either.

In this room, her schoolroom, they had taught her the culture and language of Tingawa; how to play the ondang, *the* stringed instrument of Tingawa; how to sing the native songs and tell the native stories; how to make and read maps, mix medicines, set broken bones, help at childbirth. These subjects were taught to all women, though nothing prevented Tingawan women from studying anything else that interested them. Since Xulai was of the royal blood, though only remotely, she also learned many of the things men were taught: the history of the world—that is, the history of Tingawa, since other parts did not really matter; woodcraft; fighting with weapons and without; the stories of the Before Time when mankind brought doom upon itself by worshipping the Great Seducers, the evil gods, ease machines. She learned of the Big Kill. The ease machines had something to do with the Big Kill, but she had not been told what. They taught her warfare theory and battle strategy. And, of course, the princess had taught her many other things that, possibly, even Bear and Precious Wind did not know she knew, things that Xulai would "understand later."

None of which had anything to do with the information they had given her just now. The only pertinent thing that had been said recently, by anyone, was that death changed things. Death had come, so it was inevitable that changes would occur very soon.

That night, when the duke, whom she had always called "Cousin," as she had been told to do, unexpectedly came to wish her good night, he sat beside her on the bed, wiped his eyes with an already sodden handkerchief, and told her he was sending her away from Woldsgard Castle.

"Now that my wife is dead," he said, clenching his teeth to keep from weeping, "now that my sweet princess is gone, we must make provision for your future, Xulai. Prince Lok-i-xan and I had planned that Great Bear and Precious Wind would take ship from Wellsport and escort you home to your kinsfolk in Tingawa. This continuing war with the Sea People makes that trip very dangerous . . ."

"Do you know the reason for the war, Cousin?"

He shook his head in confusion, his set speech interrupted by this. "Ah. Well, they want men to stop fishing, to stop sailing, to stop swimming in the sea—for all anyone knows, stop playing on the beaches as children. We have few translators, and those we have are uncertain about most of what the Sea People say or mean by what they say."

"So we don't know?"

"We really don't, no." He pocketed the sodden handkerchief and took up his speech once more. "At any rate, the overland route through the great forested mountains north of Kamfels, followed by sea travel between the islands that scatter the Blue-Ice Straits, is lengthy, arduous, often fatal. The great ice bears that were thought to be extinct have returned, far larger and fiercer than before.

"The far southern sea route, however, is still open. It requires a long journey east, then an even longer journey southward before one comes to a safe port. From there, one plays a kind of floating hopscotch from little island to little island. The so-called 'new islands,' those that have come up from the bottom of the sea since the Before Time, make such journeys shorter, though some are little more than exposed pours of cracked lava. I'm told one can sail across the southern end of the ocean to the western continents without leaving sight of land of one kind or another. We have decided, Precious Wind and I, to attempt that journey but to do it in stages, gradually and carefully. Luckily, there are good places to perch along the way, and you . . . will be safer away from here—"

"Because Prince Rancitor is still after you to marry Alicia, Duchess of Altamont, isn't he?" interrupted Xulai. "But you don't want to."

He glared at her as though he had been suddenly attacked by an unknown and fabulous kind of animal, asking angrily, "Who told you that?"

"Don't be angry at anyone, Cousin. No one told me, but I overhear people, *duxa devo duxa,* saying this little thing and that little thing. They say the prince is pushing a match between you and the duchess Alicia. I've seen her from the orchard, where the wall runs along the road. Sometimes she goes past on the way to the Shrine of the Kraken, or to take a boat across to Kamfels, to visit her brother, though people say he never invites her. Sometimes I think she must be staying somewhere nearby, for she goes by every day. She looks at this castle and I can see the hunger in her eyes. She would like to swallow it all, down to the last hen in the yard. By marrying you she could get whatever it is she hungers for."

"I am not sure it is she who hungers," he muttered, running his hand across his face in bewilderment. "It may as well be Prince Rancitor. He's in his thirties now, and they say he has grown in both greed and girth."

"Were you indeed close friends with Duke Falyrion?"

The duke took a deep breath. "He was closer to my father's age than mine, but his son Falredi and I became good friends. Before my mother and father died, Falyrion and his first wife and his son and daughter often visited here. The father and son came for the hunting; Naila and Genieve came to keep my mother company. Falredi was much like his father. He would have been a wiser leader of Kamfels than Hulix has been. Of course, Hulix was only a child of five when Mirami went to Ghastain. I suppose Kamfels lacks the kind of society she enjoys . . ."

"Cousin, did you ever meet her?"

"Who? Mirami?"

"Did you ever meet her?"

"I met her, certainly. My father had died that year, but my mother and I went to their wedding. It was not then so difficult a journey; the fjord was not so wide; we went back and forth a good deal."

"What was she like?"

His face contorted, a twisted smile. "We were surprised when we saw her, for she was the age of his children, a very young woman. But she was very beautiful, very . . . charming."

"Your voice has a 'however' in it, Cousin. *However,* what?"

He shrugged in discomfort. "However . . . Mother and I didn't like her very much. Of course, we had very much liked Naila, Falyrion's first wife, and we had grieved over her untimely death. It seemed very soon for him to remarry, so my mother and I were a bit upset with him and not much moved to love her."

"But she was charming?"

"All the charm seemed to us to be . . . learned. A surface gloss. She did not seem to speak from the heart as . . . as my darling princess always did. My mother died that year, not unexpectedly. She was in her late forties when I was born, her only child. But all that happened thirty years ago. It's old history, surely not interesting to you."

She shifted uncomfortably. Being interested in particular non-child sorts of things was as much a puzzle to her as it was to others. It was like the twinned reflection she saw sometimes in the mirror, herself, but not herself: simultaneously a child and someone older. Now she must say something only an older person would say, because it was important.

"Take great care, Cousin. Something says to me that you should be warned against Alicia."

"Warned? By you, child?"

She thought about this for a long moment. "Cousin, if a hostile army is seen crossing the river, does it matter who brings the news? Is the army fewer and less well armed if it is seen by a child than if it is seen by the captain of the guard? A warning is a warning. If it is true, does it matter whose mouth it comes from?" Her voice faded and she pleated her skirt between her fingers, considering how strange this all was. She had planned to have Abasio with her when she talked with the duke, for he could explain things to her, but her cousin's coming at bedtime this way had been unforeseen.

"Children sometimes like to make up stories . . . ," he offered.

"Not only children, Cousin. You should hear the stories the men in the stables make up when they don't know I'm listening." She laughed, a childlike laugh. "To hear them tell it, each of them is the greatest lover of women the world has ever seen." She laughed again at the distress on his face. "I was not offended, Cousin. Precious Wind told me all about males and females a long time ago, and there are enough stallions in the paddocks and rams, bucks, and bulls in the pastures to make the lesson clear. I know people of any age like to make up stories, but this is not a story I would invent. Remember, I spent hours with the princess, your princess. She talked to me, Cousin. I loved her. She taught me much. Perhaps these are her words I am telling you, but it comes to me as a certainty that if you ever marry Alicia, you will be in great danger. I think the duchess wishes to bring the castle of Woldsgard and all the lands of Wold to her brother the prince."

For a moment he did not reply. "She cannot," he whispered at last. "My men of business have seen to that. I hold the lands of Wold in my own right directly down the lineage of Huold! It was no gift from King Gahls that he may dispose of as he likes. It is mine to give as I see fit, and I have forestalled such a move as you foresee by already having given it. The mountains adjacent to the fiefdoms of Orez have been given to those fiefdoms. The arable lands of Wold from the foothills of the Ice-fang range to the rivers Wold and Wells have already been transferred to Prince Orez, and the prince will defend the gift with his life and his armies. He is half brother to King Gahls, junior but wiser, and he is not fond of Mirami or besotted with Prince Rancitor. He has been closer to the struggle than has his elder brother. The king likes feasts with much eating and drinking, he likes to watch performers and parades of men in gilded armor, he likes jesters and courtesans, but he has no heart for battle. The king knows, and I know, that the armies of his younger brother, Orez, are better armed and better trained than his.

"You may be right as to motives, but thus far, Alicia and Mirami have preferred to gain by seduction and subterfuge. I am her target, yes, but she will find me an elusive target, for it is my intention once you are gone to leave Woldsgard Castle for a time. If no one knows where I have gone, no one may be pressured into giving my location."

"Not even I, Cousin?"

"Particularly not you, Xulai. You are safer if I am in a place far from you and no one knows where that place may be! I have no son to guard Wold, so I have chosen Orez as my heir. He inherited his own lands as I did mine, from his mother's lineage, which goes back to the time of Ghastain. He chose an intelligent, energetic woman as a wife, and they have several intelligent, energetic sons and daughters to succeed them. I think he and his family are safe from the witches . . ." He stood up, strode about angrily, pausing to ask, "You have seen my birds, Xulai?"

"Yes, Cousin." Of course she had seen them, circling the tower top in a winged cloud, bright in the dawn light, like flung rubies at sunset. She had seen them in the lofts, feathery bundles stalking about on pink feet, cooing. She and the duke had been there together.

"We who use them do not talk of it much, but you know they are mes-senger birds. For many years I have exchanged messenger birds with Prince Orez and with the abbot at Wilderbrook, as well as with the west-ern fiefdoms along the sea and certain other places, such as the safe harbors to the south, Merhaven and its neighbors. Merhaven is where

Falredi's sister Genieve has made her home—when we were younger, she and I thought, perhaps . . . but once I had seen Xu-i-lok, I could no longer think of anyone but her. Various people send me their birds in wicker cages carried by riders; each bird is identified by a bracelet upon a leg. I send them mine in return, each one identified as mine. We exchange information privately by loosing a bird, knowing it will fly home.

"By these means, Hallad, Prince Orez, who was the friend of my father before me, has extended an invitation to you: if anything should happen to me, you may seek refuge with him and under his protection either at Chasmgard or in Etershore itself. You're not going in that direction, but his writ extends south, as well, into the small southern duchy near Elsmere that I mentioned. Merhaven was the dowry of his mother. I have heard it is a pleasant place and I have given him certain treasures to pay for whatever you might need, as I have also done with the abbot. I do not know the abbot well. He seems well regarded, but he is only human—as is the prince. Either might fail you, but it is unlikely both will do so. I would trust Orez with my life, and with yours. He will know of me wherever I am.

"Now, pay close attention. Here is a list I made for you. Here are the signs of the birds and the names of those signs written in Tingawan."

He stared at her significantly. "You understand?"

"If I am where birds are kept, and if I wish to send a message, I find a bird with the right symbol on his leg. I put the message in the little tubes as you have taught me, and I set the bird loose."

He smiled at her, looked for a moment as though he might have wanted to hug her, but withheld this spontaneous reaction, substituting another approving smile. "Memorize the signs. Then destroy the list."

How long has he been planning this? She shivered inwardly at the depth and detail of the arrangements that had been made. For her alone? No. For the soul of the princess? Oh, yes. She bowed her head, saying, "You are generous, Cousin."

"I do not feel generous," he said angrily, looking away from her. "What I have done is barely adequate, tucking away bits and pieces, here and there, like a squirrel hiding nuts! If it were within my power at this moment, I would equip an armada to carry you to your people, to Prince Lok-i-xan, whose power is far greater than that of Mirami or any of her family. That is not possible, but it is possible for you to make a southward journey by way of the abbey to Merhaven, near Elsmere. If not immediately, then presently you may take ship there and sail the southern route to Tingawa. If something happens to close that route, in time you will be old enough to withstand the rigors of the north. In either case, you will use the treasure I have sent in either place to make your way home."

She felt an inward pain at this. Twice he had told her he was sending her home, and each time it made her hurt, with a strange, persistent aching. She swallowed deeply, searching for something else to speak of, turning the strange discomfort aside for the moment.

He did not let it rest. "One thing only, Xulai. One thing more important than anything else in the world. More important than I am, or Wold, or any of the rest of us. *You must get to Tingawa!* Somehow. However long it takes. You must get there. It is not just for the soul of my beloved. It is not just because of my promise to her father. It is not for any simple, easy reason. It is a matter far more important than that could ever be! You must take my word for it that it is far, far more important! Promise me! No matter what other thing intervenes or interjects itself, no matter how tempted you are to go aside from this journey, no matter what seems more important, more urgent! Even if your best friend is in danger, even if you have a husband or child who is threatened, even if you are aged and walk with a cane before you can complete the journey, you must get to Tingawa! Promise me!"

He held out his hands. She put her own into them and bowed over them, shaken to her heart at the vehemence of his words. "I promise you, Cousin. I promise you."

After a moment's silence, he said, "They know, in Tingawa, that the princess is dead. They know I am asking you, that is, the Xakixa, to make this promise. Both she and they required it of me when we were wed. Precious Wind was sworn to keep it. Now you are sworn to keep it." He paused for a moment. "I must tell you something troubling . . ." He shifted uncomfortably.

She leaned forward and placed her hand over his. "Tell me whatever I need to know, Cousin."

"Great Bear was sworn to serve Xu-i-lok. When he was sworn to service, we all thought, well, when . . . if the princess died, you would return to Tingawa immediately. If she did not die, you would stay here in her service while Great Bear and Precious Wind might return to Tingawa as they chose. We all knew Great Bear would choose to go home. He had already paid a part of the bride-price for the woman he had chosen. At the time, she was only a child, named Legami-am, but of a very good family. It was something of a coup for Bear to have betrothed her and there was plenty of time for little Legami-am to grow up before she and Bear would wed . . ."

"Ah," she whispered. "But it has been a very long time."

"It has been a very long time, longer than anyone could have foreseen. She is older now. They have sent messages to each other, they have seen each other's pictures, they have been lauded, one to the other, by their families. Now Great Bear is afire to go home and start a family."

"But we *are* going to Tingawa."

"You are going by a long, slow way. Great Bear is not happy about that. Also, while in the service of Xu-i-lok he could not earn the prizes he had been earning at the battle games. He is a poorer man for having made this commitment, and I will not let him lose by his faithfulness. Half a year ago, Prince Orez sent three men to the abbey. They carried a very large reward I had given him for Bear and Precious Wind. It is more than enough to make up Bear's bride-price. I will tell Precious Wind about it before you leave."

"Why did you not send it now, with us, Cousin?"

"Better three hunters from Etershore, dressed shabbily, not worth the robbing, than a well-manned group of wagons from Woldsgard, Xulai. Such wagons are bait for snoopers and spies, some of them very clever. You will be looked over more than once on the way. The men from Etershore carried the treasure in gems, light in weight, easy to hide, and the abbey is accustomed to such. We know the funds are safe, waiting for them, for the men brought me the receipt on their way back, signed by the prior. I will give it to Precious Wind before you go. Neither she nor Bear will lose by their honorable commitment. Still, I wanted you to know the source of Bear's discontent. He will get his treasure when he steps on the ship to Tingawa and not before. I believe him to be honorable, but we all know the danger of giving Bear any treasure so long as his . . . habit may come upon him."

"I will be aware, Cousin. Does Precious Wind know this?"

"Yes. She knows part and will know all before she leaves. And she knows Bear well, and therefore understands the need. She calms him, but still he . . . frets."

"How do they know in Tingawa that the princess is dead?"

"I sent birds to Wellsport and Etershore. Sometimes a small boat is blown across the sea by storm, and we send messages on the return voyage. Despite that, I am positive the Tingawans knew of it the moment it happened." He turned slightly, staring out the window into the west, as though to find that far-off land. "If I learned anything about the Tingawan people from . . . from her, it was that these *knowing* senses of theirs are very real. Perhaps only some of them are so gifted. Xu-i-lok certainly was. I think Precious Wind is, also."

He went to stand at the window, saying thoughtfully, "This business of being a soul carrier seems to be spoken of quite openly. The custom is generally known of in your land, and yet no one in Norland knows much about it. Not about it or about you . . ."

"Some in Norland know some things about Tingawa, Cousin," Xulai blurted. "The duchess has a spy here."

He turned to her, face drawn. "I know. Cook knows. The scullery maid. She's not the first. She stays in the kitchen or up in her cubby beneath the roof, and Cook sees to it that she learns nothing at all. Your name, perhaps. Why you came here. Who your protectors are. And that's all. She does not know anything about my disposing of the treasures of Woldsgard, and you must not talk of it, Xulai, not with anyone, not even with your Tingawan protectors. What they do not know, they cannot say. The important thing is that you and they are to go away from here, staying here and there in safe havens until your journey can be completed."

"Where do I go first?" she breathed, her own eyes swimming. "Where, Cousin?"

"Ahh," he said, leaning forward to put his hand on her shoulder. "To Wilderbrook Abbey, child. Precious Wind will go with you, of course, and others you know and trust. Bear will go with you, at least as far as the abbey, though he'll probably leave you there for a time while he scouts the trail south. It's been decades since we've heard from anyone who has actually traveled that route, and we feel it needs to be reconnoitered before you set out on it."

"If he will go, may I ask Abasio, the traveler, to come along?" begged Xulai.

"Traveler?" He seemed dumbfounded. "Who?"

"The man with the dyer's wagon," she said. "He's staying in the yard. I wanted you to meet him today, but there was no occasion for it. He tells the most wonderful stories, and he told me the other day he wanted to see the great falls."

"How could he have come here without seeing them?" he asked sharply, with a suspicious glance out the window that looked down upon the castle yard.

"He came through the northern forests, then down along the south side of the highlands to Ragnibar Fjord, through the Stoneway, and from there down the road that comes past the gard. He has told Bear all about it. They have exchanged a good deal of information about the northern forests."

He stared into a dusty corner, thinking for a time. "That's amazing. I'd like to talk with him. We've had no visitors coming that way for a long time. Did he mention trolls?"

Her mouth dropped open. "Trolls, Cousin. He did, indeed. He says there are far too many of them past the Stony Mountains but that they do not seem to reproduce. I always thought they were mythical."

He laughed, a brief bark, half amusement, half self-mockery. "So I've always thought, but some years ago my birds brought me word that an age of myth had begun again in the east."

"East, where?"

"Beyond Norland, over the Great Stony range, on the far side, where the plains begin. Oh, it was some years ago. I was told there were trolls, and giants, and griffons, and . . . any other creature you might care to mention. We here in the west heard of a great evil building in that area. It was said a great sorceress had flown into the sky to retrieve the secrets of the ease machines and return them to earth. I confess, some of us were more than a little worried over that possibility. There seemed to be a dreadful kind of inevitability to it, but either she never went or she never returned.

"Of course, that was when I was much younger. Before . . ." *Before she died.* He blinked back a tear and cleared his throat. "Later we heard the evil had somehow been vanquished, though it seems to have left a hole to be filled by the next dreadful thing."

"Trolls?"

"I haven't been there. Perhaps your traveler has. Ask him if he would talk with me. He is your friend?"

"More like family, I think," she murmured. "He seems very close, as though I had known him before, somehow. He says he would love to see your birds."

The duke smiled at this, thinking: *If Precious Wind says the man is harmless, and if the child enjoys his company, why not? She'll have others around her to guard her. Surely, quickly, she must be taken to the abbey. Too much danger gathers here.*

"If he wants to see the birds, send someone to bring him to the bird towers tonight, or come with him yourself. And let him accompany you to the abbey, if he likes. The place is known to be kindly and hospitable. They have a wonderful school there; the teachers are drawn from everywhere in this world, even from Tingawa. You will have youthful companions. It will be pleasant for you, I pray."

"When do I go?"

"Day after tomorrow, early in the morning. And, dear child, should anyone meet you on the trip and ask how old you are, you will say you are seven . . ."

"Is that how old I am?"

"It is how old you look, though you may be . . . a little older. I am told that Tingawan women age very slowly. Though some girls here in Norland marry as early as twelve or thirteen, Tingawan women do not become marriageable until they are around twenty years old. I want you to look and act as young as possible for your own protection. The younger you are believed to be, the more inconsequential you will seem."

They sat quietly for a time, hand in hand, before Xulai murmured, "If Princess Xu-i-lok died of a death curse, Cousin, it took a long time achieving its purpose."

His hand clenched around hers, hurting her, and she cried out.

"Ah, I'm sorry, child, but it hurts to hear you say it. Yes, it took years. We fought it, Xu-i-lok and I. It may be that she fought it in ways I don't know of. I have friends who comprehend these things, and they tell me the princess had powers and strengths of her own. The curse could not be broken, but it could be resisted, so we fought endless sorties against it, countless divagations, continual feints and retreats. I let it be known at the beginning that Xu-i-lok was my betrothed and my beloved, that I would keep her beside me so long as breath was within her. Every season that she survived was a small victory. She bade me keep her alive as long as possible." He wiped his eyes again. "She said if it were only to annoy the one who had planned this, it was worth living to do so. She said that given time enough, we might do more than merely annoy . . ."

Xulai sighed deeply, aware that a dreadful oppression had risen from her heart. She had not been guilty of keeping the princess in pain, nor had her cowardice undone the princess's will to go on living. "She knew she was cursed."

"She knew before I did. It was a day or so before we were to be wed. She came in from walking in the woods and told me it had happened. I remember it as though it happened this morning. She was carrying a trowel and her hands were muddy. She had been mucking about, she said, among the forest plants. They fascinated her, and she had been exploring. She was near that old temple—you may have seen it—when the knowledge came to her. She had that Tingawan way of seeing things, knowing things. I should not have been surprised, earlier, at the questions you asked, for it is a talent your people share, that knowing without being told."

"My people?"

"Her people and yours. The Tingawan people of the Thousand Isles."

THAT NIGHT, XULAI TOOK ABASIO up to the bird lofts, introduced him to the duke, and left them there. After an awkward few moments, they decided they liked each other, and Abasio, reading the signs of grief, said some things that surprised the duke, who returned with some knowledge that much surprised Abasio.

"You've actually seen the waters?" the duke asked.

"I have. And I've heard more than I've seen."

"When my wife's father was here with us, he told me it was going to be . . . very bad."

"For those of us who breathe air, that's what they say."

"Your acquaintances in the Edges? I'm told that wise men believe it's happened before and it wasn't that great a catastrophe."

"It has happened before, but not like this. Before it was just melting ice from the poles. These are far greater waters rising. But there's still some time. A lifetime or two."

"A lifetime. Of a mouse? Or a man?"

Abasio smiled. "I was told there were enough lifetimes for a plan to work itself out, if everything goes as it should."

The duke stared at him in frank astonishment. "Who under heaven told you . . ."

"A man I met. Not a Norlander, I think. He came to find me, he said. He didn't say who sent him or how, he just pointed me in this direction. I think he sent me to Xulai—though . . ."

"Though?"

"He did not tell me to expect a child."

Justinian stared over his head blankly. "Child or not, you'll go with her?"

"Oh, yes. I'll go with her." He would, though the idea was very unsettling and he could not find the reason.

WHEN XULAI LEFT ABASIO IN the tower and was alone in her room, she surrendered to all the emotion she had so far refused to feel and let herself weep for a loss so enveloping that there was room for nothing else. She would miss the Duke of Wold and the princess, yes, but the one was as he had always been; the other had gone past grieving; so what she grieved for now was the loss of her world, her home, every accustomed corner of it, gardens, animals, trees, the entirety of the place that had been hers.

There were places in the forest and along the river she went into as though they were well-loved rooms, full of pleasure and peace; mornings with Horsemaster, watching the colts in the paddock; countless afternoons in the haylofts above the stable among the mother cats and their kittens; evenings in a certain tree copse near the swamp where the bell-like call of a blue-plumed bird and the shush of wings over her head were daily benedictions. These places had become as much a part of her life as were her hands, her feet, her eyes! Losing them felt as though she was being stripped of her skin, of her heart, of her mind, of her senses.

Since babyhood she had relished the noise and bustle of the castle, very much like a town with its various trades and the coming and going of crops and supplies. Though she had not had friends among the children, there were others she knew well. She knew the shoemaker, his wife, the farrier and his brother, the hostler and his mother, the armorers, the maids and footmen, the stewards of the various large estates within Wold. She knew the farmers, their fields, their woods, their animals. She had spent untold hours with Horsemaster, first learning to ride, then learning everything else he would teach her. Wold's Horsemaster was known as far away as Wellsport, and though he did not share his secrets with many, he had shared them with Xulai. Her roots ran deep among all the Woldsgard people, and now those roots were to be ripped out and burned, the ashes whipped away by the wind. So she gave herself to grief and wept, her hand in her pocket curled protectively around its tiny inhabitant.

From nowhere came black and white Bothercat to leap upon the bed and curl up by her stomach. Spotted Vexcat crept across her to find his place at the back of her neck. They purred, two cats but only one loud purr, rhythmic as breathing, a constant hum, like the hum of bees in the summer meadow, the hum of the wind in the young copses, the hum, perhaps, of the stars where they spun through the night. She fell into the hum, the purr, while her tears dried and she slept.

In the morning, when she awoke, the cats had departed and the chipmunk was sitting on her pillow, grooming its tail. She thought cats and chipmunk had grown accustomed to one another. Now she greeted chipmunk and offered the pocket of her skirt. She had decided that it did talk. If stones could talk, little rodents could talk. Her cats didn't, but then, perhaps they had nothing to say that could not be conveyed by a snarl, a hiss, a purr, a pleading meow. She wouldn't mention it to anyone else, but she would accept it for herself. Chipmunk stayed beside her, a tiny companion, while she washed all signs of tears from her face and later, while she made herself respond sensibly when the duke informed her of the details of her journey.

"Be careful, my lord," she whispered at the end of his instructions. "Be very careful."

"You don't hate me for sending you away?" he whispered in return. "You understand?"

"Oh, yes. I understand." And, in truth, those two words were all that mattered, for he gave her such a smile of confidence and fondness that she secured the memory of it against her heart as though it were a golden locket.

She took the rest of the day to say good-byes, starting with the people and creatures of the stable. When she arrived in the stable yard there were four vehicles being packed for her journey: a wagon, a dray, a large closed carriage of the type called a company-trot, and a lighter, open one often called a hop-skip. Half a dozen castle servants were fussing over the dray and the 'trot. Her hand was in her pocket; the chipmunk nibbled at it and the feel of the tiny teeth made something blink in Xulai's mind. She stood frozen for a moment, then went to find Horsemaster (always so addressed), who was speaking with Wainwright (who merited an equivalent title, as Wold had only one of each).

"Well, there you are," Horsemaster said as she approached him at the back of the stable where he was bent over a great heap of harnesses. "Thought you'd be down." He stood to his full height, which wasn't much above his full width, a brown and ruddy rock of a man, red haired and with wonderfully white teeth.

"Horsemaster, Wainwright, this will be my first journey outside Wold. Well, the first one I'm old enough to know about. Are such journeys easy? What kinds of things go wrong?"

Horsemaster laughed his dry laugh, one that sounded like winter weed stems rubbing together. "You mean other than people behavin' like jackasses?"

She grinned at him. Let him take it as humorous. "Well, you've told me much about that already. What about other than that?"

"Well, there's animals runnin' off or goin' lame . . . ," he began.

Wainwright interrupted. "Then there's wheels doin' more or less the same. Then there's axles breakin'. Those things happen more often than landslides or floods or trees fallin' on people, all of which I can remember happenin' one time or another."

She nodded to Wainwright. "My cousin Justinian knows your men will check the wheels and the axles very carefully early in the morning, before we go. He knows that as Wainwright you have probably even provided a spare wheel and axle for each wagon or carriage in case of accident."

Wainwright's eyebrows went up. His lips pursed. He was silent for a moment, staring at her. "Aye," he said at last. "I would imagine someone's done that."

"That makes me feel so much better," she said. "Everyone says I'm timid as a chipmunk"—she flinched, for she had been bitten through her chemise—"but knowing you take such care makes me less so." She turned back to Horsemaster. "Tell me, why do horses run off?"

Horses ran off for a good many reasons, each one of which evoked a story that reminded Xulai of other stories and taught her a few things Horsemaster had not mentioned to her before. It was an hour or more before she returned to the castle bearing a sack full of grain and herbs, after which she spent an hour or two in the kitchen with the cook.

"You say we need honey," said Cook, shaking her head. "As it happens, I have new honey from Hives Town, along the river."

"And this grain," said Xulai. "And these herbs . . ."

"Well, I never . . . ," said Cook. "What a combination!"

With the baking done, she spent the rest of the day helping Precious Wind and Bear. Most things, small and large, that they would need during the journey and afterward had been foreseen and provided for. There were even new clothes for Xulai, made large enough that she could grow somewhat before she would need to cut into the lengths of fabric they were taking along. They also had linens and weapons to pack; Precious Wind had her traveling desk and Xulai the large wicker basket she had adapted for the cats, affixing a latch so the lid could be closed tight enough to keep them inside in an emergency.

"So you're set on taking those cats?" demanded Precious Wind with a scowl at black and white Bothercat, who had just leapt across her desk, throwing all her papers into confusion.

"My cousin said the abbey allows it. I fixed the basket especially for them. It's so I won't be lonely."

Precious Wind's face changed. "You will have me, Xulai. You will have Bear, and Oldwife, and Nettie is going along to keep us all decently dressed."

"Neither you nor Bear curl up next to my ear at night and purr," Xulai said firmly. "Oldwife says she's incapable of curling; Nettie would be embarrassed. Bear is far too much the warrior to curl, and it does seem an unlikely posture for you to adopt." She cast a glance at Precious Wind, whose eyebrows were threatening to hide themselves completely in her hair. "Your eyebrows are telling me you think the curling may not be essential. I grant you that, but the purring is, absolutely." As it was, for several reasons. Under the thick padding of the cat basket, she had sewn her treasures: several gifts from the princess, now inside the little box from the forest temple, along with another thing.

When she donned her traveling dress early in the morning, the chipmunk was already in the pocket announcing itself with a high-pitched chitter. Below, the travelers were already assembling in the stable yard. Xulai's fear of loneliness lifted a little as she actually saw her escort assembled. They were all people she knew well: Oldwife Gancer, gray haired and dark skinned, somewhat stout and wrinkled as a winter apple; Bartelmy, the fletcher's son, a crossbowman, so fair as to be almost silver haired, keen eared, brown from the sun, green eyed, like a sight-hound in stance and movement, lean, alert, and nervy. He would drive the chestnut pair hitched to the hop-skip in which Oldwife and Xulai would begin the trip. Behind them four black horses drew the wagon with the brothers Willum and Clive Farrier driving. They were nephews of Horsemaster, and Xulai knew them well from the stables, bulky, muscular men, heavy across the shoulders as a team of oxen, much of an age and alike except that Willum was yellow haired and balding while Clive wore a long, copper-colored braid down his back.

Next came the heavy dray, pulled by six mules and driven by Pecky Peavine and Black Mike. Pecky was a cousin to Bartelmy, a small man with the family's pale hair and green eyes, a beaky nose, and a perpetually smiling mouth. Pecky had been raised on the castle farms. He was good with growing things, quick with his hands, weaving and willowy as his name, his arms and legs thin but roped with muscle. Black Mike was from the workshops and the smithy, called black because he was: hair, beard, eyes, and skin. He was a grandnephew of Oldwife Gancer, and he could fix anything, or build it from scratch. All the men but Bartelmy and—probably—Bear were as likely as any other to drink too much and play the fool occasionally (so said Oldwife), but otherwise, they were dependable as daylight.

Behind the dray was the company-trot, the larger, closed carriage carrying only Precious Wind and her friend Nettie Lean on one seat, all the rest of its space filled with traveling supplies. The Great Bear of Zol would drive the four horses. Nettie was a widow: graceful, wide-mouthed, blue eyed and auburn haired. She had raised her widower husband's sons by his late wife, had lost them when they set off to seek their fortunes, and then had lost her husband as well. She had no other kin but an aunt off at Wilderbrook Abbey, or so she thought, though it had been years since she'd heard from Aunt Belika. She and Precious Wind had formed a strong friendship in the last several years, as had all the others, except Bear, who tended to hold himself aloof as befit bears in general. The others respected his strength and skill too much to cavil at it. Either that or they were too wary of his temper and his touchy pride. Everyone knew everyone else and his family, everyone was amiable, so there'd be no quarrels to make the trip more difficult. Nettie was not attracted to any of the men, nor they to her, and Xulai felt this was no accident. The duke had thought of this as he had thought of everything else. The trip was to be made quickly, peacefully, and safely. Xulai might go on grieving her loss for some long time, but she was not to be aggravated by dissension among her people or be lonely for familiar faces.

Added to this entourage was Xulai's horse, Flaxen, on a lead rein behind the hop-skip.

So, Xulai thought to herself: *six men, four women*—she was slightly surprised to be counting herself as a woman—*ten horses; six mules; one small riding horse; two cats traveling in their large, well-padded basket with the latticework lid carefully fastened down; and one tiny, secret chipmunk that neither Oldwife nor Precious Wind would have countenanced for a moment if they'd known about him. Or her, perhaps. It could as well be a girl chipmunk.*

Justinian, dressed all in the deep purple he had worn since the princess's death, went to the back of the line and there spoke to Abasio, who had just pulled his wagon into line. Justinian had had a long conversation with him the night before; now he shook his hand, then turned and came forward, speaking to each one of his people and waiting until each one of them had nodded in agreement. He was telling each one of them what he had told her. She was being sent away to take the soul of the princess back to her people.

"Xulai is of an age to be in school, and the school at the abbey of

Wilderbrook is known to be a good one; you will stop there at least until spring makes the mountain roads less dangerous. While Bear scouts the southern trail for the following spring, you will remain at the abbey to take care of Xulai and see to her needs while she is at school. Her care is a debt of honor that I as Duke of Wold owe to my wife's father, the Prince Lok-i-xan, Tingawan ambassador. Do you understand?"

And each of them said yes, they understood. The duke had chosen from among his people none who were not reliable and steady. Each of them was fond of Xulai, and though they would not say it, some of them might have been grateful to be leaving Woldsgard, for by this time everyone knew of the cloud that hung over the place. Beyond him, she saw Abasio's wagon pull into line behind the dray. He saw her and lifted his hand in salute. Blue neighed and flopped one ear.

Justinian returned to the carriage and leaned in to kiss Xulai good-bye. She grasped his hand and jumped down, drawing him after her. He leaned down at her gesture, and she whispered, "Cousin, some time ago, while the lady could still talk, she said she was leaving something for me. Do you know about that?"

She saw his jaw clench, and for a moment she thought she had been wrong to remind him. Then he put his hand under her chin, saying, "Hidden in the false bottom of the dray is a flat, rather large crate, tightly fastened and sealed. Inside is the case holding whatever it was she left to you. She never told me what it was. She arranged the matter with Precious Wind, and I have given instructions that it is to be put into storage for you at the abbey." He frowned. "I fear someone may be curious about what is in it . . ."

She spoke, surprised by the words coming from her mouth. "Why, Cousin, it is only some of her court clothing in lovely silks and embroideries. The princess, your wife, set them aside for her soul carrier, as a thank-you, thinking I might someday grow into them or have them made over into something smaller before returning to Tingawa. I will wear them with joy in memory of her." Precious Wind had told her that. Long ago. Long, long ago.

His face lightened, and he actually smiled, an expression at once fragile and mysterious, though with great longing in it. "You will never wear anything more becoming than what you are wearing now. I like that color on you." He lifted her back into the carriage, taking some time to straighten her cloak. Oldwife took her hand and pulled her close. Bartelmy spoke quietly to the horses, and they moved away. Xulai could not stop herself. She leaned over the side to look back, seeing him with a kerchief to his face, weeping as he stared after her, almost as if she had been the princess instead of a mere Xakixa. Would he remember what she looked like? If she grew up, as Oldwife seemed to believe was possible, maybe she could have her portrait made and send it to him so he could know what she had become.

"He noticed what I was wearing," she said in wonder, looking down at her ankle-length, sleeveless surcoat of fine wool striped in blue and brown—the brown from brown sheep, the blue from white fleeces dyed with woad—at the long, silky sleeves of her ivory gown, at the fine woolen cape around her shoulders, at her new and very shiny brown boots. "He noticed."

"You are a very nice-looking girl," said Oldwife Gancer, her own old wrinkled eyes suspiciously teary. "The duke has always thought so. He told Dame Cullen Crampocket that Nettie was to be allowed to make what she saw fit out of whatever fabric she liked, no pinching of coin. He said the same to the shoemaker. Bartelmy himself went to Wellsport to buy leather and fabric. His Grace said your clothing was a parting gift, there would be no stinginess in it."

Xulai felt a great, horrid wave of sadness. "I will never return, will I?"

Oldwife did not answer immediately, as though trying to think of some soft thing to say without lying. She shook her head sadly and pulled Xulai close to her in a sympathetic hug. "Not unless something unexpected befalls our neighbor to the south. She's possessed by something mad, or devilish."

"Don't our people talk to her people?" Xulai asked. "Isn't that how neighbors usually find out what's happening next door?"

"They talk with us, and we with them, of livestock, crops, and of their families, but we learn nothing of her, for she never speaks with her people. She leaves all that to her stewards, and they're as bad as Dame Cullen, pinch lipped and wary of spending a word out of kindness. Altamont is enough to keep any twenty women busy with the farms and the dairies and the villages and game parks, to say nothing of the forests, so why she lusts after Wold, the Wasting God alone knows."

By midmorning they had crossed the streamlet before Netherfields.

Oldwife looked up the valley, remarking, "There is never a time, winter or summer, without flowers blooming at Netherfields: hellebore in winter, then winter jessamine and aconite, narcissus and wild iris behind great stretches of crocus, and then all the flowers of summer. In the autumn the roses and asters go on until the snow, and then the shining holly clusters its red berries along the walls. Always something blooming or fruitful there, where they laid the lady."

"*No,*" said a voice in Xulai's mind. "*It's only where they laid her body.*" Xulai heard it clearly, stunningly, a familiar voice, but within a moment she had forgotten it.

They had packed lunches for this day's journey, eating them as they went, Xulai remembering to put a crust or two into her pocket for the chipmunk. The chipmunk had no name as yet, and she had been puzzling over what it might be called, but nothing fitting came to her.

In early afternoon they passed through the village of Hay, and in late afternoon the village of Halter, towns named for the fodder and the harness each was known for. Just as the sun melted upon the peaks of the Icefang range, they arrived in Hives, the honey town, and stopped for the night at the oldest inn, the Queen's Skep, where they were fed roast chicken with mashed parsnips, fresh cheese, salad stuff from the garden, and cream pudding with raspberries for dessert. Abasio went to his wagon to sleep. Five of the men slept bedded in sweet hay in the loft of the stables, while the three women and Xulai spent a comfortable night in a large, warm room with Bear stretched monumentally upon his blankets across the threshold outside.

The next morning they drank strong tea with milk, ate puffy fried bread with honey and sweet butter, then rearranged themselves among the wagons and were on their way early. They stopped at noon near a shallow ford that crossed one of the small streams flowing down from the Icefang range to distribute a lunch of bread, sausage, and fruit before going on. As evening approached, the land to their left fell gently away, and they looked down onto the lake called Riversmeet, where Woldswater Running and the river Wells joined. The Wells, flowing westward, was the larger and the more tumultuous, pouring down from the east beside the upward-sloping east-west King's Road. Their own north-south road crossed it over a humpbacked bridge of eight piers and seven arches.

"By Brimgod the Elder, some idiot has blocked the bridge," growled Bartelmy as he pulled up the horses.

At the highest point of the bridge a wagon sat atilt while several men struggled to get the left rear wheel back on the axle from which it had parted company. Beyond them, two spans of oxen shifted from foot to foot and lowed to one another in shared complaint. The stone bridge was old, its center high enough above the river to allow small boats to pass beneath. The already narrow way across it was further constricted by low, moss-mottled parapets at either side. Not even a man on foot would get by until the oxen moved their wagon.

Xulai had been riding on the driver's seat next to Bartelmy. Bear, since he had kept watch the previous night, had slept during the day, lying in the open carriage with his head in Precious Wind's lap. Now he roused himself and joined Bartelmy in walking forward to offer help, which offer was rejected with some indifference by the apparently struggling men.

As they returned, Bartelmy said softly to Bear: "Beyond the bridge is the crossroad where we'll turn east, provided those men ever finish what they're doing . . ."

"Which seems to be making a great deal of prancing about and very little progress," commented Bear.

"They are making heavy work of it," Bartelmy agreed. "I think that's the fifth time they've tried to get that clench pin through the axle slot."

"There's dust hanging over the roadway west," Xulai remarked from the wagon seat. "As though a number of horsemen passed not long ago."

Bartelmy muttered, "They didn't pass. There's no dust eastward or south. If they came here, they turned around and went back."

Precious Wind murmured, "West lies the sea and Wellsport. A goodly town, Wellsport."

"Certainly," said Bear. "Full of stews and taverns. A good place for agents of the Sea People to sneak in, for one purpose or another, in a ship . . ."

"No ship the signalers have told us of!" Bartelmy said.

"Where are the signalers you speak of?" Xulai asked.

Bartelmy climbed into the wagon, pulled her to her feet, and pointed to the west where the unseen riders had gone. "See that high peak west of us? The one where the sun glints red from the snow still lying on it?

That's Mount Ever-Ice, and on the peak there's a signal station, fire at night, sun reflected from mirrors in the daytime. That station stands above Wellsport, a free town on a deepwater bay that is governed and maintained by the Shippers' Syndicate, the so-called Port Lords, who deal in cargoes that cross the seas . . . or once did so.

"North of Wellsport lies the delta of the river Wells, a great tract of fens and mires riven by streamlets, most of it low and swampy, full of fish and birds. The place is called The Marish, and at the northern end of it, where the hills begin, there's a small bay full of fishing boats with the little town of Wellsmouth perched on the slope above it. Wellsmouth is occupied mostly by poulterers and fisherfolk, and it lies on the side of Wellsgard peak. That station is manned by the Boat People, who swear allegiance to Prince Orez's second son, Earl Murkon of Marish. He has a manor at the high end of the town. Of course, that's as it was. The water's rising closer to us than before, so the marsh has probably moved this way.

"On north from there, four other mountains make a curve around the north coast. Chasmgard, above the depths of Bone's chasm, where Orez's elder son, Defiance, Count Chasm, dwells with his grandmother, Prince Orez's mother, Vinicia, the Lady of the Abyss—"

"The old girl keeps her seat there still, though she's ninety if a day," interrupted Bear.

"Next comes Combesgard," Bartelmy continued. "Above the steep treelands of Halescombe, ruled by Hale Highlimb, Treelord, and manned by the foresters of Prince Orez; then Valesgard, above the wider Northern Valleys where the Free Knights breed the prince's horses and keep the signal fire; and finally, Woldsgard Pinnacle, at the northwestern tip of Wolden lands, due west of where Krakenhold used to be. There the duke's Men of the Mountain keep watch. The Icefang range blocks the duke's vision of the peaks to the west, but he can look a little west of north from the Great Tower of Woldsgard and see Woldsgard Pinnacle, day or night. If a ship comes toward the port, within the hour it's first seen, your cousin the duke knows of it. If a ship comes up the river Wells, be sure he knows of that, also. Not only that it comes, but how big it is, how many men aboard, and likely, what they're carrying."

"Not only him," snarled Bear. "Altamont can see it as well." He stretched himself like a huge cat and turned to watch the men on the bridge as he moved through one of the exercises he and Xulai often had done together. This one was called the Dance of the Herons, one of Xulai's favorites, and she longed to get down from the wagon and move with him to work the kinks out. Doing so would attract attention, however. Not a good idea.

She reminded herself to be as childish and unexceptionable as possible, turning to stare back the way they had come. From the bridge, the high tower at Woldsgard was invisible, the mountain peak behind it scarcely less so. Then, as the sun fell, they saw a star blooming on the mountaintop.

"There," said Bear softly. "A signal for the duke."

"But none on the other mountains," said Xulai, who had been looking for one.

"Too much glitter from the sunset to see," said Bear. "It'll be dark soon! Will we still go a way east before stopping?"

Bartelmy replied in a voice full of annoyance. "When I went over the trip with His Grace, the duke, we planned to go several miles that way, yes, not wanting to stop on Altamont ground, but with this delay, it'll soon be dark, and the beasts are already tired. Last time I was by here there was a clearing with a brook about a half mile farther on. It's still a good distance from the Old Dark House . . ."

Ahead of them the men on the bridge cried out and slapped one another on their backs. Waving to Bartelmy and Bear, they went slowly down the arc of the bridge and turned into the eastward road, slowly, very slowly.

Bartelmy cast a look first at the creeping ox-drawn wagon, then at the darkening sky and said, "If you've no objection, Bear, we'll pick the nearer campground."

Bear examined the sky for himself, shook his head, murmured an assent. Bartelmy clucked to the horses. They crossed the river, went past the crossroad and not far beyond, around a short curve. There, to the right, through a lane of large trees, they found a small, grassy clearing. Along its far side, a cheerful streamlet rushed north toward the Wells. Willum and Clive came into the clearing, parking the wagon and the dray, one at each end of the hop-skip to form a U shape. Pecky Peavine drove the large 'trot across the open end of this arrangement, leapt down from the seat, and gathered rocks to make a cook-fire place near the stream before fetching a net to the stream itself. Black Mike found a place to dig a privy trench, put a folding lady-seat over one end of it, set a canvas sidewall around it, and went to gather firewood. Meantime, the other men removed the harnesses and hobbled the animals before turning them loose to graze.

Xulai—thankful to be off the hard carriage seat—walked out to the road and the few hundred paces back to the curve. The traveler's wagon was a little way down the road to the east, facing the way they would go tomorrow. Abasio stood beside it. When she approached he put his hand on her shoulder. "I think I'd best not be seen in your company along here. I'll see you tomorrow." He patted her shoulder and cheek, got onto the wagon, and clucked to Blue, who took them a distance down the road before commenting, "Has you confused, does she?"

"I have no idea what you're talking about," Abasio replied, fully aware of what Blue meant. He was not the kind of man who would find a child . . . attractive in that way, yet every time he saw her, his mouth dried and he shivered with a need to . . . to do something about her. He could not, would not, allow himself to define the something.

"Ah," grunted Blue. "Well, when you figure it out . . ."

Behind them, Xulai swallowed deeply. She had rather hoped he would stay with them tonight. Though the glen was pleasant and the little brook was cheery, it felt false, like a picture. As though it had been arranged. She returned to the campsite to rummage for the large sack of horse biscuits she had asked Cook to help her bake before they left. Emptying some of them into a smaller bag, she went from horse to horse, offering a biscuit to each, breaking some into pieces so they would smell, taste, and relish what they were eating. Distribution ended with Flaxen. Xulai leaned against his side fondling his soft ears while he whickered at her, giving him a second biscuit to make up for the long day's travel with no petting.

Precious Wind and Nettie Lean were setting their pans on the folding grill over the fire Black Mike had made. Pecky Peavine brought in five large fish and a number of small ones. By this time Bear had made a nest of blankets laid over the thick grass between the two large wagons.

"Is that for me?" asked Xulai when she returned from the horses.

"Of course not," said Bear. "It's for Precious Wind, but she'll no doubt let you other females share it."

"Why in among the wagons that way?"

"With the men sleeping under the carriages at each end and the wagons at either side, there's protection for you by us armed creatures if needed . . ."

"Armed?" asked Xulai. "I didn't realize . . ."

"Pistols, swords, bows, and crossbows, Xulai. Writ of the king allows us pistols when traveling where wolves may be found."

"And of course you have your knives," she murmured.

"The long and short of it is—we do." He grinned, patting the various places where both the long and short blades lived. "Should it rain, you can shelter beneath the wagons or in the 'trot. If it doesn't rain, you'll have the nest, the sweet night air, and, just to be safe, someone on watch."

"Do you always do that when you travel?"

"We do, Xulai, when we travel. Whenever we think other people are around and we don't know who."

"Or when there's an unusually long delay at a bridge," she murmured. "Or a dust cloud that came from the west and then suddenly turned around and went back, made by someone unidentified."

He stared at her, scratching his ear and narrowing his eyes. "Exactly. Aren't you going to let those poor cats out? I can hear them crying from here."

"Oh," she cried as she ran to the carriage. "I was . . . thinking about something else."

Bothercat decided the pile of dirt that came out of the privy hole was the right place to dig another. Vexcat agreed. That business disposed of, both began a game of creeping and pouncing on each other or on Xulai. When the meal was ready, Xulai moved herself and the cats into the nest, where they could share her fish and she could finish off with apples, cheese, and a slice of bread from home, both bread and cheese shared with her pocket creature.

Later, when Precious Wind covered them with a light blanket, three creatures were asleep in a heap, and the fourth was hidden in a pocket. Precious Wind went looking for Bear. She found him kneeling beside the road, his hand hovering over the wheel tracks.

"Did you eat? You've been somewhere else for a time."

"I ate while walking. Out on the Wellsport road, I saw tracks of several horses, ridden hard, that came to the crossroad from the west. They slowed, then walked east along Riversmeet and on to the top of a little hill where one can see a good distance farther. Then, turn about, same horses walking to the crossroad, then ridden hard back the way they came."

"As though to see if we had passed?"

"Which we would have done save for that desecrated ox wagon. Those weren't the only tracks. Earlier than that, one horseman came north from Altamont, rode on north, past the bridge, on to the top of the first hill, where he could see a good way toward the town of Hives, then returned in a hurry. Then, on top of those hoofprints, I found the tracks of those oxen coming south from Altamont. They stopped here. The oxen had time to browse off the roadside foliage; it's bitten fresh. They waited here until the single horseman returned to say we were coming, then went across the bridge, turned around, and came back this way with no motive other than to remove a wheel, block the bridge, and prevent us from going on. I feel nothing in the tracks, but then, even though many Tingawans have that talent, I have only a little of it."

"Well, I have a small talent in that direction," said Precious Wind, standing tall and staring back through the trees at the quiet glow of the fire, burning itself out among its stones. "And what I have of it makes me edgy."

He said calmly, "Well yes, but any unexpected change makes us feel that way, doesn't it? At least two groups of people expected us to turn onto the Royal Road and go some way east; one set was disconcerted that we didn't, the other prevented our doing so. Perhaps we should have gone on. Still, we'd have had to make camp in the dark. Besides, Bartelmy knows the animals better than any of us, and no doubt he was right about their being tired."

"We set a watch?"

"As prudence undoubtedly dictates, yes. I'll take first. Tell the others I'll be waking one of them."

She returned to the clearing, glancing over her shoulder at the stooped form behind her. Bear was still studying the road. He was apprehensive, or at least as much so as Bear ever allowed himself to be.

Nettie, Oldwife, and Precious Wind joined Xulai in the nest, where Precious Wind told them what Bear had found. Willum and Clive put their blanket rolls under the wagon; Pecky and Black Mike unrolled theirs under the dray. Bear ambled around the camp while Bartelmy lay down under the carriage he had driven. The fire died down. Bear covered the coals to keep them for morning and prevent the fire spreading if a wind came up. When the place was silent except for rhythmic snores from under the wagons and an occasional whicker of a horse moving about among the trees, Bear took his seat in the carriage and set himself to wait.

The rose moon floated up gradually over the eastern trees, casting its pale light into the clearing, only a few days past full. In the western sky, a toenail of ivory moon dropped toward the last glow of sunset. The rose and green moons were said to be artificial. Constructions made by mankind in the Before Time. Bear did not know whether he believed that or not. Occasionally a night bird called. Insects in the trees made a rhythmic stridulation, gradually falling silent as the moon sank beyond the mountains. The birds quieted. The horses stopped talking to one another. Bear sat up straight, shaking drowsiness away. Night moved toward its center: no owl, no bat, no sleepy bird meant it was unusually, *unseemly* quiet.

All of which changed in an instant. Something howled in the woods. A horse screamed, then another and another. More howls, more screams, noises of breaking branches, then a flash of lightning! A thunder of hooves, all the horses, all the mules, gone, away, faster than one might imagine! Precious Wind was standing beside the carriage, her firm hand on his knee.

"We thought there'd be something, and that was it," she murmured in a cool tone of very slight annoyance. "It wasn't wolves."

"No," he mused. "Wolves don't break hobbles, and neither do lightning bolts."

"What now?" she asked.

"Wait until light," he said between clenched teeth. "Horsemaster has his horses trained like homing pigeons! They'll be all the way back at Woldsgard castle by morning!"

"Never mind," said a small voice.

He looked down to see Xulai standing just behind Precious Wind, her eyes glued half-shut with sleep.

"Just go to sleep, Bear," she said. "You, too, Precious Wind. Likely the witch has done all she's going to do. By morning, the animals should all be back, right here." She yawned and turned back the way she had come. Giving Bear an incredulous look, Precious Wind went after her.

"So you're not worried about the horses?" Precious Wind asked.

Xulai spoke as though from a dream. "I'd be more worried about the thing she sent to chase the horses, but I think something—maybe a chipmunk or something—killed it." She trudged to the edge of her nest, falling drowsily into it beside the sleeping cats.

Precious Wind's usually expressionless face bore a look of astonishment. "So a *chipmunk or something* killed it?"

"So she said," said Oldwife Gancer from among the blankets.

"What was *it*, and what might that *something* have been?"

Oldwife shook her head slowly, brow furrowed. "Someone sent something to prevent our leaving here. Someone else sent *something* to do away with it. You know, Xulai is, ah . . . distant kin to Xu-i-lok. And she was a granddaughter of someone very famous in their country."

"I know. But she's never before—"

"I'm just saying maybe she's got some family talents, is all. If people'd let her be, they'd prob'lya known that by now."

Precious Wind returned to the nest, Bear to his carriage seat. Though he wakened several times during the night thinking he heard horses on the road they had crossed, all was peaceful. In the morning all the mules and horses were back, trailing the ends of their severed hobbles and showing embarrassment in equine fashion, studiously chomping with their noses near the ground, tending to graze near Xulai while avoiding the eyes of those who harnessed them.

Precious Wind took Xulai to a private place among the trees and asked her to explain.

She flushed uncomfortably. "I'm not really sure. Remember I asked you if you thought I was carrying Xu-i-lok's soul yet?"

Precious Wind said, "Yes. So?"

"You said I likely was. I asked because—I've been having these strange thoughts and ideas that seemed to come from . . . from someone else." She fell silent, fumbling with the buttons of her coat. She was not going to say a chipmunk was talking to her. She had firmly decided that was one thing she was not going to share.

Precious Wind patted her shoulder. "Just tell me, Xulai. No matter what it is, you have nothing to be embarrassed about." At this comforting, too-consoling voice, Xulai felt the strange feeling again. As though she wanted to snarl or shout, though she had never in her short life snarled or shouted. "I'm *not* embarrassed!" she said, in a voice a trifle more loud than her usual one. "That is, I don't think so. It's just, things jump out at me when I least expect it . . ."

"Things?"

"*Fumitos. Velipe vun vuxa duxa vevo duxa.* My cousin the duke said we would pass near Altamont. That's a little thing. He said the duchess might be curious about anyone who was associated with Princess Xu-i-lok. That's a little thing. Another little thing I know is that the duchess has had a spy in Castle Woldsgard—"

"How do you know that?" asked Precious Wind, trying to keep her voice very level and calm.

Xulai took a moment to decide among unrelated truths and came up with a plausible selection. "The duchess travels along the road. I've seen her, even though she hasn't seen me. I overheard her telling someone."

"You told the duke?"

"He already knew. The spy knows about you and Bear being at Wold, too. And she knows about me, of course. But that's all she knows. Still, these little things assembled in my head and a picture came to me. No. It was more a *likelihood* than a picture, a *probability* of the duchess getting very close to us. Not merely close, but close while we were upset or uncomfortable. You know . . ."

"While we were at a disadvantage," Precious Wind offered.

Yes, that was it! "Exactly. Well, if we were to be put at a disadvantage, something would have to happen to us while we were traveling . . ."

"Something?" Precious wind cocked her head.

"Something going wrong. So I asked Wainwright and Horsemaster what kinds of things go wrong when people travel. Horsemaster said aside from people behaving like jackasses, it's usually a matter of horses running away; Wainwright said it was usually axles and wheels. So I suggested that the duke just knew he'd look at the wheels and axles very carefully right before we left. It seemed . . . appropriate."

"Appropriate," said Precious Wind, her eyebrows rising slowly into her hair. "And?"

Xulai murmured, "Wainwright found two wheels that had been tri-fled with, not very expertly, he said, but enough to cause us trouble. The spy is only a kitchen maid, and she probably didn't have the tools to do much damage, and he had time to fix the wheels and to put spare parts for each in the dray."

"And the horses?" Precious Wind demanded.

"People say Horsemaster has all his stock enchanted. He doesn't really. He's just trained all his stock to come to him because he regularly feeds them biscuits which they like very, very much. They are fed only at Woldsgard, or by him personally, so anywhere else they happen to be is non-biscuit country, and if they are away, they hurry home to biscuit country as soon as they can. So, Cook and I baked a great many Horsemaster biscuits for them. I've been feeding them some along the way whenever we stop. That made whatever place I am biscuit country. We must continue doing it, of course. They have to understand that biscuit country travels with us, and only us."

"You have more of the biscuits?"

"Enough for a few days, and enough ingredients to make more. I know how to make them, even over a campfire. We should see that they get biscuits from us, no one else. All the horses and mules ate them last night, and once they calmed down when the thing quit chasing them, they came back to us."

"What thing was that?" asked Precious Wind.

Xulai staggered slightly, as though she had encountered something unpleasant. "I don't know. I couldn't . . . *I couldn't see it!*" She shivered. "Maybe something happened to it? Maybe it ran into a . . . protection, or something."

Precious Wind put her hand on Xulai's shoulder, squeezed it gently, and swallowed, trying to moisten her very dry mouth. "It bothers you that you couldn't see it?"

"I should have been able to see it, don't you think? I saw most of the rest of it!"

"Some things are hidden more deeply than others, but the important thing is the animals all came back. I wouldn't worry about whatever the *rest of it* was." She took a deep breath. "Are you prepared for other eventualities as well? Something we should know about?"

Xulai shook her head slowly, tiredly. "I don't remember. It was all very strange and uncomfortable." She stopped, holding her chest as though it hurt to breathe. "Though maybe it would be a good idea to put all those broken hobbles away in the wagon. If the horses were only loosely picketed, we can say we thought it was only a windstorm. I'd rather pretend it was a windstorm. We shouldn't mention the thing, whatever it was. And, Precious Wind, please don't tell Bear."

"Whyever not? Don't you think he needs to know?"

"Something tells me . . . something like that other telling, it says no, he shouldn't know about me, about this thing that happens to me. Just you and me, Precious Wind. Nobody else should know anything about that."

"And you think the duchess is going to drop in for a visit?"

Xulai reached for the reassurance of Precious Wind's hand. "Wasn't that what it was all about? Giving her an excuse to look at us."

"Yes, but I don't think we'll wait for it to happen here, on her home ground." Precious Wind moved toward the men to give them quick instructions, getting a brief argument from Bear.

Pecky filled in the privy. Xulai stamped down the disturbed earth and covered it with a few fallen branches while Precious Wind watched, wondering. Willum and Clive moved quickly to hide the broken hobbles and finish the harnessing. Black Mike rolled up the bedding and stowed it in the wagons. The kettle boiled; Nettie filled the tea mugs; Black Mike drowned the fire; Oldwife passed out bread, cheese, and fruit as everyone climbed upon or into the vehicles.

"You're putting her in the open carriage?" Bear asked Precious Wind. "She looks very tired."

"Oldwife will be with her. There's going to be a confrontation; we both know it. She is far too tired to have it last longer than it must, so let's get it over with. She will rest better once it's done. And, Bear, I'm going to drive."

He started to object, saw her face, changed his mind, and went to switch drivers about. Precious Wind leapt lightly into the driver's seat of the hop-skip, Oldwife and Xulai behind her, in plain view of anyone who wanted to get a look.

They retraced their way to the crossroads and turned eastward. They had not gone far before Bartelmy, at the rear of the procession, heard the pounding of many hooves behind him. At once he began to whistle

a lively air. Pecky joined in, then Black Mike. Precious Wind turned
to look over her shoulder, saying, "Company arriving," barely keeping
herself from gaping in amazement. Behind her on the carriage seat a
tiny child was playing with a kitten. Xulai was a child, yes, but . . . but
she wasn't this child. This one was a mere toddler, a child of three or
four snuggled against Oldwife's side, a rounded little face, deathly pale,
a blot of dark jacket and flow of striped skirt, all perfectly solid and in
keeping, except that bordering the little figure was an area of shattered
vision, not a vacancy but a perfectly appropriate blotch of brown leather
(the carriage seat), a fringy bit of rose color (Oldwife's knitted shawl),
and a spread of light brown cloth (Oldwife's broad skirts), all correct,
yet all subtly and worryingly wrong, as though the areas were reflected
from somewhere else, the reflection bordering the child perhaps covering some larger being.

Oldwife looked ahead blindly, as though she did not see. Precious
Wind faced forward quickly as the approaching horses came at a gallop.
They broke into two groups, surged around the last carriage, and raced
along the road on either side, sped by the first wagon, wheeled and
blocked the road—some twenty of them, half with bows and half with
lances, though their arms were at rest. Among them was one woman
riding sidesaddle, her long, black skirts trailing almost to the ground,
her pale, perfect face as still as though carved of stone, her lips angrily compressed, her eyes slitted, watchful, voracious. Beside her a tall,
darkly bearded man on a huge black horse towered over them all.

Precious Wind pulled the team to a stop and adopted a posture of
servility. It made her look fairly witless, which was often useful.

The woman rode forward, stopped beside the carriage, and leaned
over.

"Well, pretty little one, where are you going?"

The child buried her head in Oldwife's breast, peeking at the rider
from behind the kitten.

"Pardon, m'lady," said Oldwife without looking at Xulai. "She's shy.
Poor little thing."

"You're from Woldsgard," said the woman. "And where are you
headed?"

"To the abbey at Wilderbrook, m'lady. This little one will be schooled
there 'til it's safe to send her home to Tingawa, where her folks live."

Xulai began to sob into Oldwife's breast. Precious Wind shivered. The sobs were authentic. The child was frightened.

Oldwife murmured, "She's sad to leave the castle. Poor little thing, she's been there since she was only an infant."

"Why?" demanded the rider, sneeringly insistent. "Why are Tinga-wans here at all?"

"Shush," said Oldwife with some severity. "You're frightening her."

"I can explain, ma'am," said Precious Wind, eager to draw the woman's attention away from Oldwife and the child. "Among our people, when one of us dies far from home, we send somebody to be what we call a soul carrier, to bring the soul of the dead back to Tingawa. Some time ago, when Prince Lok-i-xan heard his daughter was so ill, he sent this child to be his daughter's soul carrier. We're just her caretakers; the old lady is her nursemaid. Now that the princess is dead, the war with the Sea People prevents our taking the child home by way of Wellsport, so Duke Woldsgard has arranged for her to be educated at the abbey until it's safe for us to go by another route. If we have trespassed in any way, we deeply apologize."

The rider smiled, a tight, one-sided smile of disbelief, and the tall man beside her said, "We did rather wonder at the number of wagons. Does one infant need all this?"

Oldwife answered with some asperity. "We do what the duke orders, sir, ma'am. And the duke does what he thinks Prince Lok-i-xan would wish. The duke says we may be a long time on the way, so we should be well provided for. That's proper respect for the Tingawan ambassador to the court of King Gahls, and our master would not want to stint what's proper."

The man, with a sidelong glance at the woman beside him, spoke again. "I'm sure the Duchess of Altamont has no wish to impede whatever the duke thinks proper."

The duchess's mouth twisted, half-smile, half-jeer. "Quite right, Jenger. We will not stand in the way of the duke's menials getting on with their journey, though the child seems scarcely worth the trouble." She hauled on the reins, turning the horse as he reared. She looked at them over her shoulder, speaking to Precious Wind. "Were you at all distressed by the storm last night?"

"Oh, indeed we were, ma'am. It caught us unaware. We hadn't tied the horses, so they bolted. If they hadn't all gathered into a herd down by the stream, we'd have been all day rounding them up."

"Into a herd? How unusual. I would have thought the wolves would have driven them a considerable distance."

Precious Wind shook her head as though puzzled. "I didn't hear any wolves, ma'am. I heard thunder, though, and that could have drowned out other sounds."

The duchess shook her reins and rode away, her mouth pinched with dissatisfaction, the tall man close beside her.

When they were out of sight and hearing, Precious Wind breathed deeply and beckoned Bear to bring the closed carriage forward. "Let's rearrange things a bit." Seeming to see nothing out of the ordinary, he lifted Xulai into it while Nettie Lean took her place in the open carriage and Precious Wind took the seat beside Xulai. With his shoulders inside the closed carriage, Bear murmured, "Armed men? That was threatening."

"Intended so," said Precious Wind, drawing Xulai close beside her. Xulai turned her white face away from Bear, too drained of energy to be able to talk. After a moment, he shut the carriage door, and the wagons began to move, at which point Xulai burst into tears.

"Now, now, now," whispered Precious Wind. "What's all this?"

"I don't know," Xulai cried. "I don't know what I'm doing!"

"You're doing very well, Xulai. You're doing remarkably well . . ."

Xulai tried to speak sensibly, but the words came out as weary wailing: "How can I be doing well? I don't understand anything! Nobody does. My cousin told me I'm going home. Doesn't he understand Woldsgard *is* my home? How could he not understand that? And last night you and Bear were very strange to me about the horses. And just now, when you turned around in the wagon, you looked at me as though you didn't even know me!"

Precious Wind hugged her close, murmuring, "What were you thinking, Xulai? When I did that?"

"I was thinking about . . ." She had been going to say she had been thinking about what the chipmunk said, about timidity, about hiding. She didn't want to speak of that. She would speak of something else, someone else. The children, yes! "I was thinking about the children at Woldsgard. How sure they were when they played at being other people, how easily they did it. No hesitation at all. No worry about it being real or not. While they were playing, they just believed they were other people."

Precious Wind held her, rocked her. "Was that all?"

That hadn't been all. It had been one little nothing awaiting another little nothing. *Duxa devo duxa.* "There was something the duke, my cousin, said. He thought it would be better if I seemed as young as possible. So I thought of playing at being a very little one, someone like Bartelmy's littlest sister . . ."

"That's wonderful, really. You imagined it so well that everyone who saw you believed that's what size you were, and it took me very much by surprise, that's all."

Xulai tried to dry her eyes. "I was surprised, too, and I really don't like being surprised. I'm tired of surprises! I wouldn't have done it if I hadn't been so tired. Now I just want things to be quiet for a while."

Precious Wind held her, stroking her back, rocking her gently with the motion of the carriage. After a time, Xulai's eyes closed and she sighed her way into sleep.

In the foremost carriage, Oldwife struggled to get a reluctant black and white cat back into the basket with his brother, meanwhile remarking to Bear, "Poor little thing. I don't know how she managed to face up to that awful woman, but it seemed to take all the child's strength, whatever it was."

Bear stared between the horses' ears at the long road ahead of them, hiding his annoyed, almost angry expression. "I'm sure it takes strength, Oldwife. Someone's."

Pursued
by a Witch

WHEN THEY HAD FALLEN BEHIND THE TRAVELERS FROM Woldsgard, the
duchess sent her men back to Altamont while she and Jenger followed
more slowly. It had long been his business to be attentive to his mistress's moods. Though he did not know why the recent encounter had
set her off, he knew very well she was in a temper.

"Now that you've seen the soul carrier," he said soothingly, "you
should be satisfied and relieved."

The duchess snarled. "I've seen her, yes, but not where she should
have been, which was where they camped! What was that nonsense
about not hearing wolves? They should have heard wolves!"

"You've told me that the sendings from the machine don't always
arrive in the form you intended." His mouth was dry, as it often was
when his mistress was upset, for her anger could turn on any convenient target. He concentrated on keeping his voice calm and soothing.
"You've told me it can happen without any purposeful intervention at
all, simply because the moon was in the wrong quarter or because the
machine is very old. You even described it to me as being like a card
game. You said even a skilled player cannot win every hand. So, since
it's obvious no one in that witless group we just looked at would have
any idea about the matter, your wolves must have been hunted down by
one of those unexpected fluctuations or malfunctions you've told me
about."

The duchess shook her head angrily. "The child can't be more than
four or five. What would she have been doing alone in the forest?"

He rubbed the back of his neck, the only evidence of frustration he allowed himself. "As I remarked at the time, your spy may have been mistaken. The castle swarms with children, and perhaps she saw one of them up to some mischief, but what does it matter? The Duchess of Wold is dead; long live the new Duchess of Wold." He forced a smile. "Your way into his heart is open if it should be his heart that interests you. Why obsess about a child?"

"I care nothing for his heart, Jenger, as you know well. And it isn't so much the child I worry about as the place she comes from: Tingawa." The duchess raised one nostril as though scenting something foul. "While Mirami and I were at the court of King Gahls, the court seer cast the bones. He warned me of a shadow in the direction of Tingawa."

"The court seer? My lady, oh, consider him. A man so old he cannot see his own face in the mirror? So feeble he needs two attendants to get him out of bed in the morning! And so, he has seen a shadow! I'll wager that he sees little but shadows! He usually delivers them in assortments: half a dozen dismemberments, a fire, a flood, perhaps an invasion of vampires or kraken." He relaxed slightly as he saw her smile.

"As he did, yes." She gestured fretfully. "Perhaps it's simply that this soul-carrying business seems unbelievable, outlandish to me. The very word 'Tingawa' sets me on edge for some reason. Is it really their custom?"

He adopted a ponderous and thoughtful expression, weighty with assurance. "Ma'am, it seems unbelievable only because it is outlandish. Tingawa is far away and many of its customs seems strange to us, though I believe we have adopted the habit of bathing in the winter, which seemed equally outlandish when we first heard of it." He smiled sweetly at her, willing her to return his smile. "I assure you it is a true custom, frequently spoken of, particularly among the noble houses. Tingawans of dynastic families have a fanatical attachment to their ancestral lands, their temples, their ancestral ghosts. They feel a continuity that is longer than their lifetimes. Part of it is merely historic but the larger part might be called spiritual."

"Spiritual," she spat. "Nonsense."

"I merely use their word. They would say spiritual. The spirits of the people who have kept the land are considered to be integral parts of that land, the very essence of the land, and if they die in some distant place, it is imperative that they be brought back to their own place, their own people. Why, even their diplomats have people attached to their legations to serve as soul carriers if that role becomes necessary."

Her Grace the duchess chewed her lip, her twisted mouth changing her face into a gargoyle's mask, harsh and unlovely. "They may say spiritual, but I say nonsense. Land is merely land; trees are trees; rivers are rivers, all of them ours to do with as we will! We have taken the world and subdued it, it belongs to us, not we to it, and custom or not, I will deal with this so-called carrier, she and those who brought her here."

He shook his head, speaking softly but urgently. "Your family and your powerful friends have undertaken an ambitious project, very ambitious. Very important. Perhaps it is so important it should not be interrupted by a child? Even a Tingawan child?" He flushed, his nostrils narrowed. "The queen, your mother, has remarked that this is a time for concentration. In my presence, she recalled a time in her forefathers' land when his people found that ridding themselves of a minor annoyance stirred up the hunters, and she has been plagued by them ever since. The hunters are still there, my lady. Be careful. It would take very little to turn a sweet-faced nothing of a child into a blessed martyr."

She turned a look of such hostility on him that he felt the cold inwardly. He barely kept himself from cringing.

"You would do well, Jenger, not to speak of my mother. Matters between my mother and me are our business, not even remotely yours."

Then, suddenly, she smiled at him, herself sweet faced and charming. "My mother would no doubt disapprove. She disapproves of most of the things I enjoy. Nonetheless, I will dispose of the soul carrier, her guardians, and any other Tingawans who may be so arrogant as to alight on Norland's side of the sea because they have no right to offend me by being here in the first place!"

The curve of her lips had almost drawn his eyes away from the frozen, empty depths of her eyes. He pretended not to see them, smiling in return. Sometimes looking into Alicia's eyes was like looking death in the face, and no easy death at that!

"Surely you are too powerful to be offended by a child! I don't understand why it would be worthwhile!" he cried, shaking his head in frustration, knowing even as he spoke that he would have done far better simply to stay silent.

She tilted her head, making a pretty face as she considered this. "The woman I cursed took her own sweet time dying, Jenger. She should have been dead years ago, the day after I put the cloud on her. Oh, I know, I forgot two of the steps in the process and got another two out of order, but it still should have been lethal enough. At least I had sense enough to have the machine make copies, many, many copies. She fought me. How many times have we camped near Woldsgard, you and I, or ridden by, so I could release a new copy of the cloud? And before you joined me, I went, season after season. I don't know how she did it, I don't know who her confederates may have been, but however and whoever, no one opposes *me*. No person, no child, no creature! I repay opposition with defeat. I repay delay with death. She thwarted me; now I will thwart her. You've said she really wanted her soul carried to Tingawa; I will repay her by seeing it does not happen. It will amuse me."

"And anything that amuses you, you find worthwhile?" he murmured.

"Believe it, Jenger, always." And she smiled again, so sweetly that he felt an instant's deadly fear. He had been her follower for some time. Sometimes, she had given him a strange, addictive sort of ecstasy. On certain occasions she had given him power. Sometimes, briefly, he had thought she considered him a friend. Occasionally, he had considered himself her friend. Briefly. Yet, most often he had been merely utilized, and sometimes, as today, he found himself playing a game with rules he did not know against a viper he could not see. He knew it was there, somewhere, its fangs exposed, its venom ready, behind her face, behind her eyes—her eyes that sometimes went empty, so that looking into them was like looking into a tunnel that had no end yet became no smaller the farther it went, a tunnel with a red light at the far end of it. There were things living in that light: ugly, sinuous movements; hard, dreadful words; a hideous, tingling laughter. Each time he felt them, his skin tightened and erupted in gooseflesh, as though he had been caught in an avalanche and was dying of cold.

It had happened half a dozen times since he had been with her. Each time, he told himself it was only imagination. Each time he was not reassured, for he knew it was real. That other place or that other person or . . . those other creatures were there, at the bottom of her eyes. Or, if not at the bottom of her eyes, then somewhere else that she saw from within herself. Wherever, whatever it was, she knew the way to it or them. Perhaps she went there sometimes, to amuse herself. Perhaps that was really where she lived in those hours and days when no one knew where she was.

He should not have mentioned the queen. Alicia hated Queen Mirami. Her own mother, and she hated her. A time or two he had thought he understood it, but at other times he did not. She had loved her father. He was sure of that. Alicia had loved Duke Falyrion with all the love she was capable of, and when she spoke of him it was with adoration, with grief and loss in her face and manner. She had said once that her mother had taken her father away from her. He had not dared ask her how.

He feigned a loose saddle girth and dismounted to tighten it, allowing her to put a little distance between them while he breathed deeply, trying to swallow the burning that filled his throat. When he mounted again, he stayed behind. The terror would pass. It always had before. It would again, he thought. He hoped. When they arrived at the Old Dark House, Jenger took the reins of the duchess's horse and led it away, forcing himself to move in a matter-of-fact way, showing no fear, watching from the corners of his eyes as she ran, actually ran, through the great doorway. He did not want to know where she was going.

She went where he had never gone: down a long flight of stairs, through an anteroom, then into a room to which only she had the key. As always, when she entered, she checked her machines before she did anything else. First, the fatal-cloud machine. She had confessed to Jenger that she had made mistakes when she used it on the Tingawan woman, years ago, forgetting some of the details her *instructor* had given her, but she had reviewed the procedure afterward, and she would not make that mistake again. Second, the seeker-mirror machine. It would find anyone, or it would reflect anyone, depending upon how it was set. Third, the sending machine she had used last night. It was very old. It had buttons on it to control "the visuals," "the sonics," "the settings," "the maps." Her *instructor* had told her it sometimes malfunctioned. She would not use it again except to send a haunting. It still worked well enough for that! Fourth was the machine that watched and protected her. That's all it did, its great bulk standing in a far corner, red eyes alert, just watching. There were other devices in the room, one that opened and shut the door, one that kept the room warm and circulated the air, one that showed her where her servants were, but the first four—no, three now—were the important ones.

Now that she had met the Tingawans, it was time to see what might be done about them—or at least one of them. From the cubicle in which she kept her precious things, she retrieved a very old package, stained by the spray of the sea, the tar of oiled ropes, the sweat of many different hands. It had been lying there for a very long time, locked away in her secret room, hidden on a shelf. Until today, she had not been moved to do anything with it, but now she opened it with hands so eager that only the iron control she held over her body kept her from trembling.

Inside were other wrappings, and still others, and at last, in a fold of oiled silk, a few black hairs obviously pulled out by the roots, a few scraps that only close examination would have revealed to be clippings from fingernails.

The duchess smiled a smile that even demons in hell would need to practice in order to achieve in such perfection. There was love of pain in it; enjoyment of torture; the rapture she felt when she observed grief and loss, especially when she had caused it; and now she could anticipate doing it all: torture, pain, grief, loss, all in one long-awaited achievement. She murmured, only to herself, "Ah, so, little Legami-am. I have all your hopes and longing in my hands, and they shall be the pathway to that large bale of muscle who guards the Tingawan girl. Bear, he is called. Well, we shall skin him. You shall summon your betrothed home long before he plans to go. It is my will that you shall summon him home. What a pity you will no longer be there when he arrives . . ."

NEAR THE END OF THE first day's travel from their camp near Riversmeet, the wagons from Woldsgard passed Abasio, who seemed to be waiting at the side of the road. Blue pulled the dyer's wagon onto the road behind the others.

When they stopped for the night, Xulai brought Blue a horse biscuit and told both Blue and Abasio about the incident in the nighttime, though Abasio had suggested Blue not talk on this journey, as it might endanger all of them if it were known a horse could listen, remember, and repeat. Xulai badly wanted comforting from both man and horse, and at the moment, they were out of earshot of the others.

While Abasio pondered the storm, the wolves, the duchess and her men, Blue munched his biscuit, mumbling, "Not bad, but they made better in Artemisia."

Xulai gave him a second one and said mournfully, "Abasio, Blue, Precious Wind says I did something else."

"And what was that?" Blue mumbled around the last crumbs of his biscuit.

"My cousin told me, before we set out, that if I looked very young, I would be thought inconsequential. And the duchess rode up to look at me, and I think . . . I think I looked like a baby."

Abasio stared at her for a long moment, forehead wrinkled in concentration. "And sometimes, do you, perhaps, think you are older than you seem to be?"

She looked up, surprised. "Sometimes. Though I don't think I do *that* very well."

He drew her to him, into a comfortable hug, a dog hug, cat hug, friend hug, anything-warm-and-living hug, concentrating on making the embrace full of consolation without any sexual overtones whatever, as those, he told himself, were his private problem. "Don't worry about it. If it's any comfort to you, sometimes I think you are about . . . oh, seventy-two."

"That old!"

"At least. And at other times, about three. I really think it will sort itself out very soon and you'll average out. You have had a very unusual upbringing . . ."

"A down-putting upbringing," she said resentfully.

"That, too. But I'm virtually positive it will soon sort itself out. Be patient."

She resolved to be patient, and the resolution comforted her for almost half an hour. That day's travel was uneventful, and that night they made camp outside the walls of a watchtower manned by guardsmen from the coastal fiefdoms.

"This is the Eastwatch Tower of Wold," the sergeant told them. He was a solidly built and placid-faced man from Chasmgard whose dark hair stood straight up in spikes every time he pulled off his helmet, which he did at brief intervals in order to scratch his head. "With Wellsport town moved high onto the slope of the mountain, with Wellsmarsh moved back miles east toward us, if the enemy takes the coast, we're probably the first line of defense."

"Wellsport moved?" grated Bear. He had not really believed this.

"The water came slow enough that the Port Lords managed to move the town. First the lower buildings, then the higher ones, a third of the way up the mountain. They kept moving the piers, too, up and up, back and back. The Port Lords are living on their fat. There's been no cargoes come over the sea for years now. Now the Marish, that's moved by itself; each year the shallow water was farther upriver to the east, and the reeds and fish and fowl all followed the shallow water. Wellsmouth town was already well up the side of Wellsgard Peak, and there's still plenty of fish and fowl in Marish for them to live on, just not so close to the town as it was."

"And north of there?" Abasio asked.

"Oh, Chasmgard, Combesgard, and Valesgard were mountain citadels to begin with, all of them well over the waters' rising. They've lost some garden lands, down near the river, but they have valleys where they can grow their food. It's only Wellsport that's had to move itself, but that does make us first in line if we're invaded. Though far inland as we are, if we're the first to see invaders from the sea, we're in deep trouble long before we catch sight of them. We're depending upon getting a signal from the beacons long before their warriors get here!"

"It might be raining," said Xulai, who had joined the men in visiting the tower. "If it's raining, you can't see anything."

"Well, that's true, little missy. So much so that we've a standing order: whenever the sky clouds over, we're to send out a line of relay riders, all the way to the crossroads at Riversmeet, or on to Wellsport if need be. They're to stay in place until the skies clear, or until they see hordes of Sea People coming down the road!" He burst into laughter. "Not that anyone expects that. I've heard they can't breathe out of water or walk on land. The sea's their place and so far, they've stayed there."

"How do they conquer, then, if they cannot come ashore?"

He pulled off his helmet, scratched his head, and said with great sadness, "By corrupting land dwellers is how. It's said they've bought allies from among us earth walkers, mercenaries from the Copf Islands and from Marshurland to the far south. It's they who take the land and then sit on it, preventing the former occupants from coming back."

Bartelmy and Abasio talked a bit more about this supposed conquest and occupation, finally arriving at the critical question. "How far from here to the abbey?"

"Wilderbrook Abbey? Well, for the next few days' travel, you've got the road winding back and forth up the cliff. It's a steep climb; the valley's over a mile above us, and your animals can't go far in a day hauling wagons. There's a dozen villages of refugees along the road between here and the top of the falls, plus more hanging in caves on the cliff, like bats. Say three or four days up the road to the top, depending on how strong your animals, how heavy your wagons, and how much the residents delay you. The falls have eaten their way deep into the cliff, into a kind of slot no wider than the falls themselves, so you'll not see them until you get there, but if the mist breaks for you, you'll see a wonder.

"Then, when you turn east once more, there's a few days' easy travel through the Lake Country—it's been dry lately, so the road is good and there'll be no swamps to deal with. In wet years, that valley's like an extension of the Dragdown Swamps. Then you'll come to Benjobz—that's his name, Benjobz, like it's King Gahls, even though there's only one of each of 'em—next to Benjobz Pond, where the Wells comes down from the highland to the north and the Wilderbrook runs in from the south. For five generations there's been a Benjobz running an inn there, where the Wilderoad comes in from the south. That's the road you'll take to get to the abbey. It's steep in places. I'd say you have twelve to fourteen days' travel from here, depending."

"On?"

"Like I said, depending on animals, weight, and whether the refugees slow you down, or whether it pours rain and the Lake Country turns into swamps. In real wet years, the Dragdown Swamps include the whole valley of the Wells and all the western slope of the mountains east of Altamont. When the slope and valley are full of swamp, travelers to Lake of the Clouds have to ride far west, high along the edges of the woods, and travel there is more difficult and more dangerous. Them's wild woods, with wilder creatures in 'em . . ."

"What sort of wilder creatures?" asked Abasio.

"I've heard some talk of new kinds of snakes, big ones. Then there's boars, always more willin' to attack than discuss the matter sensibly. Nothin' worse than you've seen before, just keep an eye out. Then, too, if you decide to visit the court, that'd take you extra time. It's not somethin' I'd recommend, by the by."

"Why not visit the court?" Xulai asked. "Is it very grand?"

"Not that, little missy, no. Just that it's been somewhat dangerous for a good while. Old friends falling out of favor. People being accused of treachery or worse."

"Worse?" Bartelmy's eyebrows rose into his hair.

"Oh, people are whispering about necromancy and such. That sister of the prince, half sister I should say . . ." He leaned forward, almost whispering. "'Where Alicia strolls, someone's head rolls,' that's what folks are saying. Not that she's there just now. Sometimes she's back and forth all the time, up and down the cliff road, doing what, no one knows, but she's stayed near Altamont more than usual lately. Longest she's ever stayed away from court that I can remember. Her goin' and comin'—it makes us nervous."

"Do you have relay riders?" Bartelmy asked.

"And good horses. Prince Orez sent us fifty horses, too, bred in Vale. He said not to put our trust in the signal fires, for the clouds have been lyin' lower of late. 'Keep watch! Keep it well,' that's what he said."

The three of them returned to camp. Xulai went to see to her animals, large and small, while considering what the sergeant had said. There was more than one way to interpret "clouds lyin' lower of late." It could have been a simple comment on the weather; it could have implied a specific threat; or it could have included both. Xulai asked Precious Wind and Bear what they thought about it, and she was interested to see Bear gnawing at his cheek as though to chew a hole in it, as he did when he was mightily displeased about something.

They began the next day's journey by crossing the bridge over the Wells and beginning the gentle climb north on a narrow road carved into the west escarpment of the highlands. By noon, they were far enough north that they could see Woldsgard, a tiny toy castle perched northwest of them on the far side of the valley. Black Mike had traveled the road before, and he taught them to locate the wide spaces on the roads above them, to keep track of wagons on the road above them, and to pull into wide spaces to let downward traffic pass.

"Down traffic's quicker," he said. "It takes less time to let them pass and makes more sense to rest the animals that are hauling up!"

At midmorning, they came to one of the infrequent wide spots, made at some switchbacks and wherever the cliff wall was slightly less steep, and Bartelmy, seeing wagons not far uphill from them, signaled a stop and got down from the wagon seat to stretch. The descending wagons made the turn and passed them, the drivers nodding but offering no conversation. Bear took Bartelmy's place; Bartelmy got into the carriage with Precious Wind. The wagons made a slow, tight turn and started back toward the south, only gradually separating from the lower road they had traveled during the morning. Xulai was beside Abasio, amusing herself by watching the traffic upon the lower road: a swineherd driving a considerable piggery; a gooseherd driving his flock down a tortuous path winding steeply westward to a marsh beside the river; a traveling tinker, well behind them, his wagon hung with pots and pans, far noisier than Abasio's wagon. Abasio had tied down all his equipment to make less annoyance for them all.

"I've been meaning to ask you a question," said Abasio. "Every time someone mentions Precious Wind or Great Bear, I wonder how they got those names. Can you tell me?"

"'Great Bear' is a title given to a warrior who has won the imperial battle games. When Tingawa is at peace, there may be several Great Bears. If Tingawa is at war, many may have perished in battle. This Bear was born on the island of Zol, so he is the Great Bear of Zol. As for Precious Wind, she says on the day she was born, a sea wind brought rain sweeping across her island to break a long and terrible drought. So she was named Xu-xin, 'Precious Wind,' as I am named Xulai, 'Precious Hope.' The princess was Xu-i-lok, 'Precious' or 'Treasure of the Ancients,' as her father is Lok-i-xan, 'Ancient Word of the Family Do-Lok.'"

"But Precious Wind is not called Xu-xin . . ."

"Here in Norland, only members of royal clans use their Tingawan names. Precious Wind says all others' names are translated into some near equivalent out of courtesy. I am related to the clan Do-Lok, and I am Xakixa, so I must use the name as I was given it."

Abasio mused on this as they passed the wall of a deep cistern being built against the cliff-side on their left, a stone wall creating a deep, curved trough, the inside of it being plastered to hold water, the whole structure held against the cliff by a net of thick ropes attached to metal rods driven into the cliff face. Farther on they could see other, completed cisterns, most with tarred canvas pipes leading upward to smaller catchments higher along the cliff.

"I wondered where they managed to get water on this cliff," said Abasio. "Now I wonder where they get that rope." He nodded toward the massive ropes to which the nets that held the walls in place were fastened. "Rope like that is expensive stuff. Since seagoing ships don't sail anymore, there can't be many rope walks left to turn out such thick cable as that."

Xulai, staring wonderingly at the huge ropes, asked, "What do ships do with those huge ones?"

"They use them for anchor cables, mostly. It takes a very large cable to hold big ships against the wind."

"And you know this how?"

His face went blank. He knew this because he had lived a life aboard ship. It had not, however, been his own life. Having lived a number of other people's lives was not something to discuss at this particular time. "I think I read about it," he said.

Xulai merely nodded. Rope did not interest her as much as the strange headdresses worn by the crews of workers, some of whom were digging out sections of the road, others of whom were filling the sections with large stones or dumping sand and gravel on them to make a more or less level surface. When the wagons approached, the people laid planks across the less level areas and stood aside with their heads down while the wagons were driven slowly across.

Ahead of them, a massive wall along the road was capped by a mud and stone village plastered against the cliff-side like a cluster of cave swallow nests: earthen houses packed close beneath deep overhangs of thatch, each little cell joined to others by twisting flights of stone steps and small, walled landings. Here the foundation walls of the houses were also held in place by heavy nets and deeply driven anchors. As they approached, they passed people carrying water from the cistern. Probably women, Xulai thought, though the figures were indistinguishable behind their robes and strange headdresses: boxes of stiffened fabric jutting forward on either side and down in front of their eyes, cutting off all vision except for a narrow view below and before them.

"You there," someone shouted. Bear pulled the horses to a halt and awaited the approach of the bulky man who had hailed them. That is, if it was a man, Xulai thought.

"You were lookin' at them!" the man exploded when he arrived at the wagon side. "Lookin'!"

"At what?" asked Precious Wind.

"Them: our people. We don't take kindly to people lookin', and her there in the wagon, she was."

"Me?" squeaked Xulai. "I was looking at . . . ah, the nets that hold your houses up. My friend was saying such rope is very hard to find. Also, your clothes are . . . we've never seen clothes like yours before." The man wore the same jutting side pieces and frontispiece and could obviously not see them. Though he spoke to them angrily, his eyes were fixed upon his feet.

"We don't take kindly to lookin'," he repeated. "House nets is our business. Clothes is our business. Can't make you wear blinders, since you're not becoming cherished, but you keep your eyes on the road, straight ahead, and you go right on through. Anybody gets in front of you, you look down."

Xulai said (without at all planning to do so), "Are you all so hideously ugly you prefer not to be seen?"

His eyes rolled wildly as he tried to find someplace to focus them without looking at any of them. "We must become beautiful." The words seemed almost to choke him, but Xulai had the strange impression he was struggling not to laugh. It came to her suddenly that he was *pretending* to be offended, pretending in order to . . . what?

"We will not be cherished by the king unless we are beautiful," the man cried in a theatrical voice. "His messenger told us others with depraved tastes would come among us to cause doubt. Evil critics and judges would come to assail us, she said. They must be kept apart from the people of loveliness. You just do as I say, go on through town, no lookin'.'"

And with that he turned and stamped away, head bent slightly forward so that he could see (in Xulai's estimation) only a step ahead of himself as he moved. Nonetheless, there was something false in his movements, false in the glance he darted behind him, as though to see their reaction. It reminded her of the children at Woldsgard who had been so intent on their play, except that this was the reverse. They had been playing pretend; this man was pretending play. They were totally different things.

The road widened for a short stretch and the drivers pulled up and took a moment to stretch their legs and engage in conversation. Bartelmy came back to ask, "Who or what was that critter, and what was he going on about?"

"I presume he was a Becomer," Abasio replied. "One who must be becoming lovely at some future time, for I saw no symptoms of glorification appearing yet. Did you think him especially splendid, Precious Wind?"

"His nose looks like a potato," she replied. "And his skin is weathered enough to serve as roofing for a barn."

"Then what . . . ?" said Bartelmy.

Xulai said thoughtfully, "Someone has told them they must become lovely in order to be cherished by the king. Possibly that person has threatened them, telling them they'll be sent back to whatever place they were driven from. Where was that, Precious Wind?"

"One of the sea islands overrun by the Sea King's mercenaries," Precious Wind replied.

"That explains the rope," said Abasio. "They're sea folk!"

Precious Wind nodded. "They were, yes. All these people are refugees that King Gahls has allowed to settle here in return for maintaining the road, but I hadn't heard anything about this *becoming lovely* business."

Xulai said thoughtfully, "Someone has set out to convince that man—all of his people, really, for they are all dressed alike—that they must become beautiful. In order to prove that he believes this, he is pretending that he is already beautiful, potato nose or not. I suppose it's a lot less trouble pretending to be something if no one contradicts what you're pretending to be."

She was thinking of the time when she had needed to be brave. In desperation she had told herself she was brave enough. She would not have wanted anyone to contradict her while she needed to believe it. She had been angry at chipmunk for disillusioning her. But this man

hadn't been angry. He'd been amused. Strange. One could play pretend with total conviction, but one could not pretend play in the same
way. His every movement spoke of mockery. He didn't believe it himself!
Moreover, he didn't intend that *she* should really believe it!

Bartelmy remarked, "The guard below said the Duchess of Altamont
spent a lot of time fiddling with these villagers. If this is her doing, what
is she up to?"

"Enough," growled Bear. "Whatever she's up to, this is no place to
discuss it. Let us do as we are asked to do and leave here without causing difficulty."

"I agree," said Precious Wind. "Someone has frightened these
people . . ."

"No, I don't think that man was frightened," murmured Abasio, who
had walked around his wagon to be sure everything was still tied down.
"I think he's making sure that if we're asked about these villagers, we
say the right thing."

"And that is?" demanded Precious Wind.

"That they wish to be cherished by the king. That they wish that
more than anything else."

Precious Wind joined Xulai on the seat of the dyer's wagon; Abasio
chose to walk alongside. The drivers returned to their teams and they
went on, each of them looking down at the road, though both Xulai
and Precious Wind glanced from the corners of their eyes as they proceeded. All the villagers they saw, even the children, were garbed in the
same fashion. On a narrow terrace at the top of steep stairs, a group of
children were talking heatedly among themselves.

"Children," remarked Abasio in an innocent voice. "One wonders
how they are conceived among such beautiful people."

"In total darkness," murmured Precious Wind with a giggle.

Xulai gasped as one of the children was accidently jostled off the terrace to fall sprawling to the next level down. He—Xulai thought it was
a boy—staggered to his feet, holding on to the wall, his strange headdress knocked askew and blood streaming from his forehead. None of
the other children had noticed he was gone.

"It's dangerous," Xulai whispered. "Even the children are dressed
that way, and they can't see what's happening around them! Shall we
help him?"

Abasio growled, "Interfering would be profitless and might get us killed."

"Not if they can't even look at us," said Xulai.

Precious Wind said, "Since they went to the trouble to warn us off, someone of them obviously did look at us. I'm sure they've arranged methods for dealing with both accidents and interlopers. Perhaps someone shouts out a location and everyone converges on that location and surrounds the miscreant so he cannot escape either their help or their blows."

"You think they kill people?" Xulai breathed, unbelieving.

"The person who set them onto this idea might expect it," Abasio replied. "Though that person would call it purification or some such thing."

Xulai risked another glance at the injured boy. He was being helped up the stairs by someone, presumably his mother, who was whispering intently as they moved. Xulai's eyes were drawn to a gleam at the side of the child's face. An earring. Adornment? In a place where people did not look at one another?

"Precious Wind," she whispered. "Look quickly. Do you see the earring in the child's ear?"

Precious Wind cast a quick glance behind them. "I see it. Gold. Some triangular emblem on it. Why?"

"Isn't it odd to find adornment on people who don't look at themselves?" Xulai asked. No one answered.

After a time, Abasio walked forward along the line of wagons and asked Bear, "Will there be more of these people?"

"Not these, precisely," said Bear. "But the guard said there were many villages up the slope. We can hope they're not right on top of the road the way that one was!"

They passed a wide spot at the next switchback, the second turn to the north, a sizeable one, already occupied by several wagons. Above it was a tower, glued to the cliff-side like a swallow's nest. A bell in the tower tolled briefly. Xulai looked questioningly at Abasio, and he shrugged. "The bell probably lets the wagons coming down know that there's traffic coming up on the road. I'd guess there's no place to pass between here and the next turn."

His guess was verified as the other wagons pulled onto the road behind them, and they traveled upward together throughout what was left of the afternoon. The sun was low as they drove north toward the next village, this one built not far from the next looping turn to the south, the seventh switchback turn the cliff-side road had made. Bear passed the word for all of them to keep their eyes on the road and do no "looking," but they were stopped once again, this time by a white-robed woman who stood in the center of the road, blocking the way, and then, having stopped them, stared into their faces as she walked along the line of wagons, stopping at Abasio's wagon.

"You are entering the village of Those Becoming Pure," she said in a ringing voice. "Do you intend to stop here?"

Precious Wind asked, "Do you object to our camping for the night just beyond the town?"

"Not so long as you are robed and do not speak to us or so loudly among yourselves that you are overheard. Sanctified robes are available in all sizes; the campsite cistern may be used for a fee; audible conversation by unbelievers is forbidden." The words were mechanical, made bloodless by repetition.

"The robes," said Bear, who had followed her on foot. "You rent them?"

"Sell them," the woman rattled off. "Obviously, once you have worn them, they are unclean and must be destroyed."

"How much?" asked Bear. "Six men, three women, one child."

"Seven men," said Xulai. "Abasio is with us."

"Ten Gahls," the woman announced.

"Good merciful goddess," whispered Precious Wind, reaching for the moneybag she was carrying. "That'd buy me a Tingawan court robe embroidered in pearls!"

When she handed over the coins, the woman accepted them in a square of ragged cloth, carefully and without touching them. She folded the cloth and put it in her pocket. "Drive your wagons to the campground to let the other traffic go on. You may pick up your robes at the vestry, the blue building on the right." She turned to stalk ahead of them.

"Her ear," Xulai whispered to Precious Wind. "When we get closer, look at her ear."

Precious Wind and Xulai were dropped off at the vestry and received a pile of robes that were neither new nor clean. When Xulai received her share, she also received a stroke and gentle squeeze from the woman's hand along with what seemed to be a wink, though it was very quick. As she pulled her own garment over her other clothing she tried to figure out what the transaction, in all its details, had meant, but was distracted when Precious Wind asked, "What is the purpose of your becoming pure?"

"Not to be sent back," said the woman matter-of-factly. "If we are pure enough, we will be so treasured by the king we will be allowed to stay."

"Who told you that?" asked Xulai.

The woman turned her face away but looked at Xulai from the corner of her eye. "That would be the one who comes. The one who tells us what we must do. She comes down from above, up from below, sometimes, often . . ." And she winked at Xulai again, frankly, with a quirky smile. "We believe her, of course. We are greatly in her debt."

They walked on to the wide, flat ledge at the turn. It held a grove of well-grown trees, a cistern, and an enclosed latrine as well as their wagons, which were in the process of being arranged according to Bear's dictates.

"It's obviously a regular way-halt," said Bear with annoyance. "The cistern collects rainwater from upslope, but there's no grazing, so we'll have to feed the animals from what's in the dray." He motioned at Pecky, directing him as to the placement of his wagon. "We could more simply have paid a modest rent than have all this nonsense about buying robes. This one is so old and worn, it's obviously been *sold* a hundred times before, despite all that nonsense about its being unclean and needing to be destroyed. I wonder if the king's traffic is halted and extorted in this fashion."

Abasio joined them in time to hear this last phrase. "What else could they be living on?" he murmured. "I saw no gardens, no fields, no animals, no craftsmen busy creating things. They need food, they need clothing, they need that heavy rope to make the nets that keep their houses and cisterns in place. Your ten Ghals probably supports both this village and the one below."

"If not all of them up and down the cliff," said Xulai.

"Speaking of king's traffic," said Precious Wind. "The woman we met wore a gold earring. So did one of the children back at the other village. I got a good look at this last one; it's stamped with an emblem, a tower with a serpent in it. Isn't a tower the king's sign?"

"The symbol of the House of Gahls has a tower in it," said Bear. "There's an eagle over it, but it has no serpent on it anywhere. Now, why would that be? Could it be a symbol that these sea refugees are under the king's protection? Or that they are of one . . . what? One sect? One heritage?"

"But under some other woman's direction," muttered Oldwife. "Some female's telling them what they have to do. Guess who?"

"What do you suppose they've decided to become pure from?" Xulai asked.

"Who knows?" Precious Wind murmured. "I have traveled in many countries, and ideas about purity vary widely. Some avoid certain words, others cover certain body parts or eschew certain colors, certain foods, certain drink. Some reject music but allow dance, others reject dance but allow music. There is nothing so delightful, so pure, so innocent or enjoyable that some group has not forbidden it. I've heard that one of these refugee groups will assault you if you let them see the bottom of your feet. It's considered a deadly insult. Before they kneel down, they hold a cloth behind them to hide their feet. Letting your shadow fall on them provokes some people, or even breathing wrong."

"How can you breathe wrong?" asked Abasio, intrigued.

Precious Wind shrugged. "I'm sure someone has figured out several wrong ways."

They gathered around their small fire. Bear snapped his fingers. When everyone looked at him, he said softly, "We'll still keep watch tonight. These people may be pure, but their purity may allow killing or stealing."

"Does he really think so?" Xulai whispered to Precious Wind. "It seems very unlikely to me. I think they're friendly but playing along with the silliness the duchess spouts for reasons of their own."

"Bear's only being cautious," Precious Wind replied. "No one ever died from being overcautious."

"How long have these people been here?" asked Bartelmy.

Precious Wind replied, "The first ones arrived in Wellsport a dozen years ago. Others followed, and more are still coming, so I've heard. All of them have been given permission to stay, though it may be the decision was made by someone other than the king."

Abasio said, "As Precious Wind says, the decision may have been made by some deputy, but from a practical point of view, it makes sense to have someone maintaining this road. The villagers are obviously controlling traffic, to avoid conflict between wagons going up and wagons coming down. Also, as steep as this slope is, any sizeable storm would cause washouts. You see they've had to build a ten-foot wall along the road and fill in behind it just to gain enough level space to put one row of houses. Then they fill in behind the first row and build another row on that, all with little alleys and walkways between."

"Like an upside-down staircase," said Xulai. "One room on the bottom, two on the next layer up, three on top of that. The cliff is very steep."

"It's steep because it's recent," said Abasio. "This escarpment hasn't been here long enough to erode. It's a strange feeling."

"Why, Abasio?"

"Oh, because where I was born most of the mountains were at least slightly rounded, and the plains were deep-cut by rivers. Most of the rock here is sharp, like daggers. It gives me the feeling I'm on some other planet."

It wasn't a feeling the others shared. The great cliff was something they knew or knew of, like the jagged peaks on the horizon west of them. The great earthquake that split Norland had happened recently in geological history, but Norland had always been this way in living memory. In either sense, however, the Becomer villages were new. Xulai stood at the edge of the camp, staring directly into it, for the way-halt was level with the top of the wall that supported the first row of houses. A path led straight from her feet to a village entry, a gateway giving on a walkway that was barely wider than Abasio's shoulders, not so wide as Bear's. Somewhere inside the structure a light-well pierced the fabric of the place, letting in a bit of sky, a faint light of evening disclosing a cross-walk where a constant flow of people went back and forth, to and fro.

The place was like a bath sponge or a cheese with square holes, little rooms and cubbies throughout, all the exterior walls perforated with windows, hung with little balconies, pierced with walkways and stairways. Narrow chimneys sprouted from wall corners, singly and in clusters, only a few of them emitting pale smoke. Flowerpots stood on roof corners, though the frostbitten vines they held trailed disconsolately down the outer walls. In summer, she thought, the little village would be interesting and gay looking. At the very top, some tile roofs fed rain into gutters that fed into cisterns at the bottom of the walls; other roofs were flat and strung with clotheslines.

"How can they live all on top of each other like that?" she asked no one in particular.

"They're island people," said Abasio from behind her. "Island people are sea people, and sea people spend a lot of time on ships. On ships, people do live on top of each other." He put his hands on her shoulders. "Come, you need supper."

When they had all eaten, they tidied the camp area before sitting together around the campfire, drinking tea, ignoring the parade of Pure Becomers who patrolled the road near the way-halt, chanting and staring. All of them wore the earring in their left ear.

"First watch mine," murmured Bartelmy at last.

"No. Mine," said Precious Wind insistently. "I slept for a while in the carriage; you didn't. We'll make it short watches, though, so everyone gets some sleep. I'll wake Black Mike."

In the night, Xulai woke. Black Mike, supposedly on watch, dozed on a wagon seat. A few Becomers still strolled by, among them the woman who had sold them their robes. When she saw Xulai looking at her, the woman smiled and came a few steps into the way-halt, where she put something on the ground, and pointed at it before rejoining the others.

When Xulai woke in the morning, in deep shadow, the dawn still pale above the cliff, she went to the spot the woman had pointed out and found a tiny loaf of sweet bread, full of raisins and spice. Both her nose and the chipmunk told her it was good. By the time the others had wakened, she and the chipmunk had eaten it all. Though normally she would have told Precious Wind all about it, she did not. The Becomers had picked her, Xulai, to smile at and wink at and bake cake for. Like most mysteries, time might explain it, but before it was explained, she did not want her guardians keeping watch on her night and day. Their customary watchfulness was quite enough. Or too much.

Soon the others woke. Every person and creature seemed well rested. The parade of Becomers resumed as they breakfasted and went on until they had relinquished their robes and were above and beyond the village on the slowly rising road. Seemingly, the Becomers could not get enough of looking at these particular travelers!

That day, Xulai spent much of her time knitting. There was nothing else to do, and she wanted to make something for Black Mike and the other Woldsgard people to thank them for their care.

During the next day, they passed through six more villages. The Sky Becomers wore all blue clothing and painted their skins the same color, for the king's favorite color was blue; the Perfect Becomers bound their bodies to change them toward an ideal form; the Song Becomers sang all their conversations with one another. There were also the Joy Becomers, a seemingly deadly serious people who invited the group to join them in sexual gratification and using mind-altering substances, following the wagons some distance on the road reiterating this invitation in voices, so Xulai felt, that were syrupy with duplicity. All the Becomers spoke of "her," the woman who told them how they were to become treasured by the king. Xulai counted sixteen or so other villages crowded into caves at various distances above the road, connected to it only by goat paths and treacherous-looking stairs. If all these were being influenced by the Duchess of Altamont, she was spending a great deal of time amusing herself with a great many people who were playing along though they were not, themselves, either amused or convinced. Perhaps, Xulai thought, this fairly innocuous game preempted other games that would have been far more painful.

Above the Pure Becomers' village, the way had grown steeper, the progress slower. The second night was spent at the eleventh switchback. Early on the third day on the cliff they came to the thirteenth turn, this one with another bell tower and space for wagons, like the one they had seen before. Several wagons and a flock of sheep were lined up on the road above them, coming down, and several other wagons, going up, had accumulated on the flat. The Wold wagons were waved onto the flat with the others by a bored-looking traffic controller, and there they sat idle while several loaded wagons and a flock of sheep went down.

"Last turn." Ordinarily taciturn, Black Mike grinned. "Fourteen times across the cliff, seven goin' north and seven goin' south, and we're up!"

By noon, looking down the cliff-side, they passed the six southern switchbacks that lay in a line beneath them. Each turn up to this point had been more or less in line with the ones above and below, but now the road beneath them continued to the south, still gently rising and shaking with a slight vibration. After a time the vibration turned into a low rumble, increasing in volume as they went until the world around them shook with continuous thunder. Opacities of fog came and went on the road before them. The drivers got down to lead the horses and mules around shrouded curves hidden by wavering, silken evanescence that twisted endlessly as they unrolled outward. Since they had only vagrant glimpses of the road before them, everyone but Oldwife preferred to walk, blindly clinging to the cliff-side on their left, watching their feet to be sure they did not approach the edge. On their right they caught occasional glimpses of the enormous cataract surging glassily over the precipice to break into a hundred separate falls on the ledges below. Momentarily, a gust of wind blew the clouds aside to let them see all the way down, multiple cascades leaping and frothing in a frenzy of foam and shattered stone.

The wind persisted long enough to disclose a colossal cauldron a mile or so below, a stone bowl licked out of the bedrock by a millennium of swirling water, maelstrom-filled from edge to edge. Fleeing this vortex, the gleaming, glassy torrent exploded through a narrow cleft in the western edge and lost itself within a wide black canopy of dripping forest, beyond which stood Eastwatch Tower, the watchtower they had left three days before, tiny as a toy.

Several wagons stood ahead of them on the road, waiting, and a bell tolled from a tower on the cliff's edge as they went onto the downward road. It was answered by a far-off echo from the tower they had passed this morning.

Bartelmy said, "I can see why there's no quicker way. What a drop that is!"

"One of the wonders of the world, I'm told," said Precious Wind. "Certainly there is nothing like it in Tingawa."

"Tingawa has mountains," murmured Xulai. "So you've told me."

"Lovely rounded mountains," said Bear in a meditative voice he seldom used. "Like the flanks of maidens, lying at their ease beneath the sun. We have rivers, too, but none so impolite as to roar at anyone."

"We camp here?" asked Bartelmy with a quick glance at the lowering sun.

"A bit farther, please," begged Oldwife, who had left her carriage to get a better look at the falls. "The noise makes my head ache. Besides, everything is soaking wet!"

They turned east. At first flickering in and out of sight before them, the road showed more clearly as both fog and noise dwindled behind them. Eventually there was only a murmur of water, like strong wind in distant trees. By this time dusk had fallen.

Xulai tugged at Precious Wind's sleeve. "I have this feeling," she said. "It would be a good idea for us to camp somewhere where we won't be seen tonight."

"A feeling?" said Precious Wind.

"Like . . . the feeling I had about the horses."

Precious Wind called a halt to the caravan and went to explain to Bear that Xulai had a feeling.

"I'd take it seriously," she said, seeing his scowl.

"I'm getting a feeling also," he said. "I'm getting a feeling that I'm not sure who we're taking where. You knew Xu-i-lok?"

"I did, yes."

"Do you get the feeling that the princess may be directing operations here?"

"You mean . . . ?"

"Who knows what I mean? If she's actually carrying Xu-i-lok's soul, does that mean she's carrying the princess's personality, her opinions? Her special kind of knowledge?"

Precious Wind looked at her feet while she composed her face. "Bear, I don't know, but I do know she gets these premonitions. About horses. About wagon wheels. About this and that. She's been right each time, so far."

"So far. Very well, we'll take ourselves away from the road."

At Bear's direction, they crossed one of the numerous little streams flowing down from the heights to their left, then turned parallel to it and left the road, not stopping until they were deep among the trees that edged the valley. Bear and Black Mike went back to the road.

"We've raked up the grass to hide our tracks," said Bear when he returned. "Here, we're close to water. There are trees and a hollow to hide the campfire. We are unlikely to be seen or bothered by nighttime travelers."

"We keep watch?" Bartelmy asked.

"We always keep watch, until we reach Wilderbrook," said Bear with a long look at Xulai.

In the night, Xulai dreamed of the monstrous roar of the falls and woke to its earthshaking thunder pounding at her. Fully awake, she realized it was not water she heard! A great many horses in a frantic hurry. She sat up, feeling someone near.

"Shh," said Abasio. "Quiet. Not that they could hear you over that stampede."

From the forest edge they peered at the roadway, gleaming silver in the light of the moon and thick with riders. The horsemen were riding from the east, toward the falls, many of them carrying torches that streamed fire and reflected from helms and gauntlets, spear shafts and armor.

"Soldiers," whispered Xulai. "Why? Where are they going?"

"From here the road goes to Altamont," said Bear from behind her. "Also to Wellsport and the Lake of the Clouds. Even to Ghost Isle and Kamfels."

"And Woldsgard," Xulai said to herself.

"How many?" asked Willum Farrier from the darkness.

"Hundreds," Bear answered.

"King's men?" asked Clive.

"Possibly," said Precious Wind.

"I think they're from the abbey," said Bear. "It's hard to see the banners in torchlight, but I think I recognize them from the ones we saw at Netherfields. They had the device and colors there. The duke told us the abbey's old and rich and it maintains a considerable force of its own."

"My poor cousin," said Xulai in a wounded voice. "My cousin, the duke."

"Shhh, shhh," said Oldwife. "Why should you worry over him? That's pure silliness."

Xulai started to speak, then caught the words before they came from her mouth. If the riders were from the abbey, they were probably headed for Netherfields, but not necessarily to build. Possibly to protect! If, on the other hand, they were from the king, they might well intend to attack Woldsgard. But! But, Woldsgard was probably already protected by an army sent by Prince Orez. The thought fell into her mind like a key into a lock.

"The troops of Prince Orez are already at Woldsgard," she murmured. "They were on the way there before we ever left. My cousin felt he could use the help."

They all looked at her as though she had turned into something strange. "Hallad, Prince Orez?" asked Bear. "Would that have been who was spying out the road near Altamont? I saw tracks when we crossed the road. A couple of riders came from the west, checked out the roads both ways, and then went back the way they had come."

"Because we weren't where we were supposed to be," said Bartelmy. "According to the plan the duke and I made, we should have turned east by then and gone some miles down the eastern road. So they watched through the night, maybe until we headed east, and then, if Xulai is right, the troops from Etershore were at Woldsgard by the time we got to Eastwatch Tower, below the falls."

"Why weren't we supposed to see them?" asked Oldwife.

"What we didn't see, we wouldn't talk about," said Precious Wind. "Is that the reason, Xulai?"

She nodded sorrowfully. "I'm sure we're not supposed to know about it, and I made a mistake when I mentioned it. Prince Orez's commander probably sent outriders to be sure we'd gone on by and there was no one else on the road. The outriders reported we'd be delayed because the bridge was blocked, so the army waited until the crossroad was clear. I hope they waited until the duchess was out of the way, as well."

"I rather imagine," said Precious Wind, "that they went by quietly, at a walk and well spaced out, shortly after we had camped, probably during or after that wolf-thunder nonsense with the horses, as well. We were far enough away that we wouldn't have heard them, and getting there at night would have made the most sense. Few travelers ride at night, and at a quiet walk they could have gone far enough north to camp without being seen from the Wells Road. Very possibly, knowing of Prince Orez's reputation for thoroughness, the last men of the troop were assigned to drag the road behind them to wipe out the hoofprints of the troop, while a few others followed them to simulate normal traffic on the road."

Xulai shivered. Had she said too much? A little, yes. They hadn't known Prince Orez would be guarding Wold. But she hadn't said anything about her cousin's plans, just that he needed help, and everyone in Woldsgard knew that. His leaving was still a secret, and so was the eventual building of an abbey, but the horsemen who had passed tonight did not look like carpenters and stonemasons. She would keep that to herself.

"An excellent decision," whispered the chipmunk from under her collar.

Eventually, Bartelmy asked, "Does this change anything?"

"We have our orders. We do what we set out to do," said Bear, his jaw clenched. "And if Xulai has no particular feelings about it, we can do it in moonlight, the hidden way. With this many riders on the road, it would be better not to get involved, however casually. Hitch the wagons. We'll move in darkness, have our own outriders, and stay hid daytimes."

Xulai forbid herself to cry. Being frightened for the duke or for her home at Woldsgard did not help. He had sent her to Wilderbrook; if she could do nothing else, she could be obedient to his wishes and keep her mouth shut. Still, she could not get his face, the way she had seen him last, out of her mind. He had been weeping, and she had felt he had been weeping for her, Xulai. He must have thought his princess's Xakixa was in danger, or why weep?

They moved onto the level road with only four of the six mules harnessed to the dray. Clive Farrier rode one mule at some distance behind them; Bartelmy rode the other well ahead of them; both outriders were far enough from the slight jingle and crunch of the wagons that they could hear riders coming from either direction. The road was almost level; the wide river wound among an endless series of ponds and small lakes that virtually filled the wide valley. The animals made good time, and the moon did not set until just before dawn. By then both animals and wagons had been hidden in the forest once more while the men moved between forest edge and roadside, raking the grasses upward to hide their tracks.

They built a small, smokeless fire, using dry wood they had brought with them in case of need. They had hot soup and tea, slabs of toasted bread with honey, then collapsed into their blanket rolls, all except Oldwife and Nettie Lean, who claimed first watch since they had slept in the carriage and were wide awake. Nettie was posted at the wood's edge, watching the road, while Oldwife sat with her sewing kit inside the woods, her back against a tree, where she would hear Nettie's signal.

When everyone was asleep except herself, Xulai eased open the basket in which the two cats were sleeping, rolled them into her blankets, and lay her face where they had been. The box the princess had sent her to find was there, close. The thing she had swallowed was . . . inside her, somewhere. Surely it could hear her if she spoke. "What should we do?" she murmured. "Is there something we should do?"

Only silence. Her eyes filled with tears as she put the cats back into their bed and pulled it close to her, one arm protectively around it, the other thrust into the pocket of her cloak, where the chipmunk slept in the palm of her hand. She had had him now for some time, but he had not grown at all. He was still tiny enough to need her warmth. Though she thought it would be impossible to sleep, she fell into a deep, dreamless slumber and did not wake until late in the afternoon when Nettie Lean shook her by the shoulder, laying a finger across her lips.

"Shhh," said the woman. "More riders."

The other blankets were already empty. Everyone was crouched at the edge of the forest, looking at the troops going by. Mounted soldiers, their guidons bearing the king's emblem: a stone tower, truncated, with an eagle above it.

Xulai crawled up beside Bear. "How many?" she asked.

"Troop of one hundred," he said. "Eight of them so far."

"How many last night?"

He tilted his hand back and forth, meaning "More or less."

"An equal force, then," whispered Precious Wind. "To join with the others? Or oppose them?" She turned to stare at Xulai. "Do you have some sudden and wondrous insight into this, pet?"

Xulai shook her head. Nothing. Except a feeling that the duke may have left Woldsgard for a time. He had said he might go, and she was sure he had gone. He had not told her where.

But he went in health, not ensorceled, she told herself. *Not cursed, as Xu-i-lok had been cursed. But then, she would not curse him in that way until she had him! And he has moved too swiftly for that.* She did not speak it. Her people had enough to worry about. The night's rest had allowed her to be sure of one thing: nothing had happened in Woldsgard that the duke had not anticipated and provided for. That anticipation was one reason he had sent her away so quickly. She had wondered at that, but it had been necessary!

They traveled at night for two more nights. At dawn after the second, they saw a ridge stretching from hillside to hillside before them, like a dike across the valley, the river thrusting its way through a cleft in its center and the road rising over its top at the left. Bartelmy rode up the rise and from there looked down on Benjobz Pond, another wide and shallow lake, this one cupped in a high, green valley with Benjobz Inn beyond it.

Once again, they hid wagons and animals in the forest while Bear sat by the fire and stared into the coals. Food was prepared, quietly. All of them but Bear ate, quietly. Finally, Precious Wind laid her hand on Bear's shoulder. "What have you thought of?"

He stirred, noticing the plate before him for the first time. Hungrily, he seized a slab of bread, drew his knife, and sliced sausage atop it, then cheese, covering both with another slab of bread. "I've thought before we go riding by that place, we need to know what's going on. Have any of you been here before? Know anyone who has? Have any kinfolk living up this way?"

Nettie said slowly, "I've mentioned my mother's sister. Belika. She's at the abbey, or so Ma always said. She cooks there. She'n' Ma didn't get along, but ever now and then, Ma got word of her."

"Ah," said Bear. "Well, now. Did you ever have brothers? Or cousins?"

"Belika had two boys, Timmer and Hout. They went down to Wellsport years ago, got in with the Port Lords, took ships for who knows where."

"Willum, Clive," Bear said. "You're now Nettie's cousins. One of you's Timmer, the other is Hout; decide which and practice using the names. Nettie, you're just who you are, Nettie Lean, joining your cousins to visit your aunt and their mother at Wilderbrook, hoping to make up for old family quarrels. Dig the cause out of your memory; create one if you can't remember, so you can gossip about it. Nothing more boring than old disagreements in other people's families. There are saddles in the dray. Each of you Farriers rides a horse—take that pale roan and the gray, they're lightest in the bone, along with that brown she-mule for Nettie. Go on down to Benjobz, ask him if he's got work you can do in trade for your lodging and food for a day or two, while the horses rest up. If yes, fine. If no, fine, say you'll camp somewhere close by. If you're asked if you've seen us, say you traveled with a bunch of Woldsgard people for a few days and left them when they had wheel trouble, this side of the falls. Get into conversation with anybody who'll talk. Say you were off the road when a whole rush of horsemen went by one night. That'd make anybody curious, and someone'll want to show off his knowledge of where they came from."

"And you folks?" asked Nettie.

"Abasio?" Bear looked at him questioningly. "It would be good if you'd follow Nettie and the men, arriving a bit later. You could take lodging at the inn to rest your horse, or perhaps find some business they may have for a dyer. You don't know Nettie and the men; they don't know you. The rest of us are going to stay right here for a day or so," Bear said. "When you find something out, one of you come to tell us about it. Once we know who all those horsemen were, then we'll decide what to do next."

Abasio nodded agreement. "And after you've been told?"

"Then each of you does what you said you'd do. Nettie and her cousins get on their well-rested animals and start up the Wilderbrook road to see her aunty. By that time, you'll be acquainted with Abasio, and he'll go along, or he'll go first and you follow or t'other way round, whatever seems most natural. If you leave before us, stop at the first good camping place and keep watch; move on each day. We may not meet up until we're at the abbey, but we'll all get there."

"We could all stop at that inn and find out the same information," complained Oldwife. "I don't like this splitting up."

Precious Wind patted her arm. "All the rest of you could stop there and ask questions, certainly, if Xulai, Bear, and I were not with you. However, there is enmity directed against the child, Oldwife. You know that. And it's against us, too, because we protect her. This plan seems the least dangerous and takes the least time."

Willum and Clive went off to the wagons, unpacking this and that to stow in saddlebags. Nettie, shaking her head, went to do the same. She was a small woman; the brown mule was the smallest one, but still shaped like a barrel, and it had been a time since Nettie had ridden anything except a wagon seat. When it came to tactics, however, Bear always had a good reason, so there was no point asking him to change his mind. She was ruminating on this fact when Precious Wind tapped her on the shoulder.

"You won't be sore from the little ride downhill from here to the inn, but you may on the uphill ride afterward. Here's some salve for anyplace you feel blistered."

"I'd feel better if Willum and Clive Farrier never touched ale," Nettie said, shaking her head. "That's an inn down there, and they can forget their own mother if they get drunk enough."

Precious Wind spoke to Bear. Bear spoke softly to Willum and Clive, his hands moving up and down their shoulders as they nodded and agreed. Precious Wind returned to Nettie. "They will each relish one tankard in the evening. Nothing else, or Bear will slice off their ears and fry them for his breakfast." She put her hand on Nettie's shoulder.

"You're sure?"

"Quite sure." She went on to whisper for some little time, while her hand massaged Nettie's arm and back. Nettie felt much better when she was finished. Xulai, watching, smiled to herself. She knew that shoulder-rubbing trick of the Tingawans. When they had done it to her, she was convinced she must obey them or die. Of course, she was younger then and didn't know how to resist it. They had taught her that, too. Later on. When she was old enough to obey out of reason rather than paralysis.

Midmorning, the three rode out, the two men in front, chatting and laughing, Nettie behind, regarding them both with unmistakable annoyance.

"Looks very natural," said Oldwife. "The men ignoring their cousin until they need her for something. Her resenting it but not saying a word."

"So Bear and I thought," purred Precious Wind. "Their relationship must appear ordinarily familial: vexed, provoked, and exasperated."

The wagon's contents had been disarranged by the Farrier brothers. Those remaining behind repacked everything and tied it down under its protective canvas. After a time, Abasio got himself upon the road, after squeezing Xulai's shoulder in farewell. She looked after him sorrowfully. The time passed much faster when Abasio was with them, with her. Bartelmy was a friend, an old friend, but he had nothing new to say to her, nothing to make her mind struggle out of the muck and look at the sky the way Abasio did.

Precious Wind and Oldwife went into the meadow where Oldwife had seen a ragged stretch of ripe grain along the trees, something left, perhaps, from some long-ago farm, the grain reseeding itself year after year. Among the tall stems of ripe wheat they found remnants of root crops, parsnips and carrots and turnips, some so huge they had obviously grown for years, but others first-year roots, young enough to be tasty. Black Mike went off into the woods, returning well before dark with a young boar over his shoulder. He skinned and butchered it in a clearing far enough away that the carrion eaters and flies would not be a nuisance before bringing it to the women. "It's only half-grown," he said softly. "Should be reasonable tender."

Oldwife and Precious Wind had wrapped the grain heads in a canvas and beaten them with sticks to break them up, then laid the canvas flat and tossed the grain in the light breeze to blow the chaff away. Now they cooked a cauldron of mixed meat scraps, grain, and root vegetables to accompany the roast pork. The meat they didn't eat would be rubbed with salt and herbs and dried beside the fire, or in the smoke, if they could find the right wood to do it. Pecky hunted for wood while Bartelmy and Bear took turns keeping an eye on the road. The only traffic was two men on horseback, headed down toward the falls at a leisurely pace.

Xulai spent the day playing with her cats, too tired to offer to help or to think—indeed, trying not to think of anything at all. Supper was eaten early, so everything could be packed, ready to go at a moment's notice. At sundown, Mike, Bear, Pecky, and Bartelmy agreed upon the order of the watch. Pecky took first turn. Xulai fell asleep almost as soon as she lay down, the basket amplifying the purrs of the kittens next to her ear.

She woke in the night. Someone was speaking to her: the chipmunk, who had not spoken for days.

"Xulai, don't worry about Justinian. He is well."

Though the chipmunk was at her ear, the words came from somewhere, nowhere, anywhere in the night. She heaved a great sigh and was asleep once more.

Morning came. By midday, they were beginning to feel edgy. There had been no report from the inn and the only creatures in the valley besides themselves seemed to be a great many sheep that had materialized out of the folds of the meadows across the road, earth-colored blobs springing up out of nothing, like mushrooms. A lackadaisical shepherd and a weary dog with its tongue out, neither in any hurry, were moving them on toward the inn. None of them saw Nettie arrive until she spoke to them.

"I was sent out to pick flowers," she said, holding out a considerable bouquet. "Some important woman is coming to the inn tonight and Benjobz wants flowers in her bedroom. I hung around while he talked. I heard him say Altamont."

"The duchess," said Bear, frowning, his teeth showing. "We move now. Nettie, go back, take your flowers, don't rush, don't give any appearance of hurry, but get your animals saddled and put them where they won't be seen by anyone arriving at the inn. All three of you leave when you can without attracting notice. Same for Abasio. We'll go past the inn without stopping. Did you find out about the first riders?"

"That first lot was from Wilderbrook," she said. "Second bunch was as we thought, from Ghastain atop the palisades. Nobody knows why or where. I've got to get back with this bouquet."

Bear summoned Precious Wind and spoke to her quickly. She nodded and ran, gathering up Xulai as she went. Everyone else was busy with harnesses. Only two horses were harnessed to the closed carriage, only two to the wagon, and only four mules to the dray. Bear drove the closed carriage, first in line; Black Mike the wagon; and Pecky the dray. Bartelmy brought up the rear with the light carriage, into which part of the wagon's contents had been piled and covered with stout canvas. When they reached the road, the men ran back and raked the grasses up, as they had done before, paying particular attention to the verges, where they scuffed out the tracks the wheels had made.

From the top of the ridge, the men could see miles in all directions. Bear raised his arm as though stretching, and the women emerged from the forest behind them: Xulai on Flaxen; Oldwife on one horse; Precious Wind on the other, leading the mule. Hidden by the ridge, the women rode swiftly across the road, splashed across the wide, shallow river, much diminished this far up the valley, then urged their mounts quickly up the sloped meadows into the forest along the south side of the valley. Once they were out of sight, Bear clucked to the horses and examined the view while they plodded down the far side of the ridge.

Benjobz Inn lay some distance beyond the pond, surrounded by green meadows and a clutter of pens, paddocks, and animal shelters of wood and stone, as well as a few carriages, including Abasio's wagon. The pond itself was a shallow oval shield reflecting the blue of the sky. The road they were on, the so-called King's Road from the King's Highland, ran along the north side of both pond and inn. On the near side of the pond the road to the abbey, the Wilderoad, came down from among the rising hills to the south. Bear drove toward the crossing, hauling on the reins to turn right over the stout timber bridge at the crossing, slowly, breathing deeply, warning himself not to hurry.

As he could not, in any case, for from both sides of the road the sheep materialized once again, bleating lambs looking for their mothers, baaing mothers trying to find their lambs. The shepherd was across the pond, talking to someone at the inn, and the dog lay beside the road, nose on crossed paws, determined to take no responsibility for the shepherd's inattention.

The horses stopped, stamping their feet, shaking their heads in irritation. The people at the inn looked up. Harnesses jingled; Bear allowed himself an epithet. The shepherd ran toward them, followed by half a dozen other men and women. Bear ground his teeth together, climbed down, made his way back beside the wagons, speaking to each driver. "No matter what happens, I want no appearance of surprise. Understand. Pretend you're a hog in a mud pit, with no opinion about anything."

Bear returned to his carriage. Help arrived to get in its own way and make the sheep mill about even more. Curious people moved along the wagons; one man in particular opened the door to the closed carriage, then shut it with a puzzled expression and walked very quickly away toward the inn.

The shepherd cursed his dog, who rose with excruciating slowness to curse the sheep before moving them off the road with one bark and several well-placed nips.

"I'm Benjobz," said a cheery voice below Bear. "Where you headed?"

"The abbey up in the hills there," said Bear politely.

"Heard there were people headed there. What's all this transport?"

Bear shook his head in peevishness that held not one iota of pretense. "Furnishings and clothes and all sorts of whatnot for a child supposed to be going up to the abbey for schooling. She got frightened into hysterics back at the falls, scared she was going to go over the edge or something, so her nursemaids took three of the animals and hired some local's wagon to return her to her cousin at Woldsgard until she settled down. They told us to take her baggage on where it'd be needed when the child finally learns to behave herself."

"Ah, so that's what's left you short of animals," said Benjobz. "It'll be a hard haul for this few."

"I know," said Bear in genuine exasperation. "We may have to double-team the wagons one at a time over the steep places."

"That's a long journey made longer yet," said Benjobz. "You want to come on over to the inn for a good meal? A little conviviality? There's many a good game in our parlor after supper, and I'm told you're a man who loves his cards."

"Who told you that?"

"Don't remember. Just some fellow you had a game with in Hay Town, said you were a good card player. Told me your name. Tingawan, aren't you?"

Bear hesitated, tempted. But Precious Wind was out there on the hills and she'd . . . No. There'd be games at the abbey. He supposed he could wait. He growled, "What I want most is to get this job done so I can get home. Once the stuff is delivered, I'm headed for the islands."

"Don't like Norland, eh?"

"I just hate this cold." Bear shivered. "Thanks for your offer, though. We may stop on the way back." He beckoned with his whip hand, and the wagons moved slowly past the gathered sheep and the curious onlookers, over a rise, down into a swale, and up the other side, swinging right around a long upward curve and out of sight of anyone Benjobzish. They went on without stopping or talking about it until well after the sun had gone down.

As they unharnessed the horses, Bartelmy asked Bear, "When are the others rejoining us?"

"Variously, I should imagine," Bear replied. "Tonight the man who was so curious about our carriages will tell the duchess what he's seen.

Then tonight or tomorrow she'll send him or someone else on a fast horse to find where we're camped and see if what her spy told her is true. After we're sure she's convinced, we'll let the women rejoin us. They aren't far. Precious Wind has good camp craft, and they have ample supplies."

"And that's why we're camped out here in the open? So anybody can look us over."

Bear began to unharness the horses. "It may be too late for somebody to come after us tonight, but I'm betting on it. And even supposing no one comes until tomorrow, he'll find us by noon at the latest, right? And he'll follow until he sees only four of us. So it's either tonight or tomorrow night."

Bartelmy sighed, sharing a glance with Pecky and Mike. "And of course one of us is always lying up there in the trees, wide awake, to see when he does show up."

"Of course," said Bear absentmindedly, as though he didn't care very much whether the duchess's spy turned up or not.

4

Becoming Xulai

NETTIE LEAN AND THE TWO FARRIER BROTHERS HAD saddled their mounts and tied them out in the forest. While they waited for darkness, they kept up the appearance of earning their keep by working for Benjobz, Nettie doing housemaid duty and the brothers putting together a row of stalls in a newly built barn. Through the barn's open door they saw the encounter between the flock of sheep and the Woldsgard wagons, particularly noticing the lopsided fellow who walked by each equipage and opened the doors into the closed carriage though the windows were wide open for him to see inside.

"Who is that?" asked Clive.

"Fellow called Loppy," said his brother around a mouth full of nails. "Says he's the cellarer. Ast me all kinds of questions about our mama, up there at Wilderbrook." He spat nails into his hand and jingled them nervously. "I told him we left her young, and that was a long time ago, and we didn't know what she'd been up to since we left. When he ast about where all we went on those Port Lord ships, I told him we warn't allowed to talk about where we went or what we stowed for fear of pirates and any of us talked about it got our tongues chopped out."

Clive considered this prying person to have taken an unwarranted interest in them, not liking the idea. "When you think we ought to go?"

"Oh, long about dusk I guess." Willum swiveled his shoulders one at a time, stretching before bending to his task once more. "After supper, when nobody'll be lookin' for us for a while."

They went on with their work, the stalls slowly forming under their hands, enough of them for a considerable number of horses, Willum thought. More than this place looked like it needed, which was interesting. Where was all this new business going to come from? Somebody had to be figuring on increased traffic coming from somewhere, going somewhere else. Such as, perhaps, traffic between Ghastain and Woldsgard, once Woldsgard was taken over by the duchess and passed on to the king, if that was what all those soldiers were off to see to.

As the sun dropped over the hill, they stowed their tools and headed for the door, only to stop on the threshold, Willum muttering under his breath.

"Whatsay?" asked Clive from behind him.

"There he is! I be dinged."

"Who is?"

"Loppy. On a horse, trottin' off purty as pie, same direction the wagons went. Now that's a puzzle. Do we head out now, like we planned, or do we wait until he gets back and see what he tells to who?"

"Or maybe stop his telling anybody."

Willum puckered his forehead and thought hard. "If Precious Wind was here, she'd say accurate information is usual more important than what's it . . . I allus forget. Arbitroosy what?"

"Ar-bi-tra-ry ex-er-cise of un-neces-sary belli-cos-it-y," chanted Clive in march tempo.

"How'd you remember that?"

"Her and Bear, they both say it all the time."

"Well, and they do, that's right. So, we just wait and see what happens when that Loppy gets back."

"We could, but Nettie says that woman's coming. The one from Altamont. Prob'ly better she don't lay eyes on us two so soon again, so stayin' or leavin', either one is what you might call troublesome."

"She never laid eyes on Nettie. Nettie was in the carriage with Precious Wind, and she had her curtain down on her side. Far's I know, she never saw the traveler man, either."

"And what's he doin?"

William laughed. "He's got out his dye pots, makin' napkins for Benjobz. Napkins with the royal crest on 'em, case some of those from Ghastain choose to spend the night. I swear, that Abasio could sell feathers to a goose."

"Well then, it's only you 'n' me better find somethin' to take us away from here from after supper 'til she's gone."

They decided on fishing. The upper reaches of the Wells were known as fishable waters, so Timmer and Hout took off after work, loudly announcing they were going fishing, giving Nettie something to complain of in the kitchen over her supper. "You'd think all the time they've spent, out there on the ocean, goin' here and goin' there, they'd have had their fill of fish!"

"How'd you do with the room for the lady?" asked Benjobz, inter-rupting her tirade.

"Clean as a new knife," said Nellie with unfeigned pride. "All the closets dusted out, the mattress turned and fluffed and made up with those special sheets and new pillows. I got the spiders cleared out and six mouse holes boarded over after I talked Hout into lending me his tools." Each time Nellie spoke, she felt deep in her innards a quiver of expectation that somebody would ask her a question she couldn't answer. So far, she'd followed Precious Wind's advice: talk too much about too little for anybody to be much interested. "I put the flowers in the vases you gave me," she remarked, going on to list the dozen or so types of bloom both by their common name and what her grandmother had once called them, ending the panegyric with a final encomium: "They make the place smell real nice."

Benjobz looked wistful. "Every time she stops here, I hope she'll be satisfied, but it ha'n't happ'nt yet."

"Where's Loppy?" asked one of the stablemen. "He owes me a pint."

"Said he had to see about some new kegs," Benjobz answered. "He gets 'em from old Whistle Snigg, him with the cooperage up the hill there toward the abbey. Told me he'd be back tomorrow."

Nettie helped with the washing up, checked the duchess's room one more time, and went out to the barn where she and her "cousins" had been sleeping in the loft, said cousins having headed upriver with great ado and furor before returning silently through the woods. Nettie gave them a sack of food she'd salvaged from leftovers in the kitchen.

"Now what?" she asked as they chewed their way through their make-shift supper.

"Now we wait until Loppy gets back, and you hang around inside there to see who he tells about whatever he has to tell."

They rested in the hay, Clive taking first watch. He woke the other two when the duchess arrived, close on to midnight, and Nettie, still fully dressed, slipped over to the kitchen, where the cook, just roused and in her wrapper, was in a temper.

"She'll have a bit of roast chicken," the cook growled. "She'll have some fresh greens and a bit of fruit. In the middle of the night she'll have a boiled potato, with sweet butter! She'll have my ladle up her thunder-shoot if she doesn't let up."

"I'll take it up to her if you want," said Nettie. "At least I'm dressed." And, in Nettie's opinion, they didn't need a fuss over cookery with the Duchess of Altamont.

When the tray had been prepared, Nettie carried it up to the room she had cleaned and rapped on the door. When no one answered, she went in, unloaded the tray upon the table, went out, and closed the door behind her. It was strange the duchess was nowhere in evidence. She could have been in the privy, of course. Even duchesses probably had to go to the privy sometimes. And strange she was here alone! The word was she went nowhere without that big man on his black horse and half a dozen armed men or more.

She returned the tray to the kitchen, waited for a time to see if the duchess would show up, then took herself back to the barn, where she found Clive sound asleep and Willum on watch from a kind of crow's nest he'd created across two rafters near the round window at the peak of the barn gable. Without bothering him, she rolled herself in her blankets and went to sleep.

Just before dawn, Loppy returned, the clip-clop of his horse's hooves clearly audible in the early morning stillness, loud enough to rouse Nettie and Clive.

"Strange thing last night," said Clive when Willum climbed down from the rafter top.

"What?" asked a voice from behind them. Abasio!

"You're a sneaky one," muttered Clive. "You finished with your napkins?"

"Finished and paid and ready to leave in the next two minutes. Told Benjobz I had to go on up to the abbey, where I've got an order for special draperies for the abbot's own audience room. Now, what was the strange thing last night?"

"Not too long after the duchess got here, here she came out in fronta the barn, 'cross that stretch of paddock there, 'mongst the trees. Big old owl up in that tree. She stands there, starin' at the owl; the owl takes off. I never saw her come back."

"I did," said Willum. "I saw her standin' out there, like some kinna statue. I saw the owl, too. It came back and flew down into the woods where she was standin'. It was still too dark for me to see into the trees, but I saw her come stampin' out of the woods in a fury, back into the inn."

Nettie shivered. "That's why she wasn't in her room when I took her dinner."

Clive muttered, "Whadduh you think happen to the owl? Foolin' with owls is bad luck, Ma allus said."

"That woman's so much evil luck, ordinary bad luck would turn tail and run," said Nettie on her way out the door with Abasio, who headed for his wagon.

She stopped at the pump behind the inn to wash her face and smooth her hair, an unnecessary neatening, for the kitchen was completely empty, the fire burned to a few embers. Nettie listened for voices, heard them, and went to stand behind the dining room door where Loppy and Benjobz were punctuating their conversation with the clink of glasses.

"I know what the duchess said, but naa, naa, it's just the four of 'em," Loppy declared. "Five, f'you count the dyer and his wagon, but there he goes now, so he's a half day or more behin' 'em. I got a good look inside his wagon, too, and there's nothin' there but his stuff: cloth and dyes and all. It's just like the big driver told us. There's no women there, and the wagons an't carryin' nothin' but house stuff."

"She'll want to know," said Benjobz. "First thing she got here, that was the question. Had we seen anybody headed for the abbey. Who and what was going there."

"What'd she care? The abbey shoun't be on her mind. Way I hear it, whas on her mind's the kingdom. She's gonna take it from King Gahls an' her mama. Mebbe give it to her brother. Share it, more likely! Or keep it for herself."

"Shhh," Benjobz hissed. "Anybody hears you, you'll have your head on the block! And he's her half brother."

"Half brother. Ha. Two boys, one girl, the queen's got, and I've seed

Duke Hulix, and the Duchess of Altamont, and I've seed Prince Rancid, and ever' one of them with the same nose, the same jaw, and I've even seed Queen Mirami, ridin' in a carriage, and there wuz her chamberlain grinnin', with the same nose and jaw as on all three. You're the only one hearin' me say that, and if you're plannin' on turnin' me in to King Gahls as a spy for the Sea King you'll get turned right back!"

"You don't know she's working for the Sea King."

"Well, if not him I'd like to know who. Stands to reason; the Sea King wants all the seaside lands held by his people, don't he?"

"He's got the whole ocean! Hasn't been a ship cross the sea in years."

"Which is just the way he wants it, so I hear."

Benjobz growled in his throat. Nettie slipped out of the place and back to the barn, seeing Abasio's wagon already some distance up the Wilderbrook road.

Willum and Clive had dismantled their crow's nest at the gable. Within a few moments, with the sun barely showing above the eastern tree line, the two of them and Nettie rode southward, inside the edge of the forest, staying hidden and away from the road until they had rounded the ridge and knew they could not be seen from either the inn or the King's Road itself.

"They'll know which way we went," said Nettie when they had achieved the road. "They knew where we were headed."

"We didn't make any secret of it," said Clive with an evil grin. "And just to reduce suspicion, I left a thank-you note for Benjobz nailed to that last stall. I said the fishin' was good up along the Wells, but now the horses were rested, we had to get on up to the abbey to see Ma, and thank you for the good food and the comfortable barn loft."

"What's this all been for, anyhow? All this splittin' up and mixin' up the trail?" Willum asked.

"Confusion," said Nettie. "That's what Bear said he wanted. He's been real strange lately, but he was clear on that. He wanted us to spread as much confusion as possible."

ACROSS THE VALLEY, PRECIOUS WIND, Oldwife, and Xulai had traveled well inside the tree line while keeping the Wilderbrook road more or less in sight to their left. Precious Wind rode first, leading the mule, with Xulai and Oldwife behind her. They didn't hurry. The forest was an old one with little undergrowth to hamper the horses. The ground was deep in dried needles and old leaves; the tall conifers and vast oaks shut out most of the light. The only young trees grew where ancient trees had fallen, heaving up their roots to leave wide, soft patches of disturbed soil, now exposed to the sun and sprung with sapling groves.

They heard birds but seldom saw them. They both heard and saw many scurrying fluff-tailed tree rats, flicking around trunks and chattering at them from branches above piled middens of dismembered cones. Some middens were yards deep around the trunks of old trees, testaments to untold generations of cone eaters who had lived and died in those particular trees.

It was a gloomy place, or would have been, Xulai thought, without the sunlit valley to their left. The nearness of light made it feel almost cozy, like an alcove in a great church, a natural chimney corner, the kind of place to which one could retreat peaceably without being disturbed. Since they had separated from their fellows a little after noon, there would be some hours of travel before they made camp, and Xulai resolved to enjoy them. During the journey, she had not ridden Flaxen at all, for Bear had not wanted her out of reach of her protectors. Even at Woldsgard, she had not ridden for several weeks before they left. Now she resolved to let Flaxen do all the work of following while she herself thought of nothing but the fragrance of the forest, the clean crispness of the air, the gleefulness of the little rivulets that chuckled their way down the mountain toward the Wilderbrook.

After a time they heard the creaking of wheels and saw the others approaching on the road below. Precious Wind clucked to her horse and they walked a bit faster, keeping up with the wagons but going no nearer them. They saw only one habitation during the afternoon, evidently a cooper's house, for his cooperage lay all about the dwelling: piles of split oak, sheds stacked with hoops and staves and the round cut tops and bottoms of barrels. Smoke from the untended forge drifted into the air among stacks of finished kegs. Of the cooper himself, they saw no sign, though Xulai thought she heard tuneless, possibly drunken singing coming from the house.

When evening came, the wagons pulled off the far side of the road onto a grassy flat and the men made camp near Wilderbrook itself. Precious Wind took her group farther into the forest, found a fallen tree with a hollow beneath it, and set up a camp of her own before starting a seemingly purposeless wander among the trees, muttering to herself.

"What are you looking for?" Xulai wanted to know.

"A place to tether these animals where they can lie down if they want to, but where they can't be seen from the sky . . ."

"From the sky?"

"Did Xu-i-lok never speak to you of watchers in the sky?"

Xulai stood with her mouth open. Yes, the princess had done that. "She had me put mirror on the windowsills . . ."

"I know, but we can't attach mirrors to the horses, even if we had mirrors, which we don't."

"Then we need to make the horses seem to be something else," Xulai said in an imperious voice, totally unlike her own. "Tie them, and I'll take care of it."

Precious Wind was moved to laughter that reached no farther than her throat. No matter how ridiculous the words had sounded, laughing at that particular voice was utterly impossible. Instead, she moved the animals into a copse of closely set trees, tied them loosely, and provided them with some of the hay and oats the mule had carried before moving away and standing, like a puppet waiting for someone to twitch her strings. It was not a role Precious Wind enjoyed or was accustomed to.

Xulai left the campsite and went into the copse to speak to the horses in earnest tones.

"What did you tell them?" breathed Precious Wind when Xulai returned to her.

"I told them they did not want to be horses, because there's a monster in the woods that eats horses. The monster doesn't bother deer, so they think they are deer, three does and a fawn."

"Deer. Why not rabbits?"

"Night eyes in the sky probably eat rabbits," Xulai replied in the imperious, unfamiliar voice. "Better a hunter not be tempted down."

"What if they whinny?"

"Don't be silly," Xulai said sharply, haughtily. "Deer don't whinny."

Wordlessly, Precious Wind led the way back to the campsite. "No fire," she murmured. "We might hide the light of it, but not the smell of it." She waited momentarily for Xulai to say something like "Nonsense, of course we can hide it," but no such words came. Perhaps, Precious

Wind thought, one might find it easier to convince horses they were deer than to convince firewood it wasn't burning.

They ate cold sandwiches and apples. Precious Wind announced her intention of going into the woods to keep watch.

"Up a tree?" asked Xulai.

"Possibly."

"Remember what you said about watchers from the sky. In Altamont, that night of the wolves, there were hunting birds in the sky. Wherever you climb, do it a considerable distance from where the men are. Whoever watches them won't look far for us."

Again, that urgent, lofty voice. Precious Wind, not trusting her own, merely nodded agreement.

Oldwife and Xulai, with the cat basket between them (while the secret chipmunk explored the intricacies of the half-rotted trunk), curled up in blankets under the fallen tree and went to sleep, though not until Xulai had spoken earnestly to the tree trunk above them, the grasses, and the neighboring trees. As Oldwife later told Precious Wind, "It was something about nothing being here but cats. Wildcats."

From her perch up a tree, well-hidden by higher branches and a good way back down the road they had just covered, Precious Wind could not see the men's camp in the meadow below, but she imagined Bear rolling a blanket into his bedroll to resemble a sleeping person before he sneaked across the brook and into the woods on the far side of the road. It was no great distance. The valley narrowed as it steepened, and at this point the edges of the forest were only about a hundred yards uphill on either side of the Wilderbrook road. Remembering Xulai's request, Precious Wind surveyed the sky, thinking it unlikely she would be able to see a flyer above her and as unlikely the flyer would see her. The last of the light had gone.

It was not long, however, until the green moon rose to cast a ghoulish light on everything. The human spy arrived on foot around midnight, a shadow barely visible against the pale packed soil of the wide wheel tracks as he crept silently along the grassy verge. Precious Wind watched as he crawled around Bear's camp, looking at it from all sides, then among the wagons, where he lifted canvas and looked under sacks of oats. He did not go near the sleeping men but turned back the way he had come.

Descending from her tree, Precious Wind went silently to the edge of the woods. The spy's horse stood at the far end of a long curve, tethered near the road, and the spy led the creature a goodly distance farther away before riding back the way he had come. By this time the green moon was high. It was said to be bad luck to be out when the moon shone green, probably because everyone looked dead in its rotting light. The green moon, so it was said, dated only from the Before Time, the time of the Big Kill.

"Somebody down at Benjobz is interested in us, isn't she?" Bear asked from behind Precious Wind's left shoulder.

She gasped. "Idiot. Are you trying to scare me out of a year's growth? I thought you'd be over there, on the other side."

"I wanted to be sure everything was all right. How's our little one?"

Precious Wind started to tell him what had happened, then stopped herself. This was, perhaps, one of those things best not talked of. What Bear did not know, he could not say. She contented herself with saying, "She's a good little traveler. Uncomplaining. She helped hide the horses and she doesn't fuss at the long ride. I think we're well hidden."

He stared at his feet for a time. "This has been a very strange journey, Precious Wind. There's something going on here, something that wasn't part of our bargain."

"My only bargain was to protect Xulai," she said calmly.

"If that is Xulai."

She stared at him in disbelief. "Why would you doubt it?"

He said bitterly, "At present, I do not. Being a Xakixa makes her unusual here, true, but why in the names of all the pantheon of Tingawa does she attract all this interest? It's not as though she were the ambassador's daughter! They told me she's just a child, a family member, true, but of a distant branch, an orphan. At home, she'd be virtually a nobody."

"She's carrying Xu-i-lok's soul."

"And what does that mean to anyone who is not Tingawan? It should mean nothing! It does mean nothing! So why all this interest?"

Precious Wind considered what she might tell him. "Well, if someone went so far as to poison Xu-i-lok, that same person might wish to destroy her soul. I think that's perfectly understandable."

He stared at the sky. "Well, the orders I was given were clear enough that I can follow them without understanding them, otherwise I might let confusion lead me into error. Whoever is stirring trouble, or for whatever reason, all we have to do is keep her safe and take her where we were told to take her. Meantime, we should make defensive moves. At this stage that means spreading confusion among her likely enemies. We're doing that, and if, as you say, Xulai cooperates nicely, I suppose that's all we can expect."

He yawned widely, gaping at the sky. "I doubt we'll be visited again tonight. You three stay in the forest one more day and we'll rejoin company at our stopping place tomorrow."

"You're sure that's long enough?"

"It will have to be. The farther up the road we go, the narrower and steeper this valley gets. Black Mike's been up this road before, taking Woldsgard birds to the abbey, and he tells me you'll only have one more day of reasonably level ground among the trees. After that, we'll need to keep to the road or let you females ride mules. They're more sure-footed."

"How's Nettie and her so-called cousins?"

"No reason to think they're not doing well. They'll travel a bit faster than we can. They should be along tomorrow or the next day with the traveler either before or after."

"Then I wish you good morning, Bear. If I'm lucky, I'll get half a night's sleep."

They parted. Bear made his way up the meadow to his men, Precious Wind to her bed beneath the fallen tree with a feeling of relief that surprised her. She did not know what she would have said if Bear had pursued the question of the interest in Xulai. The answer she had given him was probably true. Perhaps she could merely have pointed out that the Duchess of Altamont did not need reasons to cause pain. Her own enjoyment in creating pain was reason enough.

They were asleep when a large owl came floating up the valley to circle above Bear's camp for some time. Four bedrolls beside a covered fire were visible. The owl, who could hear a mouse move a single whisker, heard breathing from each one of them. She moved over the forest seeking other life, finding some creatures visible, birds mostly, and other creatures only detectable by their breathing or small movements, in hollow trees, under a fallen trunk, in a copse of trees. She flew down among the trees, searching. Nothing under the fallen tree trunk but a family of wildcats; nothing in the copse but deer.

Blinking slowly, without volition, the owl flew back down the valley to Benjobz Inn. In the forest beside it, she lit upon a low branch. The woman before her stared into the owl's eyes. The owl, unable to move, thought of what she had sensed. The woman stared more intensely, hurtfully, digging deeply. The owl was first gripped by terrible uncertainty, then by terror, then by hideous pain as the woman snatched her feathered neck, grasped her head in one strong hand, and twisted . . .

Pain over, everything over, the feathered body dropped to the soil, where Alicia, Duchess of Altamont, stamped upon it furiously before striding back to the inn. Alicia really preferred liars. People who lied to her gave her excuse to terrorize and torture them, but the damned innkeeper had told her the truth! The child and her nursemaid had gone back to Woldsgard! They must have gone by while Alicia was taking her alternate route from Altamont, the route that nobody knew of but herself and Jenger, and a few of her guardsmen. So she had missed the ones going to the abbey and two mounted troops as well, both of them headed toward Wellsport; so said the innkeeper.

It was infuriating. Of all things in life, she loved having her own way, but it pleased her more to have it when someone else opposed it. It didn't matter whom she was vying against, or even whether they knew they were vying. It could be a bet on cards, a horse race, a plot to take over a kingdom. Any of these could involve an opponent who was fun to squash like a bug or even more fun to deal with deliberately, torturously, at excruciating length, best of all if they didn't know why! The delight of their seeking a reason, their frantic attempts to understand! Their despair when she told them there was no reason. So amusing when they realized she needed no reason except her own desires. She had looked forward to dealing with a lying innkeeper, looked forward to pursuing an irritating Tingawan presence, even to the very walls of the abbey. The innkeeper hadn't lied; the girl and her caretakers hadn't gone to the abbey, though possibly, only possibly, the man called Loppy might learn otherwise.

She would wait for Loppy to return before she gave up all hope for the amusement she had planned. And even if it were true, it would mean only a slight delay before she could find the girl and her guardians and kill them all. Perhaps when she returned to Altamont she would create a new Big Kill, one of her very own. Or perhaps she would wait until she went to Woldsgard, as wife of the duke. She would make him watch. Though it might work best to wait until she was his widow. Before he died, he could spend endless days tortured by her description of the deaths that would follow his own.

WILDERBROOK ABBEY WAS DECEPTIVE AT first appearance. As the re-united animals, people, and wagons came up the last pastured hill toward it, they saw first only the clustered bell towers fingering the sky. When they were a bit nearer, they saw a massive structure extending for a mile or more behind an even longer, though lower, wall. As they came still closer, they saw that the wall had its foundations at the bottom of a huge, circular depression in the grassland, one that curved away from them on either side, circling the abbey and continuing beyond it into the forest. The walls, for they were multiple, were very high, dotted with guardsmen along their lengths; the lands they enclosed were extensive; the depression was very deep—too deep, too wide, and too water-filled to be crossed except by way of a bridge.

There were several bridges. A leather-clad man on horseback beck-oned to them from the outer end of the nearest one. As they turned toward him, he motioned toward the drawbridge and portcullis be-tween the fourth and fifth of the huge stone piers that supported the structure. As they approached, the drawbridge rumbled down. The mounted man led them across, ironclad hooves and iron-sheathed wheels beating a reverberating tattoo upon the timbers. The narrowly grated portcullis rattle-clanged up into its recess in the thick wall, just high enough to clear the wagons, barely allowing time for Abasio's wagon to follow the rest before it thundered down behind him. Once through the wall, however, all this noise had gained them access to only a wide, curved corridor between the outermost wall and a taller, inner one that was no less heavily guarded. The two walls had a wide space between them, enough that they had no trouble turning the wagons to the right to follow their guide.

"There are three ring walls," the man called over his shoulder. "None of the gates are in a line. Different gates and bridges go through into different parts of the abbey. The outliers told us you were coming, and you're expected down this way." They went along the gentle curve for some time, passing various lowered portcullises before another gate presented itself on the left. When entered, it folded them between two walls, as before. This time they turned left for a short distance, then right through a gate leading onto a paved court, only a tiny corner of which was needed for all five wagons.

Xulai opened the carriage door and slid wearily down, followed by Precious Wind and Oldwife. Even after Nettie and the Farrier brothers had rejoined the party, Bear had maintained the fiction that the other three women were not with them. Each night they had slept apart, either in the carriage or in the woods. Each night, some animals had been separately picketed. One night, when Precious Wind had asked Xulai if she wished to tell the animals they were deer, the child had said, "No, why would I want to do that?"

"You did it before."

"I did? I don't remember that. Why won't Bear let us sleep nearby?"

"Don't ask me to explain it," Bear had said rather sharply. "Just humor me by pretending not to be with us for a day or two more." In truth, he found her an uncomfortable presence, easier to manage thinking about at a distance.

Now people bustled around the wagons. From the top of a flight of stairs, the prior, glittering with gold embroideries, came down to introduce himself and welcome them. He took Xulai by the hand, and she had to force herself to leave it in his grasp. It was not rough, it did not hold too tightly, but something about it made her feel revulsion.

His voice was deep, full of charm, his smile almost believable. "We're glad to welcome you, Daughter. The Duke of Wold and our dear abbot are old friends."

Xulai had watched him descend. He was of middling height, about the age of her cousin Justinian, though he walked swiftly, surely; his hair was white, but there was a lot of it, as neatly trimmed as the beard that rimmed his narrow face; his eyes were watchful. His robes were actually white but the golden veil attached to his high crowned hat and the gold embroidered stole hanging down the front of his robe made him glitter in the sunlight. Xulai found herself wondering if he went anywhere without them. To the privies, perhaps. If such a man used a privy. "I am very grateful for your welcome, sir."

"Elder Brother," he corrected her, with his ever-so-slightly stingy smile, his hands stroking the fall of gold along his robe. "That is what we all are here, brothers and sisters, elder and younger, who make sons and daughters of the youngest ones. Some of us are given to books, some to music, some to the land, some to crafts, and some to arms. The abbot himself is Eldest Brother, of course."

"Was it your people we saw riding toward the falls?" she asked. "Did my cousin send word of some kind?"

The prior looked up, his eyes focused on something beyond her, brow furrowed, "Well, I . . ."

"If you know, please tell her," said Precious Wind a bit snappishly. "She'll worry over it if you don't."

Xulai flushed. She hadn't meant to ask him anything. She wished she hadn't. "If it is supposed to be a secret . . ."

The prior licked his thin lips, obviously deciding what to say. "By all the spirits and virtues, no, child. I just don't want to upset anyone need-lessly. I believe the duke sent word to the abbot saying he had an . . . an intimation that Woldsgard might be attacked. He asked for reinforce-ments from us. He said his people have been at peace so long, they have grown fat and lazy and may have forgotten how to fight."

"Had he any intimation of where this attack might come from?" asked Bear.

The prior licked his lips again. "Perhaps something was said about Kamfels."

He's lying, thought Xulai.

Bear and Precious Wind shared a glance. "Siblings at war?" mur-mured Precious Wind, too softly to be heard by anyone but Bear. "Is the Duke of Kamfels teasing his sister again?"

"Or perhaps helping her," whispered Bear. He looked deeply into the prior's eyes. "Elder Brother, your people would have been there only shortly before a great number of the king's men. The two troops were separated by only half a day."

The prior nodded, his mouth twisted, as though he had bitten into something sour. "Well, yes, so we heard. In any case, the troops of Prince Orez were there before either of us. Our men went back to Neth-erfields, and the king's troops went on, I believe, to Kamfels. Perhaps Justinian, Duke of Wold, intended a show of force. Though I believe he informed us later that the rumor he had heard might have been false, a feint, perhaps, to keep Wold off balance, or to diminish the strength of his friends by moving men into places they were not needed."

And that is a lie, thought Xulai. *The rumor was true, and the invading force came from Ghastain, but . . . what were the men from here supposed to do? Fight them?*

"Oh, we do hope the duke did not weaken his friends," said Precious Wind with sham concern.

"No, no. The abbey has not been weakened and any of our people not needed in Netherfields will soon return."

Before anyone else could speak, Xulai said in her most childish voice, "Do we have to talk now, Elder Brother? I know you're very busy and we are very tired."

The prior nodded, grateful for her interruption. "Of course you're tired. From the look of all of you, you would probably relish baths and something besides camp food. Our brothers and sisters have everything ready for you and you'll talk about any of these other matters with the abbot himself tomorrow."

He beckoned. A pair of white-robed, blue-veiled people came toward them, trailed by a brown-robed brother. "Will you all please stay here with Brother Rahas"—he indicated the brown-robed one—"just long enough to sort out the baggage you need? Then, Brother Pol, when they're unloaded, if you'll show the men the way to the stables, help them care for the beasts, and then show them the way to the men's baths and their rooms? Sister Tomea will take you to your rooms. Xulai, Daughter, we don't have your permanent quarters ready, but you'll be comfortable in temporary ones."

"Elder Brother?" said Xulai in a voice dripping with weariness.

"Yes, Daughter?" he replied, his eyes still focused somewhere else.

"The lady who died at Woldsgard left some of her beautiful court clothes for me to have when I am grown. They're in a crate in the bottom of the dray. They're all sealed up so moths can't get at them, so please, ask your people not to open the crate. Can it be put away somewhere until I'm older?"

The prior leaned forward, reached out with a vague motion, as though to pat her shoulder or head, abruptly withdrew, and called out: "Did you hear that, Brother Rahas? You'll take care of it? Good."

The brown-clad brother nodded agreement, then went among the horses, looking them over, while other brown-clad people began unpacking the wagons and stacking the goods as Oldwife directed. When the things they would need immediately were separated from the rest, Sister Tomea led the new arrivals and half a dozen brown-clad porters up the steps onto the terrace, right along it, then left through an arch, down a corridor that became a long cloister with numerous doors on the right, one for each of the arches on the left that opened upon a garden full of fruit trees, roses, and a tall, plashing fountain. At the end of the cloister an iron gate blocked their way. The sister unlocked it, carefully locking it behind them as she remarked, "This is a secured area," while proceeding toward another gate that stood open. Beyond this was a wide foyer with several heavy doors, one of which opened into a cozy, many-windowed room with padded chairs and an iron stove. In addition to the entry door there were two others, one leading into a small courtyard, one into a hallway separating two bedrooms and a steamy room almost filled by a huge wooden tub.

"How'n all the world do you keep that warm?" asked Oldwife of the sister. "Must take fifty buckets, at least!"

Sister Tomea smiled. "Outside that wall is a pipe that comes from a hot water spring deep under the abbey. It runs in and out constantly, keeping itself warm. When we want to clean the tub, we block the inflow and let it cool before we run the water off into the gardens."

"You have these all through the abbey?" asked Precious Wind.

Sister Tomea shook her head. "Not all through, no, but enough of them that everyone has access to a tub. Here in the secure guest quarters, there's one bath for our lady guests and one for the men. The men must share theirs, but since we have no other female guests at present, you ladies will have this one to yourselves until your house is ready."

"Our house?" asked Xulai.

The sister nodded. "There are a number of houses by the back wall, in the enclosed meadows. Originally they were built by certain families who wanted to live here at the abbey."

"Or who wanted their elderly men and women to live somewhere else," said Oldwife, clenching her teeth.

Sister Tomea hid a quick grin. "That's as may be, ma'am, and I'm not saying it's always untrue, but as it happens, no one has been housed in any of them for some time. One of them is being newly paneled and cleaned. No doubt the abbot thought it would be more convenient to have all your party together and both a stable for your animals and storage for your property. That way, you'll have some privacy without brothers or sisters or children from the school walking over you and around you all the time." She smiled as though delighted by this idea. "And you'll be a bit farther from the bells. They take some getting used to . . ."

She was interrupted by her subject as a great bell rang high above her, the initial bong succeeded by a multitoned peal. "First supper warning," said Sister Tomea.

Xulai asked, "What is the building with the towers?"

"It's where we worship and sing. Actually I should say it's where we sing in order to worship."

"This is very nice," said Xulai. "Please tell the abbot and the prior we are very grateful."

As Sister Tomea went out into the hallway, closing the door behind her, Precious Wind cried, "Bath first," stripping off her clothes as though they were a fruit skin, leaving them where they fell, and striding naked toward the tub. Nettie, though still fully dressed, hesitantly went after her.

Oldwife and Xulai returned to the sitting room where the porters had stacked their baggage, including the cat basket, which rocked violently atop a pile, threatening to fall any moment. Xulai let the animals out, and they followed her to the outside door. As soon as it was opened they darted across the small area of stone paving to the garden planted around its edges. Bothercat went on complaining for some time while casting irritated looks at Xulai. "This is all your fault," he was saying. "I've never been so ill treated in my entire life."

"That was unlike you out there," Oldwife said, "interrupting the prior."

"We were all saying too much," Xulai said. "We don't know him. We got here and we were tired and we stopped being careful. Besides, he told a lie."

"What lie?"

"He said my cousin told them it was a rumor, a feint. When did he do that? He was gone before the troops got there. I was watching the prior's eyes. His eyes are cold, and they flicker when he tells a lie."

Oldwife stared at her, through her, shaking her head. "Go along to the bath, child. I'll keep an eye on the cats, and when you younger creatures have finished, I'll have a wash. I'm not such a one as you Tingawans for the submerging of my whole naked self in company with other naked selves. In fact, I'm surprised at Nettie Lean!"

Woldsgard also had a bathtub, not unlike the ones in the abbey, built by the duke for Princess Xu-i-lok, who had refused to behave as barbarians did by either sponging with a cupful of hot water or staying dirty all winter. Xulai and Precious Wind had used it frequently, and Xulai got herself into the tub almost as quickly as Precious Wind had done. Two smooth wooden benches were fastened to the walls of the tub, one higher than the other, and the two of them sat with water up to their necks while Precious Wind hummed and splashed. Nettie, however, was still undressing, garment by garment, finally lowering herself slowly into the tub and simply sitting there, wide-eyed.

"They do this in Tingawa?" she asked Precious Wind.

"Oh, yes," she replied. "We certainly do. Daily, or more often. Of course, it's not such labor as it is here. It's warm there. The water tanks are heated by the sun . . ." She hummed a bit more before climbing out of the tub, applying soft soap to a gourd sponge, and scrubbing herself all over before filling a bucket from the tub and rinsing the soap away. The water ran away into a gutter around the edge of the room and out through the wall.

Precious Wind sighed with pleasure as she climbed back into the tub. "That's the way we do it in Tingawa, so we don't ever sit in dirty water. This one is built so well that I wager the Elder Brothers had a Tingawan guest who suggested it and drew the plans."

Nettie followed her example, then Xulai, who was having a hard time staying awake. Finally, and not without a regretful look at the still steaming water, they wrapped themselves in large towels and returned to find Oldwife unpacking their clothing and distributing it onto shelves or into the carved chests under the windows of each bedroom.

"Each of these rooms has two beds. I've put Xulai's things in that room with mine." She pointed to the smaller room. "Nettie, you and

Precious Wind can share the other. Everything we brought is in the chests or piled on the shelves. You can rearrange it to suit yourselves." And with that she disappeared to take care of her "bit of wash."

Xulai's clothing had been laid ready on the bed: a white linen, knee-length, short-sleeved undershift and drawers with a drawstring top; clean stockings that were held up by being laced through the eyelets in the bottom of the drawers; and an ankle-length, long-sleeved gown with tiny ruffles at the wrists and neck. *Aside from being badly wrinkled, the clothing was decent enough to be seen in public,* Xulai thought. Folded on the lowest shelf was the striped, sleeveless coat she had worn when they left Woldsgard. She had others, but this one reminded her of her cousin saying it became her, and she was busy doing up its thirty buttons when Oldwife came in.

"Put on your better shoes," said Oldwife as she dried her face on the ends of the towel draped around her shoulders. "They're beside your bed. Those others look like you've been slopping pigs in them." She rummaged in her own chest, finding a clean cap and long apron, as symbolic of her status as any of the veils and stoles worn by the abbey people were of theirs.

When all four of them returned to the sitting room, Sister Tomea was waiting for them. She smiled at them, put her finger to her lips, and turned to face the door. Somewhere a bell rang. Sister Tomea bowed her head. It rang again and again, seven deep, reverberant sounds with silences in between. After the seventh, she opened the door, remarking, "During the ringing of the supper bell it's customary to recite our thanks. The noise and hurry in the dining hall give us no time for reverence once we're there."

They went back the way they had come, alone as far as the locked gate, which was again locked behind them, then as part of a stream of people that broadened as they moved along the cloister and broadened yet more in the shorter hall beyond. Upon the terrace they became part of a slowly moving swarm, people thronging in from every direction and thrusting themselves through the enormous quadruple doors of the dining hall. Some wore leather; some were cloaked in black, others in gray or brown, many in white with stoles and veils of various colors. The children, who wore no particular dress, darted in and out of the crowd, some of them glancing curiously at Xulai.

Xulai's group found Bear, Bartelmy, and the other four men waiting for them at a table at the far back corner of the room, quite near an enormous open hatch with an even more enormous kitchen behind it. Xulai sat down and stared into a vast space full of sweat- shined faces and running legs. "Cart!" yelled someone in a deep bass voice. "Coming," cried someone else, and the cart plunged across the vast kitchen impelled by three tall boys. Within moments the same cart was at the open hatch, and the boys were unloading its contents: stacks of dishes, arranged in ranks and files. Behind them, other carts went to and fro, and in the background blades glittered as something or other was carved up by a whole phalanx of cooks. "Eggs," shrieked a high voice. "Coming," cried another, and a cart darted by loaded high with baskets.

Xulai turned to look behind her. Across the room, in the opposite corner, another such hatch fronted another such kitchen. A bell rang. Sister Tomea rose and went to the hatch, where the towers of dishes were lined up, returning swiftly with a stack of ten. Xulai counted the people from other tables who were rapidly picking up stacks of plates. About one hundred people. One hundred tables in this half of the dining hall. The tables each seated ten, with a bench on each of the long sides and one chair at each end, and there were only a few empty seats and very few empty tables. Two thousand people, not counting the fifty on the dais at the far side.

"It's quickest this way," said Sister Tomea as she passed out the dishes. Each time the bell rang she took another of them to collect something from the hatch: Precious Wind to collect mugs and jugs of milk; Bear for salad; Nettie for a platter of meat; the others for various bowls and baskets until all the fetching was done. By the time the cake platter was set in the middle of the table, all plates were full and the hall was aroar with people chattering, bowls and platters thumping, utensils scraping and clattering. Each of them had been given a folding knife, a folding fork, and a folding spoon, though some at neighboring tables ate with their fingers and some used two slender sticks, like pinchers.

Sister Tomea had seated herself at the center of one bench, where Willum and Clive had made room for her. "Normally, I won't eat with you. I'm just with you today to show you how to find your way and what the rules are. Eldest Brother feels it's important that no one be exempted from doing what is needed for the life of the abbey or the earth." She made the two-handed sign that meant "holy work," two fingers of her right hand walking across the back of her left hand, down her middle finger into the future. "That means we don't have servers, and everyone takes a turn in the kitchen, even the children who are old enough, though the cooks are specially trained to ensure the food is good. Same with the laundry, the gardens, the stables, and so on. The experts run each thing, but everyone has a turn at providing the less-skilled labor. The best helpers are often the ones trained to take over later on.

"The utensils on this table are provided for you. When you are finished eating, lick them clean, wrap them in your napkin, and take them with you when you leave. Remember to bring utensils and napkin to the next meal. Use the napkin until it's too dirty to use, then drop it off in the basket by the door and pick up a clean one. The wrapped utensils will fit easily in a pocket. If you prefer others, by all means bring them with you, so long as they can fit in a pocket. No one carries bare knives in the abbey, and we only furnish them once.

"When we finish eating, we pocket our utensils, stack our dishes on the trays stored under the table, and carry them back to the scullery as quietly as possible." She reached under the table, pulled out a large tray, and pointed to another huge hatch to the left of the kitchen hatch. "What comes from the kitchen is clean, what goes to the scullery is dirty. Don't mix up the two. It's considered impolite to yell or talk too loudly, but we can converse quietly right up until the abbot or next-eldest rises and gives the concluding blessing.

"After the blessing, don't stay seated. There'll be another seating for dinner within a very short time, so it's important to clear tables and get out promptly. It's easiest to clear the tables if at least three people do it—there are three trays under the table. Always unload the trays at the scullery and bring the empty tray back to stow under your table. The trays have your table number painted on them. No one else will unload them for you, and you'll find clearing without trays a bother and getting trays back if you leave them even more so. Never let just one person do the clearing; it's not polite."

She looked around the table to see that they understood before continuing. "People are split up into tens, but families generally sit together or at adjacent tables. Children sit with their parents or guardians. Children who have no parents or guardians at Wilderbrook sit with their group leaders or teachers. Because you have all come together, Elder Brother says we are to treat you as a family. You will have this table, number twenty-three, at each evening meal. The number is carved into the top at each end. The morning and noon are different. We don't all rise at the same time or finish morning chores at the same time, so anytime within two hours after the breakfast bell, we go to the kitchen hatch, pick up what we want to eat and drink, sit wherever there's room, and take our own dishes to the scullery. Same at noon."

Willum interrupted his eating to ask, "Will us hostlers have kitchen duties and such?"

"It depends on how long you'll be staying," said Sister Tomea. "Hostlers would probably be asked to help in the barns and stables or on the farms. And, of course, if people are assigned to work at a distance from the abbey, they pick up packed lunches at breakfast and they aren't expected until evening. If the duty means you can't get here for evening meal, or have kitchen duty, you'll be given a tag to hang on the chair at the head of the table. If you're sick, the infirmarian will send someone to hang it for you. That way when a tallyman comes through, he knows who's missing and why."

"Missing?" asked Precious Wind doubtfully. "Perhaps one simply isn't hungry."

"If you aren't on duty and don't have a permit from the infirmary, you're here at evening meal," said Sister Tomea. "If you're not hungry, you can always do without or take your share to eat later, but you're here at mealtime. There aren't many requirements here at Wilderbrook Abbey, but that's one of the most important ones. We have to know where people are, and this is the easiest way. If someone is missing, and we know he was on wood detail, we may find him under a fallen tree somewhere. If a tallyman comes to a table, and you have a family member who's feeling unwell, you can tell him the reason, but the person who tells the reason is responsible for the person after that. If you say your brother is sick, then you're responsible for getting help for him if he gets sicker.

"Also, everyone is given a shift for supper. You've been given one bell as your meal assignment, first seating, one bong repeated seven times. Other seatings have different bells. There are bells for other things as well, emergencies, fires, report for duty. You'll get used to hearing them.

Serving three meals takes about ten hours, two each for breakfast and lunch, more than six for supper. One crew does breakfast and lunch, another crew does supper. Tonight there will be three other seatings after this one."

"That's eight thousand people," said Xulai wonderingly.

"Eight thousand if we're full. Actually, none of the seatings are completely full. We have about six thousand in this arm of the abbey. Temporary guests don't eat here. Passersby are fed in the guest arm at the north end of the abbey, just inside the northernmost gate in the outer circle. It's near the guest housing. We don't really want people in here who are just passing through. It's too confusing for them."

"You said, 'in this arm of the abbey,'" said Black Mike. "There are others?"

Sister nodded. "Well, for instance, there's food service in what we call an anytime arm at the south end, inside the southernmost gate between walls two and three. Anytime service is for the soldiers and guards and people doing other kinds of work where they have to eat when they can. Some kinds of work you can't just put down and walk away from because it's lunchtime, you know? Then there are the separated arms, back in the mountains, some large, some small. Forestry has a couple. The farms have a dozen or so. Military has several. Those places have their own kitchens. That's where the men who went to Woldsgard came from."

"Why do you call them arms?" asked Xulai.

Sister Tomea laughed. "Because there are hands at the end of them, busy doing things. Only the choir has no arms, just voices."

All of this was a good deal to take in. The huge dining hall was noisy but not deafening, despite the chatter going on. Xulai took note of several tall, rangy individuals with long gray hair who mounted tall daises at each corner of the room and made rapid notations on a chart. The talleymen, said Sister, each one responsible for a certain block of tables. When almost everyone had finished and was just sitting there, dishes stacked, the tallymen went to the dais where the abbot sat, handed him their tally sheets, and retreated. The abbot summoned several of the men and women waiting near the table, handed out the lists. When they had departed, he leaned forward and struck a bell. Immediately everyone rose, heads bowed. The abbot said a few words, both the sound and sense of them lost in echoes, struck the bell again, and everyone moved, most of them streaming toward the doors, others, those on kitchen duty, toward the scullery hatch.

"What did we eat?" asked Oldwife as they left. "I was so caught up in what you were saying, Sister, I didn't notice."

"Lamb stew," said Nettie. "A dish of grain with herbs and onions. A dish of carrots, beets, and parsnips, chopped fine and cooked with butter, vinegar, and sugar. Where do you get butter and sugar, Sister?"

"Butter from our own cows, sugar from the southlands or honey from our own bees. We trade wool and leather for things we can't grow here. Our own orchards produce cider and vinegar."

"Ah," said Pecky Peavine. "We also had greens, bread, milk—very good milk—and some fruit. Everything good, though Mike was saying he'd have preferred beer."

"He may have that," said Sister Tomea. "Those who wish it may bring it to evening meal or may have it in their own rooms. The cellarer will be available in the morning. He keeps beer and wine for sale."

"For sale?" asked Xulai. "Do all these people get paid?"

Sister Tomea said, "All sworn members of the abbey get a personal allowance to spend as they see fit. On books. On wine. On fancy clothes or weapons to wear when they're off duty. People who are traveling through or lodging here or studying here pay for their housing and food. We presume they have their own money for wine or whatever. To its members, the abbey provides only needful things: shelter, food, clothing, warmth in winter, education and training and the means to stay clean."

"And how does the abbey make money?" Precious Wind asked.

"We have many profitable endeavors. The abbey's products are well known. Our school is famous. People pay to have their children educated here. People pay for the foods we produce, the crafts we create. They pay for the armed men who protect their caravans on the desert, their curricles on the road, their caravels on the sea—though that's not frequent these days. They hire the guides who take them through places like the Lake of the Clouds. The lodging for the ten of you has been paid for by Justinian, Duke of Wold, as has Xulai's schooling. The abbot would not ask that we labor without pay, not even for friends."

"Yet one would suppose you have many friends, all around the world," said Precious Wind.

Sister Tomea smiled, a small, catlike smile. "I do not presume to say it is true, but one might suppose that, yes. Now, one more thing before I take you back to your rooms. Those of us with blue veils and stoles are responsible for the hospitality of the abbey. You are guests, and we are the ones who see to your needs and comfort. If you need something, ask any of us blues, or ask any brother or sister to find one of us for you."

"Your colleague in brown is assigned to the stables?" asked Bear.

"He is a brother of the soil, which includes the stables, the barns, the farms, the tillage of the earth, the animals, the use of their manure on the land, the wagons and carts, the maintenance of roads, the building of walls. The green brethren are the planters and tenders of trees, pastures, and crop land. Red stoles are our healers. One of our many educational arms is the college of healing. Gray robes with hoods and black bands are architects and planners who see that we have irrigation channels and drinking water and that our refuse is properly disposed of so we don't generate illnesses. Black robes are scholars and teachers. Helmed men are among our warriors. Those who are leather clad or those with leather aprons are craftsmen of one kind or another: potters, woodworkers, carpenters, masons. Scholars and craftsmen wear an insignia on the left shoulder that tells what they do. Only our singers wear unadorned white. The abbot and prior and other members of the council wear gold.

"Now, are you ready for a night's rest?"

Xulai nodded, heaving a great sigh of relief. She wanted nothing more than to sleep, preferably for a long time, and she could see from the expression on Precious Wind's face that she agreed. There was something she needed to talk with Precious Wind about, but . . . she could do it later. Bear led the menfolk off in another direction while Xulai and the women followed Sister Tomea, finding the route of corridors, gates, and cloisters almost familiar.

Xulai had thought of reading something—there were books on the shelves of their sitting room—but when she entered the room she staggered, overcome by weariness so deep and punishing that it was like a sudden sickness. Without a word, Oldwife and Precious Wind led her into the bedroom, where Oldwife helped her undress, pulled a night-gown over her head, and tucked the covers under her chin.

"Oldwife, is my face dirty?" Xulai murmured.

"Would I have let you go to dinner with a dirty face? Why would you ask that?"

"Ever since I've been here, it's like people don't look directly at me. They sort of stare over my shoulder."

Oldwife tucked the blanket more closely. "You're just tired. Go to sleep now."

Fat black-and-white Bothercat came to curl near her shoulder; spot-ted Vexcat stretched along her side, the unvarying rhythm of their purr-ing floating her even deeper into stillness.

The older women left the room, shutting the door behind them. From Xulai's cloak pocket a small black nose appeared, whiskers twitched, a head emerged. It was not a very large creature, but it was most certainly a good deal larger than a chipmunk.

XULAI DREAMED. SHE HAD BECOME a tree, a tiny one, roots clipped, limbs clipped, wired into a strange, lopsided shape and planted in a shallow bowl. She was very happy in her bowl, but something had happened to it. It was cracked.

"Broken," someone said firmly. "It cannot be mended again."

Xulai felt for the crack with one of her roots. The sensation was like feeling for a loose tooth with her tongue, feeling around the break, the hole, fascinated by the rough underside of the tooth and the tenuous fragility of its connection to her. Her root pressed into the fault. Under the increased pressure the bowl cracked wide; a piece of it fell outward. Her root went sliding after it, searching for something. Soil. Deep soil.

She found it. Ecstasy came as energy flowed upward from the earth. She sensed more of it waiting in every direction. There was room for her roots to move, to ramify. There were no boundaries. She flexed her limbs and the wires around them loosened the tiniest bit. She put out a bud and slightly extended a leaf.

"Enough," said someone into her ear, stronger than a chipmunk voice, more forceful. "Enough for now."

She wanted to argue, but it was too much trouble. It had been such a long, long day . . . trip . . . life . . . time.

XULAI WOKE IN THE MORNING with the memory of her dream quite clear. It stayed with her as she sat up, waking the cats, who had been curled against her side. Yawning, she fumbled her way to the washbasin, trying to hold on to the dream as she washed her face, combed her hair, still half-dreaming as she put on the clothes she had worn the evening before.

Oldwife's bed was empty. She had risen early, as she always did: up with the chickens, as she herself said, and to bed with them also. Before leaving the room, Xulai thrust her hand into the pocket of her cloak, which was hanging on a hook beside the door, and stood very still, eyes wide with shock. Very slowly, she withdrew her hand and stepped back. A nose emerged, whiskers, two black eyes considerably larger than chipmunk eyes, two small round ears, then a body that came out a bit at a time and kept on coming. Front legs, a long, brown belly, back legs, a long, long tail. On the bed, the cats sat up, ears pricked, and watched very carefully, without moving.

"Cookies and grain did very well for chipmunk," the creature said. "I will need meat. Or fish. I can also make do with eggs."

"What?" she asked. "I mean, who?"

"Suit yourself." The creature nodded. "I'd suggest a name that's not species dependent. It'll save you changing it every little while."

"Species?"

"This one? I'm sure it's the weasel family. Perhaps mink, or ferret, or perhaps a young fisher. Ah, yes, that has a certain resonance. A young one, not fully grown. Don't worry about it now, just remember the eggs."

The creature disappeared into the pocket of the cloak once more, and Xulai, her eyes still wide with surprise, trailed by cats, went into the sitting room and across it to open the outside door for them. When she turned, she found Oldwife and Precious Wind sitting by the woodstove where the kettle steamed, staring at her, their teacups unregarded in their hands.

"What?" she said testily.

Oldwife said in a strangled voice, "Child! Why, you don't look like yourself!"

There were no mirrors in the bedrooms but there was one in the dressing area of the bathroom. Poised before it, Xulai stared at a stranger. No. Not a stranger, just someone unfamiliar. It was herself, but she looked thinner and much less childish. Precious Wind came in and peered over her shoulder.

In a voice totally lacking surprise, she said, "Well, overnight you've grown up a bit."

"Overnight?" Xulai cried angrily. Change was one thing, but this was something else again! "People don't grow up overnight."

"Of course not. What I meant was . . . I think you have ordinarily appeared much younger than you really were."

"This is the same dress I wore last night! It fits. It fit me yesterday and when we left Woldsgard, so I obviously haven't grown!" She stamped back into the sitting room, angry for no reason she could name. "Nettie made me this dress ages ago. It still fits. So I can't have grown any. Where is she? She'll tell you."

Oldwife and Precious Wind shared a glance, then Oldwife said coaxingly, "Nettie is visiting with her aunt. She never measured you when she made your clothes, Xulai. She just took a piece of cord from your shoulder to the floor and knotted it, then one from the middle of your neck to the shoulder, from the shoulder to the wrist, around your waist, around your chest—come to think of it, she recently changed that one . . ."

"My chest?" Xulai put her hands inside the long striped coat to feel her chest, strangely soft. "I have . . . I have breasts?"

"I don't know," said Oldwife. "I never saw breasts on you, and I'll guess you never saw them, but then, maybe both you and we were only allowed to see a little girl."

"You all stay here," Xulai muttered. She went back to the mirror and stripped off the clothes she had just put on. She had breasts. They were not large; Tingawan women didn't have large breasts. But they were definitely present. She raised her arms, felt of her groin. She had hair growing both places, dark and silky. Precious Wind had explained this long ago in the bath at Woldsgard. Precious Wind had told her all about women and how they changed when they were no longer children. Women did the moonblood thing, too, that monthly thing. This could not have happened overnight, and yet she would have sworn yesterday that she had no breasts, no hair growing on her body.

In the mirror she saw herself shaking, though she couldn't tell whether it came from anger or fear. Panic, perhaps. She wanted to cry or scream. She put her clothes back on, awkwardly mishandling the buttons with trembling fingers. It would have been pleasant to curl into a ball on her bed and pretend this was not happening. She had known persons at Woldsgard to do that when confronted with unpleasant reality. Farmer Gilsek's widow did so after he died, Old Fennig, who worked at the forge, when his son ran off. Curling up in a ball hadn't helped either of them, so it was unlikely to help her. She took three deep breaths and concentrated on the Way of the Turtle, an exercise Precious Wind had taught her when she was very young and excitable. The Way of the Turtle was slow and placid and very, very quiet.

She went slowly back to the sitting room, where she poured, very slowly, a cup of tea, keeping her hands still, her mind still. When she had seated herself and sipped at it, very slowly, she said in as calm a voice as she could muster, "I have breasts. I have hair on my body. It didn't come overnight, so I've been like this for some time. But you two haven't seen it? Last night in the bath, you didn't see it, Precious Wind?"

"We didn't see it." Separately and in unison.

Xulai tried to set the tea mug onto the table and succeeded only in spilling it on the floor.

"Sit down," said Oldwife to Precious Wind in a firm and commanding voice quite unlike her usual one. "Xulai is upset and she's obviously got to be told, and since the ones mostly concerned are here and she's already upset, this seems as good a time as any. Where are the men?"

"Gone to breakfast," Precious Wind said. "We won't be disturbed for a while."

Xulai put her cup on the table and folded her hands in her lap, trying desperately not to be angry at them, any of them, or all of them! "If there's something to be told, I believe it may be past time to tell it!"

Oldwife wiped her lips with her handkerchief and took a deep breath.

"Justinian, Duke of Woldsgard, and Xu-i-lok were in love. No, no, listen, don't flounce! I'm telling you. I have to start at the beginning. They were like two birds on a branch, giddy with happiness. They were betrothed and set a date for the wedding, but they did not wait on the wedding to love one another, and by the time the wedding date arrived, Xu-i-lok was several months pregnant.

"On the morning they were to be wed, she went walking in the woods. She returned white in the face, crying to Justinian that she had been cursed with death and with barrenness, that is, that in the future she would never become pregnant. She cried and laughed and cried again. The laughter was because she was already pregnant, though the one who cursed her had not known that. I was in the next room, making up their bed. I heard it all. I heard her laugh and cry, over and over . . ."

Her words came out, all in a train, as though rehearsed a thousand times, Xulai vaguely realized, as they no doubt had been.

Precious Wind caught Oldwife's glance and took up the story: "She and her father were staying at Woldsgard. The two of them together determined they could defeat the curse. By focusing all their power, they could defeat it for Xu-i-lok, but not for her unborn child. Or they could protect the unborn child, but not Xu-i-lok.

"Xu-i-lok shut herself up in the shrine room she and her father had set up at Woldsgard. She was in there three days. When she came out, she said she had consulted the spirits of her people, and she told Justinian she chose to save the child. I heard her arguing with her father. He wanted to save her. He said she could have other children. She told him something that I didn't overhear, and he stopped arguing. However, Xu-i-lok said that in order to protect the child, no one could know there was a child."

"You're talking about me," said Xulai, white faced. "You're talking about *me!*"

Precious Wind shook her head, held up her hand. "Don't say anything yet, Xulai. Just listen. Xu-i-lok stayed in her rooms. She and the duke had two marriage ceremonies, one performed by people from the abbey, one by priests from Tingawa. They did them both quietly, privately, with only a few trusted friends as witnesses. Shortly after that, it became known that she had fallen ill. After that, no one was allowed to see her but the duke; her father; Oldwife, who has midwived hundreds of babies in her lifetime; and a couple of Oldwife's sisters. When the child was born, that is, when you were born, Oldwife and her family smuggled you out of the castle and took you up to the Gancer home in the farmlands toward Karf.

"The ambassador, your grandfather, was with your mother when you were born, Xulai. I was there, a trusted friend, part of his entourage, which was a large one. Among the larger entourage was a fan waver or serving girl, a rather silly young woman, a remote cousin of a cousin of the ambassador's family. Her name was Bright Pearl. She surprised no one by falling in love with a Norland lad, a farm boy whose family supplied Ghastain with vegetables. He was in Karf visiting relatives. Bright Pearl married him and went to live on his farm, east of Ghastain. When the ambassador, your grandfather, returned to Tingawa, when he learned that the curse on your mother might be fatal sooner rather than later, he let it be known that the child of Bright Pearl would be Xakixa for his daughter.

"And what did Bright Pearl think about that?" snarled Xulai.

"Nothing at all. She never knew anything about it," said Precious Wind. "She was off in the country with her Norland farmer; she changed her name to plain Pearl—there had never been anything particularly bright about the girl to begin with—and subsequently bore him three sons, all of whom are still raising leeks, parsnips, and potatoes to supply the city and court of Ghastain. We keep an ear open for news of her or her family. She died several years ago during an epidemic of lung disease that swept through several villages. She never knew anything about you or your parents; she never had anything at all to do with the court. No one here in Norland knew what your grandfather told the people in Tingawa. There may be someone there he has trusted with the truth, but I don't know who that might be. The world believes you are Bright Pearl's daughter."

"And I . . . I was with you all the time?" Xulai said to Oldwife.

"With me and my two older sisters. They both died years ago. The only ones in Norland who know the truth about your parentage are Precious Wind and your father and me."

"Bear doesn't know?"

"Bear was sent later," Precious Wind said. "The . . . the sea wars began to be more troublesome, and your grandfather thought at that point we might need some rather personal kind of protection on the way to Tingawa. Bear has been told the Bright Pearl story; he knows nothing about your real parentage. You're just Xulai, daughter of Bright Pearl, an obscure family member who is no longer living. Lately, he's started thinking Xu-i-lok may be haunting you. He believes you use a Tingawan name only because of your function."

"But he thinks I was sent from Tingawa."

"He was told to *say* that about you! Actually, he believes you are Bright Pearl's child and were born here. He believes it is better if you do not know about her, for children have odd notions, sometimes, and go off hunting for fathers and mothers they would be better off without."

"Didn't he think it odd that I didn't grow up?"

"He was told you retained the childish appearance as a protection. To keep you safe. A kind of disguise. Which is true."

"Bear is tired of being protective," Xulai said. "He's talking a lot about getting back to Tingawa."

Precious Wind frowned. "I've heard him. Your father sent money here for him . . ."

"I know. He told me. Money for him and for you. Do you have the receipt, Precious Wind?"

"I do."

"Who signed it? Whose seal is on it?"

"Why, I suppose—"

"Please. Look. Now."

Precious Wind retreated to her room, came back with a folded bit of stiff paper. Xulai looked at it and paled.

"What's the matter?"

"The prior signed for it. This is his seal. I saw it on his finger. I think he's an evil man, Precious Wind. He has already lied to us. Please, do not give this receipt to the prior. Until we find someone here we know to be trustworthy, do not give it to anyone."

"I was going to tell Bear today that his bride-price is here, waiting for him."

"Precious Wind, I have a bad feeling about it. My father said it was a great deal of money, a small fortune. He thought Bear should not have it until he was on his way to Tingawa. It could have been tempting to someone. Let us be sure it is here, waiting for him, before we raise his expectations."

Precious Wind considered this. She had never thought that there might be someone inimical at the abbey! All in all, it might be wise to wait a few days while things were checked. She said slowly, "Bear's preoccupation is a troublesome development that none of us foresaw. I suppose I have the authority to tell him he may go on to Tingawa. That might be the best thing to do . . ."

Xulai stood up. "How long ago did you bring me to the castle?"

"Fifteen years ago," said Precious Wind. "You were almost four then, you are almost twenty now. In Tingawa, eighteen to twenty is the age of puberty. Until today, you looked about . . . seven. It was only an appearance, a glamour. Tingawan women mature more slowly than the women of Norland, so it was not greatly remarked upon . . ."

"Oh, it was remarked upon," grated Xulai. "Dame Cullen said I was a dwarf. Even the duke never called me daughter!"

Precious Wind did not let herself sympathize, though she felt the sadness. She said imperiously, "Think, Xulai! The appearance of babyhood helped keep you safe, as the princess and her father intended. If the duke had called you daughter, you and he would both be dead by now. Only his pretense kept you alive."

"Didn't they know that I had to grow up sometime?" she cried angrily. "What would have happened then?"

"You were supposed to be in Tingawa long before that happened," snapped Precious Wind. "As was I! No one lied about your being the soul carrier; you really are the soul carrier. Bear and I were to remain with the princess as long as she was alive, and then we were to return with you to Tingawa. The princess lived longer than *anyone* thought she could. Somehow, she learned or foresaw that you could not get to Tingawa safely, perhaps for a very long time. She told me this years ago, and she also told me she would provide for you another way."

"What way?" demanded Xulai.

Precious Wind shook her head. "We don't know. She looked into the future, she said. She didn't tell us how or why, or, unfortunately, how long it might take. Lately, Oldwife and I, we have supposed she gave you something of herself."

Still angry, Xulai said, "I honestly do not know what you're talking about!"

Precious Wind murmured, "On the way here, when you provided that the horses would not run away, when the duchess made a point of seeing you and all she saw was a baby. When you told the horses they were deer, the tree that it hid wildcats . . ."

"You think she did that?"

"No, we think *you* did that. We think she somehow endowed you with some of her own abilities. Don't ask me how, because I don't know. She wouldn't tell me. Perhaps she couldn't. It may be simply that you inherited an ability she had that she herself didn't understand. She did say, however, that it would be safer if no one knew who you really were but Oldwife Gancer and me."

"Don't be angry at us," Oldwife begged.

"I'm not angry *at* you," Xulai cried, wiping at the wetness on her face. "I'm just angry! I don't know who or what I am. I don't know how much of me is me and how much is someone else. I don't know if these parts of me will last or vanish overnight. I know everyone was just trying to protect me, but . . . I never called her Mother. Shouldn't I have at least called her Mother?" Furious tears streamed down her cheeks and dripped from her jaw.

"Did she ever ask you to do anything you didn't do?" Oldwife asked.

"Yes! No!" Xulai beat at the wall next to her with both fists. "The last thing was hard, I couldn't do it for a while, but I finally did. I did it the way a seven-year-old child really would have done it, with fear, and delay, and even avoidance. If I'd known how old I really was . . ."

Oldwife cried, "You couldn't know because you couldn't act the part! You had to think you were a child! You had to believe it! Oh, they stuffed your brain with all kinds of things, numbers and languages and history, but nothing about . . . being a woman, because you had to think you were a child. So long as you looked very young, people wouldn't talk about things when they were around you, man-woman kind of things."

"Oldwife, I heard about all that from the loft in the stables."

The old woman bit her lip. "Well, she . . . your mother tried! She wanted to keep you safe! If you did everything she asked, then she knew you loved her, and you've got to know she loved you! She died to protect you, Xulai. She suffered for years to protect you. And you've got to know the duke loved you, because he helped her do it! Not only them, Xulai. Precious Wind has given all those years to protecting you, and so have I. Anything that urgent, anything that terrible and painful, there's a reason for it. The princess had a reason, be sure of that. If, like they say, she saw the future, she wouldn't have sacrificed her life, loving Justinian the way she did, if there hadn't been a reason."

"But what reason? If I was part of it, shouldn't she have told me?"

Brow furrowed, eyes squinted, Oldwife considered this.

Precious Wind said carefully, slowly, "I think she felt you would be safer if you didn't know. Either she knew you would discover it when the time was right, when you really needed to know, or you would be informed in some way. There is something in your future that makes you terribly important."

It was too much. The tears went on streaming and she wept in Old-wife's arms as the old woman murmured, "You really did the things we saw you do, Xulai. You talked the horses into thinking they were another kind of animal. You talked a tree into hiding wildcats. You figured out something about the duchess that nobody else knew. So, maybe while you were inside your mama, she put a little bit of herself into you. Or maybe it was already there, just because she was your mama. A different part of your brain, maybe. You haven't taken hold of it yet, but it's there."

"Is it there always? Or will it leave me, too?"

"You know I can't answer that, Xulai."

They had reached an impasse. After a few moments' silence, Precious Wind said, "One thing I think we'd better agree on. We don't mention this to anyone here at the abbey. No one saw anything of what happened in the forest except we two. No one saw what happened on the road except we two. We should not talk about it even among ourselves in case someone is listening."

Oldwife Gancer said, "Whyn't you go to breakfast, Precious Wind? Maybe you can bring Xulai'n me a bite. They don't count people at breakfast, and this child needs a little time to settle without being angry at the whole world."

"Precious Wind," said Xulai, half choking on the words. "Could you bring me half a dozen eggs, please? Boiled eggs? Or meat of some kind?"

Wordlessly, eyebrows almost at her hairline in puzzlement, Precious Wind left them. Oldwife fetched a towel and mopped first Xulai's face, then the spilled tea before pouring another mugful and putting it carefully into Xulai's shaking hands.

"So how old am I?" Xulai muttered.

Oldwife patted her shoulder. "As we said, somethin' like twenty in Tingawan growth years, whatever that means."

"I don't understand this," Xulai cried. "What do I do next? I don't know what to do! I don't know how young women that age act!"

"There, there, child, now, well, you just go on being what you are. Precious Wind and I, we'll school you about the body business. Tingawan women don't get to that until they're about your age, and you already know about it. You're a Xakixa, you came here to be schooled, so you'll be schooled. Between the duke and those Tingawans, you've been well taught already. You speak their language and ours. You read, you write, you know all manner of things. As for not knowing how to act, you act more grown-up than most adults at least half the time! You've always been that way. Maybe now you need to learn things that people wouldn't normally teach a child."

"What do we tell Bear?"

"He knew you had some kind of protection woven around you. We'll tell him it was time for it to wear off, that's what we'll say."

"The prior saw me. The sister saw me. I was in the dining room."

"Last night I told Precious Wind what you said, about people at the abbey not looking directly at you, you know. We think they didn't see the child at all. She said they were seeing another you. We weren't, because we were used to seeing Xulai the child and Precious Wind says that's the image we were accustomed to. When you walked into this room this morning, though, there was no more child. Not a bit. Whatever it was, it was set to wear off when you didn't need it anymore."

On the outer windowsill, next to the outer door, Bothercat walked back and forth, tail lashing. Xulai went to let him and his brother in, trying to think of something, anything else. "What are we going to feed the cats? They can't go to the dining hall."

Oldwife went into her bedroom and brought out a package. "They'll have to settle for Woldsgard dried camp stew, just the way they did on the way here. I'll just break it up and put a little boiling water on it. Nettie will find something else in the kitchens if we run out."

Cats winding around her ankles, Oldwife prepared their food, holding the bowl aloft while the mixture cooled. When she resumed her seat, she asked, "Are you over being upset with everyone?"

"No," Xulai replied. "I am upset with everyone and everything, including myself. I don't know who this new person is. Is she pretty or plain?"

"You look a young lady, certainly. If there's any more changing to happen, it won't be much. As for talking and acting, I'd ask Precious Wind about that."

"You were once a young lady!"

Oldwife looked down, memories flooding in: Rising at dawn to milk cows. Bent to catch the light of fire at night as she sewed clothing. Her shoulders straining under the weight of full buckets from the well, her hands blistered from the hoe, wielded to keep the garden free of weeds. "Oh, no, child. A very long time ago I was a young woman, and that's a very different thing. People expect a young woman to be useful and work hard. For young ladies, expectations are much higher in some respects, far lower in others."

"Sister Tomea will be surprised."

Oldwife took a deep breath. "Yesterday, the way they spoke to you, I had the feeling they were seeing you differently than you were used to. I think they saw you pretty much the way you are today. It would make sense for everyone here to see you just as you will be while you're here. And you haven't seen the abbot yet, though you're supposed to do so this morning." She squeezed Xulai's hand. "Every girl who changes from child into woman feels strange, but the strangeness will pass. It really will."

Xulai shut herself into her bedroom to think this over. She knew this particular change would not pass. The strangeness was not merely a matter of age. It was greater than that, different from that, stranger than any of her companions had even considered. Sadly, it had come without a directory that might have defined what might happen, how she might behave, even what she might become. Recent experience indicated that when dangerous things happened, when the possibility of being maimed or killed seemed imminent, some protective knowledge would simply happen, without being summoned, even if she didn't want it. It would come! It would ride over her like a warrior on a war-horse, hooves pounding her own will into the earth, no matter what she wanted! Even if she would rather die, it wouldn't let her.

Not that she could conceive of really wanting to die.

"Weasel?" she called. "Fisher?"

Ears, a nose, eyes came out of the pocket of her cloak. "You forgot the eggs."

"Precious Wind will bring them. She'll be back before long. It's just . . . did my mother provide you? As a helper maybe? And what are you?"

"I don't know who provided me. I remember waiting a long time at the temple for someone to come. When you came, I knew you were the one. I'm your helper, guide, rescuer. Just now I suppose I am a fisher. I can move rather fast. I fit through tight spaces. I can't keep up with a horse, however, so if you're taken away by someone on horseback, you might expect to meet a bird shape instead of a four-legged one. Hawk, I should think. They're very swift. If you're in a dungeon or something of that sort, it might be most anything. I think I might be a whole tribe of gophers, perhaps. Or even a bear." He sounded rather pleased at the bear idea.

"All different?"

"Different shape, but always one thing. That's why I said I needed a name for you to call when you need me. No telling what form I might show up in, but always able to communicate. And always needing to eat!"

"You were the thing I swallowed? You couldn't have been. You came before I swallowed it."

"I was part of the box, but what you swallowed was something else." The sinuous creature disappeared into the pocket. Xulai sat on the side of the bed, struggling to think calmly. She felt she might have accepted all this more easily if she had the right to reject whatever thing or being might come shrieking out of her brain or heart or wherever it was hiding. She could have accepted it better if she could command it, tell it to go away.

However, she told herself in a kind of bleak despair, even if she couldn't command the future, she would like to command her own memory so she could forget that Xu-i-lok, despite her protective knowledge and skill, still had perished at the evil will of the Duchess of Altamont. And of all the people she wanted at this moment, she most wanted Abasio. If no one else could explain herself to herself, he probably could. Or he could help her find out. If he didn't already know.

An Awakening

WHEN PRECIOUS WIND RETURNED FROM THE DINING HALL, she brought a basket of hot bread, half a dozen boiled eggs, a ball of soft cheese, and several apples. "I have told Bear and the others," she said. "It will spare you having to explain or react."

Xulai took this in the spirit it was meant and thanked Precious Wind for her thoughtfulness. She went to her room to eat by herself, in order to think; actually she and the fisher thought together. Avoiding emotional subjects, they decided he would be called Fisher. This had a certain reference to water, which for some reason pleased the creature, and fishers were not common animals, which was acceptable to Xulai. Having eaten two eggs, Fisher returned to what he referred to as "his" pocket, carrying the uncracked eggs to eat later. Xulai returned to the living room.

"Bear reminded me that the abbot wanted to talk with us this morning," said Precious Wind. "Particularly with you, Xulai."

"Why not?" Xulai answered, managing to keep her voice level and staid, though she still roiled inwardly like a stormy sea. She could not remember ever having been this emotional before. She could not remember, in fact, feeling anything very strongly except affection and fear. She had loved the princess, had respected her Tingawan minders, and had found comfort and affection from Oldwife, who had taken out splinters and removed thorns and bandaged scraped knees. None of those feelings had been desperately ardent; they had required nothing but an obedient passivity. The one time she'd been asked to do something really active, she had almost ruined it. Now she thought it a pity she couldn't have been angry a lot sooner, for anger demanded something of one! It demanded action! Response! Naturally, now that it was very difficult *not* to show how she felt, showing any emotion at all would be unwise.

She took a deep breath. "Meeting the abbot can't be any more difficult than the morning so far." She stood up and straightened her skirts, attempting a placid smile. It felt stretched, as though her lips wished to snarl and resented being refused the opportunity.

Precious Wind nodded. "Brother Aalon will guide us. He'll be here shortly."

Oldwife begged off the meeting, so it was only the two Tingawans and Xulai who followed the brother on a lengthy route that included several locked gates guarded by helmed men and ended at a heavy door with a knocker in the shape of a kraken. Their guide rapped three times. The door opened, apparently of its own accord, and they found the abbot, a small, clean-shaven man, head haloed with a mist of white hair. He was dressed in a simple white robe and seated behind a huge writing desk in a simple chair from which he rose as he beckoned them forward.

"Ah. Here is a partial contingent from the Woldsgard group. Your associates have nothing to share with me?"

Precious Wind bowed gracefully. "They're trying to get themselves and the animals settled, Eldest Brother, so we're the delegation."

"Thank you, Aalon," said the abbot. "There are some comfortable chairs in the little room down the corridor, if you don't mind waiting to take them back. We shouldn't be long."

The brother bowed and withdrew as the abbot gestured them toward a group of chairs around a table that bore a dozen little cups and a steaming pot over a candle warmer. "You'll like this," the abbot murmured. "Real Jen-tai. Last year's." He poured and distributed the cups from a lacquer tray.

Xulai sniffed the steam from the cup. Flowers. And hay. And something like piney woods. She sipped as the others were doing, no one speaking at all. Perhaps it was a Tingawan thing they hadn't told her of, this silent sipping. More likely it was an abbey thing, for surely over all those forgotten years she had been told everything there was to know about Tingawa!

When his cup was empty, the abbot sighed and turned it upside down on the tray. The others followed his example.

He said, "Now. I need enlightenment. I have received messages from my friend Justinian, but he has never gone into any detail. He has never sent me a messenger or a bird with anything beyond a hint."

This was not what Justinian had told her! Xulai took a firm grip on her tongue and said, "Details can kill. Messengers can be tortured. Birds can be shot with arrows."

Both Bear and Precious Wind stared at her in surprise. She returned their stare. She had no idea how to go on except . . . to go on!

The abbot nodded, his face grave. "Well, there is no bowman in this room. I did gather this trouble centered on Altamont. What do we know and what have we heard about Alicia, the Duchess of Altamont?"

He was looking at Precious Wind, but it was Xulai who answered, spontaneously, in the strange, peremptory voice she had used only a few times before.

"I will be happy to tell you what we know about the duchess, if you will tell us what is known about Huold the Fearless."

The abbot gave her a look of amused surprise, then went to the door, opened it, and called to Brother Aalon. "Call Brother Wordswell, Brother Aalon. It seems we need him."

"He's probably in bed, Brother. He spends most of his nights in the library."

"Well if he is, wake him."

They sat without speaking, Bear almost visibly steaming, Precious Wind regarding Xulai with a strange expression, half amusement, half concern, while Xulai herself sat suspended, in a kind of mental cobweb, thoughts going off in all directions and ending nowhere in particular. The abbot gave no hint either of discomfort or of what he might be thinking.

A rap came at the door, which opened to admit a very tall, gray, thin brother in wrinkled white robes and a disheveled golden stole, his golden headdress so far atilt it was in imminent danger of sliding down over one ear. He had obviously dressed in a hurry. His furry eyebrows struggled with each other over the bridge of his beaky nose, and his lips were pursed in annoyance. The wrinkles around his mouth indicated the expression was habitual.

"Sit down, Brother Wordswell," the abbot said invitingly. "Will you have tea? No? Well then, sit comfortably while this young woman tells us a tale and asks you for some information afterward."

Xulai folded her hands in her lap. "The abbot asks what we know about Alicia, Duchess of Altamont. To speak of her we must first speak of Mirami.

"Falyrion, Duke of Kamfels, had a wife, Naila; a daughter, Genieve; and a son, Falredi. Naila died. Not long thereafter, Falyrion married Mirami, who bore him a daughter, Alicia, and a son, Hulix. Then Falyrion died and Falredi succeeded to the ducal throne of Kamfels. Then Falredi died. Mirami's son Hulix succeeded him as duke. Mirami left Kamfels to her toddler son, under the care of a steward, and took her daughter, Alicia, to the court of King Gahls on the King's Highland. It is my understanding that the king calls his court, city, and the surrounding area Ghastain.

"Strangely enough, over the preceding few years, King Gahls had been married three times. All three of his young, healthy, virginal wives died soon after marrying, suddenly, strangely, and childless.

"King Gahls then married Mirami, who very promptly bore him a son, supposed half brother to Mirami's other children, though likely they are full siblings sired by her chamberlain and constant companion."

Bear half rose. "Xulai!"

She waved him down imperiously. "Alicia grew up and was given the duchy of Altamont. It was then suggested to Justinian, Duke of Wold, that he should marry Alicia, Duchess of Altamont. He, being already betrothed to a Tingawan daughter of the clan Do-Lok, refused this honor, and his wife-to-be was cursed on their wedding day. She later died strangely and childlessly, and the duchess Alicia is now trying to force a marriage with Justinian.

"One ducal husband and one ducal stepson dead in Kamfels, three royal brides dead in Ghastain, one ducal bride dead in Wold, all dead! And, after all these convenient deaths, one of Mirami's children is heir to the throne of Ghastain; one is Duke of Kamfels; one is Duchess of Altamont; and all three of the children, Rancitor, Alicia, and Hulix, are evincing considerable interest in Wold and the castle of Woldsgard.

"That is what we know about the duchess and her mother. Oh yes!

It is not impossible that Naila, Falyrion's first wife, was an even earlier target."

She looked up. Silence. Three pairs of eyes focused on her, three jaws slightly dropped. Brother Wordswell was staring at his hands. "I'm sorry," she said in an unapologetic tone. "I thought you wanted me to speak."

"How old are you?" asked the abbot.

"It seems I am about twenty," Xulai said with a slightly twisted smile.

Bear said disagreeably, "Twenty going on sixty-five."

"I had been told you were somewhat younger," murmured the abbot.

"What an odd coincidence!" Xulai replied, managing a smile. "I had been told the same thing. For some no doubt suitable reason, I was treated as though I was much younger and was enabled to look and act the part. I suppose it was a kind of protective coloration provided by the Tingawans who selected me as Xakixa. Now it is evidently time to give up that particular pretense. It's a relief to me, in a way, for it helps me understand why I've been troubled for quite a long time by feelings that did not seem suitably childish."

After a long moment's silence, the abbot said, "It's strange no one else has noticed these coincidences in Mirami's life."

Xulai nodded. "There has been some notice; covert, I should imagine. And there's no real reason anyone should have taken overt notice. The events occurred over a period of years and in separate places. The births of Alicia and Hulix came some years before the deaths of Duke Falyrion and Falredi; there was at least a year or so between the deaths of each of King Gahls's three young wives; the birth of the heir to the throne came years before Alicia was given the lands of Altamont and began her assault upon my . . . lord Justinian. And there were years, long years, after that before Princess Xu-i-lok died.

"To anyone hearing of these, they would have seemed separate happenings, one thing at a time, but I heard about them all at once, in the space of a few hours. It was like hearing a song, each verse with the same refrain. Death. Barren wives. Mirami." She looked down at her hands, then up into the librarian's quiet face. "Elder Brother, what do you know of Huold the Fearless?"

"And how did Huold get into this matter?" Wordswell asked.

Xulai had briefly thought she might tell the abbot about her real parentage and what she had learned about the duchess during her nighttime mission in the forest of Wold, but upon considering last night's meeting with the prior, she had decided against it. She was not entirely sure he could be trusted, and those things had been Xu-i-lok's secrets, her *mother's* secrets. She would keep them until she knew it was no longer necessary. The story she could tell was true in most of its elements, and it would do well enough.

"The road to the Stoneway, north of Wold, is little used. I often sat in one of the orchard trees along the road, well hidden from any passerby, a quiet place where I could read or merely sit and watch the birds. One day the duchess went past on her way to visit her brother. She passed very slowly, stopping here and there along the way, eating Wold with her eyes as I had seen her do before. I heard her remark to her companion that she intended to find something on Wold lands that Huold had left there. I wondered if that might be why she is so set on my cousin marrying her. So she'll have the right to scour the lands, looking for whatever it is."

"You never mentioned this to me," said Bear, his eyes slitted as they were when he was angry.

She smiled sweetly at him, ignoring the answering heat his tone had ignited. "Bear, I beg your pardon. It happened just before the princess died. If you'll recall, everyone at Woldsgard was grieving and distracted. Then this journey began, almost overnight, and there's been no time to talk quietly of anything at all. The trip has been long and tiring and dangerous, and it was more important to get here safely than to discuss the devices of ancient heroes, which, in fact, I had forgotten about until this morning."

"But since it did come to mind," the abbot said thoughtfully, "you thought it might be useful to know about it."

"Yes. Exactly. Who was Huold, and what was it he hid or left or buried on the lands of Wold, assuming he did any such thing?"

"The thing he supposedly took into the Icefang range during his last journey," said the abbot, cocking his head and staring at his librarian.

Brother Wordswell wiped his lips, shrugged, looked over the company searchingly, then settled himself. "Throughout all his many conquests, it was said that Ghastain wore or carried a mysterious thing of limitless potency which gave him great power." Wordswell shifted in his chair, head rotating back and forth slightly, as though glancing through an index on the wall that no one else could see. "It was said that this whatever-it-was allowed him to prevail even when the odds were against him, even when vastly outnumbered, even when he attacked heedlessly, without planning. The post–Before Time historian Thrastus Danilus tells us that as Ghastain's reputation grew, so did his pride. He thought himself invincible. He coveted the world!

"During all those years, Huold was his faithful and beloved companion, many times wounded in Ghastain's service. He was sometimes called the Arm of Ghastain. We learn from the historian Barkamber that when Ghastain ran out of other places to covet, he amassed an armada and sailed westward to seize the isles of the Sea King. Barkamber quotes the stories of that time, which tell us that the Sea King called up the power of the deep. Waves taller than the tallest tree rose from the depths; Ghastain grasped the thing of power and called upon it, but it was of no use. He and all his men were drawn down into the sea.

"Only one man returned from the armada of Ghastain: Huold, only thereafter called the Fearless or the Heroic. He arrived at Ghost Isle on the back of a great silver fish. There's an interesting mosaic of it, as a matter of fact, in the castle of—"

"Just the story," interrupted the abbot. "Please."

The librarian frowned, trying to remember where he'd left off. "Ah. He told the people of Ghost Isle that he stood beside Ghastain when the great wave came. He said that he leapt into the sea himself and grabbed the fin of the great fish, riding it into the depths to save his leader and friend. Down he went, away from the sun, the air, farther down, where the only light was the green luminescence of living things. He reached for Ghastain's extended hand, from which something trailed upward. Then a huge tentacle rose like a serpent from the depths to snatch Ghastain away from him. Huold said this was one of the arms of the Sea King himself. Just as it took Ghastain, Huold managed to catch hold of the thing that trailed upward from his hand: supposedly the sacred thing, the powerful thing, the whatever-it-was.

"He told the people of Ghost Isle that the whatever-it-was supposedly gave him the power to ride the great fish to the anchorage in Ragnibar Fjord. There he found a man to serve him, a mountaineer, and they two together set out south—this was long before the Stoneway was cut through—with the intention of traversing the Icefang Mountains. Woldsgard did not exist then, of course. That whole area was wilderness.

"So far, most stories are in agreement. From that point on, the stories diverge. Most of them agree that Huold went south, to the place where Woldsgard was later built, and from there headed west into the mountains. Many of the stories mention the place now known as Marish, for the ruins of an ancient temple, a Hag's temple, lie near there, and Drawlip of Thrattlemere writes that the sacred thing was said to have come originally from there. Others say this is ridiculous, that the miraculous thing belonged originally to the Forest God, or the Hag Goddess, or any of a dozen other deities. Various other writers claim that Huold had sworn to Ghastain that he would return the thing to its place of origin, but this may merely be an attempt to explain why he went off into the mountains as he did."

Wordswell nodded to himself. "Up to Huold's arrival at Ghost Isle—a place now drowned beneath the sea—everything concerning the mysterious relic is unsubstantiated. Then we begin to find some undoubted and documented happenings. It is undoubted truth that some people from a settlement on the site of the place we now call Wellsmouth took a wagon into the mountains to cut wood, and there they found Huold's servant half-frozen just inside the complex of caverns now called Chasmgard. He told of Huold's arrival on the fish and said he had lost his master in the mountains during a storm. He couldn't remember when or how long before.

"Later on, the servant was questioned, repeatedly, carefully, by people from the abbey that existed then, a forerunner of this abbey, though not on this site. The servant knew nothing of the thing, the sacred thing, whatever-it-was of legend. After they left the Ghost Isle, Huold had never mentioned any such thing to him. He was asked where they had been going. To a place to return something, he said. What had they been going to return? He didn't know. What had Huold worn? Had he worn a bracelet, a ring, a belt, a torque, a pendant, perhaps? Had he carried anything in his kit? Did he wear a band to hold his hair; did he carry a knife? Did he carry anything closed, like a leather bag that the servant had never seen the contents of? To all such questions the servant said no. No, he had carried nothing the servant hadn't seen, worn no gem, necklace, pendant, ring, anything of the kind. The only knife had been one they both used, and so on."

"Then it could be anything," said Xulai. "It could be a word, a phrase, words to be written or carved, a map to something that would be found in one place and taken to another. It could be anything or nothing."

The aged brother reached up to push his high headdress into a more securely perpendicular position before allowing himself to nod. "Yes. It could have been anything or nothing. There was no one left to clarify the matter. Both Huold and Ghastain were gone. Ghastain had set governors over his conquered lands, to rule in his name, under his law. When they learned of Ghastain's death they kept his legal system, but they began to rule as kings in their own right. King Gahls is the tenth generation of such kings ruling in Norland. He and his forefathers conquered many of the smaller lands—conquered them, or married into them, or allied with them and swallowed them. Altamont was separate until the duchess took it at the order of King Gahls. King and duchess may have a difference of opinion as to its ownership now. Kamfels and the lands of Hallad, Prince Orez, are still separate realms."

"And Wold," said Xulai firmly.

"And Wold," agreed Brother Wordswell. "And Elsmere and Merhaven. Before he set out to conquer the Sea King, Ghastain promised Huold all the western lands, to him, to his children, into perpetuity. At that time, those lands included those now held by Wold and by Prince Orez. The promise was no momentary sentiment. It was a serious matter. The deed to the lands was written, witnessed, and sealed in the presence of agents from the institution which preceded our abbey. It is included among the documents from that time. It is still here. I've read it."

"So he had children," said Xulai.

"Before the sea adventure, Huold had one grown daughter and six grown sons. All his sons had predeceased their father, killed in various bellicose expeditions, so when Huold vanished, only his daughter, Lythany, was left to come forward and claim the western lands. The abbey ruled that she was the legitimate heir rather than any of Huold's supposed grandsons, including several born when Huold's sons had been so long absent or dead as to make their fatherhood miraculous if not impossible. The eldest of these grandsons, the Direking of Chandar—

an unknown person from a place that no longer exists—is claimed by Queen Mirami, however, as an ancestor."

Xulai smiled a cat smile. "Clever. I hadn't heard that."

"It is said King Gahls brags of her heritage, but then, the king brags about many things of questionable provenance and doubtful value. It is certain, however, that both Prince Orez and Justinian are of the twelfth generation of Lythany's line."

Silence grew in the room, broken only by the crackle of the fire as four people pondered the possibilities inherent in what they had just heard.

Bear scratched his head, stretched his neck as though it troubled him, and said, "Possessing this thing, whatever it is, would be a . . . strong argument that one was the real inheritor, but in twelve generations, this thing has not been found?"

"Likely it has never truly been looked for," said the abbot. "Remember: what Wordswell has told you is a story some hundreds of years old. Such stories grow in the telling. They are embroidered with fancy and colored with all manner of miraculous detail. When all who knew the heroes as mere men have died, the stories continue, swelling mere men into mythic heroes, expanding mythical heroes into demigods. Reasonable men who read history always discount about ninety percent as fiction."

Brother Wordswell nodded. "This is true, but some of the facts are indisputable. Huold did vanish, and his daughter—"

"What was her name, again?" interrupted Precious Wind.

"Lythany," said the old man. "Which is our form of her real name: Lythaiene, which means 'truth prevails' in the language of the time. Lythany took the lands and ordered the building of the fortress of Woldsgard. It was she who ordered the cutting of the Stoneway in order to make travel to Kamfels easier. She was a good steward of the land and an enlightened ruler of the people who came to settle it. She was the first who forbade slavery. She settled various lands, some of those now held by Prince Orez, on her nephews and nieces; she married a member of her own tribe; she had two children of her own. Her daughter was Yvein, called the Songbird, and her son was Harald Axearm. Harald inherited the lands of Woldsgard, and Yvein married into a great family to the west from which Prince Orez is descended. I have the family trees in my library . . ."

"Our library," corrected the abbot with a chiding smile.

Wordswell's lips crimped themselves into a deprecating moue. "Certainly, Eldest Brother, it is ours, except that I seem to be the only one who is dragged from his bed to answer questions about it. At any rate, Justinian, Duke of Woldsgard, is the twelfth generation in direct descent from Huold himself. He is also descended through both Harald and Yvein when the two branches of the family were united through marriage several generations later. And if you ask whether Queen Mirami's claim to descend from Huold is provable, I can only say that it can't be proven from any source we know of. In fact, no one even knows where she came from. She was first noticed as a protégé of that strange fellow, the one at Altamont . . ."

"The Old Dark Man!" said Xulai. "Great Bear has mentioned him."

"And Huold came from where, originally?" asked Bear.

"There are as many stories as tellers," said Wordswell. "He was born of the gods. He was born of a virgin who had been shut up in a cell for twelve years. He was born of said virgin because the sun god came in through the little window of the cell and impregnated her. And so on and so on.

"There is no record of the name 'Huold' before his time, so we cannot say what language the name comes from. It has no cognate in any language we know now. Ghastain was Angrian, a harsh people from the far southeast, far beyond the Big Mud, where the deserts are. It is possible Huold was also Angrian. Since the waters rising have changed things over the last centuries, we no longer see the Angrian people."

Xulai said, "So, since we have no idea what this thing was or is, and yet the duchess is energetically seeking it, we must at least allow for the possibility that she has found out or has some hint of what it is or that it might justify her mother's claim. I overheard her say something about things discovered in the Edgeworld Isles . . . in a library there . . ."

Wordswell shook his head dismissively. "Our scribes and copyists have been through all the island libraries a dozen times over the past two centuries. I doubt there is anything there that we have not copied and brought here."

Xulai said casually, "They've seen the vaults below? Deep vaults?"

Wordswell laughed. "Oh, my gracious, that again! The deep vaults holding the last of the ease machines. My daughter, if I may call you that without offending you, the stories about vaults below this place and that place have been told for hundreds of years. The Edgeworld Isles are coral islands; do you know what that means?"

"Precious Wind taught me, yes. They are islands that grow on the shells of little creatures that build up over the centuries, often on the tops of old volcanoes. When the seas rise, they grow to the surface; when the seas fall, they protrude above the waves."

"And where, in all this growing and sinking and unsinking, can vaults be created? Caves are found mostly in mountains where running water eats out caverns in the rock."

"I see." Xulai smiled. "I supposed that if they existed, they had been dug out in the Before Time, perhaps in the time of the Big Kill. I suppose even coral could be dug out and then the hole made waterproof."

"It probably could, but I have heard the stories as long as I have lived, and as yet, no one has found such a vault. Just as I have heard that this thing of Huold's in time of need will come up 'out of water' and call to those it will serve."

"If it is an evil thing, perhaps it is calling to Alicia?" the girl murmured. "And from the story you tell, it is an evil thing."

"Why do you think so?" asked the abbot.

"If Ghastain wielded it, slaughtering all those people, it must have been . . ."

The abbot leaned forward to take her hand and she looked deep into his eyes, blue eyes: kindly, clear, and guileless. "If it existed at all, it may have been completely neutral, Xulai. It may be merely a source of power like the one that underlies us here at the abbey. You have seen the great pit in which the abbey is built? It is the result of something huge, some enormous sky stone that fell long, long ago at the end of the Before Time. Some say that this sky stone and its companions is what put an end to the Big Kill, for there were great earthquakes then. Mountains were heaved about, some made higher, some leveled. The enormous tableland we now call the Highlands of Ghastain was thrust up. Norland was created anew, half of it shorn away to the west. Some remnants of that great stone lie beneath us.

Our forefathers drilled down to it and hot water came up! It takes heat from the stone, even after all this time, and we use the heat for cooking and keeping warm and bathing. We try to use that power for good. If we were ever overrun by an army of evil, however, no doubt they would use it for ill. Power is power as the sun is the sun, the wind is the wind. The villager blesses the rain as it falls on his crops; the pillager uses it to cover his approach. It is the wielder who determines the good or evil."

Xulai would have asked for more information about the power that underlay the abbey, but the abbot had already risen and crossed to the door, where he called for Brother Aalon. Though it did not seem enough time had passed, they heard the heavy stroke of the single bell, *dong! Dong! Dong!*

"Lunch bells," said Bear. "We'll collect the others at the meal and decide what to do next." He set off down the hall.

Xulai, lingering while the others departed, turned to the abbot and took his hand. "Eldest Brother. For my sake, please do not tell anyone what we have talked of here. Not anyone, even your close associates."

He nodded, a crease between his eyebrows. "It would be better not, I think."

"Not even *your very close* associates," she said again.

He nodded, looking slightly puzzled. "Not . . . ?"

"Do you remember Justinian sending a large amount of treasure to the abbey to be kept for two of his loyal servants?"

"Oh, heavens, Daughter, I don't handle things like that. You'd have to ask the prior."

She stood for a moment, transfixed, before murmuring, "Please, sir. Do not mention to the prior that I asked. Promise me you won't."

His puzzlement was plain, but he whispered, "I won't, if you ask it, but—"

"I promise to explain, later." She pressed his hand and left him greatly troubled.

"SISTER TOMEA WANTED TO TAKE you to the school this afternoon," said Precious Wind as they finished their lunch. "She said she would come to fetch you at midafternoon. In the meantime, she's suggested we go have a look at the house we're to occupy."

"I've already been there," said Bear in an offhand tone. "I can guide us."

"When did you go?" Precious Wind asked. He merely shrugged and set about assembling the rest of their group, who then followed him on a winding way through corridors and plazas and more corridors and cloisters, and at last into a tunnel through the eastern shield wall. They stood with the abbey behind them looking across wide parkland scattered with groves and shrubberies and grassy stretches, occupied by a scatter of young people playing a ball game and a clutter of grazing sheep watched by a few indolent dogs. Graveled paths led here and there.

Bear gestured at the expanse. "This is a protected park for the abbey's children, a place where people can walk or play at sports. The Wilderbrook begins over on the south side, and they've brought a bit of it under the wall to make a swimming place. They've built a ball field and playground on the north side, and there, east"—Bear pointed—"that's the back wall."

The gray outer wall curved in from either side behind a cluster of dwellings that varied in size from small to quite large. At one of the largest—built of gray stone much like the wall, the roof covered with curved tiles of rosy clay—a crew of workers was busy replacing broken roof tiles while another crew dumped carts of gravel in the area outside the front door.

"That is supposed to be ours," said Bear as he went down the path that led the considerable distance toward it.

"We'd get plenty of exercise going back and forth," remarked Oldwife in a grumpy voice.

Bear said, "Well, if we live here, we can eat here . . ."

"If we do the cooking," grouched Oldwife.

"Which means we don't have to go back and forth much," Bear continued, "except for Xulai getting to and from school. She can ride if she likes. There's a paddock outside the school."

"Actually, the walk would be good for all of us," remarked Precious Wind.

Inside, the place smelled of damp plaster and the sour-milk odor of new paint. A spacious sitting room was on the left of the entry hall and an equally large dining room on the right. Behind these were several small offices, a kitchen, several pantries, and a rear door opening out toward the wall. From the dining room a corridor led to men's quarters on the right, including a bathtub room. From the sitting room, similar quarters extended to the left for the women. In back, between the house and the looming gray of the abbey wall, were several stables, a paddock, a hay barn, and storage buildings for wagons and carriages, all built of stone, all with the same tiled roofs.

"Someone went to a lot of expense just to go off and leave this place," said Nettie.

"It feels funny," said Bartelmy, taking Xulai's hand helpfully as she approached the steps, in his usual manner, only to drop it quickly and duck his head. "Sorry, m'lady."

Xulai snapped, "Oh, for all that's holy, Bartelmy, you can take my hand without apologizing. I am still the same person. Oldwife says so. Precious Wind says so."

"She's still the same person," Oldwife verified. "Just at a bit higher boil."

Most of the rooms were at least partially furnished with benches, beds, chests, and armoires. The dining room held a long table and carved chairs for a dozen diners. The furnishings inside the building were solid, though dirty, as though they had not been used in a lifetime or more.

"You said we can eat here?" asked Xulai, running her fingers along the time-, dust-, and spider-gummed carving of a chair back. "Instead of in the dining hall?"

"If we choose to," Precious Wind said. "Personally, I think the dining hall is a better idea for a while. It will let us meet people. We won't meet anyone if we stay back here all the time."

"Except that's a long trek on a full belly," said Oldwife. "On the other hand, we won't need to be all the time scrubbing pots and pans."

Xulai examined the dirt on her hand with an inexplicable revulsion. She was used to getting her hands dirty, but this dirt made her uneasy, nonetheless. As she went from room to room, the vague agitation did not abate. To the eye, it was a very pleasant house, but she did not wish to occupy it. She could not explain why, but she did not want to live there.

"It will be some time before it's ready, won't it?" she asked.

"They're working very hard at it," said Precious Wind from the window where she was watching the scurrying workers outside.

Xulai went to stand beside her. "I think we should tell the abbot not to hurry. We're very comfortable where we are, and I need a little time to get used to the school and the abbey, and living close to it for a while will make it easier."

"The men and I are in separate quarters at the abbey," Bear said from behind her in a disapproving tone. "That has its disadvantages."

"There is no reason for you to be in separate quarters," Precious Wind remarked as she moved toward the door. "We noticed there are no other women in the women's quarters. Until more long-term female visitors arrive at the abbey, surely some of you could stay next door, down the hall."

"I'll inquire about it if you like," said Bear with a strange searching look at Xulai. "I hope you don't expect to delay for very long, however. I'd hate to offend him."

Xulai managed to smile. "No, not long. It's just that I've had . . . am having enough changes to last me for a while, Bear. Tell him I need a little time to adjust before we set up housekeeping."

They walked slowly back along the path. Ahead of them the wall of the abbey itself had alert guards at every gate and spaced between, and again Xulai felt that strange revulsion. She turned, catching Bartelmy's eyes, wrinkling her nose. He nodded. He felt the same way she did.

When Sister Tomea came to fetch Xulai later in the afternoon, she did not seem at all disconcerted by Xulai's appearance. "You look better," said the sister. "More rested. That's wonderful. Will you go to the school with me this afternoon?"

With clenched teeth, Xulai nodded, forcing a passable smile onto virtually rigid lips. "Sister Tomea, one of the members of our party is not actually a part of our entourage; that is, he is not in the employ of the Duke of Wold, but he is a personal friend of mine. I'm speaking of the dyer whose wagon accompanied us to the abbey. I'd like to see him when you have finished with me this afternoon. Can that be arranged?"

"Of course," she replied. "I recall someone mentioning he's housed with the craftsmen over near the stables. He has, seemingly, a great affection for his horse." She smiled widely at this, as though it were both unusual and funny.

"I think he's a lonely man and the horse is his only real companion," Xulai said, finding it not at all strange that Abasio would want to stay very close to a horse that talked.

"Do you want him to come to your quarters?"

"Actually, I'd rather go to his, if that's permissible," she said. "He's a wonderful storyteller, but those who share my quarters won't necessarily share my enjoyment of them and they deserve their privacy."

Sister Tomea nodded her head sympathetically. "I'll send him word that you'd like an invitation. He can ask one of us to guide you. This evening, perhaps?"

"This evening," she agreed as they stopped outside the office of the person in charge of the abbey upper schools, a woman named Solace. With Sister Tomea sitting nearby, Sister Solace fixed Xulai with two penetrating black eyes and asked, "What have you been taught thus far?"

Xulai took a deep breath. "The skills of literacy, ma'am. I read and write well in two languages. I read musical notation; I play an instrument, not very well . . ."

"She is modest," said Sister Tomea. "Her Tingawan friend says she is quite good. Better than at singing."

Xulai, with a wry smile, agreed. "Yes, much better than at singing, though I can whistle rather well. I have learned much of the history of Wold and some of the history of Norland and the other surrounding places as well as the history and customs of Tingawa. Bear—that is, one of my mentors—has taught me basic mathematics, nothing very advanced as yet. I have learned a good deal about weapons and how to handle them, and Precious Wind has taught me about herbs and healing. I also know something about the management and structure of a large estate. My cousin, the Duke of Wold, had me observe much that he did in that regard and explained how things work." And the princess had taught her much else that she would not mention.

"Ah. What do you know of the Before Time?"

"Oh, ma'am, do any of us know very much? I've heard the stories. Men were foolish and did foolish things, they did not respect the earth, they worshipped the ease machines and the world punished them by becoming barren. The blanket of air was withdrawn, the Hot Times came when the sun burned everyone, the great ice continents melted, and the waters rose. That was the First Waters Rising. Then came the time of the Big Kill, when people died by the millions. Plants could not grow. Many peoples and types of animals and plants did not survive. I did not know until recently that a great sky stone or stones had fallen then. The abbot says they did, bringing great earthquakes and changing the map of the world. That was the Time When No One Moved Around . . ."

"We say the Time of Darkness," said Sister Solace. "A second dark age."

Xulai went on. "I learned that when people resolved never again to worship the ease machines, the world relented and let things grow once more, though the land area is much reduced from what it was before. This new inundation will reduce it further."

Sister Solace said, "I'm told it is because some great aquifers remained sealed in solid stone from the beginnings of the earth, and now the waters have found ways to get out. At least that is what your friend the traveler says. I met him at lunch today. He says people far to the east of us in places called the Edges found it out. I didn't have time to ask him for any details. Now, what else have you learned?"

"I've learned that people have become more numerous in a few places: here and in Tingawa, though east of us, where many survived on the other side of the great desert, where those Edges are you spoke of, they have recently had a plague that has reduced their numbers greatly. There are supposed to be people living across the great waters to the south. Until the Sea People made war on us, ships transported cargoes back and forth from there."

Sister Solace nodded thoughtfully, then turned to Sister Tomea. "We will take a few days to find the classes that will help Xulai best. I will do that myself. At her age it seems unnecessary, but will a Tingawan chaperone be coming with her?"

Sister Tomea looked inquiringly at Xulai, who smiled and replied, "Precious Wind would do that only if such a thing were customary with other students in the . . . you call it the upper school?"

"Yes. Our schools take children at age three to . . . eighty or more, I suppose. We have no universities that stand alone. Teachers are rare beasts. We find they thrive best in a supportive environment, whether they teach toddlers or adults. As for chaperones, we've had a few Tingawan women with chaperones, but not for some time. The war with the Sea People has separated us."

So it began. For the rest of the afternoon, Xulai moved in Sister Solace's shadow, in and out of classrooms, always quietly, at the back, for the most part unnoticed by students ranging widely in age. Late in the afternoon, they returned to Sister Solace's study, where they were given tea.

"I hope you heard something that particularly interested you," Sister Solace remarked, handing Xulai a cup. "It's dreadful when a student simply is not interested."

Xulai nodded her thanks for the cup. "I was particularly interested in the discussion of the oceans. It seems there are many books about things that happen there that most of us do not know about. It seems, also, that there is a great deal known about genetics—mostly in the Before Books, of course—but I'd like to know more about that. I was fascinated by the teacher who was telling the students that all of us, mice, men, fish, horses, have genetic plans that are much the same, and it's only the little valves that turn one thing on and another thing off that make us different."

She nodded, writing things down. "Very well, we'll turn you loose in the library among the books we have on oceans and their dwellers and what is still known about genetics. We don't have the devices and equipment to do the things the Before people did, but at least you'll get the idea. All students are expected to ride, run, walk long distances, and use various weapons, including guile, for someone's life or safety may depend upon it, so there will be some active periods in each day. If you come across a subject you would like to know more about, come to me, and we will arrange it. I'd like you to teach Tingawan to a handful of students who need to learn the language. Will that do?"

Xulai said, "Except the teaching part . . ."

"Oh, you'll do well at that. These are very young students, children at the age when learning a language is like learning to breathe. You'll enjoy it. Tell them stories in Tingawan, translate, repeat; they'll be telling them to you before long. If you don't know any stories, ask the school librarian for some children's books."

That evening, not long after supper, one of the blue-veiled men, a sly, foxy-looking fellow, arrived with an invitation for Xulai to visit the dyer in his new quarters. As Precious Wind got up, prepared to accompany her, Xulai pressed her back into her chair. "No, Precious Wind. I just want to see what he's working on and hear a few stories. I'm safe enough here in the abbey and someone will bring me back."

"Are you sure?"

"I am. Sister Tomea insists I'm quite safe and since I'm no longer even a pretend child, it's time I find my own way about."

Precious Wind settled into her chair, though Oldwife Gancer shook her head in slight dismay. Giving them no time to formulate an argument, Xulai took a package from a chair by the door and slipped into the corridor behind the blue-veiled man.

"I'm Brother Derris," he told her cheerfully, looking her over from head to toe as though he were thinking of buying her. "I work mostly with visiting craftsmen and their animals. That's why they sent me. I like that friend of yours. He's a strange one."

"He's traveled very widely," Xulai commented. "I'm sure he's full of stories."

"As a hive is full of bees, that one! We all like to hear him talk. Here, I'll show you the short way."

"Can you show us the way into the—what do you call them, the grounds in back of the abbey where the houses are?"

"The Parkland. Oh, right, you'll be living there. I can do that. You want to show them to your friend, right?"

"I thought it would interest him, yes."

"Easy. Here in the abbey, there's always a dozen hard ways to get anywhere but at least one easy one. That's us blues' job—learning the easy ones." He grinned a carnivorous grin and set out almost at a trot.

They found Abasio's wagon parked next to a small stable where Blue was comfortably installed. Inside the wagon, the little stove held a steaming kettle. Abasio, on first seeing her, let his hand drop in surprise. It struck the hot kettle and he drew it back with an exclamation.

Blue whinnied, drawing the blue's attention. Xulai shook her head warningly, and Abasio took a deep breath before bowing and saying, "Welcome."

"Good fortune," she replied, bowing even lower.

Brother Derris declined the polite offer of tea and said he would be back shortly to take them into the abbey grounds. They said nothing until he had joined a group of other blue-veiled workers at some distance from them.

Abasio stared at her, saying softly, "Well. Was yesterday's Xulai the true Xulai, or is today's . . . ?"

She took a deep breath. "Abasio, which do you prefer?"

"I told you," said Blue. "I said she was no kiddy-widdy for all that glitter around her making her look like a baby."

"Do I look different?" she cried.

He looked her over carefully from several angles, hiding his relief. He had not been out of his mind when he had seen her as an older person. This was the truth! Thank God.

He said, "I was having some trouble . . . relating to you. I kept having these . . . rather unsuitable feelings."

"That's a good phrase," she said. " 'Unsuitable feelings.' I've been having those for some time now. Several years, at least."

"About whom?"

She blushed. "Oh, not really *about* anyone. Just . . . free-floating feelings. Then you came, and they became . . . more unsuitable."

"Since when?" he asked, startled. He had prided himself on his propriety.

"Since the night you took me under your cloak in the woods at Woldsgard. The night the Duchess of Altamont was there."

Abasio mused. "Feelings that may have . . . frightened you?"

"Well, no. Actually, I was mostly feeling surprised because I *wasn't* frightened. Not with you there. And yet . . . I did not feel as I did when Bear was protecting me from . . . crowds of people or horses. Logically, I should have had similar feelings, shouldn't I?"

Blue said, "Oh, no. No. Here we go! This is another one of those fated things, isn't it? Now we're in for it!"

Surprisingly, his voice was as muted as theirs, or so Xulai thought. Perhaps he did not only speak but had horse-sense as well.

"I don't know, Blue, and you're not helping," snapped Abasio.

Xulai kissed Blue on his nose. "Would you mind if your friend and I just . . . find out what's happening?" She was examining her mood, finding it inexplicably . . . what was this? Joyous?

"Your mother must have been a lovely-looking woman," said Abasio. The joy was stifled.

"Oh, well. Let me tell you about my mother and father," she said through her teeth, beginning at once to do so. It took some time, a few tears and refills of tea, and Blue's head was hanging over the rail of the corral before she finished. He was, thanks be, silent.

Abasio mused, "You figure she gave you this ability to make people see you differently."

"You evidently didn't see me differently."

"Oh, yes, I did, but your image kept wavering because I knew I was seeing falsely, if that makes sense. I've got a magical helmet, a kind of library that leads me toward the truth, most of the time, so I know what seeing true feels like." He smiled as he said this, a sad, rather longing smile. "It's not magic, really, but I call it that. I came by it through a lovely lady I knew once. Her name was Ollie, and her destiny was higher than either of us wanted it to be. She went to meet that destiny and could never return from it, but she left me the magical helmet, and she's . . . in it, maybe the way your mother is in you. Perhaps you just don't know how to . . . listen to her yet, or talk to her."

She found this thought too strange to contemplate at the moment. "No one knows who I really am except Oldwife, Precious Wind, and me. Bear doesn't know. The men don't know. They'll know I look older and Precious Wind will tell them something or other, but don't you or Blue tell them anything else. Oh, and I brought this." She handed him the package she had been carrying.

"What's this all about?"

"I knitted these scarves on the way here as a kind of thank-you to the men who came with us. With winter coming, they'll be useful, and will you give one to each of our men? Please. They seem shy of me, especially Bartelmy, so you tell them I much I appreciated their help. Then there's something else! I want you to see this house we're supposed to live in. It troubles me."

Abasio went to summon Brother Derris from among his friends and from there followed him around the corner of the stables, through a couple of doors, down a long tunnel, and up a flight of stairs that led out into the light. They were in the enclosed meadow with the forest side behind it. The sheep were beginning to lie down for the night.

Through the foliage from the scattered groves, the roofs of the distant houses made geometric shapes against the blank gray of the wall.

"I can bring her back to my place," Abasio told the brother. "Will you be there?"

Brother Derris nodded. "If you're not back before dark, I'll come looking for you."

They walked away from him, around a copse of trees, and then around another, finally seeing the house, which stood open to the dusk, the rooms still light enough to see by. They wandered through each room of the house and out the back to the row of outbuildings—woodshed at the far left, then stable, paddock, barn with hayloft, then pens for goats or cows. The wall was just behind the paddock, frighteningly close. They turned and went into the house again to stand inside the front door, where they looked at the abbey across the open ground, its rear wall crowned with guards.

"No guards!" he said.

"That's it!" she exclaimed, immediately aware of what had bothered her. "There are no guards on this wall. It's right up against the forest; anyone could come over it. If someone wanted me out of this house, they'd take me out like a snail out of a shell."

"The abbey might have outliers, guards out in the woods who'd give an alarm."

"Enough to stop an army? Enough to stop that man who was with the duchess?"

"The one you turned into a baby for?"

"You heard about that."

"Oldwife mentioned it. Then got angry at herself for doing so. I had to swear silence. I've been doing that a lot lately . . . Hush!" He held up his hand, then grasped her arm and pulled her back inside.

"What?" she whispered.

"Your two Tingawans are coming out to take a look at the house. Do you want them to know we're here?"

She shook her head. For some reason, she did not.

"Where are they least likely to go?"

"The barn," she guessed.

They slipped out into the barn and up the ladder into the loft. The hayloft door faced the back of the house; on their right, a small, dirty window looked out into the paddock. The hayloft door was half-open, and the two of them lay in old hay, dry and virtually odorless, no doubt years old. A little time passed and Great Bear and Precious Wind came out the back door of the house to stand peering at the wall.

"I simply think it's odd that all these houses are empty," said Precious Wind in Tingawan. "The houses seem very susceptible and unguarded out here."

Abasio looked at Xulai, eyebrows raised. She put her finger across her lips, mouthing "Later."

"I inquired," said Bear in the same language. "There's a whole army of abbey soldiers encamped back in those woods. No one could approach the wall without their knowing. I wouldn't go otherwise."

"I don't think you should go at all, not just yet. I think that your leaving us is oath-breaking, Bear. You swore to stay with her until she reached Tingawa."

"You told me a long time ago that the duke would reward us well for our time with Xulai. Well, now we're here. Did you get a full purse for yourself? No. Neither did I. I asked the man who shows us around to find out whether we had something here waiting for us. He asked the prior. Prior said ask this one and that one, and they all said there was nothing here for us. Now, if that's all I mean to the great duke, I think the years I've already spent are enough!"

Silence. Then, very tentatively, Precious Wind asked, "Why didn't you wait for me to join you before you asked about it? You know Justinian doesn't lie."

"The great Justinian! Pfagh! What I swore I would do was scout the trail south of here, and that's what I'm going to do. There's no oath-breaking in that. The only difference is that when I get to Merhaven—isn't that the refuge harbor that belonged to Prince Orez's mother?—I'm finding a ship for Tingawa. I'll send a message, first, that it's safe to continue the journey, and that's my sworn duty, done!"

"Bear, give me a day or two!"

"That and no longer. I feel Legami-am calling to me. You don't know what it's like, Precious Wind. She's in my nostrils, in my eyes. I seem to see her, everywhere. Feel her in the bed with me at night. I smell the scent of her. Every night I dream about her. All day she's there, on my shoulder, whispering my name . . ."

"But who will guard Xulai?"

He snorted. "She seems to do very well by herself."

Precious Wind's voice seemed stiff and unnatural. "It still seems unfaithful . . ."

"I have more lives than one to be faithful to! You are not the eldest son of a family who expects you to produce the next generation for the clan. I am. You have three brothers who have taken care of the next generation generously. I haven't. I have a wife waiting for me. I long for her. I need her. And she needs me! I didn't know it could happen like this, her voice, the touch of her hand, beckoning, begging, suddenly, out of nothing! This job has stretched on long enough! I didn't swear to spend my life on it. The scouting trip is the end of it. Even when I return to Tingawa, there is yet a great part of the bride-price to be earned before we can marry."

This time her voice was angry. "Bear, you'd have had your bride-price twice over from what you've been paid if you hadn't gambled it all away! I can straighten out the matter of the duke's reward. Justinian would not lie to me, Bear. You must let me set it straight!"

He made a gesture of rejection and they moved back into the house. After a time, they saw Precious Wind walking back across the open ground toward one of the abbey gates, shoulders slumped in dejection. Bear was not with her.

"Stay here," hissed Xulai. "Don't move."

She was down the ladder in a flash and out across the ground toward the house. As she approached a young tree, she heard footsteps and Bear came out of the house once more, this time striding across the paddock toward the wall. To Abasio, watching from the loft, Xulai disappeared. She simply vanished. There was a young tree growing against the wall of the house next to the spot where she had been standing, but she herself was gone. Shaking his head in bemusement, Abasio moved to the window over the paddock to get a better view, cursing silently at the filth on the window, which prevented his seeing clearly.

At the wall, Bear stopped and whistled, three notes, repeated three times. After a moment, the whistle was returned and someone's head appeared at the top of the wall. There was conversation, which Abasio could barely hear, as the window was not only dirty but tightly closed. The conversation between Bear and the visitor was brief. The head disappeared. Bear turned and went alongside the house and back toward the abbey.

When Abasio reached the loft door, he saw Xulai standing against the wall of the house beside the small tree, tears streaming down her face.

He slid down the ladder and went to her, whispering, "You disappeared!"

"I thought he couldn't help but see me!"

"He didn't. He went right by you!"

"It felt weird. I wanted to vanish; I felt something happening to me; my skin tingled, like I was retreating into the background. What did you see?"

"Shadows, like a little tree against the stone. You're crying! Why?"

"He's selling me, Abasio. Bear is selling me!"

"Shh. Tell me what he and Precious Wind were talking about."

"Some time ago my father gave Prince Orez a small fortune to be sent here, to this abbey, to be held for Precious Wind and for Bear. The prior signed a receipt for it and the messengers brought the receipt back to my father. Before we left Wold, my father gave it to Precious Wind. She has it." She buried her face in her hands, pressing them together as if to hold her head in place.

"All Bear knew was what Precious Wind told him, that he would be rewarded for his long and faithful service. He probably expected to get it before he left Woldsgard. Certainly he expected to get it here. So, he asked someone if there was something here for him, and the person he asked went to the prior and received word that there was not. He is very angry."

Abasio pulled her to him, hugging her closely. "Knowing Bear, Precious Wind probably intended to get the payment from the abbey but not pass it on to Bear until we were on a ship headed for Tingawa. Any earlier than that, he would lose it all."

"I know. That's what I told Precious Wind."

Abasio murmured, "Bear's weakness for wagering is almost legendary! I knew that about him within hours of the time we met at Woldsgard. One of the stablemen told me he won two gold pieces from Bear betting on which flea crawling up his arm would bite him first."

"I know all the reasons, Abasio! But we should have told him something! Reassured him! I thought Precious Wind would have done that, though maybe she didn't want to get into a fight over it now. Bear is very angry and it would cause a great trouble if he went after the prior, because we *know* the prior has lied to us."

Abasio nodded slowly. "Yes. That may be part of her thinking. There's no doubt another part. Any man who can be bought once can be bought again—by anyone else who pays more. Precious Wind may suspect he's involved in some scheme. She sounded shocked and wary to me. Who was the man at the wall?"

She shivered. "The man at the wall was Jenger, the duchess's man. He was with her when they stopped us on the road. Bear told Jenger he'd get me into this house quickly, so they could come over the wall and take me. He said to wait until he left on his scouting trip south, then they could get me out of here with no trouble."

"You're sure he was the Duchess of Altamont's man?"

She nodded, wiping her face with the backs of her hands. "Oh, yes. Both times I saw his face clearly. I heard his voice."

Abasio took his arms from around her and stood away, thinking. "There's something going on here that doesn't make sense. When did this man, Jenger, have time to make any agreement with Bear? When did he have time to get here? We only arrived yesterday. Bear was with the other men the entire trip from Benjobz Inn to here, and he hasn't left the abbey today. I can see the gates from where I'm staying, near the stables, and he didn't go out on a horse."

She shook her head hopelessly. "Could it all have been decided before we left Woldsgard? If I hadn't made the horse biscuits, we'd have been there on Altamont ground when the duchess came the next morning. Maybe Bear meant us to be there."

Abasio walked back and forth, mumbling to himself, finally stopping to say, "No, no. I don't think so. I saw him then, during the trip down the valley and that episode at the bridge. He was genuinely irritated. I don't think he had been *bought* before that. The story he told us about this house being safe because there are troops in the forest, however—that may be something we can check. Either Bear lied, or he was careless in what he said, or—"

"Or the abbot will confirm that there are troops . . ."

"But we'll have to confirm what the abbot says," he said grimly.

She clung to Abasio, feeling that if she let go of him she would fall into some kind of abyss. "Bear was my teacher, Abasio. He was almost what I thought a father would have been. He's been with me since I was a little child. How could he!"

"Hush," he said. "We're moving too quickly . . ."

She remembered, all at once. "My . . . my mother said that. She said one may neither accuse nor exonerate until one knows for sure. It was one of her *fumitos,* her sayings."

He managed a grin. "Very wise. There is another possibility. This could be Bear's attempt to play his own game against the duchess."

She shivered, feeling something cold and hard form inside her, like a rod of iron extending from her legs up into her brain, as though she had swallowed a poker without knowing it. She had known Bear for a very long time. She had never known him to be dishonorable. Cynical, but there was much in life to be cynical about. "How do we find out? We must know which it is!"

"First, you must forget what you have just heard and seen—"

"I can't. Not possibly."

"Not forget, but behave as though you are not aware. Then, you must leave it to me to find out what his intentions really are. This all seems terribly sudden, terribly unexpected. Almost as though . . . something, someone, is pushing him."

"Oh, when he was talking to Precious Wind, he said his betrothed is calling to him! And he won't talk to you. Bear is terribly proud. He doesn't talk to people about personal things."

"No, and trying to get him to talk would destroy my reputation as a wandering news carrier, a vendor of what's happening elsewhere, a general odd-body who dyes napkins and is otherwise ignorant of everything important." He hugged her to him, trying desperately to ignore the fact that she felt frighteningly like another young woman he had held this closely, this desperately. His reverie was abruptly broken by a squirming something between the two of them. He drew back just as an unexpected creature erupted from Xulai's cloak pocket.

"I may be indeterminate," said the fisher, "but I'm certainly not incorporeal. If this man is close enough to you to hug you like that, then he should certainly be close enough to know about me."

Xulai managed to suppress hysterical laughter. She whispered,

"Abasio, this is Fisher. He was bequeathed to me by my mother. That is, she's the likeliest one to have done it, though neither he nor I can say for sure. He is a kind of advance warning system, or a guide if I'm lost, or anything else that's helpful."

"And it really is helpful," said Fisher, with some satisfaction, "to know to whom one can safely go if the person I am protecting has to be rescued from a dungeon or saved from being killed. Obviously, that will not include the man Bear. Not now."

"No," agreed Abasio, seeming totally unsurprised that he was being addressed by a member of the weasel family. But then, he had come from a country that had had a good many talking animals, creatures left over from the Big Kill, when men had played with genetics as a child plays with blocks. "No, for the time being, at least, I'm your safest bet. I'll work the other end of the conspiracy. Either this is really a trap to catch Xulai or Bear is laying a trap for the duchess. Whichever, the duchess doesn't know me at all. I'm a stranger, and strangers, particularly when drunken or sleepy, can overhear all kinds of things."

"Abasio, remember what Nettie said! The duchess was at Benjobz Inn when Nettie and the Farrier brothers were there, spying. They stayed out of sight, but you were there at the same time, making royal fripperies for Benjobz. She might have seen you, and Jenger may have been there, too."

He cast his mind back to his visit at Benjobz Inn. Though he thought he had not been seen by the duchess, certainly she might have seen his wagon. And mentioning the duchess raised the interesting question of how she had managed to get to the inn at the same time they did without having been seen on the road. The winding road onto the heights allowed one to see people two days behind on the road, but they had not seen her. This would imply another route. What possible other route? Up was up; it could not be turned over to run downhill, and he had never heard anyone mention any other route up or down than by the falls, which was invariably fatal!

He took a deep breath, trying to clear his mind. "First things first. I won't let the wrong person recognize me. You go about your business as though you know nothing. Tomorrow I'll check out the disposition of troops. The men I'm housed with know a lot about who is where and what's going on. If the troop business was a lie and Bear lied to

Precious Wind about it, that's a bad thing. Then we'll have you ask the abbot about the security of the houses and see what he says. If he backs up the lie, that will be a worse thing. Then we know . . . Well, we know we have to get out of here. The two of us can travel more quietly than a whole wagon train of equipment and people." And maybe he'd have to leave his own wagon and equipment behind, he thought. His wagon was beloved. He and Ollie had traveled in it. However, it was uniquely identifiable.

"And what if the troop business is not a lie?" she asked.

"If it's not a lie, then you may have a chance at some schooling after all."

She took a deep breath. "The schooling is secondary! It was to be a way of passing time. My father made me promise to get to Tingawa. He said even if I was so old I had to walk with a cane, it was imperative that I get there. He said it was the most important thing I had to do with my life, even if I did nothing else."

He stared at her. "Ah. So there is a little wheel inside the big wheel, or t'other way round. You're saying that your physical arrival in Tingawa is the primary thing, no matter what else we do?"

"Yes. We have to do that, and as soon as possible."

Fisher stuck his head out of her pocket. "Her understanding is correct. Those are my instructions, also."

Abasio sighed deeply. "Even so, sudden moves are often mistaken. Innocent or guilty, it would be good if Bear went away before we do." He laughed harshly. "It would also be very good if what's-his-name, Jenger, got himself killed before we leave. And it would be simply marvelous to have more information. So, while we're finding things out, talk about the new house with people at the school. Someone may know why they have all these houses vacant, all at once."

She nodded, wiping her face on her sleeve. "There's one more thing, Abasio. There's a big crate under the wain. It's supposed to be court clothes the princess left for me. Actually, it is court clothes, but there's something else in there. The princess told me about it years ago. If I leave, I have to take it with me."

"What is it?"

She shook her head. "I don't know. It's small; it's in a blue wrapper.

Precious Wind said it's some kind of helper for a traveler, and it sounds like we're going to be traveling."

"Don't worry about it," said Fisher. "I'll get it."

"Weasels don't chew their way through wood!" said Xulai.

"Rabbits do. So do beavers. I think I can manage whatever type of teeth may be necessary. A small package wrapped in blue. I don't suppose you know where in the package it is?"

"One corner of the crate bottom has a red mark on it. It's in that corner."

"You'll be safe enough while you're at school, so I'll get it then. I'll bring it to Abasio. He can hide it in his wagon."

She cried hopelessly. "I hate all this."

Abasio reached for her again, more carefully. "So do I, love, so do I."

The word he used pierced her. At Woldsgard, only Oldwife had used that word to her. Not Precious Wind or Bear. Not her . . . her father or mother. For long moments she stood in his arms, simply stood there, momentarily but perfectly at peace. At last she stepped away.

"Do you call many people 'love'?" she whispered.

"One other, once," he said, smiling at her. "You don't mind, do you? I promise not to ravish you or embarrass you in front of other people."

"Who was she?"

Abasio sighed. "I . . . it's hard for me to talk about her. Some people, including yourself, Xulai, whoever you are, aren't really describable. It is possible for me to introduce you to her. She left me all her memories and a great deal more in that magic helmet I told you about. Next time we have a little time, all right?"

It was growing dark, so they ran to the abbey walls to find Brother Derris waiting for them. "You must have measured every room twice," he said. "People were getting worried about you!"

"My fault," said Xulai offhandedly. "We were talking about some of the places Abasio has traveled, and the time just got away from us."

"You watch that storytelling," said Brother Derris in a serious tone. "You'll make a bunch of us want to go off and become news-travelers, and the abbot'll have a fit!"

So, laughing, they returned to the wagon, where Xulai said she could find her own way to her rooms and Brother Derris departed. She accepted a cup of tea, petted Blue and told him what a fine horse he was, then went to her rooms, where she was surprised to find Bear with the women, all of them turning to stare at her.

Precious Wind said, "Bear had us quite concerned about your being late, so he spoke to your guide, Brother Derris. He said you'd gone out to see the house."

From somewhere in her belly, Xulai felt a strengthening fountain rise, warm, calming, flowing into her head, out her arms into her fingertips. "Oh, yes," she cried gaily. "We did start to. But then we decided to see the swimming place that Bear told us about, so we started to go there. Before we got there, we met a dog, one of the sheepdogs, and Abasio sat down to pet the dog, so I sat down, too, and the other dog came over and lay down beside me, then Abasio started telling a story about a dog he'd met in his travels, and the next thing we knew, it was almost dark. So we ran all the way out to the house, beçause I'd promised he could see it, then we ran all the way back. Brother Derris met us. He said he worried about us—no, he said *people* worried about us; was that you, Bear? Just because it was getting dark?"

Bear's face, which had been stony, perhaps a little fearful, relaxed a little. "Well, it was late."

"But surely you knew we were all right," Xulai said pointedly. "You were the one who told us it was perfectly safe, Bear! We're going to be living right there, and it was nice to get a feel for the place."

Precious Wind shook her head. "You did say it was perfectly safe, Bear. She's right. There's no point in being upset about it. If we're going to live here for a time, we have to get accustomed to the place."

"Right," said Bear with an unconvincing smile. "I'm sorry to have upset you all, but I am not accustomed yet to thinking of Xulai as a . . . grown woman."

"Who perhaps should not be gallivanting around with a grown man we don't know very well," said Oldwife pointedly.

Xulai went to hug her. "Then you must get to know him better, Oldwife, because I like him very much."

THAT NIGHT, XULAI DREAMED. THE dream began as the other dream had begun, herself a tiny tree in a tiny, constricting pot. The roots sought a crack; the pot broke; the roots reached for fertile ground and the tree grew. She felt herself growing. From the bottom of her trunk, four great branches reached out and up, each with twigs innumerable sprouting in all directions, leaves flourishing. Then, deep in the taproot, she felt something. It was newness without a name. It had no scent, flavor, or feel, no dimension or shape; it made no sound. It was like a demand that moved upward through the tree, the root first, then split and ran first along the fronts of two branches, then across the back. It paused, then ran across the tops of the other two branches, then returned along their bottoms before going upward into that part of the trunk that grew above the branches to the very top, permeating the tree until it was part of the tree, existing in every way the tree existed, inseparable, indefinable as any particular thing and yet new: an arrival.

In her dream, she wondered at it, wondered where she might find it, like locating taste on her tongue or smell in her nose. Perhaps she could feel it the way she could feel movement in her own body. If she moved a finger she knew it . . . and yet, if the movement was effortless, how did she know the finger had moved? She would not know. If the movement was unconscious and without effort, as when she turned over in her sleep, she would not know she had moved. She would know that her body moved only if and when she did it intentionally or it was done to her while she was conscious enough to be aware of it.

So this new thing, this permeation, might do things without her knowing it? Or it might do things that she would recognize only if she had intended them to happen?

"It's yours," a voice whispered. Perhaps it was Fisher's voice. Perhaps it was someone else's. "No one else can use it. No one else will do anything with it. Only you, when you need to."

THERE WERE SEVERAL TAVERN-LIKE PLACES at the abbey where the men and women of various kinds and professions could get together to drink beer or ale or mead or cider and tell stories and hear what news was to be heard. Abasio had found out where all of them were and which people were likely to go to which ones. That night he went to the Warrior's Helm, where the troops quartered nearby were said to congregate along with other people of the heartier and more physical professions. Horsemen went there. Stone layers went there. Abasio bought himself a pitcher of beer and sat at a corner table, where he soon attracted three or four other thirsty people willing to talk about what they were up to or planning. He heard about the new irrigation system for the vegetable gardens that lay just outside the south walls of the abbey and the several dams and holding ponds that would have to be built or had already been built. He heard about the disaster at the old iron mine, where three men had been trapped and rescued only after some hours of frantic labor.

"Oh, where's that?" asked Abasio.

He heard about the improved armor that the smiths had devised for the troops who had ridden off to Netherfields, or ended up there, for some evidently had thought they were headed to Woldsgard, but Prince Orez was already at Woldsgard, so that hadn't been necessary.

"Oh, is that so?" said Abasio.

"Bird-loft keeper says so," said his informant. "He hears about the messages that come through, hangs around a little, you know, while people are reading 'em. Don't think he's supposed to, but he always has, and he keeps us up on the news."

"That's the way of it most places," said Abasio.

"That's him over there," said the talkative one. "The old fellow with one arm. Used to be one of us."

"And 'us' would be . . . ?"

"The boys and me, we're armor. The old fellow there was a fine soldier, they tell me. Of course, he was younger then."

When the talkative one left, Abasio worked his way over to the corner where the bird-loft man was sitting. He introduced himself, offered to buy a drink, and told the man he'd heard about him.

"Abasio's my name. I'm a traveler. Justinian, Duke of Wold, mentioned you, but I'm sorry, I've forgotten your name . . ."

The old man laughed. "They call me Winger. Acshurly it's Whinger, Solomon Whinger, but Winger stuck, 'cause of the birds, you know. They called me Solo Winger 'cause I only had one wing left."

Abasio laughed enthusiastically. "Well, the duke spoke highly of you. He showed me his bird lofts when I was there. Wonderful man, beautiful lofts, too. I asked him how many birds he had; he said he supposed he had a thousand or so."

"Woun't doubt it," said the bird man appreciatively as Abasio filled their two mugs. "He gets word from all the Orez sons 'n' the prince 'n' the places south, 'n' the abbey here,'n' mor'er less everwhere."

"It's a long list." Abasio nodded. "I saw all the signs on the wall that tell where the birds come from. That's a lot of different places." He had not only seen the list but copied most of it while the duke was busy taking messages from this one and sending messages by that one. "They fly great distances, don't they? I don't suppose it would make sense to have them fly anywhere nearby."

"No sense atall," said the birdman, wiping foam from his upper lip. " 'Fa man c'n ride it in an hour or so, no point sendin' a bird. 'Less it's just backup, makin' sure the word gets where'ts goin'."

"Your troops use them, though, I suppose. Justinian said he used his whenever his troops were away from the gard."

"Oh, if they're some distance, yep. If they're close, they're gonna be in and out fer meals any old how, no point sendin' birds."

"Is that so? I assumed they'd have field kitchens, you know: 'Like it or not, that's what we've got, all's in the pot and at least it's hot.' That was what we said about it."

"Nah, no field cookin' 'less they're more'n a hour's ride away. 'Fthey're close they're in 'ere fer breakfas', grab a pack lunch t'eat when they can, back fer dinner in shifs, then out t' do whatever needs doin' if anythin' needs doin' at night. No armor's bin movin' round at night since those pillagers stole stuff when we were buildin' the watchtower on the south end."

"Only the one watchtower?"

"No more needed. Forest east's got wulfs and lions more'n trees. An' they say it's full o' were-critters and witch-wings. There's trip wires 'n' threads movin' mirrors t'flash sunlight 'f they get stepped on. No vis'tors or pillagers comin' that way. Y'go up belfry you'll see the road north far down t'ward Benjobz, 'n' there's 'n old watchtower in t'forest that'd see any army moving.

"On the west, there's a strippa forest, but where't slopes there's milesa wicked country, break-leg rocks and scrub, no good nowhere. They used to be mines, 'n' the place is fulla holes and shafs, half of 'em hid by downfalls 'n' brush. No army gets through there 'thout losin' half itself and makin' a racket, and that's 'fit's dry. 'Fit's wet, stay out! South, though, sighta the road's cut off the way the mount'ns lie, all stacked like a decka cards, so they built a watchtower out there, oh, lessee, it'd be fifteen years ago. From there y'c'n see a full day's travel south. Anybody comin', half a dozen birds go out t' armor 'n' they head whatever way the message says."

"How about behind these walls?"

"Armor here, ahind the walls? They'd hol' the wall likely f'rever. Nope, any army come to fight t' abbey, it could'n sneak up on us, and by the time they got set to come at us, there'd be our men behin'em doin' their own sneakin'.'"

"So you don't worry about people sneaking up on you through the trees! I'm glad to hear that. On the way here, I heard some strange sounds in those trees." Smiling confidently, Abasio did not mention a forest that was a barrier to an army might be excellent cover for a small band of abductors. Instead, he changed the conversation to a history of strange sounds and what they'd turned out to be, then to a history of strange smells, likewise mentioned a few bird keepers he'd known back over the mountains, told a few jokes, gathered in another small audience, and left Solomon Winger awash late in the evening with confidence the old man wouldn't remember anything much about their conversation. Only later did he chide himself for confidence unwarranted.

That night he thought he knew that *if* there were troops out there behind the abbey wall to the east, that fact was not generally known, and only *if* they were there would they be taking their meals in shifts in the abbey itself, not in the dining room where Xulai and her people were served, but in one set aside for armor.

Now all he needed to do was find out where that was.

Xulai had made it clear to her minders that she intended to go out in the evenings by herself, perhaps to one of the gathering places, perhaps to visit Abasio, perhaps to climb the stairs to the walk on top of the walls, as many residents did to enjoy the sunset. Though Nettie Lean was full of cautions, both Oldwife and Precious Wind seemed to have decided it was either for the best or unavoidable.

So, that evening when Abasio explained what he needed to know about where the abbey's troops were fed, Xulai leaned toward him and spoke in a low voice. "I already know about that. They told us the first day we were here. For travelers who are just passing through they have what they call a *guest arm,* guesthouses and a dining room, on the north end, just inside the northernmost gate, between the first two shield walls. Then there's what they call an *anytime arm* at the far south end, between the second and third shield walls, and that one provides food service for troops and other workers on local duty. It's a kind of come-and-eat-anytime place for people who don't have the kind of jobs they can just stop doing and leave on the stroke of the clock. You know, like medical people, animal doctors, people watching brick or charcoal kilns, people like that."

"And there's access from inside the abbey?"

"So I was told. If we're looking for troops from outside, however, I imagine it might be easiest to see who uses the outside gate. It's fairly easy to tell who's military. They wear half-armor almost all the time. When they come out, maybe you could follow them. Can you follow people? I mean, without their knowing?"

"I've been known to," said Abasio, reminded of a certain talking coyote who had been an excellent tracker. He mused for a moment or so, then said, "I haven't had Blue under a saddle in a long time, but if we leave, it'll have to be on horseback. The wagon is too recognizable to take very far, though I'll have to leave in it."

"Blue's pretty recognizable himself. That strange gray-white-black combination really does look like blue . . ."

"It won't after he's dyed black," he said. "Any more than that pretty yellow horse of yours will look yellow when he's been dyed brown and had his tail cropped short. Can you braid your hair really tightly and get it on top of your head under a cap? We need to find you some boy clothes, too, so we can travel as older and younger brothers. Meantime, I can saddle Blue and we can do some exercises out on the meadow at the south end of the abbey while I watch who goes and who comes."

"And I?"

"Do you know all the location signs your father used for his birds?"

"Yes," she replied. "He gave me a complete list of them."

"Since it seems things here at the abbey aren't as straightforward as we'd thought, it would be good to know who and what places the abbey stays in touch with. Ask to visit the loft keeper here. His name's Solo Winger. Tell whoever you ask that you spent a lot of time in Justinian's bird lofts and would like to see the abbey's. I wrote down all the signs I could remember from Woldsgard," he said, and dug a bit of paper out of a pocket.

"If you're wondering, I already know Merhaven is on my list."

"Good enough, but we still need to find out if Winger has birds from anyplace that Woldsgard doesn't." He sat back for a moment, thinking. "Even if Bear left here and a message came from him saying the way to Merhaven was safe, we couldn't rely on that information. We would need to make our own inquiry of Merhaven."

"How would we get an answer if we were on the way?"

"That's why I want to find out what birds they have here. If they have birds from someplace between here and Merhaven, we could take a Merhaven bird with us and ask them to reply to the in-between place. If there is one."

Xulai said fretfully, "There are so many puzzles."

"Quite a few," he said, ticking them off on his fingers. "There's the waters rising, the Sea King, the enmity of the duchess and probably the prior, the unknown status of the abbot, the inimical posture of King Gahls, the oddities of the refugees upon the long road to the highlands, the status of Benjobz and his expanding stables, and how in the devil did the duchess get to Benjobz and her consort get here to the abbey the same time as we did?"

"Without being seen on the road. All this is my fault," she whispered. "I've got you all involved in this mess . . ."

"Oh, Xulai! Nonsense. You'd have to be three times your age to have caused half that many snarls! My whole life has been full of puzzles! They were puzzles just as convoluted as these, and many of them happened back at a time when I was barely conscious of them. Somehow, I survived, and we will survive this time as well. Meantime, ask questions, casually. Someone must know why all these houses are vacant. See what you can learn from the bird man. And . . . do you suppose that librarian—what did you say his name was?"

"Wordswell."

"Do you suppose he knows anything about the Sea King? Like who or what or where he is? Like who or what constitutes his armies? Little details like that?"

IT WAS ALREADY LATE, BUT Xulai had gained the impression that Wordswell spent most of his nights at the library, so she asked for a guide to
take her there. On the way, they encountered the prior, who stopped
them.

"It is late to be wandering, Daughter." His tone was admonitory.

"I have an errand at the library, Elder Brother. Also, do I need someone's permission to visit the bird lofts? The duke mentioned that you
have fine ones and that I should see them while I am here."

He raised one nostril in slight distaste. "Ah, I can't imagine why.
The man who keeps the birds, a creature named Winger, is a simpleton.
Certainly he is illiterate, so you are unlikely to get sensible information
from him. However, if your guardian has recommended it to you, there
is no reason why not. By all means, go when you like."

He nodded magisterially and went off down the corridor, while
Xulai and her guide continued to the library. "He doesn't think much
of the bird keeper," remarked Xulai.

"Nor of anyone who gets their hands dirty," said the guide. "Prior,
he's a very superior kind of man. Got all that gold on him so we all know
it." And his left eye flickered in what might actually have been a wink.

Once at the library, she sent the guide to tell Precious Wind where
she was and that she would be back shortly. Wordswell was indeed
among the stacks, high among the towering shelves, perched on a
ladder, a book propped half-open before him.

Xulai called, "Don't come down, Elder Brother. But would you direct
me to whatever books might tell me something about the Sea King?"

He ignored her suggestion that he stay where he was and clam-
bered down as though he had spent all his life climbing things, trees
to begin with, no doubt, followed by anything vertical that was of interest.

"I can tell you more quickly than the books can," he said in a half
whisper, throwing a quick look around the vast room to see if anyone
else was there. "I wouldn't, ordinarily, but I sometimes get these feelings
about passing on information. A kind of itch; one that says, 'Tell this
person about X,' or 'Tell this person about Z because he needs to know.'

I felt very strongly the other night that you needed to know about the Sea King, so I've been burrowing."

"That was very kind of you."

"Well, it may have been. Or it may prove to be regrettable. One never knows, does one? Tell the wrong person the wrong thing, and it's a disaster. Still, one must chance it at times. At any rate, the Sea King: He is of the cephalopod race. His reputation parallels or is equivalent to that of the kraken. Of course, the kraken is supposed to be mountainous in size, and the Sea King is said to have conversed with human beings; it's unlikely that both are true—I find it difficult to visualize speaking with a mountain. He is said to have arisen sometime within the last several thousand years—I mean the Sea King, not the kraken—as we have no record mentioning him before that time, though krakens go far, far back in time. We have no idea whether the Sea King has been one individual during all that time or a succession of individuals. We don't know if there are any others like him. Or her. We say 'Sea King,' but it could just as likely be a queen. He or she issues orders through human servants who live on certain islands in his or her domain. When the abbey sent emissaries to meet with him or her, it was with these human representatives that they met. The humans retired at intervals to receive directions from the Sea King, but our ambassadors never saw him or her.

"We know a few things he or she has done. He or she has offered an enormous reward to any persons or creatures who invent ways to clean up the great chancre in the Western Sea. The chancre lies south of Tingawa and some way east. It is a continent-sized human junk pile left over from the days of the ease machines, and it is proving impossible to get rid of. It is poisonous. It leaks into the oceans. It is extremely difficult to dismantle into parts. The latest effort has been to determine whether the whole mass or large chunks of it can be moved over a chain of submarine volcanoes which *might* be able to incinerate it. Whales, I think, were to be the motive force—whales and possibly some sailing ships on the surface. Meantime, the Tingawans are trying to determine if the incineration would cause more trouble than leaving it alone or possibly towing it over one of the ocean deeps, weighting it down, and then causing subsea avalanches to cover it.

"We know the Sea King has done everything possible to keep ocean-going traffic and fishing at a minimum, so the chancre cannot grow and sea populations cannot be wiped out by nets. Wooden sailing ships are tolerated because they are what is called *biodegradable.* That means they rot. Rot is good. It is very important that things rot. No doubt whatever force created life included rot as a necessary concomitant. Presumably, we can have steamships if they rot properly when they wear out. Our records tell us of steamships in the far past and we still know how to make steam engines—we have one in the laundry here to wash the linens, as a matter of fact. The abbot said it really wasn't an ease machine because it uses natural steam, from the great rock below us—but we are forbidden to carry certain cargoes or have ships made of metal or moved by any kind of engine that burns what was called *fossil fuels.* Of course, such ships or cargoes are virtually impossible to create in these days. Oil is rare and far too useful to burn. No, the old ease-machine ships are gone, along with all those who knew how to run them.

"All in all, everything the Sea King has done seems to me to be perfectly sensible and justifiable from the point of view of any sea creature, though it's made life inconvenient for a good many humans. I, however, having read everything available, cannot imagine any reason why the Sea King would make it difficult for you to travel in a small sailing vessel, islet to islet, to Tingawa. The Tingawans are said to be on a good terms with the creature."

"So if I can get safely to Merhaven . . ."

"You should have no difficulty going west from there. Getting to Merhaven itself is the problem. We have reports of brigands, of wandering bands of lawless men, of patrols sent by King Gahls who kill first and ask who you are later, and of strange creatures no one has seen before emanating from the Old Dark House in the woods south of Wold."

"All the way up here? On the heights?"

"*Here* isn't that far," said Wordswell with a frown. "It's not noticeable except on a map, but the abbey is almost directly east of the Old Dark House. From Lake Riversmeet, the road to Wellsport runs almost true west, but the road to Eastwatch Tower and then up the heights gradually swings to the northeast. At the top of the falls, the road runs southeast for a way toward Benjobz, but it gradually turns due south. The Wilderbrook road from there continues south to begin with, but it winds around a lot and the abbey is actually west of Benjobz. The four points—the Old Dark House, the top of the cliff road, Benjobz, and the abbey—make a squashed rectangle, and the side between the Old Dark House and the abbey is by far the shortest side. To the west, beyond the strip of forest we can see from here, the land steps steadily downward with no great cliff to climb and no great waterfalls, either."

"Then why in the name of good sense do people use that dreadful road up the cliff face near the falls?" asked Xulai.

"Because the slope west of us was once mined for metal. It's like a huge sponge full of shafts and bores and holes that collapse without warning, besides being poisonously barren because of the chemicals that were used either in the mines or in processing the ore. You've heard of the Dragdown Swamps? That's just another name for what that huge sponge turns into when it rains for a long time, or when we have heavy snow in winter and it all melts at once. It's evil country. It's begotten many evil stories. People say that some of the old mine ease machines are still alive down there, that they can be heard talking to one another."

Xulai stood with her mouth slightly open, as though to give the ideas her mind was being flooded with a route to escape. After a long moment, she murmured, "So, if a creature knew of a safe path through this dangerous country, he or she could get from the Old Dark House up here to the abbey in a relatively short time?"

"Oh, my, yes, if he or she knew a way."

Xulai would not have bet a flibbity-bit that the Duchess of Altamont did not know a way, which meant Jenger knew it, which was why Jenger had been able to talk to Bear across the wall of the abbey.

"Anything else?" asked Wordswell.

She nodded, her face serious. "Can you lend me something on cephalopods? The most authoritative thing you have from the Before Times."

"You do know the books are not supposed to leave the library."

"Can you check to see when was the last time anyone asked for any of them, or it, or whatever?"

Wordswell stalked across the room to a large file full of tiny drawers and began pulling them out, one, then the one below, then the one below that. "Cephalopods," he murmured to himself or to her or to the air. "Cephalopods. The oceanic biology teacher spent about a week in here reading up on them . . . about ten years ago."

"No one since?"

He shook his head, giving her a conspiratorial look over the tops of his spectacles.

"I doubt anyone would miss one book, would they?"

He blinked. "I doubt they would. Things get mis-shelved from time to time."

"Just one," she said. "The best one."

"You understand it's a copy of a copy. The original would have been dust by now."

He moved the ladder, went up the ladder, came back down the ladder. The book was encased in an oiled wooden box that fit it very tightly and excluded almost all air from around it. The book inside was bound in leather and printed on a special kind of paper that lasted for a very long time. The title shone in gold on the cover: *Cephalopods*. Below it was a design of tentacles, twined around one another like a thousand noodles, and from the center of the design, two very human-seeming eyes stared at her, glinting in the candlelight. "I think I'm supposed to do this," said Wordswell. "I have such notions."

"If it's any help to you, sir, I think you are supposed to give it to me." Wrapping it loosely in her coat, she left the library and returned to Abasio's wagon, somewhat surprised at knowing the way, less so when she realized the fisher had been directing her all along.

The trouble with reading secretly was that she was very seldom alone. While Oldwife would think little of her having a schoolbook to read at night, Precious Wind would be curious, and she might mention it to Bear. Strangely enough, Abasio was still sitting by the fire, as though waiting for her.

She unpacked the book. "I need to read this."

He leafed through a few pages. "You'll need a very long time."

"You said you had a magic helmet that was a kind of library. I thought, maybe . . . And you said you'd introduce me to your love."

He sat staring into the fire for some time. "Her name is Ollie. The library is like a little helmet that takes you into another world. It has Ollie's whole life, her mind, her feelings in it. It also has the minds and feelings of every other person who ever used it and of all those who used other libraries like it. Information was shared among them. So, if you ask it a question, it has to be very, very clear what you need to know, because if there's any room for doubt, you can end up exploring fascinating information for weeks or months, until your body dies for lack of food or water or sleep, so you need someone by you to pull off the helmet after a reasonable time. I know Blue's pulled it off my head more than once. I think I can put the book into the library for you easier than you can; all I have to do is make my mind a blank and look at the pages while I turn them, ignoring temptation at every turn." His mouth twisted, as though he had tasted something both wonderful and weird. "It's a long book, so it may take a while. I can start tonight if you'll leave it with me."

Xulai considered this for a moment, nodding finally. "That would be best. Then I can return Wordswell's book, and when I'm with you, or when we're traveling, I can find out what might be helpful to know about the Sea King." She sighed, handing him the box almost regretfully, for she had been looking forward to reading it herself. "I met the prior on the way to the library. He says the bird keeper is an illiterate simpleton. And then my guide almost winked at me and said the prior had all that gold on him to show how superior he is. The abbot doesn't wear gold at all, does he?"

"Not that we've seen."

"It makes me wonder, Abasio. All that glitter. And the fortune my father says he sent. I wonder who really received it here at the abbey and where it is now. There's another very important thing: Wordswell told me something about the Old Dark House and what the land is like that lies between it and the abbey . . ."

When she had finished quoting the librarian, Abasio stared first at her, then at Blue, who had been leaning over the paddock fence to hear the entire story. "Which tells us a good deal," said the horse. "They know a way to get here quicker."

"To get here, and no doubt to get to other places as well," Abasio said, frowning. "We must be sure to keep that in mind."

The
Dragdown
Swamps

OVERNIGHT, HEAVY WEATHER CAME TO THE ABBEY AND to most of the surrounding countryside. Snow fell from black clouds that boiled suddenly from the west, one of those freakish early storms that would melt away long before autumn was over, though not as quickly as it came. In the meantime it meant tall drifts of snow, cold, wind, ice underfoot, much stamping of feet, building of fires, shoveling of walks and wall tops so that guards could keep watch without freezing their feet.

In the Old Dark House, the Duchess of Altamont was infuriated by the weather. When the eastern slopes of Altamont became spongy (as the Old Dark Man had described them), her attempts to move quickly from place to place became at first uncomfortable, then dangerous, and finally impossible. When the old mines were dry, there were underground routes she could use, old tunnels where ponies swiftly pulled carts along rails, old elevators that still functioned when valves were turned to fill shafts with water, thus raising or lowering floating platforms in others. Some of the old-time miners or their sons still stayed in the huts nearby to be sure the ponies, the carts, and the elevators kept working, for their livings, their lives, and the lives of all their kindred depended upon the duchess's getting what she wanted as soon as possible. From various places in these ancient systems, some actually under the upland valley of the Wells west of Benjobz Inn, others near the abbey, she could dispatch her servants, including Jenger—though he would have been dismayed, even frightened, to learn that she thought of him in the "servant" category, for he had been in the habit of assuring himself he was important to her. In truth, only Mirami was important to Alicia, because Alicia feared and hated Mirami more than she feared or hated anyone else.

From the mine shaft opening in the forest near Benjobz Inn, Alicia could travel within a few days to the court of King Gahls to "consult" concerning the family business. To Alicia, consultation meant receiving her mother's instructions without question or complaint. When the area was flooded, however, the shafts became wells, and the slopes became drowning pits, mortally dangerous even to those familiar with them. When such times seemed imminent, the old men used the elevators to lift themselves and their ponies to their huts on higher ground. While the shafts were flooded, nothing moved for a time, and even Mirami understood this. While Mirami could do many things others thought impossible, she could not control the weather. "Yet," she laughed when this was mentioned. "I can't do that yet."

The duchess had returned to the cellars of the Old Dark House after her almost wasted visit to Benjobz, arriving as the rains began. They were followed by heavy snow in weather just warm enough to let it melt continuously. The combination had made her usual ways impassable, and it was during a temporary lull in her preoccupation with the Tingawans that she overheard two of her servants in the castle above talking with one another. They were chattering about Justinian having left Woldsgard and the fact that Wold was now occupied by the army of Hallad, Prince Orez, while another army, this one from the abbey, had settled itself for the winter at Netherfields.

Among Alicia's rages, the one that followed was one that might possibly have been assuaged by totally destroying everyone within several miles of the Old Dark House and applying curses to their descendants for the next seven generations. Fortunately for the locals, she had overheard these remarks through an air duct while she was sequestered in her secret room set deep in the rock below the Old Dark House. What she overheard so blinded her with rage she was unable to remember the "key" to the door that always locked itself behind her. The key was a lengthy coded entry tapped onto a transparent plate that was ancient, badly abraded, and possessed of some hundreds of symbols that changed their arrangement each time they were called up. In the time it took her to quiet herself, remember the key, then find the symbols required in the specific order required, she also had time to recall that Mirami was deeply concerned with Justinian's movements. Justinian was part of the family project, but Alicia had not been concentrating upon the family project because of the Tingawans. She took a few moments to think it through. If she were to avoid her mother's criticism, which was often accompanied by painful consequences, it would be wise to inform Mirami of the current situation immediately.

Mirami's mirror was in the mirror room, next door. It was early in the morning. Mirami might still be abed, or she might be at breakfast. Alicia went to stand before it and say, "Show me!" The mirror cleared to show vague shadows, perhaps a table, one person more clearly, evidently eating a meal. Alicia murmured very softly. One mirror seeing its target would not transmit words, but it would creak a little. One of the shadows looked up, nodded slightly, and went back to the meal. Alicia pulled a chair in front of the mirror and waited. The mirror followed that one figure through the meal, through the transit of several dim corridors, and into its own, locked, mirror room. The image became three-dimensional, and Mirami spoke. "What is it?"

"I have just learned . . . ," said Alicia, going on to quote what she had, in fact, just learned. With the two mirrors linked, they could hear each other very well.

"And why were you not aware of this sooner? What were you doing?" Mirami demanded.

Alicia had had time to polish her excuse. "A train of wagons went from Woldsgard some days ago. You told me to be aware of movements there. I thought I should find out where they were going and why. It seems a Tingawan soul carrier, some puling infant, was among the people. They said they were going to the abbey, where the child will be educated until she can complete her journey to Tingawa."

"And Justinian was not with them?"

"I thought he might be in a closed carriage, so I followed them. It turned out he was not. Just the girl and some servants and several wagons of furnishings and supplies, and the child didn't even make it to the abbey. It seems she had a fit of some kind and turned back. The servants are now saying, however, that the duke left Woldsgard in the care of Hallad, Prince Orez, and armed men from the abbey are in possession of Netherfields."

"And you knew *nothing* of this?"

"Not a word until today. On the route I traveled, I did not see the troops."

"And you have not visited Justinian?"

Here, Alicia was on solid ground. "You told me to leave him alone for a while after the Tingawan bitch died. I have done so."

"Seemingly I instructed you wisely. You are not known for your warm, consoling personality. Why are you concerned about this soul carrier? Though we will dispose of Tingawa eventually, the Tingawan religion need not concern us."

Why did she care, really? She attempted an explanation: "Something about the Tingawans itches at me."

"Were they insolent?"

Without thinking, she blurted, "Their existence on our lands is an insolence!"

Mirami's eyes narrowed as her lips smiled, such a smile as a serpent might make contemplating dinner. "When you wish to be affronted, Alicia, which, I may say, has been your preferred mood since we left Kamfels, you manipulate any chance word into an insult, any unconscious facial expression into an offense, any casual yawn into a deadly provocation, and no matter how slight the slur, you always pass a death sentence on the miscreant." Her voice lowered, she whispered, a whisper like a knife. "Even when it is impolitic and stupid to do so!"

The duchess flushed. At this moment, she still felt that killing everyone for a mile in every direction would have been soothing. It would have been gratifying. No one ever served Alicia perfectly, and sooner or later she always rewarded imperfection with blood and pain. It made her happy. At least, this was the label she gave a certain draining feeling, as though all her furies were running out of her, leaving a strange satiety behind. It was a little like the effect of wine, or the juice of poppies, or that vanishingly rare sensation of sexual exhaustion. Though the feeling never persisted, she called it happiness.

The image in the mirror smiled again, an utterly ruthless smile. "I see your thoughts all too clearly, Daughter. Unfortunately, you have never learned to hide what you feel. You wish to kill someone, several of them, perhaps everyone within reach. But think a moment. Killing the populace of Altamont would leave you without farmers, horsemen, servitors, cooks, seamstresses, and smiths. The ones you have now are well cowed, too frightened to leave, but if you kill them, you will find no queue of eager but subservient lackeys to replace them."

Mirami frowned, lifting one nostril as she did when she was raging silently. "The Old Dark Man left Altamont to me, my dear. When I no longer needed the castle or the things he left me—the things in the cellar, my dear, the ones I have yet to learn to use—I let you live in the place while we pursued other ambitions."

"Mother, I know . . ."

"Oh, yes, indeed you know. You knew you had your own ambitions, and you used our dear Rancitor to get title to the place. I *have not* made a fuss about that, *not yet;* it did not seem worth my while, but the fact that I *did not* does not mean I *cannot*! When the Old Dark Man left me or died or whatever he did, he had lived a hundred and fifty years. Using what he taught me, I think I can manage at least that long myself. If you will choose to be wise instead of silly, I may help you to do the same. If you choose otherwise, I can always reclaim Altamont for myself. I have the means to do so. So, my dear, while you think repopulating Altamont might be only an inconvenience for you, please consider that I would find it more than merely annoying."

Mirami's anger was quiet where Alicia's was furious, but it was as lethal.

Alicia pinched her lips, nodded, said nothing. She had learned long ago that any pain she could inflict, her mother could equal. Mirami was saying quite clearly that Altamont could be reclaimed when its current owner died, a death she could easily accomplish.

Mirami snapped: "Tell me, Daughter, what is our business?"

"Our business currently requires that I marry, by one means or another, Justinian, Duke of Wold, because my mother, the queen, wishes to take over the lands of Ghastain and Wold, plus all those now held by Prince Orez." She knew the litany well.

"Exactly. That is still our business, despite this departure by the duke. I need to consult with others. Can you come to court?"

Alicia did not want to go to the court. She was safer where she was.

"Only by the long way," she said, temporizing. "It would take a long time. The Dragdown Swamps are with us again. There is one route that may possibly open to the tower near the abbey within a few days, but it may be very dangerous." It was the way she had returned to Altamont from Benjobz Inn before the snow came. It was the way she had sent Jenger back to the Vulture Tower just as the storm began. She was not at all sure he had ever arrived there. She did not greatly care, though it would mean making new arrangements for the Tingawans if he hadn't. Well, she would need to do that anyhow. Later. And if Jenger had perished on the way, one of the archers would do as a substitute. She'd been watching a particular one. He was nicely built. He had a usable body, a properly servile manner.

Mirami nodded. "Well, you may wait until the way is safe. We have time. Send men by the way you mention to learn whether or when it can be used. As soon as it can be used, come to me here." The mirror went blank.

The duchess did not move or speak. She knew the trick of blanking the mirror but continuing to listen in order to learn what the person at the other end might say. She did not betray herself with a sound. She merely stood, very quietly, in her deep, warm room, surrounded by things that clicked, lights that turned on and off, other things that hummed and buzzed in combinations that conveyed nothing to her. In one corner the watcher loomed; very occasionally it clicked, buzzed, hummed as it watched her.

The thing that watched her! They had been living at Kamfels, she and her father and her baby brother and Mirami, except that Mirami sometimes went to Ghastain. Mirami had friends there. Alicia liked it when her mother went away, because then she could have her father all to herself. He was so handsome, and everyone liked him. Hulix was just a baby with a nursemaid, and he didn't get in the way. Sometimes her father put her on the horse in front of him and they went riding. She had pony of her own, too, but riding with Father was more fun.

One night, she was wakened by a sound. When her eyes opened she saw a great, tall shadow carrying a little light that shined up onto his face, a face like a skull, only shadows for eyes, a mouth all teeth, wide and bony. That was the first time she had seen the Old Dark Man, and she was frightened. "I'm a friend of your mother's," he said. The voice was a surprise, calm and pleasant, flowing

into her ears like syrup, full of sweetness. "Get dressed," he said. "I'm taking you
to visit the place your mother grew up, the Old Dark House."

"Does Father know I'm going?"

"No. Your father doesn't know. No one knows."

"They'll know I'm gone."

"No, no one will know you're gone. You'll be back before they wake up."

She didn't know how he took her. He was holding something like an egg. He
clicked it and they simply walked out of her room and into another room through
flashing things that looked like mirrors. Zing, zing, zing, flash, flash, they were
there.

"These are the cellars of the Old Dark House," he said.

"They aren't very nice." The stones were cold, the ceilings hung with
webs. "They have spiderwebs."

"That's because no one can come down here to clean. No one comes here but
me and my family. Your mother is part of my family."

"So I'm part of your family?"

"You are."

"But I'm really the duke Falyrion's daughter, you know. He's my father."

"Really?"

"Really. He is."

The Old Dark Man smiled a very curious smile. "And does he love you
dearly?"

"Oh, yes, he says so."

"Ah. Well, I have deep regard for you, too, Alicia. I'm going to teach you some
wonderful things, but first you have to learn that you will not tell the duke and
you will not tell your mother."

"Mother says I must tell her everything."

"Everything but this. This is our secret."

She had objected, and he had hurt her, only a little; the scar hardly
showed, just enough to convince her that she should not tell her father,
should not tell Mirami. Then he had instructed her: the large mechanism in the corner was there to watch and protect her; she must let
the large mechanism see everything she did when she was here; this
mechanism was used in this way; that mechanism was used in that way.
He called them mechanisms, not ease machines. During their visits—
always at night, always when Mirami was away—he had moved several of

them onto a low bench where she could use them easily: the seeker-mirror mechanisms; the fatal-cloud mechanism; the sending mechanism. He had shown her how to connect the seeker-mirror and the sending mechanisms together to make a haunting. She had wanted to send a haunting onto Mirami, but the Old Dark Man hadn't let her.

Mirami never knew that Alicia had visited the Old Dark Man. He had always come for her after dark; he had always returned her before anyone knew she was gone. In later years, Alicia had sometimes wondered if he had moved her at all, or whether he had perhaps not directed her to dream everything she had learned, had seen. Later, however, when she became Duchess of Altamont, when she took possession of the castle, when she went down the stairs and opened the secret door, using the key on the screen as he had taught her, everything had been just as she had seen it as a child. Everything that had happened between her and the Old Dark Man had been real and was still a secret.

One of the things he had taught her was to keep her accounts balanced.

Now, instead of raging, Alicia thought very carefully of the account she kept with Mirami. Mirami had questioned her, then ordered her, then given her a specific time in which to comply with the order, as though she, Alicia, were a servant! She had also ridiculed Alicia's manner, her style, her way of being. None of this was unusual, and the Old Dark Man had told her how to cope with it.

"Comply. Comply in a timely manner. Then do something that Mirami would not like at all if she knew of it. Be sure it is something to your benefit, not hers. Be sure she does not know of it. That way, my child, your accounts will always be in balance."

Alicia thought she had been about seven years old when he had told her that.

"Your mother will always think she controls you. You will always know she does not," he had said. "You will take pleasure in that. Your accounts will balance."

Very well. Now it was time to balance the accounts. Mirami was getting out of hand, and it was time she had something else to think about. Alicia went to a cupboard, opened it, found a small box sealed with wax, cut the wax away, and opened the box to disclose several tiny boxes inside, each carefully labeled, several with the letter M, a couple with the letter C, for Chamfray. Chamfray was her mother's "chamberlain." She took a C-labeled box and carried it to the machine she had used to kill the woman at Woldsgard. A rack nearby was filled with small skull-shaped receptacles, rounded at one end, angled like a jaw at the other. The contents of the box—a few hairs, a few scraps of skin—went into one of the receptacles; the receptacle fitted into a little port in the fatal-cloud mechanism, clicking into place with a sound like a key turning in a lock, *scrun-chick*. She entered a certain code, then another one, thinking carefully as she did so. There would be no mistakes this time, even though this was only the second time she had used it. Since that time she had done it badly, she had studied the instructions, over and over. This time there would be no mistake. Finally, satisfied, she pushed a red button. The mechanism hummed. After a time, it stopped humming and clicked again as a small, cylindrical capsule extruded itself from the bottom of the device. The capsule was smooth, without markings except for the fine line that girded its middle, a line indicating that it would probably unscrew or uncap at that point. It was almost exactly the size of the tube one would attach to a pigeon's leg, to carry a message.

The loft was four stories above her, and she relished every step of the climb. At the top, she sent the loft man away and took time to lean in the window, judging the weather. It had cleared completely; the skies were blue and warm; it was early in the day. She picked a large, strong-looking bird from the Ghastain cage, a bird that would make the trip well before nightfall. She held it gently, stroking it: such a nice, nice strong bird. The loft keeper at the court of King Gahls would open the capsule to get the message out just the way the loft keeper at Woldsgard castle had sometimes done when she sent a new copy of the cloud. They had never caught on to that. Stupid of them! One of Justinian's cleaners, the one who swept out the lofts, had been bribed to provide a few pigeons. Though there had never been a message, she had sent copy after copy!

No copies this time! This one had been made correctly; once would be quite enough. The lofts in Ghastain, up on the highlands, were part of the castle itself, close to the living quarters of those who dwelt there. Close enough. The cloud would find Chamfray, all by itself. She returned to her cellar empty-handed, humming.

The little box lay where she had left it. The last time Alicia had been at court, she had taken hairs from inside Chamfray's cap. Hairs with their little roots attached, the only kind that the mechanism could use. With that Tingawan woman, she had taken a fragment of glass from the edge of a wine cup. It was the only material she had, the only she could obtain! And then she'd made mistakes. Instead of killing swiftly, cleanly, it had been like cutting the Stoneway, chip, chip, chip. Like bleeding someone to death a drop at a time! It had taken far too long. If she'd been able to get some other material, she could have ended it earlier, but the princess had been too well guarded.

She would do it correctly for the other Tingawans, too, when she got around to that. Mirami had no idea that Alicia could use the Old Dark Man's machines. Mirami knew he had the machines, but she had never been taught to use them. It had amused the Old Dark Man to keep her in the dark, to educate Alicia without her mother knowing of it. Mirami thought the Tingawan princess had died from poison because that's the way Mirami always killed. Though Mirami did not kill for pleasure, she did it easily and without pity when it suited her. If it suited her plans to kill Alicia, she would do that just as easily.

When Mirami found someone more talented than someone already in her employ, the former employee usually died, though sometimes they simply disappeared. Children were no different. Alicia had once overheard her mother say that children were merely anchors for attaching oneself to men one wished to use. Well, Mirami had already used Falyrion, so the children she'd had with Falyrion were disposable. She hadn't finished using King Ghals, so Rancitor was in good odor at the moment. Hulix, however, would not last long as Duke of Kamfels. Alicia had read her mother's attitude toward him. He was only a pawn, holding a square until someone else moved in and took him. Alicia had long ago decided not to be another pawn.

The Old Dark Man had come for her and found her weeping.

"What's this? Why are you going on like this?"

"Mother. She killed him. She killed my father. I saw her."

"Your father?" He made a strange chuckling sound. "You mean Falyrion?"

"My father, yes. She killed him."

"And you loved him." His voice was serious, calm, but with something sharp in it.

"I do love him! And I can't say anything to anybody or she'll kill me."

"Yes. Probably. But you remember what I taught you about keeping your accounts balanced?" He chuckled. "Usually what she does is of no concern to me, but I have a special need for you, Alicia, so I have taught you how to keep yourself safe. If you have paid attention?" He had tipped her head, glared into her eyes. Still sobbing, she had nodded. That night he didn't take her anywhere. That night he went away without taking her anywhere or doing any of the things he sometimes did to her. The "procedures" that hurt. Sometimes they hurt a lot, but learning to use the mechanisms was worth it!

No doubt Mirami had killed a lot of people before she killed Falyrion, but the deaths had never touched Alicia. Her father's death was different. She had seen her father lying on the bier. His hands were cold. His face was still. He wouldn't take her riding anymore. He wouldn't show her how to fish or read her stories of the Before Time. He wouldn't take her for surprise picnics into the forest. Mirami could kill whom she liked and Alicia didn't care, but Mirami had no right to kill Alicia's father. This death she would not forgive. That was when she really paid attention to the Old Dark Man's strange words. That was when she really focused on keeping her accounts balanced, in order to be safe, yes, but that wasn't the only reason.

She hadn't been blamed for Justinian's flight, so she could assume she was still safe, still in reasonable favor. Her meetings with the Sea King's ambassadors would remain secret. It was clever of the Sea King to hide them in the refugee villages, among the Becomers! One day, however, when she had time to search Wold for what the Tingawan had hidden there, the Sea King would put such power into her hands that Mirami would no longer matter. Until that time it was expedient to set the Tingawans aside and at least pretend to attend to family business.

This thought led her to wonder why, since the family business was so important to Mirami, with all her spies and agents and little people passing on bits of information, she had not foreseen Justinian's leaving. She always seemed to know everything before it happened, but she had not known this! In fact, such immediate action was utterly unlike Justinian's usual behavior. He was slow to act, usually. He liked to think about things. Perhaps the cursed Tingawan princess had made his plans for him before she died! More than merely perhaps. She had done so! If

Alicia needed a reason to hate Tingawans, that was a sufficient reason!

Of course, Mirami had not foreseen that the Sea King's people would approach Alicia, either. Mirami had not foreseen that Alicia might prefer to have plans of her own. Mirami was not omniscient. Cheered by this, Alicia drummed her fingers, crossing things off her mental list, eventually coming to the subject of her most recent annoyance: Jenger.

If he had reached the Vulture Tower, he was now arranging to abduct the Tingawan females and assassinate the one called Bear. If he succeeded, well and good! The prisoners could be kept at the Old Dark House indefinitely. A few times she had kept prisoners alive for years. Well, almost alive. And if Jenger had not succeeded, it really didn't matter, because the Tingawans could be killed later. She could simply send a pigeon to the Vulture Tower, telling Jenger to return to Altamont. This would tell her if the route was safe for her to use.

However, Mirami had said they had time and Jenger had been behaving very oddly of late, not as amusing as usual, more subdued. Perhaps he suspected he was about to be replaced. Servants who reached that point were sometimes driven to play games of their own. Well, since a little delay was allowable, she would wait a day or two before sending archers by the same route Jenger had taken. The shafts would be a bit drier by then; they could report on the condition of the tunnels when they returned and they could bring Jenger back with them. As a matter of fact, they could take a pack animal or two and bring back everything in the tower. If Jenger had been playing games, there would be some evidence of it.

Busy with these plans, she left her secret room, which locked itself behind her. Also behind her, she left the remaining hair and fingernail fragments from Bear's betrothed in far-off Tingawa, along with the hairs she had obtained from Bear's barber in Wold. The current haunting would go on for a while longer before she had to strengthen it. Bear's hair in the seeker, the girl's hair in the sending machine, the two linked. Wherever he was, her essence would be all around him. He would be smelling her, hearing her, feeling her. Alicia could let that situation alone for the moment.

AN UNINTENDED RESULT OF ALICIA's temporary abandonment of her devices was that the ghost possessing Bear weakened and for a few days,

Bear—who could not scout the way south until the roads cleared some-what—stopped lecturing Xulai about moving into the house at the edge of the abbey lands. Xulai gave thanks for this, however tempo-rary it might be. She was finding the weathery days an interim she had needed, a few days to get used to herself before she and Abasio needed to act. Also, Abasio had time to get the cephalopod book into his li-brary. He said it was a leftover from a time when nanotechnology had been able to do remarkable things. Not all ease-machines, he claimed, had been evil.

Xulai found this to be true when Abasio put the strange helmet on her head and she entered the library, where she met Ollie. Ollie was "the Orphan," who had been—no, who *was*—Abasio's love. Xulai spent so much time in the helmet with Ollie, walking and talking and drink-ing tea—all of which seemed completely real—that she came to regard Ollie as a close, loved friend, someone she could tell everything and anything to, how she felt, how she didn't feel, how angry she became at some things without knowing why. Ollie understood them all. Ollie had felt many of the same emotions for the same reasons. Ollie was glad Xulai had met Abasio. She hoped they would be friends, even lovers if they liked. In the world of the helmet, she said, jealousy just wasn't interesting enough to bother with. Living people had short lives and didn't have time to love many people—nor love them well—but when one was immortal, as the people in the helmet were, one could love one or a dozen or a hundred others. Immortals had time to love everyone they found compatible. There were many people in the helmet besides the Orphan, all of them living very genuine and consequential lives in their strangely wonderful, inconsequential world.

That evening, she sat in Abasio's wagon, telling him of all this, his arm around her as it often was, his cheek against hers. She said the word "love," and his arm tightened. She turned toward him and met his lips. She thought dazedly that it was her first kiss; Oldwife Gancer had told her about first kisses, waxing romantic for such a practical person. It wasn't a surprise, was a surprise, was a fantastic, wonderful surprise—especially that she did not have to decide anything at all. What hap-pened after the kiss was a silent clap of thunder, something that should have shaken the sky so that everyone heard it, though later it seemed no one had either heard it or seen the lightning that preceded it, the luminous, effulgent air that seemed to burn without heat, the fiery air that held them at the center of a great crowd. She had felt them, the people, felt their eyes, calm and studious and concerned, and yet they two had been quiet and private as though they had hidden themselves in the depths of a forest while it all happened, and after a while, happened again. They did not even speak of it. They did not need to speak of it. They knew what had occurred and how it had been witnessed; they were sure of that, though not sure why. The whole thing was simply too much for a why.

"Do I need to tell anyone?" she whispered. They were lying on his bed, covered by a feather quilt.

He was lying dazed beside her, conscious of the immensity that had come to surround them from some strange, evanescent, utterly unidentifiable source. He summoned consciousness with some difficulty and made a slightly shrugging motion with the shoulder her head was lying on. "Do you feel you should tell someone?"

"No," she said. Though she might tell Precious Wind. Sometime. If it mattered. If, for example, she found herself—pregnant. Well and well, so, if she were, they would decide what to do on their way to Tingawa. She had sworn to get there; this would not interfere.

Later that evening she returned the librarian's book. "Did you find what you needed?" he asked her, aware of her eyes for the first time. They had a depth to them he could not quite—"perceive" wasn't the right word. What was the right word for something one knew was there that one could not sense in any normal way? All he could do was repeat himself: "Did you find what you needed?"

"I'm sure I did, Elder Wordswell. I'm sure when I find out what it was, the answer will be there."

"You've copied the book?" he asked, astonished.

"Oh, the book. Yes. Someone is remembering it for me," she said, astounding him yet further.

Virtually overnight, the drifts melted down; Abasio took Blue out onto the fields south of the abbey and rode him a bit, asking him please to fancy it up so they wouldn't look like idiots. Blue said fancying it up would make them look more like idiots, but he did it anyhow. Blue had met fancy horses; he knew what horses could be trained to do. If the man wanted prancing, very well, prancing he would get, and dancing with this foot, then that foot, so that any observer would get a very false idea about what kind of horse Abasio was riding. Such horses had been trained out of having any minds of their own. Blue had no time for such horses, though he had plenty of time to notice that during their riding sessions no men in armor went into the anytime dining room.

"When are you going to dye the horses?" Xulai asked that evening.

"You don't have school tomorrow or the next morning, right?"

"It's a holiday they have here, a kind of feast day."

"Both mornings I'll go out where I've been exercising Blue, you'll come along on Flaxen, and I'll pretend to be giving you some pointers on riding. That's to get people used to your being out there. The second night, I'll hitch up Blue and drive the wagon away south. I've found a place to hide the wagon where it'll be safe, an old half-fallen-in building, maybe a cabin or barn, in a small hidden canyon with a little stream in it. The wagon will fit inside. I've already cut some trees to hide it. I'll change Blue's appearance that night and pack the things we'll need for the trip. I rode on south the day before the storm; there's a farmer southerly a few miles who had a mule for sale. I bought it and told him I'd pick it up in a few days.

"The morning after I go, you take Flaxen out to the field, just as we'll have been doing. There's a corner of the field where you can't be seen from the parapets. You'll move in and out of that area several times, then from that area move into the trees. Circle the fields, stay inside the trees, and go on farther south, parallel to the road. When you can't see any part of the abbey anymore, not even the tower, you can get onto the road, but keep watch and get off of it if anyone's coming. I'll meet you along the way.

"I've bought some boy's clothes, ostensibly for my nephew. You'll need a name. Think of one that pleases you. The clothes are already in the wagon. Anything else you need to take, you'll need to smuggle down to me over the next couple of days."

"The mule will carry what we can't?"

"Yes, but we should still keep our belongings light. You won't be a girl, remember, and we both should look a bit scruffy and travel worn—decently clean, but not polished. I've found a cap that'll cover your hair if you can braid it up."

"I've been practicing."

"Now, one final thing: It's been my experience that no matter how good a plan is, things can go wrong, so one should always have another plan in place, just in case. If anything happens to delay you, I'll wait with the wagon! One day, two, seven, whatever, I'll wait with the wagon. If you need me or need to let me know something, can you send your friend?"

"If I knew where you were, certainly," said the fisher, sticking his head out of Xulai's jacket pocket, which was deep and wide enough to hide him completely, though he had grown some in the last few days.

Abasio nodded. "You heard what I told Xulai. Follow the road until you're well out of sight of the abbey. Look for a long straight stretch with outcroppings of red rock on the right-hand side. It's the first red rock you'll see. Directly across from the third outcropping, on the other side of the road, you'll see three big pine trees in a straight line. Right now there's a pile of brush I cut and stacked between the leftmost and middle tree. I'll spread it around to hide the wagon tracks when I take the wagon in. Behind the brush, follow the tracks.

"Now, that's if you're delayed. If I'm in the wagon and everything is all right, there'll be a straight line of flat stones between the first and second tree, where the brush is now. I figure if anyone takes me out of there, I'll have a chance to scatter those stones with my feet, or Blue will. If the stones are scattered, go away."

"Or hide and watch, or creep around and see what's happened," said Xulai.

He looked at her face for a long moment before he nodded. "You've been taught."

"Oh, yes," she said. "I've been taught. I didn't realize how much I'd been taught. Some of it I must have practiced alone, in the woods, without realizing what I was doing. At school they were quite surprised. In the personal attack class I was entered as a women's level seven. Most students, of course, start as a one."

"How many levels are there?"

"Nine. Bear is a nine. Men's nine. Men are simply bigger and stronger than women, so women have to be quicker and cleverer than men. When I thought I was a child, I wasn't nearly that good. About a three or four. Well, it wouldn't have been appropriate for a seven-year-old to be any better than that, would it?"

The following morning she woke before dawn, not out of anticipation or excitement but because she was in discomfort. Perhaps she
had the cramping feeling Precious Wind had told her to expect as part
of this whole woman thing. If what they had told her was correct, she
would have to do something about the resultant messiness also, but that
idea was driven out of her head by a moment of really horrible, very
intimate pain. She started to cry out to Oldwife, who snored gently in
the other bed, but as suddenly as it had come, the pain passed, all the
tension let go, and she relaxed, very peacefully, feeling as though she'd
had several glasses of wine or some gentle, lovely euphoric.

She lay quietly, enjoying the feeling, until the first pale light lit the
window. She threw back the covers and got out of bed, turning as she
did so to inspect the sheets. They were stainless, white, except for a
small spot of moisture on the bottom sheet. At its center lay something
very familiar to her. It was spherical, mostly blue. Like a marble or . . .
very like the thing her mother had told her to swallow.

"I've laid an egg," she said to herself, fighting her sudden urge to
giggle uncontrollably. Or scream, also uncontrollably.

The fisher was on her shoulder, as though he had materialized out
of nothing. "Think of it as a . . . jewel. Hide it where it will be completely
safe," he said. "And be sure, wherever you are, you take it with you. Don't
speak of it. Don't lose it, whatever you do."

Gritting her teeth, shutting her lips tight together to prevent herself from saying anything, asking anything, she considered the problem. Jacket wouldn't do. Clothes wouldn't do; those changed every day
and bumps would be noticeable. She could put it in an undershift. She
would make a tiny pocket in an undershift. Even boys wore undershifts,
though theirs were shorter than the knee-length ones girls wore. All her
undershifts had wide hems, to allow for letting down as she grew taller,
or so the legend would have had it! She'd put it in the hem, in back,
where it would be between her legs when she sat down and wouldn't
make a noticeable bump. And she'd have to make a similar pocket in
every undershift, so she could put the . . . jewel in whichever one she was
wearing. And she had to do it now, while Oldwife slept.

The mending basket was on the shelf. It had scissors, thread, needles. A slit in the hem took only a moment; the strange little orb slid
inside. Then four stitches on each side to hold it there, and the needle,

already threaded, was thrust through the underside of her jacket collar with a long length of thread wound into a neat figure eight around it. Just in case she needed to do more sewing or for when she had to hide the thing somewhere else.

The fisher sighed, an almost human sound of relief. "If it happens to you again, hide that one, too. Always. Hide them. Always have them with you."

"I think it would be considerate of you to tell me what they are," she said almost angrily.

The fisher fidgeted, making little motions with his head and shoulders, like a bewildered person trying to remember something. "I don't know," he whispered in a sad, hurt voice. "I've been put here to guide you, when you need guiding, but I don't know what to say about anything until something happens and then, suddenly, there are words there. I've told you all the words that came to me this morning. There isn't anything else."

Just as there had been a tiny child in the carriage, on the road. Just as there had been horse biscuits when conditions required them, or horses becoming deer.

"I feel like a chess piece," she said angrily. "Move here, move there. Whose game are we playing, Fisher?"

He did the shrugging thing again, looking so sad, lost, and bewildered that she took him into her arms, sat on the edge of the bed, and petted him as she would have one of the cats. While he didn't purr, the warmth of the contact seemed to comfort them both. He did not feel like a mere thing. He was alive, furry and breathing. His nose was leathery and warm. His eyes were bright. However he came to be, he was hers.

She went to find Precious Wind, who was still asleep. Xulai touched her lightly on the shoulder. "Wind?" she murmured.

"I'm here."

Xulai beckoned, whispering, "I need to tell you something."

Precious Wind put on a robe and they went out into the little courtyard, where dew hung heavy on the grasses and the dawn birds were complaining sleepily.

"It's about Princess Xu-i-lok."

"Your mother."

"That's still hard to think about and sometimes I can't say it."

"Let it go. What about her?"

"Before she died, she sent me out at night, alone, to get something for her."

"And you did?" Precious Wind's eyes were wide, her face eager.

Xulai had thought of telling the whole story and had decided against it. She did not want to mention Abasio or tell anyone just yet what they meant to one another. She wanted people to think of him as they already did: a wanderer, an innocuous stranger, harmless and unsuspected of anything. "Yes. I was afraid. Terribly afraid. It took three tries, but I found it for her. It was a ball of something, like a candy, and when I brought it back, she told me to swallow it. I did, and I think that's when the changes started, I mean, in me."

Precious Wind shut her eyes and breathed deeply as though deciding how to react. "It's possible you were staying in childlike form through some method that needed an antidote to reverse itself."

"I suppose, but that's not the important part. While I was out there, in the woods, the duchess and that man, Jenger, came. A spy had told them that a child was going out into the woods at night. I was hidden. They didn't see me. They stood there in the woods and talked together. She wanted to find something that Princess Xu-i-lok had hidden, or the thing that Huold had carried, and she said the Sea King had offered her a reward for either one of those things."

Precious Wind frowned. "The Sea King? You're sure she said exactly that?"

Xulai put her hands across her eyes and concentrated on remembering. "Not exactly, no. She said the Sea King's *ambassador* offered a reward. The Sea People had found a vault full of machines under the library at the Edgeworld Isles. The duchess was to receive the machines as a reward, and Jenger said he thought she already had machines."

Precious Wind exhaled suddenly. "Ah! What did she say?"

"She said she only had a few. She had a little machine that made . . . clouds of tiny things that could seek out any one person and kill them— if she had the pattern for that person."

"Pattern?"

Again she struggled to remember. "Code. Maybe that's the word she used. Code. She had taken my mother's code from the rim of a wineglass at the court, and she'd sent the cloud to eat that pattern, cell by cell."

Precious Wind scowled fiercely. "Yes. That's what Xu-i-lok thought. Your mother knew what had happened. We had no defenses ready because until that moment, we didn't know anyone had rediscovered that power! We decided to call it a curse because most people find it easier to believe in magic than to believe in reality. If they're religious, they get used to magical thinking as children and go through life believing in fantasy instead of facts. Ah, well, poor things, they have to cope somehow. Besides, we didn't want the duchess or her mother to know we had any information about them."

"We?"

"We, the clan Do-Lok of Tingawa, who appointed me to guard you."

"Not Bear?"

"No, not Bear. He guards you, too, but he doesn't have the information I have. Bear is only a warrior, not a technician."

"And a technician is . . . ?"

"Someone who has some understanding of machines and science and what they can do. Is that all you wanted to tell me?"

Xulai had wanted Precious Wind to tell her something! About Bear. She could not bring herself to ask. She shrugged, saying, "No. The most important part is, while she was standing there, a little gust of wind blew a branch and caught some of her hair. And when we—I left—"

Precious Wind pounced: "We, Xulai?"

We? Well, yes. She didn't want to talk about Abasio's having been there. "A tiny chipmunk had taken refuge in my pocket. There were predators about so I left the little thing in my pocket. When we left, I saw that the branch had pulled out some of her hairs. I wrapped them in a handkerchief and brought them back with me. I thought I should tell you about them."

"You're sure they were hers, not Jenger's?"

"They were hers. I saw her brush away the branch, the same branch I took them from, and Jenger was standing some distance away the whole time."

Precious Wind seemed to be looking into a great distance. "Will you give them to me?"

"Gladly." Xulai fetched the box from her pack, took out the handkerchief-wrapped bundle of hairs, and put it into Precious Wind's hands.

"Tell me again what she was to be rewarded for."

"If she found whatever it was that Huold carried. Or if she found something that the princess . . . my mother had hidden. I think what she had hidden was already in my pocket. My mother had told me where to find it."

"Did I ever talk to you about the mirror defense?" asked Precious Wind in a faraway voice, as though she was speaking from some other place.

"You and Bear both did. It's when you reflect an opponent's strength or tactics back against him so that he beats himself. It sounded complicated."

"Sometimes it is," said Precious Wind, yawning. "I'm going back to bed. You?"

"Breakfast. Then I'm going riding with Abasio."

PRECIOUS WIND DID NOT GO back to sleep. She went as quickly as she could to find Abasio. She told him one thing and another that he had not known, that no one else had known. "If I am not here, not available, do as you see fit with this information," she said.

He bowed, agreeing, and she left him to handle his astonishment as well as he might. Then she returned to her room and went back to sleep.

WHEN XULAI FINISHED BREAKFAST SHE took Flaxen out onto the meadow, where she and Abasio and the two horses, Blue with studied insouciance and Flaxen with as much astonishment as any ordinary horse could manage, went through their paces quite long enough to let everyone on the walls or on the road see them at it. They moved in and out of the corner of the pasture that was hidden from the ramparts. Meantime, they observed what Abasio had observed before: no one in armor went through the anytime gate.

"It'd be good to check the abbot, if you can figure out how," he said to her softly as they rode back to the abbey gate nearest the stables. "Have you had a chance to talk about the houses at the school?"

"I have," she said. "I should have told you last night. None of the people I talked to knew anything about them, though one girl said her uncle used to live in one of them. I asked Sister Solace, too. She said the houses were built all at one time by a group of people who had been living in Ghastain before Mirami arrived and weren't happy there after she came. It made sense to me, for they all look rather alike, not like houses built years and years apart. Sister Solace said some of the people who lived in those houses moved on, farther south where the winters are warmer, and some of them eventually went back to Ghastain because they had family there. She didn't know if they were still there. The thing that's interesting is that no one stayed there very long and no one else has ever used them."

"We really need to know whose idea it was to house us back there," Abasio said. "How about Solo Winger, the birdman? Did you get a list of his signs?"

"I know what they are and where they go, all but two of them. I've written them out for you." She burrowed in a pocket for a much folded list. "I memorized the two new ones. Brother Winger said they were the abbot's private signs, so he wouldn't know where they went or to whom. One is a sign like a house, you know, a square with three lines making a door, and a triangle for a roof. The other one was two curved lines, hunched, like a vulture's wings, with another curved line at the top making a head. My father didn't use either of those two signs at Woldsgard, though he used many of the others that Brother Winger has. There isn't one for anyplace between here and Merhaven, but if we need to, and if we're in a place that has pigeons from those places, we can send a message to Hallad, Prince Orez, in Etershore, or to whomever he has in command at Wold."

"Are we quite sure Woldsgard is securely in Orez's keeping?"

"Oh, yes. The loft man told me messages have come from Woldsgard sent by Hallad to the abbot, asking about us, wanting to know if we're well. And the abbot has sent answers. I know that's true, because the abbot asked me if I'd like to add a message, and I did."

"What about Bear's claim about the troops supposedly outside that wall?"

"As for asking the abbot to verify what Bear said, I'll just ask him. I'll tell him I was thoroughly convinced until Bear got upset with my being late that night we were out there, so I want to be very sure it's safe, not to worry my people."

All of which she managed to do, almost by accident, by meeting the abbot and his librarian Wordswell on his way to lunch. She greeted him pleasantly, then asked him the question, just as she had phrased it to Abasio.

"Oh, you'd be quite safe, my dear. Well guarded. Yes. All manner of troops around here and there. Tell your people not to worry in the least." And he scurried off, leaving Wordswell behind.

"Word to the wise," said the librarian, who had laid his hand lightly upon her shoulder as the abbot disappeared into the crowd. "The abbot really doesn't know where the troops are. If I drew him a map, he wouldn't be able to show me where they were, or how many. He's a good domestic organizer, and he manages people quite well because he's kindly and fair, but strategic matters are not his interest or his strength. He feels safe because his commanders tell him he is. I feel safe here at the abbey because I know the commander of the abbey home force. He's the one who commands the men on the walls that protect me. If I left the abbey, however, I'd want a word with the other commanders, just to know where I could get help if I needed it."

"So the abbot may either have been lying, though I think he's incapable of lying," said Xulai to Abasio, "or he may have been telling me what he has been told is the truth."

The rest of the day Xulai spent taking her things, a few at a time, to Abasio's wagon. Underwear. Shoes. Boots. She had two cloaks, undifferentiated as to gender. Books, three or four. She couldn't take the cats, obviously, and this caused some pain that she sat down and cried over for a time, even though she knew they would be perfectly all right. Oldwife, Nettie Lean, and Precious Wind would look after them. All of them were fond of cats. There was the little box from the forest. She would keep that in the deep pocket of her cloak to remember her mother by. It was remarkable, considering all the freight they'd brought, that she was taking away so little.

During her last visit to Abasio's wagon, Fisher told her he'd brought the blue thing that had been hidden under the wain. "I may have snagged something inside that crate, because I had to burrow around to find something besides cloth, and it's all gold embroidery and whatnot in there. The only thing that wasn't cloth was a package, just a tiny one. I wasn't sure it was blue until I got here and Abasio said it was. Fishers don't see color."

Abasio said, "I've made a little space under the wagon floor and hidden it there, right behind an axle." He showed her where it was and how to get up the board that covered it. "Have you brought everything?"

"All I could think of," she said. "See you in the morning."

"You're crying."

"Am I?" Her face was wet, but she hadn't known it.

"What is it, Xu?"

"It started when I knew I couldn't take the cats . . ."

"Perhaps I'll be an acceptable substitute. I'll practice my purr."

She shook her head. "Then it's Oldwife and Precious Wind and Nettie. They'll worry so. I hate doing this to them."

He held her close, thinking. "Who here is completely trustworthy?"

There was only one name she could think of. "The librarian. Wordswell."

"I've made a sort of friend out of Brother Solo Winger. I'll ask him to lend me a few of the abbey birds and a little cage to carry them in. I'll tell him it's so I can send a message to Oldwife and the rest of you telling you about my trip. I'll tell him if I send a message he shouldn't give it to anybody unless Bear has already left the abbey . . ."

"Tell him it's because you and Bear don't get along!"

"Right. We don't get along and I'd just as soon he didn't know where I'm going. Then, when we're well on our way, we'll send a note to Wordswell to deliver to Precious Wind, telling her . . . something. It can't be the truth because someone might get it out of her."

"We'll say I've learned there's a threat against my life and I've gone into hiding."

"If you know as much as you seem to about armament, you must have good survival skills. Precious Wind would know that, wouldn't she?"

"Even Precious Wind says she worries because I'm untested. She's right. I know what I should do, but I don't have the habits of doing it. Oldwife will worry, too."

"And you'll be armed when you ride to meet me, promise."

"Of course I will." They sat for a long moment, side by side, Abasio thinking of things he knew very well he wanted to say to Xulai, she thinking of things she wanted to say to Abasio. Neither of them spoke. If they began they would not stop the telling, and there was too much else going on.

The following morning, they exercised the horses once again, then parted, casually, where others could see them, and again privately with much the same wrenching, uprooted pain Xulai had felt on leaving Woldsgard. Abasio went to visit Brother Winger with a bottled gift for the old man and couple of messages to be sent "later." He left with a supply of grain and three abbey pigeons in a cage. Brother Winger had no difficulty in promising not to deliver any message he received from Abasio if Bear was still at the abbey. Bear had not endeared himself to the residents to begin with, and of late it had been rumored that he was named Bear not for his valor in battle but because he had a temper like one.

Abasio spent the rest of the day greasing axles, packing odds and ends, tying things down. Toward evening, he said he thought he'd travel on south, see what the country was like down there, and since he liked traveling by moonlight, he'd go this evening. He said good-bye to this one and that one, drove out the gate just before the night watch locked it for the night, and jingled away down the road. Once out of sight, he tied down everything that jingled and went on quietly. By morning, he and Blue had maneuvered the wagon into the old, wrecked house, masked it with leafy branches, and made themselves as well hidden as a wagon, horse, and man could be.

In the abbey Xulai kept to the plan and set out toward the stables to go practice her horsemanship with Flaxen. As she turned into one of the corridors that led to the stables, she encountered Derris, the guide. "That fellow, the dyer, he left something for you. Told me to invite you down to get it this morning."

"I was going down to the stables anyhow," said Xulai, wondering a little at this oddity. "I need to exercise my horse before school."

"Well then," he said, leading the way. "There's a shortcut through here. It'll save you some time." He led her through a couple of doors into a long, empty, and silent corridor.

She didn't see the sack that came down over her head and body and only smelled the terrible smell for one conscious moment before her mind went utterly blank. In that moment, however, she heard Derris asking, in his cocky voice, "Twelve gold pieces, wasn't it?"

And Jenger's voice: "Well, since you've already shown me the secret way out, here's your pay, boy." Then there was a stifled cry, followed by Jenger's quiet laughter.

When she next knew anything, she was riding a horse, backward. It took her a moment to realize she was tied on Jenger's back, a rope around her arms, another around her hips, a third around her legs. The sack that covered her prevented her seeing anything, but it did let the air through so she could breathe. A tiny, cold nose touched her cheek.

"Fisher," she breathed.

The nose moved up and down, a nod.

"Can you get out of here?"

Another nod.

"Find Abasio and tell him what happened. Or . . . maybe we should wait until we get where we're going so he'll know where—"

"I can find you anywhere," breathed Fisher. "I'm part of you. I always know where you are." He slipped down her body, between her feet, found the small hole left when the drawstring was pulled closed, and slipped away.

Evidently his going startled the horse, for it shied to one side. Jenger cursed. "Damned nag. Keep on the path or you'll have both of us into a drift up to our necks."

She could see some light through the sack, not much. He must have carried her out of the abbey in this sack. She had done nothing, nothing to defend herself! She had been taken totally by surprise. Precious Wind would be ashamed of her. Her eyes filled at the disgrace of it, and she turned her head to wipe the tears against her shoulder. As she did so, the light dimmed. Straight ahead and up a little was brightest. Either before or after noon. Time would tell. As it did. The light decreased as they went on: she was no longer facing it. They were headed west.

Xulai tried to do what she should have done when she met Derris. She should have been alert, ready for anything. Right now that meant staying motionless. This did not seem to surprise her captor. Perhaps whatever he had used to make her unconscious was supposed to go on acting for some time. In fact, it was still acting, for she was vaguely aware that being fearful would be more suitable than being disinterested and very sleepy. Fear, however, refused to materialize. So she told herself she would wait it out and did not fight the drowsiness that slid her into sleep once more.

AT THE ABBEY, WHEN XULAI didn't show up at the school, someone was sent to inquire. During the ensuing search, Derris's body was found. The houses behind the abbey were searched. Oldwife told them what Xulai had been wearing: her riding clothes, a split skirt, a jacket, boots. Oldwife had no reason to think of counting underwear, shoes, or cloaks. Bear made his presence loudly known everywhere, looking in corners, on roofs, in unlikely places others might have missed. Precious Wind watched him out of the corner of her eye. Something in his activity felt like pretense, as though he were acting. And yet, when he heard Xulai was gone, he had been truly surprised. She did not like any of it, not Bear's announced intention of leaving them, not this oddness in his manner, not his talk of the bride-price he had to raise before he could marry.

Had he planned this to happen? Had someone paid him to let it happen? She thought not. He had seemed truly surprised when he heard she was gone, so he had not planned it, or, more likely, had not planned it to happen *yet*!

"It's possible she decided to go on to Merhaven by herself," he declared at the end of the day.

"No," cried Oldwife. "That is *not* possible. She would not have left us without a word."

"She spoke to me once of doing just that," said Bear. "Even though it may seem unlikely, I'm going to ride south. There are plenty of others searching here."

They argued, Oldwife and Nettie Lean positive that Xulai would have done nothing of the kind, positive that the murder of the young guide showed she had been abducted.

"It shows only that abduction may have been attempted," said Bear. "Such an attempt would be the very thing that would push her onto the road herself, to get away from whoever it is."

"Without her horse?" cried Precious Wind in exasperation. "You're saying she went on foot?"

"It's easier to hide without a horse," said Bear. "We taught her that! In any case, it will do no harm to check. If I don't find her in a few days, I'll return."

This last statement was certainly false. He had no intention of returning. Precious Wind was convinced he had merely found a convenient argument for doing what he had intended to do all along, but she said nothing. Saying anything would only put her in danger and do nothing to help Xulai. Better to let him think he was above suspicion.

Early the following morning, she was standing on the wall of the abbey, half-hidden behind a crenellation, when he went out the gate and rode south at a steady trot. She became aware that an old, one-armed man was standing beside her.

"Do you think he's coming back?" he asked, not waiting for an answer. "That man left a lot of enemies."

"Why is that?"

"Me'n the men figure he's so used to winning fights, he thinks he's meant to win everything. He plays cards like a drunk. Stupid. He loses. He gets mad, says things, threatens people. Nobody'll play with him anymore. We're glad to see him go."

Precious Wind reflected that his habit had not been that bad when they were at Woldsgard. Something had set the man off, far off. She hoped he was riding out of trouble, not into it.

In the bird tower, without a word to anyone, Brother Solo Winger picked out a pigeon from Woldsgard and another from Etershore-Across-the-Water. He took from his pocket two messages left with him by Abasio, inserted them into the little tubes, attached the tubes to the pigeons' legs, and let them go. He read them first, of course. He always read everything, going and coming, including the abbot's messages that were marked personal. In Winger's opinion, it was high time somebody caught on to what either the abbot or somebody close to the abbot was up to. And wasn't this business at Woldsgard going to be interesting!

XULAI CAME TO AGAIN AS she was thrust down on a stony surface, a raised surface, a bench or table. Before she could catch her breath, the sack was pulled up from her legs, which were abruptly shackled to the wall. Hands were next, then the sack came away from her head. The man, Jenger, stood looking at her.

"Why did you do that?" she complained in her most childish, feminine voice. "That's not a nice thing to do at all."

"I thought you were the other one," he snarled. "The little one! She wants all you Tingawans, but especially the little one. How many of you are there? You're not the one who was driving the carriage."

"There are five of us." Misleading him even a little was well worth doing. "The little girl and Yellow Bamboo have already gone to Elsmere, then there's Blue Pearl and Great Bear, and me, I'm the cook."

"And what's your name?"

"I'm Green Bamboo. Yellow Bamboo is my sister."

Jenger felt both anger and fear at hearing the child was gone. He hadn't spoken to Bear about the child in some time, but the duchess still wanted her more than the others. Now the whole situation had changed!

"Well, we'll see what my employer has to say about this. You're not the one I'd arranged for, but she's been so busy twisting your Bear's mind toward his girlfriend in Tingawa, I was afraid he'd head south before we concluded our deal. Your Bear promised he'd have the child where I could get her within a day or two. He didn't tell me she was gone."

"She's been gone since a few days after we got there. She's in Elsmere by now." Let them search in all the wrong places, she thought. They'd probably find Bear. At least they'd have a fight on their hands.

He grabbed her arm, checked the shackle to be sure it was tight, then the other arm, then each foot, letting his fingers move up her leg, under the split skirt she'd put on for riding. "I can't take you to my employer for days. I barely made it here myself. I can send a bird to ask what she wants me to do with you, though I already know what I'm going to do with you tonight." He sniggered, a nasty sound. Xulai had heard the same snigger from a stable boy who had made some remark about her to the Horsemaster. She had never seen him again, though the Horsemaster had mentioned that he had been "unsatisfactory."

The intrusive hand was getting far too close to certain hidden weaponry. She chose to distract him. "Your employer? Who is she? And why would she want to do anything with me? She doesn't even know me."

He sat back, looking both sulky and fearful. "Doesn't matter. She wants all Tingawans in her territory dead, and since you're not the girl or the driver that she plans to play her games with, she'll probably tell me to drop you down a shaft somewhere. Don't despair, though. It's a long night. We'll have some time together."

He went away, locking the door from the outside. She looked at the room, built as a cell. When Jenger went out, she had had a glimpse through the cell door. The tower door was lower, with something built at the side of it, a tank of some kind, and the tower floor was shiny and wet. The cell level was three or four steps up from the tower floor, probably so the cell floor would stay dry. The door was heavy timber, banded with iron; the two straight walls and the one curved wall were stone; the floor was stone. The ceiling was too high to reach, even if one were free to try. She was in a stone box with only three irregularities: the door, the stone bench she was shackled to, and the high, grilled opening that admitted a dull but fiery light. Fading red. Past sunset. Same day. The fisher wouldn't have had time to find Abasio.

"Not as a fisher," she said aloud, surprised by the sound of her own voice. "As a hawk, he'll be there by now."

Certainly if he could be a fisher, he could be a hawk. He had started out as a chipmunk. Perhaps it was all a vain hope. No matter when the fisher or the hawk or the whatever got to Abasio, Abasio could not grow wings. He wouldn't have time to get here before Jenger decided to amuse himself, and the thought of that amusement sickened her. Precious Wind had told her about rape. How to defend against rape. Difficult to do with one's arms and legs shackled. It had taken Jenger almost a full day to get here from the abbey, and Abasio was a good bit farther away than that.

She pulled against the shackles. They were iron, with their anchors deeply buried in the wall. Her hands were far apart, so one hand couldn't free the other. Same with the feet. She had weapons hidden on her, but she'd been too dizzy and stunned to use any of them, and Jenger hadn't even looked.

"What is the first thing?" she asked herself.

First thing always: restore mind.

Strangely enough, Bear had taught her that.

Close eyes. Shut off all surroundings. Make mind shallow, peaceful, like puddle of water, calm surface, like mirror, unmoving. Still. Concentrate on mirror, picture self in mirror. See oneself as one is: hand, shackle, hand, shackle, foot, shackle, foot, shackle. What is reality in this situation?

When she'd been with Precious Wind and Oldwife, coming through the forest, what had been the reality of that situation? Something winged might have been looking for them. What would the winged thing see, or smell, or . . . ?

If they were in the open they could be seen, certainly. If they were under cover, they couldn't be seen. They could be smelled, but only carrion birds hunted by smell. They could be heard. Owls flew at night, and they hunted by sound. Vultures hunted by scent. Eagles and hawks hunted by sight. It would be night, so most likely it would be an owl. Horses didn't sound like deer, they breathed differently. She had to convince the horses they were deer, just for a while: they'd have to lie down instead of sleeping standing up. Deer often lay down, horses more rarely. They wouldn't eat while they were lying down, so there'd be no munching noises. They'd crush the greenery a little more, however, lying on it, and the smell of the crushed forbs would reinforce the idea of animals lying on them, if smell mattered. Sound would, so their breath would have to come a little faster; smaller animals breathed faster. Then, too, the trees' trunks would be a little warmer lower down, as would the soil around the roots, which meant the sap would move differently in the trees around them. Probably birds could not hear sap move. The horses had emptied themselves just before they'd reached the grove, so if smell mattered, the smell was over there, not where they were among the trees.

So she had reached into horse minds, searched deeply to find their monsters—every creature has its own monsters. She had evoked their possible presences, convinced the horses for their own safety that they needed to lie down, not eat, breathe lightly. Hide. Be quiet.

As for Precious Wind and Oldwife, that part was easy. She'd actually had cats with her, actually had a chipmunk whose job was to tempt the cats into moving around a little, while the cats themselves made little cat noises. Wildcats weren't that different in smell from other cats, if that mattered. The tree they slept under was dead, and there'd be the same warmth beneath it from cat bodies as from human ones. The owl would hear the chipmunk moving, hear the cats, sense the warmth perhaps. She remembered staying awake a long time that night, mentally telling Oldwife not to snore, and on that night, the old woman had breathed almost silently.

In this case, hands and feet in shackles, she didn't have to convince a tree or a horse or an owl. She had to convince herself.

What was the reality of her situation?

Her hand was too big to come through the iron bracelet.

Why was it too big?

Because it had all her fingers on it.

Suppose she could convince herself it didn't have all the fingers in one row like that. Suppose the hand had only two fingers, the little finger and the ring finger. In her mind she saw them separating from the rest of the hand. *Too bony to separate? Bones are too real. Convince yourself the bones are flexible, like a willow wand.* She could feel it happening, feel the hard bone deciding to become more supple. Somewhere down her arm another brain was actually telling her hand what to do. It wasn't her brain, not her big brain in her head, but another, smaller brain, down the arm, one of several little brains like a string of beads down her arm, a little necklace of brains saying, *Let's pull our arm out of this shackle very gently, softly, then let the other part of the hand become equally soft, equally pliable, and out it slides, slippery, easily,* the two parts of her arm caressing one another, rubbing away the soreness where the shackles had chafed the wrists. . .

We dreamed this, she told herself. *We dreamed of the tree branches splitting just like this. The roots reaching down and the branches splitting. . .*

Now, now the other hand, it's already moving, the hand splitting painlessly, the wrist opening down the center, the flesh rejoining seamlessly, the arm bones gone, all gone, the arms coming out of the shackle, out of the sleeve. Now the feet! Too bad, feet are in boots, so we have to divide inside the boot and leave the boot behind when we come out of the ankle shackle. Now the other leg. Now all that's left is the head, but we don't need to worry about the head, the arms and legs can unfasten the thing that's holding the head. No key, just a pin in the shackle, quite enough to hold a prisoner unless the prisoner has eight extremities and a skull that has suddenly gone soft and malleable and a lot of little minds up and down her body and has decided to leave the clothes where they are as her body oozes out of them, then off of the bench, across the floor, then, slowly, up the wall beside the door, effortlessly up the wall to a position over the doorway.

In the room at the top of the tower, Jenger thought of using the signal flags that sometimes worked when the shafts were flooded. He hadn't signaled her yet. She didn't even know he'd made it up the slope, much less that he'd had time to bribe the boy at the abbey and make off with anyone. It had been a bit touchy getting up here. The shaft held more water than he liked to see. No one else would use it; that was sure. Not until it had drained a good bit more. Well, then. He had to let her know and there was no wind to stretch the flags so one could tell them apart. The flags wouldn't work. Even if there were enough wind, it was already getting dark.

He sat down at the table and tried to write a message. The words wouldn't come. Each time he finished he threw the thing away. He kept thinking of her eyes, the woman downstairs, her eyes. She had looked at him as though she didn't believe he existed, as though she could not be convinced that he could be as he was. The woman's eyes held no endless, deadly tunnel as did the duchess's eyes. Instead there was a calm, fearless, reasoned judgment there. A cool judgment: no hatred in it, simply an assessment as to value, likelihood, possibility, reason. Those eyes knew that nothing existed without reason, and since they found no reason for his being, the eyes had decided Jenger did not exist.

The damned Great Bear of Zol thought Jenger existed! Jenger had found a reason for Bear. Money was his reason, money to pay off his bride-price. And for Mirami, power was a reason. Mirami knew he existed. And Alicia had found a reason for him. He gave her what she liked, did the things she liked. The duchess thought she wanted power, but it was pain she really wanted. Pain and fear. People with money existed. People with power existed. People who could inflict pain existed. But the woman downstairs discounted him, disbelieved he *was*.

He wrote again. *"The Tingawan child and the driver have gone on to Elsmere. I have one of her servants, not the driver we met. What do you want me to do with her?"*

He went to the Dark House cage and picked out a pigeon, glanced at the window, and realized it was already fully dark. The pigeon wouldn't fly at night. He'd have to wait until morning. If the duchess wanted the woman brought down to the Old Dark House, he'd return some of the Vulture Tower birds to the Old Dark House at the same time. The cage was too full. Too many messages had come from both the Old Dark House and Ghastain, and he hadn't had a chance to send any of the birds back. Very few travelers cared to go to the Old Dark House, even if well paid to do so. He rolled the paper and placed it in the message tube, leaving it on the table. It would have to wait until morning.

He was tired but he wasn't ready to sleep. He couldn't stop thinking about the eyes of the woman in the cell. Eyes could be changed. People who did not accept reality could be forced to accept reality. Perhaps if this woman knew more about him, she would disbelieve less. He had changed people's opinion of him in the past. He had pursued, won, delighted, then terrified, then killed or worse than killed. It was part of the game Alicia had him play, part of the game Alicia had played with him, too, only she had most often been the one to pursue, win, delight, and now and then, to terrify.

A mirror hung on the back of the door in the room where the cages were. He looked into it, trying to see into his own eyes. He couldn't see anything. Perhaps he couldn't believe himself. He would have to make himself believable. First he would change the mind of the woman downstairs and then he would come back and look again. Either that or get on his horse and ride as far as he could as fast as he could, which would do no good at all. The duchess would find him, somehow.

It was a good thing he hadn't taken the little girl. He wouldn't have dared touch the little girl. The duchess had said she had far worse things than rape to do to the little girl and she wanted those things to come as a lovely surprise. He had not seen her torture a child before. He was not sure he could bear it. But a woman the age of the one he'd taken prisoner shouldn't be that surprised. Even if she were virgin, she should have heard of the things that some men had been taught to enjoy, guessed at those things. She had no right to disbelieve that he existed!

He went back down the stairs. Back in the mining days, the old tower had been both the communication center and the punishment tower, for workers who didn't do what they were told to do. It was called the Vulture Tower because of the carrion that had lain around it. Vultures nested near carrion, when they could. Back then there had been flag towers all up and down the slopes to exchange messages. They'd used runners, then, kids with long legs and good lungs. Before. When things were normal. When things weren't disbelieved.

He unlocked the cell door and opened it. The afterglow was almost gone. He could barely see the woman across the room, lying limp against the far wall, her clothing sagging. He had just a second to register that the clothing actually looked empty before something swung toward him from above, something gray that closed on both sides of his head at once, clamping tight on his head, closing on both his arms and wrapping around his body and upper legs so he couldn't move. He barely had time to think that he was bound as she had been bound, helpless as she had been helpless, time to realize there were two huge eyes in front of him, looking at him, and between them, a beak, like a vulture's beak, that opened, wider and wider. The top of it entered his forehead; the bottom of it came up under his chin, thrusting through into his mouth, piercing his tongue. He felt his face tear like wet canvas, felt it rip away from his skull with a terrible sound, a spongy tearing sound, forehead, eyelids, nose, cheeks, ears . . .

He couldn't scream because something boneless slithered down his throat and stopped his breathing. Very soon, his heart gave up the battle.

The thing decided to dispose of Jenger. Better if nothing were found. It oozed its way down the few stairs to the tower door, through the outside door, and into the dusk, dragging the carcass behind it. From downwind came the calls of a wolf pack.

Moving swiftly, the thing towed Jenger's body away among the trees, some little distance from the tower. It found a cliff, a straight drop onto a little plateau, a difficult climb for a man, not too difficult for a wolf, a badger, for tiny scavengers, for vultures, crows, mice. The thing paused to chop the legs and arms into pieces with its strong beak, to crush the skull into shards with a rock held firmly in its tentacles, to rip the rib cage, spine, and pelvis into fragments and then let the remnants fall. The thing stayed where it was for a long moment, as though thinking, before emitting a cloud of fragrance or stink or mere aroma, depending upon what might attract the sensors downwind, four legged, two legged, no legged at all. The cloud dissipated, moving away on the wind toward the place where wolves had howled.

The thing returned to the tower. There was quite a bit of blood on the floor, door frame, and door itself, some on the wall, the steps, the tower floor. The stone cistern at the side of the room was fed by a rainspout from the roof. It had rained recently. The cistern was full. The bucket sitting inside the cell was dipped and sloshed across the cell floor, dipped and sloshed across the cell wall, emptied repeatedly over the thing itself, then over the steps, the floor of the tower,

the doorstep leading outside, sloshed again and again until all the blood was
washed away. The thing retreated. Went away.

IN THE DAWN SKY, WINGS high above located the tower and plunged
toward it. Wings became fur. The fisher found Xulai sitting in the
room at the top of the stairs, her arms on the table, her head on her
arms, so deeply asleep she could not be wakened. A nearby plate held
crumbs of bread, a bit of cheese. The cupboard the food had come
from stood open in the corner. A half-empty bottle of cider stood
beside an empty mug. The fisher left her and slithered through a quick
reconnoiter of the entire tower and the area around it. Xulai upstairs,
one horse in the stable, and several cages of pigeons in the tower were
the only living things around. Fisher became winged again. From the
sky he could see the man and the horse who had traveled all night to
get here. Fisher, winged, cried out and dropped once more, landing on
the man's shoulder.

When Abasio arrived, Xulai was still as Fisher had found her. Abasio
put his arms around her and pulled her close. She was shivering but
still deeply asleep. She had not been injured. There was a blanket on
the bed. He looked at it, considered some of the things Precious Wind
had recently told him, and rejected using it for anything at all. Instead,
he fetched the blanket he had brought with him. He wrapped her in
it. He opened the door to the other room widely, its mirrored back
banging against the wall. He opened all the cages so the birds who
homed here could feed and the birds who homed elsewhere could fly
away, propping the outside door open so it couldn't close on them. The
biggest cage bore the hunched shape of a perched vulture's wings. Vulture Tower. One cage had the house sign on it, obviously the Old Dark
House. Those were the two new signs Xulai had seen at the abbey. He
left the room, shutting the door behind him without seeing or being
seen by the mirror on its other side.

Blue was waiting with the other horse. Abasio would not stay a
moment longer than necessary, for Xulai's captor might have summoned others or might himself return. There might have been another
horse. He might merely have gone a short distance away by foot. They
left the tower and went back the way they had come, Xulai cradled in
Abasio's arms on Jenger's horse, Blue following, almost sleepwalking.

They had to circle widely not to be seen by the abbey watchmen on the walls, but by late evening, Abasio had hidden all of them in or near the wagon, where a small, virtually smokeless fire in the little clay stove made it warm and comfortable. There was room between the wagon and the back wall of the old, wrecked house for the two horses to stand or lie at ease. Abasio had spread straw in the space, and the little stove warmed this temporary stable as well.

He looked Xulai over carefully while she slept, his touch seeming to be of no concern to her. She was not injured anywhere except for a chafing of her wrists from the shackles he had seen in the cell, shackles still closed, locked. She was not bruised except on the upper arms and around her hips where she had obviously been bound on the way to the tower. The bruises were not extensive. Her clothing, complete with hidden weaponry, told him she had been taken totally by surprise but not interfered with in any way. She had been taken, chained, but not abused, and her captor had disappeared. There was something sewn into the hem of her undershift, but it didn't feel like a weapon. He let it alone.

He held her as she slept, and she did not move in the circle of his arms. In the night there was another light snowfall that he knew would erase all tracks of people or things around the tower. In fact it did that, as well as the tracks of the wolves that had carried every fragment of their feast far away to other, scattered places and the tracks of the vultures and crows, the weasels, raccoons, skunks, and other small carnivores that had scavenged the site when the wolves had gone.

When Xulai woke, late the following day, she said Jenger had bribed Derris, killed him, and taken her. She could not remember what had happened after Jenger had left her in the cell. There had been something in it about deer, or changing reality, but she couldn't remember what it was. Abasio, looking deep into her eyes, saw something there he had not seen in her before. He had seen that same look, however, in the eyes of people and speaking beasts who had survived terrible battles and did not want to remember what had happened.

He concluded that whatever had happened to Jenger had been done by someone else. Perhaps Xulai had seen it happen or heard it happen. People did not get that expression in their eyes if they had been horrified only in their imagination.

SOLO WINGER RECEIVED A MESSAGE from Abasio. On the outside, it said, *"Deliver to the librarian, Elder Brother Wordswell, no one else."* On the inside—Solo had become an expert at unsealing messages and resealing them—it said, *"Derris was bribed by Jenger, a servant of the Duchess of Altamont, to help kidnap Xulai. Previously Jenger conspired with Bear to kidnap Xulai, but her reluctance to move into a house near the back wall delayed those plans and Jenger grew impatient. Xulai overheard some of this conspiracy but does not know Bear's true intentions in the matter. Jenger has disappeared. Xulai has been rescued. The bird-sign of the house is the Old Dark House of Altamont. The bird-sign of the vulture is the sign of the Vulture Tower west of the abbey. These places may well be linked through old mine shafts. The bird keeper told me these were signs used only by the abbot. I question this. Whose idea was it to house the Tingawan party near the back wall, which is unguarded, where they might be easy prey?"*

Solo Winger carefully resealed the message, tucked it into a pocket, and impatiently waited until nightfall. Wordswell was known to work in the library at night. He did it, Winger thought, in order to be uninterrupted, and he was confirmed in that opinion by the old man's brief expression of annoyance when he was interrupted.

Winger handed over the note and moved away to let Elder Brother Wordswell read it. He did not leave; there might be an answer, after all.

"I suppose you read this," said Wordswell in a dry voice.

"Why, Elder Brother . . . ," Winger began in offended tones.

"Don't give me that pigeon shit, Solomon Winger. You read everything that comes through that tower."

"Sometimes thins ak-see-dentully come unsealed, like."

"The man asks a good question. Whose idea was it?"

"A message from Old Dark House come while them ladies from Woldsgard wuz on their way here, them an that Bear an t'other fellas. A message went back 'n' forth, two, mebbe three times, in fack."

"From whom?"

"Who d'y'think from *whom* brought 'em to me? Who brings everthin'? Who sees everthin' afore the abbot gets a look? Who takes everthin' the abbot sends and reduz it? Hm?"

"Did they start fixing up that house before or after those messages?"

"Can't say's I took notice. I guess sumbuddy'd have ter ast the crew adoin' it."

"I suppose you have no idea how the person who sent this message managed to get an abbey pigeon?"

"Well, and you think I wunn't know where's my own birds? Course I do! He ast for three. I guv him three. He said he wannud to let the lady know how he'uz doin'. He said the old one, but I figured it wuz the young one he reely had on his mind. She's a nice girl, and I figure she'd care 'bout how he was doin'."

"Misuse of abbey property . . . ," mused the librarian.

"Misuse, pfff. Dang good use, I figger," said Brother Winger. "Don' I hear you tellin' people alla time now-lidge is pow'r? Well, now you got some now-lidge you dint have afore. And it's bin goin on for some years."

"I suppose you have copies?"

"Man c'n s'pose anythin', 'fhe wants."

Wordswell actually smiled. "Come back and see me at midnight, Brother Winger."

WORDSWELL WAS AN ELDER BROTHER but not the eldest. He held in his hands what others of the elders, male and female, would consider an accusation of the abbot's complicity in crimes of kidnapping and murder—that is, if one did *not* know that the prior handled virtually all the abbot's messages and appointments. The elders did know. They would not consider the messages proof of the abbot's complicity; they were as likely as the librarian to suspect someone else. What proof might there be? Two cages of pigeons in the abbey bird loft with certain signs. The allegation that these signs were of Altamont and of an old mining tower could be proven. A party could be sent to the old mining towers to look for evidence of that same sign; it might be found somewhere, on a bird cage, for example. Wordswell himself had authority to send someone to explore that possibility.

But that didn't prove the existence of this Jenger. It wouldn't prove there had been any message sent by the abbot or received by him or by some other person in the abbot's stead. Unless, that is, the abbot or that other person kept the messages he received, in either case in their personal quarters. There would be some difficulty searching there! Though there might be copies in the mining tower itself of messages sent and either copies or the originals of messages received! Now would be an excellent time to explore that possibility, for the Dragdown Swamps still covered the slopes westward and it was unlikely there was anyone there to take notice.

What a pity the writer of this message had not taken time to search for messages or to say that he had done so and there were none. Though if there had been none in the tower at the time of the rescue, it meant nothing. Pigeons might have arrived there after the rescue. Besides, the writer of this note had been preoccupied. He said the girl was rescued, but he didn't say what condition she was in, injured perhaps, perhaps . . . sexually attacked. Wordswell's face showed a moment's fury before he purposefully smoothed it. He liked Xulai! If someone had abused her, Wordswell hoped fervently that person was dead.

He found a particular book of maps. They had been drawn years before, when the mining of the western and northern slopes of this massive highland had been at its height. He noted the round red circles that denoted towers, the spots that indicated communication-flag poles, the round black circles that meant shaft entries, the dotted lines that meant underground tunnels, layers of them shown in different colored inks, one atop another. At the top of the slope there were three red circles. One, far south, was merely a ruin. It had been undermined and collapsed a lifetime ago. Wordswell had seen it. Another stood farther north. If the duchess were indeed involved in this abduction, the chances were that she or her agent would have used the middle tower, the one closest to the abbey. Less than a day's ride away. The one around on the northern slope was closer to Benjobz.

There might be a chance of finding evidence of the duchess's complicity, though after Xulai's brief dissertation on the career of Queen Mirami, evidence against the duchess seemed unlikely. The woman was old in villainy, well schooled, no doubt. If all that Xulai had said was true, Queen Mirami and her daughter, perhaps Prince Rancitor, also, and the Duke of Kamfels, were of a measure far beyond Wordswell's power to comprehend. They frightened him.

Then there was the matter of Xulai herself. Her people were grieving, the old woman most seriously. She had not been at meals recently, though of course, the others may have taken her food. He decided to make a quick call upon her, which he did, taking the message.

He found Oldwife Gancer much worse than he had feared: pallid, weak, so deeply troubled as to be incapable of caring for herself. He told the women, Precious Wind and Nettie Lean, that he had a message for her to be delivered privately, and they agreed, reluctantly, to leave him alone with her.

"Oldwife Gancer," he said. "I have a message from Xulai."

"Who're you?" she grated.

"Someone Xulai trusted," he said. "Someone who could receive messages without other people knowing. Can you read, lady?"

"Of course I can read," she said. "All us folk at Woldsgard were schooled!"

"The message is delicate, be careful with it, don't tear it."

She took it in her cupped hand, drawing herself up in surprise, her eyes alight. "Why, it's one of those pigeon things! Duke Justinian was always sending off those things. Many's the times I've sat in the loft with him and Xulai watching those birds . . ."

She took it from his hand and unrolled it carefully with trembling hands, turning it until it was right-side up. "This isn't Xulai's writing."

"It's Abasio's writing," he said. "The dyer. The man with the wagon."

She was still reading, her mouth falling open. "Bear? Bear did that? Oh, why would, why . . . he was like a . . . like an uncle to her, or a big brother would have been. Why would he . . ."

"Money most likely," said Precious Wind from the door. Her voice was bitter. "Sorry to listen, Elder Brother, but I was worried for Oldwife."

He gestured for her to enter and shut the door behind her. "This message is secret. You must not tell anyone here about it." He handed the message to Precious Wind. "You see what it says about the abbot."

Oldwife cried, "That nice old man! He sent such a sweet message telling us to keep up our spirits. Why would he . . ."

Precious Wind looked up from the fragile paper, her face quite still. "I don't imagine Elder Brother has any certain *whys* yet, Oldwife, or any certain *whos*, either. He looks to me like a troubled man who has just learned something that's upsetting him a good deal. Why would that be, sir?"

He grimaced. "Not having known this was going on, of course. Not knowing for sure even now. And not knowing what to do. Each of us elder brothers and sisters has some departments or offices that we control as far as manpower and material allocations go. The bird loft is one of mine, ostensibly. Actually Brother Winger runs it very cleanly and simply, and I seldom have reason to question anything he does. Now he tells me he's known of this correspondence for some years! Though he works hard at giving the impression of an unschooled and ignorant man, I have had my doubts about that. I've suspected for years he reads everything, but he's never said a word about it until now. I find what he tells me more troubling than I can say. From what Xulai told us about the duchess, she is a very evil woman. I cannot imagine why the abbot would have anything to do with someone like that, especially since she apparently has evil designs upon the Duke of Wold, who has been a friend of the abbey for decades. Why, this abbey maintains Netherfields. It is this abbey that guards the graves of Wold!"

"Who puts an abbot in power?" asked Precious Wind.

"We all do, all of us, elder brothers and sisters. It is an election."

"How many of you?"

"A hundred or so, not all of them working here at the abbey, of course."

"So getting them all together secretly wouldn't be possible, would it?"

"Getting any ten of them together secretly would be impossible," he said. "And before I even tried, I'd have to have real evidence, not just a note alleging things. You know, various of us do things in the abbot's name. Because something is addressed to the abbot, it doesn't mean he necessarily sees it. If Abasio were to come back here, with the girl, she might know more about it, she could give evidence, but . . . I don't even know how to reach him."

"And he wouldn't bring her back here for anything," said Oldwife through her teeth. "She wouldn't be safe here, and that Abasio, he'll keep her safe. That's one thing I know is true. He'll keep her safe. He loves her, that's why. I saw his face, I did. He loves her. Don't even know if he knows it yet, but I know it!"

"Do you think the abbot was alone or a part of this conspiracy, I mean, here in the abbey?" asked Precious Wind. "Or someone else, using his name?"

He shook his head. "Who knows? I don't keep track of him, who he sees, who he talks to most. I know almost everything goes through the prior."

"Maybe she promised him Netherfields," Precious Wind offered.

"The abbey already *has* Netherfields, or will, when the duke passes on. I have the documents on file! He willed Netherfields to us years ago!"

Precious Wind put her hand upon his shoulder. "Then maybe she promised him the duke would pass on sooner. Sir, forgive me, but you seem out of your depth here. I have some knowledge of conspiracies and their ilk. Will you let me help you? Will you let it go for now and do nothing?"

"I was going to send someone to that tower, to see if there were copies of messages or originals from the Old Dark House . . ."

"You know what tower it is?"

"I'm assuming it's the closest one, northwest of here at the crest of the slope. There's a fairly well-used track through the woods near there. We cut timber in that area, though we don't go all the way to the crest as that is Altamont land."

"Well, let it wait for now. Xulai served as a representative of the Tingawan ambassador and his daughter. In a sense, I, too, have that representation. I have a duty both to him and to the Duke of Wold. Since Bear and Xulai are both gone, I need to consult with our embassy and with Prince Orez about what we should do next.

"I have been given a location within a day or so of the abbey where I can meet a person associated with our embassy, or more properly, a person who knows a person associated with our embassy. I'm going to go ask for advice. I'm fairly sure I'll be told to stay here, awaiting further events, but there may be some useful suggestions or information. It may be suggested that we simply go on to Merhaven, since Xulai knew that was our eventual destination. On my way back, I'll check the tower myself.

"So, until I return, please, don't do anything at all! There may be some innocent explanation and bothering the elders may prove unnecessary. By the way, how does one go about making an appointment with the abbot?"

"Oh, you'd go through the prior's office. Everything goes through the prior. Messages, requests, orders, all that. Our dear abbot would

work himself to death if the prior didn't take some of the load away."
Wordswell gave her a look that was half-gratitude and half-confusion,
his habitual mode of thought betraying that even yet he had not considered the full implications of what they had been saying. He pressed her
hand in departure.

That night, amid the crowd after supper, she saw the prior and asked
him if he could arrange an appointment with the abbot.

"I'm leaving the abbey for four or five days. When something like
Xulai's disappearance happens, I have a protocol to follow as a representative of the ambassador, and I don't want anyone to worry over my
absence or misinterpret it."

"A protocol?" mused the prior. "Is it anything we can help you with?"

"No, Elder Brother. I am merely required to report things like this
in person."

"I can offer our birds . . ."

"You have no birds to reach the person I must meet. In fact, I do
not know the person's name. I know only that I have been told to go to
a certain place where someone will recognize me and they will tell me
where to go from there."

"Somewhere a few days from here. Now that is curious."

"Isn't it! My people seem sometimes to make a fetish of—what
should one call it? I hate to call it secrecy. 'Discretion' is perhaps the
better term. They believe that important things should be discussed
quietly by those who need to make important decisions rather than by
a hundred voices in as many different places. It does give us less to talk
about." She smiled at him, her most winning smile, practiced until it
looked totally genuine.

"Well, if that is all it is, I can tell the abbot you're going."

"Protocol again, Elder Brother. I am required to tell him myself.
I will have to tell my contact that I, personally, have told the abbot of
Wilderbrook Abbey that I have gone and for what reason. In that way,
we maintain a chain of information. The abbot will know I have gone;
I will know that he knows because I have told him face-to-face; my contact will know because I have told him I have done so; the person my
contact informs will know that all this has been done because I will tell
him, face-to-face; and so on. We are not allowed to say, 'But I told so-
and-so to tell someone else.' No offense meant, Elder Brother."

He mused, managing with some effort to achieve the appearance of someone truly intrigued by a new idea. "Not allowed. Well, indeed! Remarkable. When I think how many times I have told someone to tell someone else to do something that needs doing, and that person claims never to have heard a word about it! A chain of information. What a very good idea!" He turned away, smiling secretly to himself. His chief work in the abbey, as he saw it, was to make sure that the abbot did not know nine-tenths of what went on and that no chain of information ever connected to himself.

It turned out the abbot was available. Precious Wind spent three minutes with him, explaining what she had called the chain of information.

"Four or five days," he said, nodding. "Well, I hope you have an enjoyable ride and get some help. I'm very disturbed by this whole matter." He was, in fact, even more disturbed by the "chain of information" idea, which Precious Wind had somehow managed to explain two or three times during a very brief meeting. It had made him realize, quite suddenly, that most of what he knew about the abbey came to him from others, and this had led him to a related, very disturbing thought: *What I know about my abbey is told to me by others, or perhaps it is not told to me by others when it should be! What is there that I do not know?*

"If I had been the abbot," Precious Wind informed Oldwife, "I think I'd have been more interested in knowing who was to be told that someone rather important to Tingawa had been abducted from my abbey. I got the impression he was very distracted about something else."

Early next morning, she packed a few things in her saddlebags, tied on several anonymous bundles, put her bow and half a dozen arrows in their case, picked the liveliest of the Wold horses from the stables, and went out into the yard. She made a slight detour along the stable where the abbey horses were kept and noted the uniform sets of tack and saddles outside the stalls. Most of the abbey's horses, she imagined, were with the troops, wherever they were stationed, but still there were a few hundred riding animals and as many heavy horses to haul wagons. When she arrived at the gate, she bid the guards good morning and asked what the procedure was for using an abbey horse.

"Some elder brother or sister signs the chit, and that's it," she was told.

She rode out to the road that led toward Benjobz Inn. Since the inn was at least four days' ride away and she had said she'd be back in more or less that time, since she had made people as suspicious of her journey as possible, she felt it likely she would be followed. Someone would want to know who in the wild forest and valleys north of the abbey was getting information from this Tingawan woman. Evading followers would be no problem. Secretly finding out what they had been told to do might be more difficult.

Midafternoon, having stopped along the way no more than was necessary, she started searching the road for fresh hoofprints. About a mile farther on she found a well-traveled track coming in from the left and fresh hoof marks continuing north. All those would hide the fact that she was leaving the road. She took her own horse off to the right, then went back to erase the few prints that might have interested followers. Leading the horse across the grasses, she went back into the forest to find a lookout, a fairly comfortable branch halfway up a large nut tree that gave her a view some miles back the way she had come. She shared the nuts and some fruit from her saddlebags with a tribe of squirrels, staying aloft long enough to make her think she might have misjudged the situation. She was about to climb down when she saw three horsemen coming far more briskly than necessary this late in the day. As they topped a hill, the foremost among them galloped ahead, reined in, and stood tall in his stirrups to see as far ahead as he could. At the distance it was hard to be sure, but the tack and saddles looked very much like those issued by the abbey.

Well and well, she thought. *If those aren't followers they are giving a very fair impression of such.* She climbed down, stood quietly beside her horse, which was busy dining on grass, and waited until hooves had passed and faded into silence down the road before she returned to the road herself.

She stayed well behind until dark, then stopped and walked on along the roadside, leading the horse, looking for a campfire. Considering the fresh hoofprints she had found, they might have found someone else's camp where they could stop. Or, she hoped, they might have given up that idea and built one of their own.

Not much later she saw the fire in a sheltered dell off to the left. She picketed the horse between two trees near two huge stones—a landmark she could not miss even in the dark—before making her way toward the flame. She slipped among the trees until she found one to stand behind where she could see three men and three unsaddled horses tied to a picket line near a campfire.

The trees were good cover; she could get close enough to hear.

There had been some mumbling as she approached. She arrived in time to hear a speech from a hulking man, weighty in the arms and shoulders, barefaced but with a heavy mop of black hair. "So, Jun, whut I dunget is wat's the dif we killer r'not. Ol Pry Eye, he wans rid of her, alri'. Why we got to fine sumplace to keep her livin'?"

"He says she knows stuff. Mebbe he needs to talk to her. So we find 'er, we grab 'er, we haul 'er off someplace, I dunno where, tie 'er to a tree, mebbe. We come ever couple days 'n' feed 'er. Prior, he says it won' take but a day, mebbe two, an' he'll com ast questions."

The one called Jun was taller than the others. When he turned his head, she saw his face profiled against the light. Knobby nose, thin lips, scant brows, long light hair pulled back and tied with a thin band of something, maybe a thong of leather. She would know him again.

The youngest one spoke. "Didy say we cudd'n have some fun wit'er?" He was only a spotty-faced youth, but he had that same knobby nose and thin lips. Jun's son, perhaps? Or nephew? Definitely at the age when women's bodies occupied a very large share of male mental capacity, if one were not a Tingawan.

"Shut, Jamis," said Jun. "We do whut the prior says. He pays us better'n most. He allus has. When he says kill'm, we kill'm. When he sez no, thas whutty means, is no. When he gives a man gold, that man stays bought! If he don't stay bought, he's usual dead inna day or so."

"But you tole me I cud kill the nex wun! I wuz jus—"

"I said mebbe an' I know what you wuz jus. You're s'pose to be hep, n'that means you do zackly whut I say do when I say do and you don' kill nobody 'less I say so."

Precious Wind slipped back into the trees to think it over. She had hoped Bear could not have been implicated in the business of Xulai's abduction because he had not had time to meet anyone who could have, in the words of the trio by the fire, made him "stay bought." Bear had not needed to meet anyone, however. The "anyone" had met him. The prior. The prior who took all the abbot's messages, all his letters, who screened those who saw him and those who didn't. When had he turned Bear around? Bear hadn't mentioned questioning the prior himself about the money Justinian had sent, but that did not mean Bear had not done so! He might well have done so that first night. Before Xulai had explained about Mirami to the abbot the next morning. Was that the real reason for Bear's annoyance at Xulai during that meeting? Anyone conspiring with Mirami or her people would not want her history so concisely spelled out.

Now she faced an ethical dilemma: what should one do about three men who killed other people when paid to do so? It would be far better if they were no longer available to the gentleman who had sent them, but it would also be better if that gentleman did not know what had happened to them. Oh, no. If they turned up dead, that would look very odd to the gentleman. Almost suspicious. Far better if it didn't work out that way.

She sat quietly, waiting until the fire burned down, until the blanket-wrapped bundles made only sleeping noises, then slipped silently into their camp carrying a single tightly sealed vial. Each man had a water flask. One by one, she uncorked them, dropped in a pinch of powder from the vial, then restored the corks. The men had no other water with them. In the morning, or even during the night, they would drink water from their flasks. The thin man would wake first. Then the bulky one. The young one last. Boys his age slept long.

The herb she had used was called Y'kwem, a small, inconspicuous trailing plant with minuscule yellow blossoms. It grew in a few places in the Ten Thousand Islands and nowhere else that she knew of. Ingesting the powdered root had the effect of reinforcing personal characteristics. The peaceful became more passive. The kindly became saints. The amusing became hilarious. The killer became a slaughterer. The herbalist who had taught Precious Wind had said, "Those who drink Y'kwem become wagons without brakes, laden with stone, each at the top of his personal hill." The word "*kwem*" meant "halter" or "brake" or "restraint." The prefix meant simply "without." No chain, no barrier, nothing in the way. Free to do as their own natures dictated. Heedless children were sometimes referred to as *y'kwem*.

Well, it was in the hands of fate. They would do as they liked. She went back to her horse between the two huge stones and led him past them into a narrow wash well hidden from the road, where she made her own fireless camp. She slept well until dawn, when she was awakened by shouting, then screaming, then the panicky whinny of horses, everything subsiding into silence.

She took a large water bottle from her saddlebag and went back to the other campsite once more, still hiding among the trees. She did not approach the barely smoking fire, reading the signs of what had happened from a distance. The tall one lay in his blankets, dead, his throat slit. Next to him, the bulky man was on his knees with a knife in his back and his hands tight around the throat of the young one. Bulky wakes up, decides to kill thin man, probably father or uncle of young one; young one sees him do it, knifes him, fatally but not immediately, and gets choked to death before Bulky dies.

Stepping softly, leaving no footprints, she went from water bottle to water bottle, emptying them on the ground, rinsing them out, partially refilling them, recorking them, returning them to their place. One would not want an innocent person to drink from those bottles by accident, even though no truly innocent person would ever suffer thereby. *So few of us,* she thought, *are truly innocent. So few of the truly innocent survive for very long.* She let the horses go, untying one end of the picket rope as if it had come loose by itself. The tie ropes slipped easily off the loose end, and the horses wandered away into the woods. Left to themselves, they would probably return to the abbey.

She stopped suddenly, conscious of eyes on her. She turned, slowly. Oh, yes, eyes indeed. She made a questioning sound in her throat. The muzzle turned toward her, amber eyes staring hungrily. Wolves. They had smelled the blood. Well. Why not? These men had forfeited the right to any sanctified burial and the herb had used up its potency. It could not make a wolf be more wolf.

"Take them," she said, staring into those yellow eyes. "Leave the horses alone!"

She went away, back to the place where her own horse waited. Behind her was the sound of feeding, the usual furor over reinforcement of status: it was the way of wolves.

She reviewed what she had heard the men say about the prior. Now she knew who. Now she had an idea why. She returned to her campsite, breakfasted, saddled her horse, and rode back to the trail that had entered the road from the west. If she was not wrong, this would be the way to the Vulture Tower.

The track, obviously the way the woodcutters went, was well traveled in its earlier stages, wagon-wide and rutted deep, though any wagoneer who tried it in snow time would find it muddy going. Precious Wind rode beside it, where the mud was somewhat mitigated by grasses. Other trails led away on either side, as wide and as mired, though not as deep. The newer the trail, the newer the stumps cut along the way. The men from the abbey were making clearings, not cutting the forest down from edge to edge, and she nodded approvingly. Clearings were good for game.

The final few side trails were only horse or deer trails, leading vaguely north or south, but Precious Wind continued west. She estimated that from the place she was now, it would be the better part of a day's ride to the abbey, and it was only moments later that she saw the top of the tower thrusting up through the trees ahead. Leaving the horse hidden, she approached on foot, stepping where she would leave no footprints. It was a stubby, cone-roofed tower, a privy built at the south side, a stable on the north, the rooftop barely taller than the closest trees. She went around the stable and found the tower had been set on the very rim of the valley. The ridge at her feet fell away a lethal though not towering distance. It ended in a stony flat with another ridge at its outer edge. These precipitous ridges alternating with wide, flat ledges continued westward, each corrugation a bit lower than the one before, a giant's washboard, the whole extending south farther than she could see. This was the west edge of the so-called Highlands of Ghastain. The cliffs went on north, around the corner, where they formed the south wall of the valley they had traveled through to Benjobz. Far to the west, all the way down, a pale line of roadway cut through the lighter green of pasture in a straight north-south line. This was the road that ran gently downward toward the Lake of the Clouds after passing the Old Dark House, its location marked only by the top of an ugly, black tower thrusting above the trees.

Everything between the place where she stood and that distant road was a patchwork of brush, broken trees, and stone—stone piled in enormous heaps or fallen in avalanches that had broken through the ridges farther down. Every flat surface reflected sunlight from barely hidden pools or pits; every slope was awash with little runnels of meltwater. Maps had told her that this vast slope ended far to the south in the marshes around the Lake of the Clouds. In its current flooded state it was the mid to northern end of the legendary Dragdown Swamps. Precious Wind felt no urge to explore it.

Inside the tower, a cistern had been built at the left of the door, the stairs at the right, spiraling a quarter turn onto a lower floor where the cells were, then on around the tower wall once more and through a hole in the floor above. The trap that closed the access was leaning against the wall, but she went up the steps as she went everywhere: very carefully, making sure no one was above her. The stairs entered a half-circle room with one window and one door. A half-full water bucket sat beside the fireplace, where a dry kettle was suspended above a pile of powdery ashes. A small cupboard stood in the corner, and she used her handkerchief to open the door to see a small store of food: bread, cheese, dried meat, dried fruit, a few potatoes, a tightly lidded box of tea, a few bottles of cider, a basket of candles—scant comfort for anyone who had to stay here long. A plate and an empty mug stood on the table along with a box holding a man's personal belongings, presumably Jenger's: a razor, soap, cloths and sponges for washing himself. Also a comb cut from tortoiseshell and a well-made brush with clumps of hog bristles set into tiny holes in a carved wooden back. Both the comb and the brush held long, dark hairs.

Carefully, still using her handkerchief, Precious Wind removed all the hairs from the brush and comb, wrapped them in a bit of paper she found on the table, and put them in her pocket. She washed the comb and the brush in the water bucket and dumped the water out the window. Then she took the handkerchief Xulai had given her, unfolded it, removed half of the duchess's hairs, and put them into the comb and the brush, winding them deeply. They were somewhat longer than the hairs Jenger had left there, though they were the same color. She used the knife to cut the hairs shorter before replacing brush and comb, restoring the handkerchief and remaining hairs to her pocket.

The narrow door let her into the loft where the birds were. She opened it only a crack, enough to see two of the cages. A large arrival cage had a door that was propped open. It held about twenty birds, the ones who regarded the tower as their home. The other cages, now empty, should have held pigeons that homed on other locations. As she moved her head forward to peek around the door, she saw the side of a frame on the back of the door.

She stepped back. A picture? Unlikely in this place. A map? Possible. A mirror? Unlikely, and yet . . . She stood in thought, thinking of mirrors and curses and a tactic called the mirror defense.

A blanket was folded at the bottom of the bed. Holding it high before her, she entered the room and draped the blanket over whatever it was, holding the blanket there as she lifted the thing. Chances are it would reflect only a particular person, but she would not take the chance. It was only hanging from a hook by a wire. She rubbed a finger against the blanket, feeling it slide easily: probably glass, so very likely a mirror. Holding the wrapped bundle, she examined the room. In addition to the cages and food for the birds, it held another small table and a little shelf of supplies: a pad of thin papers sewn together along one side with strong thread; a spool of the same thread, to tie the messages when they were rolled; a box of little message tubes; pens; an inkstone; a water jug.

She wrapped the blanket into a package, using the thread to tie it fast. Moving quickly but carefully, she went down the stairs and out to the privy. It had a board seat, but it was hinged as she had thought it would be. The pigeon droppings had to have been disposed of somewhere and this seemed the likeliest place. She heard nothing when she dropped the bundle into the evil-smelling pit, which meant it went straight and very far down, as it would if this were a natural fissure in the stone. The deeper, the better.

With the mirror gone, she felt somewhat more at ease as she went back to the cage room, where she shut the cage door and sorted among the birds to see whether any carried messages. Three of them did. She removed the tiny metal vials from their legs, putting the vials in her pocket. Another vial, capped, lay on the table, and she took that one as well. She would not take time to look at them now. If the thing she had dropped down the privy had been a mirror, someone might be trying to look through it from the other side, and that someone might already be on the way here. There were scribbled papers in a small box on the table; she rolled them together, tied them, and put them in her pocket.

Finally she took away the props that held the cage door open and broke the door in a way that could appear to have been an accident.

Abasio had been here; presumably he had freed the birds in the smaller, empty cages along the wall where birds for various destinations were kept. With the arrival door broken, any birds still here or still to arrive would not be trapped inside.

Downstairs, she stopped to examine the cell, looking closely at the shackles. Xulai might have been held there, and when she rubbed the shackle with her handkerchief there were stains that might have been of blood. She did not know if the stains were old or new, but they could not stay there if Xulai's blood was in them.

She returned to the loft to fetch several message papers and a candle, noticing as she picked up the pad that it bore the impression of an earlier message. That one and several beneath it she thrust into her pocket with the others. Downstairs again, she lit one of the papers with her flint lighter, lit the candle from that, and carefully held the shackles in a fold of her cloak as she burned the edges and the surfaces of the cuffs, including even the chain links that might have pinched flesh. The leg shackles were clean. Xulai had been wearing boots. She searched for hair, skin, anything that Xulai might have left behind. Nothing. Xulai had been fully dressed; her hair had been braided; it would have been unlikely that anything was left behind. Still, Precious Wind went over the top of the stone bench, inch by inch, over the wall behind it, over the floor itself, all of which were very slightly damp, as though they might have been washed. Perhaps they had. Abasio was no fool.

She tossed the candle down the privy and made sure the seat was down. On the way back, she rode through the trees, not coming near the trail until she had passed the first woodcutters' trail. Even so, she stayed alert, stopping every now and then to listen for the clop of hooves. She was almost at the road before she heard them, just in time to slip away once more into the forest.

Four mounted archers. She had seen them before as part of the mounted group that had stopped them on the road when they first met the duchess. She did not want to be on a road that those men might take. She did not want to be near enough that they could hear her horse if he whinnied. Far better to be behind them than before them. She crossed the trail and rode southward through the woods until she found a little glen where it would be safe to leave the horse. She tied him on a long rope near a grassy patch. No one would hear him but he would be close enough that she could get to him quickly. She took food and a blanket, just in case she had to spend the night, and returned the way she had come, this time cutting westward to intercept the trail to the tower.

She found it and followed it until she was near the tower itself. Four horses and two pack animals were picketed among the trees. Two of the men were outside.

"There's no sign of Jenger anywhere out there," said one. "Me'n Gabler have been all over the place. His horse is gone and there's nobody outside, alive or dead, not anywhere close, and there's no birds circling to show where a body might be."

His fellow nodded in agreement. "Well, one thing, he let all the birds go. There's none here except tower birds. None for the House. None here for the queen. None for the duchess's friend at the abbey. No sign of a prisoner. No sign anything happened to anybody, no blood, no nothing."

"Why did she send us here anyhow?" the first speaker asked.

"To bring him back to the House. She says he's been actin' funny."

"You think he's tryin' to disappear? People try to disappear, she finds them."

The other man dropped his voice. "How does she do that?"

"Nobody knows, and I'm not gonna ask her."

"She said bring him, bring anything that belonged to him. Clothes, that kind of stuff."

The one who had searched the tower said, "I've got everything in a sack: his clothes, his comb and brush, his razor. She doesn't want the food, does she?"

"She said everything! You better figure that means everything."

Both men went inside. Precious Wind stayed where she was. In a few moments the two who had gone inside came out again with new burdens, there to be joined by two others, one from the privy, one who came from the forest beyond the stable. They conferred in low voices for a few moments, then, shaking their heads, they arranged the bags on the pack animals, mounted up, and rode slowly back along the track.

Precious Wind retrieved her horse and went back to the road, arriving in time to see them riding away northward on the Wilderbrook road. She counted the days. Day one, Xulai had disappeared. Early morning of day three, a message had arrived saying she had been rescued on day two. Day three, she herself had set out and had spent one night observing the abbey men who had come after her. Three days. The archers had arrived here on the afternoon of the fourth day. If Jenger had sent a message the minute he arrived here with Xulai, it would have been late that night or the morning of the next day before it was seen by the duchess. If the archers had set out at that moment, they still would not have had time to get there by road today. So, they came another way, or they had been dispatched earlier—or some combination of those factors. They had been sent because Jenger had been acting funny.

And how would the duchess have known that except by the mirror? Precious Wind knew how the special mirrors worked. They were made by a machine. Each of a pair of mirrors had a unique pattern based on the genetic codes of the two individuals. Tingawans knew about that. The two could speak to one another through the mirrors. In each case, what one reflected the other showed. When Jenger stood in front of one mirror, the other mirror looked out at the duchess. She saw him, he saw her. Yes. She had looked back at him, read his expression, seen what he was doing, how he was acting. He didn't need to be looking at her at the time. He didn't have the mechanism to start up the mirror; she did. She could look through and see him, if he were within sight of it, without his knowing it.

All it required was some cells from the body of each of them, plus the machines to prepare the glass, and the knowledge of how to use both. Pity she hadn't kept the mirror. Perhaps she could have done something to send a false picture to the duchess since it no doubt reflected only to her. Best not! Too dangerous. What she had already done might well be sufficient.

"The mirrors utilize a power source. What passes between the mirrors are transient energies. They are not spirits or ghosts," her Tingawan teacher had said. "They never *were* anyone themselves. They are neither good nor evil. They are merely little vortices that for a time have a separate existence. If exactly the same pattern exists in two different places, what happens to one set of energies will influence the other, regardless of the distance between."

The lecture had not ended there. The teacher had gone on: "Using a similar technique, one set, while remaining complete, may have an additional pattern element included that changes or warps it so that it will eventually be unable to hold together. The warped element destroys the complete pattern, that is, the person from whom the pattern came."

"You could kill someone with it?"

"Yes. If you knew how. If you had the pattern. If you had the machines. The augmented pattern would have to be held in a kind of suspended animation until it was released in close proximity to the target. It does not last long enough to seek its matching pattern over a great distance."

That was how the princess had been killed. Before she became so weak that she could not talk, when they all thought the attack had been thwarted, the princess asked Precious Wind to explain what was happening.

"Long ago, we found some ancient machines in Tingawa . . ."

"I knew about that, but no more than that."

"In the Before Time they had a disease called cancer. Parts of one's own body began to grow and attack other parts. It took them generations to learn how to fight it. Among the machines, we found one that we think might have originally been used to fight that disease. It could reproduce the code for individual people, or animals, or anything living. Our people experimented with the patterns of simple plants. To the pattern of the plant, they added part of the pattern of bacteria that killed those plants. The combined pattern sought out the plants and killed them. In the Before Time, if the pattern had been of the cancerous cells, they could have added something to kill them and only them. We saw the danger, the temptation. We put the machines where they could not be used. We never have used them.

"I believe that there, in the Old Dark House, some old machines had survived. I think the duchess first took your code, then added something that would feed upon it. She carried it with her. She probably drove by here in her carriage—she often did that—and she set it free outside the castle."

"How did she get my pattern?"

"She obtained something of yours somewhere, somehow, perhaps at court: a few hairs from your brush, perhaps. A napkin you had used to wipe your mouth at dinner. That's all it would have taken."

"But you helped me defeat it!"

"I can't explain that. Perhaps the machine she used is faulty. It must be very old. The ones we found in Tingawa were very old. Or perhaps she did not understand how to use it correctly."

They had not known then that the machine had made copies. They had not known then that defeating the duchess once meant nothing—they would have to defeat her hundreds of times.

When they learned this, Precious Wind had cried, "We can defeat it again. You can go back to Tingawa! Far enough she can't follow you."

"Xulai has to be here! Everything says she has to be born here and live here. I stay here for Xulai. She is too important to us to do anything else."

Still, they had fought. They found things to disrupt the vortices. If the princess mixed her saliva with the blood of a chicken or the foam from the back of a horse, then applied this mixture to the back of a mirror, then bits of that mirror set in windows attracted the vortices and the varying patterns in those mirrors trapped them, weakened them. When the mirrors were melted, the energies were dissipated, that copy was defeated. Even different genetic patterns could distract them. A sprig of yew the princess had breathed on, a line of chalk she had held. The patterns could be weakened by those who had some understanding of what was happening, but they could not be stopped without the machines. They could not stop the duchess without risking Xulai. They could never risk Xulai.

Nor could they learn anything about the duchess except what everyone knew: The duchess was Mirami's daughter, Falyrion's daughter. She had been given the duchy by the king. They could learn nothing about the Old Dark House except what everyone knew: The Old Dark House had been owned by the Old Dark Man. He was not there anymore. He had been there when Mirami was a child, but he had gone away or died. He had been called a wizard, a monster, a vampire. People had feared him and still feared him even though the Old Dark Man must have died long, long before Alicia was born.

In Tingawa it was said that the Old Dark House must be totally destroyed, burned to the ground with every device that could be found within it. That would certainly be done, some way, some time. But not today.

Here at the Vulture Tower, Precious Wind had learned nothing new; she had only verified assumptions she and the princess and Justinian and Lok-i-xan had made long ago. There were still riddles piled upon riddles, and it was not a conundrum Precious Wind could solve now. Her story to the abbot and the prior required that she spend at least two days more away from the abbey, and it would be wise to stay somewhere other than the Vulture Tower. If she could get archers here in such a short time, she might send them with the thing, the vortices, to go looking for Jenger. If they searched for cells of his body, there would be plenty of them where the mirror was now. Her own hair was, as usual when she was on a mission, tightly braided, smoothed down with oil, and covered. Long hair was a disadvantage in combat and a disadvantage if any hair, long or short, fell into Alicia's hands. Precious Wind had worn gloves and used her handkerchief to hold things. She had not put her mouth to anything. She had not used the privy. She carried a little folding shovel among her supplies and was neat and hidden as a cat about her own droppings. She remembered her surprise at Xulai hiding the privy, that morning when they left Altamont lands. Who had taught her that? Well, it didn't matter. The only cells anyone had left in the Vulture Tower had been Jenger's, and possibly the bowmen's. Jenger, so far as Precious Wind could see, was nowhere to be found.

IN THE WAGON INSIDE THE dilapidated house hidden in the forest south of the abbey, Abasio was tending to Xulai. She had worn the library helmet almost constantly for the last several days, and he had to take it away from her from time to time to be sure that she ate something. Each time, she seemed better, less haunted by whatever it was that had happened. He had decided he would wait and find out what had happened to her from the helmet itself rather than make her talk about it. He had done so, finding the memory but not the truth hidden in the memory. She didn't know what she had done. She couldn't remember what she had done. Ollie could not help him. Understanding would have to wait.

Xulai had asked for his sewing kit and made some arrangement with her clothing before letting him wash the things she had been wearing. In between feeding and cosseting Xulai, he carefully copied a map from a book the librarian had loaned to him, a large book, unsuitable for carrying on a horse. He also made over Jenger's horse, giving it a shorter mane and tail and some large white spots on the chest and forehead. Doing it right took time, for he actually bleached the hairs rather than merely painting them. Blue was now black, which he deeply resented but understood. One afternoon, Abasio rode him south to fetch the mule he had bought, leading it back to the hidden wagon. As soon as Xulai was fit to travel, he wanted to be on the way south, and since he might have to stay off the road, it would be a slow journey.

He still had two pigeons and a sizeable sack of grain, but he couldn't carry the birds on horseback, so he'd release them before he left. Perhaps it would be a good idea to send a couple of misleading messages in the meantime, and he spent time composing these, sending them two days apart. One, directed to Wordswell, said, truthfully, that Xulai was recovering from the shock of her abduction and asked him to send that information on to Hallad, Prince Orez, at Woldsgard. Winger would read it first, of course, but that was no matter. It would get to Wordswell and so would the message to the prince.

The next message, to the abbot, said Xulai was being sent to Woldsgard under the protection of men sent by Prince Orez. That would confuse whoever saw it.

The morning after the last message had been sent, they set out, two men on horses, leading a pack mule, one of the men quite young. The older man had reddish hair and a short beard and mustache; he rode a black horse with white blotches. His name was Bram. The younger man wore a large cap of a kind often worn by farm people of the area. His name was Chippy, and he rode a plain black horse. In midmorning, they met a group of riders coming from the east, a couple of traders and their families on their way to Merhaven with a number of hired men along as guards. Bram, being charming, received an invitation for him and his shy young brother to join them.

The Old
Dark House

THE ARCHERS RETURNED TO THE OLD DARK HOUSE by the same route they had taken earlier, arriving early in the morning. The duchess had been watching the road from the tower, and she met them in the forecourt of the castle. Their leader dismounted and bowed deeply.

"We didn't find him, ma'am. He wasn't in the tower, and we didn't find him anywhere near it. His horse was gone. The birds were gone, except for the ones that home there—"

"The prisoner?" she demanded.

"We didn't see a prisoner, ma'am. We didn't see any sign there'd been a prisoner. No sign of food or blood or . . . anything in the cell, ma'am. Usually, if there's a prisoner, shackled, there'll be . . . like . . ."

"Piss," she said. "And stink."

"Nothing there, ma'am."

She glared. "Did you search the area, look for a body?"

"Oh, yes, ma'am. First thing we did. We didn't have the manpower to make a search over all the forest, but we took a good look everywhere nearby. We found some old bones on a little shelf below the tower where he maybe gutted and butchered a deer, but the bones were just bits, brown, chewed. Nothing that looked human."

"You brought back everything?" she asked in a razor-edged voice.

He said placatingly, "Everything but the furniture and the birds, ma'am. We didn't have cages for the birds or a wagon for the furniture, but we can go back and get them at once if you want us to."

"No," she snapped, thinking that someone else would have to occupy the tower and the birds could be fetched then. It did not occur to her, as it had not to the archers, that caged birds would have no one to feed or water them in the meantime.

"Just carry the sacks downstairs for me."

So they did, down the crooked flight of stones into a kind of anteroom where there was nothing to see, though the archers pointedly looked only straight ahead. No one worked for the duchess without quickly learning that curiosity killed in the Old Dark House. When they were gone, she emptied the sacks onto a workbench. A few items of clothing. Supplies for messages: papers, pens, ink, the little tubes the messages went in. A sack of food: dried meat, cheese, a few bottles, some stale bread. His personal things. A comb, a brush with several of his hairs caught in the bristles. Well. Upstairs in her bedroom she had several of Jenger's hairs. He had left them on her pillow, and she had saved them carefully. These were fresher. She would use these.

She unlocked the door to the room with the machines and went to the fatal-cloud maker. The angled receptacle went in with a tiny click, and she noticed once again how much the receptacle resembled a skull, rounded on one side, angled like a jaw on the other, with a row of little protrusions that looked like teeth. This always amused her. When the device had finished and extruded its cylindrical capsule, she stroked it for a few moments. It had been foolish of Jenger to run from her. His horse had gone, so obviously he had run from her. Well, between her seeker and cloud machines she could deal with Jenger no matter how far he had run. Unfortunately, she would have to use the seeker to find Jenger before she could use the capsule. But then she said to herself, "Vengeance deferred is often sweeter! The capsules will keep almost forever!" The Old Dark Man had told her that a long time ago, his own bony and deep-set eye sockets seeming bare and empty as a skull.

In one corner of the secret room, behind a huge square pillar, the Old Dark Man had lined a stone cubby with narrow shelves on which his "very important books" had been ranged. The cubby was too small for him to enter, but his huge hands at the ends of his long, ropy arms could pluck out whatever book he needed. When Alicia had come to the Old Dark House as its owner, she had found the book alcove empty. It made a perfect repository for her most precious things, however, and the cubby was not too small for her slender body. She went there often to admire and caress her memorabilia: her father's gold ring with the sapphire seal lying upon a tiny satin pillow; a lock of his hair; a tiny ivory easel with a miniature of the duke Falyrion in gilded armor on his favorite horse. She had taken the ring from his finger while he lay in his coffin, his initial carved into the seal inside a ring of laurel. The lock of his hair was tied with a bit of the ribbon that had trimmed his shirts. He had given it to her when she asked for it. The miniature was a copy of a large portrait that had hung in the hall at Kamfelsgard. Mirami had been away at court when Alicia had hired a traveling artist to paint the miniature, paying for it with a ring she had stolen from Mirami's jewel chest, a ring Mirami had never worn and had never missed once it was gone. Beside these things, she kept a book she had made when she was only six or seven, several stiff pages of pressed flowers and leaves from the hidden place above the pool where her father swam and a linen undershift he had worn against his skin. She had taken it from his room long before he died. She believed it still smelled of him. He had given her the little gifts on the same shelf: a brooch, a lace shawl folded into a neat packet.

On the shelves below were other things, necessary but ordinary things: a bottle of ink and a few writing brushes; the written instructions for using the slaughterer, the seeker, the mirror maker, and the sender; a card with the key-code for the doors written on it, in case she forgot; a shallow tray that until recently had held a dozen copies of the cloud she had made to kill the princess. Once she knew the princess was dead, she had thrown them away. Now she labeled Jenger's capsule with a J, dipping a brush into ink to do so, and placed it in the tray. If she ever made any capsules for other people, it wouldn't do to get them confused.

When the Old Dark Man had brought her there as a child, not only these shelves had been packed with books, but there had been hundreds more in the rooms upstairs. When she returned there from Ghastain after becoming the Duchess of Altamont, she had been able to get into the room without trouble. She had remembered the key-code that let her open the door. She could swear no one else had been in that room, but all the books had been gone. The devices had still been there: the slaughterer, the seeker, the mirror maker, the sender—though that disappointing device was useless now. There were other devices here, of course: the big machine in the corner that watched her through its red eyes, the one that showed her where her servants were, their lights shining in the dark, their innards making small, satisfied noises: *click, whiz, purr.* All of them had been there. The doors had still been tightly locked, no one had disturbed the place, but she had found no books in the Old Dark House at all.

Mirami didn't have them. Mirami hated the Old Dark House; she had never come there after the Old Dark Man had died. Besides, Mirami did not care for books, and Falyrion's books, her father's books, were of a different kind. He had collected books about battles and hunting and the keeping of game and dogs and horses. He had some about swordplay, too. Fencing. He had been an excellent swordsman. Alicia had wanted to learn the skill, but he had told her no, it was only for boys. Girls needed their beauty, he said. Men were only made more interesting by a few scars, but it would never do to have her pretty face scratched and ruined.

Her father had no scars, but he was wonderfully interesting even without them. He was beautiful. His hair was sun gold, his eyes were sea blue, his skin was copper, all over, face, body, legs, arms. Those were his colors, the ones he wore, gold-and-copper-plated armor and a blue and gold tabard and blue trappings on his horse. He was tall, and strong, and wore wonderful clothing with lace and jewels on it. He rode like a . . . like a centaur. There had been instructions for making a centaur in one of the Old Dark Man's books. Half-man, half-horse. She was glad her father was only man. When he and his men went swimming, they stripped from their clothes and Alicia, hiding in the glen above the pool, could admire his body. Falyrion's body was beautiful. All men were made alike, all men thought their pricks were beautiful, Mirami said. It might be true that they thought that, but it wasn't true in fact. They had the same parts, maybe, but the parts could be ugly or beautiful and the assemblage of all the parts of a man could be very, very different from one man to another. There was no man in the world as beautiful as her father. Each time she came into this closet she felt again what she had felt when she lay there in the grass above the pool, wondering what it would be like to be held by her father without all his clothes in the way—without all their clothes in the way.

She had always known that Mirami killed people. She had not

known Mirami was going to kill Falyrion. She would have warned him if she had known, but she hadn't known. Mirami had poisoned him. She poisoned people all the time. People who were in her way. People who offended her. She had many different poisons. The Old Dark Man had taught her about them when she was young. She knew poisons that couldn't be detected, poisons that had no smell, poisons that would lie inside one for days before acting, poisons that would simply stop the heart and others that would weaken people and take whole seasons to kill them. And when they died, Mirami was never there, never anywhere around.

Mirami had poisoned Alicia's father, and when Alicia learned of it she had shut herself in her room for days, raging, weeping. At last she had calmed herself by remembering the Old Dark Man's words about balancing the accounts. She stopped grieving for her father where anyone could see her. She was mute. She listened politely when Mirami told her what the family business was. Mirami said she had killed Falyrion because she and Alicia and Hulix were destined to take all the lands of Norland that didn't belong to the king and give them to the new king, who would be Mirami's son and a new brother for Alicia! To do that, however, Mirami had first to marry the current king and bear him an heir. And, to do that, she had to be a widow.

But they would then be the mother and sister of the king of Ghastain! Mirami said it as though she were giving Alicia a present.

Alicia had listened to all this, not only to the words but to the voice, the tone. Her father's death was in the words. Her own death was implicit in the tone. Raging at Mirami might well have meant her own death; Alicia did not want to die, so she did what the Old Dark Man had told her to do—nothing. She had been unresponsive, which Mirami had not understood at all.

"Aren't you excited at the idea of ruling a great country?"

"Yes, ma'am."

"You don't show it."

"I think maybe it's better if I don't. Show it, I mean. You don't want people to know about your plans, do you? So I shouldn't look . . . excited, should I?"

Mirami had given her a long, thoughtful look. "No, Alicia. You're quite right."

Mirami had been giving her long, thoughtful looks ever since, but Alicia had managed to stay out of real trouble by staying as far from her mother as she could. She and her mother had gone to Ghastain as soon as Hulix became Duke of Kamfels. It wasn't hard to stay away from Mirami in Ghastain. Mirami spent most of her time at court, where she would be seen by the king. The king liked to have something going on all the time, festivals, and parades, and dramas, and tableaux. The king liked to get dressed up; Mirami liked to get dressed up; being dressed up meant endless hours with wigmakers, dressmakers, jewelers, and shoemakers, looking in mirrors. They both liked to look at themselves in mirrors, and they found endless fascination in trying things on, so it was easy for Alicia to be otherwise occupied. After her mother married the king, it was even easier. Alicia had her own quarters, her own maids. And then Rancitor was born, and as soon as he was weaned from his wet nurse, Alicia decided she would be his friend. The Old Dark Man had told her that friendship was even better than love as a way to use someone, so she made a friend of Rancitor, and he loved her, more and more the older he got, especially when she started teaching him some of the more pleasurable things the Old Dark Man had taught her. Rancitor did not mention these things to others, because it was a secret. And when he was six (without telling Mirami, because it was a secret) he asked the king to give Alicia the title to Altamont.

Even after she was Duchess of Altamont, Rancitor expected her to stay in Ghastain, and since Alicia's own plans depended on Rancitor, she spent a lot of time at court. She didn't like him at all, really. He was rather like Hulix, though more like Mirami. He liked her, however, and he liked the man-woman games she taught him to play. And now, of course, he was old enough to play them with others, for which she was thankful. The things she had taught him to enjoy gave her no pleasure. It was of no matter. The games had bought her Altamont. The games would buy her other things. Meantime, Rancitor's quarters were probably the safest place she could be in Ghastain. The servants brought his food there and she shared it with him, only pretending to eat or drink when at table with others. If she bought something herself, in the market, then she could eat it. She wore gloves most of the time, because some poisons entered through the skin. She sneaked into the servant's bathhouse at night, never bathing in the one reserved for the women of the court. She kept the curtains pulled shut in the room she used. She opened doors and drawers with a metal hook concealed in her sleeve, for poisoned needles could be positioned in places where people might put their fingers. Often she covered her own hair with a wig made of other people's hair. One of the things the Old Dark Man had taught her was never to underestimate enmity. Anyone could arouse enmity. Beautiful women were not exempt.

Rancitor's quarters, however, where their games had been played, were undoubtedly safe. Mirami had no wish to destroy Rancitor until after King Gahls was dead, and possibly not even then. *"It's often better, my dear, to be the one who props the crown, rather than the one who wears it."*

Mirami had begun to say that she wanted to live as long as the Old Dark Man had lived. The Old Dark Man had claimed to be a hundred and fifty years old: a century more than Mirami had lived already. What would she do with all that time once the king had swallowed up all the lands of Norland? What would amuse her then? Alicia had wondered this many times and the only answer that seemed satisfactory was the conquest of Tingawa. That had to be it. Mirami had said the Tingawans would be killed, so she must have been planning to take the army of Ghastain—King Gahls called his army the army of Ghastain—across the sea to the fabled lands. Mirami would do what Ghastain had been unable to do! Probably that was it. Mirami planned, in time, to conquer the far west. Except that Mirami would not have the time.

In a few days, Alicia would have to obey her mother's summons. She would go the way the archers had gone, taking them with her. By that time, Mirami's friend Chamfray ought to be at the point of death, but it could not possibly be blamed on Alicia. Mirami didn't know anything at all about the fatal-cloud machine.

PRECIOUS WIND SPENT TWO DAYS idling in and around the Vulture Tower, careful always to sleep far enough away from it to avoid surprise. Staying near the tower allowed her an unforeseen opportunity. Precious Wind had always been fond of wolves, possibly because they had always seemed if not fond, then certainly tolerant of her. The experience with the men who had followed her and ended up killing themselves, thereby attracting wolves, had not been totally new to her. In Tingawa, as a child, she had befriended a wolf pack living in a mountainous territory at the edge of the huge continent that extended for thousands of miles westward through dozens of other territories and kingdoms. When she came to Norland, she had hoped to learn whether these Norland wolves were similarly inclined toward friendship. Though she had spent years in Norland, there had been no opportunity until now, for Justinian's stockmen and their huge hounds kept wolves well away from Woldsgard.

The previous night she had heard their howls approaching. They were closer tonight. Very possibly they had scented her horse. She put the gelding in the stable of the tower and shut the sturdy door. She was growing fond of the beast and did not want him troubled. She rubbed his shoulder and told him to relax and ignore anything he might hear. Then she stood inside the open door of the tower and waited.

The pack leader entered the clearing in which the tower sat, looked around it, saw her. He made a quick, breathy sound, a kind of whuff, not surprise, not fear. He was saying, "I see you. We see you."

Precious Wind replied in kind. "I see you, too." Then she sat down on the step of the tower and ostentatiously licked her hand, paw.

The pack leader approached. Behind him she saw ten or a dozen pairs of eyes peering from among the trees. They stayed where they were except for one big-footed, big-eared youngster who half staggered out of the trees toward his father, who promptly turned and bit him. The pup yipped and went back where he belonged. The pack leader came closer, sniffing.

Precious Wind rose, went slowly into the tower, and tugged something out onto the doorstep. Wild pig, fresh, shot that day, first arrow from her bow. She had been a bit worried about that. She was woefully out of practice.

She pulled the carcass into the clearing and sat down on the step again. The pack leader circled it, half circled her, circled the pig again. The youngster came out of the forest again and sat there, head cocked. His mother came to crouch beside him. Other shadowy forms squeezed out of the forest, halfway, a quarter. Eyes didn't blink. Precious Wind took out her knife, went to the carcass and cut a piece of meat, tossed it to the youngster. His mother pounced on it, put her feet on it, sniffed suspiciously. Finally she licked it. The pack leader put his nose to the place she had cut, licked the blood, turned, made the same whuff as before, giving the pack permission.

Crossing their trail behind them could have been interpreted as a move to trap or encircle. Precious Wind moved to the side of the clearing opposite the one the wolves had come from. She stood by a tree while they ate. There was the usual baring of teeth, asserting of rights, the usual "this one eats first, that one last," but the carcass was of a well-grown boar with meat enough for all of them. She'd found a whole piggery of wild ones north along the ridge, rooting up old crops from another of those abandoned farm places they'd found on the way to the abbey—old crops, reseeding themselves, turnips and parligs gone wild. Good pig food. She'd had to drag the carcass here. Horses not used in battle or hunting often objected to dead cargo. The horse had dragged it to the door, however, and she'd been able to roll the carcass into the tower.

While the pack was still eating, the pack leader broke away from the melee, licked his jowls, his paws, shook himself, came over where she was standing, cocked his head. She held out her hand. He sniffed it, made a sound in his throat. The female came over, sniffed in her turn, and was followed by every member of the pack, the big-eared young one last. There were two other young ones. Nine adults and the lead female's latest litter of three. This was probably the pack that had disposed of Jenger, if, as she suspected, either Abasio or someone else had killed him. She hadn't found a body, the archers hadn't found a body. The only bones were scraps that could have been any kind of bone, pig, deer, no nice bulbous skull to identify a human. The archers had supposed Jenger to have ridden away, but the absence of a horse was meaningless. If a horse had been here, Abasio would have taken it when he left.

The following morning she returned to the abbey. All the way there, she saw shadowy forms inside the trees, keeping pace with her. They wanted to know where she was, where she might come from again. Meals didn't usually come that easily; human friends seldom came at all.

WHEN PRECIOUS WIND RETURNED TO the abbey, she went first to Wordswell, laying before him everything she had found at the tower. They opened the four message tubes and read the contents. Jenger, with the help of "our friend at the abbey," was directed to abduct Xulai by any means possible. Jenger was directed to kill Bear or have him killed. Jenger was directed to kill any Tingawan he could lay hands on, with the help of "our friend at the abbey." The last message, the one that had not been sent, they read together. "The Tingawan child has gone to Elsmere. I have one of her servants, not the driver we met. What do you want me to do with her?"

Precious Wind said, "The first three of these are in one hand, that of the duchess: they were sent from Altamont to Jenger. The last one was no doubt to be sent from Jenger to Altamont. He didn't send it. It may have been too late in the day. He may have intended to wait until morning, but something else happened. Obviously Xulai lied to him about who she was. When Jenger first saw her, she appeared to be a child."

"A child? That explains it! That first night when I saw her, it was like looking at two people in the same body. I've seen that illusion before, but rarely."

Precious Wind smiled, shaking her head. "She has always been . . . changeable. More so recently. Now, Elder Brother, if the prior has been sending messages to this Vulture Tower and to the Old Dark House, which Solo Winger can testify he has done, I think these messages from the Old Dark House make it clear the friend in the abbey referred to was the prior himself. These make it clear he was conspiring with the duchess to kill various members of the Tingawan group entrusted to the abbey by Justinian. Just as a matter of interest, Justinian recently sent funds here for the keep of his people. Did they come to you?"

"They were taken by Justinian's messenger to our treasury, which is kept by an elder sister who is completely trustworthy. Receipts were given to the messenger, and copies of them were given to me."

"I rejoice at hearing this. Now, some time ago Justinian sent three men carrying a substantial amount that was to be given to me and to Bear when we left here for Merhaven. Justinian did this because he did not want Bear to receive his reward much before he left, lest it be diminished in the intervening time. Do you know about this?"

"I do not. Our treasurer does not. Your friend, Bear, was inquiring about it."

Precious Wind took out the little bag that held her valuables and retrieved the receipt Justinian had given her. Wordswell stared at it, teeth clenched.

"I never thought . . . the prior was that interested in . . . treasure. I thought he was most interested in power."

"Money is a good way of creating power, Elder Brother. Your prior finds money useful. I can testify to the fact that the prior paid three men to follow me when I left a few days ago. Their instructions were to kill me."

Wordswell's face became drawn and gray in an instant, as though someone had knifed him and his blood had drained away. "He paid to have you killed."

She nodded.

The old man sighed, shrank as though in pain, murmured beneath his breath before saying, "His position would not allow him ample funds to pay for something like that without his taking money from some un-authorized source. I presume you . . . evaded the men."

Precious Wind thought it wisest to say very little about the incident. She shrugged. "People who do that sort of thing are violent by nature and tend to be quarrelsome. I thought their actions upon the road were somewhat suspicious. I hid myself and my horse where I could overhear them. They began to fight among themselves, and in their argument they mentioned the prior, the payment, and the fact that they would kill me. They also disputed as to who would have that pleasure, attacking one another violently. Having heard this, I simply avoided them and went in a different direction. However, I did see that they were wearing the livery of the abbey, and I haven't seen them since I returned. It may be they are still out there looking for me, but it would be wise to find out what other men in the abbey might be accustomed to being sent on such errands."

She waited until some color returned to his face before continuing. "You asked for proof of his misdeeds, and these notes are your proof. I myself fetched these notes from the Vulture Tower. I myself saw what was there. The Duke of Wold put this receipt in my hands. It would be wise if a few trustworthy elders knew what I have told you so you will not be alone in your knowledge."

"While you were away, I spoke to the abbot. He asked if I had proof."

"Well, now we do. I will see the abbot next. Will you come with me?"

He nodded, voiceless.

They went to the abbot and laid before him the messages referring to "our friend at the abbey."

The abbot sighed deeply. Lying was foreign to him. Subterfuge was foreign to him. He felt deeply troubled. "I have been a foolish old man, haven't I?"

Precious Wind said, "No, sir, you have been trusting."

"Things have been happening I should have known about, but I didn't. Things happening to my brothers and sisters, without my knowledge. Wordswell has been telling me. I find it so hard to believe."

"I know. But we will solve that problem."

The abbot sighed. "A message came, while you were away. It said Xulai had gone back to Woldsgard under the care of Prince Orez." He took it from his pocket and showed it to her.

Precious Wind knew Xulai had promised her father she would get to Tingawa as soon as possible. She considered it very unlikely that the message was true. *Trust Abasio to keep stirring the pot,* she thought with mild amusement. "Has the prior seen the message?"

"No. The loft keeper brought it directly to me."

"May I have it?"

"If it is wise," he whispered. "You can do what needs doing better than I."

She put the message in her pocket. "It is wise. I'll take care of it. Don't be troubled, Eldest. For your information only, I don't believe she's returned to Woldsgard. The message was sent by the man who rescued her. He did it to confuse matters and to help him keep her safe."

"What does your embassy want to do about Xulai?"

Though she regretted the necessity for it, guile came easily to Precious Wind.

"I am to stay here for a short while, awaiting developments, and then, if there are none, I am to go south through Elsmere, to Merhaven. In the meantime, however, Wordswell and I, some of our people from Wold, and the good trustworthy people of the abbey will solve this dilemma. Do not speak of it to anyone except those Wordswell suggests. Let us work on it."

The abbot gave her a pitiful look. "I thought, perhaps, I should confront our prior. Explain to him that what he is doing is wrong, contrary to our beliefs!"

Precious Wind put steel into her voice. "Abbot, if you do that, you condemn Xulai to death! The man sent murderers after me, murderers after her. If you say anything to him about it, you ensure that next time he will be successful!"

"Murderers . . ." He turned ashen.

"Read those messages again! That is what the 'friend at the abbey' was expected to do. Murder."

Wordswell said, "Put it out of your mind, Eldest Brother. She is right. The prior doesn't need to be told what he's doing. He knows very well what he is doing and he relishes it. Do not risk other lives in an effort to save his conscience. He has none. You have not yet been foolish, only too trusting. Do not now be foolish!" He turned to Precious Wind. "Show the abbot the receipt, Precious Wind. Read it, sir. The prior claims no knowledge of it. You realize the abbey must make this amount good?"

"Some of it may be found," said Precious Wind. "Let's not worry about that just now."

The abbot had tears in his eyes. He bowed his head. "I will say nothing. I will say nothing. You have my word."

Precious Wind retreated to the library with Wordswell. "Keep an eye on him," she said. "His kindness may kill us all."

"Not if we can get him moving on something to distract him; not if we can wind it up quickly."

"The men who came with us from Woldsgard move in the same circles as the men who were sent after me. They're all horsemen, workingmen; they drink beer, they talk, things are said that our men from Woldsgard can hear and remember." She was quiet for a moment, thinking. "The prior believes if the abbot dies, he, the prior, will succeed to the abbacy without any trouble at all. I must leave it to you to see that particular thing does not happen. I understand you will need to speak with dozens of people. Do it as quickly as possible."

"We have already begun—the abbot and I—to sort out some of the more . . . apparent problems such as our troop movements. Other meetings are scheduled. What are you going to do with the message the abbot gave you?"

"See that it reaches the prior and that he thinks he has seen it first. To do that, I will need to talk to your birdman."

Together they went to the bird loft. Precious Wind gave Abasio's misleading message to Solo Winger, who scanned it rapidly.

"Yeah. So? I sor it when it come and I guv it to abbot."

"We'd like you to pretend it just came today. Let the prior see it."

He fixed them with clever eyes. "So tha's the way of it, hah? That chap with the wagon, he's puttin' down a smell trail."

"In the wrong direction," said Precious Wind. "If you don't mind misleading the prior."

"Oh, tha's one clever, clever fellow I woun't mind misleadin' right over a cliff. You know the abbey armor is comin' back from Netherfields?"

"I didn't know," Precious Wind said.

"Abbot sent a bird. Came up here hisself to do it. Armor's t'come home. Says there's not enuff food an' stuff for them at Netherfields."

"I should have told you," said Wordswell apologetically. "Even though we didn't have what the abbot considered to be conclusive proof, he and I have been doing what we can to sort out the worst of the mess. We'd heard from Woldsgard that the troops from Ghastain have gone on to Kamfels and that Hallad, Prince Orez, occupies Woldsgard, so the abbot recalled our men from Netherfields. He told them to go back to the southlands where the brigands are."

Winger nodded. "S'right. Abbot sent 'em south. They go by Altamont, Lake o' Clouds, then east, back where they started. Most of 'em. Abbot left a few there in Netherfields jus' in case any armor comes back that way from Kamfels."

Precious Wind managed to keep her face placid. Too many people were going south. Abasio and Xulai were no doubt headed that way. Bear was headed that way. Now the army of the abbey, and did anyone know whether the commandant of that army was part of the prior's plans? Well, there were many ways of laying a false trail!

Precious Wind lingered outside the dining hall when her dinner bell rang. The prior was also fed during the first night meal. She managed to be in front of him, to look up and see him, to let a smile light up her face as she greeted him. He was not as well schooled. Just for an instant he looked terribly surprised, even dismayed.

"Elder Brother, I'm so glad to see you. I know you were interested in our embassy's analysis of the situation here." She shook her head. "They're very concerned. They've told me if there's no immediate message here from Xulai herself, I'm to go on to Merhaven. Before I leave, I want to tell you about our people from Woldsgard. The two women and the men, except for Bear, who left earlier, may take advantage of your hospitality for a time. The duke told me he had already made recompense to the abbey for their care. Once I have gone, however, all the Tingawan presence will vanish, and you can quit worrying about the diplomatic consequences. I know you've been concerned."

By this time the prior was in command of his face and able to offer her an expression of polite concern. "Oh, indeed. Concerned, of course, certainly. There will be no problem about the people from Woldsgard. I'm told one of the women has found an aunt here, one of our cooks. She has offered to work for us if we have work for her. The elderly woman is welcome to stay, of course, and the men will be useful."

Precious Wind had no doubt of it. Black Mike, Pecky Peavine, Bartelmy, and the brothers Farrier were going to be very useful. If anyone could find out who among the abbey's men were confederates of the prior, those five could. Meantime, she needed to take a few hours' rest and have a little talk with Oldwife and Nettie Lean. But before that, there was one item of unfinished business.

She went out the little gate at moonrise, giving the guard her word she would return within the hour. She was carrying a sack of scraps she had begged from the kitchen, saying she was baiting traps. She walked out into the night, across the grasslands, down into a hollow. She put her hands around her mouth and howled.

They came out of the forest, all of them, and behind the pack a few loners, strangers to her, who sat to one side, not daring to come closer. Sons of the alpha wolf that he had chased away. Two females. The nucleus of another, related pack. She emptied the big sack for the pack and let them sniff her again, memorizing her smell. With the pack leader, she laid her hand, very briefly, upon his shoulders, then walked away to the place where the loners sat. The smaller sack would do for them. Just meat scraps, bread with meat juices on it, cheese that may have gone a bit moldy, nothing that would hurt them and more food than they found on some nights by themselves. Pig was good, but both boars and sows had tusks and were very good fighters. Deer and wild cattle would feed a pack for days, but they were swift or horned or both, and not easily come by. Rabbits were quick, shifty, and had very little meat on them. Smaller critters were hardly worth the trouble unless they could be caught by dozens. The loners sniffed her as well. The pack leader came to get her and walked beside her as she went away. She knew they had made an agreement. They would follow her south. She would hunt food for them. If needed, they would hunt men for her.

ONE OF ALICIA'S SERVANTS TOLD her an army was approaching on the road that went through Altamont to the Lake of the Clouds. Alicia called for her horse, her guards, and went to meet it. The commandant rode forward and bowed graciously. "My lady, we ask your pardon for this intrusion. We will not trespass on your property except to use the road so far as the Lake of the Clouds."

She pretended surprise. "Why, where are you coming from, Colonel . . ."

"Colonel Sallis, ma'am. We were told our people at Netherfields might be in some danger and rode to their relief, but it is we who were relieved." He smiled, an honest smile. "Netherfields is in the care of the abbey, as you probably know. I am told by the people there that on the duke's death, it will pass into our care in perpetuity. They have long known of this in Netherfields and at the abbey, but it is recent knowledge for me and those who sent me. We have left a small contingent there to cope with any incursions, and Hallad, Prince Orez, has pledged his help. So, we are returning to our camps east of here. There are brigands enough there to keep us busy."

"Then I wish you a quick journey, Colonel." She managed a smile that felt adequate, turned her horse, and went back the way she had come at some speed. The colonel, left in the dust behind her, frowned. The smile had not reached her eyes. Something he had said had surprised her. Or offended her, perhaps. And what could that have been? He had been as gracious as it was possible to be.

The troops, four abreast, passed the short road that led upward to the hill where the Old Dark House loomed. Its towers peered at them from above the trees, and the colonel very suddenly decided that they would go as far as possible before camping for the night. Strangely enough, there was no griping among the men, who seemed as eager as he was to put the Old Dark House behind them. He later learned many of them had heard stories from those at Netherfields, stories that explained very clearly why Justinian had thought it wise to leave his home.

Behind them, Alicia spent the daylight hours considering what she might do with this knowledge. If Mirami had known of it, she wouldn't have asked the prior to send men to Netherfields, because Mirami owned the prior, the prior would soon become the abbot, the abbot would control the abbey, and Netherfields would soon be the property of the abbey! All this was part of Mirami's plan. The question remained, why hadn't the prior told them this? Was it possible he had not known? If the documents had been negotiated at the abbey some years ago, the current prior might not have been involved. Suppose he didn't know?

Well, he should know. She, Alicia, would tell him. Tell him and tell her mother, both at the same time. She made her way to the bird lofts, humming under her breath. Surely there was something happening here she could use to her advantage. Pity about Jenger. She would have liked to talk it over with him.

SOLO WINGER RECEIVED A MESSAGE from the Old Dark House. He knew exactly which pigeons he had sent where, so he knew exactly where each one was coming from. When he took it from the message tube, he saw that it was sealed and the prior's name was written on the outside. He smiled, unsealed it, read it, then danced a little jig around the loft. It was early evening. He would have to wait a while. The best time to reach either the librarian or the Tingy-away woman would be late evening. The prior usually retired to his own suite early in the evening, shortly after the dinner hour. He had the habit of drinking wine then. The servants said he was a long, loud sleeper, full of snores, snorts, and heaving about. The women who made his bed said he tore it apart in his sleep, every night. They wondered if he had bad dreams.

Solo Winger did not speculate about the dreams. He thought it likely the prior had no conscience that bothered him enough to have bad dreams. More likely he had dreams of glory. More likely his thrashing was his arms flung out demanding that this one or that one be beheaded. Ha.

When the last of the diners left the hall, when darkness fell, when peace descended on the abbey, he went to the library and gave the note to Wordswell. Though unsigned, it was obviously from the Duchess of Altamont.

"I am told by Colonel Sallis that Netherfields becomes the property of the abbey on the death of Justinian. Since you can be the abbot very soon, perhaps it is time to ensure your election. Send now the material I have previously asked for."

"What does she mean 'material'?" Wordswell asked.

"That woman, the Tingy-away woman . . ."

"The Tingawan woman, Precious Wind."

"Her. Yeah. We need her to tell us."

Wordswell and his crony crept through silent corridors, stepping into dark doorways when necessary, finally knocking on Precious Wind's door. Nettie Lean had moved into Oldwife Gancer's room, to care for her, and Precious Wind had a room to herself.

"What does she mean by 'material'?" Wordswell asked when she had read Alicia's message.

She nodded. This was verification of the long supposed. "She means something taken from the abbot's body. Fingernail clippings. Hair pulled by the roots. A vial of spit. Even, I think, something from his seat of comfort."

Wordswell's face showed his disgust. "She can use this to . . . what?"

"Kill him," she replied. "Oh, don't make a face, old bookworm. You've read of such things, I'm sure of it."

"In the olden days. In the Before Time . . ."

" 'At's where the she-devil's from, some old afore time," grunted the loft keeper.

"Well, she can do it now, if she has the machines to do it with. Which she has."

"What are we to do?" asked the librarian

"Who barbers the prior? Who shaves him?"

"His manservant."

"And when his manservant is . . . ill?"

"He would use the abbot's manservant. At least, he has in the past. So do I. The abbot has shared a servant with me for many years. He thinks it foolish to have a man sit idle just in case the abbot should want a cup of tea."

"Ah." That was no help. "I doubt the prior would use someone else to go sneaking about in the abbot's quarters. He would want to do it himself."

Solo Winger snorted. "Prob'ly. Likes to keep 'is 'and in, does prior."

"Then we must let him. How reliable is the servant you share with the abbot?"

"We trust him with a blade at our throats every day."

"Do you trust him to keep a secret?"

"I have heard that a secret can be kept between two people only when one of them is dead."

"That has always been my strongly held conviction." Precious Wind stared into the distance. Still no help. "Well, are the abbot's quarters locked when he is not there?"

"None of us have locked doors."

"So much for that, then. Could you find some reason that the abbot's quarters should be cleaned? I mean cleaned of every hair, every particle of dust, every spider's web in every corner? Rugs beaten into submission. Walls swept. New mattresses. Floors waxed. Linens changed."

"If the abbot went away for a little while, yes. That's usually when the cleaning people choose to do what you describe. The abbot has not been away for over a year, so it's probably time his quarters were cleaned."

"Can you manage to get him away from here for a few days, having previously arranged for his quarters to be cleaned as I have suggested, but without the prior knowing about the cleaning part?"

"Cleaning is not the prior's concern. One of the other elders takes care of that function. And yes, before you ask, the elder in question is completely trustworthy."

"Then you and the abbot should go on a little trip of inspection of something innocuous that's discussed publicly and loudly. Talk about a trip that will take just a few days. And no one should tell the prior about the cleaning."

"What are you going to do?"

"Something we can't trust anyone else to do, Elder Brother. Remember, a secret can be kept between two people only when one of them is dead, and I rather enjoy your company and that of your friend here."

Wordswell managed a shadowy smile. The loft keeper's face was frankly jubilant.

Two days later the librarian, the abbot, and one or two other elders set out to make an inspection of the improvements around the southern watchtower, including the arable lands and irrigation systems being constructed there. The librarian was going because he needed to be sure the records were being kept correctly, and for the past two days this had been a matter for continuous semipublic discussion among him and the abbot and half a dozen other brothers and sisters, often within the prior's hearing. The trip would, in fact, be longer than had been discussed, during which time still other elders would learn about still other matters. That part had not been mentioned where it could be overheard.

While the abbot was away, various cleaning, laundry, furniture-polishing, and woodwork-refinishing people—all with covered hair and gloved hands—did an unobtrusive but thorough turnout of his quarters. Drawers and cupboards were scrubbed. Dust was eradicated. Spiderwebs, never numerous, became nonexistent. No flake of skin was left unswept, no used handkerchief or slightly soiled bit of clothing—indeed, no item of clothing, used or not—was left unlaundered. Floors and furniture shone. Windows were cleaner than when first installed. A small mirror, the only one the abbot allowed himself, was polished. When all was done and inspected, the door was shut and two watchers took up inconspicuous posts where they could see it.

That evening, while the prior was having his evening meal, the abbot's door was opened again, and a slender figure moved through his quarters, slightly disarranging the bed linen, opening a book and leaving it at the bedside, depositing a few hairs upon the pillow, a few more in the perfectly clean brush on the shelf below the mirror, a film of dust and a few fingernail clippings on the desk, together with the scissors that might have clipped them. A used washcloth was deposited beside the basin. A used handkerchief was placed in the laundry basket. In addition to the newly added material, clothing in the wardrobe was slightly disordered; a pair of new, unworn slippers was left on the floor beside the bed. It had been ascertained that the abbot did not moisten a finger to turn pages, so a few of his books were carefully shaken out the window, wiped, shaken again, and laid on the desk, the places marked by used toothpicks.

The depositer of this detritus then examined the room carefully.

It was quite a neat room, with only that minor untidiness one might expect. This figure departed. The two people who had been quietly chatting in the hall outside—to be sure the third one was as uninterrupted here as she had been earlier in the prior's quarters—hid themselves again where they could watch the door.

At dusk, Solo Winger told a messenger that a message had just arrived for the prior. The messenger delivered it. The prior, remembering the abbot was absent, felt the timing of the message was extremely opportune.

Later that same night, when everyone slept except the guards on duty, another person entered the abbot's quarters, this one carrying a lantern and a tiny bowl. The person went from place to place, searching diligently, finding and putting into the tiny bowl almost all the bits and pieces the earlier prowler had left behind: Hair from pillow and brush, skin fragments shaken from a washcloth, fingernail clippings, even a scraping from the handkerchief, the toothpicks marking the books. No one was visible in the hall outside. The person was, so he thought, completely unobserved.

Still later that night while Solo Winger, with an empty bottle on the floor beside his bed for verisimilitude, pretended sodden slumber, the prior arrived in the bird loft. He selected a bird from the Old Dark House cage and attached a message tube containing all the material taken from the abbot's quarters. He thrust the bird into the night. The same pigeon, not at all interested in flying around in the dark, returned almost immediately to the home cage. The home cage was crowded with birds moving about, eating, cooing, fluttering; one more coming in through the hatch was not noticeable. In any case, the prior was preoccupied with another message, this one to the court at Ghastain. Though the prior thrust this bird into the night as well, it too returned unnoticed.

Solo knew not only his own birds but also every other bird in the loft. It didn't matter what cage they were in, he knew where each one would home to, and the birds that would fly to the Old Dark House and to Ghastain were temporarily in the cage labeled Merhaven! When the message sender had departed, Solo Winger rose, withdrew from the abbey cage the two abbey birds that had message tubes on their legs, removed the tubes, and returned the birds to their fellows. He made a copy of the message that accompanied the bits and scraps of skin and hair: "*By the time you get this, there will no longer be any Tingawan people at the abbey. They have all departed.*" He then spent a few moments sorting out-of-place birds into their proper cages before transferring the skin-and-hair message tube to an Old Dark House bird. He would let it go first thing in the morning. It wouldn't have flown until morning anyhow.

He read the message to Ghastain carefully, word for word.

"*For Queen Mirami: A Tingawan girl believes you have an interest in five deaths in Kamfels and Ghastain. The girl has returned to Woldsgard under the protection of Hallad, Prince Orez. Since your armor is in Kamfels, perhaps you can be of assistance to her. There are no longer any Tingawan people here at the abbey. They have all gone.*"

Solo Winger decided he should not send this one until Wordswell and the Tingy-away women had seen it. He put it behind one of the stones in the wall along with a great many copies of other messages sent and received. When the abbot returned, along with the librarian and the others, he would give it to them. They could decide what to do with it.

THE COURT OF KING GAHLS was known for its luxury in an age when a mere sufficiency satisfied most. The lands on the high plateau were fertile and well watered. Food was easily grown and harvested. There were lakes, streams, and marshes full of fish and fowl, forests full of game, fields full of grass on which sheep and cattle grazed and grew fat. The market gardeners did well, as did the poulterers who provided eggs, the dairy farmers who provided milk, cream, cheese, and butter. The court was the center of all provisioning, each circle around it feeding on the ones farther out. Hay from the outermost provided winter fodder for cattle in the next; the beef fertilized market gardeners in the next; the fancy vegetables and fruit fed the court, which paid for everything in minted gold. The gold came from the mines in the mountains, which were owned by the king. So long as there was enough of everything, everyone benefited. The system was more or less closed. Though the king's coinage had spread throughout Norland, barter was still widely used elsewhere than in Ghastain itself. People who raised food traded it for wood, people who cut wood traded it for food, both traded to people who wove cloth. Coinage was reserved for things one could not trade for: fancy things, imported things, silks from beyond Tingawa, furs from the high north mountains, even a few manufactured things from the Edges at the center of the continent. These things delighted the court of King Gahls in Ghastain, which is what he chose to call both the city and its surroundings after he took the throne.

The city had not merely accumulated, as do most cities; it had been designed. Streets lined with well-built shops and houses and stores radiated from the center of the city, joined by circular roads that spiraled inward from the four city gates. Four simultaneous processions, one entering at each point of the compass, could, and frequently did, wind their way toward the castle at the center. The castle was not a walled fortress but an architectural triumph surrounded by a paved mosaic plaza, decked with towering spires, with stained glass windows that jeweled the refracted light, with enormous bronze-sheathed doors hammered into images of Ghastain and Huold and all the mighty warriors of past times. Inside were marble floors and columns; walls hung with tapestries; furniture made of rare, fragrant woods imported in some former time, before the Sea King had stopped the ships from the east. Windows reached from floor to ceiling, flooding the rooms with light. At night, velvet curtains were drawn across them to keep out the chill. Stoves were built into the walls, and when the weather turned cold, their isinglass windows glowed with heat. All was warm in Ghastain, all were well fed in Ghastain, all were well clothed in Ghastain, all were at the service of the king. And the queen.

On this day, however, the queen was not satisfied with the service she was receiving. Her chamberlain, Chamfray, was seriously ill, and the physicians who served the king could not tell her what it was he suffered from.

"He has no fever, Your Majesty. He has no sign of illness beyond this weakness he complains off. His skin, his heart, his lungs, all appear normal. The weakness may be subjective rather than real. We have no way to test it."

"The weakness is real," she snapped. "I do have ways to test it. He drops things. He stumbles. He gets dizzy."

"He is an elderly man, Your Majesty. The symptoms you describe are those of age. Age is not an illness. It is . . . simply inescapable."

Mirami did not believe it was inescapable. She had learned as much from the Old Dark Man. She took certain drugs herself, created them herself from the sources she had been taught to use. She had given those same drugs to Chamfray. The Old Dark Man had told her the drugs were good only for the one they were designed for originally. She had not believed him at the time, but now she was concerned. She wished she had his books. Alicia had said there were no books in the Old Dark House when she went there. What could he have done with them? The secret to the drugs had been in the books; she had seen the books, seen him referring to the books when he gave her the drugs for the first time. "Only for you, lovely," he had said. "Only because you are so beautiful."

Mirami was well aware she had been created to be beautiful. She had often thought on the matter of beauty. What was it? Why was it? Why did one person think another beautiful, while a second person did not? Why did one person admire a view, a building, a costume, while another did not? Alicia was beautiful and she, too, had been created to be that way.

Well, Chamfray was not beautiful, but he was useful. She depended upon him. He knew everyone, all their secrets, where they were vulnerable, where pressure could be applied. He remembered everything that had ever happened to anyone. He collected stories as porcupines are said to collect fruit: he rolled in it and it stuck to him! As yet, she had found no one who could take his place. Hulix hadn't the brain. Alicia was too . . . shut in. Closed. Though she knew Alicia was clever, very clever, she couldn't tell what Alicia was thinking, and how could someone be trusted when one didn't know what they were thinking? Rancitor was still a boy. He was thirty-one now, but he might always be a boy. He wasn't interested in anything but women and hunting and leading parades. He loved to lead parades in full armor on any one of his huge horses. He loved to lead dances, especially in costume. He loved to lead young women off to bed. As his mother, she had had to dispose of some of them when her son had finished with them, daughters of influential people! A terrible accident, people had said when a body was found. She had fallen off a cliff. She had drowned. She had been trampled by horses.

Rancitor's tastes were odd. She wondered where he had picked up such habits. None of the men Mirami had known had had such leanings. She had forbidden him to take women from the court. She had explained the dangers. A milkmaid, fine. A farmer's daughter, fine. A servant girl, fine. Nobodies, do what you will, a bit of gold will quiet the families. But people of influence? No. She needed such people as friends. Or would soon enough, when King Gahls died.

She went to Chamfray's room. He was lying down on a low couch near a window that looked out upon the plaza and the fountains. Men were sweeping the leaves that had blown in overnight. The day was mild and pleasant.

"Are you feeling better?" she asked with real concern.

Chamfray considered the question, moving his limbs as though testing symptoms. "Not better. No, not really. I think it's some kind of passing thing, you know, something I've eaten, probably. We had that shellfish last week, remember, from Ragnibar Fjord."

"Mussels from the coast. They were packed in ice. Hulix sent them. He said he had enjoyed them."

"Perhaps they came a bit too far. Or the ice was bad. I've heard that if ice freezes from contaminated water, the ice itself is bad."

"Contaminated?"

"Something bad in it. Something that died or was rotten. Where did Hulix get ice?"

"There are high mountains near Kamfelsgard where the ice never melts. People go up and cut great chunks of it with a saw, wrap them in straw, and haul them down the mountain. They put it in a special house at Kamfels Court, a kind of deep cellar where it stays cool, then they use it all summer to keep things cold."

"Ah. Well it was probably the ice. An ice bear probably peed on that particular bit."

She regarded him with something very like fondness. He wasn't a handsome man. Too large a nose, too heavy a jaw, and terribly ungainly. But he was as dependable as the sunrise, and she admired him. The thing she most admired was that he never showed emotion about anything. It was so much easier to deal with life if one didn't have to consider emotions. Of course, Alicia was like that, too, except for her rages. Perhaps it was a useful way to be.

"What are you thinking about?" he asked. He always wanted to know what she was thinking, what she was planning.

"Alicia. I can never tell what she's doing or going to do next. I know she's full of anger at the world, always has been. She was born that way. Sometimes I think the Old Dark Man made a mistake with her; there's too much of him in her."

Chamfray made an amused sound. "Some of me, too."

"Some of you, some of me, some of him. Alicia doesn't know that, though, so be sure not to—"

"I never talk to Alicia about anything. She prefers it that way," Chamfray said.

"So do I. She gets very strange ideas. She seems to be cooperating in the family business, just as one would expect, but then she goes off on these strange tangents about totally insignificant things. Now she's all upset over the fact there are a few Tingawan people up at the abbey. As though it mattered!"

"The princess was Tingawan."

"Yes, she was. And what difference does that make? We own Kamfels and Altamont, we almost own the abbey, and the Thousand Islands are a thousand miles away."

"More than that."

She threw up her hands. "Exactly. At this time of our lives, Tingawa has nothing to do with us or our plans or anything else. It will be years before we turn to Tingawa!"

Chamfray stretched his lips in what passed as a smile. "Yes, Mirami, at least that."

"Well then, let the silly little Tingawan girl do her soul-carrying duties, let her servants take her home, and let us get on with our business!" She heard her voice rising and stopped, hand to throat, listening.

"We're quite alone here," he said. "The way the doors are arranged, no one can hear from the hallway or from below us in the plaza. Are you really concerned about Alicia?"

"It's just that I can never tell what she's thinking. She's like the Old Dark Man. I could never tell with him, either. I still can't understand why it took so long for that Tingawan woman to die. Not that it mattered. It didn't set anything back. We're not ready to do without, you know, yet." She never spoke the name of the king. It would not do to be overheard discussing the king, particularly doing without the king, and what one did in private, one might do without thinking in public. She and Chamfray made it a practice not to mention him by name at all.

Chamfray mused, "Tingawans are skilled physicians. The princess probably had excellent care, strengthening care. Exactly what did Alicia use to kill her?"

"I never asked. She gets pettish if I ask. She says she knows what she's doing."

"She did use poison?"

"Of course. That's what the Old Dark Man taught me to use, and he taught her as well. He told me he would, when I left there. 'You'll have a daughter,' he said. 'I'll teach her what she needs to know.' I suppose he did, though she never went there. I think she lied about not finding any books at all. I think he left books for her in the Old Dark House. He said it was always wise to be elsewhere when people sickened and died, and poison was the surest way to do that. He had a wealth of knowledge, the Old Dark Man."

"I wonder that he died at all, even at his age. How did it happen?"

"It's odd you should ask. I was trying to think earlier today when it was I knew he had died, what the sequence of events was. When Alicia was just a baby, he told me he was leaving possession of Altamont to me; he wrote to me saying so. He never mentioned it again. Then after Hulix was born, when Alicia was about eight—I remember, because that's when I killed Falyrion and Alicia turned odd—some travelers came through with the news that the Old Dark House was empty, that the Old Dark Man was gone. I went there. It was closed, locked. He had never given me a key. No one was seeing to the castle itself, but the farmers were still farming, the stockmen still raising their cattle; everything was going on as before. They told me everything was being managed by an agent who worked for the Port Lords in Wellsport. The Sea King hadn't yet completely shut down the shipping, but the Port Lords were already looking about for other ways to earn a living. They said they had no instructions regarding my taking the place. None at all. Well, I had his letter telling me the place was mine, but after looking at that dreadful, gray, dead pile of stone, I decided not to bother with it. You and I had other things going on, as you remember."

"So you don't really know that your Old Dark Man is dead."

"What else? He was already ancient, and he's gone. When Rancitor spoke to the king, when the king had Alicia made duchess and gave her title to the place, the people in Wellsport gave her the keys and told her to take over. She was still very young, fourteen, I think. She didn't go there for several years. She wouldn't have gone at all if the Old Dark Man had still been alive."

"Did you ever wonder about him?"

"Wonder how?"

"When you speak of him, he seems to be a very strange, almost unearthly kind of creature, and I find myself wondering if he was really human. Do you think he was?"

She stiffened, her face suffused with blood. "I saw him, Chamfray. I saw quite enough of him, head to toe, uncovered. He was just like all other men. Taller, that's all. Very dark skinned, not brown, more a dark gray, but just like every other man. All men are more or less alike!"

Something about his last question had disturbed her, so he waited for a time before asking, "And you haven't had any reason to go there since?"

She took a deep breath. "No. As I said: it's an ugly, uncomfortable pile of stone. The cellars were full of spiders and rats. The rooms were piled with books and ancient papers. As a child, I lived in the little gatehouse. I had a nursemaid, then a governess. I had a tutor. I even had a riding master. It was warm in the little house. It was clean. The food was good. Every time I went into the Old Dark House, I spent the whole time either shivering or rat catching. No, I've not been back there since Alicia went there." Of course, she hadn't spent the whole time shivering or rat catching. There were other things the Old Dark Man had required that had been far worse than shivering or rat catching. "Why do you ask?"

He shrugged. "Alicia was always fussy about things. She was quite willing to kill any servant girl who didn't do the dusting properly, so I was just wondering how she could bear to live there, if it is as you say."

"She has no doubt cleaned it up. She may even have redone the inside of it. It wasn't dilapidated, just terribly dirty and uncomfortable. Altamont has plenty of income. Alicia may even have left the Port Lords in control and be living off the income from the farms and herds. Most of the produce is sold in the fiefdoms along the coast anyhow, and if I had the place, that's the way I'd have done it."

They said nothing more that day. The next day, Chamfray was worse, and worse yet the day after that. A week later he died. The doctors asked if they could cut him, to find out what had killed him. Mirami told them yes, for she wanted to know. They told her it looked as though he had melted inside. They had no idea what could have caused it, nor did she. None of her poisons did any such thing. The doctors said some fungi had spores that became liquescent in the same way; perhaps he had eaten something contaminated by a fungus. Mirami was too upset to ask whether such fungi grew upon mountains where ice was cut.

A BIRD BROUGHT A MESSAGE from the abbey to the Old Dark House. It contained the material Alicia had asked for, and she made the proper use of it, sending the resultant little capsule to the abbey just the way she had sent the same kind of capsule to Ghastain. A long time ago she'd found out where the bird towers at the abbey were, quite close enough to the abbot's quarters.

Later that day, she received a message from her mother asking her to come to Ghastain. Mirami was feeling lonely, as her old friend Chamfray had died. Before Alicia rejoined her mother, however, she had one thing to take care of. Since she intended to deal with Jenger eventually, she needed to have the seeker device start looking for him. The hairs she had kept in her bedroom would provide the material. Wherever Jenger's particular code was found, the machine would show it as a red light on a map. The map was huge. It covered the entire continent. Alicia had no idea where the Old Dark Man could have found such a map, but she did know the farther away Jenger was, the longer it would take for the seeker to find him. If she set the seeker in motion before going to Ghastain, it would have her answer by the time she returned.

Since the Old Dark Man had gone, she had used the fatal cloud on three victims: the princess, Chamfray, and the abbot. She had one prepared for Jenger. It was in her little cubby, ready to use when she found him. Now she would create two more. Another one of Jenger, for the seeker to use in finding him. And on mature consideration—that was a phrase the Old Dark Man had often used, "on mature consideration"— one tube would go with her to Ghastain. She had collected the material for this one in Kamfels years ago, after her father died . . . had been killed! Just to keep her accounts balanced with Mirami.

When Solo Winger received a bird from the Old Dark House carrying a message tube that was a bit different from the usual ones, he did not open it. He had been warned to watch very carefully for anything from that source. He waited for a proper time and took it to the quarters of the person he continued to call the Tingy-away woman. She took it into her hand, looked at it closely, and nodded.

"I'll take care of it, Brother Winger. Believe me, it will do none of us any harm. By the way, if the abbey needed to be out of touch for a while with either of these places, the Old Dark House or Vulture Tower, what would be the best way?"

He thought about it. "The bes' way'd be some fool kid cleanin' after the birds leavin' cages open, so alla House anna Tower birds got out an wen' home. They c'd sen' here, but abbey cudn't sen back. And they cudn't sen' much 'cause I keep a count. I know zackly where my birds is. House's got two, Tower's got none, Ghastain's got three."

Precious Wind looked him squarely in the eye and repeated words the prior had used: "I don't suppose an illiterate simpleton like Solo Winger could arrange for that to happen?"

Solo Winger grinned only inwardly as he replied with perfect enunciation: "Oh, anyone as stupid as I might get awkwardly inebriated and commit some unconscionable impropriety. God knows, all total ignoramuses are known to be completely irresponsible."

Later that night, Precious Wind placed the little capsule on the stone floor outside the prior's door. Through that door she could hear the snorts and snores of a man deeply asleep. She stepped on it, crushing it, closely observing the wisp of fog that came from the crumbled thing. It swirled, swirled again, and promptly went under the door. Precious Wind smiled to herself. *So much for sending three assassins after me, old man. Tingawa is a very old country. It has forgotten more about assassination than you blundering Norlander conspirators will ever learn.*

She had arranged a meeting with the men from Woldsgard this evening, after Oldwife Gancer and Nettie Lean would be asleep. The old woman was recovering from her grief over Xulai and had come to believe the girl was well, somewhere, and would in good time be restored to them, so she'd been eating and sleeping better. Nettie was keeping close watch on her. Even Precious Wind had come to believe Xulai's return was not impossible, in time, and if the old woman dwelt in that hope, she would not cast doubt upon it. Provided that this abbey nastiness was cleared up, including finding each and every man the prior had corrupted, or perhaps simply co-opted. She went to her meeting with that firmly in mind.

The five Wolds men were in one of the abbey gathering places, those tavernlike places frequented by both men and women who work all day and have either too little or too much family life to keep them at home. The five were known to be old friends, so no one would question their being together with another old friend from the same place. They drank beer. Precious Wind disliked beer greatly, but it was a drink that would draw no attention whatsoever, so she put the mug on the table before her and pretended to take a sip every now and then, trying not to breathe the sour smell of it.

"So we've been asking," said Bartelmy in a low voice, though his face smiled and his eyes crinkled as though he were telling a joke.

Bartelmy had it in him to be a good spy, she thought, unlike Black Mike, who always looked as though he were about to assault someone.

"We've been asking this, asking that, what kind of work we can do to make ourselves useful. I've been saying I'm a good bowman, do they need a good bowman. Mike says he's a good one to keep order if order needs keeping; you know the kind of thing, Precious Wind."

"And?"

"And I've had a sergeant or two say I might find a place with the abbey armor, and another fellow said the watch has openings, and like that. But Mike, he had a nibble from someone saying a certain high-up person has occasional very-well-paid work for people who aren't afraid to get their hands dirty."

Mike lifted his mug and muttered around it, "So I asks, hands, or something else? And the guy gives me a look and says, so if it was something else? And I say, I'd hafta know what, because I don't mind doin' to, but I don't want to be done to. Like that. He said he'd be in touch."

"So then," Pecky said, "Mike gave me the nod, and I followed the guy to see who he talked to, which was a certain bunch of men in the watch. Altogether, there's about twenty of 'em. All single. They all live in one of the dormitories, and I said to myself, well, now, their living together makes it a lot easier to know who's involved with 'em."

"And?"

"And it's just them. All of 'em. We can't find any one of 'em who isn't."

"So me'n Clive, we've been gettin' acquainted with this one and that one," said Willum. "I hear from each and every one, prior's a man who pays well."

"Don't push it," said Precious Wind. "Let them come to you. And don't worry if they don't come to you. The prior may have a change in plans." She gave them one of her rare and radiant smiles, toasted them with her mug, set it down, and left them.

Black Mike switched his empty mug for her full one and drank it down. "We'll do that, lady," he said to no one in particular. Sometimes he dreamed about Precious Wind. He was not enough of a fool to attempt making any such dream come true.

PRECIOUS WIND MADE A SHOWY bustle, going hither and thither at the abbey, telling people she was departing soon. Off to the southlands. Off to find a ship from Merhaven. Going to return to her native land. Farewell, good people. And so on. Meantime, she was concentrating on leaving no loose ends. In making a mental inventory of everything she had done, heard, thought, and planned, she came at last to the large wooden crate that had been secreted in the bottom of the dray. Bartelmy showed her where the dray was, where the crate was, and she found the corner that had held the ideogram with a hole gnawed neatly through it. Xulai's furry friend could well have done the gnawing.

"She's with Abasio," said Precious Wind to herself. "He rescued her. If she had had the thing with her and had read the instructions, she obviously wouldn't have needed rescuing. The thing would have brought her back on the wings of the wind. So, she didn't have it. The thing isn't in our quarters so she didn't leave it here. Abasio left the abbey before she did, which means he could have had it before he left. If he didn't unwrap it and read the instructions—which I'm fairly sure he would not have done, as it was hers, not his—he wouldn't carry it around. So, he'd leave it in his wagon."

She wandered restlessly through a cloistered arm of the abbey, staring at the fountain at its center. The dyer's wagon was more than merely distinctive. It was unmistakable. If anyone, Bear, for instance, saw that wagon in Merhaven . . . If one of the duchess's spies saw it . . . well, the duchess had never seen the dyer's wagon in the same group as Xulai. Abasio had had better sense than that. Nonetheless, both Xulai and the wagon had come from the same direction and might be linked in the duchess's mind, so chances were very good that Abasio and Xulai had left the wagon behind. If they hadn't thought to take the package with them, which was very possible considering that Xulai might have had a hard time during her abduction and Abasio was thinking about her, rather than anything else, then the thing might still be . . . in the wagon.

So where was the wagon? Abasio had reached the tower in time to rescue Xulai and, possibly, probably, kill Jenger. This meant he had not been more than a day's journey away, which meant he had taken the wagon less than a day's journey south of the abbey. This indicated he had not been far off the road where he had hidden the wagon and waited for Xulai.

Precious Wind went to the library and, in the absence of her friend, Wordswell, asked one of the other librarians to provide her with a map of the surrounding countryside. There were several. She spent the afternoon pondering them. Farms were shown. Dwellings were shown. Ruins were shown. She drew a careful mental arc, one day's ride, from the Vulture Tower south, not far from the road. Included in that arc were half a dozen farms, a few ruins. One, in particular, caught her eye.

"What does it mean if there's a little triangle by the name?" she asked.

"Means the family died out," said the young woman who was helping her. "Some of the farms and mines and things around here were leased by the abbey to certain families, oh, generations ago. So long as the family wanted to go on, the abbey let the leases alone. They were always leases whereby the family paid in crops or wood or metal ore or something, not money. But if the family died out, we would note it on the maps and in the books. It meant in future we could include that land or whatever in the abbey plans."

"This shows a house," said Precious Wind.

"It shows where there was a house. It might be empty or fallen in or even disappeared."

Precious Wind nodded, thanked her, and returned the maps to their proper folders in the proper drawers. She had mentally marked three possibilities that met her criteria as to distance and location. She chose to take the hop-skip they had driven from Woldsgard. It was a vehicle that could be drawn easily by one horse on the level, but she felt two, hitched tandem, would be better for hills. Though quite small, the hop-skip was large enough to carry a significant load of supplies: a small tent, blankets, food, some oats for the horses, water bottles, and her saddle. She might need a saddle; there were places a wheeled vehicle could not go. Willum and Clive had modified the harness so it could be either a single or tandem hitch. Two horses would be better, in case one might grow lame.

She supplied the little carriage and made a tearful farewell to Old-wife Gancer and Nettie. Though Nettie had been happily surprised to find Aunt Belika both able and willing to forgive old arguments and joyous to have a niece, she still considered Precious Wind a good friend and was sad at her leaving.

"When I find Xulai, Oldwife, I'll send you a message; I'm taking some pigeons from the abbey. I'll be able to let you know that she's well. You know she has to return to Tingawa."

"It's just, since she's gone, and now you're going, I'd like to go home," said Oldwife.

"To Woldsgard?" This should not have surprised Precious Wind, but it did. It was a loose end she had not thought of.

Oldwife had her reasons. "To my little house there, yes. To my kin-folk. And the men, they'd like to go, too. Bartelmy was telling me. Probably Nettie as well, though I'm not sure."

Precious Wind shrugged mentally. This would only take a day or so more before she could leave, and it had to be done. These people were her family as well as Xulai's. She hugged the old woman, saying, "There's no reason you shouldn't go. I'll talk to the men now. They may want to leave some of the furnishings here, no reason to labor taking them back. They have the dray, the company-trot, and the wagon. All the horses and mules are still here except the two I'm taking and except for a few up-and-down miles north of the abbey, it's all downhill from here until you reach the Woldsroad. Xulai's horse should go back to Woldsgard. When she returns, that's where she'll go. It was home for her."

Oldwife broke into tears. "It was home for her. I heard her . . . her . . . the duke telling her he was sending her home and I saw her poor little face. Poor thing. Where did he go, do you think?"

"None of us know, Oldwife. He wasn't going to endanger anyone by telling them where he was going or if he would ever come back. But there's no reason you and the men shouldn't go home. The man here has pigeons for Woldsgard. I'll send Hallad, Prince Orez, a message saying you'd like to come home. He may even send an escort for you."

This new complication did take another day, as she had to wait for the librarian and the abbot and the other people in their party to return from their tour of inspection out and around the South Watch Tower. Upon their return, they learned from the prior's servant that his master was very ill.

Precious Wind arranged a meeting with Wordswell that night, hoping she could tie all the loose ends into one bundle and place it in his lap.

"They say the prior's ill," said Wordswell. "Do you think he is seriously ill?"

"I think he'll die," said Precious Wind. "Probably in a few days."

"How very sad," said the librarian. "Will anyone here particularly miss him?"

"If I were you, I'd pay particular attention to anyone who does," she said, handing him the list she and the Woldsgard men had compiled. "The men listed here will probably miss the pay he's been giving them to do murder and mayhem. It's possible there are others, but we doubt it. Might be a good idea if this bunch went somewhere else for a while. And maybe didn't come back."

"And the three who followed you?"

"They haven't returned. It's not unusual for that kind of men to disappear rather than confront the anger of the person who sent them."

"Really." He regarded her with something like awe.

Precious Wind nodded. "It has been known to happen, yes. I have one more burden to place upon you. Oldwife Gancer, possibly Nettie Lean, and certainly the men from Woldsgard would like to go home. Actually, Bartelmy would probably like to go hunting for Xulai, but it's best he not do so. He was sweet to her when he thought she was a child, as little maids and men sometimes are, but nothing can come of it, so best he go home and find himself another sweetheart. He's a lovesome boy and will not want for takers. So, I'd like you to send a message to Hallad, Prince Orez, telling him they'd like to come home and asking if he would care to send an escort."

Wordswell smiled. "Prince Orez should be advised they're coming, certainly, but I think the abbot will send an escort from here so they can leave promptly. It's a round-trip either way, for them or for us. I think we'll send about a hundred men, including the ones on this list. The officers in charge will know that this . . . how many, twenty . . . can be left at Woldsgard. We will already have sent Woldsgard our suggestion for dealing with them."

"I agree that Prince Orez's men will find it less difficult to dispose of them than their own mess-mates might do. The Woldsgard folk may take their freight back. It'll be easier than when we came, it's downhill most of the way."

"As you say," he murmured. "And what of you, Precious Wind?"

"I am going to hear evensong in the abbey tonight. I am going to hear morning psalms at dawn. Then I am going to hitch up my horses and go south, to Merhaven. Solo Winger has given me pigeons. I am taking a little carriage so I can carry the cage and their food. I will let you know."

"Take half a dozen birds," said Wordswell, feeling unaccustomed tears gathering in his eyes. "Let us know how you fare. And, Precious Wind, if you can . . . let me know what all of this was about. It wasn't about a Xakixa, a soul carrier, I know that much. That foul woman in Ghastain and her daughter, they may have thought it was about them and their machinations, but I know it wasn't. I would hate to die not knowing what the reason was for it all."

"My friend," she said, controlling a strong urge to hug him, "I know you for a brave and honest man. I have written here what it is all about." She handed him an envelope, sealed with her own seal. "You may read this, but only after I have gone, for I may not answer questions and you will be full of them. Read it once I am out of sight and then destroy it, burn it. I hope you will not die for many, many years, but when the time comes, you should not die unsatisfied. To my mind, the worst thing about death is not knowing how the story ends. And, who knows, we may yet meet again. I may even be able to tell you how it is working out."

Precious Wind was usually kind, but she had a streak of cruelty in her. She knew it and sometimes grieved over it as a character flaw. On the other hand, some of the things she needed to do could not be done without a certain simple cruelty, and she tried never to gloat over it. The prior, however, had infuriated her, for he had gloated in the same way that the duchess gloated. A hot little flame of superiority and entitlement had gusted off both of them. Each of them had breathed a sly little wind of greed. The duchess was out of reach, but it would be good to tell at least one of them that it had been noticed.

She found the prior's servant and asked if she could be of any help to the prior. Tingawans, she said, were schooled in medicine and perhaps she could help.

The servant inquired. The prior, in great pain and considerable fear, would clutch at any straw.

Precious Wind arrived to express her sympathy. "It is a pity Xulai is not here," she said when he had told her what he could of his symptoms. "She was far better than I as a physician."

"She was only a girl," the prior panted. "I don't understand."

"Oh, it's partly learning, sir, but it's partly talent, inborn. She would have known many cures that I do not. Especially since the only thing I know of that fits the symptoms you describe is impossible. Such symptoms as you have are said to have been caused by a mechanism that has not been known since the Big Kill. It could use such things as hair and fingernail clippings and spit to create a . . . what was it called? A virus? Something of that kind. The virus would find the pattern of the person it was created to find, and it would destroy that pattern. The person would simply melt away." She shook her head in emphatic negation. "Nothing known today can do that! Such mechanisms no longer exist!" Looking deep into his horrified eyes, she reached forward to pat the hand that quivered uncontrollably upon the blanket.

"Now, if I could find the duke's treasure that he intended as a reward for me, and for Bear, I might be able to hire the one person in all Norland who can cure that disease I mentioned! It would take all that treasure, believe me. The remedy is known to be effective but it is hideously expensive. However, that's simply fantasy. Since we know it can't be that illness, that cure wouldn't help. I'm sure it's just a winter cold. Nothing serious."

She gave him her mostly kindly, brilliant smile and left him, testing her conscience as one might test a tooth with one's tongue, to see if it ached. It did not.

Behind her, in the prior's quarters, the prior thought dreadfully of things he had not considered before. Of the fact that the abbot had been away recently; of the fact that when the abbot went away, which he did rarely, his rooms might have been cleaned. Of the fact that his own rooms might have contained the very things he had found in the abbot's quarters. Of the fact that Tingawans were said to be subtle and secret and knowledgeable about many things.

Surely not. Surely not. It could not be. The Tingawan woman who had just visited him was not that clever. None of those people from Woldsgard had been that clever except perhaps for the girl herself, and she hadn't been here. Well, there were others on the road south to take care of her if she went that way. The one called Bear. He was there.

No, it had to be that woman, at Altamont. She had done it. Perhaps she and her mother were cleaning up after themselves. Or, more likely, the duchess was conspiring against her mother! No love lost there, she had made that clear. So, no love lost the other way, either. And Mirami might know of a way to cure this! To stop it! Stop it happening!

He called for his servant. He wrote. He asked that the message be sent to Ghastain.

His servant returned. The boy who cleaned the bird lofts had mistakenly released all the birds for Ghastain. They had no way to reach Ghastain except by messenger.

The prior wrote again and sent for one of his special men, those who did particular jobs for him, such as ride very long distances very fast on the relay horses that they'd been sending to Benjobz recently, for Benjobz was going to be a waystation for vastly increased traffic when the abbey and Wold were brought into the king's lands.

The servant returned. The particular men the prior wanted had been sent to do a reconnaissance of the road down to Benjobz Inn. There were said to be brigands in that area, molesting travelers, and the abbot had sent a hundred men from the abbey to seek out their camps along the road while escorting the people from Woldsgard home. The men the prior wanted were with them.

The prior asked the servant to get a small box from the hidden compartment in the top of his armoire and take it to Precious Wind. Ask her to come see him.

The servant left with the box, and no one came to replace him.

The prior thought furiously. He tried to get out of bed and couldn't. His legs folded under him. He vomited blood all over himself. He felt a hideous pain. Both his men and the duchess had killed easily, often, but none of them had ever mentioned causing pain. As he passed from screaming to throat-blocked silence, from agonized thrashing to excruciating immobility, it seemed impossible to him that he was alone in this room and no one came to offer him any of the drugs that he knew, *he knew*, could be given for pain.

He opened his eyes, at the last, to see Wordswell standing at the foot of the bed, regarding him with solemn sorrow not unmixed with satisfaction, and *he knew* the omission had not been accidental. If it had been the abbot standing there, he would not have allowed his prior to suffer this torment. The abbot was too kind. But the abbot didn't know. The prior had made sure the abbot didn't know . . . about a lot of things.

ON THE ROAD WEST OF Benjobz Inn, the troop from the abbey cantered down the road, not so fast it would lose the wagons that followed, not so slowly as to bore the armored men who took every opportunity to scour the nearby forest for the brigands who might be there. Oldwife Gancer and Nettie shared the wagon, driven by Bartelmy. Each of the menfolk wore one of the gay scarves Xulai had knitted for them, the fringed ends trailing over their shoulders. They were going home. Of them all, only two deeply mourned the fact that Xulai would not be there when they arrived: Oldwife, for a near daughter lost; Bartelmy, for a near sweetheart, ever dreamed of, never really gained.

On the road south of the abbey, Precious Wind drove her little carriage at a great pace, the wolves keeping even with her inside the shade of the forest. Sewn into her garments were the contents of the box the prior had sent to her, the gems that had made up virtually all of the treasure Justinian had sent. She had been surprised. Considering that the prior had had the treasure for some time, he had used remarkably little of it. He hadn't even thought to ask the return of his receipt.

ON THE ROAD TO MERHAVEN, a group of travelers had come to a pleasant meadow between the road and the shining crimson surface of Red Lake, some distance to the west. The lake received a good deal of its water as runoff from red clay country, giving it its name. The travelers had set up their usual evening encampment, little tents, little wagons, a few campfires with kettles hung above them. Off to one side two brothers had built their own stingy fire, cleared their own patch of ground on which to erect their own two-man tent against the wet, if any.

"I wish I had some idea of what's happening back at the abbey," said Chippy to his bearded older brother. "Don't you . . . Bram?"

"Hearing nothing is sometimes better than hearing bad news," said the older man, the one scratching at his beard. Though it had been growing for days, he wasn't used to it yet and it itched him continuously. They had traveled with a considerable train of folks headed south along the main road to Elsmere, lagging at the rear of the procession, not so far back as to look separate from it, not so close as to involve them in unnecessary conversation. Occasionally they would move aside for a faster-moving horse, an abbey messenger or some post rider in a hurry. They'd passed a number of posts on their way. Blue always whinnied at the corrals and received a whinny in return. Chippy's horse was more laconic, and their mule brayed only when he didn't get the oats or horse biscuit he expected. Along the way, Chippy and Bram had managed to get hold of the necessaries to make horse biscuits almost as well accepted as those the Horsemaster had made back in Woldsgard, though there were a couple of herbs that no one seemed to know of.

They had come far enough south and far enough down the mountains that late autumn was still with them rather than the winter that had taken the highlands around the abbey. There had been no more snow, only a few light rains. When the group stopped each night to make camp, there was still plenty of edible grass for the horses and mules. The group was large and well armed enough to discourage any wandering bands of ruffians. They did have some elderly folk, however, and some women who weren't accustomed to travel, so they made slow time on the road. Dawdling, Chippy called it. Safe, said Bram. Better slow and easy, part of a sizeable group rather than quick and easy prey, part of nothing.

There had been nothing remarkable about the journey except that Chippy had several times produced another of the strange little orbs, each time without the pain the first one had caused, each time discovered in the morning in the blankets he had been wrapped in. He had sewn them into the undershift as they were found, not bothering to mention the fact.

Their current campground was observed, to the amusement of its inhabitants, by two enormous eyes that peered at them from above a ridge of mountains west of them, beyond the lake. These were the two pinnacles of Frog Eye Mountain, two sheer, polished stone surfaces that shone with reflected light and were capped with forested ridges that much resembled eyelids. Their attention was drawn, however, to movement on the road, far below them, where an indiscriminate black dot had become a dot with legs and then a dot with arms as well. The rider had familiar characteristics.

Chippy sighed. "That's Bear, isn't it?"

"Looks very much like him."

"He won't know you. You look completely different with a beard, specially a black one."

"Unfortunately, you haven't grown a beard."

"I think I can if I set my mind to it," Chippy said. "I've been worried we might run into him. I hoped he'd gone on to Merhaven and taken a boat from there, but here he is coming back. I'm going behind a bush."

Chippy actually went behind several bushes, as people who were traveling occasionally had to do, taking out the little folding shovel with some ostentation just in case someone looked back. There was no need at the moment, for the only digging Chippy/Xulai was doing was deep into him/herself. The hair follicles were there. Everyone had them. On women they usually made a soft, invisible down, but with proper concentration . . . though not too much, because the others had seen her clean shaven this morning, every morning. She considered having all the hair on her head fall out but decided against it. If it took this much effort to grow stubble, how long would it take her to grow her hair back?

When Chippy returned to his brother, Bram looked at him and

nodded. "Not bad. Your hair's a lot darker than mine. You look a villain. Like Black Mike."

"Black Mike's a nice man. You always said so."

"You might lengthen the mustache just a little, especially at the corners of your mouth. You have a very . . ." He stopped, censored what he had been going to say, substituting, "distinctive mouth." He went back to staring at the approaching rider.

Chippy concentrated on his whiskers. "Better?"

"I don't think he'd know you. If he sees you. I'd recommend going in the tent."

The horse approaching was within hailing distance, close enough to see that Bear was frowning and angry.

"I wonder what he's upset about now?" murmured Bram.

"He was going to take a boat to Tingawa. My guess is he couldn't find one."

The self-appointed caravan leaders had ridden off onto a level bit of grassland and begun to arrange themselves and their wagons for the night. Bram and Chippy, as was their custom, took themselves and their horses off to one side, not far, unsaddled the horses, and took the packs off the mule, letting the animals roll and scratch before giving them their ration of oats. Meantime they pitched their own little tent. Fisher, who rode in Chippy's cloak pocket during the days' travel, went through the tent and out the other end. There were small dirt hills a bit farther into the field. That meant burrowers, which meant fresh meat, and Fisher was of a mind to find his own rations and stay out of Bear's way.

Bear had talked with this one for a time, then that one, then made the rounds of the others in the group. Before long he came stalking over to Bram, Chippy having made himself scarce in the tent.

"Where from?"demanded Bear.

"Us? My brother'n me?" said Bram in quite a deep, unfamiliar voice.

"Yeah. Got any news from anyplace?"

"None I know of. Came from a place east of Ghastain, know where that is?"

"I do. Up on the highlands. You come past Benjobz?"

"Yeah. Din stop. Got no money to be payin' inns."

"Where headed?"

"Where the rest of 'em's headed. Elsmere, then down t'Merhaven. Got a cousin there name Rabbik needs help carpenterin'. No work where we was."

"There's armor coming up this road."

"From where?" Bram asked, leaving his mouth open to swallow the answer, looking purposefully half-witted.

"Abbey troops. I met dispatch riders coming ahead of the troops. They say they went almost all the way to Woldsgard, then got called home. All a mistake."

"Well, tha's armies," said Bram. "My pa says left foot never knows what right foot's doin' in a army."

"It's light yet," said Bear with annoyance. "Think I'll make a bit more distance before I give it up tonight. Went all the way to Merhaven to get a ship. They got a ship. Will they let me take the ship? No, they will not! Ship's reserved for a certain person. They won't let me use it unless I'm with the certain person, so I got to go all the way back to the abbey and see if they've found her."

"Was she lost?"

Bear flushed. "In a manner of speaking. She may be back by now. Maybe. Or if she's not, her friend'll be there. The friend would be all right. They'd let her have the ship. She's from Tingawa. That's who the ship is for, either of the women from Tingawa, but not me!" He belched an ugly gust of laughter. "I'm from Tingawa but oh, no, not me."

"Good luck," said Bram. "Hope you find 'em."

"Oh, I'll find 'em."

When the retreating horseman had gone over a hill, Chippy crawled from the tent. "No need for the whiskers," he said. "But I know how to do it now. I can do it quicker next time. Fisher's hunting his dinner."

The older brother was staring after the retreating horseman. "He's looking for Precious Wind. That worries me a little."

"I don't think we need to worry about Precious Wind," Chippy said sadly. "I'm just sorry for Bear. He was . . . he really was a good man. If they'd let him alone, he still would be."

8

Merhaven and the Sea

WHEN PRECIOUS WIND RODE SOUTH FROM THE ABBEY, she kept in mind the direction and placement of the three ruins where Abasio might have hidden his wagon. When the first appeared, a group of half-collapsed buildings off to her right, she at once discarded them as a possibility. The area was too clearly visible from the abbey walls. Looking back, she could see individual guards moving back and forth atop that gray mass, stopping occasionally to use their distance glasses. Seeing people use them always made her wonder why it was that some things had survived from the Before Time while others had totally disappeared. Even in this barbaric place and time, Precious Wind reflected, people made glass and ground lenses, though the ones made in Norland were poor compared to those made in Tingawa. Glassmaking had survived, smelting ores and working metal had survived, though many alloys recorded in the histories were now almost impossible to make. Electronics were no more. Architecture had retreated to a time far more ancient than the centuries just before the Big Kill. No building reached higher now than the towers of the abbey: stone could not be piled on stone interminably, not even with so many flying buttresses that the buildings seemed half-air. Abasio had spoken of much higher towers far to the east, now half-drowned, but Precious Wind had never seen such things.

Her second possible location was identified only by an overgrown road leading away to the right, but the piles of rotted wood and rubbish at its end could have concealed nothing larger than a mouse's nest. Only the arrangement of the piles in vaguely rectangular shapes spoke of their having been a dwelling, a barn, perhaps a cowshed or stables.

The third possibility noted on the map was to the left along a straight section of the roadway, the only straight section for some miles. When she came to it, she noted the outcroppings of red stone on her left, like a dotted line, and when the road eventually veered to the right, she knew she had missed the ruin shown on the map. She turned the hop-skip, went back almost to the start of the straight stretch, and let the horses stand while she walked along the edge of the forest. If she had not known the wagon must be there she would not have found it as readily. The wagon, with all its paraphernalia, was inside the three-walled wreckage of a house, the drooping roof covering it from the sky, chopped limbs and small trees camouflaging the gap where the front wall had once been. The horse had simply walked through the open side and out the back door, leaving the wagon sitting under the roof, composedly untroubled, its pots and vats tied down, its window and door neatly closed and locked.

Now what? She was looking for a thing she had seen only once, years ago, when she had taken it from the hands of its keepers to wrap both the thing and its sheaf of instructions to be placed among Xu-i-lok's court dresses: a stiff blue packet holding a gadget about the size of a hen's egg. Where would Abasio have hidden it? She picked the lock on the door and went in, examining everything carefully and in great detail.

At the back of the wagon, a bed stretched all the way from side to side, long enough for a tall man, wide enough for two sleepers. Either Abasio and Xulai had slept together or Abasio had made a bed on the narrow floor. Precious Wind considered the implications of this, finding a slight embarrassment in the presumption. The relationship between the two was, in one sense, none of her affair. In another sense it was of overwhelming importance and interest to an enormous number of living people and would have been to a greater number long dead. She set the matter aside. If there was nothing one could do to affect a situation, it wasted energy to think about it.

The outside edge of the bed had legs that folded flat beneath it; the back edge was hinged against the wall. When the front side was tilted down, the mattress was held in place by straps. Flat against the wall above the bed was a hinged worktable, and when it was folded down, it revealed a window. The bed, slanted down as it was, left space beneath the table for the worker's legs. Precious Wind smiled with real enjoyment at the ingenuity. The workmanship spoke of a craftsman's hands coupled with a nimble, sagacious mind. He had been the son of a farmer's daughter, she had been told, and his father had been a leader of men—not a particularly evil man by the standards of his time and place, certainly not a good man, but an intelligent one.

Forward of bed and table, cupboards lined the sidewalls, every one of them full of the tools, supplies, and implements that were, she supposed, essential either to the dyer's art or to Abasio's survival. A tiny, double-walled stove was built into the cupboards on the side opposite the door, with spaces open at the bottom to allow cool air to flow in, be warmed, rise upward and out a vent above. Atop the stove was an iron kettle, its base fitting snugly into a recess so that it would not slide or tip. The smokestack was carefully held by metal brackets away from the surrounding wood. Every detail spoke of care, and time, and thought. She herself could have lived in this wagon quite comfortably. The only thing she would have done to improve it for herself would have been to add books and a musical instrument, for there was no sign of either books or music, though Abasio had seemed familiar with both. Perhaps he sang to himself.

The roof and floor were made up of full-length tongued planks laid lengthwise, front to back. She saw the only exception when she kicked the mat that lay just inside the door. In that one place, above the right front wheel, a short piece had been inserted. Before she trifled with it, she went outside and crawled under the wagon. As she had thought likely, the wagon was double floored, for these boards ran from side to side. It was probably double roofed as well, with the cupboards on the side walls fulfilling the same insulating function, keeping out winter's cold and holding the heat from the little stove. Back inside, she found a sharp chisel in one of the cupboards and pried until the short section shrieked out of its place, revealing a floor stuffed with straw. When she probed into it, carefully, with a knife blade, she found the bundle she had wrapped in Tingawa, years ago.

Precious Wind bowed her head to let sudden and unexpected tears fall onto the thing she held. She let them flow. Inevitably, some days were harder than others. The ones when nothing much happened could be harder than days in which every moment was spent in conflict and confusion. Being at war kept her from remembering. When threats came from every side, one stayed on perpetual alert, one assessed, one decided, acted, moved on, over and over. *Zagit-gaot* and *rakit-gaot*, senders and doers of evil, had given her little time to mourn for Xu-i-lok. Her kinswoman. Her *nariba-ama*, treasured sister. They had grown up together. When Xu-i-lok knew she was dying, it was Precious Wind she had asked for. It was into Precious Wind's protection she had given Xulai, and thereafter Precious Wind had been Xulai's protector, guide, watcher, teacher, mother, aunt, older sister. Oldwife had helped, of course, fulfilling a grandma's role, and Xu-i-lok herself had done what she could with what strength she had. No one had guessed she had enough to last as long as she did. Perhaps Precious Wind had helped her live that long, for Xulai. Perhaps Xulai herself had helped, more than she knew. Xulai. Xu-i-lok's child. Lok-i-xan's granddaughter.

Precious Wind had sworn protection for Xulai, not merely privately, as she had been asked to do, but officially, at the temple, with Lok-i-xan sitting cross legged on the witness bench. In Tingawa, oaths were taken seriously. One might be killed trying to fulfill an oath, there was no disgrace in that, but being forsworn while still alive and able to fight was a disgrace to one's clan, a disgrace washed out, if at all, only by one's own blood. The validity of an oath was a matter for the priesthood. If an oath maker was brought in, still alive but crippled past movement or intention, the priests could declare the oath fulfilled, or they could refuse to do so, thereby moving the oath onto the family of the oathbound. Precious Wind had never thought of breaking her oath to Xu-i-lok, and she was still bound by it. Additionally, privately, Precious Wind had sworn vengeance, no oath necessary, and there was much of that yet to do. She had also laid a mirror curse upon Alicia, upon Mirami, to reflect the evil they did back upon them. So far as she knew, the duchess was as yet untouched, her mother was as yet untouched. Mirror curses were not magical or supernatural in any way. They were merely statements of intention, communicated to the universe: *This person has done great evil. Let evil return upon them. If they hunger, do not feed them. If they are drowning, let them drown. If they thirst, let them go dry.* Though the duchess and her mother had not yet been repaid, so far they had been robbed of their prey! Xulai was in hiding. Justinian had gone so quickly they could not track him.

Months before she left Woldsgard, Precious Wind had reminded Justinian of what must be done prior to his leaving. Every room must be cleaned to the walls. Every curtain, every blanket, every carpet, every tapestry. In the bird lofts, every door to every cage, every fragment of dust. From the stables, every piece of harness he might have touched, every saddle. In the armory, every bow, every sword. In the wine cellars, every bottle he had racked. At Netherfields, the very place on the floor of the nave where he had lain the night after Xu-i-lok's entombment had to be scrubbed. No trace of him could remain.

At the princess's direction, he had shaved his head years ago and had since worn a cap or a wig made of dead men's hair. When he trimmed his beard or cut his fingernails and toenails, he burned the clippings in a little clay furnace Precious Wind had made for him. Almost invariably, he ate his meals alone, scrupulously cleaning the dishes when he had finished. When in company, Precious Wind herself watched everything he touched and later saw to his wineglass, his dishes, the fork he used, the knife he used, the napkin he used. This had not endeared her to Dame Cullen, but then, nothing endeared anyone to Dame Cullen. It was enough that Dame Cullen hated Altamont with sullen ferocity. It was enough that Cook and Dame Cullen and the other household people knew they were protecting the duke and thereby protecting themselves.

"May all holy things assure he left nothing behind the *zagit-gaot* could use to find him," Precious Wind muttered now, angrily wiping her eyes. She had not had time to mourn before, and she did not have time now. One day, in Tingawa, when the light burned over the name of Xu-i-lok, she would cut and burn a lock of her hair, put the ashes on her brow, and mourn properly.

She stripped the wrapping away from what she held and unfolded the closely written sheets around a dark red ovoid, rather shiny. The device was an *ul xaolat*, a "thing master." On one side were four shallow depressions, like fingerprints, and one's hand folded naturally around the *ul xaolat* with a finger settled into each depression. Precious Wind had brought the *ul xaolat* from Tingawa to be given to Xulai when she was no longer a child. She, Precious Wind, should have retrieved it and given it to Xulai that first morning at the abbey, when the girl looked into a mirror and saw herself as a woman. On that day, however, Xulai had been angry and upset, which was absolutely the wrong frame of mind for anyone to be introduced to this dangerous device with all its complicated warnings and instructions. Besides, Precious Wind had believed their little group was safe in the abbey. Foolishly, she had believed! She had regretted it since! Her own teachers had often said that the moment safety was presumed was the moment when one was most in danger, but that day she had pitied Xulai, that day she had wanted the child to have time to get used to herself. "My fault," she murmured, not for the first time. "My fault. My error. Mine the blame."

She put the device into her pocket, put the table back up against the wall, lifted the bed, smoothed its cover, put the short board back into the floor, replaced the mat, relocked the door, folded the sheets of instructions into a deeper, more secret pocket, and returned to the hop-skip and her journey south. She was days behind Abasio and Xulai. If she did not catch up to them before she reached Elsmere, she would find them in Merhaven, probably with Genieve, Justinian's old friend, Falredi's sister.

For a moment loneliness had overwhelmed her and she had found herself longing for Bear's company, forgetting, just for that moment, that Bear was no longer her—anyone's—friend.

IN GHASTAIN, QUEEN MIRAMI HAD held a dinner party to welcome Alicia to the court once more. Alicia had not been at court in a very long time, and it never crossed the queen's mind that her daughter might have been involved in Chamfray's death. Though Mirami was sly and clever, she had never been imaginative. She had been taught the use of poisons and told what to do with them, and what Mirami had been taught made up the sum total of *the way things were to be*. If she had been taught to kill in a certain way, it was because that way was the only right and appropriate way. She had never killed at a distance. She might occasionally use a disposable person to put some powder in a bowl of soup, but she was always nearby, pulling the strings. Even when disposing of King Gahls's three wives, she had come to Ghastain, secretly, disguised as an old woman, to do the thing properly, and she always thought of herself as a person who acted alone, fully capable of making and carrying out plans without help. Blinded by this view, she had never seen that Chamfray's seemingly casual comments and advice had contributed enormously to her success. She thought of him only as a companion who had a soothing effect upon her. Since his death she had found herself overtaken by a strange feeling that she only gradually identified as loneliness. She had never been lonely before. But then, Chamfray had always been there. Even back when she had been at the Old Dark House, Chamfray had been there. When the Old Dark Man had sent her to Kamfels, the Old Dark Man had sent Chamfray with her, to be her helper.

There was no lack of company in Ghastain. There were always people about, people courting favors, people eager to earn her thanks, but she could not speak freely with any of them. Hulix did not have enough brains to take Chamfray's place, and though a number of brainy persons frequented the court, she knew she could trust none of them to support her aims and ambitions. The only one who had the same motives was Alicia. Chamfray had pointed that out, suggesting that Mirami and her daughter might be of great help to one another if Mirami would treat her daughter as she treated Chamfray, with something approaching friendship.

Mirami had not really liked that idea. To her mind, her children were creations, things to be used, even to be used up if necessary. They were game pieces to be moved hither and thither. The Old Dark Man had taught her this, and he had helped her create those children. Mirami had not enjoyed the process, but she had understood the necessity, and Chamfray had helped her tolerate all that had to be done. He had been generally useful, he had her interests at heart, and it would do no harm to follow his suggestion. If Alicia would be her friend, it might be pleasant. For a time, at least. Until she found another Chamfray.

For this reason and no other, Alicia was welcomed with unfamiliar solicitude. She was given the same suite she had occupied before, but nothing remained of its former comfortable shabbiness. The rooms had been refurbished in what Mirami had assumed were Alicia's favorite colors. It was only a guess on Mirami's part, for she had never taken trouble to actually inquire about Alicia's favorite anything. She simply remembered that, given a choice, Alicia often picked clothing or ornaments of copper, or gold, or blue. Mirami had no idea why; she never asked herself why about anything. If she had known why, perhaps she would not have made the mistake of using them. As a consequence of her ignorance, when Alicia entered the suite and saw the blue carpeting, the fabrics woven with copper and gold thread, the gold-leafed headboard and chairs, the wall panels, each beautifully painted with an ornate copper urn holding varied bouquets of fantastic blue and gold foliage and flowers, she did not even see the room. Her mind filled with thoughts of her father and how she had lost him.

When she met her mother for tea in the queen's private suite the morning after her arrival, she was in no conciliatory mood. She went with the intention of begging off that night's party. The queen's new chamberlain had come to tell her about it, and since Alicia did not intend to eat anything provided by her mother, any dinner party would have presented a problem. Morning tea, however, she could manage. She came equipped with a small jar of her own tea, said it was something she had been taking for her headaches, made it herself in a separate pot with fresh water, refused cakes on the grounds of a wholly fabricated stomach upset occasioned by her recent arduous travel, and settled herself to be lectured in Mirami's usual manner on her lack of enthusiasm, her delays, her inability to get Justinian thoroughly into her clutches.

No such lecture ensued. Instead, Mirami merely smiled and drank tea as they sat in the pleasant breeze that came through a window slightly open to the terrace. Outside, fountains conversed in a constant burble and chuckle accompanied by flute songs being played somewhere nearby. It was too late in the season for flowers, but the breeze brought scents of pine and cedar. Inside, the room was warm, thickly carpeted with jewel-toned rugs and provided with furnishings chosen for bodily comfort. Mirami, dressed in a loose, red throat-to-ankle gown, seemed unusually relaxed and, to Alicia's surprise, when she began speaking, spoke not of Alicia's failings but of Chamfray, of his company, his comments, even his humor. She spoke of his endearing clumsiness.

"He could not enter a room without knocking something over. He could not pick up anything smaller than a water pitcher without dropping it, and if it were a water pitcher, he would spill the contents." Mirami laughed softly. "I miss him greatly."

"I would have thought you would be infuriated," said Alicia, uncertain as to where this conversation might be leading.

"Oh, no. I didn't have to pick up after him, there were servants to do that. I never expected him to be graceful. That certainly wasn't what he was good at."

"It was said at one time that he might be your . . . that he might be closer than . . ."

"You mean a lover?" Mirami laughed, choking on her tea, so that a little of it spurted into her lap. "No, no, my dear. I had no desire to be handled by the world's clumsiest man! I can't imagine Chamfray making love. Ha. It would be like being mated by a blind bull! Or one of those animals from the Before Time, the very awkward tall ones with spots. Haraffs, was it?" She giggled.

Mirami did giggle occasionally, as part of whatever seduction she had chosen to be involved in, but Alicia had only once before heard her mother giggle, and the sound made her mind blink into an abrupt abyss of darkness. Herself in a dark hallway. A closed door. Behind it, her father and Mirami, and that same giggle.

Then it was light again, and Alicia gulped for breath—unnoticed—as Mirami continued.

"No, the very idea of being loved by Chamfray is ridiculous. No. He was a friend. People like us, my dear, people who are engaged in very lengthy, dangerous, but profitable projects, can allow themselves to have few if any friends. The ones we do have are precious to us."

Alicia would not have thought her mother had any friends. She would, in fact, have laughed at the idea of her mother needing friends. It was a concept worth exploring.

"If you benefited from his company, Mother, how did your friendship benefit him?"

Mirami gestured aimlessly, "Oh, I kept him in luxury, of course. He was fond of expensive things to eat and especially things to drink! He was quite a connoisseur of wine and brandy. He liked books, *old* books, and those are expensive as well. He loved music, and I was able to hire musicians to play for him almost daily—I've kept some of them on! Do you hear the flutes? I became used to the sound and now I miss it if it isn't there. Also, because he was so tall and awkward, he could be really comfortable only in furniture made to his measure. I gave him such things, and he enjoyed them. I used to see him in his own quarters, spread across a chair I had had made for him, listening to his musicians and drinking wine. One could almost hear him purring."

"Ah," said Alicia, nodding thoughtfully, deciding to risk a dangerous comment. "Then the rumors that he was Hulix's father are totally false."

The queen did not explode in rage. She actually appeared thoughtful, as though considering the matter. "Needless to say, we do not allow such rumors to circulate, but I don't suppose they are *totally* false, no. The Old Dark Man took genetic material from several sources, and Chamfray may have been one of them. I have no idea what particular material was used for what purpose, but we had to ensure the child would be a boy. We needed a boy, you know—to inherit."

"Once the duke Falyrion and Falredi were gone," said Alicia without expression.

"Exactly." Mirami smiled at her daughter, delighted at this understanding.

Taking a sip of tea, Alicia swallowed carefully to quell the bloom of fire that had erupted beneath her breastbone. "I've always wondered how you so easily captivated King Gahls."

Mirami gave this some thought. "I think it must have been the hair, my dear. He loves long, dark hair. Many of the women in Ghastain are those pallid, milky northern types, hair the color of sand, skins like sour cheese. The king's mother was dark, I believe. Men often marry women like their mothers. Men often respond to certain scents that evoke memories of them, as well. There are still women here who remember his mother. I found out what she wore, what she perfumed herself with, and then I used the same colors, fabrics, scents. Her colors were flame colors, often in combination: reds, ambers, yellows. Her scents were lilac and lavender; can you imagine anything less subtle? Oh, yes, and cedar. Let's see, there were two other ingredients: lemon blossom and ambergris. There are lemon trees in the conservatory, but I have very little ambergris left. It really has no scent of its own, but it holds the others sweetly together. The Old Dark Man gave me a lump of the stuff decades ago. It comes from some sea creature and is sometimes found along the shore."

"How well did you know the Old Dark Man?"

Mirami frowned, her nose wrinkling, as at a bad smell. "I could not say I *knew* him at all. No one ever really knew him. He was there, in the Old Dark House, as far back as I can remember. For some reason, I think my mother had left me in his care for a time, and then something happened to her. He had promised her he would care for me and he did. I had the usual serving people around me. At first I had a nurse-maid, then a governess, and a teacher and a riding master—though the riding master soon gave up on me! I do not like horses! The Old Dark House itself was dreadful, of course, he cared nothing for beauty or comfort, but I had the little carriage house, and it was quite nice. Later, he exacted a price for my upbringing. I paid it over time. It seemed worth it, and I thought I would forget the unpleasantness. I do, most of the time." She leaned forward and touched Alicia's knee gently. "But I miss having a friend, Alicia. Chamfray said it was my fault that you and I were not friends. I hope we can be."

Alicia lifted her cup, letting it hide her surprise as she made the lightning decision to respond in kind. "Oh, Mother, I'm so glad!" The words were too quick, too unrehearsed to be wholly believable, but evidently their very spontaneity made them sound convincing—at least to Mirami, who began to chat. They "chatted" for some time. Alicia had on occasion listened to other people "chatting," but she was certainly not accustomed to doing it herself, and she found it difficult—much more difficult, actually, than killing people. One had to listen to idiocy, sometimes about people one did not know or care to know, and respond to idiocy with idiocy. One repeated oneself a lot, over and over. The other person or persons repeated themselves, over and over. No information was actually exchanged. What had the beekeeper at Kamfels called it? Hive noise: the buzz that went on in the hive, meaningless as breathing, but no less significant.

By the time they parted, Alicia was tense with the strain of it, but Mirami seemed well pleased. She had taken Chamfray's advice. Alicia would be her new friend. If she had to kill off her new friend at some point, it would still have been comfortable to have had a friend for a while. Dutifully, she reminded herself of something else Chamfray had said: if Alicia was to be a friend, Mirami must not be so critical of her. One didn't criticize friends. Not where they could overhear.

Alicia went back to her own rooms and became lost in concentration over the emergence of a totally new idea. Mirami was a very beautiful woman, yes. She was also fifty—no, fifty-five years old. Alicia was at least equally beautiful, and she was seventeen years younger. Mirami had been a very young bride. If Alicia said she was thirty-two, no one would dispute it. Also, during those strange childhood journeys to the Old Dark House she had had the advantage of being instructed by the Old Dark Man in matters that went far beyond how to poison people and how to make sure one had a male child. Alicia—since her father had died—had often resented being female, but at this moment she was glowingly grateful for being a woman so that neither Chamfray nor the Old Dark Man himself had *contributed* to her birth. She actually felt pleased and satisfied at that. These were unfamiliar though interesting emotions, not unlike the satiety she felt after a slaughter. If Mirami could be believed, Alicia might be able to make her own place in court society without having to be alert to observe anti-poison precautions at every moment. If Mirami could be believed! It would be foolish, of course, to believe her much, or for long. It would be unforgivably stupid to take what she said at face value, though one might act as though one believed her for a day, perhaps a few days, if one was careful.

And, of course, a lot depended upon whether Justinian was totally beyond reach! If he were, if Alicia's marriage to Justinian were no longer possible, Mirami could change her intentions in a moment. Although . . . Wasn't it possible Alicia might make another, loftier conquest that could prove easier and much quicker than Justinian? Couldn't Wold be obtained later on, in some other way? Well, easy enough to find out!

When in company at court, she had almost always dressed in subdued colors, so as not to be noticed with particularity, so as to fade into the crowd. Today, she went into closets she had not used in years and brought out youthful gowns she barely remembered. She sent for dressmakers to modify and retrim her garments so she could appear in the bright colors the queen had mentioned. She summoned the queen's hairdresser and had her own hair arranged loosely, girlishly. Standing before her mirror, she decided that over her underclothing she would wear only the dress, no jewels. No jewels at all. Not at her neck, not at her wrists, not in her hair. None at all.

She had jewels. The Old Dark Man had left jewels in the Old Dark

House. Her father had given her jewels. Mirami had many and wore many; she often glittered, so Alicia thought, like a parade horse. Though most of the women at court would consider going without jewels to be an admission of failure, Alicia had observed something interesting about gems. Gems were sexually enticing only to women—or boys—who were being bought and paid for. When a man saw gems on a woman, he knew the woman could be or had been bought—or had merely been well paid when she was younger, as Mirami had been. Women really wore gems in order to impress other women.

Alicia did not care how other women regarded her. She did not want the king to look at her jewels. Alicia preferred that the king should look at the skin of her bosom, delicately rouged; at the depths of her eyes, enlarged and enhanced; at her willow-slender waist, the delicacy of her hands and ankles. She would not blind him with the hard glint of gems attesting to former owners or masters. No. No jewels. She would definitely make him look elsewhere.

IF PRECIOUS WIND HAD USED the *ul xaolat*, the thing master, to summon a transporter, to move herself, she could have gone from one place to another in an instant. It was one of the things the device could do, allowing its holder to escape almost any danger. One had to have a clear mental picture of where one wanted to go, however, and that place had to be within a half a day's travel by ordinary means. She could not use it to go to Tingawa or to Woldsgard unless she could concentrate on a chain of locations in between. It would be impossible to use the device to cross an ocean! One wave looked like every other wave. She could not even use the device to get to Merhaven, for the terrain ahead was totally unfamiliar to her. Besides, she did not intend to leave the wolf pack behind.

All of which did not mean the device was useless! The *ul xaolat* could also be used to summon a hunter, which meant the time normally used for hunting could be used for travel. Each morning of their journey she had placed one finger on the device in her pocket and spoke to the air, directing the *ul xaolat* to summon the hunter and have it find a legitimate prey animal—it would not attack anything that looked even remotely human—and leave it where she and the pack would arrive by the time dusk fell.

Each day she had driven until the sun went down, stopping only once to rest and water the horses. As dusk fell this evening, as on every other, she and her pack came upon their evening meal lying near the road. Last night had been deer. Tonight it was pig. She pulled the carriage off the road and called to the wolves. The hunter stood at the edge of the trees, visible only as a wavering of the air. If one knew what one was looking at, one could make out the evasive shimmer of manipulating talons and penetrating lances. One might see a faint haze surrounding it when it lifted into the air and went off on whatever hunt had been ordered. Mostly, it went totally unnoticed, but the wolves knew it was there. She walked among them, soothing them. Precious Wind wanted the wolves to recognize the servants of the *ul xaolat*—the hunter, the carrier, the transporter—and to know these strange things belonged to her, that they would not, could not, harm the wolves.

While they feasted, she unharnessed the horses and gave them their evening oats. The wolves still made them too nervous to eat. They shifted and swiveled on their picket lines until the wolves had eaten their fill and she had sent the pack away.

For some things, horse senses were keener than those of mankind. For some things, wolf senses were keener than those of mankind. A man would not notice the smell of a wolf pack; a man would not notice the slight glimmer of the hunter, except for one man perhaps, one man on this side of the sea.

As a child, Mirami had lived in the Old Dark House, supposedly with the Old Dark Man. From what was said about him, he may well have known about such ancient devices. However, the Old Dark Man had disappeared before Mirami left the place, and Mirami was not known to have used any ancient device. However, Alicia had used them. She had used an ancient device to kill the princess. That fact had caused much puzzlement and argument in Tingawa. How had she obtained it? How had she learned to use it? They were forced to assume Alicia had found the thing and its instructions in the Old Dark House. However she had found and learned how to use the other devices, Alicia's usual mode of travel proved she had not used a thing master. Even if she had, the *ul xaolat* would not have killed humans for her, and Alicia was not interested in a weapon she could not turn upon humans.

The problem of Alicia deferred, the problem of wolf feeding solved to her satisfaction, she had turned to another. Day after day she had ruminated over it: what was she to do about Bear? The problem had been bothering her since the first evidence of his betrayal, back at the abbey. She would not have thought him capable of dishonor, even impatient as he was to get home to Tingawa. Considering everything Precious Wind had learned and now suspected about Alicia, Duchess of Altamont, however, it was possible his betrayal had been forced upon him. In that case, killing him would be an injustice. If the woman could use genetic material to make mirrors, to send killing clouds, she could use them for creating obsessions, for faking the presence of someone, the calling from someone. The only problem with this idea was how Alicia could have obtained material from Bear's betrothed. No ships had come from Tingawa in years!

As she picked each part of her argument apart, however, she realized there would have been no difficulty in obtaining the materials if they had been sent *before* all sea traffic stopped! Bear had been at Woldsgard for over a decade. His presence there was well known. The fact that he was betrothed was general knowledge, and some ships had arrived shortly after he did.

That would mean, however, that Alicia had intended to dispose of all Tingawans from the beginning. Her malice had not been directed at the princess only.

So, Precious Wind thought, *if I accept that Alicia is quite capable of indiscriminate hatred toward all Tingawans, if I accept that she wants all the Tingawans dead, as her messages to Jenger have made clear, what is her motive for all this?*

If one wished to understand the enemy's strengths and weaknesses, one had to understand motives, and Precious Wind could not find any sensible motive: Alicia had never been to Tingawa; she would not profit in any way from Bear's death or Precious Wind's death or the death of a Xakixa. There was a motive for Xu-i-lok's death, granted, but why the rest of them?

Was Alicia looking ahead to a time when she and her mother would rule all Norland? Did they wish to free Norland from all foreign influences even before that time came? Even supposing that Alicia had been promised some gift by the Sea King's ambassador, the question was still not answered. Tingawa, almost alone among nations, had been a friend of the Sea King for generations.

There was one answer to this, of course. In Tingawa, in certain circles, when one was completely puzzled, one put the question, "Who stands behind?" Who is the cause behind a cause, what is the motive behind a motive? If one asked that question, one assumed Mirami and Alicia were only tools, that something or someone else was the puppet master. Clan Do-Lok had not considered this. Precious Wind had preferred not to consider this, but now she felt it had to be taken seriously. She had to assume someone or something else had set Alicia into motion for a reason, however obscure, insane, or ancient that reason might be. If that motive had been planted in ancient times, then Alicia or her mother, or someone else, could have sent for the materials to enchant Bear years, even decades ago. They could have arrived on the same ship Bear had first arrived on.

If this were the case, she could acquit Bear of having sold his honor. He might be no more guilty of betrayal than Xu-i-lok had been of her own death.

So . . . if Precious Wind encountered him on this journey, what should she do? For the moment, think of something else, clear her mind. She did so, and slept.

By the following afternoon she was traveling east. The road curved south just ahead, where it entered the cut in the southern edge of the highlands that took the road down a long ravine toward the sea. The mountains to her right had given way to flat tableland, and as she looked across the level plain to the southwest she saw two huge, mirrored eyes staring at her over the edge of the highland, startling her into pulling up on the reins before she realized she was seeing the great convex bosses of stone that faced the two peaks of Frog Eye Mountain. The eyes were still glossy after untold ages of weather. She smiled at her own surprise. She had heard of them, seen them on her maps, and they were indeed as strange as they were reported to be. Some said they were polished by ghosts or spirits of the forest. Who- or whatever kept them shining, they were amazing.

She flicked the reins and had just brought the horses back to their easy canter when she saw a lone rider emerging over the lip of the Cut, just ahead of her. It was a very large horse carrying a huge bulk, a powerful shape unlikely to be anyone else. He must have started back from Merhaven almost immediately after arriving there to be so far north! She prayed he had not seen, or not recognized, Xulai and Abasio upon the road.

In that instant, all her doubts reconciled and she decided upon on a course that would provide for Bear's redemption, possibly for his life, while at the same time not requiring that she trust him. That she could no longer do. *He must believe Xulai is dead,* she reminded herself. *He must not go near the abbey, for a number of people there know Xulai is alive.* Even if she sent a pigeon to warn the abbot and Wordswell to keep silent, the warning might not shut all mouths. The people from Woldsgard would, by this time, be at least halfway home, so they would not speak to Bear, but others might. Bear must be focused elsewhere.

She spared a quick thought for her followers. She did not want Bear to know about the wolves, either. It was not yet noon. They shadowed her well within the woods that still covered the hillsides to her left. They would not approach her when someone else was with her. The hunter device was far ahead.

She flicked the reins and speeded up a little. She and her pack still had to reach their dinner by sunset tonight and she would lose whatever time she spent talking with Bear. She must keep their conversation brief, saying she could not linger. She remembered to smile sadly when he approached, letting her face tell the story before her lips did.

All for nothing! Bear was bursting with words even before he arrived, shouting at her, telling her she must come with him immediately to Merhaven, telling her she must let him take the ship that had waited there for Xulai. Had she found Xulai? He pulled to a breathless halt beside her.

"Dead," said Precious Wind flatly. "She is gone."

He stopped. Hope leapt within her at this cessation. Would he grieve?

Ah, but he did not stop long enough even to sorrow!

Too quickly, too eagerly, he said, "Well then, there's nothing we can do. There's nothing to prevent our going home."

"I'm afraid there is," she replied in an icy voice that wiped all eagerness from his face. "My oath, for one. I was sworn to exact vengeance upon those who killed Xu-i-lok. And now upon those who took Xulai.

That would be the duchess Alicia and perhaps also her mother. You were also sworn, Bear, sworn in the temple, by the priests. If the Great Bear of Zol returns to Tingawa without having done his sworn duty, he will be known to be forsworn and the family of his bride will not have him."

Bear had been so involved in his own urgencies he had forgotten the fringing details of his oath. Being known to be forsworn had not occurred to him; he had never considered it, and in his driving need to go home he had forgotten that the princess's death was the beginning of an ancillary task, not the end of the journey. It had been too long! It had taken too much time!

He said as much, angrily, with evil words cast upon the priests who had sworn him.

"I don't recall any limitation being placed upon us," said Precious Wind when he had run out of fury. "In any case, it's now a matter that can be dealt with in a timely fashion. We know who was responsible. Alicia, Duchess of Altamont, is now either at the Old Dark House or at Ghastain. There is a Tingawan embassy in Ghastain. You have an excellent reason to go there. When I have finished certain tasks I am required to perform, I may have time to join you there. If not, you will find me in Merhaven. Even if you include all the travel needed to get to Ghastain and back, you should be finished before winter is over. The trip home will be easier in spring. I dislike winter storms at sea."

"What do you have to do?" he asked, grasping at any straws that would force her to go to Merhaven at once.

"I have certain duties to perform for Xu-i-lok's father that may not be discussed with anyone. Listen to me, Bear, look at me! You may not go near the abbey. They suspect you of having conspired in the abduction and murder of Xulai."

He glared at her, mouth open to answer but no words coming out, his face reddening. Both his face and his silence damned him.

"I know this is nonsense," she said in a soothing tone that hid her disgust. "I know you would not be forsworn in that way. We both know no Tingawan Great Bear could possibly do so, but we have no time to spend in allaying their suspicions. You must pass the abbey without being seen. You must go to our embassy in Ghastain and find out whether the duchess is in Ghastain. You must tell our people that she was the mover behind the abduction and death of Xulai. Alicia is the daughter of the queen. The people of Ghastain will not act against the duchess except with the queen's or king's permission, which I doubt would be given. You can, however, consult with our people as to proper vengeance. Also, I have something for you and something that must be taken to them."

She burrowed into her pouch and removed Justinian's receipt. "The duke sent a treasure to the abbey six months ago, to reward you for your faithful service. Here is the receipt. We found that the prior had stolen the money." She held it before his eyes and waited. His flush vanished. His face turned pale, ashen.

"He did send it. My bride-price."

"I told you he had sent it. Yes, your bride-price, and more than that. It is not lost. The prior is dead, and the treasure is being recovered and sent on to Merhaven. It should be there by the time we are ready to leave." She burrowed a hand into her pocket and removed the three messages that had been sent to Jenger in the Vulture Tower, the three she had brought back from there and had carried ever since Wordswell had returned them to her. "These are in the handwriting of the Duchess of Altamont, Alicia, daughter of Queen Mirami. The first directs her servant, Jenger, to abduct Xulai. The second directs him to murder you. The third directs him to murder any Tingawan he can get hold of." She sighed deeply. "It was your abrupt departure after Xulai's disappearance that led the people of the abbey to suspect you, but let me say again: we do not have time to deal with their accusations now. You must avoid the abbey. They have an army and you cannot fight an army."

Bear did not speak. The news that Jenger had received orders to kill him coupled with the fact he had been wrong about Justinian had, for the moment, frozen him. When he spoke, it was in a whisper. "Xulai. You found her?"

"I received word from those who found her," said Precious Wind. "I went to the place where she was held and wept at what I saw there."

"How did you get these?" he demanded, holding the messages out to her.

"I found them in Jenger's things at the Vulture Tower," she replied. "He had been killed, possibly by wolves." It was certainly possible, though she thought it unlikely. "I would have sent them to our embassy by messenger bird when I arrived in Merhaven."

"You won't," he said.

"Won't?"

"Arrive in Merhaven. Well, not the old Merhaven. It isn't there anymore. What's left of the town has been moved uphill. They aren't even building permanent piers anymore. They're building floating ones that can be hauled up the slope as the water rises. Our shipping office there has only the one ship, the *Falsa-xin*, the *Daywind*, and they refused to let me take it. They said only you can take it. Or Xulai."

"Well, ship or no, my messages must be sent to Tingawa and Merhaven is the only place I can send them from. Meantime, you must find out where Alicia is. If she is at Ghastain, give these messages to our embassy, and they will make appropriate decisions."

"And if she's not there?"

"She'll be at the Old Dark House. You know where it is. How you exact vengeance is your business. Remember how she works. Guard yourself."

He stood there, very like a bear, standing but weaving slightly, as though he found balancing on his own feet very difficult. She knew he was weighing all that she had told him. If he went back to Tingawa, he could not lie to the Do-Lok family. They had truth tellers among them who could read a lie as another would read words on a page, so he could not claim to have fulfilled his oath if he had not. Standing there, so at a loss, so worried, he seemed to her almost pitiable.

She said softly, "You've been in a great turmoil, Bear. It may not be your fault. Alicia may have obtained genetic material from Tingawa, from your betrothed. She may have used this to send a ghost of Legami-am to haunt you, to twist your mind, your nerves . . ."

"All night," he whispered. "Not so much lately, but before there wasn't an hour she wasn't in my head. Whispering. I thought it was her, hating me because I had been so long away. I love her, you know. As Justinian loved his princess, I love her. I am Tingawan, too, Precious Wind. And all the time it was that . . . that foul bitch . . ."

"The duchess hates Tingawans for some reason we know nothing about. We don't need to understand or explain it, but we do need to repay it in kind."

He put the messages into his pocket, thrusting them deeply as he sighed, a longing sigh. He said, "I may as well go to the embassy. I'll find out what's going on. If I can, I'll return to Merhaven. It's still a port. When I was there, I carried a greeting to Genieve from Justinian. He had told me long ago if we ever went there to find her house and to greet her for him. Her house is across the bay, high on the hills, so she has not had to move it. She will no doubt invite you to stay with her while you are there. She invited me, but I was too occupied trying to find a way to get home."

"Poor Xulai," murmured Precious Wind.

Bear said, "She was a nice child, but I never understood what all the fuss was about her. Some baby Bright Pearl had. Babies are cute enough, like puppies. As a baby, she was a nice little thing. There at the abbey, though, she was a real . . . well, high and mighty, acting like royalty because she was a Xakixa. Just daring the world to take her for ransom. I suppose something went wrong with the payment for her."

"Is that what happened? She was taken for ransom? Because she carried Xu-i-lok's soul?"

He flushed. It was obviously what he had been told. "Why, of course. What else?"

"No, Bear. No ransom was asked. They took Xulai to torture her and kill her."

His eyes went wildly off to the side. His body went rigid. "That's . . . crazy."

"That's the duchess Alicia. It's what she does. She cares nothing for souls."

He turned away, saying at last in a strangled voice, "You know as well as I do the souls come home, eventually. Even if Xulai didn't get to Tingawa, Xu-i-lok's soul would get there."

"And Xulai's?"

"Hers, too. Eventually."

"So if there's no one to carry your soul home, it doesn't worry you."

"I'm a warrior, Xu-xin. Many of us don't have Xakixas. We have a saying. It's not how we live, it's how we die that matters." He laughed harshly.

She nodded. "That must be of comfort to you." She breathed deeply. "If I am not in Merhaven when you return, I will leave word where you may find me."

He did not bid her farewell. He got on his horse and rode away

north, not looking back. For a moment she had a pang of guilt. She had
lied only about Xulai being dead. But she had misled him and . . . and,
all too tellingly, when she had done so, he had not grieved for Xulai. She
had thought the old Bear would have grieved, and perhaps he would
have, for the child, but not for the woman she had become. He had not
known, or perhaps had chosen not to know, what her fate was to have
been. She feared she had seen the last of him as he rode over a little hill
and disappeared. She had hoped for some other memory of him.

From within the edge of the forest, the wolves saw her moving once
more. They got to their feet. They would have to hurry to get to their
dinner before it was fully dark.

AT THE PALACE IN GHASTAIN, Mirami's dinner party had been a success.
Rancitor had been there, enchanted by the daughter of a new ambassador to the court. Mirami had reminded him that his freedom from
restraint depended upon treating the girl courteously and making no
sexual overtures. She also dosed his food with something that would
keep him politely calm. King Gahls enjoyed himself. Alicia was there, of
course, sweetly gracious, not trying to outshine anyone, no jewels at all,
which Mirami thought a little too inconspicuous but generally sensible
of her. No point in attracting attention and making other courtiers jeal-
ous of oneself. The king admired her. He told Mirami what a lovely
young woman she was. Of course, her own daughter, what would he
expect?

Actually, Alicia's campaign to fascinate the king had moved along
quite nicely. He had invited her to sit at his side at dinner, Mirami on
the right, Alicia on the left. He told her she might use his name, Karios,
instead of "Your Majesty." When Mirami was out of hearing, moving
about among her guests, Alicia asked the king if he were not concerned
about the kingdom, having only one heir. He had not thought about
this. "Well," she said soothingly, "of course, Mother is really too old now
to have other children. We will all pray that Prince Rancitor stays well
and healthy and lives to succeed his father only in the great fullness
of time." This left the king feeling vaguely discontented, thinking that
Mirami really should have had more children for him.

Several times in the days that followed, they had ridden out to the
hunt together, the king and Alicia. Mirami did not care for riding, but

Alicia rode very, very well. Her father, Duke Falyrion, had taught her. As they were returning from the hunt one day, the king was told by a messenger that the Tingawan embassy was closing its doors and departing.

When he shouted that they could not do that, there were trade negotiations under way, he was told the emissary would call upon him the following day.

Alicia was with the king when the emissary arrived bearing the three messages sent by Alicia to the Vulture Tower.

"These were received by the abbot of Wilderbrook Abbey. It was thought proper that you know of them . . . if you do not already know of them."

The emissary put the messages in the king's hands and bowed very slightly, the bow known in Tingawa as "the bow deprecatory," recognizing the king's position while expressing that the man who held it was dishonored; he turned on his heel and left, showing the king his back.

The king didn't recognize the subtlety of the bow but understood a turned back when he saw it. When he unrolled the messages, he shook his head in confusion and thrust them at Alicia. "Where did these come from?" he demanded. "How do I find out where these came from?"

Alicia, taken by surprise and herself furiously angry, made herself concentrate as she stared wide-eyed at the all-too-familiar writing. "That's mother's writing," she said firmly. The writing was indeed very like her mother's writing. Mirami had taught her to write, after all.

"What should I do?" gasped the king. "If this is known . . . There are people here from Wellsport who have invested heavily in the sea trade. We have been negotiating to resume that trade. The Tingawans can obtain the permission of the Sea King; we can't. If the Tingawans refuse to deal with us . . ."

"I have no idea why she would have done this," said Alicia. "It is ridiculous. But you must tell the embassy you have affirmed that Mirami did kill the princess Xu-i-lok, and you must tell them that you will take care of the matter yourself."

"But she could not . . ."

"I know, I know, dear Karios, but you must save yourself! You'll have to tell them she did it, then seem to get rid of her so the emissary may convey to the family Do-Lok that suitable vengeance has been taken. They must think that she is dead."

"What may I do? Shall I have her killed? The scandal would . . . my heir!"

She fastened on that idea. "A scandal might affect Rancitor's position as your heir," she agreed. "We must avoid that. Tell the Tingawan people that. Tell them you must manage it without throwing doubt on Rancitor's inheritance. Tell them you will lock her up while deciding what must be done. As for her, tell her to be calm, that we're working it all out. I need to consult with people I know, to decide what is best. And forgive me, dearest Karios, if I leave you for a few days. I must be gone before you lock her away, understand? I must not be here while she is still here . . . you do understand? It cannot be said that I attempted to influence you. We must think of my dear brother, your son, your heir! We must think of Rancitor!"

He thought he understood. He wasn't sure, but he thought he did. Alicia would protect Rancitor. Alicia would somehow deal with Mirami. He had depended on Mirami to deal with things for such a long time. Would her daughter take Mirami's place? Oh, that would be very good. He would like that.

The little capsule Alicia had prepared for Mirami was in Alicia's suite, in her jewelry box, down at the bottom wrapped in a silk handkerchief. She had her servants ready her horse and arrange her escort. Just before leaving, she went to bid her mother a fond, temporary farewell.

"There's been some news of Justinian. I'm going home by the quickest route. I'll be back as soon as I can."

Outside her mother's door, she dropped the capsule out of the fluttering, distracting handkerchief and stepped on it firmly without anyone seeing it. She almost regretted doing it! Now all of the little clouds she had made were gone. Well, someone else would no doubt need putting away. She wondered who it would be as she ran down the marble stairs to mount her horse and ride away.

BEAR HAD STAYED IN GHASTAIN after delivering the messages to the embassy, spending most of his time watching the castle. He had wagered with himself whether the king would have Alicia killed publicly or privately, and he was astonished to see her riding out with a group of archers. He followed them to the southern cut in the highland cliffs, where the road went down into the valley toward Benjobz. She had either escaped or blamed it on someone else, he thought, shaking his head in something almost like admiration before following at a discreet distance. He never went anywhere without saddlebags packed; he was quite ready to take to the road. The emissary had mentioned receiving messages from the abbot that referred to the Old Dark House, to the Vulture Tower, to the plot against Xulai. The messages Bear had brought piled proof upon the abbot's allegations. Bear had been pleasantly surprised when he learned that his own name had not been mentioned except as a victim! He was not implicated by anything written from the Old Dark House, the tower, or the abbey. He was free to act. He saw it all very clearly. His duty was plain. The Old Dark House was where the evil had begun and thrived. He would follow the duchess to her lair and put an end to it. Then he would meet Precious Wind in Merhaven. They could all go home.

BRAM AND CHIPPY, BLUE AND Fisher, plus the previously unnamed horse and mule now known as Greedy and Ears, reached the border of Elsmere and took one more day to arrive at the new Merhaven, pausing above it at the top of a last gentle rise before the long descent into the sea. Below them, a new town spread across the flanks of the mountains and along the shores of an expansive bay, a bay vastly wider than the ones shown on their maps and extending southward to a dim shoreline above which a separate town was perched.

"Merhaven and South Merhaven," murmured the horse.

The map had shown Merhaven as a single town that had made an arc along the gentle slope of the bay's north side, nearest them, and extended along the narrow shelf edging the eastern, inner curve.

Abasio pointed toward this inner curve. "That side was steeper. There was just a narrow shelf beneath that wing of the town; water covered it. They couldn't move up, so they moved to the far side of the bay."

"They've cut a road to join the two," Xulai said, following his gaze toward the curved gash that had been chopped into the steep eastern slope and around it onto the southern shore. Though the evening light was fading, the new road showed as a lighter ribbon against the green of the hill.

Below them, wooden piers protruded into the water among a clutter of the small fishing boats that had plied the bay and the nearby shorelines of the ocean for generations. One large, seagoing ship was moored at the end of the longest pier. Though it bore the pennant of Tingawa, no one moved upon it or near it. The other little ships had men around them; nets were being strung up to dry among the spars and masts; people were moving about along the piers, along the shore, up and down the unpaved streets of the new town. Evidently there had been time to salvage building materials from the drowned town, for many of the newly built structures were of brick or stone. Abasio guessed they had been taken apart piece by piece and reassembled. That the reassembly was temporary was evidenced by the fact that none of the houses had gardens, none had landscaped surroundings. They had simply been plopped down on hastily leveled plots of ground, road-ways scraped out leading to them, and only time would tell whether they would stay settled in place or be pulled into pieces to be reassembled again, somewhere higher.

"Genieve," said Xulai. "Falyrion's sister. That's where we ought to go."

"What's the name of her house?"

"The Watch House. It's supposed to have a watchtower."

Abasio pointed across the bay. "Over there, the white one. It's the only one with a tower. And it hasn't been moved; it's been there all along. Look at the trees around it."

It stood straight across from them, alone, a white house behind a buttressed wall, the whole a massive white fist, one tower sticking up like a finger raised to test the wind.

"There's supposed to be a Tingawan something here," Xulai said. "Precious Wind told me. It's an office of some kind; not an embassy, that's in Ghastain near the court of King Gahls. Before the Sea King declared war, a lot of ships came here from Tingawa."

"A commercial office," he said. "Do you want to try for the Watch House tonight? It's getting on for dark."

"There's only one road around the bay," she replied. "We're not likely to get lost."

"If they have a stable and hay, I vote we go there," said Blue.

"I could go take a look," Fisher offered.

"Good idea," said Abasio.

Wings took off in a flurry; a dark arrow sped across the sky, over the waters, losing itself in the distance. Abasio got out his glasses and focused on the distant tower. "Where would he go?"

"To the stables," she replied. "That's what Blue is concerned about."

"Justifiably," snorted the horse.

"They must be behind the house," Abasio said. "I can't see where he went."

They moved slowly down the hill through an evening hush. Below them, people were going home. Chimneys were beginning to smoke. Near the curved sliver of moon, one star gleamed brilliantly against the blue. A flurry of wings came again.

A hawk settled on Xulai's shoulder to defeather and refur itself. Fisher said, "Stables, hay, oats, only one horse there, room for half a dozen. Somebody's in the house, there's smoke from the chimney."

"Let's ride for it," said Abasio.

They trotted down the hill, angling to their left to arrive at the road around the bay without going through any part of the town. Once on the narrow though well-graded road, Blue broke into a canter, Greedy reluctantly following, grunting with each footfall. Ears was made of more resilient stuff, following silently without making a fuss about it. He was lightly laden. They had eaten almost all their food, and the mule carried only their blankets and tent together with a few odds and ends. It was full dark when they reached the far side of the bay and started up the hillside. The moon sliver and the star shine reflected just enough light from the hard-packed surface of the road to keep them on track. Though the gate was shut when they arrived at the white wall, a lantern lit the bell rope beside it.

Xulai assayed a couple of well-spaced clongs. After a time, the door of the house opened, and a man came out. He had bowed legs, a scruffy beard, a napkin tucked into his collar, and an expression of honest annoyance.

Xulai headed off the annoyance in a clear, carrying voice. "Is this the home of Genieve, daughter of Falyrion, Duke of Kamfels?" The man gaped without saying anything. "If so, tell her, please, that a messenger from Justinian, Duke of Wold, is at her gate and begs her hospitality."

"Let them in, Dobbich," a deeper voice cried from the open door. "Let them in at once."

The man shut his mouth and opened the gate wordlessly, letting his jaw sag again as they entered. The woman in the doorway came toward them, looking up at them with amazement. She saw a bearded man, a boy with some kind of animal on his shoulder. Neither of them was Justinian. A messenger, someone had said?

Xulai slid down from Greedy's back. "You are Genieve? Justinian's childhood friend? I am Xulai, his . . . messenger. We are . . . traveling alone to avoid being taken by . . . By what, Abasio?"

"By very nasty people," he said, dismounting. "Madam, we thank you for any kindness you can offer. It has been a long, weary way here."

"Justinian?" she begged. "Is he . . . Is he well? And his . . . his wife?"

After a moment's pause and a deeply heaved sigh, Xulai said, "Princess Xu-i-lok is dead. The duke has gone into hiding from the same people who killed her and who have driven us this long way. We have no reason to think he is not safe and well. It was he who sent us here and told us to find you in the Watch House."

She beckoned them in. "Dobbich, go find Mrs. Bang and tell her we have guests who are hungry and not fussy about food." She smiled at them, obviously trying to be welcoming while deeply worried. "At this time of night, given your obvious weariness, I presume that's true."

"Very true, ma'am," said Abasio.

"Of course, the livestock are more particular," said Blue.

The woman turned in astonishment. "Did I just hear . . ."

Abasio glared at Blue. "Yes, ma'am, it's a very long story. Blue can take himself and his friends to the stables, but they'll need some help shedding those saddles and packs. If you'll take my young friend in, I'll see to the animals and join you shortly."

"There's hay there," she said, "though we're a little low on oats. We rely on my late husband's farms to keep us in provisions, and we have not sent a wagon for some weeks."

"Farms?" asked Xulai.

"Over the ridge, back there in the hills a bit. He owned several farms, yes. Those of us who have hill farms are managing quite well. They're located in high valleys, and they've always fed Merhaven whatever it couldn't take from the sea itself. We have grain and hay and vegetables, mostly root crops now. We have milk and cheese. Of course, the fishermen bring in full nets. Fish of both shell and fin are plentiful and getting more so." She pushed the heavy door open and led Xulai inside. The floors were tiled with red clay; the walls were as white inside as out; the rooms were warm. Xulai laid her hand on the floor. That was where the heat was coming from.

"Hollow tiles," said Genieve. "Justinian and I used to talk about all the ancient technology that we'd lost. He had many old books. This is a very ancient system. Some ancient people—I forget their names— heated their baths this way. There's a fireplace outside, and it's arranged so the hot air goes through the floors inside and then up a chimney. Several of the families up here have copied it. Justinian sent me the plans in a letter when I wrote to him saying how chilly it was here in winter when the wind comes in from the sea."

Xulai smiled. "Abasio heated his wagon in a similar way. He, too, has old books."

"Is Justinian all right, really?"

"I believe so," said Xulai honestly. "Truly, Genieve, I believe so. He's simply gone where he can't be bullied or used in any way by the evil people Abasio spoke of. We traveled as two brothers and Abasio grew a beard so no one would recognize us. I'm supposed to take that ship down there and sail to Tingawa. It is my father's wish that I do this, as soon as I can."

"Your father?"

Xulai stared intently at the woman across from her. Her father trusted this woman; she would also trust her. She laid her hand on Genieve's, saying softly, "Genieve, I am Justinian's daughter, Xu-i-lok's daughter. You must not tell anyone. Not your servants, not your friends. To the rest of the world, I am only his messenger, but he would want me to tell you the truth."

The woman merely sat for a long moment, mouth open. "Did he tell you that we . . ."

"He told me that you were his dearest friend. He told me that if he had not met my mother, you and he might have married. He could not help himself, Genieve. The match between him and my mother was a thing fated. Truly. And you must not mention to anyone that I am his daughter because everyone related to him is marked for death. Self- ishly, I would like to avoid that, but evidently my survival is important to many others as well."

Genieve sat down, shaking her head. "But no one knew he had . . ."

"No one knew he had a child. Exactly! Genieve, even I did not know I was his child until after my mother died. I didn't even know she was my mother. I have grieved over my ignorance, but it was a secret, kept close, and we must go on keeping it. If anyone asks, I am simply a Xakixa—do you know what that is?"

She murmured, "I've heard of it. There are Tingawans here. They have spoken of the custom."

"Good. Then you say that's what I am. That's why I'm returning to Tingawa."

"This man with you—who is he?"

"His name is Abasio. He is a good man and a good friend who has saved my life several times. My father trusted him."

Abasio chose that moment to enter the room, pay his respects to Genieve, and make brief explanations. "We must get to Tingawa. The last ship is here, and we must take it. Do you have any idea where the crew or the captain may be?"

"They are staying in the building that was occupied by the shipping office when the ships came in here. Before the waters rising made everyone move. They moved the shipping office, of course, but it's still the building nearest the piers."

"How long ago was it that the town was moved?"

"Two years ago. The piers have been moved twice since. They are about ready to move the wooden buildings again. They will not move the stone ones again. From now on, all buildings will be built on runners that teams of beasts can move uphill. When will the water stop rising?"

Abasio shook his head, choosing to be soothing rather than truthful. "No one seems to know exactly. The people in Tingawa probably know better than we do. That's another reason for our journey there."

"I wish someone would find out and tell the poor people who live by the sea. It's a wearying thing, moving a town! Everything is so strange! Some of us rode out recently, down around this arm of the mountains, to take a look at the Big Mud. You know of it?"

"A marsh, isn't it?" Xulai asked. "I've seen it on maps. A huge swale, the size of a country, that accumulates rain and stream water, south of here."

"It was a marsh, yes. Full of ducks and stilts and storks and other wetland creatures, huge, as you say. Not a good place to get lost in. It has always been separated from the ocean by a seaside desert of low dunes, smaller than those on the Great Dune Coast, but the same kind of loose sand, moving with the wind. Now, at high tide, the ocean cuts through the dunes and runs into the Big Mud. It's no longer merely a marsh. It has become a huge shallow lake! Some of the men said it is larger in area than the Highlands of Ghastain. Each tide washes more of the dunes away."

Genieve sounded more annoyed than troubled. Xulai followed Abasio's lead, merely nodding while swallowing her surprise. It was better for the good lady to be annoyed than frightened to death.

There was a knock at the door, and a very wide, white-aproned woman came in, her hair done up in a twisted kerchief. "Since you said they wasn't fussy, ma'am, I've warmed something up."

"This is Mrs. Bang," Genieve announced. "Please go with her and have a warm meal. We'll talk again when you've finished, and meantime I'll see to having rooms readied for you."

She went away, shaking her head slightly, worrying at the idea of Justinian away somewhere, in danger. Abasio and Xulai went in the other direction.

Across the bay, on the ridge they had left only an hour or so before, a small carriage surrounded by an orderly pack of wolves arrived. Carriage and driver sat there for a moment while the driver stared at the rising waters and across at the pale blotch on the hillside that was all she could see of the white-towered building she was looking for. After a time, she detected the road to her left and she and the wolves started down the hill toward the road that led around the bay. No doubt there would be some game in those forests across the way that would feed her charges so she would not have to frighten the lady of the house.

In Ghastain, Mirami was forbidden to leave her quarters, over her vehement protests. The following morning, when the king went to question her himself, she lay on the bed, barely breathing, a terrible smell coming from her with each exhalation, like rotten meat. At first, when closed in this suite of rooms yesterday afternoon, she thought she had caught Chamfray's illness. Then she had wondered if the illness had not been directed at them both. Briefly, she had thought of Alicia, but she knew of no poison that did this, and very shortly later she was barely conscious and could say nothing. King Gahls fidgeted and fussed; one of his advisers suggested that this felicitous coincidence be put to use and the Tingawan emissary be summoned as witness. The emissary came to see that Mirami was obviously dying; she had not even the strength to deny she had killed Xu-i-lok when the question was asked. Though Precious Wind had long ago told them the truth, the emissary pretended to be satisfied. Bear was not the only vengeance seeker who was now following Alicia on her way back to the Old Dark House. Several very highly trained attachés to the embassy were keeping both Bear and Alicia company on the way.

In Merhaven, late at night, when no one was moving about in the town, the shipping office of Tingawa in the person of the ship's captain received a delegation: Precious Wind, whom he had met long ago; Abasio, whom he had not; Xulai, whom he knew of but had never met. The ship must be readied to leave, he was told.

"Except for food stores, the *Falsa-xin* is ready. It has been ready for almost twenty years," the captain growled. "My hair was black when we arrived here. The crewmen were young. We are older now, some of us have died; they've been replaced. The sails and cables have rotted; they've been replaced. We have a new mainmast. Last season we hauled her up onto the beach and scraped her bottom. I have almost renamed her *Baywind* instead of *Daywind*. Everything is as I promised my lord Lok-i-xan, head of Clan Do-Lok. We do not break oath."

"You will need hay," said Abasio. "I'm taking my horse."

"Ridiculous," said the captain.

"Either he takes his horse, or I don't go on the *Daywind*," said Xulai firmly. "Then you will have broken oath."

The captain took a deep breath and bowed slightly. "Of course, ma'am. Hay." He should have expected this. Clan Do-Lok never did the thing expected. "Just one horse?"

"We had another, and a mule. They will be cared for here."

"You will need a good deal of meat," said Precious Wind. "I'm taking a dozen wolves."

The captain grimaced and looked at Xulai, his mouth agape.

"Yes, she is," said Xulai. "I'm taking my fisher, as well."

The furry thing on her shoulder wiggled its nose at the captain and remarked, "Actually, if you can do some fishing en route, the wolves and I can probably do very well on fish. Fresh fish is preferable to salt meat, certainly."

Though imperturbability was one of the requirements of command, the captain took a moment or two to admit to himself he had heard the creature speak. "Give me a day or two," said the captain. "We didn't plan on livestock. And, as for the wolves, do they need to be . . . caged?"

"I shouldn't think so," said Precious Wind. "Not so long as they don't get really hungry."

"About . . . sanitation?" the captain went on doggedly.

"The wolves will poop where I tell them to poop," said Precious Wind.

"The horse likewise," said Abasio, trying to control laughter. "Have you a poop deck?"

"I don't poop at all," said the fisher in melancholy tones. "For some reason, it isn't necessary for me." Then, seeing the four pairs of eyes fixed wonderingly on him. "Well, one likes to experience everything, doesn't one?"

"No," said Abasio firmly. "Fisher, there are many things you don't want to experience. Loss, grief, pain for a start . . ."

"Weariness," said Xulai. "Trouble, hatred . . ."

"Sending former friends into danger," said Precious Wind. "Be content, creature. You are better off than most of us." She turned to the captain. "Sir, aside from these unexpected quadruped guests, we will put you to no trouble. But, please, put it about in the town that you and your men are weary of waiting and have decided to return to your own country. Say nothing about anyone going with you."

The captain frowned at her. "And how do I explain hay?"

"Say you've purchased a couple of fine horses to take home with you. Tell people they've been stabled over at the Watch House. The lady Genieve will confirm it, if anyone asks. As for whatever meat we take, it could be for the crew, and the fisher is right. Fresh fish is preferable to salt meat."

"It's strange," said the captain, "but the oceans are not as salty as they were in my youth. It's easier now to soak salt meat and make it palatable."

They left the captain and rode back to the Watch House.

"Is it true, about the oceans not being as salty?"

Abasio nodded. "The deep waters rising had no salt in them. One could almost drink the ocean water now."

Genieve awaited them. "When will you go?" she asked.

"A couple of days," Precious Wind replied. "Will you come with us, Genieve? You would be welcome."

She shook her head. "I knew you would invite me, but no. No. My people are here. My children and grandbabies live nearby. They depend upon me. I will stay with them. I think it's likely the waters won't come much farther, not in my lifetime, at least. I remember Justinian telling me about Tingawa. The islands are mountainous, I know, but still, they are islands. Will you find any land left there, when you return?"

Precious Wind answered. "Tingawa also extends onto the neighboring continent, ma'am. Much of that area is mountainous. The low-lying islands were being depopulated even before I left there. Those left are not so heavily populated that there would not be room for all Tingawans on the continent, if it becomes necessary."

"Still, I will remain here with my family and my people. They were my husband's people, and before he died, he passed his duty toward them on to me."

"As it should be," said Precious Wind approvingly. "Now, it may be that Bear—you met him, he brought you Justinian's greeting here some days ago?"

"The big, angry man. Yes, he did."

"If he returns, tell him we have gone but that another ship is coming for him from Tingawa. We cannot wait for him, but we will not abandon him or our people who are at our embassy here in Norland. Tell him to wait for us here. But do not talk to him or anyone about the ship that is leaving. Do not say we went aboard it. The captain got tired of waiting, and he left. He bought a couple of horses. You've been stabling them for him. He took the horses with him. Everyone in Merhaven will have heard of that before we go. Can you trust your people to stay silent about our having been here?"

Genieve nodded, saying in a serious voice, "Only Dobbich and Mrs. Bang are here just now. Both are trustworthy. And when your friend comes, he may stay here with us. I will give him the message."

And that was all there was of it. A few nights later, the ship sailed in darkness, with no one to witness Blue's difficulty getting through the door of one of the four little cabins opening onto the deck, now his stable. Three other cabins were for Precious Wind, for the wolves, and for Abasio and Xulai together. The wolves greeted the straw-bedded little room they were to use as a den with suspicion. Precious Wind threw a blanket upon the straw and lay down upon it. They lay down around her. If she was there, they were satisfied. When she knew the wolves were comfortable without her, she would sleep in her cabin. There was no hurry. She could sleep anywhere.

There was no moon. The sky was overcast. Men at the capstan trudged silent circles, first to pull up the anchor that held them near the pier and then to pull the ship away from the pier by winding up the fat cable that led to a second, larger anchor sunk far out in the bay. Abasio pointed the big cables out to Xulai, reminding her of the rope nets holding the cliff villages in place. When they were above the larger anchor they trudged again, coiling that rope into its cable tier and hoisting the anchor into its chains. The captain gave his orders in a low voice; the seamen did not shout or whistle as they loosed sails and tugged them to catch the offshore wind, turning the ship and tacking it slowly out of the bay. When morning came, the ship had gone west beyond the edge of the world, and only one woman, standing alone in the tower of the Watch House, had seen it go.

FAR OUT IN THE WESTERN sea, as the sun rose, Xulai came on deck to see a familiar figure standing at the rail. She stopped, breathless, as he turned.

"Father!" The word she had never used came without thought. She threw herself into his arms, feeling his wet face pressed to her forehead. "Where have you been?"

"Xulai, Xulai, Daughter, oh, if you knew how long I've wanted to call you that . . ." They clung together wordlessly.

Finally, she managed a coherent thought. "But here? Why didn't we travel together? Why didn't we—"

"Shhh. We couldn't." His arms tightened around her. He held her away from him, looking into her eyes. "So many things I wished for that I couldn't . . . Couldn't let you know who you were. Couldn't let anyone know. Couldn't show you any affection more than I might show a stranger. But I've been here, child. I started the journey two nights after you left. Hallad, Prince Orez, arrived that same night to keep Woldsgard safe. This is where your mother told me to go, to keep me safe and to confuse things." He wiped his eyes, half laughing. "Oh, didn't we spend decades confusing things! I've spent so many years making false trails I may never be able to travel openly anywhere!"

"How did you get here?"

"I came south, within easy distance of the Old Dark House but west of it, along the mountains. A couple of my Men of the Mountain from the high north were with me for most of the trip, scouting ahead, cleaning up our trail behind. That's one route, close behind the Old Dark House, where they'd never suspect I would go! From there, day by day, I kept on through the forests to the Lake of the Clouds, then east to Elsmere and on to Merhaven, and then, at night, onto this ship. Years ago, Xu-i-lok wrote a letter for me to carry, telling the captain what to do with me. I have been just another of the seamen for some time now. Every now and then they have to take the ship out into the sea to be sure it's still seaworthy. I am actually learning how to set sails and which rope to pull when they yell at me. It took some getting used to, being yelled at."

"You came all that way alone? But you didn't go to Genieve?"

"It was best so."

"Why didn't we go to Tingawa years ago? Why didn't we bring my mother? Why—"

"Shhhh." He drew her over to a covered hatch and sat her down upon it. "We followed plans, dear one, plans centuries in the making. Plans made by the clan Do-Lok. Oh, child, they've been trying to solve this one for over a hundred years."

"What 'this one'?"

"The problem of what mankind does with the waters rising. What does he do when there is no more dry land, dear heart? Oh, not in my lifetime or yours, but soon after. No way to stop the waters rising. No way to go back to the planet we used to have. No way to undo all the things we did wrong. Clan Do-Lok has been trying to work this one out for a very long time. You're part of the solution, as was I. First Xu-i-lok and I, the man who loved her, to create you. Then you and Abasio . . . we had to wait for Abasio. He was a person they knew had to exist, somewhere. Statistics, they said. Statistically, he had to exist! First they had to find him! Then they had to get him to Woldsgard. We couldn't leave Woldsgard until that happened. And it might not have worked. You might have hated him. Oh, I was so thankful to meet him, there at the gard, to know you liked him."

"Love him, Father."

"Even better then, my child. Even better. Oh, so good to say that something is going well! Precious Wind, she was part of it, a good part of it. Even Blue, the horse, he's turning out to be part of it too. And you had to be old enough to understand and strong enough to endure . . ."

"To do what?" she cried.

"To create a new human race," he said. "People who can live in the sea."

"And all this terror, this being frightened, was *planned*?"

"No. None of the horror was planned, not by *us*. Just as the water goes on rising, so there are forces on earth who don't want us to survive. That much was known. We *did not know* who they were! Where were they? Why were they? Those things weren't known then and aren't really known now. To begin with we didn't know about the duchess or her mother. We still don't know where they got their powers or their ideas. Decades ago Prince Lok-i-xan sent someone to cross the Stony Mountains and locate the man who *statistically had to be there*. He turned out to be Abasio, but they had to locate him and send him in our direction. He had to come and meet you. It had to be voluntary."

"Voluntary," she cried. "Are you sure?"

"I'm absolutely positive. The only thing anyone suggested to Abasio was that he go to Woldsgard because he might find something interesting there. Precious Wind came to Woldsgard voluntarily, and Oldwife Gancer was already there, and I went away when my beloved died, and I knew you would come to Merhaven. I knew I would go with you."

"And Genieve?"

He smiled sadly, shaking his head. "I haven't spoken to Genieve. I know Genieve will stay with her children, her people. We cannot recover our youth, so why make her suffer yet again? Or that may be only my vanity speaking. She may have forgotten me long ago."

"No, she had not. But she did choose to stay with her people," Xulai said in some confusion.

"Genieve was always dutiful. And, though people always seem to value what they lose more than what they have, I think, she loved her husband very well. All in all, then, my decision was a good one. Now, take me to meet your companions, the new ones, with four legs."

She took a deep breath and decided to stop asking questions for a while. She had not yet half absorbed the answers she had been given.

"I can introduce you to Blue, Father, though he is seasick, but only Precious Wind can introduce you to the wolves."

ALICIA AND HER ESCORT ARRIVED at the Old Dark House four days after leaving Ghastain. They had ridden hard to Benjobz Inn, taken a meal and short rest there, for the horses. Men could be terrorized into staying awake, but horses could not, and flogged horses sometimes stumbled, hurting or even killing their riders. Even Alicia bowed to this necessity. From Benjobz her nearest hidden shaft was not far; the horses went back to Benjobz, the people made the trip down the shaft to the ancient rails and trams, which was fearsome but quick. The underground tram ride from east to west was downhill the whole way, ending at another shaft only one day's ride from the Old Dark House, and there were always horses kept stabled nearby. She dismissed the men at her gate and went on into the house by herself. No one answered her call. There was no one in the house at all.

Raging, she went to her cellar, opening the door with her code and flinging herself headlong down the stairs, not waiting for the door to close behind her, not seeing Bear, who had caught it in his huge hands and was holding it open. The men from the embassy had found Alicia's secret route, and they had not rested at Benjobz but had come straight on.

Two Tingawans stepped around Bear and blocked the door open for him. He had realized he was being followed some time ago and had invited the other Tingawans to stop hiding from him in the interest of time. He knew trained assassins and warriors when he met them. It was well they were trained, for the underground way had been terrible, dark, and seemingly endless.

Now the foremost among them gave him a grim salute. "Together," he said. "Now we take vengeance on the woman who killed Xu-i-lok and ordered the death of Xu-i-lok's daughter."

Bear froze, for the moment unmoving. "Daughter?"

"Xu-i-lok's daughter. Xulai. The granddaughter of Lok-i-xan."

Still he was motionless. *The granddaughter of Lok-i-xan.* And he had been too stupid to see it. He had stood there on the road, on his way from Merhaven, talking with Precious Wind, naming Xulai as a mere Xakixa. Ignoring all the time, the attention, the treasure that was spent in caring for her. Calling her the daughter of a nobody. Of course they had said she was, to protect her, from people like himself! A mere Xakixa. *Whom he had sold.*

He seemed to hear Precious Wind whispering to him from across the wide sea. "*Oh, Great Bear of Zol! As though her parentage should have made any difference!*"

In the room below, Alicia was inspecting her devices. She had left the seeker device working to find Jenger, and now its screen sparkled with red dots, dozens, hundreds of them, spread in a great circle around the Vulture Tower, and more of them leading south, fading like a comet's tail. How could he be spread over that wide a distance?

The answer came to her. Wolves: they had torn him apart, eaten him, and shat him out as they traveled away; merely wolves. No need for the little capsules, the seeker mirror, the hunt. He was gone. She was momentarily angry, as momentarily amused: poor Jenger. He certainly wouldn't have foreseen that!

She turned to her household devices, a simple screen with lights that moved among the various rooms to show her where her servants were. It was completely dark! There were no servants anywhere in the Old Dark House. They were not anywhere in Altamont that she could find upon her map. She screamed, "Where? Where is my cook, where are my maids? My archers? Where have they gone?"

A voice came from behind her, gratingly, slowly, mechanically. "Master said send them all away."

She turned. Brighter lights than usual gleamed on the huge device in the corner, the one that watched her and made little noises.

"What master?" she demanded. "Who told you to send them away? And what right do you have to send anyone anywhere?"

"He is my master. I do what he says do," the machine said. The words did not come from any organic throat or mouth, she knew that. Devices could not feel. They could not be threatened, any more than horses could. She forced herself into something approaching calm. "Who told you?"

"Old Dark Man told me."

"Old Dark Man is dead."

"No." *Hiccup hiccup.* "Not dead. I make sure not dead."

The hiccup sound was almost laughter. In that instant, she heard a sound above and behind her, on the steps. She turned and saw Bear poised there, his face twisted in hatred, a sword in his hand. A half scream came from her throat, cut off by a shout from the machine.

"In corner, quick! I protect, quick!"

Without thinking she darted into the cubicle behind the pillar, bumping the shelves so that their contents rattled, rolled, fell. Her precious things! She grabbed for her possessions as the machine moved. It couldn't move, but it did move! It thrust itself across the opening, completely blocking it, preventing Bear from coming near her. She had walls all around her, three of stone, one of metal. She heard Bear shout, heard other voices. Tingawan voices! Men's voices! A grating sound came from the device blocking the cubicle, a creaking, as of old, unoiled hinges.

She knelt to pick up her precious things, brushing aside the fallen capsule, crushing it beneath her knee as she moved to retrieve the lock of her father's hair. She choked down hysterical laughter. With Jenger spread all over the Dragdown Swamps, all over the heights, she certainly didn't need that anymore. Strange to see him spread on her map like that, everywhere, a cloud of him! She actually chuckled. A cloud of shit instead of her neat little cloud of . . . death. She turned to her father's linen shift, brushing it off, folding it carefully. The little portrait, so handsome, so wonderful. She set it carefully on the shelf, the shift and the lock of her father's hair beside it. Where was his ring? Where? She fell to her knees once more, searching the corners.

Continuous sounds came from beyond the barrier, in the cellar, cries of pain, feet running up the stairs in panicky haste, yells of fear, rage, pain! There were people out there. Bear hadn't been alone. After a long time, silence fell, absolute. Not a whisper, not a creak, not even the little hum of the watcher. Only a silence that stretched, stretched, went on and on for a long time. The watcher had shoved its huge bulk tight across the cubicle, like a metal wall. Only a thin slit at the top let in the light, the air. No one could get in to hurt her. Of course, she could not get out, but it would let her out when it was safe, she was sure of that. The Old Dark Man had said it would protect. The mechanism itself had said that. She sat down on the floor, leaning her forehead on her knees, moving in discomfort. The ring. Falyrion's ducal ring. She was sitting on it.

Carefully she wiped the dust from it, replaced it upon its cushion, put it in place upon its shelf. She was astonished at how exhausted she felt. Well, of course, she and the archers had not really slept in three days.

More time went by. Her father, Falyrion, had always said, "Sleep when you can. Eat when you can. You may not be able to do either later on." She had found this to be true. She took her father's shift, pillowed her head on it, leaned back against the wall. She could smell his scent, still, after all these years.

Later, new sounds wakened her, the heavy footfalls of someone coming down the stairs and moving about. The watching machine creaked, turned slightly, but remained against the cubicle. She dozed again until the sound of the machine woke her as it rolled away.

She gathered her precious things and clutched them to her breast, struggling to get up and out of the cubby. She was stiff. She hurt. Her stomach hurt. She peered into the gloom. The room was almost unlighted. She could see one body on the steps. Not Bear. Someone else. No sounds, and then a voice she knew.

"Alicia, my dear."

She turned. She knew that voice. *She did not want to hear that voice!*

He was there, leaning slightly on the huge machine. It had opened to disclose a place inside it, a kind of cocoon, a padded, man-shaped cocoon, like a coffin . . .

"It seems I had picked a good time to be wakened," said the Old Dark Man. "Just in time to save my dear daughter."

She glared at him, lifted her hands. She held Falyrion's things, her father's things, in her hands. "I'm not!" she screamed. "I'm not your daughter. I told you! I'm Falyrion's daughter. He was my father, not you, not you."

The enormous head turned; the huge jaw dropped enough that the thin lips of that wide, wide mouth could curve into a parody of a smile, like a horizontal slit in a melon, empty, mirthless, horrible. He did not laugh. She had never heard him laugh. His brows were like a cliff, his nose a promontory. He was monumental, ashy gray, old as time. His voice was the sound of rusty hinges, creaking doors, lids of rotten coffins.

"Falyrion? Is that what your elder sister told you?"

"I have no elder sister!"

"Mirami!"

"My mother!"

"Oh, well, yes, both your mother and your elder sister. Both my daughter and your mother. You are the tenth or eleventh generation of creatures I have made to serve me and bear the next one in line. My first daughter was your great-great-great-how-many-greats-grandmother, and my next daughter from her was one great less, and so on until your mother, and from her, you, my daughter, will bear me my next daughter, who will be my first daughter's so-many-greats-I-have-not-recently-counted-them-granddaughter, and on, and on, and on . . ." He made a noise: "*Heh, heh, heh.*"

Was it meant as a laugh? "I don't want you for a father," she screamed, beyond herself, outside herself with rage. "I want him. I want him. She killed him. Your daughter, she killed him. So now she's dead. I killed her. I won't, I won't, I won't do that with you anymore, I won't help you create someone else. You didn't create me. He was my father. I know he was. I know he was. She said he was."

The voice changed, the face changed, stilled, became even more skull-like. "Mirami? Dead? Why?"

"Because she killed him. He was mine and she killed him."

"I still needed her!" the huge voice howled. "She is my flesh! I need my flesh! You had no right to interfere in that way." The Old Dark Man stood away from the machine. "Hold her," he said.

Quick as the strike of a snake, the machine reached long arms, like tentacles, like cables with hands at the ends, hands that took her and held her.

"You will do whatever I tell you to do," howled the Old Dark Man. "You have been overeager, undisciplined. In future you will do only what I tell you to do! You will be impregnated. You will give me another one of you, for later! Then you will give me flesh!"

He came close to her, staring into her face. Horrid sickness bubbled up inside her; a flood rose in her throat. She dropped the things she was holding, her father's things, to clutch at herself, to clutch at this sudden opening inside her, like a great thrusting flower of horrible pain, pushing up, swelling, bursting, petals going into every part of her! She writhed in the machine's grasp and vomited, a great spew that drenched the Old Dark Man. Blood. Blood on the linen, the ribbons, blood on her precious things . . . her father's things.

"What is the matter with you?" the Old Dark Man said, glaring at her. "Are you ill?"

"No!" she screamed defiantly, as honestly as she knew. "Just sickened at the thought of you."

The pain came again. Past the machine, on the floor, she saw the shattered fragments of a capsule. Jenger's. It was Jenger's. It had to be, that was the only one left. She had used the machine five times. First was Xu-i-lok. It had been long ago, not done well, but done. The woman had died, finally. All right. And the second time she hadn't made any mistakes. The second time was Chamfray. She'd attached the capsule to a pigeon's leg and sent it to Ghastain. Whoever took it from the pigeon and tried to open it would have squashed it, and released it, and the pigeon loft was close enough. So that one was all right. Then her archers had brought Jenger's hairs from the tower; she'd used those to make one for Jenger. That's the one she had left here. Then one for the abbot. The prior had sent the materials and she'd made it and returned it by pigeon inside the message tube. He was dead by now. All right. Then she had made one for Mirami. The one she'd kept material for ever since her father died. She'd done that one right, taken it to Ghastain herself. She couldn't have mixed them up. Unless she'd mixed Marimi's with Jenger's before she left for Ghastain.

If she'd done that . . . if she and Marimi were sisters, genetic sisters, maybe . . . maybe it had been close enough to kill her! No, and it wouldn't have acted this soon, would it? It had only broken a short time ago when she saw Bear . . .

She reached up to brush her hair from her face, remembering that night with Jenger, poor Jenger, he was gone, and she had brushed her hair away from the branch that . . . the branch that . . . did it catch her hair? *Because someone was out there in the woods.* No. It had been dark. Too dark. No one had seen, no one could have seen. Besides, it was too quick. *The capsule had only broken a little while ago.*

No. No, the capsule broke before she fell asleep. She had been so tired that she had slept a long time. A long, long time. If the capsule had been Mirami's, it wouldn't kill her. Make her sick, maybe, but it wouldn't kill her. *Unless those hairs had not been Jenger's hairs . . .*

It was the last coherent thought she had. She never heard the Old Dark Man raging through the cellars of the Old Dark House. She never heard him screaming at her, asking her what foolish, foolish thing she had done to allow her own methods to be used against her. "Mirror defense," he cried. "Didn't I teach you about mirror defense?"

Later, he left the place in a rage, like a spout of black fire. Generations he had bred to hate Tingawa! Generations to kill those who had foiled the aims of his makers! Now it was all to start over. He would have to do it all again!

EYES FROM THE FOREST WATCHED the Old Dark Man go southward through the trees, a blazing black shadow, faster than anything natural could move. Eyes in the forest looked down at the Great Bear of Zol, lying dead among the leaves. Bear had been a great warrior. The thing that had defeated him was a greater warrior, but that thing was only partly human, and not the greater part.

The emissary from Tingawa leaned down and put his hand on Bear's body, bloodied as it was. "I am of your people," he said. "I respect your clan. I will carry your soul to the clan of Zol in Tingawa. You are not forsworn and I will be your Xakixa."

He sat there for some little time, his head bowed, while the soul made up its mind to come with him. It was very confused and ashamed. The confusion often happened in battle. Men did not really expect to die. He guessed where the shame came from. Poor warrior. He had been tempted past his strength. The emissary kept his hand in place, forgiving whatever the cause had been. When the emissary knew, finally, that the soul had come to him, he arose and went into the Old Dark House. The monster he had seen would return here. The monster needed these machines, these devices. They had made the mistake of waiting for him before. They would not make that mistake again.

The emissary had brought weapons with him to vaporize this house and all it contained; ancient devices, partly discovered, partly remade, that would make it impossible for flesh to live on this ground for a very long time. He stood looking at Alicia's body for a long moment. The machine that had protected her had been left without instructions. It clicked and hummed as though troubled. He took a flame weapon from his clothing and burned the inside of the device, crisped it, broke the wires, the linkages, wrecked it. Whatever else he did, this must be done first, this thing must be disabled. He would not wait, not even while he and his remaining men took time to check through the monstrous house. Both the machine and the woman's body would vaporize, along with everything else, but he would not gamble on their getting it done before the creature came back.

They spread out, working their way upward room by room, floor by floor. They had newly created tools that helped them find hollows, secret rooms, all the places where the books were hidden. They had known there had to be books. He and his fellows scanned them rapidly, looking for particular things, particular subjects. He took those that would be useful, including a few that were extraordinarily interesting. The others he tossed about so that they, too, would be destroyed atom by atom. They were obscene in their love of pain, in their gloating over death.

In the deepest vault of all they found something stranger than anything they had found before, and they left the ways to it open, so that this, too, would be totally destroyed.

When they had gathered the things they intended to save, the emissary set the devices carefully, calling his remaining companions to help him from time to time, to double-check, to be quite sure. They few and the rest of the embassy staff, who had already begun the journey to Merhaven, were the only Tingawans left in Norland. They had stayed out of the conflict, for this duty had to be done and they could not risk being killed before it was done. If the monster hadn't gone away, they would have had to use other devices from outside the Old Dark House, devices that might not have been as effective. The creature had gone, so they could do this part of the job right, do it as they had been trying to do for generations.

When they had finished, they went swiftly southward along a hilly road, toward the Lake of the Clouds. From a hilltop, they watched the bulbous cloud of fire and smoke that rose on a stem of flame above the heart of Altamont. They had allowed for the light evening breeze, which would spread the dust only so far as the ancient tunnels, the old shafts, the elevators, the towers. The dust would not reach farther than that, but that far it would reach. No one would go there again. He had brought pigeons with him to carry messages to the abbey, warning them away from Altamont, warning the world away from Altamont, warning them about the Old Dark Man, warning the world about the Old Dark Man. Without his coffin, his womb, his preserving container, he would not live long, but the terrible truth was he need not live long to do great damage. One day was too long. A year would be an eternity of destruction.

In the morning, they began the trek south and east where they planned to meet the other embassy staff on the road. They would all leave Norland together. They would not leave until they had consulted with the clan Do-Lok. There might still be things left to do here in Norland.

ON THE SHIP, LIFE SOON settled into a routine. Blue slept at night; the wolves prowled. First thing in the morning all four-legged passengers came out on deck to empty themselves in a designated place and have the resultant mess hosed overboard with the water that was pumped from the bilges. Precious Wind and Abasio then saw to their feeding: oats and hay for Blue, meat—often fish—for the wolves. While he ate, Blue leaned against the rail and thought of the trail he had traveled on the way to Woldsgard, thus keeping his mind off waves, water, and the fact that if he did not think of something else he would be seasick. Meantime, the wolves prowled around the ship if they needed additional exercise, after which they retreated to their den, where they lay about in snoring piles until evening came, when the whole process was repeated. By the tenth day, the sailors—who had very slowly grown accustomed to wolves—commented that there were no more rats on the ship. Precious Wind thought this unfortunate, since hunting rats had given the wolves something to do, and restless wolves would likely be discontented.

Remembering hiding-and-finding games she had played as a child, she hit upon the idea of hiding bits of dried meat about the ship for the wolves to find at night, and the sailors offered to do the hiding for her, in the holds, mostly. She allowed this, warning them that what a wolf could smell, a wolf would get at, one way or the other, and it would not be a good idea to bury the bait in places they did not want wolves to dig their way to. She also conducted races between various pairs and offered for discussion the idea of giving each member of the pack a name. The resultant discussions passed many hours for both men and wolves as names suggested by wolves were often impossible for humans to replicate; names suggested by humans were often unpleasant to wolven ears.

"Captain," she asked when she began to run out of ideas, "is the equipment I left aboard when you brought me here still in the hold?"

He nodded. "That was a long time ago. It's there. Do you want it brought up?"

"I'll need a place with good light to work in. The devices are solar powered."

"Aside from the deck, the best light is in where the horse is. There's room in there for you to set up a worktable, if you like. If the horse won't mind."

"The horse won't mind," she said. "In fact he may be very helpful."

Blue was interested. "What are you going to do?" he asked when the men had set up her table and she was busy unpacking the little machines she would work with.

"I'm taking the first tiny step in attempting to let the wolves learn to talk."

He snorted, asked, "How are you going to do that?"

"Same way they did with you. Or with your father or mother. They discovered or created an equine voice-box cell for horses. They took genetic snips from humans, the parts that give them the parts of the brain associated with language, the vocal cords and throat, and the tongue. Then they took centuries or so to figure out how to meld the two physiologies and how to insert the genetic instructions into the reproductive system of horses."

"Centuries?"

"Well, each new horse baby took almost a year to be born, then it had to be exposed to language, which meant people around it all day talking. Then if it didn't work—and the first few dozen times it didn't work—the people doing it had to figure out why it didn't work, then they had to start over. I say 'they,' but of course there was a different 'they' every thirty or forty years. There was no way to hurry the reproductive part. It takes patience."

"I have noticed my tongue is not like most other horses' tongues."

"Yes, the tongue has to change some while still not interfering with your normal eating habits. It's all very complicated. We've succeeded with horses and dogs—that's how I know we'll be able to do wolves. There are only minor differences in the genetics, but . . ."

"There was a talking coyote in Artemisia."

"So Abasio said, yes. Dogs and coyotes can talk; wolves are next."

"Who will teach them to talk when they're very young? Their parents can't."

"Well, sometimes we've been able to change adults. If we can change the pack members, they'd teach the young ones. Otherwise it would be whoever's around."

"And when you have talking wolves, then what? Will that stop the waters rising?"

She stared at him for a long moment. "Blue, nothing we know of will stop the waters rising."

"Then what good is it?"

She sat down on a hay bale and gazed at him thoughtfully. "If you had the choice to change what you were and go on living—let's say you could turn into a whale—would you do it?"

"My other choice being what?"

"Drowning."

"Oh, I'd whale-ize. Sure. At a full gallop. Are you proposing to do that to me? A whale seems a bit large."

"No, we're not proposing to do anything to you, because at the rate the waters are rising, you'll live out your life on land, and so will the wolves. But you have offspring, colts."

"Foals; colts are male, fillies are female. I have offspring, yes, here and there."

"You'd like the idea that your descendants could . . . whale-ize, wouldn't you? If it was that or drowning?"

"I'd like the idea, I think."

"And you'd like them to talk? Can yours talk?"

"Some of them, but not all. Speaking doesn't breed true. With some mares yes, with others, no."

"Well, if they could, they could tell us what they prefer. Wouldn't that be an advantage?"

"To a whale?"

"Isn't it an advantage for a race of creatures to be able to tell us it wants to be saved instead of just having us do it? Isn't it an advantage to any creature to have a voice, language, and hands to manipulate things?"

"You mean, considering what mankind has done with all three of those great gifts?" He whinnied laughter.

She flushed. "Too many of mankind are fools, but not all. The waters rising may be the salvation of mankind, in fact. So we believe."

"And you're going to arrange it so whales would have hands?"

"A voice, a language, and manipulators of some kind. Whales and dolphins already have their own languages, but no one else can speak it. The easiest way to solve that may be the way we've done it already: create simple translators. Anyhow, that's why I'm trying to give the wolves a language. I like wolves. I admire wolves. And horses."

"Horses do not admire wolves."

"I know. I realize that herding herbivores cannot admire packs of carnivores. I'm hopeful that the time will come when no creature with a developed brain will ever kill any other creature with a developed brain. We have always had two aims. First: to save humanity and as many other dryland living species as we can. Second: to make every intelligent creature mentally and physically capable of language and capable of talking to every other intelligent creature."

"All creatures are intelligent."

She threw up her hands, crying, "I know. We know. It's impossible to save them all, so we started with those that either have a language or that we can give a language."

She turned away from him, her shoulders sagging, and he knew this was a grave trouble to her.

He said, "Well, fish aren't very intelligent, and we'll all have to eat something. If the world is underwater, that means either fish or seaweed, and I don't think I'd do well on fish."

She sighed, nodded, conceded. "We've been arguing over that for several generations. One group of us has been experimenting with vegetable body parts for humans, hoping we could live on sunlight, soil nutrients, and water . . ."

Blue turned his head to stare at her, his mouth half-open as he considered Abasio with branches. "What would that look like?"

"The volunteers looked like themselves with green wings added on. It worked, but the vegetable system is so much slower that the volunteers had to spend most of their time just sitting in the sun. If they were awake, thinking took up most of the energy they were accumulating. Moving was very slow and difficult. Talking was at a rate of about one word a minute. When we took the wings off them and let them go back to eating, they described it as a kind of dream world. Ideas were slow; images were slow; they couldn't even hear speech—it went by like a burst of sound with no meaning in it. Some of the volunteers came out of the experience convinced that trees think all the time, it's just so slow that we can't detect it.

"We're still working on the possibility that people could sleep in the daytime while they accumulate energy, then take off the wings and work at night."

"So, I'm right. If you don't turn us into vegetables, carnivores will have to eat fish and herbivores would eat seaweed."

Blue stared out through the door while she attached and assembled tiny parts in the light of the window. He was trying to imagine talking with wolves. How does food talk to someone who is hungry? Does a hungry person want to take time to talk to food? If they could talk to one another, could they still eat one another?

He mused, "So you'll grow vocal cords in the wolves. Then you'll teach them to talk. Then you'll see if they actually can. Then you'll ask them if they want their young born able to talk?"

Precious Wind picked up one assembly and attached it firmly to another, setting the linked devices into the sunlight. A tiny wheel began to spin. She said, "That's the last step in the process, inserting the right sequence into the reproductive organs. Once we find the right sequence."

"Keeps you from being bored, I suppose," said Blue. "Keeps you from feeling seasick. I'd like to make a suggestion."

"That being?"

"There's a thing called a . . . wampus? A sea thing. It's about my size, I think. Abasio read me a book about it."

"I think you mean walrus," she replied, starting a new assembly. "But they need dry land to have their babies on. A lot of the creatures that were originally land animals that returned to the sea and evolved further while in the sea still need dry land to bear children on. Walruses. Seals. Sea lions. All those. Whales and dolphins bear their young in the water, but they have to boost the babies up to the surface to breathe until the babies learn to do it themselves."

"I'd prefer to think of my foals as turning into something like the wampus, if it came to that." Blue brooded over this for some time, forgetting completely to be seasick. "Or a very large herbivorous sea otter that could live on seaweed. They make nests in the weeds and lie on their backs in the sun. That looks very pleasant to me. I remember rolling on my back as a colt. It was comfortable." He went back to his railing, so full of thought about sea creatures and eating seaweed that he forgot to be seasick for the rest of the day.

OUT ON THE DECK, JUSTINIAN was continuing his conversation with his daughter while Abasio listened from where he leaned on the rail. He had never really seen the ocean until now, on this ship, and he found it endlessly fascinating. He found equally fascinating the things Justinian was telling Xulai. How he had loved Xu-i-lok. How they had met. How they had been married. How frantic they had been when they found out she had been "cursed," though they knew it hadn't been a curse. Whoever had done it had done it badly but repeatedly. If it had been done right, the princess would have died within a season instead of lingering all those years. How they found out it had been Alicia. What they had learned about the Old Dark House.

"The Old Dark Man sounds like an ogre to me," Abasio commented.

"I met a few, back in the wild lands. At first I thought they might be trolls, but trolls weren't intelligent. Both were the results of unhindered genetic experimentation, and I'll bet your Old Dark Man was the same, at least partly. Why does he want to kill Tingawans?"

Precious Wind, who had finished assembling her devices, emerged from the cabin with Blue behind her. "Now that you're talking of the Old Dark Man, there's something I have to tell Xulai. Well, tell all of you, actually. May I interrupt you?"

Justinian nodded and gestured toward a large, square hatch cover where they could sit near one another. As the others arranged themselves, Precious Wind sat down, her booted feet neatly together. From her pocket she took a red, ovoid object and a sheaf of papers, holding them before her. "I found this where you hid it in the wagon, Abasio. I should have given it to Xulai long ago, but I put it off."

"That's not like you," said Xulai chidingly. "You don't put things off."

"You had just learned who you were and how old you were, and I thought any additional responsibilities might be crushing. It was to ease your life that your mother left you this," Precious Wind replied, holding up the red oval she had been holding: "This is *ug ul xaolat.*"

"What is it?"

"In Tingawan the words mean 'a thing master.' It has a number of 'things' that it can order and direct. You can speak to it or simply press it with your fingers to summon a hunter, or to move very swiftly to a place of safety, or to have something carried to another place. Whatever thing you want, this master summons it. It can move you faster than a slaughterer can move. It is why it was entrusted to your mother, so she could escape, if necessary. Unfortunately, this device could not protect her from the peril that came upon her."

"Why has it not been used since?" demanded Xulai, in that voice they had heard only a few times before. "Why has it not rid us of this monster?"

"It was not designed as a weapon. It was meant to be used by scouts, by people moving in the wild. It helps in getting across steep canyons, up and down cliffs. It will carry equipment. It will kill prey, but it will not kill anything that looks human."

"Unfortunately, our monster does seem to look human," said Abasio almost angrily. "And we have no immediate need to be transported across a canyon. Was there something else?"

"Yes, a great deal else." She sighed. "Be patient," she said. "It is a long story. I will tell it not as we discovered it, in bits and pieces, but as a whole, as it happened.

"Late in the Before Time, humans everywhere had divided into tribes, clans, sects that were constantly at war with one another. Each group hated others because of the language they spoke or the god they worshipped or the color of their skin or the food they ate or their personal habits. Few of their hatreds were based on reality; many of them were brought into existence by people who used something called 'media' to whip people into frenzies of hatred. All these hatreds resulted in violence and death.

"One or two tribes among them, we're not sure which ones or how many, put all their ingenuity to work and developed terrible weapons to kill their enemies. There was nothing new in the killing, only in the weapons themselves. Some of the brilliant technologists did a prideful, stupid thing. They invented killing machines that could . . . smell intelligence."

"Smell?" cried Abasio.

"We call it that. The machines could sense intelligence. These men, whoever they were, sat down together and codified their own beliefs. They wrote them down precisely, defining the words they used, making them explicit. A set of beliefs might go something like, '*We believe in Oog, the only true god. We believe women were made to be inferior to men and take orders from men. Oog rightfully directs some men, Oog's high priests; only those men may rightfully direct other men; all men may rightfully direct women and children. Women's task is to have children and obey men. Oog directs that all Oog-believing men convert or kill all other men who do not believe in Oog or the rightfulness which Oog asserts. Women and children who refuse to believe in Oog must be killed.*'

"In order to belong to their faction, their group, their tribe, their clan, Oog people had to believe exactly what was written down, all of it, just as it was written. Then these inventors recorded the brain waves of those who believed these things. We think they averaged them in some way, and the resultant pattern was called the 'pattern of acceptable belief about Oog.' They put this pattern into their new machines."

"So the machines would believe?" cried Xulai. "Machines?"

"No," said Abasio, feeling sick. "So the machines would recognize what thoughts about Oog were allowed."

"Exactly," said Precious Wind. "The inventors then directed their machines to kill anyone whose thinking about Oog did not match the pattern."

Justinian got up and went to lean over the rail, his face ashen. "What one man may devise, another may steal," he said.

"Exactly, again," said Precious Wind through her teeth. "What one may devise, another may steal or reinvent. The slaughterers were very hard to build. We know each one used the brain and body parts of a human volunteer. Only volunteers would have the basic mental pattern. Before long there were dozens of slaughterers going about the world killing people with differing ideas about Oog. Then a group decided that a different language should be banned and anyone thinking of a word in that language was killed. Then a group decided that certain foods should be banned, so anyone thinking about that food or raising that food was slaughtered. Then certain ideas about sex were held to be anathema, and those who thought about those things were slaughtered.

"When the slaughterers had killed off languages A through L and all who worshipped gods 2 through 100, and all who raised parligs, and all who thought about unusual sex practices, some of the zealots refined their objectives. Each in their own region had killed most of those who had *different ideas,* but there were many still alive who thought mostly about other things. They didn't think about Oog or any other god, they had never raised parligs, they didn't really *think* about sex that much, so the tinkerers decided that instead of killing people who held incorrect ideas, they would kill all those who *did not hold the correct ideas.* The devices were told to find all those who did *not* think P or Q and kill them."

"All," grated Abasio. "Not merely men."

"In their pride, the original creators of the killing machines did not realize that intelligence permeates all living things to some extent. The machines were taught to smell intelligence; they smelled it in all living things that did not think P or Q, including animals, birds, bees, ants. The result is what we now call the Big Kill."

"When it was over," said Abasio, "ninety percent of all creatures living on land were dead. Only creatures on remote islands survived. Some of them."

Silence gathered. Eventually, Precious Wind said, "As I said, each slaughterer was made from a volunteer. Back then they were called 'terrorists.' Each slaughterer began with a real human being, a real human brain, though very little of the human being was left when they were completed. Some of the personality survived. Each of the creatures had a name, for example. The tissues that were removed from the original human being were banked for their future use during *maintenance*. Human cells had to be renewed at intervals. The slaughterers mimicked humans in being able to reason, plan, move, adapt. They had memory. They could remember, if vaguely, who they were, what they had done, who they had been. In their folly, their creators had made them and their associated devices self-maintaining, self-repairing. They had been given a very long lifespan. However, they did have to have periodic maintenance, and each one had a maintenance device to which he—they were all male—retreated from time to time for renewal.

"There were a few rebel scientists at the time who fought against the slaughterers. They found out how the creatures were made. They could not destroy them because the killing machines moved around too swiftly. So the rebels retreated to some secret redoubt and developed a way to reach the part of the whole system that did not move around: the maintenance devices. They found a way to change the routine of the maintenance devices so that when the slaughterers went to be maintained, they would be kept in perpetual maintenance. They were not dead, but they were immobilized. In the words of the men who did it, they were 'stuck in the maintenance loop.' If those rebel scientists had failed, or if there had been a few more of the slaughterers, all life on earth would have died except trees and grass."

Justinian murmured, "Why doesn't everyone know about this?"

Precious Wind said, "The few humans who were left knew how most of the race had died. They knew why. They probably wanted to forget it. In any case, it became taboo to speak of it on the theory that speaking of it might make it happen again. In a few generations, the truth was forgotten. The killers became the ogres of future fairy tales. The historic episode came to be called simply 'the Big Kill,' a terror that had happened at the end of the Before Time."

"But you of Tingawa learned the specifics," said Justinian. "When?"

Precious Wind sighed, turned her head from side to side, the cords of her neck standing out. Xulai reached out and massaged the drawn muscles. "Yes, Precious Wind. When?"

"A century or more ago, in Tingawa, our people discovered an ancient vault below one of the Ten Thousand Islands. It contained ease machines."

Abasio barked laughter. "The wonderful subterranean vault of legend?"

She shook her head. "I know, I know. This is a story we have ridiculed for generations, though it persists in the public imagination. We ridicule it honestly now, for it is true that there are no more such vaults and the one we found is now empty. It was a cavern in a volcanic island, not a coral island. We believe it was the same cavern where the savior rebels worked, the ones who stopped the slaughterers, because that's where we found the maps that gave the locations of scores of vaults around the world."

"Around the world?" cried Abasio. "The whole world?"

"On every continent of the ancient world, Abasio. It took Tingawa a full century to find them all. We destroyed them all, along with most of the machines, devices, mechanisms we found with them. All the devices were originally made in the Before Time, when men flew to the moon, when they signaled other worlds around distant stars, when men could engineer the infinitely small in both genetics and electronics to affect even the monstrously large. Truly, they did marvels then, but none of these marvels profited the human race. All of them were for nothing. The earth had already collapsed under the ravenous appetites of too many humans; its ecosystems had been destroyed, its oceans were all but dead, its atmosphere dilapidated so that its sun bathed the surface with deadly radiation. It is hard to imagine, but the environmental situation was so desperate that the sea dwellers and even some land dwellers welcomed the Big Kill."

"I was told the environmental situation actually caused the Big Kill," said Abasio. "Men trying to get rid of other men to make room for their own kind."

"Where did you learn that?" asked Precious Wind.

"Someone in the Edges, I think." Actually it had been from the library helmet. It was all there. First the Big Fat epidemic, the mass starvation, the barking asthma, the lethal skin diseases, then the rich retreating to enclosed redoubts with filtered air, filtered water. And finally, the assault on the redoubts by those who had no redoubts. Air could not be filtered if the air intakes were blocked with bodies. Solar power did no good when millions laid themselves down on the grids. Not everywhere, not all at once, but enough, when added to the work done by the slaughterers, to make a very big kill indeed.

"That could be true. The Big Kill did leave the people who remained more room in which to breathe, though many of them moved near the poles, where the radiation was less severe. They ended up living mostly in caves, coming out only at night. Many groups lost the ability to read, write, or build. It was a darker age than any that had come before. Now we call it the Time When No One Moved Around. Indeed, men did not move around. There was nowhere to go.

"Here and there, mostly in caves or underground redoubts, an abbey survived. In Tingawa, certain monasteries survived, also underground. In such places, we lived like moles. From what Abasio has told us about the Edges, it is probable that some learning survived there. It is certain that in Abasio's Place of Power there were deadly technological survivals. In abbey, or monastery, or Edge, learning was kept alive, ancient things were stored away, and people held the hope there might be an eventual enlightenment.

"When we discovered the ancient vault below the island—"

"How long ago?" Abasio interrupted, wondering vaguely if there were some alive who could be blamed for all this.

"Well before any now living were born, Abasio. The vault we found had monitors showing locations, scattered across the entire world. At first, we didn't know what would be found at those locations. Up until then we had not given our full attention to the records stored in the vault. They were in old languages, hard to decipher, and we had thought we'd get to them later. The new findings demanded that we do it immediately. So, while some of our people tried to find the places being monitored, others of our people burrowed into the accounts, the procedures, the reports.

"The places weren't easy to find. All were very well hidden. When we found the first one, we realized we had discovered the slaughterers that committed the Big Kill. Each one of them was still being monitored by some kind of everlasting atomic device; each one was dormant but still capable of being wakened to kill again. The old technicians had caught them in the so-called maintenance loop, but they hadn't been able to destroy them." She held up her hand, quelling Abasio. "Don't ask me why because I don't know. No one knows. Personally, I think they simply couldn't get to them, not the way the world was then. By that time, people who tried to go anywhere usually died trying it.

"Difficult or not, we of the clan Do-Lok determined to destroy them utterly. One by one, over a long, weary time, our people found and demolished them. As each one was shattered, one of the ancient monitors went dark. Now only one of them registers the existence of the last slaughterer. We knew from the first that this one was different, for it showed movement where the others did not. We knew where the maintenance machine had been, but we *could not find it or find where the creature was!* This one, unlike its fellows, had never been completely dormant. It had either been designed differently or it had adapted in ways its creators never considered. The monitor didn't tell us where either the maintenance device or the slaughterer could be found. It told us only where they had been a hundred years before."

"As though the inventor was looking ahead, preventing his creature from being found," said Justinian bitterly.

Precious Wind nodded assent. "Very possibly, Duke of Wold! A hideous joke from the remote past! We went to the place it had been a hundred years ago—a deserted city along the Great Dune Shore, south of Orez's country, north of Elsmere. We asked questions. Was there a monster here a century ago? Do you know where it went? Men do not live long enough to remember, but sometimes there were local legends, old records. We picked up clues as we went. We tracked the creature through time: to the Big Mud southeast of Merhaven, onto the Highlands of Ghastain, then down toward the Lake Country. Eighty years ago it was here, seventy years ago it was there. We found it, finally, some twenty years ago when Xu-i-lok was stricken by a technology that should no longer have existed!

"You have asked why Alicia and her mother hated Tingawa. They hate Tingawans because they were created by the Old Dark Man to hate the land and the people who destroyed the other slaughterers, and also, perhaps, because in Tingawa there is much intelligence that does not conform! Or, perhaps, merely because they are out of reach."

"The war with the Sea King!" cried Xulai in sudden enlightenment. "It was to keep Tingawa safe from him."

Precious Wind heaved a great breath. "Yes. The fictitious war with the Sea People was to keep the slaughterer away from the islands. There had been some slaughterers near Tingawa, but we'd already destroyed them. The Old Dark Man, however, had been created to be more adaptable than the others. It was a new and improved model. It could move its maintenance device from place to place. It did not kill indiscriminately. It made plans. It deferred killing so it could kill a better target. It had not struck at our embassy. It did not strike at me or Bear, not until recently, after the princess died, and it struck at her through its creations."

"Mirami and Alicia," said Xulai. "Both of them. The creature made them, taught them, trained them."

"Directed them," said Precious Wind. "So we believe. The thing can think a century ahead, and its long-range plans would involve Tingawa directly. So far, we hope, the creature remains ignorant of our larger concerns."

"Do we know anything else about it?" Abasio asked.

"Prince Lok-i-xan's group believes that its flesh part dies periodically. It is thought that perhaps it reproduces itself, over and over, using egg cells from some human female coupled with its own DNA. Rebirth, however, would not explain the fact that this particular monster remembers where it has been and what it has done in the past. It has a continuous memory. It knows who it is and what it has done and what it plans to do."

"I doubt it is reborn," said Abasio. "Repaired, yes. Maintained, yes. It may grow spare parts using cellular material, yes. Or the flesh of the original volunteer may have been divided up to be used at maintenance time. And maybe it hibernates in its maintenance cocoon from time to time, like a toad encasing itself in mud until the next rainy season. It could live for millennia that way, coming back for a while every century without actually being reborn."

Precious Wind said, "The cellular material could have been its own. Each slaughterer we found held only parts of the brain and a small amount of the living body tissue from the original volunteer."

Xulai said, "Then my grandfather may be right about its using cells from women."

"Perhaps he grows bodies he can harvest from," said Precious Wind. "We've considered that. We now know the creature came to the Old Dark House before or at least during Mirami's childhood, and we didn't know that much until Mirami left the place and married Falyrion. She actually spoke of her childhood. Word began to circulate about the things she said. We had people everywhere listening for tales of ogres, monsters, ghosts. By the time we figured out that the creature that had lived in the Old Dark House might be the creature we were seeking, Mirami had left and the Old Dark House was empty. Our agents went there very soon after Mirami left the place. It was closed up, locked. We can deal with locks, even highly technological locks. Some of the people from the embassy took part in the search and know more about it than I do.

"I do know the first thing they looked for was one of the maintenance containers, something like the ones we had found in every other case: a large easy-to-open case about waist high, shaped like a huge coffin, the top made entirely or partially of glass, with various dials and controls on the outside, a man-sized vacancy inside, and a place on the side of it to insert the tubes that held whatever the monster needed to go on living. There was nothing resembling that at the Old Dark House. The cellar did have several small devices and machines and one large, upright machine that seemed to keep the environment properly warm and ventilated. Little lights and sounds on the smaller devices made our people believe some of them might be still functioning. We found cartons of maintenance tubes there, so we assumed the maintenance container had been moved, as it had been many times before. We thought the creature would return for the books, or some of the maintenance tubes, or some of the other devices; when it did, we didn't want the creature to know we'd been there, so we left no sign.

"Many of the people who lived in the area claimed to have seen the creature, it, him, in recent years. The same people also told our people they had seen a unicorn, a goblin, and a sleeping giantess. The unicorn turned out to be a goat with one deformed horn; the goblin was a midget; the giantess turned out to be a small hill.

"We left the place undisturbed and kept watch on it, hoping the thing would return. If it did, we would destroy both place and creature. If he did return, which we now think probable, it was by some way we could not trace."

"Just a minute!" said Xulai. "Some way you could not trace?"

"We were keeping careful watch on the place."

"But what did you just tell us about that thing mother left me? That it could transport people from place to place in an instant? If it moves that fast, presumably no one can see it happen."

Precious Wind was shocked into silence. She had not thought of this! No one had thought of this! "Of course," she said at last. "Of course, it may have had *ug ul xaolat*, a thing master of its own." Her face was gray. She felt ill. "We believed that the Old Dark House stood empty until Alicia was named duchess and reopened it."

"But if the creature had been there, somewhere, and if he had one of those gadgets, he could have gone to Kamfels and brought Alicia back to the Old Dark House, even as a child," said Xulai. "Perhaps repeatedly."

Precious Wind only nodded. Oh, yes. He could have.

"Then that would have been how she learned about the machines!"

Justinian, seeing the sickness in Precious Wind's face, drew their attention away from her. "Falyrion and I spent less time together after he married, but we still rode and hunted together from time to time. He talked about Mirami. She told him she was born at the Old Dark House, so she must have had a mother there, but no one ever spoke of her. Falyrion thought she was very beautiful, very interesting, but he was puzzled by her as well, puzzled by the children she bore him. He was fond of the girl, baffled by the boy. Now that Xulai has told me she killed Falyrion and his son, as well as others, I understand his puzzlement. How my friend would have hated fathering such . . ."

Xulai frowned. "Chances are he didn't father either one of them. No. But Mirami doesn't slaughter indiscriminately. One would think . . . but no. She always has a specific reason for killing someone. Unless she has killed people we don't know about."

Precious Wind said, "The fact that the creature has suspended general slaughter has been discussed by Clan Do-Lok. They think the creature has gone beyond its original function and has set itself some other goal."

Justinian asked, "Is this believable in a machine?"

Precious Wind smiled ruefully. "So we wondered, as well. But the creature was made from a human being, and such reasoning might not be beyond its capability so long as the end result is *more killing*, for killing is what it was designed to do. All its satisfactions, all of what one might think of as its *comforts*, are supplied during its maintenance, but it can have maintenance *only* after it has killed."

"It earns pleasure by killing?" murmured Xulai.

"So we believe. In this case, the Old Dark Man has allowed some of the work to be done by its creations, its Miramis and Alicias and the many others before them that we know nothing about."

"Just a minute," said Abasio. "If its satisfactions come from killing, how do killings done by others satisfy it?"

Precious Wind said, "All the ones we found and destroyed were in maintenance cocoons. They had been there for many centuries. It is possible that this last slaughterer, realizing it would be dormant for a long time, created others to kill *while* he could not kill. Others' killings were not instead of his own, they were merely supplementary. Perhaps he even intended to create others who would go on killing after he, it, eventually died."

Xulai remarked, "And, if the women are its creation, they hate Tingawa without needing a reason. If one or both of the women are still alive, will they come after us?"

Precious Wind shook her head. "Their immediate ambitions were for Norland . . ."

"No," said Xulai, contradicting her. "Alicia had larger ambitions than that. I heard the duchess, remember. There in the forest, that night, she talked about finding something for the Sea King, and how he would give her machines, and how much power she would have."

"Are you sure you remember that correctly?" Justinian asked.

Abasio said, "I was there. The duchess and Jenger talked about finding Huold's talisman or whatever Xulai's mother had hidden in the forest. In return for either of those things, the Sea King was going to reward her with machines, but it was the Sea King's *ambassador* who promised, not the Sea King himself."

Precious Wind said, "The few ancient machines left in Tingawa are guarded, protected, kept from doing damage. They will not be used to reward anyone."

"You told me about one at the embassy," said Justinian.

Precious Wind nodded. "It could not harm anyone. We call it a far-talker. It dates from far back in the Before Time, to an innocent age, long, long before the slaughterers. It is so simple that we can actually make more of them quite easily. It allows messages to be sent through the air, but it needs both a sender and a receiver. The priests allowed the ambassador to take one of each of these to the embassy so our people could summon a ship if they needed to go home. When Lok-i-xan returned to the islands, he left it with the emissary, for the same reason."

"Is this something they can carry with them?"

"Yes. It's a small thing, no trouble to carry in a wagon or cart. Its power can be provided by someone cranking it. I know the emissary has wearied of talking to King Gahls and plans to leave for Merhaven. Once they know this ship is gone from Merhaven, they will use the far-talker to ask for another ship. Since the embassy also communicated with Merhaven by pigeon, our captain may already have asked for a ship for them."

"Is there one of the devices on this ship?" asked Abasio.

She nodded.

"Can you talk to the embassy and find out what's happening?" Abasio asked. "It might be helpful to know. If this creature is as you've described, it might follow us by sea, and that has me bothered. I dealt with similar but totally separate critters years ago, near the Place of Power, and the death toll was very great."

Precious Wind sighed deeply. "We believe the creature cannot travel under the sea. It was built to ape humankind. It breathes air."

"So do human beings," said Xulai in a strange, faraway voice. "Humans can't travel underwater either. So they build ships."

"And we have prevented ships from crossing the sea."

"How were the other monsters destroyed?" asked Justinian.

"They were inside their maintenance containers. We used explosives and both creature and maintainer were blown to bits, then the bits were raked up and molded into concrete, and the concrete was taken and dropped into the depths of the deepest parts of the sea. The Old Dark Man's maintenance device will probably have been destroyed by now. The monster itself can also be blown to bits, if we can find it! We need to know where it will be at a given time."

Precious Wind sighed and turned toward Xulai. "Among the things this master can do is to transport you, very quickly, away from danger. It can, therefore, be used to escape from peril."

Xulai first nodded, then shook her head. "Our lives are complicated enough, Precious Wind. You keep the thing master and put it in some place where it cannot send one of us off into the sea by accident. We all need to think of something else for a time, but let us be very careful to tell whatever ship goes to Merhaven that it must not bring back an evil barnacle upon its hull."

Full of discontent and unwarranted guilt, Precious Wind took the device away. It might be useless so far as Xulai was concerned, but it had been very beneficial for her wolves. And the wolves might well be very beneficial to everyone concerned.

IT WAS SOME DAYS LATER, in the predawn darkness, that a wolf woke Precious Wind and pulled her garment with his teeth, telling her to come. On deck, all the wolves were assembled, staring across the sea. They had heard something, she thought. She could not hear it. The men on watch had heard or seen nothing. She woke the captain, who climbed the mast and turned his glasses in the direction the wolves were facing. "I see a light out there," he called. "Watch! Run up the signal lights!"

The watchman ran the lights up the mast, and the captain hung them there, one green; one red, above it; one white above that. The sails were shifted so the other light, far ahead of them and to one side, was in the direction of their movement. The captain stayed aloft, after a time returning to say, "They've hung answering lights. She's our sister ship, the *Axan-xin* from Tingawa. The *Night Wind.*"

Precious Wind went to her cabin, where Xulai saw her busily writing something. Everyone else hung across the railing waiting, seemingly interminably. Eventually, along about dawn, when the ships came within sight of one another, Precious Wind joined them. When they were within shouting distance, the captain of the *Axan-xin* shouted that he was coming across.

"I know him," cried Precious Wind excitedly. "He is the Gull of Caspos, so called for his ability to ride out storms at sea. We were schoolmates once."

A small boat was lowered and came skimming across the calm water, rowed by six of the men from the *Night Wind*. Indeed, the captain and Precious Wind remembered one another, for there was much hugging and giving of introductions, and bowing to Xulai and Justinian.

"We are three days out of port, and we knew you were on the way," said the Gull, whose name was Bunjasi-velipe: "Protector of Knowledge."

"His whole name is Bunjasi-lok-koularka-velipe: 'Protector of *Ancient Seagoing* Knowledge,'" said Precious Wind, as an aside. "Just call him Bunja. It's easier."

Bunja had news. "We're on our way to Merhaven to pick up our people. We received a far-talker summons from the emissary. All the members of the embassy staff, those still living, are assembling in Merhaven. The *place* is destroyed." He looked a question. "I presume you know which *place*. And, Xu-xin, I am sorry to tell you, but your friend Bear has been killed. The emissary is Xakixa for him. The emissary told me to tell you Bear did not die forsworn. I don't know why that is important, but the emissary said it was."

"Ah," said Precious Wind, grieving. Her grief was echoed by Xulai. Both of them felt both sorrow and a kind of shamed relief. Bear had not been forsworn. His memory would not be soiled to those who had known him.

"How?" they asked in one voice.

"*Ul monga-paf,* the thing we do not mention, killed him. It killed several of the embassy warriors as well. *Ul monga-paf* escaped. It moved like lightning, so quickly it could not be seen.

Xulai looked at Precious Wind, who nodded. The thing had an *ul xaolat*.

Cursing silently, Precious Wind asked, "And we are expected?"

"Lok-i-xan knows you are coming. They are in council, debating how *ul monga-paf* is to be killed. Again, it has gone away and we do not know where."

"Were the women mentioned? The queen, Mirami, and her daughter, Alicia?"

He smiled grimly. "Oh, yes! Cleanse them from memory! Those evil ones are dead! The oldest witch died in the castle in Ghastain of some quick, terrible disease. Her daughter died in the same manner in her cellar at the place. Where her machines were. Where Bear died."

"The Old Dark House," said Abasio.

Bunja made a gesture of revulsion. "*Gol mongapaf!* We do not mention that, either. It is no more. It is gone."

Precious Wind had a very strange expression on her face. "Just a moment! When Alicia died, when her mother died, did anyone describe the illness?"

He nodded, face screwed up in revulsion. "They had a smell, like rotted meat, like one long dead, vomiting of blood, much blood."

Precious Wind held up her hand as though to say, *Don't talk, let me think.* "Is it possible *ul mongapaf* got any of that blood on it?"

Bunja considered this. "As the emissary described it, it would have been hard to avoid. He said she spewed blood everywhere . . ."

"Ah," said Precious Wind. "Then let us get to Tingawa as quickly as we may. That information may give us a way to find the thing!" She took a paper from her pocket, folded and sealed. "Bunja, old friend, I have written here something I need you to take care of for me when you reach Merhaven. Read it when you have time. Justinian's old friend Genieve lives there in a place called the Watch House. She can help you find someone reliable to do what we need done." She put it into his hand and folded his hand around it. "It's important. If you cannot find Genieve, find someone else. And do not forget to have your divers examine your hull before you leave Merhaven. It has been suggested the thing we do not mention might possibly make some kind of oxygen device and attach itself, like a barnacle, to the hull of a ship. If so, tell them not to notice it, not to touch it, to use the far-talker first and talk to me!" She leaned forward to kiss his cheek. "We will see you soon in Tingawa, Bunja. Sail safe. Be well."

THE FEW REMAINING DAYS OF the trip, though they seemed endless, were in fact very swift, for the winds held true. They began to pass little islets that had been, so Precious Wind said, sizeable islands fifty years before. They passed between two mountainous and still sizeable islands that marked the entry to the Tingawan Sea. The capital city of Ushiloma al Koul, Great Mother of the Sea, lay before them. It had obviously been recently moved. As in Merhaven, there were buildings on skids, and the piers were floating. They saw the umbrellas even before they reached the pier, tall, fringed, golden umbrellas.

No, Xulai told herself, they were parasols. Parasols were the symbol of nobility in Tingawa. Precious Wind had told her about them when she was only a child. "Here, in this world of Norland, a crown is put onto the head of a person at a coronation, making that person the king. Both the act and the ownership of the crown can lead crowned heads to the belief that they have some inherent right to rule. In Tingawa, the parasol, a symbolic shield against evil, is held over the head of the leader by representatives selected by the people. The ruler is thus always reminded that power is not inherent but is granted and can be taken away."

The ship docked. The walkway went down onto the pier. Two parasol bearers came aboard to stand at either side of the walkway. "This honor is for you," said Precious Wind. "You have to go first, then Abasio, then Justinian. Then the rest of us."

Xulai went first, suspended in time, suspecting that all this business of honoring was silly, believing at the same time it meant much to those who gave it, thinking that this land could never be home, wondering at the same time whether it might not be more of a home than any she had yet known. Those holding the parasols came with her. Well, her mother had been a princess. Perhaps that was enough reason. She made herself stand up straight and walk gracefully as Precious Wind had taught her. Precious Wind had also told her who the man at the end of the walkway was: her grandfather, Lok-i-xan.

He smiled at her, leaned forward to kiss her gravely upon her cheek, gave her his right hand and Abasio his left. He nodded at Justinian and Precious Wind, then turned and led them down the pier toward the city.

9
The Sea King

LED BY LOK-I-XAN WITH XULAI ON ONE SIDE, Abasio on the other, they proceeded away from the sea on a wide boulevard lined with silent, smiling people. The boulevard ended between two ornamental pillars at the bottom of a broad, conical hill where a slightly narrower road made a gentle turn to the left and began spiraling upward. This road was also lined with people, some Tingawan, many in costumes of other lands that Xulai had heard of or read of, others who looked totally unfamiliar. Lok-i-xan did not let go of her hand for a moment, and she quickly came to understand that this long walk through the city, among the people, was a kind of . . . what could one call it? An adoption. If she read it correctly, the head of Clan Do-Lok was saying that she and Abasio were of his kindred, that Justinian was also of his kindred, and that was that.

"You have questions," he murmured halfway up the hill. "I can hear your brain sizzling. Are we walking you too quickly? There is yet some way to go, but we can stop to drink tea."

"That would be . . . very nice," she agreed. The distance and the climb weren't wearying her physically, but the entire experience was beginning to overwhelm her. It didn't seem to bother Abasio, but then, he'd been traveling here, there, and everywhere for years. He was used to being confronted on every side with new sights and sounds. He simply strode along, nodding to the crowds, smiling at anyone who smiled at him.

Lok-i-xan turned his head very slightly toward one of the parasol carriers, who promptly fell back, spoke to someone in the procession, then resumed his place. The person spoken to fell in behind Lok-i-xan, who murmured, "Next tea stall for five, please."

The runner went forward up the rising road like a sight hound after a rabbit, zipping around the bend. In moments he came back into view at the center of the road, bowing and gesturing to usher them forward to the right.

If there had been people against the hill along that particular stretch of road, they had been moved away. Now there was only a bright awning over a table and five chairs before a stone-lined hollow containing a fiery little stove and shelves laden with pottery. They sat: Xulai, Lok-i-xan, Abasio, Justinian, Precious Wind. The parasol holders moved away and began a slow dance on the road, the parasols twirling, the feet pointing and leaping. A brilliantly robed old woman came from the hollow, her steps timed to coincide with those of the dancers; she bowed and set cups before them, poured tea from a pot shaped like an elegant dragon, and was replaced by two equally brilliantly robed women who also danced as they set bowls of tiny cakes before each of them.

Xulai realized she was hungry. They had come into port early in the morning; no one had bothered to eat. There had been a last-minute complication before they left the pier: the business of seeing that Blue and the wolf pack would be provided for during their absence, which had to be settled before any of them could take part in the procession.

It was this furor that Lok-i-xan referred to when he leaned toward Precious Wind and asked, "Are your animals settled, Xu-xin?"

Xulai noted that he spoke Norlandish, well-sprinkled with Tinga-wan words, and, of course, he used Precious Wind's Tingawan name.

Precious Wind swallowed before answering. "The wolves weren't happy at being left alone. That's what all the howling was about. Neither was Blue at being left with them. That's what all the kicking and whinnying was about. He says herbivores don't take kindly to carnivores in bunches. So, we have Blue stabled in a building by the pier and the wolves will stay aboard until I am there to take them to the place we'll prepare for them. A couple of the sailors have become friends with them, and they'll stay, too, until we get the other arrangements completed."

Lok-i-xan cocked his head, smiling the least possible smile. "Wolves, Xu-xin? A whole pack of them?"

She flushed. "I foresaw a need, Your Wisdom."

He cocked his head at her. "Ah, well, we have learned to respect your foreseeing. I am surprised at the horse! I didn't know any of our technology was available on that continent."

Abasio said, "It may be a survival, Your Wisdom." He had been told this was the polite form of address. "When I was younger, I sometimes passed among walled areas surrounding the old cities. The places were called Edges. Precious Wind—that is, Xu-xin—likens them to the abbeys and monasteries that served as repositories of old knowledge elsewhere. My native area was generally a barbarian state . . . no, one can't call it a state. Perhaps 'a loosely federated group of tribes' would describe it better. Still, I believe your technical people and the people in the Edges would likely speak the same language."

"Xu-xin has mentioned your regard for the people south of you."

"Yes. The people of Artemisia . . . They lived very simply but I had the feeling they knew a great many things they didn't share with or even mention to others."

"Perhaps I will have the opportunity to meet some of them," the older man said musingly. "Artemisia. Ah."

"They would greatly treasure that opportunity," Abasio said sincerely. The people of Artemisia would treasure it, and Abasio wanted to witness the meeting.

Xulai swallowed her sixth cake. She had counted them, not wanting to seem greedy, for though they were delicious, they were very small. It had taken all six to make her feel more like herself. Across the road, the people stood quietly looking at her, at the dancing feet and twirling parasols, at one another. The audience did not point or murmur. Even the children were quiet, simply standing there, looking at one of the tea drinkers, then another, then another, and so on, as though they were memorizing every feature, every color, every garment.

There was little more talk. Seeing that Xulai's fingers had stopped conveying cakes from dish to mouth and that the others seemed satisfied, Lok-i-xan reached for her hand. "Shall we go on to the citadel now?"

They went on as before, around the back of the hill, up toward the front again, and so, having made one complete upward-spiraling circuit, they came to the gate of the citadel, directly in line with the boulevard below. From where they stood, a long, steep, and completely empty flight of stairs descended all the way to the bottom, where the people still stood, still smiling, still silent. Lok-i-xan turned, raised his arms, and bowed. Every person in the far-flung crowd returned the bow, still silent as ghosts.

Lok-i-xan called out something Xulai couldn't quite catch the meaning of. With myriad voices but one phrase, the crowd replied. While some of them stayed where they were, others broke away into little groups and wandered off, talking among themselves, laughing, a cheerful babble rising from people who had enjoyed the whole experience.

"What did you say to them?" she asked.

"I told them you said thank you for the welcome. They said, 'Be one of us.' Here, we feel silence is the best greeting. Any bird or monkey can chatter, any wagon can make a noise upon a street, but to stand silent, to observe, to remember, that is recognition, don't you think so? Of course, with children, concentration takes some teaching. Children too young to be quiet stay at home on these occasions."

"Quiet makes fewer demands on the ones they're looking at," she agreed, suddenly thankful that the crowd had not cheered and waved things at them. "It allowed us to see them, really see them, more easily than if everyone had been shouting. I will remember the tea ladies' robes. They were beautiful. I will remember the cakes, and the children, the young man who ran to the tea kiosk, the dancers. Everything was . . . elegant."

"We admire and revere elegance," said her grandfather. "Even in simple things."

They turned and went inside to more elegance. Abasio noted both the lack of ostentation and the very high level of craftsmanship. He also saw, with some surprise and considerable interest, that the doors seemed to sink into sockets that would very probably make them waterproof. The four of them were escorted to rooms at the end of a corridor where sliding doors could shut off the corridor itself to make the area completely private. Their baggage had already been brought from the ship by some quicker way, unpacked, and put away. Lok-i-xan left them in their common room to get settled.

Two walls of the common room opened into bedrooms, two on each side. Each had an adjoining bath with a small, gently steaming tub and all the other accoutrements Xulai had come to think of as being essentially Tingawan. The third wall, across from the door to the corridor, held floor-to-ceiling windows that separated them from a walled garden. Xulai leaned against the window to look out at the gnarled tree at the garden's center. It looked old enough to have lived a few thousand years. A bird's nest rested on an ancient, twisted bough. Old and new. Water flowed into a pool rimmed with sparkling sand. Wet and dry. The rock at the roots of the tree was covered with thick, green moss. Hard and soft. There were probably a dozen other oppositions brought into harmony in the garden; she would no doubt find all of them in time, and she would be told the garden had the word "harmony" in its name. The Garden of Harmonious Waters. Something like that. Very Tingawan. She returned to her bedroom, hers by virtue of her own belongings having been hung in the beautifully carved wooden wardrobe or folded into drawers or otherwise appropriately distributed.

Her room adjoined the next one, and as she stared accusingly at the adjoining door, Abasio opened it from the other side. "You're . . . peeved?" he asked, looking from her to the door and back.

"It just seems that everyone assumes . . ."

"I don't think so. The two rooms on each side simply have joining doors. I can ask Precious Wind to trade with me."

"I don't want you to have another room, I just think . . . everyone knows everything about me, you, us."

"They probably do," he said cheerfully.

She moved fretfully away from him. "It's . . . I feel I don't have any private things, not even my thoughts!"

He took a deep breath and sat down on the bed, bouncing a little. Very comfortable. After a moment's consideration, he said, "Let's see. We've talked about many things on this journey, but we never talked religion. Do you believe in a deity?"

"One who fiddles with people, you mean? One who saves this one while condemning a thousand others to painful death? That kind of deity?"

"I was supposing a much more benign one. My question really is: if you *did* believe in a deity, would you be annoyed at the deity knowing you?"

"Presumably the deity would have created me, so it would know me. There'd be no point in my being upset about it."

"Exactly." He put his arms around her rigid form and held her lightly until the steel framework she had summoned relaxed and she felt rather like flesh again. "Exactly," he repeated when she leaned into him, breathing against his throat.

"You mean the ones who know all about me did make me?"

"Not quite from scratch, but I think it very likely they had a part in your design. I also think they've had a very large part in bringing me into your life, and I absolutely refuse to be even slightly upset about that. It would be the basest sort of ingratitude."

"I have to go back to the port," Precious Wind announced vehemently from the open common room door behind them. "I can't bring the wolves here, and I have to talk with the people who are finding them a place with someone they trust. I had a forester in mind and they're locating him for me. He has a . . . I suppose you'd call it a royal preserve. Clan Do-Lok doesn't pretend to royalty, but they make very sure certain places are kept in their original state as long as possible. Then I have a meeting with the ministers, to talk about the creature that killed Bear. None of us slept well last night. I suggest the rest of you take a nap, if you can. This afternoon, Lok-i-xan is taking you to meet the Sea King . . ." She stopped, aware they had not been listening. "Abasio! Xulai!" she cried. "Did you hear me?"

He turned, taking Xulai around with him so he didn't have to release her. "One could not fail to hear you, Precious Wind, but you are correct in supposing we are not listening. You may have said you were very busy and were going back to the port. We accept that, just as we would accept anything you propose. Did you not create us? Have a good time. Pet the wolves for us."

She glared at him before realizing he was making fun of her. "You're tired. Sorry. Have a nap." She made a "what's the difference" gesture as she departed.

Xulai giggled. "She's the deity that created us?"

"Not all by herself. I get the impression that you were the result of a very long, difficult group effort, into which I have fallen as a more or less accidental but, one hopes, welcome inclusion. Some bit of the pattern they needed but had overlooked to begin with."

"Did she imply we should take a nap?" she asked innocently. "It has been a long morning."

"Does a nap appeal to you?"

She shut the doors, rejoicing to find there was a formidable latch on the inside.

WHEN PRECIOUS WIND RETURNED FROM the ship, she brought with her the captain of the *Falsa-xin* and the forester she had spoken of. All of them took a meal together in their common room, where the wall of windows had been moved aside to join the room and the garden. The table was set with a variety of foods, some hot, some cold. There were various things to drink as well, some familiar, some strange. Precious Wind identified certain dishes and argued amiably with the captain and Justinian about where they had originated. She and Justinian decided that Blue should have a stall in the citadel stables. It would still leave him and Abasio farther apart then they had been accustomed to being; on the other hand, the forester had spoken with the stable master, who thought Blue might enjoy meeting some of the talking mares treasured by Clan Do-Lok.

As for the wolves, the forester had approved a restricted preserve with an unused building where Precious Wind could set up her laboratory. They discussed the details of who should do the moving and when it should be done. Xulai and Abasio said very little but smiled quietly as they ate. After everyone had eaten the fresh fruits that concluded the meal, the captain and the forester departed.

Precious Wind said, "We have a few minutes." She gave Xulai an up-and-down look before saying with a meaningful intonation, "*Your hair very much needs combing.* We're meeting your grandfather for the Xakixa ceremony."

Xulai turned in surprise. "No one said—"

"I know. They told me just before our meal. Just neaten yourself. You don't need to change your clothes, and it won't take long. My lord, both you and Abasio are invited to come along. There's not a great deal of ceremony about it." She left them to "neaten themselves," returning a few moments later to escort them down yet another very long hall to a small, bench-lined room where Lok-i-xan awaited them.

They sat on the benches along the walls and the room moved.

"We're going down!" Xulai exclaimed.

Her grandfather nodded. "The way we came today is the formal route, for festivals, for memorials, for state funerals, for greeting an ambassador, that kind of thing. Sometimes newly married couples make that walk to be sure everyone knows of their changed status. You know, former sweethearts, estranged relatives: we have those, even in Tingawa. The stairs are the penitential route, for people apologizing to their god or their clan, or the emperor. The emperor doesn't actually live here, but his throne room is here, so it's regarded as an appropriate venue for formal occasions. He avoids such occasions whenever possible."

"What does he do?" asked Xulai.

Lok-i-xan drew a thoughtful breath. "Ah. Well, emperor is a hereditary personage. Tingawa has always had an emperor, and most of them, the very best ones, did very little. One of the problems with hereditary positions is that sometimes among such families marriages are made for political rather than genetic reasons, and the resultant children show no talent whatsoever for the role they are expected to play, or, indeed, for any sensible or productive role whatsoever. We had one emperor who sniggered, not occasionally but constantly. We had one whose muscles jumped and another who was so greedy he had to be carried everywhere he went. They were, in order, Glon-xan the Giggler, Tabi-xan the Twitcher, and Frukito-oox the Fat. So, as you can imagine, we really prefer that hereditary personages not be allowed to do much. The current one is very pleasant. He breeds ornamental fish and presides amiably over court occasions."

"Interesting," said Abasio. "You were telling us about the rooms that go up and down."

"Yes. As I was saying, when we need to move about on ordinary, everyday business, we go up and down in these ascendables. They are moved by wind power. I am told such things were customary in the Before Time, in those great tall buildings they had. This citadel hill, if you stripped the soil away from the outside, is actually a very similar building: the 'hill' has been hollowed out over the centuries and except for an outside layer of landscaping is now totally occupied with offices, along with a hospital, and laboratories for our scientists. It has dozens of entrances at ground level where the stables are. The Clan Do-Lok citadel takes up the top floors and the Clan Do-Lok shrine is about halfway down; we're going to stop there, then we have another appointment . . ."

As he spoke, the room stopped moving and the door opened on a dimly lit corridor. Lok-i-xan's face changed in a moment. It lost all animation, leaving only a mask that spoke of weary self-control. It was an expression that Abasio recognized from his own mirror, years ago, and he barely stopped himself from patting the leader of Clan Do-Lok on the shoulder as he left his seat to lead them down the hallway. He thought that at some time, it might be appropriate to pat Lok-i-xan, but Abasio did not feel he had that right as yet. He wondered if he ever would.

There were doors, branching corridors, and alcoves along the way. In one of the alcoves a small group of elderly Tingawan men and women had gathered to await them.

Xulai, alert to feelings around her, felt the tension, the sadness.

Precious Wind put her hand on Xulai's shoulder, squeezing it slightly. "It's all right. You remember what we told you?"

"The tablet with my mother's name."

Precious Wind hugged her and stood silent. The door was opened from within. They entered the shrine.

Abasio had seen shrines before. Artemisia had shrines. In the city where he had lived during his youth every gang had had a shrine. Since Ollie was taken from him and from the world, he had worn the library helmet to visit shrines of the world through many ages of the world. There were shrines of one kind or another in virtually every city or town he had visited on his travels. None were like this.

Light came into the cavern here and there, glowing softly from behind a stalactite or through a tissue-thin curtain of mineral that had obviously flowed into place, molecule by molecule, over centuries of time. This was natural light, reflected downward, possibly angled and directed by mirrors so that it fell precisely upon this place and that place, giving just enough illumination to see the corridors extending into the black distance, each corridor barely lit by tiny stone lanterns that sat atop small stone tablets—thousands of tablets, thousands of lanterns, some dark, most offering a single, tiny glow. They were ranged in rows along the walls, on shelves, around pillars. Behind them the walls shone wetly. The thin slick of moisture that covered them glowed softly; the filmy pools that gathered on horizontal surfaces gleamed.

Abasio thought that if he half shut his eyes he could believe he stood on a mountaintop at night surrounded by a heaven full of stars. Xulai, next to him, sighed. He looked down into her troubled eyes.

"Where?" she whispered.

He took her hand, kissed the palm. "Xu-i-lok knows. Just ask her."

She breathed deeply. Of course. Xu-i-lok would know. "Mother," she whispered to herself. "I have brought you home. Tell me where to go."

It was the tiniest of tugging—the tug a spider's web might have made—but she felt it. To the right. Past a line of tablets, another, to a group tiered against a wall. To the second tier, back, no, farther back. Many of these were unlighted. Many of these were the tablets of the living. Back. A little farther right . . . And there it was: engraved with the characters that were her mother's name, furnished with the tiny stone lantern, three legged, three open sides, an ornately carved top in the form of . . . of her fisher . . . and other creatures including a hawk, a chipmunk. Xulai breathed a sob in, out, as she laid her hands upon the stone. The room had been quiet, broken only by the scuff of slippered feet, the brush of fabric, but now it was utterly silent. Within the stone lantern a firefly glow began, like a bit of luminescence on the sea, like the vagrant reflection of a star in a pool, pallid, softly silver, becoming green, then bluer, brighter, a little larger. Xulai held her breath. Suddenly it was a white-hot flash that lit the entire cavern before fading to become softly yellow, a candle light only, fading until it glowed steadily among the thousands of Clan Do-Lok.

"The flash . . . ," Abasio murmured.

"We believe," whispered Precious Wind, tears running down her cheeks, "that when that happens, it means the knowledge gained by the returning soul has been shared. This shrine is not for thousands of individuals. What is here is not many little flames. What is here is one clan, one flame, the knowledge and history of one people. And those like Lok-i-xan can consult it, can benefit from it. He talks with her now."

And indeed, he was beside the tablet, his hands upon it, murmuring. Abasio thought he was saying good-bye, but the words he heard were not the Tingawan words for farewell. Seeing the confusion in his face, Precious Wind wiped her eyes and said, "He's not saying good-bye. He's welcoming her home. And now I can mourn her!"

He noticed that she had found a place to burn a lock of her hair. The ashes marked her forehead. As Precious Wind moved away, Xulai came to sit beside him, tears in her eyes as well. "I'm glad she's home. It's just . . ."

"What, love?"

"My fisher is gone. He hasn't been with me since we came."

"Ah," he said after a moment, understanding. "It was part of her."

"Yes," she agreed, half smiling through the tears. "I hoped he was part of me, but I guess he was part of her. I wish I knew how she did it, how she created it and left it for me. The fisher shape was carved on the top of her lantern along with a dozen other animals. She was like me, like Precious Wind. She loved animals."

"My love, I think you and she love all living things."

XULAI STAYED IN THE SHRINE with Lok-i-xan. Precious Wind, Justinian, and Abasio went outside with the other Tingawans who introduced themselves as people who had known the princess when she was young. They had come to witness. "Whenever a Xakixa comes, some of us are here to witness," they said. "So we can be sure the soul has returned."

"Tell me about the shrine," Abasio begged. "That cavern is ancient."

An old woman answered. "Oh, yes. It was the first burial place of Clan Do-Lok. Our dead were burned on pyres nearby, and the ashes were put in the cavern along with the name stones. The little lanterns were traditional, only symbolic. Then, long, long ago, the lights began to come. At first, just a few. Then, more and more, some of them very old, back as far as there were name stones. Once we had seen the lights, we realized what was happening here. It has always happened, probably; wherever people have had their own land, their own surroundings for hundreds of years, the souls have remained there, so once we knew, beginning then, as soon as a baby was named, the family made the stone and brought it here. It continues today. If the person dies here, the light comes. If someone dies afar, the Xakixa brings them home. Not the body, that doesn't matter."

"For everyone?"

A very old man shook his head sadly. "No. Sometimes, young people, you know, they think if something is old, it's worthless. They don't love their land or care for it. They go away not only in body, but in spirit, and those who go away like that, they hardly ever come back." He sighed. "But, at the same time, we know they never were one of us in spirit, so we have lost nothing but the love and care we gave them, and that was their due, stay or not. Some believe their spirits go somewhere else, some other world, but that's silly. A soul stays where it is at home. If it has no home, it just goes out, like a candle flame. That's why we must save our world, so the souls of all the people who love the world will have a place to be."

Without meaning to say it, Abasio blurted, "And what will you do with the waters rising?"

The old woman smiled. "This was a mountain with a cave in it; now it is a waterproof building the size of a mountain. Do-Lok will build a tower on top, as high as is needed, if one is needed. The cavern will remain. I have heard talk of building a boat that goes underwater to get to it . . ." She sighed, half smiled. "We'll think of something."

"And the other clans?"

"Each clan has done this in their own way. On some islands, their shrines drowned, but when divers looked inside, the lights were still there. They're not fire, you know. They're the kind of light one sees in the ocean. Now they have divers who carry down the stones of the newborn. Later, if there is a Xakixa, the diver brings up the stone, the Xakixa lays hands upon it, and then the diver takes it down again and there is light in those caverns, under the sea."

The other witnesses were smiling, nodding, yes, that was the way of it. Light in the caverns, under the sea. Only a few clans had people who could actually consult with their ancestral spirits, they said, so caverns under the sea were all right for most of them.

IN THE SHRINE, XULAI AND Lok-i-xan sat together on a stone bench, hand in hand.

"Grandfather," said Xulai, "will you tell me about elegance? You said Tingawans like elegance, even in simple things."

"Ah," he said. "Didn't Precious Wind ever tell you the story of the emperor's garden?"

She shook her head.

"Long ago there was an emperor. We call him E'loms Los Velipe Umvok, or Elvuk for short. Emperor Elvuk loved gardens. Before he became emperor, he traveled widely, looking at gardens. He collected books about gardens. He collected plants and trees, and when he became emperor, he decided to create the most beautiful gardens in the world. He hired gardeners. Of course, gardeners have their own ideas about things, and this one and that one offered opinions. Elvuk did not want their opinions, so he made them wear blinders and told them they had only to dig where he said to, plant where he said to, fertilize as he said to. People came to look at the gardens, and Elvuk found nutshells and candy wrappers, and so he planted a hedge that grew thirty feet high and where there wasn't a hedge, he had builders build a wall.

"His garden grew; it matured; it was beautiful beyond all his dreams. He kept it carefully locked so no one could pick a flower or throw litter. The gardeners weeded in blinders, so they couldn't see anywhere except where they were weeding. Whenever they trimmed anything, the emperor told them where to cut. The emperor knew it was the most beautiful garden in the world, and the emperor loved it.

"Came time, as it always does, and the emperor died. Death came for him, and death said, "Tell me what you have accomplished so I can assign you the proper job in the next world." And the emperor said, "I created the most beautiful garden the world has ever seen."

And Death went away to look at his records. And he returned, saying, "I'm sorry, but I find no record of your garden anywhere. No one has seen it. No one has enjoyed it. No one has been benefited by it. If it really existed, you didn't even leave it behind. If it was behind that tall hedge and wall, there's only a weed patch there now."

The emperor sighed. "Well, assign me to create another."

"Sorry," said Death. "But our garden is already almost perfect, it grows more so with each proper gardener who arrives."

"I am one," said the emperor.

"Of course, and we do have a proper job for you" said Death. "Here, put these blinders on so you can pull the weeds properly."

Xulai thought about this for some time. "The story says that elegance has to be for everyone?"

"No. The story says that *if* one creates something *very good,* it *becomes* an elegance only when other people can enjoy it. If one keeps it to oneself, it can be a talent, a skill, an amusement, but it can't be an elegance. No elegant singer sings only to himself. No elegant sculptor puts his work in a dark cave. No elegant baker hides his cakes in a closet. No hoarder can create an elegance; he can only be an Elvuk."

"If it has to be very good, then elegance is always expensive, I guess."

"Oh, if it's a thing, the thing itself might be expensive, yes, but even if so, it need not be hoarded. A thing can be very good and cost almost nothing. So, if I have a vase by Um-minchox-di, who was the greatest artist in porcelain the world has seen, I may have acquired it for almost nothing, before he was well known. Or I may have spent a treasury on it. In either case, to become an elegance it must be kept in a place where everyone can see it, where some child who is the next Um-minchox-di can take inspiration from it. If I hide it away, it is as nothing, and, metaphorically speaking, I do not want to wear blinders and pull weeds in among my kinsmen during our afterlife."

"You have a vase by Um-minchox-di?"

"I do. That was his nickname as a child—Um-minchox-di. 'Small Muddy Boy.'"

"He made things out of mud?"

"As a toddler, yes. And when he achieved artistry, he took it as his name. I don't even remember his real one. It says 'Small Muddy Boy' on his tablet in the clan shrine."

"And how do I translate the emperor's name, E'loms Los Velipe Umvok? Great one without . . . ?"

"'Largeness without wisdom number one.' Just call him Emperor Big Stupid the First."

She grinned. "So the tea and the dancers were an elegance even though the people along the road didn't get to drink tea."

"It's the same tea everyone drinks every day and the same cakes everyone has on holidays. The *elegance*, the interesting and unusual part, was you and Abasio and your father. That's what they came to see. And they got to see the parasol dancers. You didn't see the dancers after we came inside, but they danced all the way down the hill and back to the pier for anyone who cared. A lot of people stayed, just for that. The dancers, too, wished to be an elegance, and so did the people who stayed to watch them."

"Precious Wind says the parasols are held over your head by ordinary people. But the dancers aren't ordinary people."

"The dancers are ordinary people who happen to dance exceptionally well. Ordinarily, the people who hold the parasols are picked by lottery; for special occasions, we use people picked for special contributions. You and Abasio and Justinian were a special occasion, so we did an elegance."

WHEN THEY REJOINED ABASIO AND Justinian, Lok-i-xan led them through busy corridors to a ground-level exit and from there to an inlet where a boat waited to take them to meet the Sea King.

The site of their afternoon meeting was on the far side of a small island out in the harbor, not a great distance from the pier where they had docked. It was unoccupied and it held no evidence it had ever been occupied. Except for the small stretch of sandy beach on the far side and a few twisted trees that had grown up in pockets of blown soil, the island was almost all stone. Chunks of it extended into the sea, great spray-slick brown boulders that hunkered in the gentle surf like the slumped backs of giants asleep in their bath. When the boat and its oarsmen had left them and gone well away from the little island, Lok-i-xan went to the edge of the sand and called: "*Xaolat . . . al . . . Koul.*"

"Master of the Sea," Xulai translated to herself. For a while, nothing happened. Xulai and Abasio exchanged shrugs. When they had begun to think nothing would happen, one of the huge boulders in the surf moved. At several places around it, other, smaller stones appeared, smooth and shining, rising briefly above the water, then sinking again as the monstrous central bulk turned and came toward the beach, where it heaved upward to lie in the shallows. Enormous tentacles coiled and uncoiled; two huge eyes opened. A voice that held its own echo said: "Welcome, Abasio. Welcome, Justinian."

"Kraken," breathed Abasio.

"Yes," said Lok-i-xan, taking him and Xulai by their hands as he had done during their walk through the city. "Come." He led them almost to the edge of the sea. The tip of a tentacle appeared. Lok-i-xan put out his hand, took the tentacle tip, bowed, gestured Abasio forward, and placed it in his hand.

Abasio was wishing Blue was with him. Blue would have loved this. He shook hands with the kraken and bowed. "I am deeply honored," he said.

The great eyes stared at them and through them. A voice full of the liquid flow of the sea said, "Welcome, Abasio. Be one of us."

"Xulai," her grandfather said, beckoning.

She stood as though stunned. Abasio saw her face, reached for her, tilted her head back. "You're all right. What's happening?"

"I remember him," she whispered.

"That's all right. I remember a lot of very strange stuff, too. Just now, I think you should meet the . . . Sea King."

He said, more loudly, over his shoulder, "She remembers you, Sea King."

"Ah," said the kraken. "She has had sea dreams. Come, child. I won't bite."

She stumbled to the sea edge, Abasio's arm around her, took the proffered tentacle, pressed it between her hands. "You . . . I think you helped me."

"It is possible I did, a long time ago."

"In which case, I should thank you."

"Among kindred, no gratitude is necessary." The tentacle left her as the great creature shifted its way into slightly deeper water. Lok-i-xan drew them back to dry sand.

"Now," the Sea King said, "sit down there where it is warm. Be comfortable." The enormous, shining bulk lifted a wet tentacle and let the sea water drip over itself. "Lok-i-xan and I have been waiting a long time for this meeting. Lok-i-xan's grandfather and grandmother and my ancestors waited for this meeting, and several generations before that! For all that time it was planned that when we met, the Sea King would make a *speech*. Every generation the Sea King practiced the *speech*! Now, it really happens, in my life! We have rehearsed this over and over, Clan Do-Lok and I, so I will explain all the things that need explaining. Still, no matter how many times we have created it, the speech is not perfect. We are always changing it, for there are always questions. You will be allowed to ask questions."

The enormous creature made a sound that, to Abasio, sounded like gentle laughter. It could as well have been the rumblings of a strange stomach or the gurgling of water in a very strange throat, but seemingly Xulai heard it as laughter, also, for she patted the sand beside her to indicate Abasio's place, then folded her hands in her lap when he sat. He felt uneasy about her. Though she seemed composed, she was dreadfully pale. Lok-i-xan and Justinian took their places to either side. After a short silent moment, the kraken began to speak:

"Long and long ago, before the time of monsters that you now call the Big Kill, our sea people learned your dryland languages. Not that we have your kind of ears, but any creature who lives in the sea learns to understand vibrations. Whales and dolphins speak in vibrations. A female drylander beside the sea calls to a child, 'Come out now, it's getting cold,' and we begin to understand what that means. We learn of coming out and going in, and swimming and drowning and being eaten by sharks. We learn the words for 'wrecking' and 'sinking.' Death we already knew about, but we learned your words for it." The great eyes swiveled sideways, and the voice murmured, " 'Death.' 'Injury.' 'Malice.' 'Hatred.' And better words, as well.

"Often, in the Before Time, drylander people used to do a thing called 'taking a cruise.' They would go from one place to another on a ship, and during the voyage they would learn about places. We could climb up the side of a ship and look through what they called a port-hole. The teacher would show them pictures and tell them words. We learned the pictures, we learned the words, both hearing and reading. We learned that this vibration meant this word and this vibration was also conveyed by this set of symbols. So we learned 'Ancient Greece' and 'the glory that was Egypt' and many such things. Later, we learned 'DNA' and 'genetics' and 'mutation.' We already knew of mutation, for man had put evil things into the sea that had changed some of us in strange ways. Some of the changes we were grateful for. Others we hated you for. It was a difficult time to know what to think about drylander-kind, for those of us sea dwellers who could think.

"The thinkers were mostly cephalopods, which you called us, and it was an apt name. We were head-footed, for we went where our brains told us to go. The cetaceans were thinkers, too, even though they were former drylanders. We decided to call your people *erotopods,* sex-footed, for you were always chasing your sex organs. Not all of you. Some of you, too, were cephalopods.

"We learned 'war.' You had many of those. Some of us, the seals and the whales, hoped war would kill you all. Some of us would have regretted that, for we had learned so much from you. That was in what you call the Before Time and the Time When No One Moved Around.

"During the not-moving time we sea dwellers made our alliance with Clan Do-Lok. Together we learned of the great waters; together we realized dryland people really would die in times to come. You would die, and all the things you had made would fall beneath the waves." It coiled, the shape conveying grief like a face flowing with tears. Its color changed to one of sadness.

"Couldn't we build boats and live on them?" asked Xulai.

"Oh, Daughter, you have momentarily forgotten. There will be nothing to build boats from. There will be no more trees, no more land. Even the mountaintops will be gone. You have a few hundred years, maybe two hundred or so. You will push higher and higher. There will be very little room, if any, left. Perhaps a few trees may live on the peaks, but not enough to build boats."

"So we have no hope," said Abasio.

"When there is no hope, one must create hope," said the Sea King, shrugging all eight of his immense shoulder equivalents. "At first the waters did not rise quickly. The channels were narrow; we had time to create hope! Clan Do-Lok had been working with Sea People for a long time: they had given some of us voices as they had done with horses and dogs; they had given us ways to write things down. When we could speak together, humans apologized for the harm they had done us; we grieved for humans' fate. We talked of genetics, and Clan Do-Lok began to breed and teach geneticists to create among both our people those who could live in the future.

"We people of the sea learned greatly from that, different as we are! Through the breeding programs, we created ways to modify ourselves as we wished and have those modifications descend to our children. Some gained voices; some acquired manipulators; some learned to write; we made repositories in the sea where much is written. Together, we and Clan Do-Lok formulated our plan. We have been at it now for several hundred years. Your mother, Xulai, was among the end results of it. Did she give you a sea egg? Before she died, before that spawn of the evil one, that *mongapaf*, killed her, did she give you a sea egg?"

Xulai stared. A sea egg?

Abasio stirred. "Xulai, I was there when you brought it to her. He means the thing she sent you to find! You brought it to her."

"I never had a name for it," she whispered.

"What did you do with it?" the Sea King asked.

"I swallowed it," said Xulai, hovering between horror and curiosity like an atom of iron between two magnets. What was it she had done?

"*Aaaaah,*" the Sea King said with a satisfaction that seemed to spread and glitter across the waves like a sunrise. "So! And after that perhaps you understood things you didn't know you knew. You heard things you couldn't have heard. You spoke the language of nature, convincing living things that they were other kinds of living things, perhaps."

Had she? Oh, Fisher, yes, but the other? She couldn't remember! "They tell me I did such things. I know somehow I got out of a prison there was no way to get out of. Somehow, the man who took me disappeared completely! I don't know how it happened."

The Sea King made a humming noise, a satisfied noise. "Perhaps you did not need to remember, not then. Nonetheless, you are Precious Hope, the daughter of Xu-i-lok, Precious of the Ancients, for those long-ago people worked on this project for generations. Most of the human genes that went into your lineage were found here, in Tingawa, or on the continent nearby. However, some needed variations were not found here, or were not found among suitable donors.

"Of all Lok-i-xan's daughters, only one had the proper genetic structure. Your mother. To beget you, she needed a human male with a certain rare genetic structure. We knew it should be found among the descendants of Huold, and that meant in or near Norland. She went there, she found the duke, together they begot you, and you were X, her precious hope. You are the first one able to create more sea eggs! The people you give them to will change, and if two changers mate with one another, their children will inherit their abilities and their children after them."

After a lengthy silence, Abasio said, "Two of a certain, very rare kind of people finding one another? That's leaving it to mere chance! We . . . that is, you should have better odds than that!"

"There must be no odds at all! Xulai must be sure that each fertile sea egg is given to a person like herself. Otherwise, we will have wars beneath the sea, hatred, species-ism, territoriality—who knows what horrors we would have. Your children will be born with the ability; they will pass it to their children."

Xulai cried, "What ability? I don't have—"

"We believe you can be a land creature when you wish, you can live beneath the sea when you wish."

Xulai cried, "No, I—"

Abasio put his hand on her shoulder, silencing her. "Just out of curiosity, what would happen if Xulai gave me one of the things?"

"It would extend your life but it would not make you immortal. Both you and Xulai will live out your lives long before the oceans cover the last mountaintops. But it will give your descendants a new life and that will give us more time to save humanity."

Xulai cried, "I don't understand any of this. But . . . but suppose I might give an egg to a woman who is a perfectly lovely woman, but she might marry someone who was a dreadful person, and then their children would be all wrong . . ."

"This difficulty was foreseen. It is all planned for! Once the man or woman has the egg, only the right kind of mate will attract them. As your mother found Justinian, Xulai. Your father has told you. They saw one another; she knew he was the right one."

Xulai found herself staring at Abasio, wondering if he felt as she did, this feeling of being herded, directed, this uncertainty whether to be relieved or furious. Here they were again, planning her life for her in a way she did not comprehend in the least, and they'd been doing it generations ahead!

The Sea King read her face, or perhaps her mind. "You are not required to do any of this. You can destroy the sea eggs and let all humans die. You can give them to others and let your own grandchildren drown. That would be a pity." It was said without expression. "However, it is your choice. Lok-i-xan says we may not take away your freedom of choice."

Xulai was still struggling with the idea. "And I suppose, if I wanted to be absolutely sure, I should let someone check the genetics and approve him. If I wanted to marry someone like . . ."

"Like Abasio, here?"

She flushed. "Purely as an example, yes, suppose I did?"

"Well, the person who sent him to Woldsgard thought he was a likely candidate. Abasio wasn't the only man he sent to Woldsgard, but he was the only right one. You probably don't even remember meeting the others. They saw a little girl and were polite, and that was all."

Abasio saw her face, wavering between fury and curiosity, and pulled her tight against him to keep her from erupting. "Was this sea egg what the Duchess of Altamont wanted to get her hands on?"

The great creature before them coiled and recoiled, expressing distaste, horror, contempt with every curl and twist. "People like that one! I wish we could ignore them. We can't. Evil must be found before it can be eradicated. We find one, that one leads us to others. As she did."

"As she did what?"

"She led us to people, places, to an understanding of what was happening. We have certain drylanders who act as our agents. They offer rewards for information, bait for people who will tell us things. This woman wanted power, so we promised her power in return for something we knew she could never find. We said, 'Find Ghastain's miraculous amulet, or anything like it, and we will give you power.'"

Xulai turned, her anger momentarily forgotten. "What was it? Where was it?"

The Sea King's great body shook, and Abasio realized he was laughing. "Ghastain's amulet was a piece of wood with an invitation carved into it. It was from Clan Do-Lok and from the Sea King—I should say Sea Ruler, for at that time it was a female—an invitation to come to Tingawa and talk over the future of all human people. The Sea Ruler sent it by a messenger, or, probably, a whole chain of them. Unfortunately, the Sea Ruler of that time had the message written in Tingawan and did not think to send anyone to translate the message for Ghastain. She did not consider that Ghastain had never lived near the sea, that he would not recognize Tingawan writing. He thought the carved words were magic."

"But . . . all Ghastain's victories? His unconquerable army?"

"He had victories, true. And he had failures, also. His victories took him even into the center of the continent where Huold or Huold's sons begat sons and daughters and where Abasio later lived. And his failures ended his life when his unconquerable army got onto ships and set out for Tingawa. He got as far as he did because he had some good luck and a particularly fine tactician in Huold, who, by the way, strongly advised Ghastain against that armada thing. We could not allow all those ships!"

"It was arrogant," said Abasio, watching Xulai carefully.

"It was stupid," Xulai agreed.

The Sea King could not quite nod, but the flexible tentacles marvelously expressed his feeling of agreement. "Ghastain was clever but he was not really intelligent. When Huold got to Ghost Isle—people say riding on a fish, which is not true; half a dozen dolphins and a whale saved him, none of them fish, really—and when he showed the amulet to the people there, someone told him the words were Tingawan. Huold was intelligent, and he found a word book! A Tingawan-Norland dictionary! Below the sea we are now developing a word book! Cephalo-drylander! Ha. No drylander will be able to say the words, but they can hear them if they stick their heads in the water! Huold struggled to work out the meaning. He spent several days sitting on the beach there at Krakenhold. Our stories say he was toasting sausages, writing, eating a sausage, pondering, then writing again. All that time, the Sea Ruler was lying in the fjord, watching and listening.

"The she-kraken saw that Huold could not believe what it said. Over and over he went back to the book, shaking his head as you drylanders do when you are confused. When Huold finally understood, he started laughing and went on laughing until he was weak and had to lie down on the sand. Then, when he recovered, he broke the amulet into pieces and threw them in the sea."

"Where did he go?"

"He traveled to the mountains above Marish and left his servant there. He himself went down to Marish. Nobody knew who he was. There was a ship readying to sail to Tingawa. Before it sailed he told the people of Marish there was a man lost up on the mountain. When they found the man, he told them the story Huold had given him to tell, that Huold was lost in the mountains. Huold wasn't lost at all; when he reached Tingawa, he was adopted into Clan Do-Lok. Justinian is also a descendant of that family through Lythany, Huold's daughter, who began Woldsgard. That's why the genetics worked out so well."

Xulai rose, shaking her head, trembling. "I can't believe this. It's so . . . it's not probable! That my father would have said nothing about this! Nothing at all, not a hint. That the princess, my mother, that she wouldn't have said anything. I don't suppose anyone else would have known. Not even Precious Wind?"

"Precious Wind knew only a part," said the Sea King. "Your mother knew a part. Your father, standing behind you so quietly now, is hearing it for the first time. Everyone would have known all about it a generation ago if it had not been for that . . . creature. Precious Wind has already told you the history of the creature. We knew that whenever Tingawan people went into Norland, something dreadful followed them, sometimes killed them. Despite all our protections, it killed your mother. We could not risk it happening to you. Secrecy was absolutely necessary, to protect you. If we could have completed our plan without Tingawans going to Norland, it would have been easier, but we could not. As it was, we took all kinds of precautions against the monster, but we didn't know he'd created assistants! Just as we did not know about the women he spawned. Just as we did not know of the devices the creature had from the Before Time. We did not know what he was capable of!"

They sat silent for a moment. Xulai moved restlessly. "I still don't understand about this 'ability' you've mentioned. I think I understand about the genetics, but not at all about this *changing*. How is it we *change*?"

"Come here," he said. "Come close."

The words were gentle but they were still a command. Something tiny within her struggled, only for a moment, before she went toward him, the great buttress of him lying there near the waters' edge, his tentacles spiraling among the stones, his great eyes peering at her, his terrifying beak motionless below though the hypnotic word flowed from it. "Come."

She went. A tentacle as wide as a tree rose from the sea, the bottom side circled with cups that had a life of their own, gaping and contracting. The tentacle rose over her, curved away, growing smaller as it tapered away, branch sized, then arm sized, then finally the tip, only the size of a finger, delicate as her own, came forward to touch her. It was chilly but not cold. It was wet but not slimy. It stroked her arm and then held her hand, taking the little finger and the ring finger and squeezing them together very softly. "Change," the Sea King murmured. "Daughter, change."

Her fingers changed. The bones went out of them. They flexed. Little circles erupted from their bottom sides. Her hand split in two. Dreamily, she remembered this feeling. She had been a tree in a very tight little pot, breaking the pot. It was the feeling she had had in the dungeon, as though her arm had split in two. Her hand split in two with little cups replacing the palm, wrist splitting in two, then the lower arm, elbow, upper arm, shoulder. At the same time her feet and the other arm were also splitting, the separations rising toward her shoulders, and she was becoming eight limbed, each limb lengthening, changing color, turning, spiraling, curving, infinitely flexible. She felt the bones come apart into pieces, tiny pieces, moving aside, encapsulating, staying there but no longer attached to one another, each capsule flexibly joined to the next. The change reached her neck, her head. There was a carapace there. Her eyes moved outward, to the sides, seeing things she had never seen before. She had no nose, but she had something that sensed a smell, things she had never smelled before.

"Come," he said, tugging gently. "You are *homocephalo-sapiens*. You are many-legged brain-holding humankind. You are a color changer, shape changer, dweller beneath the sea. And yet you are still humankind, still female, and inside you, in that organ you call an ovary, you are creating more sea eggs."

Behind her, Abasio pulled every fiber of himself into a tight bundle, wound it with cords of self-control, and made it stand still. Rigid as iron, he saw what she became and how she had become it. The helmet had recorded what Xulai had felt and seen during her imprisonment in the Vulture Tower, yes, but that had been as observed from inside herself. That had been mostly . . . feelings! That he had accepted, how she felt, how she reacted, but the helmet had not shown him what she became, how she became it. Now there was no more mystery about how Jenger had died. Now there was a new, more important mystery, about himself! How would Abasio react to this? His first reaction, rigidly controlled, had been to flee, to refuse to accept, refuse to understand or want to understand. How long did he have before she would come back? How long did he have to talk sense to himself? What form would she come back in? Psychologically wavering helplessly between love and revulsion, mentally trying to make sense of the story he had heard, bodily he stood utterly rigid, a man carved from stone.

Meantime, Xulai had been tugged into the sea, into the shimmer and the curl of the sea, the foam and ripple, the shush and pull, the buoyancy, the bounce, the tremble, the shift, the constant movement and life of the ocean. One of her arms picked up a shell, curled around it, opened it, delivered the contents to her beak. Oyster. Very nice. She had never tasted such freshness. But, but, wasn't this akin to murder, to killing one's. . .

"It's all right," said the Sea King.

He was speaking. She heard his Tingawan words through the water. The vibrations were felt through her skin. "There are things that think and feel and there are things that don't. We try not to eat the things that do. Except for certain very evil ones. Those we go after in groups and some eat them with considerable ceremony, but it is not obligatory."

She thought she nodded. Perhaps she nodded.

The tentacle tugged again. "Swim. See."

He went ahead of her, huge but buoyant, tentacles trailing, she a tiny copy of him, propelling herself through the waters, a balloon with fringes trailing behind. She caught a tentacle tip around an arm of coral and spun to rest, eyes fastened upon the complexity and glory of the reef, jeweled with thousands of brightly colored fishes, ornamented with corals of myriad shapes, dotted with fringe-shelled clams, swarming with eels, starfish, urchins. A tiny octopus crept from a hole in the reef, its little tentacles like a fringed skirt. It greeted her as a child might greet her on the street. "H'lo. Who're you?" She introduced herself. The baby giggled and withdrew into its hiding place.

"One of my offspring," said the Sea King with a certain satisfaction. "The females of our new race come here for sperm packets and sometimes leave their egg packets close by."

"Sperm . . . ?" Xulai felt herself flushing.

"Our males who have language do it no differently than we cephalopods have always done. Our males have always given a sperm packet to the females." He chuckled. "Your people call this an 'arm's-length transaction.' We find it sensible. Intelligent! You already know what we think of your way! All that . . ."

"Yes," said Xulai, not wanting to get into *all that*. "I know."

He continued. "Our females store the sperm, sometimes for a season or more. They use it when they have eggs ready, when they have found a safe place to attach them to the seafloor where the young will not be threatened. Of course, as Sea King, I have issued an edict concerning our young. Each creature with a mind knows they are not to touch them. The scientists have given us what they call disincentives. Our babies do not taste good."

Xulai turned toward him and met the eyes of a dolphin, head and body tilted in the water so it could see her better.

It warbled, in Tingawan, "Is this your drylander daughter, Sea King?"

"It is," he rumbled.

"Swim well and swiftly, sea daughter," said the dolphin. "I will tell my people."

"He speaks our language," she murmured, watching it swim away. There was something strangely fringed about the flippers. Were those fingers at the edges?

"Those of us Sea People who speak, speak a language we have chosen to speak. We have our own languages as well, but we chose a simplified Tingawan to become the language of the sea. Dryland Tingawan has many more words than are strictly necessary. We are not writing a thesis here. We seek only to communicate!"

Across the bulk of him she saw something very strange. It looked like, it seemed to be . . . "What is that?" she asked, pointing with several tentacles.

He laughed, that deep, interior gurgle. "That is the dolphin's joke. They said, because I am a king, I must have a castle. The corals grew it for them. Corals don't talk; I don't know how the dolphins told the corals what to do, but they grew me a castle! The dolphins had seen castles, here and there, where men live near the coast. When they had built it, the eels liked it very much, so they moved in. So, the Sea King has a castle full of eels."

It was true; the place crawled with them. It actually seemed that one huge eel went up the entire height of the structure, and she had to stare for a moment to realize it was actually a tail at the bottom, several middles of eels at various places in between, and one quite large head at the top.

"I suppose everyone in the sea knows about it," she said. "Your castle?"

"I suppose," he said.

"There are people, refugees," she said. "They say they are refugees from you, Sea King. They live on the great cliff of the highlands of Ghastain. Each of them wears an earring, a tower with what I thought was a snake winding through it."

"I know. If you look very closely at what they wear, there is a little line of waves at the very top, hardly visible. That tells you the crest is an underwater tower with an eel wound through it. Those people are not refugees from me, Daughter. They take refuge from the sea. Their islands have been drowned, but I did not drown them. They are partly Tingawan, but the islanders have a different culture, a different language. We, Clan Do-Lok and I, asked them to settle there, to be an army, if we ever need an army. Some of our best geneticists are among them. They keep us informed of what is happening. They send messages to Wellsport and the dolphins bring them to Tingawa. They tell us who goes where. We offered them sea eggs in exchange for their help."

"But there were no sea eggs then."

"They know that. They live in hope, as we do. The Duchess of Altamont amuses—that is, amused herself with them, or they with her. They have sent messages to tell us she is dead, her mother the queen is dead. King Gahls is alone now. He is not an intelligent man. He will go on having parades while the water rises."

"Gahls is not alone enough," she replied. "Rancitor is Mirami's son. He has evil blood. I'm sure the Tingawans know that. He must not become king."

He shrugged enormously. "Forget it for a time. For this little time, simply enjoy the sea."

He went to the castle and she turned aside to admire a marvelous fish. When she turned back, the Sea King had disappeared.

He did not reappear. Disoriented, she turned, turned again, finally called out. "Sea King!" She was looking at the last place she had seen him. And he emerged, there, from the background, laughing at her.

"How did you do that?"

"How did you do it? When you became a little child?"

"Precious Wind told you! I never knew how I did it."

"You took the color of the thing you wished to be, the color of the background."

"I was wearing clothes!"

"When you change, you are like water. You can leak through your clothes, tiny bits of you, like needles, holding the color of your background. I cannot do that, but then, I don't have to."

"You planned that!"

He laughed. "It was totally unforeseen. Precious Wind said you had done it. It took us a long, long time to figure out how."

Precious Wind knew about it. Well, let it be; she did not really believe it. It had surprised her at the time, but it had felt much more like a mental thing to her, something she did with her mind, not her body.

Together they explored the coral-flowered, fish-gemmed castle, from its laughably porous dungeons at the bottom to its towers just below the water's surface, one of which held a flagpole that waved a tiny red seaweed pennant. It was tenanted by great numbers of the Sea King's children, safe from the eels because they did not taste good. After a time—short or long, she didn't know—he reached out a tentacle and together they moved back toward the beach. Once there he thrust her toward the sand and moved away. "Change back." It was only a whisper, but it was a command.

And she did, as she crawled onto the sand. Her head had not split, it had merely become flexible. Bits of skull joined together. Starting at the neck, her body came together and buttoned itself up like a long shirt and pair of trousers, though her real shirt and trousers lay on the sand where she had slipped out of them on her way into the ocean. All the little bits of bone slipped together like the oddly shaped pieces of those sawn puzzles Bear had made for her when she was little, locking together, knitting into solidity. The little subordinate brains up and down the tentacles encapsulated and hid themselves. Her flesh melded. She looked for a seam on her arm and could not find one.

Justinian and Lok-i-xan had turned and walked away when she came from the sea, whether from politeness or some less pleasant feeling, so only Abasio, still rigid as stone, widened his eyes as he saw her dress herself. Her eyes passed over him blindly, as though he were not there. He shivered. Apparently he didn't exist; she had forgotten the entire world in which he existed.

When she turned toward the sea once again, the Sea King had moved a good way offshore. "Come to the edge of the sea and call my name if you need me," he said.

"What is your name?"

"Just say you want to talk to your father," he called, disappearing below the surface of the sea. "Or call for the Sea King."

"Your father?" Abasio breathed from close behind her. He had had to force himself to approach, even though most of his fear had vanished when she had become Xulai once more. He put aside any contemplation of how he would feel about, how he would deal with, whatever other form she might choose or keep in the future. Let it alone. Don't think of it. Deal with it, if at all, later on.

Xulai sighed, aware of him. This was Abasio. Yes. Abasio. He was there, steady, calm . . . like her other half. Had he been afraid? She could hear his heart beating, too quickly. He had been afraid. For her, or for himself? For both of them, probably. Of course he had. So had she. She reached behind her to take his hand. She leaned against him.

"All my fathers, Abasio, just think of all my fathers. Justinian is my father. Clan Do-Lok is my father. The Sea King is my father. I probably have a dozen mothers. Generations of them. Hundreds of years of them. Are you frightened, Abasio? I am quite definitely terrified, but I'm so stunned, I can't feel it yet. I'm afraid I'll be afraid, dreadfully afraid, when I do."

He made a shivering sound, a fragile, brittle exclamation that was not quite laughter and not quite a shriek of terror. He made himself put his arms around her and draw her even closer. "Yes, I was . . . am frightened."

"Do you know why?"

He could not answer immediately. At last he took a deep breath and said, "I decided it was because I thought you might not come back at all, or that you might come back as something else entirely. Which is what you may have done."

She thought about it. "I worried about that, too, but no. I'm me. I was me even when I wasn't. It was like getting out of bed and stretching and finding all my bones weren't necessary, and dealing with that perfectly well while at the same time something inside me was screaming that there was something terribly wrong. It was like one of those dreams where you're flying, and you know very well if you fall, you're dead, but the flying is nice, so it's half terror and half exaltation. You know? Part of me was scared to death, but meantime, the rest of me was just enjoying it. I imagine your frightened part was doing the same thing mine was, but you didn't feel the other part. Assuming we both have the same parts."

"Can I do that? Change like that?"

"If I understand what he was saying, evidently all it takes is a sea egg. I gave you one a long time ago. In Merhaven. What did you do with it?"

"I swallowed it. When I was with you in the princess's bedroom, that first night, I got the very strong feeling your mother wanted me to do what you were doing, so when you gave it to me, I did it on faith, I guess. But I haven't felt like changing!"

"Well, neither did I feel like changing. Not until I had to. I dreamed it at least twice before I actually did it; then I did it to save my life, there in the Vulture Tower, but I couldn't remember doing it. Did you get what the Sea King said about Ghastain's amulet?"

"It was an invitation to join the party."

"And Huold did! The amulet wouldn't have done anything for the duchess, even if she'd found it. Before Huold went to Tingawa, though, he left descendants we know nothing about. Some of them, obviously, were in the part of the world where you were raised. One or more of them were your ancestors."

Abasio considered his mother and his father, the Drowned Woman and the Gang Leader. At least one of them had been a great-great-great-how-many-greats-grandchild of Huold the Heroic? How utterly unlikely that was! "And our part in all this is . . . ?"

"Our part came about because Xu-i-lok was the first woman, *the only woman,* who would be able to lay the sea eggs after she mated with . . . with someone who had the right genetics. Well, so . . . after she and my father . . . got together, she became pregnant with me and laid the first sea egg. She did it about the same time that . . . *creature* at Altamont sent her killing cloud! My mother hid it. She hid it and kept it hidden until I was old enough . . . or you were strong enough to help me find it. If she'd had time to create other sea eggs, all this wouldn't have been necessary!"

He nodded slowly, thoughtfully. "But, since there was only one egg, you were her only hope. Precious Hope. Your mother wouldn't have chosen all those years of pain if there had been another way."

"But it was still only a hope, because then they had to find you! They needed to find a mate for me with the right genetics, just as my mother had needed to find my father. Because they needed one more. Oh, I hope she knew I was going to be a girl. If she didn't know, how she must have worried. If I'd been a boy, it wouldn't have done any good, because there'd have been no more sea eggs."

He put his arms around her, pulling her close. "But you were a girl, for which I am very grateful."

"Yes. I am female. And I've laid a dozen sea eggs, and I've given you one, and I'm producing more of them, so now we have enough to give others. And if the sea egg you swallowed works, we will have children who can change and our daughters will also be able to lay sea eggs. Our children will live. Any couple that we give sea eggs to will live and their children will live. We start by giving them to men and women, then they connect with one another. The right women. The right men."

Her voice tightened and she shivered in the circle of his arms.

"You hate that? Being controlled?"

She looked into his face, so familiar to her that she might have always known it. "No. Abasio, no, I really don't. I hate the *idea* of being predisposed, prearranged. But I don't hate the reality, not now. I hate the thought I could not choose, but I would not have chosen differently. It's a dilemma, isn't it? Precious Wind says it's how all young people feel when they grow up. They do not wish to be like their parents, and yet very often they end up choosing to be like their parents."

He held her close. "I've never asked you, Xulai. Do you love me?"

"I loved Xu-i-lok. I love Oldwife Gancer. I love my horse. I loved Fisher. I would not have lost any of them. I would rather lose myself than lose you. Should it be more than that? How do I know?"

"So you want me with you? Always? So you'd grieve my loss? Would you leap between me and certain death?" He laughed harshly. "I would answer yes to any of those questions about you, though I'd prefer not to find the last one necessary."

"Well, do you love me, Abasio? Will you come under the sea with me? Will you chat with my sea father and live as part octopus?"

His face clouded. "How do octopuses . . . you know?"

She laughed at his expression. "It's what the Sea King calls 'an arm's-length transaction.' As soon as he said it, I remembered it was in the book I borrowed from the abbey library. The males give the females a sperm packet. The females store it inside themselves, then they use it when they get ready to plant their egg packets. I absolutely know there has to be some biological incentive, some hormonal or sensory drive, but the Sea King spoke of it as though he were . . . simply being accommodating. 'Here, madam, you seem a pleasant cephalopod, please accept this with my compliments.' "

"Isn't it nice to have the choice of methods?" Abasio croaked from a throat suddenly tight and painful.

She drew away from him. "I'm not sure we have that choice. Sea-egg people will evidently be part human, part octopus-who-talks, but the Sea King is all octopus-who-talks. The only humanity he has is in the design of his vocal apparatus. I don't think *his* children can change. With the waters rising, there'd be no point in that."

"So when there is no more land, how will *we* procreate?"

She shook her head. "Well, if we're not totally different, we sea eggers, I can think of one possibility. I had the idea when the lady served tea . . . Precious Wind and I used to drink tea at Woldsgard. The foresters cut chunks of ice from the glaciers up in the Icefangs, and we kept the ice in an icehouse and in summer we had iced tea. And thinking about ice made me remember reading that the north and south poles were frozen. And I wondered if they wouldn't still be frozen with the waters rising. That's where the walruses and seals have their babies, don't they? Won't the ice bears and the penguins and the other creatures who live in those cold lands go on living there? And didn't men used to live in those snow lands? Couldn't men still live there? In the coldest parts, couldn't people even make ships out of ice?"

He thought about this. "You mean, people who are given sea eggs could live out of the sea, or they could live in both places? Or just go there to procreate?"

"I can imagine us going north to have babies. We build a hut on an ice . . . raft, is that what they call it? And it floats south, and by the time it melts, we're ready to take the baby underwater. Something like that." She sighed, her face crumpled in dismay. "I killed Jenger. Now I remember doing it. I even remember why, though it was the part of Xu-i-lok in me who actually impelled me to do it. If he had raped me, if he had impregnated me, it would have ruined everything. It could not be allowed to happen, so I, she, killed him. I did it by taking a sea shape even though I was on land. The Sea King was out of the water a lot of the time today while we talked. So, we should still be able to take sea shapes and live out of the water part of the time. And if someday so much water freezes at the poles that the oceans go down again, then there would be a place for land creatures, wouldn't there? If we keep seeds. If we keep animals, or their patterns. If we keep Clan Do-Lok's laboratories on the ice when Tingawa is covered with water?"

"I think Clan Do-Lok has made provisions for its laboratories, even underwater. I worry more about Precious Wind's wolves."

"She might have thought of it. Precious Wind thinks of most things."

They sat longer. Abasio was searching himself for feelings of revulsion, rejection, or fear, finding vague shadows, nothing he could not manage. Xulai was remembering the ocean, the sheer, bubbling delight of the ocean.

Abasio said, "If you're distributing sea eggs, I think Artemisia might be one place to start—after Tingawa. I think you'll find a high proportion of the right kind of people."

"The right people! The refugees," she cried. "Abasio, the Sea King told me who they really are . . ." She told him what she had learned, including the winks and nods given to her while they were climbing the great cliff. "So many people, counting on us, depending on us, and we still don't know what we do about the monster. He's still intent upon ruining everything, and I'm so afraid he actually can! If he can detect those who have been given sea eggs, he'll kill them. He'll kill them all."

Neither of them could believe otherwise, and they sat in baffled silence, side by side, unmoving, until they looked up to see Xulai's father and grandfather rounding the end of the little island and returning slowly along the sand. Their faces expressed what Abasio had felt earlier: intense curiosity mingled with extreme apprehension. Xulai and Abasio stood up and went to greet them, seeing the older men's expressions change and soften as they came nearer.

"It's all right," said Justinian. It could have been a statement or a question.

Xulai took his hand and drew him close between them. "It's all right." She reached up to pat his cheek. "We're not totally comfortable with all this. We're nowhere near understanding all this. We're not sure we can manage it. But we're not afraid of it."

Over her father's shoulder, she smiled into her grandfather's eyes and he bowed to her, to Abasio, and turned away so they would not see his tears.

"So you met the Sea King," said Precious Wind. "I never have. What did you think of him?"

"A very large, very smart creature who looks nothing at all like a human being," said Abasio. "And who, nonetheless, seems very humane."

They were dining in their common room, the food brought to them, they were told, by the same people who served those of Clan Do-Lok who lived in the citadel. Many of the clan had homes elsewhere, but those who did live there shared a common kitchen and people to provide their daily needs. Abasio, who liked to know people's names and what they were like and where they lived, found himself frustrated at not seeing any of the same people twice. Each meal, it seemed, new people arrived, served them, bowed pleasantly but not at all obsequiously, and departed. Precious Wind said that because everyone wanted to see them, the opportunity was being passed around.

When their intimate group was left alone, Xulai took from her lap the small box that she and Abasio had taken from the forest so long ago. She set it on the table and opened it. It now held the twelve sea eggs she had cut out of her undershift that evening after returning to the citadel.

"I had thirteen," she said. "I gave Abasio one in Merhaven. He swallowed it. I want you and Clan Do-Lok to decide who gets these. You know your people better than I do, and these will change six men and six women. I hope to heaven they'll come out even when they are recognizing mates and that none of them need to run off across what's left of the world to find someone."

"Why didn't you tell me?" Precious Wind asked, staring at the little box as though at a miracle. "We've been waiting, wondering. I told everyone, all the workers and planners, they were not allowed to ask you! Oh, this is wonderful. Once there are several couples, the number of sea eggs produced will increase exponentially. Within a year, we could have hundreds or more . . . what shall we call them? Sea-fertile people?"

"Let me be sure I understand this whole thing," said Abasio. "A woman who is given a sea egg can produce sea eggs. Her female children cannot, however, unless their father has also received a sea egg. Xulai can produce sea eggs because her mother could and because Justinian's genetics were already the same as the sea egg would have given him, right? It's the same with Xulai and me. Justinian and I couldn't change into . . . another form without the eggs, but we could father children who could." He shook his head. "Sometimes I have a little trouble remembering what part of the situation is which."

Precious Wind nodded. "If both father and mother have had sea eggs, or if one of them has and the other is already genetically compatible, then their children, male and female, will be sea fertile as well as able to change. Being able to change will be critical as the waters' rising goes on. So, since genetic compatibility is very rare—we were lucky to find Justinian, but it took years and a number of false starts to find Abasio—our first priority is to increase the number and distribution of sea eggs as quickly as possible."

Xulai said, "Also, the distribution must be as wide as possible, assuring that both men and women all over the world get them. No people or group should feel they are being left out. Assuming each sea-fertile woman produces as many as I have, each woman should pass on at least a dozen every year. By the time the waters' rising has completed, all children should be changeable."

Precious Wind nodded in agreement. "We will take the first ones produced by Tingawans back to Norland with us. And, if we give each one to a new candidate as soon as it's produced, alternating between men and women . . . How many, Abasio?"

"Hundreds. The first year. When I think how far they had to go to track me down, and to find Justinian, though . . ."

"You can forget that. That was different. We didn't have a sea egg for any of the men then," said Precious Wind. "We had to search Huold's lineage for a genetic match. Once we had sea eggs, however, we no longer needed to fret about that."

Abasio was still worrying the problem. "I understand Justinian having the right genetics, but my family was never anywhere near Norland . . ."

Xulai said, "Huold had seven sons. Both he and they traveled all over the map, Abasio. Women liked him and he liked women. If you could trace it back, you'd find that your mother or father or both had Huold as an ancestor. And the line may have inbred several times, as well. As soon as we have a few sea eggs to distribute, we want to take them to Norland. But, Precious Wind, we can't ignore the threat of that monster . . ."

Precious Wind made a face. "I know. Clan Do-Lok has been talking about it. They'll want to meet with the emissary as soon as he gets here. He's the only one who's actually seen the thing. It killed Bear plus several of our best fighters, and quite frankly that terrifies us because it means it's going to be very hard to trap the thing or kill it. It hates Tingawans, and we'd rather set a Tingawan trap in Norland than here, for obvious reasons. It might decide to destroy the whole country if it were here, and maybe it actually has the means to do so. We don't know what it's capable of. However, I don't think our people will like the idea of you or any sea-fertile woman going into danger. They want to figure something else out."

They left it at that. The following day, Xulai joined Precious Wind in providing the sea eggs to a dozen young Tingawan men and women, all very serious, several of them seeming to be in a state of exaltation. Xulai wondered at this until she realized that, of course, these were to be the parents of the whole race. It would be a very great honor to have been chosen. They were eager to question her about how she had felt.

"I felt strange," she said. "I think you may, too. Try very hard just to relax and let it happen, because otherwise you'll upset everyone and they'll wonder if they've chosen the right people."

As it turned out, she had given this advice to the wrong people. The scientists who had run the program descended upon the poor young people with a battery of tests and hours of questioning. The young people, already struggling to adapt, felt irritated and unresponsive, and this in turn made the questioners doubtful, itchy, and more demanding. Precious Wind wanted to compare this with Xulai's experience, and she began going back and forth with suggestions and questions.

Xulai, suddenly aware of what was happening, went furiously off to find Lok-i-xan.

"Grandfather, your people are very smart and very interested, and they chose the twelve people by doing all that preselection stuff, testing for compatibility and so on, but now instead of trusting their process, they're fiddling with it, and they're driving the young people crazy. If anyone had treated me like that, I'd have jumped off a cliff! You've got to make people leave them alone!"

"Tingawans are not perfect," he said, half-amused. "Most humans behave in the way you have described, particularly people who have spent a large part of their lives on a single project. They have a great deal invested in those young people and, unfortunately, they regard them as experimental subjects."

"Well they'd better disregard them as such," said Xulai emphatically. "That was the one thing I really had trouble with. I could face danger. I could stand confusion. I even managed to deal with betrayal, even though it still makes me cry every time I think about Bear and what he did, but it was the idea that people were herding me like a goat or sheep that I really objected to."

This meeting ended with her kissing her grandfather and promising to hold her temper.

"And I promise to keep the experimenters away from the subjects," he said.

"They're not *subjects*!" she snarled, forgetting her promise. "You see, even you're doing it."

Precious Wind and her colleagues were instructed to leave the sea-fertile people alone. Left alone, each one of the twelve managed to cope, either alone or with one another's help. Over the next few days there was a good deal of group talk and group strolling and group eating and drinking tea, often with Xulai and Abasio. Within ten days six couples had coalesced from within the group, and Precious Wind had started to relax and spend more time with her wolves.

"WE'LL HAVE TO TAKE A ship to get back to Norland, won't we?" Abasio commented to Xulai as they lay on their comfortable bed, looking out into the garden. "Blue was asking. He's just recovered from being sea-sick last time."

Xulai murmured, "We can't really talk about going until you've made the sea change."

His mind balked. He felt it happen. He'd seen Blue balk like that, stop dead when there was nothing much in front of him, and the comparison bothered him momentarily. "Why is it dependent upon that?" he asked. "You didn't do it until you had to. Perhaps I won't be able to do it until I have to, assuming it works at all. I'm the first male they've tried it on, remember."

"That's why," she said rather sadly. "You're the first one, and we have to know it works before I'll go back. Why should I go, otherwise? Danger. Possible death. For what? I had a dream last night. I dreamed we got there and you couldn't change. If you can't change, it means giving eggs to the men may not work. You and my father have never changed even though you can supposedly father children who can change. Grandfather says the change part comes only from a sea egg. We need at least one man to change so we know they can!"

"It's the sea egg that has the cephalopod genes in it, right?"

"Right. And I'm proof they work on at least one woman. Will it work on all men, or just some men, or any men at all? We need to know for sure. If it only works on ones like you and my father, then it presents another problem. Of course, Father's going with us, too. You're the only two we know of who are genetically . . . apt. If the eggs won't work by themselves, we'll have to put you both out to stud. If that's the way it has to be, I've got to be emotionally prepared for it."

"You'd put us to what? *You've* got to be prepared! By all that's . . . You've been talking to Precious Wind!"

"Well, so? She just wants me to know what's going on."

Abasio rose and took his cloak from the back of the chair. "I'm going to see Blue," he said.

"Abasio . . ."

"What!"

"Put on your trousers first."

"It's a compliment," said Blue. "I don't know what you're so upset about."

"Being put 'out to stud' is what I'm upset about. To talk that way about me, and about her father!"

"You're looking at it from the wrong end. Usually, when horses get old, it's, 'Well, time for the knackers, old fellow.' Being put out to stud is like the gardens of paradise."

"I am *not* old. You don't know what it's like. You didn't see what she turned into. What I'd have to turn into . . ."

"No, and I've been meaning to speak to you about that. It's time I found out about what's going on. My race is involved here as well as yours."

"Very well. You're perfectly right." Abasio opened the stable door and bowed him out. "Come on, we're going down to the shore. You can meet the Sea King."

"From the shore!"

"Certainly from the shore. The shore is on an island, however. We'll have to take a boat to the island."

"Oh, no, no, no more boats! I've just gotten over being—"

"It's not really a boat, and it's not far. You'll just have to put up with it if you want to know what's happening."

They went to the shore, where Abasio found a flat-bottomed barge sort of floating thing. He wasn't sure what one might call it. A barn door with an edge around it, maybe. There were a good many seaside hangers-about available, several of whom were willing to row, scull, or pole the barn door out to the island. Blue was maneuvered aboard with some difficulty. He made the trip with his head down, refusing to look at anything but his feet. When they arrived, Abasio led him around the island and onto the little beach, where Blue kept on walking.

"What are you doing?"

"I'm walking. I'm going up and down this strip of sand in order to convince my insides that I'm on solid ground. Horses need solid ground. They need solidity. Stability . . ."

"Which is no doubt why they're kept in stables."

"Very funny, I'm sure."

Abasio left him walking and went to the edge of the water, mentally rehearsing the words he had heard used before. When he had them well in mind, he shouted over the sea at the top of his voice, "Xaolat al Koul!"

Nothing happened for a time, then a dolphin came speeding toward the shore, thrashed himself up onto the sand, and asked, "You're calling the Sea King?"

"Would you tell him, please, that Abasio would like to see him? I need to . . . discuss things with him."

The dolphin squirmed back into the water and sped away. Abasio sat down to wait.

"He could be otherwise occupied," said Blue.

"He could be very far away," said Abasio. "We'll wait."

They did not wait long before the middle stone of a group of three just offshore began to move slowly toward them. The great mantle protruded above the waves, the huge eyes looked them over, the abyssal, echoing voice said, "You wanted to talk to me?"

"Yes, if you don't mind," said Abasio. "I'd like to introduce you to—"

"Ah. A horse. I have seen horses. What is your name, horse?"

"Blue," the horse replied, clopping down to the waterside. "In certain lights this combination of black, gray, and white looks blue. Sometimes they call me Big Blue. You've seen horses?"

"Along the edge of the continent, yes. The horses there have been discussing what is important to them, so that if they are sea changed they will retain their essential equinity."

"Horseness is important," agreed Blue, nodding. "What have they decided upon?"

"They say speed is important to them. They say grazing is important to them. They say mating is important to them, though the stallions seem to believe it is more important than the mares do."

"Oh, mares," said Blue, shaking his head. "They always have to be whinnied into it. Or . . . subdued."

"Why, Blue," cried Abasio in an outraged voice. "That's *rape*."

Blue snorted. "I have long observed that human people do not care what they do in front of livestock, and believe me, what some humans do during mating makes horses look absolutely . . . gentle by comparison." He stalked away and stood, front legs crossed, nose up, facing the sea.

"Isn't Abasio your friend?" the Sea King asked him.

"Friends do not call their friends rapists," said the horse without turning around.

"I'm sorry," said Abasio. "Really."

"You are getting more judgmental," said Blue. "You need to watch that. Elderly people do get more judgmental."

"Elderly!"

The horse turned to the Sea King. Pointedly ignoring Abasio, he said, "I should think hooves will be important. And teeth, for fighting."

"Will it be necessary for you to fight?" asked the Sea King.

The horse looked embarrassed. "Usually there's one stallion to a herd of mares and young," he said. "Which stallion is a matter of who has the best hooves and teeth, usually." He thought for a moment. "Though . . . with the waters rising, eloquence may become more important. It is with people like him." He snorted in Abasio's direction. "He probably just *talks* them into it."

The Sea King asked, "Is mating strategy what brought you to talk with me today?"

"No, certainly not. Abasio came to talk with you today because Xulai doesn't want to go back to Norland until she's sure he can do whatever it is, change into something."

Abasio interrupted. "I told her maybe I couldn't do it until it became necessary. She didn't do it until she had to, but she says it's pointless to go without knowing . . ."

Blue snorted again. "But she wants to know he's seaworthy before she goes for a cruise on him."

"Blue! Really!"

"Well, she does. And I don't blame her."

"Let it go for now," said the Sea King in a thoughtful and very soothing tone. "You sound very tense. You need to relax, Abasio. Do you swim?"

"I swim human-style, yes." He had learned as a child, in the river. On the farm.

"Well, if Blue doesn't mind waiting—and I think there's some grass among the rocks at the back of the beach—you can get out of your clothes and come swim with me. One of the shell fishers left his face mask last time he was here. Over behind those stones, I think?" He pointed a tentacle. "Yes, that's the one. It was one of the oystermen I believe, or maybe an abalone-ist or a mussel-eer. At any rate, he won't mind your borrowing it."

Abasio dropped his clothes behind the rock and donned the mask before somewhat apprehensively walking into the sea.

"Just swim alongside me," said the Sea King. "I want to show you my castle."

"You have a castle?"

"It's a joke. I told Xulai all about it. She thought it was very funny." He started away, rather slowly, letting Abasio thrash along behind him, turning his head every stroke or so to gulp air. They went out beyond the nearer rocks, not really very far. "Can you dive just a little so you can look?" said the Sea King.

Abasio took a breath, dived, went back up to laugh, then came down again.

"I didn't build it," the Sea King said through the water. "The dolphins did. They talked the corals into doing it. Though frankly, I don't know how a creature that doesn't have any brain at all can be talked into doing something. It took them quite a while; corals don't grow overnight. The dolphins may merely have put food here, where they wanted the corals, I mean. Corals will grow toward food. The eels came all by themselves . . ."

Abasio had gone up for a breath. He came down again.

The Sea King continued. "There are lots of little deep holes in the castle for my children. That is, I suppose they are mostly my children. The other males of my species don't come into this area, out of respect, but many of the females choose to anchor their egg cases here."

They swam over the castle, seeing in the doors of its narrow tunnels many tiny octopi, who greeted them variously: "Who're you?" "It got hans!" "Whasit?" "Wasse doin?" "Whasitname?"

The Sea King replied, "I'm your father, yes he has hands, he's a dry-lander, he's swimming, his name is Abasio."

"Already very vocal," said the Sea King with satisfaction as they moved away. "Breeding true, almost all of them. Come along, I'll show you some of the laboratories."

They dived deeper and Abasio was amazed to see lines of huge transparent bubbles anchored to the floor of the bay, each occupied by one kind or another of unfamiliar creatures.

"These are third-generation seadogs," the Sea King said proudly.

"They have skinny tails," Abasio exclaimed. "Not very good for steering."

"For wagging. Notice the articulation of the front and rear legs. Sitting and wagging were specified by the canine design committee."

"The design committee?"

"Of dogs. It seems to be a species thing."

"How do they breathe?"

"See the gills all along the sides?"

"They have fur."

The Sea King sighed. "Yes. They felt strongly about fur, as well. The fur does rather hide the gills. It cuts down their swimming speed as well, and the large ears are no help. In time, perhaps they'll give the fur and ears up, though seals seem to have kept the fur with no problems. Seals are still dryland birthers, of course, which these will be, too. We can't get away from that just yet. Young mammals have to suckle."

"Whales manage. And dolphins."

"Yes, but they've mastered that whole business of pushing the young to the surface to breathe, over and over. You know, whales have developed kinship or friendship bonds between mothers, daughters, and sisters so that one helps the other for the first few days until the single baby does it instinctively. Dogs, however, have litters, six to ten at a time.

It presents an entirely different problem, and we haven't figured out how to handle that yet."

"They have flippers instead of feet."

"They can walk on them very nicely. If, as I understand Xulai has suggested, there are ice floes in our future, the seadogs might bear their young on ice floes as seals and walruses and otters do now. Ice floes melt rather rapidly, however. They might not last long enough."

"Sea King, Xulai has been talking about ice, yes, but not simply ice floes. I am told there is still more or less permanent ice as one goes to the far north. People used to live on that ice in the Before Time. The new oceans are less salty than the Before Time oceans. They should freeze even better than the old ones did, and Xulai wondered if there might not be room for people to live there. Out of water."

"I don't think we've ever considered it," the Sea King said in a shocked voice. "And I thought we'd considered everything. It would help the seabirds, as well. Though, actually, we have a lot of seabirds already, but we'd like to adapt parrots and ravens, since they are linguistically advanced. Ducks, swans, and other swimmers will have no trouble, but Lok-i-xan tells me his people grieve over the loss of chickens. They have tried, but chickens do not wish to adapt. Pigeons, on the other hand, do." The Sea King sighed deeply and changed the subject. "Did Xulai tell you about the meaning of the earrings on the refugees?"

Xulai had only mentioned it, so while they swam, the Sea King told Abasio all the details, between stopping here and there for more sight-seeing. When they arrived back at the beach, Abasio heaved himself out of the water and lay on the sand, feeling rather achy.

"I'll leave you now," said the Sea King. "Oh, by the way, Abasio, for the past few hours, I've been carrying the face mask you borrowed. Would you mind putting it over behind the rocks when you've put your clothes on?"

Abasio felt for the mask, felt of his face. Abasio looked at what he was feeling his face with. Abasio yelled, not quite a scream, and began to choke.

The Sea King swarmed up the sand and shook him. "Breathe!" he commanded. "Change! You know you can. You have! Now change back!" He grabbed two of Abasio's adjacent tentacles and pushed them together.

Somewhere inside Abasio a bell rang, or a switch clicked, or a survival trait came screaming out of a cave, and the two tentacles joined. Arms and legs squirmed and thrashed. Bones clashed together like cymbals. Sounds fell on him like rocks, like metal, clanging like gongs. Sight, two of everything, jiggled, tumbled, coalesced. He felt as though he were being mangled, drowned, crushed, smothered, squashed, and then he gulped air.

Blue, who had galloped as far back on the beach as was possible when he saw the two creatures coming out of the sea, tiptoed back and sniffed at Abasio, who screamed again.

"Well," Blue huffed. "You're making made a great deal of fuss over nothing."

"I shall be happy to see how well you do when it comes your turn," said Abasio in an acid tone as, carrying the mask, he went to reclaim his clothing.

XULAI AND PRECIOUS WIND WENT to interview Blue before choosing to believe Abasio's version of affairs.

Blue confirmed the episode. "Yes, he did. Yes, he did it without knowing it. Yes, the Sea King tricked him into it by making him think about something else. That's it. And he made entirely too much fuss about it."

"So it took the sea egg," Xulai said to Precious Wind with an enormous sigh. "And it did work."

Precious Wind repeated it, like a mantra. "Yes, it took the sea egg, and now we know for a fact that it works. Thanks be."

SEA EGGS BEGAN TO ACCUMULATE, some from the new sea-fertile females, some from Xulai. Everyone was waiting for the emissary to arrive. They needed the information the emissary had before they could complete their plans. While waiting, Xulai and Abasio took their first sea change together, exploring the Sea King's castle and spending some time playing with the Sea King's children. Infant octopi were not, strictly speaking, compensation for Xulai's fisher, but they had a charm and attraction of their own. Blue came to the waterside to meet several of them but refused to repeat the adventure after one octo-child clamped itself firmly upon his nose and refused to let go, even after it started to dry out and Abasio and Xulai had to regrow frantic fingers so they could remove it safely.

"It's a boy," said the Sea King apologetically. "My sons are curious and exploratory, like all males. I'm thinking of setting up a school."

"Schools are only for fish," muttered Blue as they left the shore. "That octo-brat needs a reformatory."

"What's a reformatory?" Xulai whispered to Abasio.

"It was a mythical solution from the Before Time," he answered. "The people in Artemisia say the people who lived in the Before Time preferred easy myths to rigorous analysis. Belief instead of reality. That's why things so often went wrong."

"Couldn't they tell the difference?"

"People can't tell the difference if they start with an 'if' statement. Myths always have an 'if' in them. '*If* people believed in *Whifflepop*, then we wouldn't have *Gloop*.' So then, instead of working on Gloop, which is the problem, they try to make people believe in Whifflepop."

"I don't understand . . ."

"A lot of young people didn't have schools that interested them. They got into trouble instead of going to school. So instead of fixing the schools, people said, '*If* all young people knew they would be locked up and punished for being bad, we wouldn't have any more Gloop.'"

"Getting into trouble was Gloop, and locking them up was Whiffle-pop?"

"That's right. So they did Whifflepop, and while they were being Whifflepopped the very worst young people soon taught all the others how to do more and worse Gloop when they got out."

"And the schools stayed the way they were."

"People preferred to believe in Whifflepop because it was easier to build prisons than to create good schools. No one expected prisons to do any good, but a good school makes demands on students and teachers and parents and communities. Prisons were easier and cheaper. A very large part of the problem was that no one tried to limit the number of children people had, so prudent parents had one or two and stupid, self-indulgent, egocentric, careless ones had however many happened. They always excused themselves by saying their god sent them, ignoring the sex that went on before their god presumably got interested. The prudent people resented trying to create schools to educate other people's huge families. Belief that their god sends unlimited children is

Whifflepop, and as long as you believe in unlimited Whifflepop, you'll have unlimited Gloop."

"So they built prisons instead."

"Yes."

"In the Before Time."

"That's right."

"I used to really feel bad about what happened to all the people in the Before Time. Now I'm not so sure. Maybe it was best most of them weren't saved."

"As the Sea King pointed out, that opinion is widely shared today," Abasio said angrily.

"No." She shook her head, unable to understand his anger. "No, Abasio. In his speech, he said historically there was discussion of whether we should be saved, but—"

"It was more than a polite discussion, Xulai. There was something the Sea King didn't include in his little speech, though he let us see enough that we should probably have figured it out on our own. You saw the seadogs?"

"Yes, I did. And they're going to transform horses, too."

"Right. They're transforming dogs to be sea creatures and they're letting them retain their doggishness. Wagging, sitting, fur, floppy ears: very dog."

"I know, yes."

"They're trying to do the same thing for horses."

"I know that, Abasio."

"Don't you think it's strange, then, that they are not transforming humans into mermen and mermaids, letting us retain our humanity? We will have dog-shaped swimmers with gills and finned feet. Maybe horse-shaped swimmers. Why must humans transform into octopi? Why not human swimmers with gills and finned hands and feet?"

She stared, stunned. "Why?"

"I think your sea father made it clear: because the sea dwellers wouldn't stand for it. They were willing to save us, but not as humans. Humans did too much damage. The only way they'll let us live is if we don't look like humans. We have to be willing to take a shape that's totally unlike our own! A shape that may even be repulsive to many of us. We have to be willing to do that before they'll accept us. Horses and dogs never hurt them. We did!"

THE SHIP BEARING THE EMISSARY and the remaining members of the Tingawan embassy staff arrived late one afternoon. Lok-i-xan arranged a meeting for the following morning, which would give the emissary time to fulfill his duty as Xakixa for the Great Bear of Zol. Precious Wind and Xulai went with him to Zol—or to the place where Zol had been.

During the long years Bear had been in Norland, Zol had vanished with the waters rising. Bear's name tablet lay in the clan shrine beneath the waves. It was retrieved by a diver, brought up for the laying on of hands, then replaced by the diver, who reported the lantern had shown light. Precious Wind and Xulai took him at his word; they would have lied about it themselves if necessary to save Bear's family from shame. Neither really blamed Bear for his betrayal, though both had felt it deeply. His end had redeemed him in their eyes, as it had in the eyes of the emissary.

This return of the Xakixa was reported also to Bear's betrothed, who paid a courteous visit to Bear's clan. The following day Precious Wind learned Legami-am was soon to be married. Out of curiosity, Precious Wind went to visit her and asked the woman—for she was no longer a girl—if she had ever noticed something missing, something personal, even if it had happened years ago.

Oh, yes, she said after considering the question. Yes. A tortoiseshell brush had been stolen from her bedroom when she was only eleven. She remembered it because the brush had been a gift from her grandmother, and she had grieved over its loss. Why?

Precious Wind told her why, and on hearing, Legami-am shed her first tears for Bear.

"I did not know," she cried. "I thought he had forgotten me."

"He would want you to be happy," said Precious Wind, though, given Bear's temperament, she was not at all sure of this. "Those of us who knew him want you to remember him kindly."

"THE MONSTER HAS TO BE killed," said the emissary. "It is of such power and malevolence that it will, if able, kill every human being on the planet. I doubt such a creature can be satisfied, and it does not satisfy the creature to know all mankind has limited time."

"Now that his home and devices have been destroyed, he cannot go on for centuries, as he has in the past," said Justinian.

"Our problem, sir, is that we have no idea how long he can go on! A decade might allow him to destroy the world. A year perhaps. How do we know? He has to be destroyed, trapped. Since his particular animosity is toward Tingawa, if we bait a trap, it must be with Tingawans."

Precious Wind and Lok-i-xan exchanged glances. Precious Wind said, "Emissary, were you able to do as I asked in my message?"

"You asked me to find Abasio's wagon and get it to Wellsport. I sent a pigeon to the abbey, to the man Wordswell. I told him where the wagon was hidden. I asked him to send good men to find it, to bring it to the abbey, and then drive it to Wellsport. I received a message in return that the wagon was on its way to Wellsport from the abbey. I do not know if it has arrived there."

"My wagon?" asked Abasio.

Precious Wind nodded. "Your wagon, yes. It is easily recognizable, and some of us have been working on a plan. Remember when we met the *Nightwind*, the *Axan-xin*?" She turned to the emissary. "The captain of that ship told me of the message they had received from you, sir. You said the monster likely could have been splattered with the duchess's blood?"

"From what the witness said, I would judge it likely, yes."

"We have a locator here in Tingawa, one of the old machines much like the one the duchess had. In itself, it is harmless. It can find someone by a genetic code. It uses the same technology that probably killed the duchess herself, in the end."

"How?" asked Abasio.

Precious Wind shrugged. "The duchess's hair was snagged on a tree—remember? When you first saw her in the woods behind Woldsgard?"

"Yes. I do remember."

"Xulai gave me those hairs. When I went to the Vulture Tower, I substituted some of Alicia's hairs for those Jenger had left in his hairbrush. Alicia used them to make a cloud to destroy Jenger, and in doing so, she destroyed herself. The clouds had to be released close to the victim. She couldn't find him to use it, but she kept it and somehow in the conflict with the Old Dark Man the capsule must have been broken. We must suppose it was an accidental release, or that she destroyed the container thinking it of no further use to her. It does not matter which."

"How do you know this?"

"From our people's description of her body. The cause of death is unmistakable. What is of interest is that I did not use all of Alicia's hairs. I have several left, enough to determine her pattern. I assume the place she died is utterly destroyed, nothing left of it at all?"

The emissary agreed. "Those were my instructions. There is nothing left of the place."

"But if that creature left that place with her blood upon him, he is carrying her pattern around. Were you in that place when she died?"

"My job was to destroy the place, the building, everything in it, everyone associated with it. I was told to stay away until I was sure of success. One of the surviving warriors was there when the woman died. He's waiting for me outside . . ."

"Can you ask him to join us?"

The warrior came in, his face, body, and arms still bearing wounds that had not completely healed. The question was asked. He sat thoughtfully, trying to recall.

"The stairs went down the right-hand wall into an empty room . . . a kind of entry room, with a door straight ahead. Inside that door, on my left, yes, there was a worktable of some kind. There were several things on it, mechanisms, I suppose. Two had round screens on them. One had a plan on it, like the plan of a house. The other was a map, yes, with many tiny red spots on it, a big blot of them, then more of them arcing away, like the tail of a kite . . ."

"If she had been searching for Jenger, it would have located Jenger's remains," said Precious Wind. "You know Norland well. Did the map seem familiar?"

"It showed roadways, dots that might have been towns, but nothing I could identify . . . no coastline. No body of water."

"I think we can assume that device was a locator," said Precious Wind, looking at the emissary, who nodded agreement. He had seen it. It was.

Lok-i-xan spoke. "One thing more before you go, warrior. Can you describe the creature for us?"

The man drew a deep breath, though it obviously hurt him to do so.

He clasped his wounded right shoulder with his left hand, tipping his head in that direction as though to relieve a constant pain.

"I can only try," he said. "It was shaped like a man. Taller than any man I have ever seen, perhaps a third again my height, and I am thought to be tall. He was thin, as the trunk of a tree is thin, and strong in that same way, as though made of layers of hard wood rather than flesh. He bled when we wounded him, which not many of us managed to do, though his blood did not run red but oozed a pale orange color. His flesh was gray, the color of dark ashes, and it seemed that his wounds healed almost at once, for the strange blood never showed for more than an instant." The man eased his position, lowered his head in recollection. "I managed to strike him with my sword, across the back of his hand. In that wound, for a moment, I saw metal . . ."

Precious Wind waited briefly, then prompted him. "As though his bones might be of metal? Was he covered in blood? Not his own. Perhaps the woman's blood?"

The warrior looked up, his face betraying a kind of empty desperation. "I thought I was seeing things. He had knocked me across the room and I was stunned, but I did see it. The memory is clear. His clothes were soaked, clinging to him, and that blood on his clothing was red, yes. Where I cut him, it glinted like metal, as if the bones in his hand were of steel."

"Anything else?"

His head went down again. "Behind him, there was a . . . Would you think me mad if I said an open coffin? On end? A kind of packing case? It was taller than he was, wider, padded inside, full of tubing and little lights and sounds. I remember thinking, *So, that's the box he came in,* as though he had been something manufactured that had been delivered there. I *wanted* to believe that!"

"Ah, yes," said Precious Wind and Lok-i-xan simultaneously.

Lok-i-xan said, "You wanted to believe he was a machine, yes, but you were *right* to believe so. Though it has flesh and needs flesh to continue working, it is mostly a machine. He was created in the Before Time. He and the others of his kind were responsible for the Big Kill. You are very fortunate to have survived him, and we are fortunate that you did so, for you have told us something of great value."

The warrior looked his question, unable to ask it.

"The thing like a packing case," said Lok-i-xan, laying his hand on the man's shoulder. "We're virtually sure he—*it* had been inside it. Not merely recently, no, but repeatedly, over and over again, we don't really know how long. Perhaps for a thousand years. The case looked nothing like the ones we found elsewhere, but it had the same function. It kept him alive . . ."

"And now his packing case is gone," said the emissary with a little satisfied nod. "Now it is gone!"

"But the thing is still alive," cried the warrior in an agonized voice. "It chased my comrades up the stairs. I got out while it was gone . . . I should have—"

"Shh," said Precious Wind. "You should have done no more than you did. Do not despair! We know it lives now, but it needs that 'packing case' to *continue* living. His time is limited, but we don't know limited to how long!" She made an aversive gesture. "Why do we say 'he'? We know the creature is male, in a sense, but we should not say 'he,' for it is not truly human. *Its* time is shortened, and we must devise a way to shorten that time even further."

They thanked the warrior and let him go—which he did standing a bit taller than when he had arrived. The few survivors would have given much to forget that battle, though they knew they never would. It had been a failure. The only thing that redeemed it was that no fault lay with those who had fought there or died there.

"Now," said Lok-i-xan. "You say we have the beginning of a plan."

"We have more than that," said the emissary. "Before we destroyed the place, we took a few things. We took another of the tubes that were used by the coffin device. And, we have a very interesting book."

"A book?" cried Lok-i-xan.

The emissary laid the book on the table before them, turning the encased pages one by one.

"Pictures," said Precious Wind. "By all that's holy! You found pictures."

"More than that," whispered the emissary. "We found the creature's name."

The Last Monster

THE RETURN VOYAGE TO NORLAND TOOK LESS TIME than had the preparation for it. Once again, the wolves had been a problem, once again Precious Wind had insisted that they were needed. Blue had been more phlegmatic than previously, though no less susceptible to seasickness. There were a number of extra passengers, Tingawan warriors, for whom room and feeding must be provided. Lok-i-xan had lamented that there was no time to prepare one of the large Tingawan ships, several of which were at anchor near the continent. The big ships had carried up to a hundred passengers, but none of them had sailed for years and fitting one for a voyage would have taken more time than they had to fulfill the plan.

Precious Wind had been laconic about the plan devised in Tingawa. It was better, she said, that it not be discussed, even among themselves. As the time grew nearer, they would go step by step, the first step being to "locate" the monster.

"I thought your locator device along with all those devices was too old and fragile to be moved," Abasio commented to Precious Wind.

"The emissary found books," Precious Wind told him. "Books with pictures and diagrams. There were even spare parts packaged in such a way that time scarcely touched them. The language was archaic. We called in our linguists. It was difficult, but we've built a new one, and a power source to go with it."

"A power source?"

"It really takes very little power. It can be cranked or pedaled as we did the far-talker. Two men can keep it running all day."

"What powers the *ul xaolat,* the thing master?" asked Xulai. "The monster uses it to move around, doesn't it?"

"It must be powered by something hidden, something left over from that former time. We don't know where it is. It could be up there." Precious Wind pointed to the sky. "They had things up there that took power from the sun and sent it to earth."

Abasio said, "And we're assuming the creature *still* has Alicia's blood on it? That seems rather farfetched to me. It's been quite a long time since she died."

She said, "It's one of the few things we're certain of. Remember the description of that coffin-shaped device the creature slept or hibernated in? Our people are certain it did all the maintenance for the creature. The device clothed it, bathed it, and—"

"You call that *maintenance?*"

She frowned. "Just listen! Remember, I told you on our voyage to Tingawa that we—that is, Tingawan agents—long ago journeyed around the world, finding the hidden monsters from the time of the Big Kill: one here, one there, well hidden, deeply buried. In each of those places we found a case with a top made of something like glass and we found cartons of metal tubes. In each of those glass cases we found a monster. Through the side of each case into the hip of each monster one of the tubes had been inserted.

"The first time our people went to the Old Dark House, they examined every corner. The cellar had nothing in it that looked like the glass cases we had found everywhere else. We knew the creature had moved its maintainer before; we assumed it had done so again. There were cartons of the maintainer tubes there, and we thought it possible the creature would come back for them. Our people didn't disturb the cellar, but they did take one tube from a full carton at the bottom of a pile. They resealed the carton, so nothing would appear to be missing.

"Our people went through the entire building. There were no clothes, no remnants of clothes, not anywhere in the building. There was no food storage, no hint that any food had ever been prepared there. There were ancient fireplaces but no sign they had been used for years, decades, perhaps centuries. In the Old Dark House itself, we found no sign that anyone had slept, eaten, washed, bathed, anything that living people do . . . except one. They found secret rooms full of books.

"This convinced us the creature *used* books and it *used* maintainer tubes, but it did not *use anything else*. Yet it lived. Yet it was clothed. People had seen it. Our people concluded that when the creature needed information, it turned to books. When it needed rest, clothing, nourishment, or what we might call 'cleaning and fueling,' it received all those things from the tubes that were stored there as part of *maintenance*.

"It was only when our people went there for the second time, when Alicia died, and found the case open did they realize that the *interior* of it was similar to the glass coffin-cocoon devices we had destroyed all over the world. This told us we might have made a terrible mistake the first time we were there: the creature may have been inside, dormant. Empty cartons could have been disposed of. Of course, equally, the creature could have been somewhere else and returned without our seeing it. It was a judgment call. It had taken us fifty years to find the Old Dark House and nothing indicated the creature was there; at that time we judged it was worth leaving the place alone to see if the creature returned."

Abasio cried, "But, Precious Wind, the damned thing is intelligent! When it came back, it would have known your people had been there!"

She sighed wearily, wiping her face with her hand. "A dog is intelligent, Abasio. I can teach a dog or a wolf how to do things that involve running, leaping, biting, howling, hunting. I cannot teach a dog to strum the strings of an ondang or read a book. I can teach a dog with vocal cords to speak several words. Dogs have distinguished among spoken commands for millennia. Mimicry is not natural to them; once they have vocal cords, it comes to them. Each creature has to learn within its own limits.

"So does this creature. I'm sure it is able to choose intelligently among successful strategies for killing people, because killing is what it thinks about. It may even be able to use books to look up ways of finding and killing people. But our people don't believe it can think about maintenance any more than a dog can decide to build a doghouse. Dig a den, yes. Build a doghouse, no. We left the place absolutely undisturbed, the dust untracked, no footprints, no smell of our being there. We wore special suits. The people who built the creature were as single-minded as the thing itself. They wanted to kill everyone who did not believe what they believed. The creature has no thoughts or memories that are unrelated to that purpose. Its program tells it to find things to kill; kill until it needs maintenance; go get maintenance; find something to kill again."

"So when it gets hungry it goes home."

"Yes. When it gets really hungry, it goes home. It inserts a new tube into the maintainer; it gets inside, closes the maintainer, and all is taken care of. While it is being fed, it is also clothed and repaired as necessary."

Abasio shook his head, hating the entire subject. "So on the basis of assumptions that Alicia shed blood on it to begin with and that the thing still has blood on it, we're ready to risk Xulai's life."

"We are taking every precaution, Abasio."

"Which you won't tell any of us about."

"That's right. You'll have to trust me and those who advise me."

"Where Xulai is concerned, I really don't trust anyone." He didn't. Abasio confessed to himself that he was in a mood. He had lost one beloved. He felt that he had spent half his life grieving. He was in a mood not to lose another and was growing increasingly afraid that it was fated to happen just as it had been fated that dreadful time before.

Xulai, meantime, had been so preoccupied with all the preparations that they were several days into the voyage before she confessed to Precious Wind it had occurred to her she might be pregnant.

"You're what?" Precious Wind snarled.

"Well, you don't need to sound like that!"

Precious Wind ground her teeth together. "No. Quite right. I needn't. It's just that, I hadn't, we hadn't considered that."

"Oh, for all that's sanctified, Precious Wind, you had to have considered that! It's the reason for the whole thing, isn't it? Aren't I supposed to have children? Aren't all of us sea-egg people supposed to have children?"

"How long?" demanded Precious Wind. "Before Abasio was given the sea egg, or after?"

Xulai shut her mouth and became very quiet, finally replying, "I'm not sure."

"When did he get the sea egg? How long ago?"

Again silence. "I'm not sure."

"Which is why I was exploding. If you got pregnant before, your child will not be a changer. If you got pregnant after, your child will be a changer. I presumed . . . I thought . . ."

"Well, all of you people who brought me up presumed entirely too much. Not one of you ever said a word about it. Not you. Not Oldwife. Not Nettie."

"We assumed you realized . . ."

"And how was I supposed to realize anything! It's customary to tell people things you want them to realize. We don't pick up tactical information through our skins!"

Precious Wind went into her cabin and shut the door. Xulai went into the one she shared with Abasio and broke into tears, from which he rescued her some time later by telling her it did not matter.

"What do you mean it doesn't matter?" she sobbed.

"I mean it doesn't matter," he said, patting her on the back. "Your first child, our first child, sea fertile or not, will live out his or her life-span long before the waters' rising covers the earth. Our subsequent child or children will definitely be changers. If our first child is not, when he or she grows up you can give him or her a sea egg and his or her lover a sea egg. Their children, our grandchildren, will be changers. At this juncture, now, today, it makes no difference, therefore it doesn't matter."

"What do you mean it doesn't matter?" shouted Precious Wind when Abasio went to discuss the matter with her.

He explained. He concluded by saying, "Since you're asking her to risk her life to help trap the monster, I think it would be very nice of you not to yell at her. It would also make my life much easier."

Precious Wind scowled. "We're taking every precaution. When we made the plan, we didn't know she was—"

"Your knowing would *not have made any difference*," said Abasio forbiddingly. "You would have had to risk her anyhow. So it doesn't matter. You can't Whifflepop it into something else so it won't Gloop. No, don't ask!"

The days at sea passed in a seemingly unending procession. Precious Wind spent most of the daylight hours teaching the wolves something that she would not talk about. Blue stood at the rail, staring over the sea while considering the future of sea horses. A few of the mares he had left behind in Tingawa would bear young ones, young ones who would be used to create a generation of swimmers. Blue wavered between pride and depression. The thought of death had never bothered him. Now it did, simply because he could not see the future he had always pictured: ongoing horse life amid pastures, mares and stallions browsing along the banks of streams, young ones racing across green meadows. Undersea life would not be like that. When he visualized what it would be like, he felt cold, unloved, his life useless, his line ended. He had no idea how similar his feelings were to Abasio's.

Justinian, between repeated climbs up and down the rigging and endless circuits of the deck, walking and running, sometimes leaned on the rail nearby, seldom speaking, never taking his eyes from Xulai when she was within view, never taking his mind from her, not even when he was asleep. He grew sadder, leaner, and more muscular with every day. Abasio watched him with concern. Justinian was not yet elderly; his body showed that, but his face showed a man past age, eternally frozen in some other time.

The Tingawan warriors also spent their days exercising, both with and without weapons, single-mindedly readying brains and bodies for whatever might occur. The captain brooded on the lack of winds. There were too many days of calm; they were moving eastward far too slowly. As though in answer to his complaint, the calm was broken by unseasonable storms that drove them along the Great Dune Coast, much farther south than they wished to go. Eventually they sighted the Icefang Mountains a goodly distance north of east while a steady north wind blew against them. Days of constant sail-shifting labor, sailing close to the wind, gaining slow mile after slow mile, brought them finally to Wellsport. There was much talk among the sailors when they came in sight of the place. Most of them had been in Wellsport in years before, and they found everything changed. The piers floated now, as they did in Tingawa. The buildings had been moved or rebuilt two-thirds of the way up the mountain, well above the landing area.

The people of Wellsport had observed the ship for over a day. Crowds of them lined the shore to watch it arrive, the first ship to have crossed the sea in a very long time. Rumor had it that ships would be coming regularly now. Rumor had it that the sea war was over. The sailors explained, Abasio explained, Justinian explained, the war is not over, the sea is still closed, this is an exceptional arrival. In the end, rumor won.

The people had decided the war was over. Xulai wondered if the people might not be right. Though she had never discussed it with either her grandfather or her sea father, there seemed to be little reason to continue the ban, if for no other reason than to expedite the movement of sea eggs among the various parts of the world where they were needed and wanted. Lok-i-xan had advised that they must be wary of too much inbreeding. In each place where sea eggs originated, at least half of them should move away into other areas with unrelated populations. Many of those were across the sea. Of course, though such places were a very long distance from Tingawa, they were not across a sea from Tingawa. Perhaps that was the real reason why ships should not travel until the monster was dead, Xulai thought.

Abasio's wagon awaited them at an inn in Wellsport, brought by a couple of hostlers from the abbey. A large number of horses awaited them in an area outlying Wellsport, brought by the Free Knights from Valesgard in Dale at the command of Hallad, Prince Orez. The "plan" was that the group would first take the wagon and the horses to Woldsgard. Then, said Precious Wind, they would go from Woldsgard to the Eastwatch Tower and from there up the cliffs of the highlands, where the villagers awaited them. Messages had gone out and replies had been received. They were expected.

Xulai carried several boxes of sea eggs, two pair of which were to be left in Wellsport and another pair in each of the Becomer villages. All the cliffside villages were close enough to one another that eggs could be shared among them. Besides, sooner or later the villages would have to relocate nearer to the sea. Everyone who received sea eggs would need to live closer to the sea. Only those who could change would parent the new race; only the sea would test who could change. This was explained to the populace by Abasio and by Precious Wind. They had to be willing to accept the change of shape in order to prove to the people of the sea that they were worth saving. The people of the sea weren't sure.

On this topic, the town was full of discussion, argument, and a few brawls.

"You wuddn catch me doin' that if the world ends t'morraw."

"You old goat, you're too old to do any changin', egg or no egg."

"Who you callin' old?"

Or: "Sounds nasty to me. Just pure nasty. Turnin' into somethin' like that. Yer not agona do that! No daughter o' mine's agona do that."

"Ma, it's that or drown . . ."

"You'd jus best drown."

Precious Wind shook her head and went to Abasio and Xulai. "They're going to have to see it happen, Xulai."

Xulai burst into tears. "I've been poked and prodded and questioned and your doctors took samples of every part of me, and I am *not* going to change *naked* in front of all those people!" Her mind was saying, *This is unbecoming. This is childish.* Her body was saying, *Don't give a damn.*

"I know." Precious Wind sympathized. "I'd feel the same, but I've figured out a way . . ."

Accordingly, Xulai went down to the shore wearing a loose garment that resembled a small tent from which her arms and head emerged. At the edge of the sand, she changed and went into the sea from beneath the tent, leaving it in the surf. While curious townsmen examined the tent to be sure she hadn't been hidden in its seams, she swam about among a small group of curious local swimmers and divers, allowing herself to be petted, stroked, looked at, and returning only when Precious Wind had spread the tent properly at the waters' edge. She slipped under it and resumed her proper form.

Abasio, who said to himself he would be damned if he would refuse to do anything Xulai was expected to do, eschewed the tent and changed right out in public. Wellsport was not a puritanical community, and nakedness was a fact of life in a place where freshwater was scarce and public baths were the rule. If the women would be offended, they didn't need to look. He changed in the surf and swam away.

Three young men of Wellsport had agreed among themselves to have some fun with him if he changed into that thing the woman changed into. In fact, they provided him with a good deal of fun they had not expected. Octopods had more arms than any three regular swimmers, and octopods could breathe underwater, which the human swimmers had forgotten, to their subsequent discomfort. Abasio was in a better mood when he slithered back onto the sand, changed, toweled himself off, and dressed in time to assist the rescue of his would-be tormentors. Once again, the explanation. They had to be willing to accept the change of shape, even into something some people considered repulsive, in order to convince the Sea People they were worth saving!

The discussions that ensued in Wellsport were not notably changed.

"I tell you no daughter of mine is gonna . , ."

"Josh, your daughter's fifty years old. Nobody's gonna even suggest it."

"Women've had babies when they were fifty. My own ma! That's de-scriminatin'."

"Maybe, but you don't have to worry about not lettin' her. Nobody'll ask her."

"An' I'd like to know why not! We're as good as anybody."

"Ah, fer . . ."

For several days most of the troop was busy with unloading and re-packing while Precious Wind and Xulai talked to groups of young men and women.

"I want to know how it feels when you're like that."

"Does it hurt?"

"Do you have to learn to breathe underwater or is it just like breath-ing air when you're born?"

"When you, you know, do you do it in your human shape or do you have to do it . . . you know?"

No, Xulai thought. *No, no, no, I don't know.*

"What happened to the baby when you changed?" asked Precious Wind. "Did it . . . ?

"I DON'T KNOW!" said Xulai.

From among those who asked the most sensible questions, they chose the two couples who seemed most devoted to one another, for, as Xulai vehemently pointed out, if they were not devoted to one another, the difficulties caused by their families and friends would separate them soon and permanently. The four swallowed the eggs. They subse-quently had endless discussions with the Tingawan women concerning the rules for disposition of future sea eggs: where, to whom, how many.

"I understand your sister's feelings, but you may not give sea eggs to your sisters and brothers."

"Your cousin breeds chickens, not people. Inbreeding in this case is not a good idea."

"It doesn't matter what your father said, you may not sell sea eggs. Anyone selling sea eggs or forcing someone else to do so will be sent to Tingawa and put in a cage at the shoreline, and stay there until death or drowning, whichever comes first. If it was suggested by someone else, that person will be alongside in another cage. Tell him we said so."

"Remind your aunt that she will be dead long before the waters rising has affected her. No sea eggs except to young people."

Xulai thought of having to repeat this over and over in every community they came to and despaired. Precious Wind seemed merely to get thinner and more tightly controlled with each passing day.

Eventually, the small cavalcade left for Woldsgard: Abasio and Xulai in the wagon, the warriors and Justinian mounted on Valesgard horses, another small wagon carrying their gear. Precious Wind rode separately, ahead of them, with the wolves. She had, she said, been training them to recognize the Old Dark Man, by smell and by sight.

"By smell?" Abasio wondered.

"The emissary picked up a bit of the creature's clothing from the cellar. The wolves have good noses. They'll alert us to anything strange. If necessary, if we get into a . . . confrontation . . ." She didn't finish the sentence. She didn't want to think what might happen to her pack if, indeed, they got into a confrontation.

Every few miles they encountered relay riders from the Eastwatch Tower of Wold, all saying the same thing. There had been no sightings on or near the road. If the information had been otherwise, the group would have retreated to Wellsport. They were not yet ready for confrontation.

When they approached Riversmeet, however, the message changed. There had been sightings, not confirmed, near the place where the Old Dark House had once been. People with distance glasses watching both from Eastwatch Tower and from villages farther up the cliff face had seen a tall dark something moving about in the forest and along the eastern slopes of Altamont. The wagon turned toward Woldsgard, extra horses were hitched, and the pace quickened. Precious Wind took the wolves uphill, into the forest of Wold. She was carrying the thing master, the *ul xaolat*. She thought it better to feed the wolves with wild game than to upset the Wold farmers by killing their livestock. Once at the gard, Precious Wind would house the wolves and feed them as she had done on the ship.

It was Abasio who first called their attention to the silence. It was summer; the weather was warm. Normally there were sounds in the forest: the young that had been born in the spring would be learning to find food and shelter and water. Some would learn to gather nuts, others to graze on grass or browse tender leaves, and all that activity was accompanied by a constant, quiet chitter-chatter of squirrels, the calls of mate to mate, the territorial songs of birds, the nighttime twitter of bats and hoot of owls, the rustle of fallen leaves or underbrush where small, furry things hunted or sought hiding places from hunters. Now, however, the forest was silent, as though every creature in it was burrowed as deeply as possible, hidden as well as possible. No creature called any attention to itself.

"I can almost smell the thing," Xulai murmured to Abasio, clenching her hands together to keep them from shaking. "I can imagine what it must have been like during the Big Kill. I find myself wanting to stop thinking so it can't find me."

"The library helmet says people took drugs then," said Abasio, putting his arm around her. "They took drugs so they couldn't think, but the slaughterers found them anyhow. We have unconscious thoughts that drugs don't stop and the creatures could find. Remember what Precious Wind told us. At the end, it didn't kill only the people who thought wrong things, it killed anyone who wasn't thinking the *right* thing."

Silently, he was thinking about losing Xulai. He would not. Duty or no duty, saving the race or the world, he would not. And if she was determined, then by all that was holy she would not go alone. Not the way Ollie had gone. Never again. Xulai would not go alone.

They stopped for the night at the Queen's Skep in Hives. They found the small town locked, as though against a plague. Justinian had to convince the innkeeper that he could safely provide for them, and later that they could open to Precious Wind, who had come to report.

"The *ul xaolat* is finding game all too easily," she said, her face twisted in revulsion. "I have never before seen hungry deer lie with their heads down, unmoving, half-starving, with browse all around them. The wolves know of the creature, as well. They can smell it. All of them turn into the wind, pointing, like trained hunting dogs. Men are dead, their families are dead, the wolves and ravens have found their bodies. We need to bring this to an end very soon."

"The power source for your locator?" Abasio asked. "Is it mobile?"

"The original device was designed to store power from the wind.

As I said, we've made one that uses human power. We can crank it or pedal it."

"The Edges had solar power," said Abasio reminiscently. *Also, the Edges had walls. And places dug below where monsters could not come. And they had weapons. The warriors that attacked the Old Dark House had weapons, and what good did they do?*

"We have solar and wind power in Tingawa," she replied. "But for this, we need the power source to be totally reliable, even if clouds cover the sun or no wind blows. The locator sends out a pattern. If it finds that pattern, a signal comes back and shows up on the screen. We need to see that signal move, so we know it's the creature, not some rag or bit of clothing or flesh it has lost or discarded." She shook her head in frustration. "I could almost use the wolves for this! They only tell me the direction, though. Not the distance. Two men can keep the locator constantly powered all day or all night without being overtired. Four can keep it running night and day. Theoretically, we could put it in your wagon, Abasio, and keep it running as we moved, but it works more accurately if it is set up and established in one place where we can determine the fewest possible . . . things in the way."

"Interference," said Abasio. "That's what things in the way are called. Like human beings. Animals."

"Whatever it or they are called, we want to avoid them. So, we plan to unpack it high atop a tower at Woldsgard and use that as our locator base. We have far-talkers with us, so the people running it can keep in touch with us."

"So you'll locate the thing; then what?" asked Justinian.

"Then we'll do something to entice it to the place we want it, when we want it," said Precious Wind. She laughed shortly. "Meantime praying it does not find us in a place we don't want it before we do want it."

"You'll look for a pattern," said Xulai.

"We'll pray for a pattern," said Precious Wind. "A pattern lets us make a plan. If there is none, our task will be very much more difficult. And I'm not telling you anything else, because we don't want anyone at all to know anything at all."

"Including me," said Xulai to her father. *I wonder if I will survive this? I really don't want to die. I'd like to have . . . my child. I'm very curious about my child. Of course, now that the sea eggs are being distributed, I'm not so important as I was before . . . They can risk me now.*

"It seems unending," said Justinian. "The Before Time, resurrected. The Big Kill, starting over."

Precious Wind put her hand on his and squeezed it. "There is only one of them left, Duke of Wold. He, it, cannot go on much longer. Mirami is gone. Alicia is gone. The Old Dark House is gone. Even if we fail, there will be an end to it."

"But at a terrible price for Wold," he said.

"And Rancitor?" asked Xulai. "If he could use flesh from Mirami or Alicia, can't he use Rancitor? Or Hulix?"

Precious Wind repeated monotonously, "There will be an end to it."

OLDWIFE GANCER MET THE WAGON at the Woldsgard gate. Xulai leapt from the wagon to hug her, seeing over her shoulder that the court-yards and stables swarmed with livestock, with wagons, with farm families, all in from the farms and behind the walls for protection.

"Oh, child, you look . . . so grown up. I keep remembering my baby. You and little Bartelmy." She broke into tears.

"Bartelmy?" asked Xulai. "Oldwife, what about . . ."

"That thing got him," she said. "They found what was left of him. That thing killed him. And it got Black Mike." Weeping, she led Xulai and Precious Wind into the castle.

Prince Orez came out to meet them, embracing Justinian as a long-separated brother. "I'm sure you know how things have gone," he said, motioning to include them all. "We feared you might be attacked on the way. We've lost too many people. The thing takes someone every night. Here, there, no reason for it. Time enough to talk about that later. Come in, there's food prepared. Our people will take care of the horses."

"One of us has a wolf pack," said Justinian.

"I know. We've received messages."

"How?" asked Justinian. "No pigeon can cross the sea!"

Orez said, "Before Abasio left the abbey, he sent pigeons to Eter-shore and here to Woldsgard saying that Precious Wind had left a far-talking device here. She had brought it from Tingawa originally and had used it to keep in touch with Tingawa since Xulai was a child. The message told me where it was and how to use it to receive messages from Tingawa. I've been getting them every now and then, only a few words, but enough so I could be sure we had prepared for the wolves. There's a little gate in the back that opens into an orchard. She can bring them in there. We've cleared out a storage building for their den. Whenever she's ready, we have meat hanging for them."

Abasio remembered the gate, the poppleberry orchard. He went to find Precious Wind, and once they had the wolves settled they joined the others in a dining hall near the kitchens.

Orez was saying to Justinian, "When you left, Justinian, we got here within the time you allowed for. We beat the troops from the abbey by several days. I was a bit confused when they showed up, until one of the commanders advised me his orders had come from the prior, not the abbot. The commander, a Colonel Sallis, was perfectly reasonable. I showed him the authorization; your people here verified it, and he realized his men weren't needed here. I told him I'd send a pigeon to get him some new orders and I asked him to take his men back to Netherfields, where they'd have room to camp and probably find some supplies. They were, I'm thankful to say, out of the way and off the road before King Gahls's men arrived."

"Not so easy with them, I imagine," snarled Justinian.

"Getting rid of the royal armor was a bit harder. I'd taken the precaution of closing the gates and having most of my men inside on the walls, with the horses well up in the hills, where they couldn't be seen. I didn't want them thinking Wold had been invaded but I did want them to know it was defended. Their troop commander was surprised to learn that Wold was not part of the king's territory. He had evidently received orders through Mirami or that old adviser of hers. I told him the king's stepson would no doubt be eager to see them in Kamfels, which was a good thing as we had no room or provisions for them here, even overnight. I'm told they camped hungry just beyond the Stoneway and took several days to get themselves over to Kamfels. The ferry couldn't handle many of them, so most of them had to ride all the way east around Ragnibar Fjord, and the road's only wide enough for two horses abreast."

"Hulix?" asked Justinian. "What's going on there?"

"Evidently he didn't need them either. They soon went back to Ghastain, most of them by the long, slow northern route along the river that runs into the fjord and then up onto the highlands by the forest trails. A few of them stayed for a while, then came back this way later. The ones who passed by here told us Hulix was very ill. You know about the explosion south of us?"

"We were told," said Justinian. "The Old Dark House was destroyed."

"Shortly after that Hulix fell ill. Strangely enough, we heard the same thing happened to the king's son, Crown Prince Rancitor. About that same time, too."

Justinian looked at Precious Wind, who shook her head. "I don't know," she said. "It's possible the same machine that . . . maintained the . . . thing also maintained . . . but that would mean . . ."

"It would mean that the Old Dark Man was the father of Mirami's children, or had a part in fathering or creating them," said Xulai. "In both cases, Mirami needed a son: Hulix to inherit Kamfels, Rancitor to inherit Ghastain. Was something in the Old Dark House helping to keep them both . . . living?"

Precious Wind looked at the scarf she held in her hands, twisting it as she thought. It had become a habit recently, this wringing of the hands, or things in hands, though not yet her mind. Better her hands than her mind! "Most organisms are self-monitoring. If our bodies need something, some kind of feedback mechanism inside us tells us we are thirsty or hungry, or need to sleep, or it adjusts the flow of this hormone or that secretion. If we suppose the Old Dark Man's creations were *not* self-monitoring, if their organs or components required adjusting from time to time, those adjustments might have been triggered remotely . . ."

"Remotely?" asked Justinian.

"Like the far-talker," said Abasio. "It is triggered by a device that converts sound or writing into waves and sends those waves through the atmosphere to another device that converts the waves into instructions, or a voice, or whatever."

Precious Wind nodded slowly. "A signal could have been sent directing some organism, or some tiny mechanism, to adjust whatever it was. If the adjustment didn't happen, the organism might fail, eventually."

Xulai's nose wrinkled in disgust. "So Mirami's brood were not human!"

"In talking about Mirami, we always thought in terms of human genetics," Precious Wind confessed. "Even though we knew the Old Dark Man was not entirely flesh, I don't think any of us thought Mirami could be partly . . . mechanical. That's not the right word. Something more refined than mere mechanics, but still . . . not flesh."

"If both Hulix and Rancitor die, it solves two minor problems," said Abasio. "Lok-i-xan will be delighted."

"Poor King Gahls," Xulai murmured. "Not an heir to his name."

"He's still not too old to get one," said Hallad, Prince Orez. "Now that no one is poisoning every attempt. He may not know just how far Mirami had gone. If Hulix dies, Kamfels can be garrisoned by my men. Perhaps, once everything . . . settles down, I'll make a visit to the court. He might be grateful, even conciliatory."

Justinian asked, "What about our defenses here? I left you little enough to work with, my friend. I'm afraid the years took their toll on Wold's readiness and mine."

"You are looking very fit and you have some good men," the prince said. "Perhaps both you and they needed only to be reminded of that fact. We've brought your Men of the Mountain into Woldsgard and sent some of the old hands north to the pinnacle; we have scouts watching your borders. And I'm not leaving here, my men aren't leaving here, until everything is settled for the foreseeable future. I understand that the future beyond that is to be strange and wonderful in ways we have never dreamed of, but we'll have years to talk of that later . . ." He marked this in his memory, to remind Justinian of it in happier times. Or to forget it, if there were none. "As to our defenses here: we are no longer threatened by prior or queen. Only the creature threatens us and we assume it has no allies. It came here long enough to kill some of our people, but it will come alone if it comes at all. There have been no recent sightings close by.

"Lately, it stays mostly in that area where the Old Dark House was and up the eastern slope from there. We've taken the advice received from Tingawa. If it attacks, the archers will shoot only flame arrows. We are told that pistols will probably not hurt it, but fire may. We have catapults that can throw bigger lumps of fiery stuff that sticks to what it hits. We also received a visit from a Tingawan armorer who came here after he and his fellows had destroyed the Old Dark House. He gave us some small cannons and showed us how to use them to fire the same kind of stuff. We've always stayed away from guns, big ones at any rate. Using them brings us very close to the ban on machines. However, they are easier to aim than catapults and since he left the things with us and taught us how to use them, we'll use them if we have to. I hope we won't need them, for your plan is to meet it some distance away."

"That is the plan, as I understand it," said Justinian without expression.

"Not that we've been told much," said Abasio.

"A secret is best kept between two people when one of them is dead," said Hallad, staring at Precious Wind. "Such has always been my understanding."

"And mine," said Precious Wind.

Abasio felt something was very wrong with the plan. This monster was not supposed to be able to think about maintenance. And yet it could think about creating subordinate creatures that would receive signals from the maintainer? It could modify the device to do that?

It seemed unlikely. Except . . . those things were related to killing. And it could think about killing . . .

LATER, IN XULAI'S OLD ROOM high in the castle gard, Oldwife grieved over Bartelmy and Black Mike while Xulai sat empty eyed beside her.

"He were just a lad," Oldwife said for the tenth time. "Just a boy. A sweet boy. No harm in him. Went out to see his folks, got caught in the woods by that . . . that . . ."

"How do you know it was the . . . the creature, Oldwife?"

"What else kills and rips and tears flesh away and then just leaves a body? Bears don't do that. The big mountain cats don't do that," she cried. "What else but that monster?" She sobbed. "Both on 'em, they wore those nice scarfs you made 'em. Both the boy and Mike. They was so proud of those!"

Xulai went to find Abasio. "Find Pecky Peavine and Willum and Clive Farrier. I knitted them each a scarf before I was taken from the abbey, remember. Bartelmy and Mike were wearing them when they were killed. They may have been smelled out, Abasio. Tell them to wear nothing they might have worn when they were with me, or Precious Wind, or Bear."

Abasio collected Precious Wind and together they found the three living men. The scarves were burned and Xulai's warning was passed on. Meantime Xulai lay curled on her bed, shivering uncontrollably. If it had smelled them out because their scarves had her scent upon them, how much easier to smell her out when she was bait in the trap.

THAT NIGHT PRECIOUS WIND, ABASIO, and Prince Orez met atop the tower. It had been tented over to protect them from rain, the side curtains open to the south and east. Below them, in a room beside the bird lofts, four Tingawan warriors pedaled slowly, evenly, to create power for the small device set on a sturdy table. They were there to discuss the plan.

"This is Alicia's pattern," said Precious Wind, holding up a little angular receptacle. "We made this in Tingawa from the hairs that Alicia left in the forest here at Woldsgard. I put the pattern in this slot and press this small lever that says 'record' on it." She pressed the lever and stepped away. "If it can read it and record it—and it did read and record patterns successfully in Tingawa—the red light at the lower left will go on."

The red light blinked on as she spoke.

"Now, the locator will make its own map outward from us, searching for the pattern of Alicia, which is in her blood, even old, dried blood. It reads the area around it and shows coastline as a dark line, river edges by a slightly narrower line. Water is blue. Land is gray. Elevations are shown as the old mapmakers showed them, very thin lines every ten feet, or twenty, or fifty, or one hundred. Here I have it set for fifty."

An image appeared. Precious Wind pointed out the clustered lines east and west, where the mountains or cliffs rose steeply. Beyond the mountains, the blue of the sea, the dark line of the coast, the narrower lines of the river Wells leading to the blue of Lake Riversmeet.

"I'll bring the edges in closer. We want to have the tower here at the top so the screen covers all the land between here and where the Old Dark House used to be. We want to keep the cliffs on the screen, as well."

They stared. Abasio stirred, laying a fingertip on the screen. "There he is. See this little light. It moves."

For a moment, they couldn't see it, a tiny dot, barely visible, a green tint. It did not seem to be moving. "What scale of distance do we have here?" Abasio asked.

"Three to four days' journey across. You have good perception, Abasio, sensory or otherwise. That odd-looking blotch is where the Old Dark Tower was, and he's very near that. We rather hoped for that. What was sowed there by the blast will help kill him, though it doesn't kill as quickly as we'd like. Once we're sure we are seeing him, we can come in closer . . ."

"Do it now. A larger scale will help his movements show up better," said Abasio.

She made adjustments. The green light grew brighter, creeping like a spider.

"So," said Prince Orez. "What now?"

"Now these men will work through the night: two men to pedal, one at a time, changing every half hour; one man to record. We have paper maps of this area, ones we made a long time ago. We have many copies. The recorder will mark on a map every few minutes where this green speck goes and how long it stays there. We'll watch tonight. We'll watch during the day tomorrow and tomorrow night, comparing the maps from night to night, and we'll do it long enough to see if there's a pattern. When we know where it goes, we will know how we can move."

That night the locator signal moved back and forth across the map; by morning it returned to a place on the eastern slope of Altamont, not far from the road that led south, to the Lake of the Clouds. Each of the next two nights a pattern repeated itself. The thing moved out onto the road, swiftly, almost instantaneously, to the Eastwatch Tower and up the cliff. One of the men on watch went to fetch Precious Wind. She had wanted to be told if the creature went to the cliffs.

She climbed to the tower, pulled her chair where she could see the little light, how it moved. "It's staying on the cliff road," she said wonderingly.

"It doesn't want to be seen," one of the men remarked. "At night, there's no travel on the road."

"But it should be able to climb. It's as long legged as a spider. I thought it would go straight up the face of the cliff between the roads."

"Ma'am, the villages are on the inside edge of the road. They're filled in behind to make a flat place, and the villages sit on that flat place. Along a village, the wall is three stories high, and the houses are part of it. There are windows in it and a few places where the little alleys come through . . ."

"I remember," said Precious Wind. "Of course."

"If it wants to stay away from people, using the road is the best bet. Otherwise it might end up waking or killing somebody and the whole cliff would be on guard."

They watched it go up the road very quickly. It ran steadily, like an engine, seemingly tireless.

"Where's it going to stop?" she murmured to herself. "It has to stop somewhere!"

It stopped at the turn in the road beyond the second village. A tiny twist in an elevation line showed the small flat surface.

Precious Wind nodded. "I remember now. It's where we camped. It's the village that's 'becoming pure,' where they sold us those old robes."

Abasio spoke from behind her. "It knows where we went last time. It knows we're going back."

"You're up late," said Precious Wind.

"I haven't been down to get up from," he said grimly. "I've been digging up bodies. Bartelmy's. Black Mike's. Their bodies are torn. Flesh missing. When Prince Orez mentioned that, I wondered what kind of weapon . . ."

Precious Wind's mouth twisted. "Our emissary watched the battle at the Old Dark House. The creature has blades in its hands. It has metal teeth. It is terribly strong and terribly fast. The emissary thought it could shoot fire."

"Acid?" he wondered. "They used to use acid in that part of the Dragdown Swamps that was mining country. It's one of the things that makes old mines so dangerous. People still use it where I came from, but the people in the Edges are in control of it now."

"We brought fireproof clothing . . ."

"Is there acid-proof clothing?"

"I'm sure there is. We'll use the far-talker to find out."

"You didn't hear what Abasio said. It can hear the far-talker," said another voice. Justinian.

She turned to stare at him, openmouthed.

The duke came into the circular room from the stairs, shook his head, made a face. "We should have foreseen that it would hear a far-talker, Precious Wind. We knew the far-talker was used at the same time the creatures were made. It may have even been used to instruct the creature originally. The pattern the creature is traveling each night is the pattern we intended to lure it into taking. How did it learn our plans? Do you have an agent here? One you've been exchanging information with?"

"We never thought . . ."

Abasio said, "When you use the far-talker, do you talk in plain language? Or code?"

"I've always spoken Tingawan. You mean, it understands Tingawan?"

"If it's supposed to be killing Tingawans, I would imagine it can. Your people found books. Were any of them books in Tingawan? If so, and if your plan intended something to happen at that campsite near the Pure Becomers, I think the monster knows all about it."

"Well, that's good, isn't it?" came another voice from the top of the stairs. Xulai.

"Good?" Precious Wind choked on the word.

"Yes, very good." Xulai was glassy eyed, obviously on the edge of collapse. "Because now we know what it expects, and it doesn't know we know, so we'll do something different. And we won't use the far-talker. Or, if we do, we'll mislead it, or we'll do what Abasio said. We'll talk in code."

"But we don't have a code," Precious Wind cried.

"We'll invent one. My grandfather is a very smart man." She laughed, a mad little laugh that made Abasio shiver. "For example, if I tell him something will not create an elegance, he will know I mean that it is a bad thing. If I tell him I have to plant a thirty-foot hedge around my garden here because vicious horses with no blinders are jumping into it and ruining all the things we've been planting, he'll know our plans are being upset. If I tell him I really wanted to use some of those old landscaping devices the old books mention, but we're going to have to do without Distancia Oratoria trees because they're spreading a disease through the air . . ."

"Allergy," said Abasio very calmly, putting his hands on her shoulders and squeezing. "That's what trees spread through the air. People sneeze."

"Allergy," she repeated, nodding, "Allerlgy. All gergy." She began to laugh helplessly, almost hysterically.

Abasio took her in his arms. "Shh, dear heart. Shh. There's an easier way. We can do as you suggested in the first place. You're correct. It is good that it doesn't know that we know."

Justinian looked helplessly at his daughter. "We can probably adapt whatever plans were made; perhaps we can just move them. Make it happen earlier or later than the creature expects." He looked questioningly at Precious Wind.

"If we're going to change plans and can't use the talkers, we need to send a messenger," said Precious Wind. Her arms were folded on the table, and her head rested on them. She seemed to be speaking to the wood. She thought she was speaking to the wood inside her own head, not to have realized . . . "And we can't do that until we know the creature is off the road and out of the way."

Xulai said, "Send a bird, Precious Wind. Those people on the cliff are your people. Don't they have birds?" Her voice was rough, barely intelligible.

"Yes," she breathed. "I hadn't even thought of that, we've been so used to using the other . . ."

Abasio asked, "Have any of the relay riders been attacked? Has any Wellsroad traffic been attacked?"

Justinian shook his head. "Orez hasn't mentioned it. The men we met on the way here didn't mention it. If it plans to trap us, it wouldn't scare us off by attacking traffic. So far, it's killed in remote places away from the roads. Places it judged it would be safe to kill some of our people."

"Then we need to modify plans, send messages—multiple, to be sure they get through—and we need to move now," said Abasio, glancing at Xulai's white face. "This waiting is driving us all a little crazy."

WHEN PRECIOUS WIND WENT TO her room that night, she found Abasio waiting for her. He held a small bundle, which he handed to her.

"In the event that Xulai and I do not return from this venture, we want you to get this to Tingawa, to Lok-i-xan. It's something from the Before Time. Something benign. I want you to use the far-talker and message him where you're leaving it, in case you don't survive. Since the monster can hear the far-talker, say it's something the monster won't care about. Horse breeding records, maybe. A recipe for baked fish. Tell him you're leaving it because you know he wants it, and be sure to put it someplace that will survive."

"Abasio, this isn't necessary. You'll be able to—"

"You can't guarantee that, lady. You can't. We all try to act as though this is going to work, and not one of us knows whether it will or not. I do know one thing for sure, and that is if Xulai dies, she won't go alone. And, maybe, I know that if I die, she won't let me go alone either. She said this morning that she's not so important now. She said that other people can do what she's doing. I know what she's thinking . . ."

"No. She can't. She wouldn't."

"She can and she might, though I'd give my life to prevent it. This package is something important. There's a letter with it, and whoever opens the package should read the letter first. Even though the thing is benign, it can kill you if you don't know about it first. Don't open the package, don't think about it now. If all goes well, you can return it to me. Promise me, Precious Wind."

He left her before she could respond. The library helmet had been a worry to him. He did not want to risk that falling into the wrong hands.

VERY EARLY THE FOLLOWING MORNING, well before it was light, a wagon loaded with hay left Woldsgard. It had a number of horses following it and a larger team than was usual for slow-moving wagons, but then, it moved a good deal faster than such wagons usually move. The men who drove it were dressed in ordinary Norland clothing, clothing that smelled very much of horse and hay, with some pig and chicken to season it. When the wagon reached Hives, the men driving the wagon switched horses and traded places with other men who had been hidden in the load. By dusk, the wagon had come within a mile or so of Riversmeet. The wagon turned purposefully off the road and was driven close to a haystack. The horses were picketed separately. The men burrowed in the hay and slept, one of their number keeping watch on the pinnacle behind Woldsgard.

Later in the night, the creature, returning home and scenting the wind between the dreadful pits on the eastern slope of Altamont and the site of the Old Dark House, smelled only horses, and hay, and pig, and chicken, and nothing of the Tingawan flesh beneath. The creature did not look for and did not see the fire atop the pinnacle, but the man on watch did. Something moved in front of the fire, dimming it. It dimmed and brightened twice. This meant the creature was moving on the road south of them. The watcher woke the next man on watch, who took his turn watching the pinnacle. Well before dawn, it dimmed and brightened once. After a pause, it dimmed and brightened once again. And a third time. The creature was well away from the road and had stopped moving.

Though it was not yet light, the horses were hitched, and the wagon moved briskly back to the Woldsroad, turning east onto the road leading to the Eastwatch Tower. It would be a long day for the horses, but the load was not exceedingly heavy and there were many more horses than were necessary. By the time true darkness fell, both wagon and horses were inside the walls of the fort. Well before dawn, the light on the pinnacle signaled again. The wagon left the fort and by early afternoon had reached the place it was intended to be. By evening, the campground beside the Pure Becomer village had a wagon lying upside down beside the road, one wheel missing, its back end pointing down the road, its other end surrounded by neatly stacked hay. The horses that had delivered it to that place were already back at the Eastwatch Tower—it had been a downhill canter all the way. The two men who had led the herd down the cliff had joined the troops manning the tower. The other men who had been in the wagon were somewhere else.

"Well," said Precious Wind on receiving a message relayed from Eastwatch to the pinnacle by mirror flashes. "It worked. Let's hope it works the next time."

"The creature was all over that wagon last night," said Abasio. "The little green light crawled around it a dozen times. It knew it hadn't been there the night before."

"The wagon was missing a wheel," Orez commented. "I'm sure the creature assumed it was a wagon headed down that had lost a wheel and its driver left it there to get the wheel fixed."

Precious Wind wished she were as sure. She asked the group to assemble in the tower, where they could be sure they were not overheard by anyone. Justinian sent word he had another matter to attend to, but everyone else involved was there.

"Our original plan was to set our trap in that way-halt, the one where the wagon is now. We had enlisted certain help from the people in the villages, a fact we never mentioned while using the far-talker. The creature expects us to go to that campground and pretend to camp there, while actually hiding out in the nearest house, which is on the same level. We've never mentioned sea eggs, so we don't think the creature knows about them. If it did, it would want to destroy the sea eggs along with all Tingawans, including Xulai. The sea eggs were in the wagon that's already there, and they are now in safekeeping in the next village uphill from the one we're looking at.

"Our people who have watched the creature and studied how it works and how its fellows worked all those years ago believe it will go to the wayhalt in advance of our arrival, lie in wait, and attack the house when it has seen us arrive.

"Our new plan requires that we not reach the village. Our new plan requires that just at dusk we arrive below the village, meet a wagon coming down, get into a very difficult mixup, a messy wagon accident that entangles us with horses and yelling men. It should take advantage of that to attack us there. The three men here in the tower will not signal the pinnacle, they'll use fireworks from here. It's quicker, it's visible, and we can signal red, blue, green, or white.

"Red means the thing is keeping to its usual pattern for that particular time of night. Whatever it usually does, it's doing. Two reds means it's sleeping, resting, whatever the hell it does when it's not moving. Blue means it is getting ready to attack us as we think it planned to do, that is, moving toward the way-halt. Two blues, it's moving toward the house at the south end of the village. Green means it is moving toward the place on the road where we wish to be attacked. White means they can't see it, they don't know where it is. If we see that, it's every person for himself.

"We will time this to happen after dark. I was reminded there's a high wall along the road on the uphill side, which is why we will have our altercation below the village."

"What's going to destroy the thing?" asked Abasio.

"You don't need to know until later," said Precious Wind. "Those who need to know do know."

THE THING THAT HAD BEEN the Old Dark Man had made itself a lair in an old mine tunnel, almost at the top of the rise, south of the river Wells. The falls was only a short distance away, and the thunder of it shook the place where he spent the daylight hours but the sound did not disturb him. Nothing could disturb him. The part of him that thought was caught in an endless loop. His body, his self, required that he do procedure A. Each day his body, his self, would try to do procedure A. Hours would be spent trying to do procedure A. His body, his self, was unable to do procedure A. His body went by default to procedure B, and more hours would be spent without doing procedure B. Default to procedure C, to procedure D. . .

The list of procedures numbered over a hundred items, but the error feedback mechanism did not allow the loop to get any longer than five items, the same five, over and over. When one was done, the loop would go back to the first one. The only thing he felt was a hideous, weakening hunger that demanded to be fed, but he couldn't be fed. His body was unable to recognize "feed," though the creature recognized it as something Mirami and those who had come before her had done. They had had to be fed. After he grew them as infants, he required a thing called a wet-nurse to secrete food and put it into their mouths The Old Dark Man had not done it himself, but back then, when he had been created, he had been given the instructions, he had observed the procedure. Later he had observed the making and feeding of solid food.

When the hunger began, when he could not find the Old Dark House, when he could not find his cocoon—that was what it was called in the schematics: his cocoon—he had tried the procedure as he had seen it. He had taken flesh, his usual nourishment, and instead of putting it into one of the maintenance tubes as he usually did, he had put the flesh into his mouth. His mouth was a weapon. It had no way to swallow, to digest, to nourish. It could bite, tear, but it could not swallow. If he could find the Old Dark House, he would find his cocoon. If he could find his cocoon, he could find Mirami or Alicia, he could rip flesh from one of them and put the flesh into a certain place in the maintenance tube and put the tube in his cocoon. Then he could lean back into its embrace and be fed, satisfied, comforted, maintained.

Each time the loop got to that place, he tried again to find the Old Dark House, find the cocoon, find his flesh providers, Mirami, Alicia. There had been others, before them, but all the ones before them had died. Gone. Without the Old Dark House he could not create others. Failing to find their flesh, he tried to put other flesh directly into the receptacle in his side where the tube connected, but it did not work. The flesh hung there and rotted. Either the flesh was wrong or the device was needed. It was the same when he tried to drink. There was no way out of the cycle. He had not been given a way out of the cycle. He could only follow it through to the end. Procedure E.

Procedure E required him to kill something. That he could always do. Killing was the only procedure he could achieve, the only satisfaction that momentarily stopped the hunger. For a moment. Only a moment. But once he had killed, he was back at procedure A again. The hunger started over.

He had observed Alicia. She had been like him. She was more like him than any of the others had been. She, too, had used killing to stop the hunger, but killing had never stopped her hunger for long. How many others had there been? He could not remember. Many. Many. Most of them like Mirami. Adequate to use for food.

Most frustrating of all was the presence of another program. He knew it was there. He could feel the program like a pressure, pushing on him. It was readying itself for use when the situation warranted, when an optimum target presented itself. Optimum target. Priorty One target. Data concerning the optimum target still came in. Data was still processed. The time was growing shorter. When that time came, the loop would stop. He would come out of the endless hunger into reasoned action! For a time he would not hunger, would not thirst, would not feel all that painful strangeness that was now his daily life. When that time came, he would be himself again. Utterly invincible.

Until then, he hungered. The hunger possessed him. He put back his great head, dropped his huge jaw, and howled. The howl went out across the world and everything with ears heard it, collapsed, and shook with uncontrollable terror.

THE THREE WAGONS FROM WOLDSGARD followed the pattern established by the single wagon that had gone before. They traveled quickly almost to Riversmeet. They stopped there. In early morning when the creature rested (two red rockets) they moved out, went quickly onto the road and as fast as possible to Eastwatch Tower, arriving there before the creature moved again. At two rockets in the morning, the wagons moved out. Precious Wind and Xulai walked beside the wagons, dropping things along the way, things that smelled of Tingawa, of themselves, of the warriors who had attacked the creature in the Old Dark House, who had destroyed that house.

"Dead birds," cried Xulai, moving a feathered body away from the road with her foot. "Everywhere. They dropped out of the sky like rain. Under the orchard trees there were dozens of them. The thing howling killed them." Her voice was remote, uncaring, as though she had gone past caring.

"I know," said Precious Wind. "Try not to focus on that. Just keep moving. Chew a bit of apple and spit it out. Keep littering the way, leaving a trail."

"I didn't get to say good-bye to Father. Where was he?"

"Prince Orez said he had to go up to the pinnacle. Something happened up there—nothing to do with all this—but he felt he needed to speak to his men personally."

"Can Abasio come walk with me?"

"He will, a little later. Just along here we want the trail to be unmistakable, not cluttered up by the smell of anyone else. We're saying 'smell' because we don't know what the real sensory apparatus is. And we're trying to keep the target specific, so extraneous people don't get hurt."

"Only us specific people will get hurt, right?"

Precious Wind bit her tongue, made herself sound calm. "If we do this right, Xulai, nobody gets hurt except it. You and Abasio will have a long life together."

"Together," Xulai agreed. "Yes, we will be together."

They walked up the hill. When Xulai was too weary to walk farther, she sat on the wagon seat next to Abasio and spit bits of food into the road while two of the Tingawan warriors walked alongside. They were dragging some of Xulai's clothing behind them. She pretended this was an ordinary trip, from which she would be returning. If it had been, she would have had a good excuse for having Nettie Lean make some new clothes. Certainly her old ones wouldn't fit her. What did women wear when they were pregnant? Would she live long enough to care?

They went around the fourth switchback and began moving to the north once more. "Two more," said Xulai.

"Two more what?" murmured Abasio.

"Two more switchbacks. The becoming-pure village came after the sixth switchback."

"How many, all together?"

"Thirteen," she said. "Thirteen turns, fourteen trips along the cliff. Last time I quit being afraid of the road collapsing after about the first six or seven traverses."

"You didn't tell me you were afraid of heights." He wanted to put his arm around her but decided not to. It was better to keep everything ordinary. Very ordinary.

"I'm not. I'm afraid of roads collapsing. All those heavy nets made me worry. I'm glad we're not going all the way to the top. I had nightmares about falling into those falls. I wondered if the duchess had some way to get up the falls, like a fish jumping or something."

"She and Jenger had their own way to get back and forth."

"Poor Jenger. There was something in his eyes, Abasio. Something that wanted out."

"I'll bet. Like a tiger out of a cage."

"No. That's how he was trying to be. But in his eyes he was like a child that's been locked in a dark closet. I saw it just before he died."

Abasio said nothing. He knew too well what she meant. He had had acquaintances, maybe friends, who had looked like that when they died. Mean, no good, violent, cruel, and when they died they had looked like children, whipped for no reason. He put his arm around her after all.

"Do you think Jenger's gone somewhere happier?" she asked.

What could he say? Nothing ugly. Not now. "No. I think he's gone somewhere where nothing will ever lock him in the dark again. Where there is no unhappy. Just birdsong and leaves rustling and the wind." There was a long silence, interrupted only by the squeak of wagon wheels. Abasio made a mental note to oil them tomorrow, maybe.

She said, "You know what we're going to do when we get up there, don't you?"

"I know what you and I are going to do while everyone else is yelling and horses are whinnying. We're going to climb the wall along the road and get down behind it."

"Really?" What he had said had sounded like actual information. "Nobody told me. I'm not sure I'm up to climbing . . ."

"There'll be a net to climb. You'll do fine. I'll be right behind you. What you can do now is watch for a couple of wagons coming down. They need to reach the way-halt where we camped just after the sun has gone down, as it's getting dark."

"Blue isn't pulling us. Is there some reason?"

"I didn't want to risk him. We didn't need him, so . . ."

"I'm glad. I hope none of the other horses get hurt."

He thought, *I hope no one gets hurt. But if other horses do, they at least won't blame me for it. Or curse me in absentia.*

Time went by. They came to the fifth switchback. Someone had built a path at the end of it, one that led away, around the edge of the cliff to the right. Perhaps there would be a new village there. More time went by. They turned the sixth switchback. They were headed north once more.

When they had gone about halfway, she remembered to look for the wagons coming down. "I see the wagons coming down."

Abasio looked high to his right, then spoke to one of the walking warriors, who sprinted forward. "We need to drag it out a little," he said, pulling on the reins. "I'll check the wheels."

All the wagons stopped, people watered horses, checked hooves, checked wheels, made considerable fuss about nothing. Above them at the next switchback, other wagons were doing more or less the same thing. One of the drivers ahead of Abasio raised his voice, shouted something unintelligible, then crawled under a wagon. Someone else shouted about axle trouble. There was some to-ing and fro-ing, this one with a pot of axle grease, that one with a hammer. There were hammer blows, voices raised. Time passed. Abasio spoke to one of the men who again went up the road to see what was happening, which stopped happening upon his arrival. The sun had set. The wagons moved again very slowly. "Look to your left, watch for rockets," Abasio whispered.

Xulai could not see Woldsgard across the valley below, but she knew where it was in relationship to the pinnacle, outlined as a greater darkness against a graying sky.

"Red rocket," she said softly. "It's moving."

"Ah," said Abasio, looking ahead of him. The wagon on the upper road was not yet making the turn. The team began the downward turn and he heard the squeal of wagon brakes as the steeper slope of the turn took hold. The cliff face hadn't enough room on it for a wide, gentle turn. The switchbacks were tight, not too bad going up, but they were difficult coming down. Particularly for a loaded wagon, which the one approaching happened to be. The brakes screamed; the horses moved against one another, bracing themselves against the load. Abasio held his breath. The wagon straightened out, the slope became gentler, the squealing eased, stuttered, faded. The wagon was now moving past the village, and it was rapidly growing darker.

"Red rocket," Xulai called. "Three of them, widely spaced, then a blue."

"My guess is that means it's really moving toward the way-halt, not up the road."

"Is that what it's supposed to mean?"

"We didn't cover all eventualities," grated Abasio. "But that's what I'd mean if I were in charge of the rockets." He edged the horses to the inside, against the wall, to miss the huge pile of wood up ahead that was blocking the outside half of the road. Some wagons had gone past it; others had slowed down well before they reached it.

The far wagons were converging. There wasn't room for them to pass one another. A loud argument broke out up in front of them.

"C'mon, love," he said. "Out of here."

He lifted her from the wagon, hustled her to the wall, and put her hands on the net she found there. "Foot up," he said, putting it there. While the noise ahead of them escalated, he came behind her, up and up and up, and over, among a dozen pairs of hands that promptly began drawing the net up from behind them. Someone took Xulai's arm and moved her into the village quickly. Abasio was beside her. The other drivers were climbing over the wall around them. They ran along a level path, into an opening, through a gate that shut and was barred behind them, up a flight of stairs, and another, into a room to their right. Then they were alone, facing a window that looked down on the road below them. All the wagons were tight against the cliff, leaving the outside part of the road bare.

Far across the valley a green rocket sparkled in the sky, then half a dozen more.

"That would mean it's right on top of us," said Abasio.

The hullabaloo below had stopped. There was no sound. Uphill, at the way-halt, something exploded; a comet flamed down the hill and landed on the huge pile of wood that had blocked half the road. Some wagons were well past it, others hadn't come that far. The fire had the roadway all to itself as it burst into leaping flame.

"There were two small cannons hidden in the wagon we sent earlier," Abasio whispered. "There were also two men who knew how to use them. They were all set up under the overturned wagon, hidden behind hay, but aimed, loaded, ready. All they had to do was fire them. The villagers had that huge pile of wood ready . . ."

The wood burned brilliantly. The roadway lit up as though by daylight. Standing in the firelight were two, no, three figures: downhill, Precious Wind surrounded by her wolves; nearer the fire the Old Dark Man, a hideous, skeleton-like figure, half-flesh, half-metal, looming against the firelight, and across from him . . .

"Shh," said Abasio, putting his hand across her mouth. "Don't."

"But it's my father," she whisper-screamed into the palm of his hand. "It's Father."

He put his mouth to her ear. "He came with the other wagon, the one that came several days ago. He wanted to. No. He demanded to."

"Jacob," Justinian called. "Jacob, do you hear me?" He was dressed in a white garment. He carried something.

Abasio whispered. "He's carrying the maintenance tube the Tingawans took from the Old Dark House."

"What is that he's wearing?"

"The book the emissary brought says it's called a lab coat," he answered. "There were pictures in the book of the people who made the slaughterers wearing them."

"If it doesn't work . . ."

"If this doesn't work, it'll be up to the wolves . . ." *And after the wolves, us.*

Justinian's voice. "Jacob, you remember me. It's Doctor Hammond. Remember?"

The Old Dark Man said, "Doctor?"

"You must be terribly hungry, Jacob."

The thing gasped, opened its mouth. "Hungry! Must finish imperative procedure so can be fed."

"You can be fed first, Jacob. We decided. You've been so effective, you can be fed first."

"No . . . No cocoon."

"That's all right. We're building a new cocoon. In the meantime, I've brought food. See here. Sit down here beside me. Open the portal. Let's give you some food."

Xulai saw the bench beside the road, just within the edge of the firelight. Justinian sat down on the bench that someone had put at the side of the road, inside the circle of firelight, not so close it would burn. Who had measured?

"Here, Jacob. Sit beside me."

Abasio whispered, "The wagons that were coming down the hill were full of archers with fire arrows. They've all sneaked out by now. They're on the other side of the fire from the Old Dark Man. If they have to shoot, the arrows will light as they come through the fire. They'll be burning when they hit . . ."

"Father will be hit . . ."

"He's wearing protection. He'll fall flat on the road if anything goes bad."

The man in the white coat said mildly, "Sit down, Jacob. Rest."

The thing staggered. Stumbled. Turned as though undecided.

"You'll have to hurry," said Justinian. "So we can finish on time. You're so hungry. So very hungry you're losing efficiency. You'll be more efficient when you have food. Come, let me feed you."

The thing sat, fumbled with its body where a hip joint might have been. Justinian put the tube into the opening and turned it a quarter turn. It made a loud *snick,* an emphatic dagger of sound piercing the utter silence. Down on the road, even the horses had stopped breathing.

The thing raised an arm. Firelight reflected from fingertips like knives. The thing turned toward the man in the white coat. Xulai tried to say, "Why, don't, don't let him . . ."

Abasio's hand covered her mouth. He bent close to her ear. "Shhh. Don't say anything. Nobody is supposed to say anything."

The thing sat quietly, watching its own hand. It was trembling. "Maintenance," it said. "Loop. Can't get out of loop."

"Doctor Hammond knows. Doctor Hammond will get you out of the loop."

The creature closed its eyes. Justinian sat quietly. The thing did not seem to breathe. Perhaps it had never breathed. After a very long time it said, "Good. Out of loop. Good. Thank you, Doctor Hammond. Soon will go kill now . . ."

Justinian got up and . . . walked . . . away . . . down the road . . . in the silence.

The fire burned. The wolves watched. The archers stood, arrows nocked. After a while, a rather long while, the creature slumped and fell from the bench. It lay still in the road. Precious Wind and the wolves came closer; the wolves spread, watching. Behind them the archers moved forward, arrows ready.

Xulai whispered, "What was in the tube?"

"Something that stopped the hunger. Narcotic, I think. Something that went to the flesh parts of the brain and put it to sleep. If we're right it won't be able to move for a while."

Men emerged from the shadows down the road carrying one of the heavy nets. The creature was wrapped in the net. It struggled feebly. The wolves darted forward. Precious Wind recalled them. Another net came, equally heavy. Twelve, eighteen, twenty-four men fastened loops through the net, picked it up, and ran toward the north, a dozen to each side, the way they had come, a practiced lope that did not hesitate or stumble.

Xulai leaned out the window. The moon had risen; there were other men waiting to help anyone who faltered; torchbearers ran alongside. In the moonlight, she could see the bearers running, onto the way-halt, then downhill, toward the switchback below, where she had seen the footpath. Torch flame burned red against the dark, descending on the path, hidden at last by the slope. She watched until the men returned without the net, still running. She could hear their panting. Someone came into the room and closed the shutters over the window. Precious Wind.

"Come," she said. "We need a barrier between us and the explosion. The pit is around the hill, down a bit. They're about to blow it up, the way we did all the others."

"Wasn't he dead?" asked Xulai.

"All the flesh that was in him is dead. The only way we know of to kill the rest of it is to blow it up and collect the pieces and pour them into a concrete lump and sink it in the deepest part of the sea. It seems to work. None of the ones we fixed that way have ever come back."

She led them into the village, into some lower floor at the very back of the village where there were no windows, no doors, and where every villager was taking refuge. Justinian was among them. Xulai ran to him. "Why did you do that?" she cried. "I thought it would kill you!"

"Not if we had learned the right words," he said in a rather feeble voice with an even feebler chuckle. "The emissary told us he took books from that place, remember. Before they blew it up. The books were very, very old. Their pages were enclosed in stuff they used to preserve paper, stuff like glass, page by page. It was a record of what they'd done. The books had pictures and names in them. The names of the people, the real people they made into monsters. Volunteers! The names of the real monsters, the ones who created the slaughterers. Proud scientists, the ones who set out to make the world pure. Jacob was the last monster, the new, improved monster. Doctor Hammond was the real monster who made him . . ."

The building shook. Dust fell from the ceiling. A few children cried, a few others cheered.

"That was the bomb," said Precious Wind. "Only a little one. Not lastingly deadly, like the one at the Old Dark House. When everything cools down, we'll pick up any scraps that may be left. We dropped the creature in a pit and put a heavy cover on it before we set the bomb off. Chances are, not much will be left to find."

The door opened. People began to leave.

Justinian said, "The emissary told me they found Doctor Hammond in the Old Dark House too. He was very well hidden in a subcellar, in a kind of coffin attached to a maintenance gadget. He had planned to wake up in a purified world, but he was very, very dead. There were pictures of him. He looked a little bit like me."

"And that's why you did it? Because he looked like you?"

"No," he said. "Maybe a little. It increased our chances of success. I really did it because of your mother. I was quite willing to . . . take the risk so long as I put an end to her killer. Alicia was only a creation of the Old Dark Man, and even the Old Dark Man wasn't as guilty as Doctor Hammond and his friends. They were the real ones."

He had, at one point during the planning, actually wanted to die during the event, but he didn't mention that. That was before he knew Xulai was expecting a child.

Xulai turned pale and gulped. Abasio helped her sit down.

She said, "I was getting very angry at you. No one told me anything. I really thought you might die. If you did, I would have . . ."

Precious Wind murmured, "It could smell fear. We needed you to be afraid. I'm sorry, but we needed you to be afraid . . ."

Abasio turned her and let her lie back against him, thanking every beneficent entity that it was over. "I didn't know that little bit of information, Precious Wind. I thought it was just that everyone thought Xulai had quite enough to deal with, and we had to do a great deal of last-minute scurrying."

Precious Wind nodded. "That, too. The creature was behaving just as the people in Tingawa had guessed it would. They said if it was deprived of its maintenance, it would have to fall into a pattern. Killing preceded maintenance. So it would kill, then try to find its maintenance location, then try to find the coffin thing, then put flesh directly into the tube portal, maybe even try to eat, then it would revert to killing again. It would gradually be weakening. We were all but positive it would work, Xulai. And it did."

"It's all just . . . it's been . . . and now I feel very strange." She relaxed against him, breathing deeply, her hands pressed firmly on her belly. "My stomach is acting very . . . strange!"

Justinian laid his hand on her belly, felt the kick. "Very strange," he agreed, smiling, deciding he was glad he hadn't had to die after all.

The Sea
Child

IMMEDIATELY UPON THE DESTRUCTION OF THE OLD DARK Man, the cliff-side villagers had stopped wearing strange garments, acting in strange manners, and advocating strange ways of becoming beloved by the king. They no longer seemed to care particularly whether the king loved them or not. Xulai, Abasio, and Precious Wind spent some time among the little towns, distributing sea eggs, and Xulai had a lengthy conversation with the woman who had given Xulai the cake on her first journey up the cliff.

"We knew the duchess was dangerous," the woman said. "We knew there was a monster; some of us talked to old people who had seen it when they were youngsters. The duchess claimed to represent the king, she claimed to express his wishes; she amused herself trying to find out how far we could be pushed. We had already decided to go as far as she wished. We kept her amused, though it was wearisome. We never knew when she might show up, so we had to play the part all the time even though she had shorter ways to go and come from the court. There are shaft entries up and down the slope at the north end of the road as well as at the top, in the Eastern Valley, so she didn't come up the cliff road often."

After the eggs were distributed, with many of the same delays and questions that had kept them for some time in Wellsport—though without the obligatory sea change—they returned to Woldsgard. There news had come, via travelers to and from Ghastain and Kamfels, that both Hulix and Rancitor were dead.

"We'll never really know what killed them," Xulai complained.

"I'd just as soon not know," Abasio replied. "Everything tied to gether, we're sure of that. Genetic patterns and mirrors and sending killing clouds, it all tied together. There may have been a device in the Old Dark House, perhaps in his cocoon, that maintained the patter of the Old Dark Man and every creature that shared his pattern. When the Old Dark House was destroyed, the patterns simply fell apart, no all at once, but inexorably. I don't need to know how. I'm just very glad they did."

"Did you get the helmet back from Precious Wind?"

"Yes. I promised her I'd let the people in Tingawa look at it."

"That's good. They can probably learn a lot."

Justinian was resuming his life in Wold. Most of Prince Orez's men had returned to their homes in Etershore or among the fiefdoms though the prince lingered, enjoying a friendship that had too long been scarred by tragedy and separation. The prince had decided that before leaving Woldsgard he and Justinian should make a trip to Ghastain. It had been years since either of them had talked with the king.

It might as well have been a lifetime, they confessed when they returned to Woldsgard. King Gahls simply wasn't interested in hearing about the waters rising. He told Hallad and Justinian he didn't believe it. It was all chatter. Mirami had told him it was all chatter. The only problems that bothered the king were that the tailor simply couldn't get his costume for the parade to fit right, and oh, incidentally, Rancitor had died, leaving him without an heir.

"I had thought of suggesting a new wife," said Hallad to those gathered at the supper table. "But I could not think of a woman sufficiently unworthy. Then Justinian told me about the emperor in Tingawa."

"The hereditary personage? The one who did as little as possible?" asked Xulai.

"Exactly. We decided King Gahls should be far too important to be bothered with trivialities like survival. So, first we told him about Ghastain adopting Huold, then we suggested he follow Ghastain's example and adopt an heir. We said he should find a bright young man among his subjects, one who spoke several languages, one who could deal with foreign dignitaries, one who could take care of all the dull business of the kingdom while the king himself saw to the important things, like parades and balls."

"Wasn't he offended?" asked Xulai wonderingly from the couch where she had lain in marvelous idleness all morning among a purring clowder of cats, Bother and Vex among them.

"Not at all. He thought it was a splendid idea. We offered to help find someone for the job, and he agreed to let us do it. If you and Abasio weren't so involved with the whole sea-egg project, I'd have suggested you."

"Someone will have to supervise Ghastain at some point," said Abasio. "There's a large population there, and not all of them are going to reject survival. We'd rather thought that someone from the cliff villages would take over the sea-egg distribution on the King's Highland."

"However," said Xulai to the prince, very firmly, "I don't think either of us is interested in running Ghastain. I'll bet you have someone at Etershore who would be perfect for the job."

"He does," said Justinian with a sigh. "And now that the monster is dead and sea travel will be allowed again, that person will have something to do. Ghastain will have more trade than heretofore. For one or two lifetimes, at least."

"Perhaps a bit longer," said the prince. "Ghastain may become a port city. They're a long way up there."

"Meantime," offered Precious Wind, "we have to schedule a trip back to Tingawa. We have to take sea eggs from Wellsport across the sea and return with Tingawan ones to take inland. Transport of eggs between populations is a necessary part of the plan."

"Artemisia," said Abasio. "I want to be sure the Artemisians are included."

"But first," repeated Precious Wind, "we need to return to Tingawa."

"She means before the baby comes," said Xulai in a slightly annoyed voice. "They want me there when it happens. Since it's the *first one*, you know."

"'They'?" asked Abasio. "What 'they'?"

Xulai stood, cats spilling on either side; threw her arms wide in a fine dramatic gesture; and trumpeted: "They, the head of Clan Do-Lok. They, the council of elders of all the clans. They, the Sea King. They, the people who have been working for a hundred years to make our survival possible!" She sat back down. "That's how Precious Wind says it."

Precious Wind flushed. "I never shouted."

"You most certainly did. You know, Precious Wind, I really thought when we'd done all the stuff we were supposed to do, people would stop herding us around like goats and yelling at us." She turned to Abasio, giving him a wink that only he could see. She sighed dramatically and whined in a pitiful voice, "Abasio."

"Poor thing," he said. "She's tired. We'll let you all get on with your councils of state."

They left, she leaning heavily on his arm.

"What was all that?" asked Prince Hallad.

Precious Wind said, "That was Xulai having a temperament. She's enjoying it. We have led her quite a dance. She hasn't forgiven me for allowing her to be so frightened during our confrontation with the monster. Abasio hasn't either. I don't grudge her getting a little of her own back, but we really do have to get back to Tingawa. It's the only place I know of that has the equipment and the trained people to handle any kind of medical emergency that may arise. No, no, Justinian, don't get in an uproar. We're not expecting an emergency. But she was right, it's the first time. We really don't know what to expect. Right now I wish we had some of the devices they had in the Before Time. X-ray machines, for instance."

"Those machines only showed bones," said Justinian with some distaste. "Her baby may not have bones."

"What do you mean?" asked the prince.

Precious Wind explained to him about changing, that both Xulai and Abasio could change. "I can't believe no one has talked with you about this."

"We've had very little time to discuss anything," Hallad, Prince Orez, said stiffly. "I was under the impression that our great great-great-grandchildren might be born with gills. I was not told they might be born without bones."

Justinian said plaintively, "If Xulai is going to Tingawa, I'd like to go with her. Can you recommend someone to stay here and keep Wold running for me?"

"You have good people of your own. Crampocket is a good steward, out he's not good with people, so you need someone else between him and the world. If I were doing it, I'd put Horsemaster in charge. He's strong enough to keep Crampocket from overdoing his economies, he knows everyone, he knows how things are done, and he's respected."

"You're right," said Justinian, amazed. At one time, he would have suggested this himself. How long had he been elsewhere? All the while the princess was ill, he had been elsewhere. Perhaps it was time to come back from elsewhere. He was to have posterity, after all, at least a few generations of it. "Will Xulai consent to inherit Woldsgard? Will she want it?" he wondered.

"It's her home and she obviously loves Woldsgard," said the prince. "But with the future of the human race hanging in the balance, she and Abasio are going to be traveling a great deal. While they're gone, Horsemaster is still a good choice. He has a son who will be a good choice in his turn. The thing you don't have is an alert and well-trained garrison. Though the need may not be great from now on, I'll leave you a good man to whip them into shape."

THE RETURN TO THE *FALSA-XIN*, still anchored in Wellsport, was far easier than their previous route through Merhaven. Blue would go. The wolves would stay and Precious Wind would stay with them. Two of the younger ones could speak a few words. She had changed them, trained them, would have let them risk or lose their lives to save Xulai. Having used them so, she would not leave them now. It would have felt dishonorable.

Justinian would go, of course. He would return after his grandchild was born. He wanted to make sure that someone approached Genieve with the offer of sea eggs for her child or children or grandchildren. Precious Wind said she would see to it. Meantime, sea eggs from Wellsport would go with the *Falsa-xin* to Tingawa. Sea eggs would go from the cliff villages to Wellsport. Sea eggs would go from both Wellsport and the cliff villages to "Ghastain," as the king still called it. "Up there," said Hallad. Precious Wind and the wolves would see to it. She still had the *ul xaolat*. Lok-i-xan had sent word that she should keep it; a reward for her service, her honor, her faithfulness. If she was to be chief distributor, it would be of great assistance to her. When Xulai and Abasio returned to Woldsgard, they would join her in making a long trip to the east, to Artemisia. In the meantime, Precious Wind would recruit travelers, guards, scouts, to make that trip easier. No, she had said heatedly to Abasio and Xulai, under no circumstances would they be allowed to go alone!

"I have never felt so well planned for," grouched Abasio.

"Now you know how I've felt my entire life," said Xulai. "Except I never before felt hungry all the time, the way I do now."

"You are burgeoning," said Abasio. "Very properly. It is my understanding that women in your condition crave exotic foods. What may I bring you?"

"Two scrambled eggs and one of Horsemaster's horse biscuits," she said thoughtfully.

"You crave horse biscuits?"

"I always did. I've eaten them since I was little," she said in surprise. "I used to lie up in the haymow in the stable with the cats, eating horse biscuits. I didn't know how to make them then, as I do now, but how would I know they were any good if I didn't eat them myself?"

There were no sad farewells. When they left, Precious Wind was already on her way to the cliff villages and Oldwife Gancer had patiently been talked out of going along to take care of the baby. Both Abasio and Xulai were worried that she could not deal with the situation. She might be too surprised. Shocked? Who knew? No, she could see to the baby when they returned to Woldsgard, "Unless the baby needs to stay in the sea," said Abasio.

That required some explanation. Nettie Lean caught on more quickly. She said she would explain it to Oldwife again and again, until as she put it, "it sunk in."

"Not, perhaps, the best word to use," said Abasio. "Very apt, but not best."

Orez was going with them as far as Wellsport, along with a good number of his men. The journey proved to be uneventful: one pugnacious boar encountered; one broken wheel more or less mended; one water bag with a leak in it; one drunken villager en route who had celebrated the monster's demise by setting up an unauthorized toll booth.

In Wellsmouth, most of them attended a previously arranged meeting with the head of the Council of Port Lords; Earl Murkon of Marish; Hale Highlimb of Combe; half a dozen of the Free Knights, down from

Valesgard; Defiance, Count of Chasm—Orez's eldest son; and Orez's mother, Vinicia, a very old woman, the so-called Lady of the Abyss. All of them wanted to meet Xulai. All of them wanted to know everything there was to know. Abasio did a changing for them, asking them to forgive Xulai, but in her condition she preferred not to. They quite understood. They were fascinated. The very, very old lady insisted upon feeling Abasio's tentacles.

"By all that's holy, I wish I could do that," she exclaimed to Orez. "My bones hurt all the time!"

Abasio explained that all the sea eggs were being used for women of childbearing age. "But, ma'am, they won't always be in short supply. Hold the thought. You may be able to lose your bones yet."

"Such a nice young octopus," she said to the prince as they departed. "Such nice manners."

There were a dozen eggs in Wellsport to be taken on to Tingawa. Both young couples were well, healthy, interested in their new lives. The young men were full of information about the sea, things they had discovered, things they had never thought of. Wellsport was advised it would receive additional sea eggs when Precious Wind returned from the cliff villages and Ghastain. Xulai was introduced to several sea-fertile couples who had traveled to Wellsport from the cliff villages so they would be able to change.

"We're going to have to set up an egg registry," she told Abasio. "The cliff village people are akin to Tingawans, so their eggs are essentially Tingawan eggs. The ones from Ghastain and Wellsport are essentially Norland eggs . . ."

"Um," said Abasio, "is that so? My my." He did not find the subject endlessly fascinating, for his mind kept veering away from the far to the nearer future. Children. Would one be able to say, "My, he certainly has your chin"? Or would one say, "His tentacles are exactly like yours"?

The *Falsa-xin* sailed on the morning tide. The winds bearing them westward were steady. Day by day the captain measured his speed, plotted their position upon his charts. Day by day they saw other ships, headed the opposite direction. The monster was dead. Trade had been resumed. Day by day, dolphins came alongside to tell them what undersea landmarks they were passing, a navigation convenience the sailors of long ago had not had the advantage of. Blue stopped being seasick, leaned his head over the side, and talked to the dolphins whenever he had the chance. They told him stories that he repeated to Abasio and Xulai. Day succeeded day. The food grew increasingly monotonous. The sailors fished. Eventually, they began to see islands, one, two, several. One morning, early, they came to Tingawa. Lok-i-xan awaited them at the pier as he had waited what seemed to them to have been a lifetime ago. This time there were only ordinary parasol carriers, and they all, including Blue, walked only so far as the bottom of the citadel steps before entering the hill to find either an ascendable or a stable.

When Xulai and Justinian left the dinner table that evening, Xulai remarking that she wanted to catch up on her sleep, Lok-i-xan asked Abasio, "I heard all about the confrontation. Was it truly as peaceful as that?"

"When I saw the creature in the firelight, I felt pity," said Abasio. "You would have, too, even though it had volunteered to be turned into a monster. It was not without guilt, but it had already been in terrible pain for . . . a very long time. It was weak—well, much weaker than it normally would have been. The kindest thing we could do for it was to destroy it."

"Justinian risked his life."

"Justinian had an *ul xaolat* in his hand and a destination clearly in mind that the monster would not be able to visualize or find. Precious Wind taught him how the gadget works. Nonetheless, he did risk his life. He was brave and perfect. He looked and sounded the part."

"Like the pictures."

"Exactly like the pictures. I don't know precisely what Precious Wind and her friends concocted to put in the maintenance tube. I overheard them talking about flesh of some kind, and some kind of narcotic. And a poison which did not cause pain."

"And the monster just died."

"It just died. Its pain went away. Perhaps it did not die totally until it was blown up, but it's gone now." He laughed, an uncomfortable laugh. "I keep waking in the night wondering if it really was the last one."

Lok-i-xan said, "Abasio, you will have many worries left in your life if you do the traveling you propose to. I believe this is one worry you can dispense with. Unless slaughterers were made that weren't on the monitors, that worry is over. I've seen all the original papers. I've seen he original monitors. Every monitor led to a vault, and every vault was cleaned out. Eventually. Just because we knew where each one was didn't mean they were easy to find! Some of them were a hundred feet down in stone. Some of them could only be reached by tunnels that opened miles away. It took over a hundred years for our people to find and enter one hundred and seventy-two vaults. We dropped one hundred and seventy-two chunks of concrete into ocean trenches. This one was number one hundred and seventy-three. It was the only one left."

"No more Big Kill."

"Not until the waters rising reach the tops of the mountains. And by then, most of us should be able to swim."

Abasio didn't reply. His life had run into more than a few ironic happenings that were the antithesis of what he had planned and expected. "Should" was a word he distrusted. Along with "probably." And "we believe." A lot of people *believed* that he and Xulai *probably should* have a child that could live underwater. He simply leaned back in his chair, took another helping of whatever it was he was eating, and smiled at Lok-i-xan.

Abasio was having his own concerns, concerns that each morning required a new analysis. Today's had been that if Xulai gave birth to a cephalopod, at least the birth would be easy as there'd be no skull to worry about. The idea did not cheer him, but nothing would be gained by sharing his own doubts. Lok-i-xan had earned his optimism. Let him enjoy it.

Lok-i-xan thought that Abasio seemed very cheerful. Well, he had earned his optimism. Nothing would be gained in voicing his own nightmares about genetics that didn't turn out right, the possible birth of monsters that either couldn't or shouldn't live! No, let Abasio enjoy this peaceful time.

BOTH OF THEM REPLAYED THESE thoughts some days later as they sat together with Justinian in a kind of anteroom in the hospital. It had been strongly suggested to them that they wait as patiently as possible *out here*, because they would be in the way otherwise, and everyone needed to concentrate on what was happening. Lok-i-xan, gray faced and weary, had not moved from his chair since he had arrived. Justinian changed chairs frequently. Abasio had not sat down.

Xulai yelled at intervals from the next room. Really, more of a scream. Really, sometimes, more angry than pained.

"She'll be glad to get back to traveling," Abasio said. "She said so yesterday. She's felt very . . . stifled."

Lok-i-xan smiled. It was the slightly condescending smile given by a man who had been a father, many times, to a man who had not. "She won't want to leave the child, not for a moment," he said. "Young mothers are all alike."

"Yes, but, in this case . . ."

"There'll be some adjustments. One has to expect that. Don't be disappointed when she doesn't want to accompany you, Abasio. Later on, when the children are independent, you'll have plenty of time to travel together."

Abasio walked into a wall and stood there, wondering if hitting his head on it would help. What would "independent" mean in this case. His child living in the Sea King's castle, saying "Whassat, who's he?" to passing fish? He could hear the voices in the next room, some men, some women, all of them "medically trained," whatever that meant. They had the books from the Before Time, and they had a lot of the same equipment. However neither they nor anyone else on the face of the planet had delivered . . . ah. What?

"Stop that!" screamed Xulai. "Leave it alone!"

Justinian turned gray. Abasio bit his lip. It bled. He found a handkerchief and polka-dotted it with red.

A voice shouted, "Another. Hold that. Don't move."

Lok-i-xan panted, "Oh, my. I wonder what—"

Someone said, "I don't believe this. I simply don't believe this."

Someone else in the next room said, "People have twins all the time. It's not unusual."

Xulai screeched what sounded like a curse. At the very least, a malediction.

The first person said, "This is unusual."

Someone said, "Of course, dogs have litters of eight or ten all the time. More than cats."

Lok-i-xan got up hastily and left the room. He looked decidedly unwell. Justinian went after him.

Someone said argumentatively, "Dogs have eight teats. Or is it ten?

Someone else said, "Shut up and hold this. You, go get a very large kettle."

"Kettle?"

"Kettle, pan, bucket, pail, whatever. Move!"

Long silence. Very long silence. Splashing sound. Abasio told himself they must be washing themselves off. Births were sort of messy, he understood. Not that he'd been present at any. Except his own, of course.

"Why does it keep doing that?" someone asked.

"Because it wants to," said Xulai angrily. "Leave it alone."

"Are we finished here?" someone asked.

"Just leave it alone where it is," said Xulai, with what sounded like an enormous yawn. "I'll let you know." There was a considerable time of almost silence, broken by small sounds. *Mop mop. Slosh. Splash. Mop.*

A very tall woman in a white garment—in a very wet white garment—came from the inner room and sat down on the sofa Lok-i-xan had been occupying for some hours. She took a small bottle from a capacious and invisible pocket, removed the top, and drank from it. It did not look like water.

"Lok-i-xan?" she said wearily. "And her father? They didn't stay?"

"No, they seemed somewhat . . . taken aback," said Abasio politely. "May one ask what is going on?"

"What is going on is . . . you are a father," the woman said. "My name is Tsu-tin. I am an obstetrician. I was privileged to be appointed by your . . . your wife's grandfather. What would that be, in your language?"

"I'm not sure," said Abasio. "I think it would depend upon the relationship. As of earlier this morning, I thought he was my friend. Under other conditions, he might be an old bastard."

The woman's mouth crooked very slightly. "Let us try to stay with the friend," she suggested. "Though given the circumstances . . . Why don't you sit down?"

"Why don't you just let me go look?" he said.

"In a moment. We're cleaning up."

A very large splash came from the other room. Someone cursed, and someone else said, "Get the mop again."

"My sons or daughters or both are causing some difficulty?" asked Abasio.

"You knew there was more than one?" she asked in surprise.

"I'm extrapolating from various comments you and your . . . assistants were making in there. Rather loudly."

"Ah. Well, yes. Your son and daughter, or sons or daughters, whichever may prove to be the case, have caused some unforeseen difficulties."

Thank heavens. Only two. "You don't know if they're male or female?"

He had said it before he thought. Well, how could one tell with an octopus? How in hell would a woman nurse an octopus? She couldn't. Baby octopi would eat . . . fishes. No little cradle. Cradles. No little stuffed animals. What did one give a baby octopus for its birthday?

After a long silence she said thoughtfully, "I don't suppose one would know male or female until puberty, no. At least, I wouldn't know. Wasn't trained to know. Someone might have been." She took another little drink and stared at the wall.

Cephalopods didn't *have* puberty. He sat down beside her. Things grew swimmy, insecure, and he felt himself teetering. The woman put her arm around him, saying, "Take a deep breath. Now another."

The door opened. A large man stood there, carrying a sizeable bucket in each hand. The woman beside Abasio beckoned. The buckets approached. A baby head protruded from each, a human baby head, each with two little eyes that looked extremely alert. Abasio shook his own head, ordering his eyes to track, focus, behave. He leaned forward. Each baby head was attached to a baby neck, shoulders, chest, and . . . tail. Long, fishy tail. Kind of bluish. Perhaps the tail was actually split . . . leggishly. Hard to tell.

Tsu-tin said, "You have two lovely merbabies. Or mermaids, or mermen. Or one of each."

He put his hands on the edges of the buckets, feeling he was about to faint. A tiny hand from one bucket grabbed a finger. Another hand from the other bucket did the same. The little heads went under the water. Gills quivered along the babies' sides.

"*Issums wussums cutest li'l fishies,*" said the obstetrician, wiggling a forefinger under a little chin. "*Isn't ums li'l darlins.*"

The little heads came out of the water. "Ga," said one. "Ba," said the other.

"Abasio," cried Xulai's voice in an annoyed tone. "Are you out there?"

"Would you mind babysitting for a moment?" said Abasio, lifting his hands and detaching his children with some difficulty. The little hands felt almost like tentacles, he didn't say. "I need to go say . . . something to my wife."

"*Wuzzums uzzums,*" said the obstetrician.

Abasio was already through the door. Xulai was lying in a clean bed, propped on a clean pillow, regarding him with an unreadable expression.

"Forgive me, please, if I misunderstood you," said Xulai in a voice halfway between fury and relief. "Did you not say that the Sea People insisted we take a shape that was . . . I think you said 'repugnant to us' . . ."

"Repulsive," he corrected.

"Because mankind had done them so much harm they would not accept us as sea creatures if we continued to look like people?"

"I was quoting the Sea King," he said. "Very accurately."

"I think you misunderstood him."

"No, I think I understood him exactly. He told me the truth."

"*Tweetums, splishy, splashy. Wheee,*" crowed the obstetrician from the next room.

"You've seen our . . . our children! That doctor out there! She's *cooing* at them. They are not repugnant."

"Repulsive."

"That, either."

"No. Darling, remember, the Sea King was talking to me. Well, to me and to you. He was talking about, ah . . . a proof of sincerity. Only humans who sincerely wanted to live as sea creatures should be allowed to have children who would be sea creatures. Actually, he never said what *those children* would look like."

She lay back, yawned, tried to open her eyes all the way but did not succeed. "You mean, it only applies to the . . ."

"I'm guessing it was a kind of selection process. I think that's the way he planned it. Or he and the Tingawans who were involved."

"You mean it only applies to the first generation." She lay there very quietly, her eyes shut, thinking it over.

It was time for him to kiss her, he felt sure. That would be appropriate. That and some comment about how . . . beautiful the children's tails were. They really were handsome children. Of course, he couldn't judge them from the waist down. He had no criteria for tails. Her eyes were opening. He shuddered. He had seldom seen so evil a smile.

"Well then," said Xulai, "since we first-generation ones can be only human on land or octopus in water, and since cephalopods don't lactate, and humans have to breathe air, and since I intend to leave with you on our next trip very, very soon, isn't it lucky we have Grandpas Lok-i-xan and Sea King to be the nursemaids." She smiled again. "Sea King especially. Two arms for each baby and one arm for each bottle. And two to hold on to a rock or something."

"*Oozums splishy sweetums*," cooed the obstetrician.

Abasio kissed his wife. He sat beside her, holding her hand until she went to sleep. There was silence in the room outside. He wondered what the doctor had done with the babies. Did merbabies sleep? And where? Had they set up a nursery with aquaria?

He went out into the room. The doctor had gone. In the buckets, the babies were asleep, their heads out of water. They seemed to have belly buttons. A little raw looking, but no cord attached. Self-separating, maybe? The gills along their sides weren't moving. Evidently it was a matter of convenience, gills or nose, either way. Great. Mother octopus wouldn't need to lactate; the babies could be fed out of water.

He decided to show the babies to Blue.

The stables weren't far, but it took him, them, some time to get there. Various people came along, to look, to admire, to recoil in surprise. It was only surprise, he realized, quite correctly. It was not revulsion. One husky warrior offered to carry a bucket. The warrior's friend offered to carry the other one. Abasio gratefully accepted. Buckets full of water were heavy. Transportation was going to be a problem. One of many.

In the stable, Blue stood waiting. "The news preceded you," he said. "I heard you were coming."

The buckets were set where Blue could put his nose in them. He snuffed at the babies, who said "ga" and "ba" at him and attempted to grab his nose. Other people gathered, both human and horse. Conversation ensued at various levels. Someone fetched several bottles of . . . "Oh wonderful! Something to drink!" Toasts were proposed. Silence abruptly fell, and Abasio looked up: *Oh, damn! Imperial parasols!*

"Lok-i-xan," said Abasio as cheerily as he could manage. "Justinian." He noticed with dismay that most of his fellow revelers were edging toward the door.

"Everyone stay as you are," said Lok-i-xan, waving the parasols away. "Someone offer me a cup."

Someone quickly did so.

"We're sorry to be so late," Justinian said. "The doctors wanted to . . . congratulate us, and they did go on and on about it." He came rather tentatively toward the buckets, putting his hand on the rim, just as Abasio had done. His fingers were seized. He smiled. His eyes filled with tears.

"Let us drink to the next generation," said Abasio, raising his cup . . . mug . . . actually he wasn't sure what it was usually used for. One of the stablemen had given it to him. It looked . . . veterinary. Silence threatened to fall heavily.

Blue said hastily, "I am reminded of a song." He nudged Abasio, cleared his throat, and sang, quite tunefully:

> *Oh, evolution is the force*
> *That pulls the culture wagon*
> *But no one really knows, of course,*
> *By which the what is draggin'.*
> *Time sometimes runs from front to back*
> *And sometimes even sidewise*
> *And oceans have the liquid knack*
> *Of daily running tidewise.*

"Ti-i-idewi-i-ise," echoed the two warriors, one of whom strummed an ondang as Blue continued:

> *Though who has tails, and wears them where,*
> *Are matters that could lure us*
> *With riddles so arcane and rare*
> *That none would ever cure us . . .*

Abasio patted his grandfather-in-law on the shoulder and, waving his glass—mug—whatever—joined in.

> *Let's not waste life deciphering,*
> *Let lore and logic scatter,*

Let love and beauty rapture bring . . .
And fish tails will not matter
And fish tails will not matter.
No, fish tails will not matter!

"Fish tails will not matter," echoed Lok-i-xan, who was very busy tickling one of the babies. "Such a big, strong boy . . ."

Abasio patted him on the shoulder again.

And Justinian, leaning over the other bucket, looked up with a glowing face. "Look, Abasio! Lok-i-xan! She has her grandmother's eyes."